SHORT NOVELS OF *Colette*

SHORT NOVELS OF *Colette*

WITH AN INTRODUCTION BY GLENWAY WESCOTT

New York, *1951*   THE DIAL PRESS

A PERMANENT LIBRARY BOOK

Contents

An Introduction to Colette

1. Sido

UPON publication of her love story of World War I, *Mitsou*, Colette received a letter from Proust.* "I wept a little this evening, which I have not done for a long while . . ." *Mitsou* concludes with a passionate communication from a little musical comedy star to her lieutenant in the trenches; and this impressed Proust especially, but he quibbled. "It is so beautiful, it even verges on prettiness here and there, and amid so much admirable simplicity and depth, perhaps there is a trace of preciosity." He could not quite believe in the sudden elevation and refinement of *Mitsou*'s style, educated only by love. And, how characteristic of the very neurotic great man! the chapter of the lovers' dining in a restaurant reminded him dolefully of an engagement to dine with Colette which he had been compelled to break, it unfortunately having coincided with one of his illnesses.

Upon publication of *Chéri* she received a letter from Gide.† He expected her to be surprised to hear from him; and perhaps she was. While Proust was a great complimenter Gide was known to be somewhat chary of endorsements. He had read the tragical tale of

---

* *Colette*, by Claude Chauvière, Paris 1931.
† Ibid.

the youngster in love with the aging courtesan at one sitting, breathlessly, he said. "Not one weakness, not one redundancy, nothing commonplace!" Why in the world, he wondered, had none of the critics compared her young hero or villain with Benjamin Constant's "insupportable" Adolphe? "It's the same subject in reverse, almost." On the whole this was higher praise than Proust's, and deservedly higher; for in the three intervening years Colette had extended and intensified her art. Gide quibbled also, or rather, he suggested that with his natural uneasiness and malicious humor, if he took a little more trouble, in all probability he would find something quibble-worthy. "I'd like to re-read it but I'm afraid to. What if it were to disappoint me, upon second reading? Oh, quick, let me mail this letter before I consign it to the waste-basket!"

It is pleasant and, I think, appropriate to begin with a glance at these two little documents of literary history. For, now that the inditers are both dead and gone, Colette is the greatest living French fiction-writer.

I know that in critical prose, as a rule, the effect of the superlative, greatest, is just emotional. It is not really susceptible of analysis, at least not of proof. Even the comparative, greater, is unhandy in any limited number of pages, as it calls for some examination of those who may be thought comparable. Greater than Mauriac? Greater than Martin du Gard, Jules Romains, Montherlant, Sartre? Yes, of course. But I have not had the zeal to read or re-read that entire bookshelf for the present purpose; nor do I imagine that the reader wants any such thorough and fanatic work. Let me not pretend to be able to prove anything. Let me peaceably point to those of Colette's merits, here and there in her work, which I regard as components of greatness; going upon the assumption that in the essentials, as to general literary standards, the reader will agree with me. Easy does it!

As it happens I can claim an uncommon familiarity with all of Colette's work. This winter, just before the editor of the Permanent Library offered me this opportunity to pay her my respects, I came into possession of the recent collected edition, fifteen volumes, seven thousand pages, two million words, in that handsome format which finally crowns the French literary life: laid paper with margins, red ink as well as black. This spring I have read everything that I missed in ordinary editions in the past, and re-read all the master-works that I have loved so dearly for many years. Thus I know whereof I speak, all fresh in my mind.

I wish we could have illustrated this volume with photographs of Colette; there are plenty, entrancing, at all ages. The first written description of her that I ever read was an entry in Jules Renard's *Journal*, November 1894: her appearance at the first night of Maeterlinck's translation of *'Tis Pity She's a Whore*, bright-eyed, laughing, "with a braid of hair long enough to let the bucket down a well with"; Melisande-like.

Rebecca West has described her in her middle age, out for a walk with her bulldog, a rich silk scarf looped through its collar in lieu of a leash. Her impression was of animal energy, fierceness, and though as a rule an intrepid reporter she declared that it rather frightened her.

I met Colette just once, in 1935, when she came to New York on the maiden voyage of the "Normandie." Her American publisher gave a cocktail party for her. She was not expected to speak English; and as I had lived in France long enough to have learned French, it was thought that I could facilitate the sociability. I was thrilled.

I remember her strong hands—serious writing is a manual labor! —and her fine feet in sandals, perhaps larger than most, rather like the feet of Greek goddesses. I remember her slightly frizzly hair fetched forward almost to her eyebrows, because (as she has told her readers) she has a square boyish or mannish forehead. I remember her delicate nostrils and her painted thin lips.

The conversation that I had been invited to engage in was not really very witty or deep. She extolled the great maiden ocean liner; how safe it seemed, how imperturbable upon the waves! She gave it as her opinion that there was nothing at all surprising about skyscrapers; man having been all through the ages a mountain-climber, a tower-builder. I then expressed my pleasure in the little conversation I had had with Maurice Goudeket, her distinguished, interesting third husband. "He is a very good friend," she said, and she emphasized friend a little. As I recalled certain bitter pages about her first marriage—the bitterest were still to come—I supposed that the designation of husband seemed unromantic to her.

Now I will furnish a sort of outline or résumé of biography. I wish that, instead, her autobiographies, the half-dozen little volumes which, taken together, are perhaps her best work—*la Maison de Claudine, Sido, le Pur et l'Impur, Mes Apprentissages, l'Étoile Vesper, le Fanal Bleu*—were available in English. All I can do is flutter in and out of that noble repository, treasure-trove, picking out bright bits, like a magpie. Though she has many reticences, grandeurs of style, and sometimes little riddles, she seems not to have left much for other narrators of her life to do, except to simplify and vulgarize.

Sidonie-Gabrielle Colette, born on January 28, 1873, in a village in Burgundy, Saint-Sauveur-en-Puisaye . . . Her father, Jules-Joseph Colette, was a pensioned-off soldier who had fought in North Africa, in the Crimea, and in the wars of Italian liberation, and lost a leg at the second battle of Marignan. Her mother, Adèle-Eugénie-Sidonie Landoy, born in Paris, was a young widow when the ex-Zouave loved and wooed and won her. It was a good marriage. She was an octoroon. Blessed France! where it may seem to handicap one in a career of serious authorship to have commenced with *Claudine*, a slightly raffish best-seller, or to have divorced and gone on the stage; but where race-prejudices are few and mild. Never have I heard any mention of that sixteenth part of Negro blood in the famous authoress' veins; only her own statement.*

Mme. Jules-Joseph Colette—Sido, if we may presume to use that abridged name which, her daughter has said, "sparkles amid all my memories"—was a woman of real force of character and un-

---

* *La Maison de Claudine* (1922), page 64 in volume VII of the *Oeuvres Complètes*, Paris 1949.

usual mind, with a gift of expression from which, doubtless, for the most part, her daughter's genius derived.

As a young girl Colette must have felt overwhelmed by her. The first independent action of Colette's life, marriage, rash and premature, was in specific rebellion against the better parental judgment. Thereafter Sido must have sensed the wrongness of impinging too closely upon her daughter's difficult life; she stood upon a certain ceremony, kept her distance. As the first page, indeed the first paragraph of a novel, *La Naissance du Jour, The Break of Day*, (1928), Colette has published a letter of Sido's old age,* declining an invitation to spend a fortnight in Paris. The excuse she gave was that her rose cactus seemed on the verge of blooming. In northern climes this rare plant blooms only once every four years, and in all probability that would be her last chance to see it.

La Naissance du Jour is a tale of the renunciation of love; Colette has portrayed herself in it under her own name; she was then in her fifties. The thought of her mother was a challenge to her; she studied herself in the mirror of her inheritance, measured herself against her mother's stature. It is like a large and solemn chaconne or passacaglia, in which the daughter's bereavement—after sixteen years!—still serves as the slow repetitious ground bass.

She began her filial tribute long before that. In *La Maison de Claudine* (1922), which is an account of the home to which the authoress of the *Claudines* came, not otherwise connected with the series—the best of the sketches are portrait sketches of the authoress' mother. *Sido* (1929) is a more formal portrait, entrancing. Even after thirty-four years in *l'Étoile Vesper, The Evening Star* (1946), there are sudden touching souvenirs: a fragment of a blue dress of Sido's, a miniature of Sido's mother, to whom Sido's father, the quadroon, was notoriously unfaithful, one of Sido's recollections of one of her other children, one of Sido's motherly criticisms, as to disorderly cupboards; and Colette has especially called our attention to them. Here as in other various texts, in fear and terrible

---

* *La Naissance du Jour* (1928), page 7 in volume VIII of the *Oeuvres Complètes*, Paris 1949.

bitterness and whatever other trouble, she evokes the great strong spirit, and despite her age—three score years and ten, no, nine—clings almost childlike. Evidently the filial devotion, half of it posthumous, has been the mightiest strand in her entire being.

2. *Willy*

THE next most important strand was coarse and incongruous, and seemingly weak; nevertheless it held her a long time. At twenty she married the noted journalist and hack-writer, Henry Gauthier-Villars, known as Willy. She was then, as he remarked some years later of her heroine, Claudine, as pure and unsophisticated as "any little Tahitian before the missionaries got there." He was, to characterize him in his own manner, the opposite of a missionary. He was a bad, clever, corpulent, somewhat crazy man. He was only about fifteen years older than she, but already the worse for wear, physically as well as spiritually. "Worse than mature," Colette said.

"The day after that wedding night I found that a distance of a thousand miles, abyss and discovery and irremediable metamorphosis, separated me from the day before."* What a painful sentence! What a beautiful sentence! All of her portrait of Willy from memory years later, is perfection. "The shadow of Priapus, flattered by the moonlight or lamplight on the wall"—then, little by little, the traits of the mere middle-aged man coming out from behind that image of newly espoused male: "a look in his bluish eyes impossible to decipher; a terrible trick of shedding tears; that strange lightness which the obese often have; and the hardness of a featherbed filled with small stones."† He was nervous, disgraceful, and shameless; foxy and comical and cruel. He was thought to

* *Noces* (1945), page 251 in Volume VII of the *Oeuvres Complètes*, Paris 1949.
† *Mes Apprentissages* (1936), page 55 in Volume XI of the *Oeuvres Complètes*, Paris 1949.

resemble King Edward VII; but in spite of his carefully dyed, extra-thick handlebar mustaches, his wife noted also something of Queen Victoria.

The term hack-writer, as applied to Willy, needs a little explaining. He was, as you might say, a wholesaler of popular reading matter: music criticism and drama criticism; and in book-form as well as journalism, revelations of his own everyday life and night-life in the somewhat side-splitting way, sometimes verging on the libidinous, with verbal pyrotechnics, especially puns; and all sorts of light fiction, something for almost every type of reader; and once in a while, dramatizations. Hacking indeed; but he himself did scarcely any of the writing! Doubtless he had what is called a psychic block to start with, but he made it work. He employed writers, several at a time, for his different types of production. He helped them. He was not at all lazy. Sometimes he seemed to want to fool them, pretending that the work of one of them was his work, and getting another to revise it, and so on. He may or may not have given them a fair share of the income from all this; they never understood his finances. Some of them had literary careers on their own in later years: Messrs. Pierre Weber, Vuillermoz, Curnon-sky, Marcel Boulestin.

Young Mme. Colette Willy's literary career began with her telling little tales of Saint-Sauveur; tales of childhood, girlhood, and school-girlhood. One day Willy suggested her trying to get some of these memories down on paper. She tried, the result disappointed him, and he discouraged her. But one day when he happened to need money he picked up her manuscript again and thought better of it. Could she not work on it a little more? he asked her. It only needed a detail of psychology here and there, a specification of emotion. Why not develop her little heroine's crushes on her girl-friends just a little further?

Young female writers, as Colette remarked years later, are not notable for their moderation; nor old female writers either. "Further-more, nothing is so emboldening as a mask." Before long Willy's reminiscing young wife was his favorite ghost-writer. He paid her

xiii

too; well enough, it seemed to her at the time, enabling her to send little presents to Sido, woolen stockings, bars of bitter chocolate. He would lock her in her room for four-hour stretches while she inked up a certain number of pages with her heaven-sent and profitable phrases, sentences, paragraphs. In her recollections of all this, Colette has expressed mixed emotions, doubtless impossible to unmix: pathos, furious resentment, and toughness toward herself—Willy locked the door, but, she had to admit, there was nothing to hinder her from throwing herself out of the window—and in spite of all, a certain appreciation of the way destiny worked to her advantage in it, *amor fati*. For thus in servitude, page by page, volume by volume, she became a professional writer. Regular as clockwork: *Claudine à l'École*, March 1900, *Claudine à Paris*, February 1901, *Claudine en Ménage, The Indulgent Husband*, April 1902, *Claudine s'en Va*, March 1903; and then a new series, *Minne*, and *les Égarements de Minne*. Willy took all the credit and signed them all.

Claudine, all four *Claudines*, had a fantastic success. Shall I attempt to say what it was like, with American equivalents, for fun? Rather like a combination of Tarkington's *Seventeen* and Anita Loos' *Gentlemen Prefer Blondes*. But also there was the factor of personal notoriety. Suppose Anita Loos had been married to, let us say, Alexander Woollcott, and he had posed as the author of it, and given the public to understand that it was the true story of her life! Also in due course it was dramatized and acted by a favorite actress, Polaire, who was, as you might say, a cross between Mae West and Shirley Temple. The name "Claudine" was bestowed upon a perfume, indeed two perfumes in competition, and upon a form of round starched school-girlish collar, and upon a brand of cigarettes and a flavor of ice cream. It makes one think of the old story of the sorcerer's apprentice, with a variation: young Mme. Willy not only brought the broomstick to life, she was the broomstick.

No wonder she has shown a divided mind about the merits and demerits of those early volumes. As a rule her references have been rather shamefaced, disdainful; and critical commentators on her work have followed suit, even I. But in truth almost any writer who had not gone on to write something very much better, would be

xiv

quite sufficiently proud to have written the *Claudines*. To be sure, here and there, they put us in mind of that once popular periodical, *la Vie Parisienne*. They are a little foolish but not at all false. They are wonderfully recreational, with all the assortment of approaches to romance, and small talk sparkling every instant.

A part of Colette's talent appears in them all right: her warmth of heart, brilliance of the senses, command of language; only none of her genius. She surely appreciates them as well as they deserve, for all her little promulgations of sack-cloth and ashes. She fought hard to get the rights away from Willy; for a while both names appeared on the title pages, then hers alone; and now she has devoted two and a half volumes of the proud definitive edition to them . . .

While she was writing and writing for Willy, intimate relations between them went from bad to worse. Halfway through the miserable marriage, or perhaps three-quarters of the way, she suddenly felt unable to stand it; collapsed in her own mind about it. She began to believe that perhaps Willy was not simply wicked but insane; a furtive kind of insanity, venting itself in little sadisms and in whims and frauds of one kind and another. She tried to pity him but she found herself unable to pity him. Presently she realized that the reason she was unable to pity him was that she had begun to be afraid of him. She has written of this with sombre moderation, with a sort of good nature, which gives one goose-flesh. "Healthy young people do not easily open their minds to fear, not altogether, not constantly. The worst tormentors have their hours of clemency and gaiety. Perhaps even a mouse finds time, between one wound and the next, to appreciate the softness of the cat's paw."* And on another page there is an allusion to something that happened finally, that she resolved never to tell; worse than anything she has told!

Whereupon she retreated to the country, to a little property in Franche-Comté called Monts-Boucons. Willy gave it to her, but

---

* *Mes Apprentissages* (1936), page 54 in volume IX of the *Oeuvres Complètes*, Paris 1949.

afterwards seized it back ... She told him that going away would enable her to get on faster with her work, his work; but there appears not to have been any vagueness in her own mind about it; it was for the specific purpose of suffering. It was what in our American life is so common, or I should say, what we have so common a term for (the French have none): nervous breakdown. It was the turning-point of her life: anguish, the first phase of independence!

In her account of this, years later*, I note one of those components of literary greatness which I have undertaken to indicate when I came to them: a sort of contradictoriness in the working of her mind; manifoldness. When reticence would seem to have closed down on her, because she is ashamed to tell the whole story, and no wonder; when her thought has failed, no knowing any longer what to think; when she feels obliged in all honesty and modesty to specify that she cannot really specify anything—then! then more than ever, compensatorily, her power of expression of emotion reaches its peak, by means of images and verbal music.

There in retreat in the Franche-Comté countryside, having on her mind day and night her problem of over-sophisticated, broken-down, psychopathological metropolitan home-life, suddenly she discovered, not the meaning, not the moral, but the metaphor, in simple nature around her; in the painfulness of nature. Metaphor singular? No, metaphors plural! all over the place; but all saying the same thing.— A superb serpent pecked to death by hens. Dark painful wasps slumberous in the ground like a minute buried bunch of grapes. Her cat undeterrably murderous without even any excuse of hunger, and the bird on its nest optimistic but obstinate as the cat approached. Her old horse so badly mistreated by its previous owner that, when she went riding, it had to be bandaged as well as saddled ...

By means of these observations she expressed the dread and disgust to which her married life had turned, more than by any outspokenness or outcry. And none of it really could be said to be, for

* *Mes Apprentissages* (1936), pages 79-83 in volume XI of the *Oeuvres Complètes*, Paris 1949.

the creature concerned, error or bad luck or injustice; in each case it was according to the given nature. Oh, likewise in her own case as the wife of Willy! She was justified in forgiving herself for her weaknesses of the past. On the other hand she could not be expected to repress in herself indefinitely a certain dire strength of which she was beginning to feel the stirrings. Both things were in her nature, in her attitude and reaction to the rest of nature and to others' human nature: awful compliance for a while, but power of rebellion after a while, even power of hatred.

But never, for her, indifference or obliviousness! This is what I call the contradiction: the creative mind embellishing what it hates; winding around what it is escaping from; rendering everything, as it goes along, in so far as can be, unforgettable. For example, that reptile and the barnyard fowl and those predatory insects and that beat-up horse: Colette kept them stored in her head for about thirty years, along with the more general concepts of early sorrow, early philosophy. As she has expressed it in the way of aphorism:—"By means of an image we are often able to hold on to our lost belongings. But it is the desperateness of losing which picks the flowers of memory, binds the bouquet."*

Nervous breakdown had done her good, as it often does, or so it seems: something in the way of a liberating effect. Suffering somewhat outweighing her natural conservatism . . . As she expressed it in later years almost cynically, she had monogamous blood in her veins by inheritance, the effect of which was a certain enfeeblement in the ways of the world. There by herself in Monts-Boucons, blood-letting! What year was that? Perhaps 1904 . . . Sometimes the chronology of her memoirs disappears in the poetry. She did not actually, entirely, leave Willy until 1906. Why the delay, when she had seen all and foreseen all, and as they say, found herself?

In more than one text Colette has declared, and no doubt sincerely thought, that it was mainly on her mother's account. From the very first day of her marriage and metropolitan life she had painstakingly

* *Mes Apprentissages* (1936), page 138 in Volume XI of the *Oeuvres Complètes*, Paris 1949.

prevaricated in every letter back to the provincial town. Perhaps Sido read between the lines, but she replied only to what her daughter chose to tell. Little by little Colette felt bound by her own spiderweb. Given what our sociologists call vertical social mobility, it is a frequent crisis in the lives of gifted young persons who have ventured to the city in search of fortune, to no avail, and then have to consider giving up and going back home: prodigal sons or daughters not even remorseful, nobodies with not even a cent or a *sou*. The prospect of burdening Sido in the financial way troubled Colette especially. Must she not have been inhibited by another point of pride also? In Sido's instant perception of the miserableness of Willy, and prediction of the martyrdom of being married to him, had she not felt some possessiveness, bossiness? It is a matter of observation that daughters often very nearly perish rather than admit that mother knew best.

But at the close of a life and career so felicitous and successful, let us not glibly say that at this point or that, things were misconceived or mismanaged. Nowadays one is apt to make too much of the spell cast by parents, and the fixation of first marriage, and everything of that sort. Especially in the lives of literary persons, planners by their temperament and training, the feelings of ability and ambition may be of more decisive effect. What caused her to set her bizarre young heart on the odd older man from Paris in the first place, if it was not the fact that he was a literary man? And after she came to hate him with her whole heart, probably it was the muse which kept her there beside him a while longer, faithful to vocation rather than to the marriage vow; only seemingly shilly-shallying, while accumulating the materials for a great piece of literature decades later.

And Willy was her job as well as her husband and her subject-matter. She has remembered to tell us that—doubtless sensing her restlessness, the gradual unfolding of her wings for flight, also the sharpening and tensing of her beak and claw—he opportunely raised her wages. The *Minnes* were more remunerative than the *Claudines* . . . It does seem to me that if I had been the author of those six volumes at the rate of one a year, I should have felt quite confident of being able to support myself by writing—also my mother in the provinces, forsooth, if called upon—even without an accustomed consort, slave-driver, agent, and front-man. But Colette did not feel confident. She was like someone learning to swim, someone who has learned, who can swim, but still depends on water-wings. And the fact is that, when at last she got up her courage and left Willy, and continued writing—an excellent volume in 1907, another in 1908—there was not a living in it. It must be admitted that she did not, perhaps could not, certainly never wished to, write any longer in the previous half-humorous best-selling style, Willy's style. She went on the stage instead.

3. Theatre

I FEEL a little embarrassment about this theatrical interlude in Colette's life; which let me deal with this summarily. I have not gossiped with any old friends of hers, nor questioned my Parisian friends of that generation for the outward aspect and general public impression of her life on stage and backstage, nor researched concerning her in the drama criticism and gossip-columns of newspapers or news-weeklies which perhaps exist in French libraries, yellowed but not yet mouldered away.

Not that I think Colette would mind if I had done so—now that she is the highest-ranking authoress alive, the pride and joy of France, the national great lady. Usually when literary folk manifest a dread of gossip, horror of investigation, like the ostrich in the adage, one reason is an exasperated proprietary sense. They want to do their own telling in their own way, with all the applause and the profit. Surely Colette is done telling: two theatrical novels, three, if we count *Mitsou*, and a volume of sketches, and various chapters in her autobiographies.

But reading all that, I find myself in a kind of quandary which (I think) must derive from ambiguity or at least uncertainty in her feeling. So much of it seems to me funny, but apparently to her it all bore connotations of resentment, misfortune, sorrow. Even when the theme is the picturesqueness of something, or eccentricity of someone, when obviously she means to make it as entertaining as possible, it is in a minor key or upon a sharp or harsh note. The theatrical way of life is lonely, and it was especially so in old-fashioned vaudeville or music-hall, with brief engagements in a hundred towns. Perhaps in young womanhood loneliness, lonesomeness, loneness, is as hard to bear as unhappy marriage. Perhaps, with a vocation as absolute as Colette's for literature, working at anything else seems an outrage.

And literary persons especially mind the impermanences of the interpretative arts, musical performance as well as acting and dancing. In Antibes on the French Riviera there is or used to be a little Roman tombstone bearing the inscription: SEPTENTRION AET XII SALTAVIT ET PLACUIT. Have I remembered the Latin as it should be? Someone named North, or perhaps someone from the North, aged twelve, danced and gave pleasure . . . In Paris in the Musée Guimet there is or used to be a little Egyptian mummy; within its angular tight leathery arms appear some dried bits of something else: it is a dancing girl clasping upon her bosom her last bouquet. Which is said to have inspired Anatole France's *Thaïs*, Massenet's *Thaïs*, and perhaps indirectly Somerset Maugham's *Rain* . . . Such are the personifications of the theatre, vanishing out of men's minds in no time, unless memorialized in writing or one of the other fine arts.

Colette's stage career began more or less by chance, in semi-public, upon occasions of that elaborated, almost laborious sociability which is peculiarly Parisian: masked balls, *soirées littéraires*, amateur theatricals. She has given us an account of a great afternoon in the garden of a noted and lovely young American woman, sapphire-eyed Miss Nathalie Barney, when she, Colette, and another lovely young American woman, red-haired Miss Eva Palmer, costumed as approximately Daphnis and Chloe, performed a playlet by Pierre

Louys.* That same afternoon there also entered, upon a white horse, costumed as approximately patient Griselda, that young Dutch or perhaps Asiatic woman, Mata Hari, whom the Germans later employed as a spy and whom the French detected and executed. Come to think of it, I do not believe that Colette's old friends have gossiped about her much; not in my time, not interestingly. In recent years I have had the honor of acquaintance with the red-haired Chloe above-mentioned, who has expounded the dualism of Greek religion to me, the balance between the two great gods, Apollo and Dionysus; but never a word about that gala garden-party.

Presently Colette got beyond the fashionable and sophisticated orbit, and took for her partner a good capable man named Georges Wague, who made a professional of her. For several seasons they appeared in various pantomimes, ballets, and sketches, most of the time on tour around the provincial cities. One of their numbers was first entitled *Dream of Egypt*, which a certain police commissioner, goodness knows why, obliged them to change to *Oriental Revery*. Their greatest success was entitled *Flesh*, and it ran an entire year. Then there was *The Bird of Night*, in which Colette wore rags and tatters, rather Sicilian-looking, and there was a third performer named Christine Kerf, and they all three glowered about something.

The iconography, especially the photographic archives, seems more evocative than the literary or journalistic record. Somewhere in a scrapbook I have pasted a reproduction in rotogravure of an early news-photograph in which Colette is making an entry, perhaps on stage, perhaps at a ball, with a panache of what appears to be real peacock-tail, borne upon the shoulders of four young strength-and-health men in jockstraps. Lately there have been published a great many such shots, old-fashioned in the comical way which may grow poetical as the years pass, and she has commented on them:† for instance, as a black cat in woolly tights with inked-on whiskers; for instance, in repose propped up on a taxidermized

* *Mes Apprentissages* (1936), page 122 in volume XI of the *Oeuvres Complètes*, Paris 1949.

† *L'Étoile Vesper* (1946), pages 316-9 in volume XII of the *Oeuvres Complètes*, Paris 1949.

head, showing to advantage those fine feet which, a quarter of a century later, impressed me. A certain art study reminds us who was the most famous, most influential dancer in the world in those days: Isadora Duncan. In at least one action photograph we are able to glimpse something of Colette's talent: a tension and a kind of blissfulness in the holding of her head and the outflinging of her arms.

The upbringing and formation of a writer as such: that is the significance of everything I have had to tell thus far. Even follies working out better than one could have calculated; even mere drudgeries serving a dual purpose, future subject-matter as well as present livelihood—nothing to be regretted unless the fatigue is too great or the life-time too short! For, as a rule, the development of talent into mastery, or even genius, is not a matter of studying to write or training to write, but of exercising as greatly as possible the entire being, senses, nerves, excitements, emotions, thoughts; only two or three habits of mind making the difference, leading on specifically to literature: the recollective faculty, conversational power, including the power of making others talk, and of course studiousness of the classics of literature and the other arts.

As we look back on Colette's life, indefatigable beyond anyone's, and not short, certainly we see that her odd, hazardous, almost scandalous young womanhood, even the years of hack-writing, even the intense unhappiness, even the years of hack-acting and dancing, all of it just as it happened was almost ideal for the future writer's purpose.

4. "*Chéri*," and "*The Last of Chéri*"

N o w please look with me at some of the result and the outcome, the writing itself; the several works of fiction included in the present volume. I will point to things and underline things, quote a little, paraphrase, and comment, and praise as best I can and dispraise scarcely at all . . . The two novels of the theatre, *la Vagabonde* (1910) and its sequel, *l'Entrave* (1913), made a reputation for Colette, quite distinct from the success and notoriety of the *Claudines*. Renée Néré, the protagonist of both, is also in some measure self-portraiture, analytical, spiritual, and not without self-consciousness. Perhaps Colette felt that this sombre presentation would counteract the foolish, girlish mask she had put on for Willy.

The curiosity about the life of Thespians evidently is international and ever-recurrent, but as a rule has not inspired novelists very profoundly. Colette, for her part, played down all the glamor of show-business, reduced it to realism, almost dispelled it. Theatre is merely Renée Néré's livelihood, while she rejoices in, then suffers from, love-relationships. I think the appeal of these two novels must have been not particularly to the stage-struck but to career-woman in general. Those were the early days of feminism, with a little host of women even in France seeking to wean themselves from domestic unhappiness by means of various labors out in the world, with very little written by way of guide-book for them, to say nothing of consolation.

It was *Chéri* (1920) which made Colette famous. Though she did not get around to writing *The Last of Chéri* until six years later, they really constitute one and the same work. It requires an unusual ability to hold a theme in mind for so long a time, ripening it, resolving it, perhaps depending for some of its elements on one's further experience as well as developing artistry.

Colette's first pairing off of novels, *Minne* followed by *les Égarements de Minne*, was just upon order from Willy; and as soon as they became her property she combined them rather imperfectly in one volume, *l'Ingénue Libertine* (1909). But perhaps this effort of reconstruction inspired her serious interest in binary form. The connection between *la Vagabonde* and *l'Entrave* is more than just the further developments in the life of Renée Néré. Over and above the explicit continuity there are recurrences of emotion, like echoes in the transepts of a large building, back and forth.

In *Chéri* and *The Last of Chéri* the double construction is handled much more decisively and strongly. There is an entire shifting of key and change of tempo from one to the other, and a somewhat different proposition in morals and psychology; yet the reader feels that all this was a part of the writer's knowledge and plan in the first place. A sweeping and agitated, sensual, humorous love-story ending in farewell, then a concentrated and solemnly instructive account of psychopathology, they are structurally perfect together, with an effect of not simply chiming echoes but of polyphonic music; with clear perspectives both in the passage of time and in the way the mind of each protagonist focuses on the characters of the other protagonists, and all according to human nature and fatality from start to finish.

Said Lawrence Sterne, of all men of genius perhaps the least masterly, "I begin with writing the first sentence, trusting to Almighty God for the second." Do you observe and compare the odd little beginnings of the various great novels? It is pleasant to do so, and it often illumines the deep-laid aesthetic and particular nature of the novelist in question. Both of Sterne's own first sentences are famous. There is a thrilling solemnity about the four and a half syllables of *Moby Dick*, "Call me Ishmael"; and the rest of the paragraph meandering along, "the watery part of the world" and so forth. The dozen words of *Anna Karénina*, thoughtful, universal, and yet simple, give an instant impression of narrative genius: "All happy families resemble one another; every unhappy family is unhappy in its own way." In due course there was struck the new note of American literary art, in Hemingway's first book, for instance, "Everybody was drunk . . ."

Now turn to the opening page of *Chéri*; the voice of the spoiled youngster addressing his aging mistress, an absurd outcry:—"Léa! Let me have your pearls!" Do you see? it is rather like theatre, sudden, in order to prevail over the incredulity and metropolitan nervousness of the audience; and poetical in the way of the stage, with more paradox than sentiment.

It is not unlike the fine opening scene of *Der Rosenkavalier*, first thing in the morning, with the dramatic soprano in or on her grandiose eighteenth-century bed, and the mezzo-soprano uttering the clarion notes of the pledge of everlasting devotion which in fact only lasts out that act. If I were in Paris, and the pleasure and privilege of a call on Colette were accorded to me, this is a question I should be tempted to ask:—Had she seen the music drama of Strauss and Hofmannsthal (1911) before writing *Chéri* (1920)? She has always been appreciative of music, and indeed in Willy's day helped with his music-criticism, and went along to Bayreuth.

No matter. The theme of an oldish woman in love with a very young man or a boy, and vice versa, is an old and fairly familiar theme; natural, insoluble, therefore persistent—except perhaps in the United States. We seem to take our matriarchy straight, in the proper context of family relationship, and more often analytically than for the expression of heartache or heartbreak.

"Léa, Léa, you're not listening to me!" the heartbreaking French youngster continues. "Let me have your string of pearls, Léa! It's as becoming to me as it is to you. Are you afraid of my stealing it?" And there, swiftly and simply, you have the three or four moral factors upon which the entire sad story turns: Chéri's childishness; and his exceeding good looks and corresponding self-admiration; and that constant concern with cash value, which was practically all the education he had been given, prior to this love-affair; and his resigning himself to having a bad reputation, not so much cynicism as defeatism.

Mauriac, a strictly Roman Catholic writer, having written a biography of Racine, situating the glorious dramatic poet in relation to baroque theology as well as classical theatre, emphasizing his profoundly troubled Christianity, inscribed a copy of it somewhat surprisingly: "To Colette, nearer than she thinks to this periwigged man."

If we give it a second thought, even in the opera-like or operetta-like first part of *Chéri* we find something of Mauriac's meaning: the suggestion that mere human nature, natural human happiness, is hopeless, that there is original sin, *et seq.* None of Colette's unhappy mortals, whether like puppets jerked to their death by pride and error, or just drawn to it by time in the ordinary way, seems to have the least sense of the eternal life, or any feeling of having to choose between salvation and perdition. But often their undeluded, unreconciled attitude as to the condition of humankind here below is quite Catholic. In the mentality of Chéri, in his plight of psyche if not within his will-power, is a readiness for religion.

Interviewed by someone, in the *Nouvelles Littéraires* if I remember correctly, Colette stated the subject of this pair of novels in plain terms without a hint of religion or even of philosophy, as follows: —When a woman of a certain age enters into a relationship with a much younger man, she risks less than he. His character is still in a formative stage, and therefore the more likely to be spoiled by their love, deformed by the failure of it. After they have parted he may be haunted by her, held back by her, forever.

This of course is what reminded Gide of Benjamin Constant's *Adolphe.* I am tempted to quote from the famous commentary which Constant added by way of preface to the third edition: as to those degrees of passionateness which a young man may think that he can arouse in his mistress without feeling them himself; which nevertheless little by little take root in him also, and injure him terribly in the uprooting. No, it would require lengthy quotation and perhaps new translation.

Chéri is younger than Adolphe, Léa is older than Ellénore. Shall I tell you the plot? It is simple: the life and love and death of one Frédéric Peloux. Chéri is his pet name, as we should say darling or dearie—the French word is not quite so belittling; we have a derivation from it in cherished. The protagonists of the older generation are all courtesans, or so near as makes no matter; and all rather superannuated and retired. The cleverest and least pleasant of them, Charlotte Peloux, Chéri's mother, has contrived, no, only facilitated his attachment to her old friend, Léa, born Léonie Vallon, known as Baroness de Lonval. Léa was in her forties; in all walks of life woman were expected to retire early then. Chéri was nineteen. It suited Mme. Peloux to have him kept out of mischief, and schooled and exercised for his future marriage, and at someone else's expense the while.

It worked like a charm. It continued for six years, quite peaceably and dignifiedly, in good understanding and good health and powerful enjoyment of sex. You may look down at it, as a kind of mutuality of the commonplace and the materialistic—bourgeoisie gone wrong—in its way it was love. At any given moment it must have seemed to everyone that Chéri was playing the inferior part. He would always take that wrongly suggestive tone; his requirement of the pearls, for example. Oh, probably his love never attained any particular height or powerfulness, except in intercourse. On the other hand, it never really diminished or altered, until the day of his death. Only his young body detached itself from Léa's old body, and only when ordered to do so.

How remarkably Colette makes us see and feel Léa's physical, sexual attractiveness, despite the emphasis on the fact of her aging rapidly: blue-eyed and rosily blond, with long legs, and that very flat back which you may also observe in Italian Renaissance sculpture, with dimpled buttocks and with somewhat exceptionally elevated breasts, long-lasting.

Colette lets her do most of the emphasizing on age herself. With one eye always on the mirror—as a normal and necessary part of the discipline of courtesanship—evidently, a good while before her intimacy with Chéri started, she had learned always to think of herself as gradually growing older. That was what the passage of time, every day, every hour, every minute, meant to her. She had accustomed herself to the prospect of finding herself, one fine day, really old, disgracefully and decisively old; and she had resolved to call a halt to love-life and sex-life before that happened. Thus, in her sorrow when it came time to lose Chéri, to let him go, indeed to help him go, there was a factor of submissiveness to fate; long-prepared, philosophical.

The gerontophilic devotion—the feeling of a young person for someone definitely not young—is a very genuine, earnest, and passionate devotion. Who has not experienced it or observed it? Only as a rule it is not to be depended on; it is short-lived, subject to sudden coldness and indeed sexual incapability; it is a fire in straw. It was not exactly like that in Chéri's case. The elder person, beloved in that way, very naturally skeptical to begin with, nevertheless as a rule is almost certain to get enthralled little by little. But if you have any common sense, good education, or worldly wisdom, you will keep your skepticism in mind even after it has ceased to have any currency in your heart. For you must be prepared to yield your young person to some other young person or persons one fine day, upon a moment's notice. Was this not what happened between Léa and Chéri, when young Edmée came on the scene? Not exactly.

For we feel quite certain that Chéri would never have decided upon, nor lifted a hand to procure himself, that pulchritudinous well-schooled impeccable creature; not in a thousand years. It was all managed by the matriarch, more managerial than anyone, and more mercenary. Edmée was the daughter of the courtesan noted among them for having put away the most respectable amount of money. It was a case of gerontocracy's having prevailed over gerontophily. And in the essentials Léa functioned as one of the gerontocracy. She cooperated in the transfer of her darling back home, back under his mother's control, and into that holy state of matrimony which, as the French conceive and practise it, certainly is a mother's province.

Miserable young man! his emotions are pathetic and profound, as we see terribly by the outcome. His heart is in the right place but he has scarcely any head. Whether in happiness or unhappiness he has not even observed exactly what his emotions were until too late; until someone else has decided things. To all intents and purposes he is inarticulate. His talk—his explanation of what is so beautiful about his eyelids, for example—is a kind of play-acting, like that of infants at a certain age; sound rather than sense. In more ways than one he is a kind of infant. In the very first instance, his passage from his mother's malicious and avaricious salon to Léa's bed and board, oh, blissful bed and sumptuous board! was but a bewitchment—and now back again, as it were the dream of an infant not yet born, from one part of the womb to another!

The comedy of the aging courtesans is as well developed, and perhaps as important, as Chéri's misery. And in their scenes together the malicious, almost joyous tone and brisk pace of the first volume continue into the second: satirical *vivace* even amid the funeral march. Once in a while we laugh at them, but more often with them, in appreciation of the fun they make of one another. It is not all unkindness. In this class of womanhood one has to be careful of old friends, in view of the difficulty of replacing them. Their main objective in their youth and in their prime having been to please men, now it is rather to find various ways of conciliating other women; talking amusingly is one way. Sense of humor keeps up their courage, and serves another mutual purpose also: helps them pretend that those compulsions which constitute their morality —competitiveness, avarice, cruelty—are not really heavy upon them; that a part of their evil is not evil at all, but only a convention, affectation and clowning.

Léa is the least amusing, but partly in consequence of that, keeps our sympathy from beginning to end. Note especially her first encounter with Mme. Peloux after the marriage of Chéri and Edmée. Upon previous readings I seem to have missed this passage; now it delights me. After absenting herself in the South of France for a season, by way of discipline and therapy, Léa has returned to town with her heartbreak not remedied, but anaesthetized, scarred over. She has reached that decision so long meditated: farewell to men, once and for all, and at once. Naturally she has been feeling dull and nervous, listless and slack.

Then, without warning, she is called upon by Chéri's mother, Edmée's mother-in-law; triumphant, and infernally inquisitive, and, yes, at the same time, sincerely friendly. For an hour Léa sits and gazes at that all too familiar face and form, the short and tight and tirelessly bestirring body, the large inhumane eyes and the glib lips; sits and listens to that lifelong chatter, petty but savage, detail after detail of the skilful, almost mechanical futility of her existence, the organized heartlessness. All of this, Léa reflects, with self-commiseration for a moment, visited upon her as a test of her strength of character . . .

And the next moment, exultantly, she realizes that in fact her character is strong enough. In the time to come as in the time gone by, she will be able to strike back. She knows, or can soon figure out, what well-turned phrase will hurt, what practised and well-timed smile will worry. And upon the instant she feels less discouraged about herself. From her dreaming of love, and nightmare of the end of love, and sloth of sorrow, now animadversion and contempt and resentment have waked her up. She feels her heavy-heartedness, her sense of having nothing to live for, lifting and dispelling. What she will have to live for is simply self-defense. Her terrible old friend, old enemy, will keep her on her marks. In the strain of losing Chéri, and in the spirit of general renunciation, she has been living at a somewhat higher level and greater tension than was good for her. Mme. Peloux has brought her down to earth. She is grateful.

Here in a small way we have a philosophic mystery: the vision of evil as giving opportunity for an exercise of virtuousness of a sort . . . I realize that my comment upon this is longer that Colette's telling. In incident as in aphorism, along with the stimulation of our senses, acceleration of our sentiments, she has the power to set our brains to work. Even as in the maxim of Montesquieu: "A great thought is one that puts us in mind of a number of other thoughts."

Meanwhile the process of Chéri's death has started, though it does not happen until 1919. Noted above, a certain lack of intellect has been ominous in him all along, predisposing him to demoralization. Stupid! or if you like, innocent! apparently he has taken it for granted that he will be able to resume amorous intimacy with his old beloved after the necessary term of concentration on his young wife. He attempts it one night; and perhaps, if he had not then noticed certain new ravages of her age, devastated nape of neck, weightiness or weightedness of cheek—he pretends to be asleep, and peeps at her with only the narrowest beam of morning light between his beautiful eyelids, through his thick eyelashes—and if she had not noticed his noticing, perhaps . . . !

Indeed they are tempted by one another even after that; later that morning. For just a moment there glimmers between them a further hope of the recommencement of love, a lunatic hope, "such as may be entertained by persons falling down out of a tower, for the time it takes them to reach the ground . . ." That is the conclusion of the first novel; a thrilling chapter. What difference would it have made if they had recommenced? Only the difference of a few more months of enjoyment, or perhaps a year, perhaps two years; down-hill enjoyment of course. But is that not the best that is ever offered anyone on this earth: prolongation, with deterioration? Also, for Chéri, the difference between suicide and a gradual ordinary death . . .

As it happens his suicide is gradual too. The entire second novel, *The Last of Chéri*, is devoted to it. No suspense; the very first page indicates to us, with many tiny touches—I count seven suggestive words, set in odd cadences—that he feels condemned to death, or has condemned himself. But he finds it a strange hard task to carry out the sentence. Even his self-absorbed wife senses something wrong with him: "white shirt-front and white face hanging in a darkness." One thing he has to overcome is his self-esteem, his narcissism; that more than anything might have inclined him to spare himself. Every time anything or anyone reminds him of his good looks, the prospect seems to brighten.

The outbreak of World War I is wonderfully timely for him, just two years after his marriage; and as long as it goes on, his morbidity does deviate into heroism. And when peace has been restored, will that not, we ask ourselves, serve as at least an acceptable substitute for happiness? No, it is the ignobility of the post-war life which strikes him; ignoblest of all, his own parent and his own spouse. Of course the real trouble, or perhaps I should say, the true pretext for the real trouble, is just his inoperative and irremediable feeling about Léa. Not infrequently, I believe, great love gets one in a habit of procrastination; so that one's grief at the failure or loss of it also rather maunders, loiters, creeps.

Notwithstanding Colette's deftness and forward-moving rhythm, she has allowed *The Last of Chéri* to be, doubtless wanted it to be, her slowest book. It has called to my mind the catchphrase of a comedian in old-fashioned burlesque years ago, one of those endlessly patient, absolutely pessimistic types prone to more or less comic accidents: "No hope, no hurry." Nothing that really deserves to be called accident happens to Chéri, scarcely even incident. We are given a fantastic feeling of being with him morning, noon, and night, while all his life is in a kind of quiet decomposition, unravelling and discoloring. We watch him as he seems to be deliberately experimenting with himself, with singular little techniques, little exercises, to turn his mind backward, to deaden himself to the present, to withhold himself from the future. It is all quite harmless behavior, only entirely unenjoyable and motivationless.

At the last he spends most of his time with an awful little old woman, the oldest of all the courtesans, called la Copine, that is, the chum or pal, who knew Léa well in her heyday. Comedy again, but this time it is not *vivace* or even *allegro*; la Copine is like a death's head wearing a wig, reminiscing all through the night, *largo*. She has a great collection of photographs of Léa, studio portraits framed and snapshots just thumbtacked up. In one of the snapshots she is escorted by one of her young lovers; not the one before Chéri, but the one before that. In another snapshot there appears in the background an elbow which la Copine declares must have been Chéri's own elbow; but he knows better, and it is only a blur anyway.

And then suddenly, when it has become almost a bore—in the scenes with la Copine Colette has lulled our minds along with a soft, almost listless humorousness—suddenly we have reached the end. Chéri has reached the point of real readiness for the little flat revolver which he has had in his pocket a long time. He bolsters it up between two pillows so that he can stretch out at ease, his ear pressed to the barrel. In his freakish fatigue of life, at the last minute he seems almost unwilling or unable to make the effort of dying. We have a feeling that his laziness might almost have saved him. The worst and most rudimentary of the forms of will-power, stubbornness, has destroyed him. We mourn over him very little.

Instead our minds run on ahead to what might possibly furnish a third volume: the reactions of those who have loved him. It is a gauge of the verity of Colette's characterizations that we can conceive their suffering in a circumstance she has not written—series of thunderclaps in their several minds, especially punishment of Mme. Peloux, and ghastly bafflement of Léa, realizing how stupid she was ever to let him go, how conventional, how lazy; and of course for them both, for all the courtesans, fear! The sudden needless passing of one so young sounding the knell of everyone older, deafeningly!

5. *Style*

GLANCING back at all the above synopsis and commentary, I have a troubling impression of having imposed on the story of Chéri an extra sordidness somehow; accentuation of the immorality, diminution of the charm. No wonder! For what, in fact, have I had to offer? Only some of its bones, no flesh and blood, nothing in the skin of the language in which it was written—none of the beauty of the way Colette writes, which is often like a conferring of her own personal physical beauty upon the fictitious creatures she writes about, even unfortunate old satirized macabre creatures like la Copine. By means of diction, syntax, cadence, she gives them all something like complexion, milkiness and snowiness, rosiness and amber, and something like sheen of hair, sometimes raven and sometimes golden, and sinew in one place and bosom softness in another, and every single lineament of things in accord with every other, according to all five senses; that is, verbal equivalents . . .

Style! that is what Colette is most celebrated for, in France, in French; or perhaps I should say, what first brought about her celebrity. Even in the early volumes, perhaps not in the *Claudines*, but surely in the *Dialogues des Bêtes* (1904) and *les Vrilles de la Vigne* (1908), she wrote like an angel; handled the language to perfection, or almost to perfection, in an inimitable though influential way.

And of course the sensuousness which I have tried to suggest is only one aspect of it. Elegance, brevity, and clarity are other aspects; and those turns of phrase, speedy and forceful and neat, and with a sense of fun, for which the French have the word *esprit*. Expressiveness above all! In the first place, the expression or at least implication of the mentality of the author, in passages where the nature of the work requires this to be rather reserved, held back— the moral temper, idealism, philosophy, and perhaps religion— unifying the lifework as a whole, that is, the mature and post-mature work; giving an effect of a peculiar or unique balance of emotions. I seem unable to think of a way of defining this in Colette's case. Will half a dozen loosely balancing words serve? As follows: an odd form of pride, which I call gloriousness; and serenity; and thankfulness; and stoicism; and a certain sharpness or asperity . . .

And in the second place, more important for the novelist as such, the rendering of nuances of the particular subject-matter, minutiae of characterization, instantaneities of the plot, with almost imperceptible touches, subtle selections of vocabulary, small patterns of syntax, even little calculated disorders. When a manner is as fine and intensive as Colette's it can hardly be distinguished from the action or emotion or thought it has to convey. On many a page her meaning really resides in the mode of utterance rather than in the terms of statement; the nuance is all-signifying, as in poetry; and it loses heartbreakingly in translation as poetry does.

Having mentioned in passing certain subtleties of this kind in *The Last of Chéri* I wish that I could examine passages in the other novels with the like or even closer application. But I know that, alas, writing about the detail and texture of writing is a mug's game, especially in English. English and American literature never having been as painstakingly wrought and self-conscious as the French, we are short of technical terms of the art. Academic critics of course invent technicalities and teach them to their pupils, but neither the general reader nor, indeed, the creative writer, understands them very well. Perhaps on the whole the best way is just to express enthusiasm simply, as one would any other feeling, rejoicing in the artistry in question, marvelling at it, pondering, with imagery more or less in the manner of the artist under consideration, and with borrowings from the phraseology of the other arts if they seem to suit.

In this way, for my part, I often compare Colette's prose to dancing. That was at the back of my mind when I declared that her years on the stage had been helpful to her in the development of her greatness as a writer. I borrow an exquisitely apt term, not, to be sure, from the kind of dancing Colette did, but from the old Italian-Russian-French tradition: absoluteness, as applied to the perfectly trained and entirely experienced female ballet-dancer, *assoluta*. A discipline and indeed muscularity altogether disguised by gracefulness, so that the eye of the beholder is deceived, the sense of reality set aside—for a split second, she is emancipated from gravity; she pauses and reposes in mid-air, stops to think in mid-air! Does this seem altogether far-fetched, as an analogy of literary style? Believe me, I could prove it, with plentiful and suitable citations, with perfect phrases suspended in midparagraph, and never for a split second failing to keep time to a general music. . . .

6. "The Indulgent Husband," and "The Other One"

TWICE, a quarter of a century apart, Colette has undertaken a most difficult or delicate theme: triangularity in marriage, by which term I mean something more than chance infidelity, something different from the regular sinfulness of adultery; some involvement of the marriage partner sinned against, condonation or acceptance for whatever reason, or perhaps inclusion somehow—in *The Indulgent Husband* (1902) which is the third in the *Claudine* series, and in *The Other One* (1929).

In the very early work the involving element, connecting link, is some measure of homosexual responsiveness between young Claudine and a strange young woman named Rézi, who presently turns out to be Claudine's husband's mistress. He encourages their attachment, with intermingled amusement, kindness, and lustfulness. To be a good novel, with this oddity and criss-crossed compounded feeling, it would have had to be very good. It is only pleasant and interesting.

For one thing, there is the dubious, perhaps illegitimate, but irresistible biographical interest: the mirroring of Colette's own youth in the immature and surely distortive creation. In those days when *Claudine* was not only a best-selling book but a successful play, played by Polaire, Willy persuaded Colette to bob her wonderful long hair to match the bizarre and entrancing little actress's. In a recent edition of *Mes Apprentissages* Colette has let us see a photograph of them, out of doors somewhere, at the races or at a garden-party: unhappy young host-writer and moody young matinée idol in strikingly similar white ruffles, like twins, escorted by their notorious elderly employer. Perhaps Willy intended only a bit of good publicity. We certainly cannot come now to the conclusion to which an excitable Parisian public undoubtedly jumped. In one of her most beautiful miniature narratives,* Colette has made her feeling about Polaire quite clear, as of great importance in her life then, in another way; no triangle. Possibly it was public misapprehension, wrong gossip, which provided her with that part of the plot of *The Indulgent Husband* in the first place. Inspiration may be the merest accident.

But in spite of her great lifelong use of experience of her own in her work of fiction, on the whole she has been less inspired by the turn of personal events, the impulse to explain or to justify her conduct, than most authors. Her life has provided her with knowledge, but in the handling of it she has been extraordinarily objective, with pride of aesthetics rather than of reputation, and with unusual educability and severe critical sense. I am inclned to think that even in her early work, when any self-indulgence or frivolity appears in it, it is because, at that time, she could do no better; she had not learned how to write those pages more seriously. *Le Blé en Herbe* (1923), her masterly novel of young love, youngest love, initiation and defloration—the modern *Daphnis and Chloe*—recapitulates one of the themes of the not quite successful *Ingénue Libertine*. I think that dissatisfaction with *The Indulgent Husband* may have been one thing that moved her to write *The Other One*. Alas, once more she somewhat missed the mark. If she were to live long enough, she might try it again, in still another volume, perhaps a masterpiece . . .

* *Mes Apprentissages* (1936), pages 89-92 in volume XI of the *Oeuvres Complètes,* Paris 1949.

Certainly the autobiographical factor has ceased to amount to much in *The Other One*. Farou, the husband in it, bears not the slightest resemblance to Willy. He is a playwright but rather, if I may say so, just for fun, like Henri Bernstein. He is a great bull-like, hard-working, tireless and tiring creature. He loves his wife Fanny very well, though he has been unfaithful to her in the way of a little relaxation now and then, as it has happened to come in handy. She has always forgiven him and relaxed about it; and now relaxation, even laxness, laziness, is a part of her nature. She seems just not capable of not forgiving, though this time it is under her own roof, under her nose. The mistress this time, Jane, Farou's secretary, has become her good friend and comfortable companion. Fanny is not young; neither is Farou, but he still seems rather excessive in her life, too much for her. All things considered she feels the need of Jane; and Farou needs her, rather more in the secretarial capacity than the amorous capacity. Fanny gets to thinking of Jane no longer conventionally as interloping mistress, rather as assistant wife; and the book comes to a close in this way, which is a kind of happy ending.

As a whole *The Other One* lacks vitality. Perhaps this subject-matter lay fallow in her mind too long. It does not lack plausibility or function or general human interest; only it is not intensely interesting. It lacks *chiaroscuro*; no brilliance anywhere in it, no deep sort of obscurity either. Or perhaps I should say, the lights and shades, the several contrastable elements, are not arranged to set each other off to best advantage. The date of it puzzles and fascinates me: 1929, the year after the avowedly autobiographical *Naissance du Jour*, sumptuous with landscape-writing, grievous with frustrated and stoical amorous feeling, haunted by Sido's ghost. Perhaps wearied by that, she went to the other extreme in the story of the Farou family; overdid the objectivity. And after it, not another volume for three years—then a spate again, the most remarkable sequence of all: *le Pur et l'Impur* (1932), the boldest of her reminiscences, all about various singularities of sex, then *The Cat* (1933), and then *Duo* (1934) . . . When we consider

xxxviii

The Other One in its place, in relation to the lifework, it is mysterious. In seemingly shallow, limpid, even glassy waters we discern greenish and bluish tones; something sunken perhaps, wreckage or treasure.

7. "*Duo*"

Duo (1934) is also a story of marital irregularity, but not condoned at all, quite the contrary; and it has an unhappy ending, as unhappy as *Chéri*, except that the dénouement comes about more promptly. The marriage of Michel and Alice has lasted a decade; a good marriage, with no lack of sexual responsiveness thus far, a happy hard-working life, working more or less in double harness in various theatrical enterprises. But, recently while he was absent in the South of France on some business venture, she gave herself to one Ambrogio, a business associate; a silliness, a mistake, to which she called a halt after about two weeks. And, indiscreetly, she has kept some improper letters from him, in a purple letter-case; and she carelessly lets Michel catch a glimpse of this, then tries to persuade him that there is not, never has been, any such object; and thus the deadly trouble starts; jealousy, the unpleasantest conceivable subject, the shame and disgrace of humankind, from the beginning of human history. No, not from the beginning, but ever since Dante or ever since Catullus . . .

"I do not believe in dénouements," Balzac made one of his highbrow great ladies say. Literature can do as well as chance, if the literary man tries hard enough. "But," she concluded, "if we re-read a book it is for the details." Colette's details are a marvel. For example, turn to Michel and Alice's breakfast on the terrace. It is the morning after the first evening of his wild jealousy and her evasiveness and defiance; after a night of extra-deep sleep, in avoidance of intercourse. Our concern about them has been well worked up, in behalf of them both: the justifiably but exorbitantly aggrieved husband, the culpable but regretful and well-meaning wife. "Man and woman, close together, disunited, languishing for one another . . ." We hope that they may soon make peace.

Wifely, there on the terrace, to make him as comfortable as possible, she reaches across and turns the coffee pot and the cream pitcher, so that he shall have the handles on his side. Without comment! A good part of matrimony is in that gesture. Then a still slumberous bee comes clumsily to the honey pot, and she will not let him swat it with his napkin. "No, let it go," she cries, "it's hungry, it's working." And the mention of those two fundamentals, work, hunger, bulking so much larger in her womanly mind than jealousy—that male mania, negative form of eroticism, which is tormenting him, destroying their marriage, destroying him—brings tears to her eyes.

Note Colette's probity in this particular. Thus she informs us of Alice's being the healthier-minded of the two, having the more constructive purpose. Michel is the sympathetic one, we suffer for him; but she is rather to be approved, less disapproved. And beyond probity, subtlety . . . Writing as a woman, with wisdom explicitly womanly always, Colette enters farther into Alice's mind and motivation than Michel's. She seems to hint at various extenuating circumstances, excuses for her infidelity. Also, I think, she makes it quite clear that, if asked, as one woman moralizing with another, she would agree with Alice that infidelity was no such terrible thing, *per se*.

In due course, remembering and understanding everything about Alice, her background, family, upbringing, and all, Colette also added a sequel to *Duo, le Toutounier* (1939)—Alice widowed, back in the family studio-apartment in Paris; a conversation-piece with two of her sisters, Colombe and Hermine, somewhat woebegone bachelor girls, career-women. Their fond curiosity brings out Alice's defects, inadequacies; their psychology mirrors hers with the greatest animation of little lights and colors. And here we note that those characters Colette knows best, and perhaps loves best, put her under no particular obligation of indulgence. Here we learn why we did not like Alice better in the former novel; what it was about her that, almost more than the fact of her infidelity, contributed to her husband's desperation. For example, a certain conceit not unusual in women, but especially brought out by tactlessness in her case; and a kind of bravery that is not real courage, only false pride and defiance. Think back! how she frittered away Michel's patience and good will by changing her story every little while: admixture of truth and falsehood, unkinder than either . . . How self-indulgent she is, doubtless always was; therein she trespassed in the first place. Worst of all, her lack of imagination; therefore she fails to say the things that might possibly have consoled the poor creature trespassed against; therefore at last she lets him have it, the entire documentary truth, crude and exciting.

Note how I have mingled tenses in all these sentences, turning from the one book to the other; years apart in the writing, only months in the chronology of Alice's life. Here once more the binary form is impeccable; the division of the material very precise and meaningful. For one thing, at the end of *Duo*, we are alone with Michel when he is planning to drown himself; whereas in *le Toutounier*, Alice allows herself to believe, and convinces her sisters (and the insurance company), that it was an accidental death.

Nevertheless she blames him, even for misadventure—hah, the fool! stumbling into the flood-water, forgetting the slipperiness of the red-clay river bank—because she loved him, still loves him, and terribly misses him. There is often a factor of anger in great bereavement. Do you remember Schumann's song cycle, *Frauenliebe und Leben?*—"Now for the first time you have hurt me, hard unmerciful man, by dying, and that struck home!" She also blames him for his proneness to tragical feeling, darkening those last few days before the so-called accident; much ado about nothing, a trait of maleness . . .

But thus she does not blame him as Colette blames him, and as

xli

we blame him. Colette shows us his abysmal pessimism, his self-destructive ardor, from the first word of the trouble. And at the end, Alice's impatient stupid entire revelation, with documentary evidence, which maddens him: he himself insisted on it; he would not take no for an answer. Neither to the right nor the left would he turn or even look; nothing else touched or excited him, only his determination to know more than he could bear knowing. The sign of Psyche! he would commit it if it killed him, and it did.

Let me also call attention to the pages about the singing of the nightingales, once to each of these miserable mortals whose love is failing. The nightingale is a bird very dear and personal to Colette. *Les Vrilles de la Vigne* (1908),* one of the first works of her own sole devising, without Willy, begins with a sort of allegory or fairy tale, two or three pretty pages. A nightingale falls asleep in a vineyard in the burgeoning spring-time, and when it wakes up, has a bad fright; for the tendrils of grave grapevine have begun to wind around its feet and wings. Therefore, thereafter, it sings and teaches its young to sing, "While the grapevine is growing, growing, growing, I'll stay awake." In French this is a near enough approximation of nightingale-rhythm . . . It expresses her feeling of escape from marriage—thirteen years of tendrils!—and of blessedly finding that she had voice and song of her own; that is, literary talent and something to express by means of it.

Here in *Duo*, in the prime of that talent, we have nightingales once more. The poor adulteress leaves the room, and the poor cuckold, sitting there by himself, begins to pay attention to a number of them, singing their hearts out, but softly, remotely; and then to a soloist, a much greater voice than the others, or perhaps only proximity makes it seem so. But how sad! how sick! Michel is not able to take any pleasure in any of it. It is as though his thoughts partly deafened him. How can a man so sad and sick partake of glorious nocturne? Only by withholding his breath, then trying to breathe in time to the music, which suffocates him a

* *Les Vrilles de la Vigne* (1908), in volume III of the *Oeuvres Complètes*, Paris 1949.

little and keeps him from thinking for a minute or two. And after-ward—one of Colette's characteristic touches, with her sense of physiology keener than anyone's!—he feels a burning thirst.

A couple of pages further on, he goes out of the room; Alice comes back. It is her turn to listen, especially to that one loud tenor voice seemingly wasting itself away in brilliance, in repetitions so insistent and variations so far-fetched that it scarcely suits her troubled heart; it seems to hinder all emotion, except its own emotion, if it can be called emotion. But, but, when the soloist pauses for a moment to catch its breath, there arises the soft chorus of the far-away singers, each for himself, each at the same time in harmony with the others—*accordés* is Colette's word, which means reconciled as well as harmonized; which also means matched, mated, betrothed. And unhappy Alice is reminded of the great spring labor going on along with the spring concert: assembling and weaving the nests, laying and hovering and hatching the eggs, feeding the fledglings; labor of the females for the most part. But not lonely; as long as they have to labor the males will not fail to serenade them!

It is one of those metaphors, extended and, as you might say dramatized—bearing as great a portion of the author's thought as her dialogue or her action—for which I love her. Do you not? Do you see what it signifies, suggests? The woman listening to those male birds, thinking of those dutiful female birds inarticulately nesting, is childless. In her joint life with Michel now stricken suddenly, in their hapless marriage unbalanced, toppling, hopeless, that important corner-stone of civilized heterosexuality is lacking: no egg, no fledgling, no real nest! Therefore, perhaps she thought of herself as free to lead a little double life for a fortnight, entitled to partake of modern single-standard morality; thus she erred in idleness, with not even watchful conscience, not even sufficiently troubling to keep it secret. Therefore . . . Go farther with this theme if you wish. Colette always knows when to stop; here she has stopped with the metaphor.

A bad thing about jealousy is the element of pornography in it: the stimulation of visioning one's darling in someone else's arms, with the consequence of desiring somewhat more than usual just when one is expected to content oneself with somewhat less—or as in extreme and morbid instances, as in Michel's case, looking backward, crying over spilt milk, desiring the past. How clearly Colette has marked this, though with no stress or scabrousness! Michel himself admits it, in a single painful exclamation, after Alice has let him read all Ambrogio's letters: one of the games of love played by those two happened to be, ah, something the miserable husband has especially delighted in, more than anything, more than life.

Another detail: whereas Alice is Parisian, Michel is a Southerner, meridional—even as Sidonie, née Landoy, and Jules-Joseph Colette. Make no more of this parallel than it is worth; it doubtless furnished their daughter with observations of the contrast of temperaments. From the first page of *Duo* it is suggested that Alice is somewhat the more intelligent or more civilized—or rather, the other way around: Michel is the more instinctive, primitive. I over-simplify ... The point is that he is not at all the type of man for whom it is normal or natural to forgive a breach of the marriage vow. But for the grace of God, but for a generation or so, and a veneer of twentieth century morals, this story might have ended in murder instead of suicide. It would have done Michel good to give Alice a beating, would it not? Yes, but perhaps he would not have known when to stop. Indeed, this might quite plausibly be given as his excuse for committing suicide: to prevent murder, or to punish himself for murderousness.

As representations of suicide, a subject most important to us, important in the symbolical or anagogical way especially: psychologists having shown us how frequently misdemeanors and misfortunes partake of the same dark frenzy, only a little less dark—the same desire to die but less determined, the same unwillingness to live, dilatory—see how the case of Michel compares, contrasts, with the case of Chéri! This is but a momentary violence, though the result is forever; an act almost of aggression, though the point of departure is true uxorious devotedness.

Whereas Chéri is bemused and benumbed, torpid, unmotivated.

xliv

Would that he had been capable of a bit of violence! Colette has given us, as one of the gravest indications of his state, the fact that he feels no jealousy of Edmée. That might have waked him up and saved him. Or, alas, he might have relapsed into his slumberousness again, gone sleepwalking away in some other realm no less lonely. For there is a curse upon him; and we feel that if he had not turned it into the channel of death it would have developed in another direction: imbecility or worse.

The Last of Chéri, from the first page to the last, is a representation of that famous so-called sin of the middle ages, rampant again in this century in more ways than one: acedia, that is, horrible languor, malignant listlessness, irremediable boredom, paralysis of soul; the intolerable sorrowfulness when the specific sorrow keeps slipping one's mind. And this is the greatest portrayal of it in modern literature. Michel is not in this classification at all. If the enraging circumstance of Alice's infidelity had not befallen him, or if Alice had kept him in blessed ignorance of it, he would have been all right.

See the mystery of morals! Although Chéri's background is so bad, all those old courtesans constituting so gross and mean and base a society—and Michel and Alice and even Ambrogio are just average inoffensive humanity—the opprobrium upon him is slighter; for the most part we think of it as sickness. Michel is the wickeder. In cases of suicide we cannot moralize upon the act itself—we do not know enough—only upon the attitude of mind, heart, and soul, just prior to it. What was in Michel's mind, heart, soul? Possessiveness, punitiveness, intermingling of lust and prudery, deafness and blindness to all the signs of Alice's love, rejection of her. In Chéri's? Only disappointment, disappointment in himself and in the crazy bad sick world—many a saint has felt as much —and fatigue and loneliness and stupor; nothing very bad, nothing unfair.

And see the indivisibility of morals and psychology! in *Duo* Alice is the healthy one. In so far as Michel's wicked intention is to make her suffer, he miscalculates, it miscarries, she is too strong

xlv

for him. Wherein lies her strength? In her dullness of mind as well as her robustness, lack of imagination as well as good nature. Her salvation and Chéri's perdition correlative in some way, but impossible to correlate . . . The fact is that neither of the two sets of values by itself—neither right versus wrong, nor sickness versus health—will serve to explain or to save humanity. We have to try first one, and then the other. And in the last analysis of course there is no salvation: everyone is deathward bound, the road has no turning, God is not mocked.

8. "The Cat"

IT OCCURS to me that I have taken *Duo* out of chronology, for no particular reason; not far out. *The Cat* (1933) is another of Colette's masterpieces, made of rather similar materials of middle-class humanity, matrimony again; matrimonial misunderstanding and mischance and fiasco. Approximately of the same length, the same shortness, I think you will agree that because it is more poetical, it tells more and signifies more per page. It has no sequel, needs no sequel.

The marriage of Alain and Camille scarcely deserves to be called a marriage; it lasts only a few months, a trial and a failure. We first see Alain still living at home with fond parents. He has a most cherished, most beautiful cat named Saha, a thoroughbred Carthurian, greyish-bluish. After the honeymoon he takes it to live with them. Marriage does not make him any the happier; neither does he make his wife happy. He lets her realize his vague sense of having made a mistake, vague longing to be back home again, infidelity of spirit. The cat seems to Camille emblematic of all that. She tries to kill it, does not succeed. But Alain cannot forgive her, nor she him.

xlvi

Do you observe how this constitutes a sort of diptych with the story of Michel and Alice? And here also, how strong and sure Colette's sense of justice is; how deft her communication of it, though never passing specific judgment! Is it by instinct, or with intellect like a precision instrument? I think it is a part of her femininity, and an attractive part, to seem to set aside claims of mere cerebration. As in *Duo* she has presented the wife somewhat more understandingly than the husband, that is, more explanatorily, with an extra perspective, a brighter light. But, thus, all the more critically! We are not in the least obliged to love the female; we are allowed to love, and to feel that Colette herself loves, the male.

Indeed, peering a little more profoundly into creative coincidence than it is proper to do, we may remark that we have heard of only one other person on earth as devoted to cats or to a cat as this young Alain; that person is old Colette herself. And as she conceived this story she may well have arrived at a part of the tension between him and his bride by asking herself, What if I had to choose between my cat and some such vain, disrespectful, disturbing new young person?

Alain's young person really is a terrible girl, a type that may sometimes incline one to despair of the epoch: so very nearly in the right about almost everything, but just missing the point; so self-righteous but so lacking in self-assurance; possessive without strength, destructive without deadliness. She has energy to burn but somehow very little warmth except perhaps in the specific conjugal connection. With a certain fatuity, as to her importance to her husband, which gradually gives way to sadness and bitterness, in the realization of her unimportance, she seems to have nothing else to live for.

Indeed we sympathize with her as to her resentment of the cat. We see that it is less exorbitant and less abstract than Michel's jealousy in *Duo*. The trespassing of Ambrogio against him was a thing of the past; and even at the time of its happening he felt no injury, not the slightest pang, no deprivation. Whereas Saha is an ever-present rival, lauded by Alain with every other breath, and established by him as a permanent feature of their married life.

But why, we wish to know, why could she not somehow gradually vitiate and exorcise the childish magic it has for her dear husband? Is there ever any point in a vain, violent iconoclasm, loudly denying the tabu and pushing down the sacred image? And if it came to the point of violence against her will, if her husband in his aelurophily suddenly maddened her, why so inefficient about it? Why defenestration, instead of poisoning or drowning? The very idea of just giving it a push, hurting it, and arousing its hatred, paroxysm of hissing and explosive yellowish eyes, which is what betrays her to Alain!

The worst of this kind of female character, we say to ourselves, is that even in violence it falls between two stools. It results not even in disaster but in muddle and mess and absurdity. But, beware! this kind of objection is valid in aesthetics, if you really prefer tragedy to comedy; but in morals it is evil nonsense. Falling between two stools is better than successfully killing cats. The reason for Camille's weakness and coarseness and confusion, and even loss of husband, is fundamental and creditable. To express it in the sentimental style, she is on the side of life. It not only enables us to forgive her, it necessitates our forgiveness.

Her dear husband really is a maddening youth, though attractive. He is as fatuous in his feeling of unimpeachable male supremacy as she in her feeling of absolute female desirability; as self-indulgent in his daydreaming and voluptuous frivolity with his pet as she in her vain commotion and pursuit of pastime. We can never feel quite happy about him, even when he is perfectly happy himself, even when he gets back home where perhaps he belongs. In the very first chapter we observed how recklessly his parents have spoiled him; marriage to Camille seemed the only hope for him. At the end of the story we cannot see into his future at all; it seems all beclouded and scarcely even tragic, just harrowing. A type that may sometimes incline one to despair of France . . .

Two thousand years ago St. Paul decided that it is better to marry than to burn; a way of stating the case which seems to start marital relations off on the wrong foot. Psychologists nowadays,

scarcely less severe, have added that it is better to be infantile—
better to disappoint a wife and concentrate on a cat and give up
marriage altogether, as Alain did—than to commit suicide. If we
agree, we are constrained to admire this young man more than the
poor hero of *Duo*. Colette seems not to have reached any absolute
decision upon this point; no aphorism that I can recall. But certainly she expects us to take Alain's cat as an emblem of child-
life, home-life, childish home-life, and of its compromise and consolation in secret: autoeroticism. No pettiness about this; nothing
belittled or made sordid or left sordid—not ever, in the writing of
this good woman and liberal writer!

Let me call your attention to her description of Saha at night,
at the beginning of the story: one night just before Alain's marriage,
on his bed, thrusting her claws through his pyjamas just enough
to worry him, with a pleasurable worrisomeness; then giving him
one of her infrequent quick kisses with her chilly nose; then seating herself on his chest while he fell asleep; and until morning,
vigilant perfect superhuman creature! seeming to fix with her hard
eyes, and to follow around and around in the darkness, the fateful
zodiacal signs, lucky and unlucky stars, which in unknowable time
and space dance to and fro over sleeping humanity. Two things
at once—it is that manifoldness which I have mentioned, as of
the time of her nervous breakdown—the littlest instance, Alain's
mere inconsequential self-provided soporific pleasure, and at the
same time, the greatest concept, great eternality and destiny even
as personified by the cat-goddess of the Egyptians.

Toward the close of the story there is another little picture of
Alain and Saha together. He holds her in his arms, rejoicing in her
entire contentedness and entire confidence in him. With the peril
of Camille's rivalry happily averted, Saha has, Alain reflects, a life-
expectancy of perhaps another decade; and he winces at the thought
of the brevity of life, the brevity of love. In the decade after that
decade, he promises himself, probably he will want a woman or
women in his life again. He does not specify Camille; he is not

such a cad as to expect her to wait for him. In any event, he promises Saha, he will never love another cat.

Yes, this love-scene of childish man and almost womanly cat seems almost too good to be true, too pretty and tender and humorous. It is a kind of happy ending. Any valid commentary upon a work of narrative art has to be in some measure a re-telling. Now suddenly I realize how much less cheerful my re-telling of this has been than the text itself. The loveliest of love-stories; at the same time a serious study of modern matrimony, yes, indeed! But the true love in question is that between Alain and Saha; the true marriage is theirs. Camille is the trouble-maker, the interloper, who makes a fool of herself and is successfully driven back out of the way. It is almost an allegory or a fairy-tale; and what truth there is in it I certainly cannot state, in the way of either ethics or psychotherapeutics.

Suddenly I am ashamed of all my stating and interpreting topsy-turvy and wrong end to. For the little pure narrative itself is preferable to any meaning one can read into it or moral one may attach to it. Is not this the profound thing about narration, the almost mystic belief of the true narrator? Its incident, description, characterization, dialogue, are the means of expression of truths that are greater, more affecting, truer, than anything that can be put in general or theoretical form. Perhaps a great narrator like Colette only pretends to be thinking about her characters, coming to conclusions about them, pointing morals—the supreme narrative device, to convince us of their reality! We are able to moralize about them; *ergo* they exist . . .

1

9. Later Life

N o w I think you have had enough of being escorted by me from page to page. If I have accomplished what I intended, you will have begun to be impatient with me, tired of reading me, eager to read the six works by my dearest author that I have criticized at such length. So I will tell you briefly a little more of her life-story, from where I left off until approximately the present, and make my bow. Colette's later life does not lend itself to lively telling the way her youth did. Somewhat as it is said of kings and queens, that happy reigns have no history, it will be understood that very great labor of authors and authoresses—this authoress' fifteen short novels and fifteen long stories and scores of very short tales and sketches and half a dozen volumes of non-fiction—is bound to curtail the materials of biography.

Briefly:—Just prior to World War I Colette married Henry de Jouvenel. She bore him a daughter, Bel Gazou, of whom she wrote enchantingly, enchantedly, at the age and stage of growth when a little human is most like any other immature animal: *la Paix chez les Bêtes, Peace Among the Animals.* Jouvenel was a distinguished and successful newspaperman. Therefore, very naturally, Colette forsook the stage and also took up the career of journalism, and after their divorce, continued in it for many years, indeed never has discontinued; presumably has had to depend on it for a part of her livelihood to this day. The literary art, in the present half-revolutionized world, does not as a rule feed its practitioner, though world-famous. While more Frenchmen read more books than we, they pay less per volume.

Thousands of pages of Colette's collected works were first printed in, if not conceived for or commissioned by, various newspapers and periodicals; including five solid years of drama criticism, in the second-thickest volume. No one has written more gravely than she

of the waste and fatigue of hack-writing, though without plaintive-
ness or pretension. But on the other hand, I think no one has managed it so well, with so much to show for it in the end. After her
autobiographies have grown familiar around the world as one great
work, perhaps her greatest, then surely some editor will select and
assemble from all her reporting, column-writing, and familiar essay-
writing, the equivalent of an important diary, notable especially for
terse, intense aphoristic passages, which surely a great many readers
will appreciate.

To this day, Colette has told us, she suffers from two recurrent
bad dreams: one of the presses rolling, and no copy; and another
of coming out on a vast vacuous platform or stage to sing, and her
song lapsing. In those old days of her acting and dancing, did she
also sing? I do not recall any mention of that . . . Which reminds
me: just for her pleasure, one year, she went back on the stage—
I forget what year, and I have not the patience to research for it, and
no matter—in Léopold Marchand's dramatization of *Chéri*, in
the role of Léa, with the famous comédienne so near and dear to
her, Marguerite Moreno, in the role of Chéri's mother.

As I remember, 1935 is given as the date of her marriage to Maurice
Goudeket, her "best friend." If that is correct they were newlyweds
when I had the honor of being presented to them in New York.
One of her most moving passages about her own life is the dialogue
with him which forms the first chapter of her penultimate autobiographical volume, *l'Étoile Vesper*. In 1941 when the Germans
were in France, Maurice Goudeket being of Jewish ancestry, they
seized him, with twelve hundred others in the same seizure, and
kept him in the concentration camp of Compiègne; and after his
liberation from that hell-hole, for eighteen months more, he lived
half free and half in hiding and in flight, preyed upon by the evil
police and bureaucracy. Colette has written of this with terse horror, and of his homecoming at least with restrained tenderness.

Also during the war she was stricken with extreme arthritis,
and has been bedridden ever since.

Beginning in 1948, continuing through 1949, concluding in 1950, the illustrious old publishing company of Flammarion issued the collected edition to which I have kept referring in this essay; prepared for the press, as its colophon specifies, with the author's watchful eye on it, and by the good offices of the author's husband. "Thus, at the conclusion of a long career," wrote the collected one in a tiny general preface,* thus and only thus is the writer enabled to compute the total accumulated weight of his lifework. At this point only is he entitled to rejoice in his own good opinion; also his real anguish commences." Anguish of unrevisability, irremediability—fundamental though much ignored principle of ethics as well as aesthetics!

In other brief sentences scattered all through the collection she has sounded the same proud, uneasy note; glanced back disappointedly but dispassionately upon every work in which she can detect unworthiness: frivolity, facility, mannerism. So many pages having been written in a great rush, of dire necessity, she is afraid of their seeming not polished enough. Here and there, alas, has she not failed to discover the absolutely suitable word, to form the perfectly felicitous phrase? Having had to depend so often on incidental inspiration, with one fortuitous commitment or another, she is afraid that the younger generation and indeed posterity may lament in her entire lifework a lack of cohesiveness . . .

Let no one laugh or even smile at her unnecessary humility, fastidious fretful apologia. Instead, let the multitude of fellow-writers hang their heads in, relatively speaking, shame; and let the shameless, the unhumble, the uneducable, despair and cease and desist from writing altogether; and let the very young with any talent, in high school, at universities, at writers conferences, on newspapers, wherever they may be, dedicate themselves with stricter and fonder vows than the usual! It seems to me that the time has come—a part of the twentieth-century being against culture—to speak out in this connection with some portentousness and intensity. In the more serious sects of religion perfectionism is a sin; and in the present

* *Préface* (1948), page 7 of volume I of the *Oeuvres Complètes*, Paris 1948.

science or semi-science of psychology, no doubt psychopathological. But in the literary art it is just method; the one and only good and sound method.

It is an essential feature of the artist temperament: pride of greatness—and heartbreaking ideal of greatness for those who know that they personally are second-rate, which keeps them from declining to third-rate or fourth-rate—taking all that has been done already as a matter of course, a matter of no further interest; climbing up on the previous proud accomplishment, not to glory in it, just to see what may lie beyond, perhaps accomplishable, if one lives long enough. From which must derive for aging artists a certain chronic bitterness, and for second-raters, a sickness at heart. For we never do live long enough. *Ars longa* . . .

It can be justified in religion, come to think of it! Bossuet, the glorious baroque theologian and preacher, explained it in someone's funeral sermon:—"We are inevitably less than our thoughts, God having taken pains to indicate by means of them His infinity." Without changing his saying much: artists by the great pains they take, and by the extent of their intelligence, always greater than their ability—along with other voices in the enormous concert of the world, cacophony of the cosmos—indicate and celebrate infiniteness. And surely there is not in the world at present a greater exponent of this than Sidonie-Gabrielle Goudeket, née and known as Colette.

We know how the aesthetic conscience and high, tender, and constant virtuosity began in her case. She has remembered a very early, very significant slight incident for us. It is in a commissioned text,* accompanying some fine color-plates of exotic butterflies, hack-writing—an account of the butterfly—collecting of her two adolescent brothers; their over-niceness and wastefulness. Every evening they would sit in judgement upon the day's catch, and relentlessly eliminate every unworthy specimen. "Thus, aged seven or eight, I learned that only beauty deserves preservation, and that the

---

* *Journal à Rebours, Papillons* (1936), pages 110-14 in volume XI of the *Oeuvres Complètes,* Paris 1950.

sons of men in their vainglory are never altogether satisfied with anything." Neither, it may be concluded, are the daughters of women; least of all, the daughter of Sido.

Supreme rememberer! how frequently, and with what youthful sensitivity, her mind still turns upon those very bygone days! Perhaps I have laid too much stress on her dissatisfaction with the style and form of this and that small part of her lifelong creation. Certainly she minds its incompletions more than its imperfections. She looks longingly at certain mysterious untouched themes, unarticulated messages; especially things about her mother. Only two years ago she wrote in the preface to *la Maison de Claudine*,* that, when Sido died, she did not depart upon any remote path into an abstract eternity, but instead "has made herself better known to me as I have grown older." Perhaps there will still be time to paint another filial portrait. She has a feeling of not having discovered everything that the extraordinary matriarch deposited in her mind. "I began this discovery late in life. What better could I conclude with?"

Which suggests that she probably is still writing, disregarding physical desuetude and dolor and whatever awkwardness and distraction. That strong hand with well-fleshed and tapering fingers and unprojecting fingernails, not infrequently photographed, poised over her desk, or reposing amid very fine sulphur-glass paperweights and other bibelots and small useful objects in elegant disorder—not greatly changed in the most recent photographs—we cannot imagine it without one of her accustomed extra-thick pens in it.

She lives in the heart of Paris, in the Palais-Royal, that extensive rectangle of not very palatial architecture built by Louis XVI's cousin Philippe Egalité who was not opposed to the Revolution, whom the revolutionists decapitated nevertheless. It is said to be the first apartment-house ever erected; that is, the first conglomeration of fairly small sets of rooms designed to be rented to independent individuals of middling income. The inside of the rectangle

---

* *Préface* (1949), pages 7-8 in volume VII of the *Oeuvres Complètes,* Paris 1949.

is colonnade, playground, statue, fountain, flowerbed, and orderly plantation of modest trees.

It suits Colette. She has the bed in which she lies bedridden drawn close to the window; and her desk is mobile, pulled up close over her knees. She sleeps very little, troubled by the usual nervousness of the aged as well as by the caprices of unrelenting arthritis, and by her genius. She works at night. Over her head hangs that electric light sheathed with blue paper referred to in the title of her latest volume, *le Fanal Bleu, The Blue Beacon.* To nocturnal strollers in the colonnade and the arbitrary garden area down below it has become as familiar as that star referred to in the title of the preceding volume, *l'Étoile Vesper, The Evening Star,* the folding star of shepherds, Sappho's star. Colette's modesty about her authorship is not constant, thank heaven; it is traversed by almost youthful gleams of natural and joyous importance, and by the sense of immortality looming. And, doubtless, composing her paragraphs about this illumination of her midnight hours, she must have thought of Flaubert who more than anyone else influenced her in the matter of style, verbal workmanship, justness of diction, melopoeia; Flaubert who kept such a regular working schedule that the bargemen up and down the Seine used his study window as a slight lighthouse.

There is a text expressive of her belief in the literary art which I love, which I will proceed to translate myself, taking great pains, not without vanity of my own style as a really more appropriate tribute to this writer whom I love than any ten-thousand word exegesis. In her young womanhood she made friends with the noted courtesan Caroline Otero, known as *la belle* Otero; a sort of friendship of curiosity to which writers naturally are inclined. When she came to write Chéri apparently this world-famous beauty—with thorough changes, from brunette to blonde, and from Spanish to one hundred per cent French, and so on—posed in her mind for certain aspects of the characterization of wonderful Léa.

And many years later, sixteen years later, she wrote a description of her, non-fiction,* in which we find, brought in with seeming casualness, oh, not a principle of aesthetics, nothing so cut and dried! but surely an article of her faith, as follows:—"That beautiful body, so arrogant in its declining years, defiant of every illness and evil frequentation and the passage of time, that well-nourished body, with plumpness drawn smooth over its muscles, with luminous complexion, amber by daylight, pale in the evening, I vowed that some day I would describe it, painstakingly and disinterestedly. We can never produce perfect likenesses of the faces dearest to us, we slip into passionate deformation somehow. And who ever will undertake to set down faithfully all the traits of true love?

"Instead we record, with words as with paint-brush, the flaming redness of outworn foliage, a green meteor amid the blue of midnight, a moment of the dawn, a disaster . . . Spectacles not notable for their significance or their profundity, but charged by us with premonition and emphasis. For the time to come they will bear the imprint of the four numerals of a given year; and mark the culmination of some error, the decline of some prosperity. Therefore it is not for us to say with any assurance that we have ever painted, contemplated, or described in vain."

GLENWAY WESCOTT

Stone-blossom,
Hampton, N. J.
1951.

---

* *Mes Apprentissages* (1936), page 18 in volume XI of the *Oeuvres Complètes,* Paris 1949.

Chéri

1

*L*ÉA. Give me your pearls. Do you hear me, Léa? Give me your necklace."

There was no response from the enormous bed of wrought-iron and copper which shone in the shadow like a coat of mail.

"Why don't you give me your necklace? It looks as well on me as on you—and better."

As the clasp snapped, the laces on the bed were roused and two naked arms, magnificent, with thin wrists, lifted two lovely lazy hands.

"Let it alone, Chéri, you've played enough with that necklace."

"It amuses me. Are you afraid I'll steal it?"

In front of the pink curtains barred by the sun he danced, black as a dainty devil on a grill. But as he drew near the bed he became white again in silk pyjamas above doe-skin mules.

"I'm not afraid," said the soft alto voice from the bed. "But you'll wear out the thread. Those pearls are heavy."

"They are that," said Chéri with respect. "He certainly didn't do things by halves, whoever settled these on you." He stood before a mirror framed against the wall between two windows and considered his reflection—that of a very handsome and a very young

3

man, neither big nor little, and with hair like the plumage of a blackbird. He opened his pyjamas on a chest that was lusterless, hard and curved like a shield: and the same pink high-light played on his teeth, on the whites of his black eyes and on the pearls of the necklace.

"Take off that necklace," insisted the woman's voice. "Do you hear me?"

Motionless before his reflection, the young man laughed to himself. "Yes, yes, I hear you. I know well enough that you're afraid I'll make off with it."

"No. But if I offered to give it to you, you'd probably take it."

He ran toward the bed and bounced into it like a ball. "Wouldn't I, though. I'm not old-fashioned. I think it's idiotic for a man to let a woman give him one pearl for his pin or two for his studs and then think he should be horrified if she offers him fifty. . . ."

"Forty-nine."

"Forty-nine then. I know how many there are. And tell me they don't look well on me. Say I'm not good-looking enough for them. Say it!" He tossed toward the recumbent woman a provoking laugh which showed his small teeth and the soft inner sill of his lips.

Léa sat up in bed. "No, I won't say it. In the first place you'd never believe it. But can't you laugh without wrinkling your nose like that? How will you like it when you've made three ugly lines between your eyes?"

Immediately he stopped laughing, relaxed the skin on his forehead and held in the fullness of his chin with the instinctive gesture of a faded old flirt. They looked at each other hostilely, she leaning on her elbow among her sheets and lace, he sitting side-saddle on the edge of her bed. He thought: My wrinkles, eh? Wrinkles are the last things she ought to mention. She thought: Why is he ugly when he laughs—he, the handsomest boy I ever saw? She reflected a moment, then made her thoughts audible.

"You know, you look horrid when you're happy. You only laugh for malice or mockery. It makes you ugly. You're often ugly."

"That's not true," cried Chéri, irritated.

4

Anger knotted his eyebrows over the rise of his nose, magnified his eyes, bright with insolence and bristling with lashes, and widened the intolerant and inexperienced curve of his mouth. Léa smiled to see him as she loved him most—mutinous but amenable, insufficiently chained and yet incapable of being free. She put her hand on the young head which shook at the yoke impatiently. She murmured as one calms an animal:

"Now, now ... What's this? What's this, now ..."

He threw himself against her big beautiful shoulder, pushing with his forehead, his nose, hollowing out his familiar place, already closing his eyes and seeking the accustomed sheltered drowsiness of long forenoons, but Léa thrust him away:

"None of that, Chéri. You're lunching with the national harpy and it's already twenty to twelve."

"Really? Am I lunching at the old girl's today? And you too?"

Lazily Léa slid deeper into her bed. "Not I. I'm off duty. I'll go drink coffee at two-thirty—or tea at six—or have a cigarette at quarter to eight. Don't worry, she'll see enough of me. And anyhow I wasn't invited."

Chéri who was standing and sulking grew radiant with malice: "I know, I know why! We're going to have high society. We're going to have her nibs, Marie-Laure, and that poisonous brat of hers."

The large blue eyes of Léa, wandering, fixed themselves: "Oh, yes. She's charming, the little girl. Less so than her mother, but still charming ... For the last time, Chéri, take off my necklace."

"No luck," sighed Chéri, unclasping it. "It would look well in the hope-chest."

Léa lifted herself on one elbow. "What hope-chest?"

"Mine," said Chéri with facetious importance. *"My* hope-chest of *my* jewels for *my* marriage." He jumped in the air, cut a dance step in space, came to earth again, butted open the curtains and disappeared, crying: "My bath, Rose. And be quick about it. I'm lunching with the old girl."

"Of course, of course," mused Léa. "A lake in the middle of the

5

bathroom floor, eight towels floating at high tide and the scrapings from his razor in the wash basin. If only I had two bathrooms. . . ." But she realized as usual that in order to obtain this it would be necessary to tear out a clothes closet and lop off a corner of her dressing room. So she concluded as usual:

"I'll simply have to be patient until Chéri marries."

She lay down again on her back and noted that Chéri the night before had left his socks on the mantel-piece, his brief underdrawers on the chiffonier, his cravat around the throat of a bust of Léa. She smiled in spite of herself at this hot masculine disorder and half closed her great tranquil eyes of a youthful blue and edged with unfaded chestnut lashes. At the age of forty-nine, Léonie Vallon, called Léa de Lonval, was rounding out the happy career of a courtesan who has become rich, of a good creature whom life has spared from flattering catastrophes or exalted sufferings. She made a secret of the date of her birth but willingly admitted, letting fall on Chéri a glance of voluptuous condescension, that she had reached the age to allow herself certain sweet comforts. She liked order, beautiful linen, ripe wines and well-thought-out food. Her youth as a courted blond, then her maturity as a rich demi-mondaine, had been carried off without a scandal or subterfuge on her part and her friends could remember a Drag-day about 1895 when Léa said to the secretary of Gil-Blas who was treating her as if she were a great artist: "An artist, am I? Oh really, my lovers are too kind."

Her contemporaries were jealous of her imperturbable good health and the young women of the fact that the mode of 1912, already fulled over the back and front, merely made a successful rallying point around her fine bust. Both old and young equally envied her possession of Chéri.

"Though, good God," said Léa, "there's no reason why they should. They're welcome to him. I don't tie him up, he goes out alone."

In this she lied by half, proud as she was of a liaison—occasionally she called it an "adoption" owing to her weakness for truth—which had lasted for six years.

"The hope-chest," repeated Léa. "Allow Chéri to marry? It's not possible, it's not—human. Give a young girl to Chéri—why not give a doe to dogs? People don't know what Chéri is."

She rolled between her fingers as if it were a rosary the pearl necklace which had been tossed on the bed. She removed it at night now because Chéri, who had a passion for fine pearls and who fondled it in the mornings, would have noted that Léa's throat, in thickening, was losing its whiteness and showing flagging muscles beneath the skin. Now she snapped the jewels around her neck without lifting herself and took a mirror from her night table.

"I look like a gardener's wife," she said with untrammelled judgment. "Like a market-gardener's wife. A Norman market-gardener's wife about to go out into the potato field with a pearl collar on. It's as becoming to me as an ostrich feather stuck up my nose—and I'm polite to let it go at that."

She shrugged her shoulders, severe with all she no longer loved in herself—a hearty complexion, healthy, a little ruddy—the complexion of out-of-doors, well suited to enrich the frank color of her blue eyes. Her proud nose was still pleasing to Léa. "The nose of Marie-Antoinette," Cheri's mother always stated, never forgetting to add: "And in two more years our dear Léa will have the chin of Louis Sixteenth." In harmony with the large eyes which wrinkled slowly and rarely, the mouth opened infrequently to laugh over tight teeth, contenting herself with smiling in a gesture which had been praised a hundred times, sung about, photographed—a profound and confident smile which never tired.

As for her body: "Everyone knows," Léa had said, "that a good body lasts a long time." She could still show it, that great white body tinted with pink, gifted with long limbs and the flat back which one sees on the nymphs of Italian fountains: the dimpled hips, the high breasts "which would hold up," as Léa said, "until well after Chéri's marriage."

She rose, wrapped herself in a dressing-robe and opened her curtains. The noonday sun entered the pink room, bright and over-decorated with a luxuriance that was out-of-date—double lace curtains at the windows, rose-bud pink silk on the walls, gilded wood, electric lights swathed in pink and white, and antique furniture upholstered in modern brocade. Léa refused to give up either this stuffy room or its bed which was something of an indestructible masterpiece of mixed wrought iron and copper, hard on the eye and on the bones. "Oh, come now, come now," Chéri's mother always protested. "It's not so bad as all that. Personally I like this room. It belongs to a period and so it must have style."

Léa smiled at this recollection of the national harpy while twisting up the loose strands of hair. She hurriedly powdered her face on hearing two doors bang and the shock of a booted foot against some fragile piece of furniture. Chérie re-entered in trousers and shirt, without his collar, his ears white with talcum powder, and ill-tempered.

"Where's my scarf-pin? This is a hell of a house. Have they taken to pinching the jewels around here I'd like to know?"

"Marcel's wearing your pearl to do the marketing in," said Léa gravely.

Chéri, devoid of humor, came up against her pleasantry like an ant against a piece of coal. He stopped his angry walking and could find nothing to say but: "Oh. Then,—look here, I'm in a hurry and want my pin and my boots."

"What for? You can't stick your pin in your waistcoat and you already have one pair of shoes on."

Chéri tapped with his foot. "I've had enough of this. Nobody looks after me here and I'm tired of it."

Léa put down her comb. "Then why not leave?"

He shrugged his shoulders rudely. "That's easy enough to say."

"And mean. Go. I hate guests who complain about the service and leave their odds and ends all over the place. Go back to your sainted mother, my son, and stay there."

He failed to hold up under Léa's gaze, dropped his eyes and protested like a school-boy. "My word can't I ever say anything

8

at all? At least you're going to lend me your motor to go to Neuilly?"

"No."

"Why?"

"Because I'm going out at two and Philibert is eating his lunch."

"Where are you going at two o'clock?"

"To say my prayers. But if you need three francs for a taxi . . . Idiot," she said tenderly, "at two o'clock I'm probably going to take coffee at your mother's. Does that satisfy you?"

He shook his head like a young ram. "Everybody abuses me around here, nobody does what I want. They hide my things on me, they . . ."

"Won't you ever learn to dress yourself?" She took from Chéri's hands his collar which she buttoned, his cravat which she knotted. "There. And that awful purple tie! It's just the thing for her highness Marie-Laure and family. And you want to put a pearl pin on top of all that? You little dago! Why not some earrings as well?"

He made no resistance; blissful, soft, vacillating, absorbed by a lassitude and pleasure which closed his eyes. "Nouonune, darling," he murmured, calling her by the name he had given her when he was a child.

She brushed his ears, straightened the blueish parting which divided his black hair, touched his temple with a finger wet with perfume and kissed him quickly because she was unable to resist the invitation of his mouth breathing close to her. Chéri opened his eyes, his lips, stretched his hands.

She evaded. "No. It's quarter to one. Run. And don't let me see you again."

"Ever?"

"Never." She laughed with uncontrollable tenderness.

Alone, she smiled with pride, heaved an uneven sigh of defeated desire and listened to Chéri's footsteps in the court of her private hotel. She saw him open and close the gate, start off with his wingéd walk only to be met by the appreciation of three shop girls, marching arm in arm by the curb.

9

"Oh, mama. He's too good to be true. Wonder would he let us touch him for luck?"

But Chéri, blasé, did not even turn.

2

"MY BATH, Rose. Tell the manicurist she may go—it's too late. My blue tailor-made, the new one. The blue hat, the one faced with white, and my little shoes with the straps. . . . No, wait." Léa, her legs crossed, rubbed her bare ankle and shook her head. "No, my high laced shoes of blue kid. My legs are a little swollen today. It's the heat."

Her maid, aged and with a lace cap, lifted toward Léa a comprehensive glance. "Yes, it must be the heat," she repeated docilely, shrugging her shoulders as if to say, "We know better. Nothing lasts forever."

Chéri out of sight, Léa became lively, precise, relieved. In less than an hour she had been bathed, rubbed with alcohol, scented with sandalwood; her hair had been dressed, her shoes had been laced. While the curling iron heated she had found time to run through her butler's account book, call the under footman, Emile, to show him where he had failed to polish the pier glass. Her competent eye, rarely deceived, darted everywhere and she lunched in contented solitude, smiling at the dry Vouvray wine and at the June strawberries served with their stems in a plate of Rubelles china, green as a wet tree-toad. A good trencherman of an earlier date must have chosen for this rectangular dining-room its huge Louis Sixteenth mirrors and the English furnishings of the same period—lofty buffets, long-legged sideboards, slim solid chairs of dark wood, almost black, carved with slender wreaths. The mirrors and massive service of silver received the abundant light of the day, the green reflection from the trees in the Avenue Bugeaud, and Léa also observed, eating all the while, the red powder clinging between the tines of a fork and half closed an eye, better to judge the polish of the dark woodwork. The butler behind her regarded her investigation with foreboding.

"Marcel," said Léa, "the wax on your floors has been sticky for the last week."

"Sorry, madame, if madame thinks so."

"Well, she does. Add some gasoline and let it melt in a double boiler. It's no work at all. You brought up the Vouvray a little too soon. Pull the curtains as soon as you've cleared the table, the heat is at its worst now."

"Very good, madame. Will Monsieur Ch . . .—Monsieur Peloux dine in tonight?"

"Probably. No *crème-surprise* this evening. Tell them to make us an ice from the juice of the strawberries. And now serve the coffee in the boudoir."

In rising, straight and tall, her legs visible under the skirt that veneered her thighs, she had time to read in the butler's discreet glance, "Madame certainly is a handsome woman," which did not displease her.

Handsome, thought Léa as she mounted the stairs to her boudoir. No more. Now I have to have something white around my face, pink underclothes and tea-gowns. Handsome. Pah! I don't have to be any more.

Still she did not permit herself a siesta in her boudoir of painted silk after she had finished with her coffee and newspapers. And it was with a face set as if going into battle that she said to her chauffeur: "To Madame Peloux's."

The alleyways of the Bois, dry beneath their new June foliage which the wind had faded, the tollgate, Neuilly, the Boulevard d'Inkermann. . . . "How many times have I taken this drive?" Léa asked herself. She counted, then tired of counting and, softening her steps on Madame Peloux's gravel path, reconnoitered to locate the sounds which came from the house.

"They're in the hall," she said.

She had powdered her face again before arriving and wrapped about her chin her blue veil which made a screen as fine as fog. And she responded to the footman who asked her to enter and pass through the house: "No, I'd rather go round by the garden."

A true garden, almost a park, isolated the whiteness of the vast villa set up in Parisian suburbs. Madame Peloux's villa had been called a country residence during the period when Neuilly was still on the outskirts of Paris. The stables, changed into garages, the dog-runs and kennels and the wash-house were still witnesses, as well as the spaciousness of the billiard-hall, the vestibule and the dining-room.

"Madame Peloux certainly got her money's worth," devotedly repeated the old parasites who, in exchange for a dinner and a glass of brandy, assembled to take a hand at besique or poker. And they added: "But whoever knew Madame Peloux to make a bad bargain?"

Marching in the shade of the acacias between the blazing knolls of rhododendrons and the rose-trellis, Léa heard a murmur of voices, pierced by the nasal trumpetings of Madame Peloux and the arid laughter of Chéri.

"As usual, he's laughing out of the wrong side of his mouth, that young man," she mused. She halted a moment to listen more carefully to a new feminine note, weak and amiable and quickly drowned out by the powerful trumpet-tones. That'll be the young girl, Léa thought. She hurried her pace and found herself on the threshold of a glass hall where Madame Peloux rushed forward, crying: "And here's our handsome friend."

The jug-shaped Madame Peloux who was really Mademoiselle Peloux, had been a dancer from her tenth to her sixteenth years. At times Léa hunted in Madame Peloux for something which might recall the chubby little blond Eros of long ago or, later, the dimpled nymph, but could find nothing except the enormous implacable eyes, the fine hard nose and a flirtatious fashion of still pointing out her toes in what was called the "fifth position" in the ballet.

Chéri, pulling himself out from the depths of a rocking chair, kissed Léa's hand with involuntary grace and ruined his gesture by: "For heaven's sake, why have you worn a veil again? I loathe them."

"Will you let her be?" interrupted Madame Peloux. "Don't you know it's not polite to ask a lady why she wears a veil? We'll never be able to do anything with him," she said tenderly to Léa.

Two women had risen in the blond shadow of the straw blind. One in mauve rather coldly offered her hand to Léa who looked her over from head to foot. "Good God, you're lovely, Marie-Laure. You're simply perfection."

Marie-Laure deigned to smile. She was a young woman with red hair and brown eyes who was able to astonish without making a move or speaking a word. She pointed out, as if by coquetry, the other young woman. "But you know my daughter, Edmée," she said.

Léa lifted her hand which the young girl accepted reluctantly. "I should have known who you were; my child, except that school misses change so quickly and that Marie-Laure never changes at all except to grow more ravishing. You're through with boarding school now?"

"Well, I should hope so, I should hope so indeed," cried Madame Peloux. "You can't keep such a marvel of grace and charm under a bushel basket forever, especially when it's only seen nineteen summers."

"Eighteen," said Marie-Laure suavely.

"Eighteen, eighteen. Of course it's only eighteen. Léa, don't you remember? This child was only making her first communion the year that Chéri ran away from school, you know as well as I do. Yes, you did, you little good-for-nothing, you ran away from school and Léa and I were both half out of our minds, poor old things."

"I remember perfectly," said Léa and she exchanged with Marie-Laure a little nod of the head—such as a good fencer makes when his opponent scores a point.

"You ought to marry her off, you ought to marry her off," continued Madame Peloux who never repeated a first-rate truth less than twice. "And we'll all dance at the wedding." She whipped the air with her little arms and the young girl regarded her with adolescent astonishment.

She's a perfect daughter for Marie-Laure, thought Léa watchfully. She has everything within limits which the mother has too much of. Soft ashy hair like powder, troubled secretive eyes, a mouth which evades both speech and smiles. She has everything that Marie-Laure needs but her mother must hate her just the same. . . .

Madame Peloux wedged in a maternal smile between Léa and the young girl. "You should have seen how well those two young people have been hitting it off in the garden." She indicated Chéri who stood smoking in front of the glass partition. He was balancing his cigarette-holder in his teeth and tilting his head to avoid his own smoke. The three women watched the young man who, his forehead at an angle, his lashes half closed, his feet motionless and joined, still seemed to be winged somehow, planing and drowsing in the air. Léa did not miss the frightened conquered expression in the young girl's eyes. She therefore gave herself the pleasure of making her quiver by touching her arm. Edmée trembled the length of her body, drew back her arm and said savagely, inaudibly: "What?"

"Nothing," said Léa. "My glove dropped."

"Shall we go, Edmée?" Marie-Laure commanded carelessly.

The young girl, speechless and docile, walked toward Madame Peloux who flapped her fins. "Already? Oh, no. But we'll see each other again, we'll see each other again."

"It's late," said Marie-Laure. "And then you're expecting a lot of people, it being Sunday afternoon. And this child isn't accustomed to . . ."

"Of course, of course," Madame Peloux cried tenderly. "You've kept her shut up so long, she's had to live so much alone."

Marie-Laure smiled and Léa looked at her as much as to say: "This time it's one on you."

"But we'll see each other soon."

"Thursday, Thursday! Léa, you'll come to dine Thursday, too, won't you?"

"I'll come," responded Léa.

Chéri had rejoined Edmée at the threshold of the hall where he contented himself by standing near her and disdaining speech. He heard Léa's promise and turned: "Good. We'll all take a drive together."

"Yes, yes, just what you young things need," insisted Madame Peloux, touched. "Edmée will sit in front with Chéri and we'll squeeze in the back, the rest of us. Make way for youth! Make way for youth! Chéri, darling, will you ask them to bring around Marie-Laure's car?" Although her tiny round feet slipped and slid upon the gravel she took her guests to the end of the path and then left them to Chéri. When she returned Léa had removed her hat and lighted a cigarette.

"If they aren't too sweet, the pair of them," gasped Madame Peloux. "Don't you think, Léa?"

"Lovely." Léa breathed in a puff of smoke. "But that Marie-Laure . . ."

Chéri came in. "What's Marie-Laure done?" he demanded.

"Nothing—except be beautiful."

"Ah, ah." Madame Peloux approved of this. "It's true, it's true. She really has been awfully pretty."

Chéri and Léa looked at each other and laughed.

"Has been?" Léa underlined. "But she's the picture of youth. She hasn't a wrinkle. And she can wear even pale lilac, that foul color which I hate and which hates me."

The large implacable eyes and the thin nose deserted their glass of brandy. "The picture of youth? The picture of youth?" Madame Peloux squealed. "Pardon me. Pardon me. Marie-Laure had Edmée in 1895—no '94. She had just run off with a singing teacher and turned down Khalil-Bey who had given her that famous pink diamond which— No, no. Wait . . . That was a year earlier. . . ." She was trumpeting at the top of her voice and off key.

Léa put a hand over her ear and Chéri declared sententiously: "It would be too much to expect a whole afternoon without having to put up with mother's voice."

She regarded her son without anger, being accustomed to his insolence and sat down with dignity. Her feet failed to touch the floor, the wicker chair being too high for her short legs. She warmed her glass of brandy in her hand. Léa, balanced in a rocking chair, occasionally glanced at Chéri—Chéri sprawled on a cane couch, his waistcoat unbuttoned, a cigarette dying between his lips, a curl hanging over his eye—and thought to herself: what a good-looking young swine he is.

All of them sat side by side without making any effort to please each other or to speak, at rest and in a certain fashion happy. Being used to each other permitted them to be silent, brought Chéri back to his native fecklessness and Léa to her accustomed calm. Because of the increasing heat Madame Peloux lifted her narrow skirt over her knees, displaying her small sailor-like legs, and Chéri angrily pulled off his cravat, a gesture Léa disapproved by clucking at him: "—Tch, tch."

"Oh, let him alone," Madame Peloux protested as if at the bottom of a dream. "It's so hot. Do you want a kimono, Léa?"

"No, thanks. I'm very comfortable."

The abandoned lack of dignity of these afternoons sickened her. Never had her young lover surprised her by day half-dressed or in house slippers. "Naked if need be," she always said to herself. "But never when I'm neither one thing nor the other." She picked up her illustrated paper and did not read it. —Like mother, like son, she thought. Put either one of the Peloux at a smart dinner table or in the middle of a field and—crack! the mother unhooks her corset and the son unbuttons his vest. They both have the souls of barmaids off duty. She raised her eyes vindictively to one of the barmaids and saw that he slept, his lashes folded down over his white cheeks, his mouth closed. The well-molded arch of his upper lip, illuminated from beneath, caught in its corners two gleams of metallic light and Léa had to admit that he looked more like a god than a beer-drawer. Without rising, she skillfully plucked a lighted cigarette from between Chéri's fingers and tossed it into the ashtray. The sleeper's hand relaxed and like drooping leaves, let fall his pointed fingers tipped with malevolent nails—a hand not exactly feminine but prettier than was necessary—a hand which Léa had kissed a hundred times and not with servility but for the pleasure involved—the perfume.

Over her newspaper she eyed Madame Peloux. —Is she asleep too? Léa liked the siesta of the mother and son to afford her, wide-awake, an hour of complete moral solitude amidst heat, shadow and sun.

But Madame Peloux was not sleeping. She held herself like a Buddha in her wicker-chair, looking straight ahead of her and sucking at her brandy with the eagerness of an alcoholic baby.

"Why isn't she asleep?" Léa asked herself. "It's Sunday. She lunched well. All her old hooligan friends will arrive at five o'clock. So she ought to sleep now. If she's not asleep, it's because she's up to something."

They had known each other for twenty-five years. Theirs was the unfriendly intimacy of kept women that one man enriches, then abandons and still another ruins—the peevish affection of rivals stalking each other's first wrinkle or white hair. Theirs was the comradeship of women with highly defined characters, both shrewd at gathering in the cash, but one was a miser and the other a sybarite. . . . All these old ties between them counted. Another tie had brought them even closer together—Chéri.

Léa could remember Chéri as a baby, a prodigy of long curls. In his infancy he was not yet called Chéri but Fred.

Chéri, by turns adored or forgotten, matured among blotchy maids and tall sardonic valets. Though his birth had coincided with a mysterious rise in the family fortune, no smart English nurse or fraülein was furnished him by his mother who called them all "money-sucking vampires."

"Charlotte Peloux, woman left over from another generation," the old tarnished dying and indestructible Baron de Berthelemy used to say. "Charlotte Peloux, I make my respects to you as the only light woman who ever dared bring up her son as the son of a tart. Woman of another generation, you don't read, you never travel, you're interested only in your neighbors and you leave your son to the tender mercies of bad servants. How perfect! What nineteenth century literary realism! It's as good as any of the worst master-pieces of the period. And to think you never even heard of them."

Chéri enjoyed all the pleasures of a shameless childhood. While he still lisped he picked up the low quips of the butler's pantry. He shared the clandestine supper parties held in the kitchen. He had baths of orris-root in his mother's tub or hasty scrubbings from the corner of a towel. He alternately endured indigestion from too much candy and cramps of hunger when everyone forgot his dinner. He bored himself, half-naked and catching cold, at the flower fêtes where Charlotte Peloux showed him off among roses wet with dew. But he managed to amuse himself royally at the age of twelve in an illicit gambling house where an American woman gave him a fistful of gold pieces to bet and told him he was certainly a little master-piece. About the same time Madame Peloux gave her son a tutor, an abbé who at the end of ten months she dismissed: "Because," she confessed, "that black robe which I saw dragging all about the house made me feel I'd taken in a poor relation—and God knows there's nothing sadder than having a poor relation about the place."

At fourteen Chéri tried boarding school. But he didn't believe in it. He loathed restraint and ran away. Not only did Madame Peloux find the energy to incarcerate him once more but before the tears and insults of her son, she added, hiding her eyes: "Oh, I won't see you cry like that. I won't see you cry." So sincere was this in-ability that as a matter of fact she left town in company with a man who was young if not scrupulous, only to return two years later alone. This was her last emotional sally.

She found Chéri thin from having grown too fast, his eyes sunk in black circles, wearing horsey clothes and talking worse than ever. She beat her breast and jerked Chéri out of boarding school. He refused to work, wanted horses, carriages, jewels, demanded enormous monthly allowances and at the moment when his mother was beating her breast and crying like a pea-hen at the same time, he stopped her with these words:

"Ma'me Peloux, don't get excited. Have no fear that I'll bring you down to sleeping on straw. For all of me you'll die in your own downy bed and with your boots on. . . . I hate lawyers. Let's just say that your purse is mine and don't worry about me or it. . . . Men friends cost nothing—a dinner and a bottle of champagne. As for the pretty ladies, Ma'me Peloux, considering that I'm your child trust me to express my gratitude by giving them no more than a mere trinket—and maybe I won't have to do the giving at all."

He pirouetted while she shed soft tears and proclaimed herself the happiest of mothers. But when Chéri began buying automobiles she began trembling about expenses again until he recommended instead to "just keep an eye on the gasoline bills, if you please, Ma'me Peloux," and thriftily sold the horses. Nor was he above checking up on the expense of the two chauffeurs. His calculations were quick and accurate, his rapid round digits tossed on paper contrasting markedly with his large laborious handwriting.

He passed his seventeenth year in turning into a miniature old man, a fussy little property owner with his nose in everything, still handsome but thin and short-winded. More than once Madame Peloux met him on the basement staircase where he had been counting over the bottles in the wine cellar.

"Can you believe it," said Madame Peloux to Léa. "It's too wonderful."

"Much too wonderful," replied Léa. "He must be ill. Chéri, stick out your tongue."

He protruded it with disrespectful grimaces and other irreverent manifestations which failed to shock Léa, a familiar friend, a sort of doting foster-mother whom he called by her first name.

"Is it true," inquired Léa, "that you were seen last night at a bar with old Lili, sitting on her knees?"

"Her knees," scoffed Chéri. "She hasn't had any for years. They disappeared long ago."

"Is it true," insisted Léa more severely, "that she made you drink gin with pepper in it? Don't you know that that'll ruin your stomach?"

One day Chéri, wounded, responded to Léa's interrogation: "I don't know why you ask me questions—you ought to know what I was doing since you were there in the little loge in the back with Patron, the prize fighter."

"That's perfectly true," said Léa impassively. "But Patron is somebody. He's no dissipated little whipper-snapper like some people I know. He has something else in his favor beside tuppenny cheek and black circles under his eyes."

That week Chéri capped the climax by staying up all night in Montmartre and at the Markets with women who called him "the kid" and "passion flower," but he found no pleasure. His head ached and he coughed constantly. And Madame Peloux who confided to her masseuse, to Madame Ribot, to her corset-maker, to old Lili, to Berthellemy-le-Desséché, her heart-breaking announcement: "Ah, for us mothers life is a perfect calvary," passed without a pain from the state of happiest-of-mothers to that of mother-martyr.

A night in June which assembled Madame Peloux, Léa and Chéri in the conservatory at Neuilly changed the destinies of the young man and the already matured woman. The chance that for the evening had scattered Chéri's so-called friends—a little wholesale wine merchant known as the young Bolster, and the Vicomte Desmond, a parasite barely of age, difficult and haughty—brought Chéri back to the maternal roof where habit had also drawn Léa.

Twenty years, a past made up of similar wan evenings, a lack of friends, also that defiance and weakness which toward the end of their lives isolate women who have loved only love, settled them face to face for one more night to be endured while waiting for another identical evening,—these two women, each suspect in the other's eyes. Both stared at the taciturn Chéri. Madame Peloux, without the force of authority to take her son in hand, limited herself to hating Léa a little each time a gesture bent her white throat, her healthy cheek toward the pale cheek and transparent ears of the boy. She would willingly have bled the robust neck of the woman where the wrinkles shaped like the girdle of Venus had begun to weigh on the flesh, in order to dye red the greenish-white lily her son resembled. Yet it did not occur to her to transplant her frail flower to the country.

"Chéri, why do you drink brandy?" Léa scolded.

"In order to keep company with Ma'me Peloux who otherwise would have to drink alone," Chéri answered.

"What are you doing tomorrow?"

"Don't know. And you?"

"I'm going to Normandy."

"With—?"

"That's none of your affair."

"With our good friend Spéleïeff?"

"You're behind the times. That was over two months ago. Spéleïeff is in Russia."

"Chéri, my dear, you'd forget your head if it weren't fastened on. Don't you remember the charming desertion dinner Léa invited us to last month after he left her? Léa, you haven't given me the recipe for those lobsters I liked so much."

Chéri sat up, his eyes brightening greedily. "Oh, yes, lobsters swimming in cream sauce. Oh, I'd love to have some."

"You see," Madame Peloux said reproachfully, "he has no appetite at all and yet he would have loved some lobsters with . . ."

"Oh, shut up," Chéri ordered. "Léa, are you seeking the shady countryside in company with Patron?"

"I am not, my dear. Patron and I are merely friends. I'm going alone."

"Oh, rich enough to go alone, eh?" Chéri tossed off.

"I'll take you along, if you like. There'll be nothing to do but eat, drink and sleep . . ."

"What deserted village are you going to?" He arose and stood in front of her.

"You know Honfleur? And the Côte de Grâce? Sit down, you're turning quite green. You know, on the Côte de Grâce that old gate where your mother and I always said each time we drove by . . ."

She turned toward Madame Peloux. Madame Peloux had disappeared. This discreet conniving flight, this fading away, was so little like the normal Charlotte Peloux that Léa and Chéri looked at each other and laughed with surprise. Chéri sat down and leaned against Léa.

"I'm tired," he said.

"You're ruining yourself," Léa said.

In his vanity he sat more erect. "Oh, I don't know. I'm still good enough."

"Good enough. Perhaps for others but not—not good enough for me, for instance."

"Too green?"

"Just the word I was looking for. Just between friends, why don't you come to the country? Ripe strawberries, fresh cakes and cream, broiled spring chickens . . . that'll be your diet and no women."

He let himself slip against Léa's shoulder and closed his eyes. "No women. Fine. . . . Léa, you'll be a real friend to me, won't you? Then let's go. . . . Women? I'm through with them. I've seen enough."

He said these things in a drowsy voice whose full soft force Léa caught with its warm breath against her ear. He had taken hold of Léa's long necklace and rolled the large pearls between his fingers. She put her arm beneath his head and, accustomed as she was to the boy, pulled him toward her without second thought and rocked him.

"How nice," he breathed. "You're going to be a real friend to me and this is so comfortable."

She smiled as if highly praised. Chéri seemed to be sleeping. She looked down at his eyelashes, shining as though damp, spread on his cheek and at the cheek itself which bore the traces of fatigue without happiness. His upper lip shaved that morning was already turning blue and the pink lamps afforded his mouth a fictitious color of blood.

"No women," Chéri declared as if dreaming. "Then . . . kiss me."

Surprised, Léa did not move.

"Kiss me, I tell you." He made his demand, frowning, and the flash of his eyes, suddenly opened, confused Léa like a lamp suddenly relighted. She shrugged her shoulders and placed a kiss on his forehead. He locked his arms around her neck and pulled her toward him.

She shook her head but only until their lips touched. At that moment she became motionless and held her breath like someone listening. When he released her she detached herself, rose, breathed deeply and rearranged her hair which had not been disturbed. Then a little pale and her eyes darkened, she turned to him and said as if making a pleasantry: "That was clever of you."

He moved to the depths of a rocking chair and said nothing while he brooded over her with a glance so energetic, so full of defiance and interrogations that she said after a moment: "Well, what is it?"

"Nothing," Chéri answered. "I found out something that I wanted to know."

She blushed, humiliated, but defended herself dexterously: "What have you found out? That your mouth pleased me? My poor boy, I've kissed uglier. What does that prove? You think I'm going to fall at your feet and beg you to make me yours? You must know nobody but young girls. Do you think I would lose my head because of a kiss?" She felt calmer in speaking and wished to show her nonchalance. "Listen, my dear," she said leaning over him. "Do you think that would be so rare among my memories—a handsome mouth?" She smiled from above him, sure of herself, but she did not know that something rested on her face, a sort of faint palpitation, an attractive sadness, and that her smile looked like those that follow on a fit of weeping. "I have nothing to be afraid of," she went on. "If we kissed again or even if we . . ." She stopped and made a gesture of contempt. "No. No, I really can't see us doing that."

"You didn't see us doing what we just did a moment ago either," said Chéri without haste. "But you gave it all your attention for several minutes. You've already thought of going further? It wasn't I that suggested it."

They took each other's measure like enemies. She feared to show a desire which she had not yet had time either to nourish or dissimulate, and she resented this youth, become chilled in a moment, perhaps mocking.

"You're right," she conceded lightly. "Let's say no more about it. Let us say instead that I offer you a nice country field for you to graze in and good food—mine, in other words."

"We'll see," responded Chéri. "Shall I bring along my Renouhard runabout?"

"Naturally, you're not going to leave it with Charlotte."

"I'll pay for the gasoline but you'll pay for the chauffeur's meals."

Léa burst out laughing. "I'll pay for the chauffeur? Ah, you're your mother's own son, all right. You never forget a thing. I'm not naturally curious but I should like to hear what you call a tender conversation between you and a woman."

She sat down and fanned herself. A moth and insects with long legs turned about the lamps and the odor of the garden because of the coming of night became the odor of the country. A gust from the acacias bore down on them, so distinct, so powerful, that they both turned as if to see it arriving on foot.

"It's the acacias with the pink clusters," Léa said under her breath.

"Yes," Chéri said. "But tonight they've stolen their perfume from the orange trees."

She watched him, vaguely admiring his having thought of such an idea. He breathed the scent that victimized, contented him and she walked away, suddenly fearful that he might not recall her. But he called and she came toward him.

She came to kiss him with a burst of resentment and selfishness and thoughts of punishment.— Wait, she thought. Now it's my turn. It's only too true that you have a pretty mouth and this time I'm going to take my fill because I want to— and then I'll laugh at you, I'll walk off. What do I care? It's my turn. . . . Now. . . .

She kissed him. They became drunk, deaf, breathless, trembling as if they had been fighting. She drew back above him, he not having moved from the depths of his chair, and she defied him half under her breath:—"Well? . . . Well?" and waited to be insulted. But he held out his arms, opened his beautiful vague hands, tilted his head as if struck and showed beneath his lashes the double brightness of two tears while he murmured words, complaints, a whole animal and amorous chant in which she distinguished her name, the words "darling," "together," "never leave you . . ." a chant which she heard, leaning over him with anxiety as if she had inadvertently wounded him.

Whenever Léa recalled her first summer in Normandy, she always said impartially: "In the way of spoiled brats, I've had several in my time who were more amusing than Chéri, also less disagreeable and more intelligent. But just the same I've never known one exactly like him."

"It's funny," she confided to Berthellemy-le-Desséché at the end of the summer of 1906, "there are moments when I think I'm sleeping with a Negro or a Chinaman."

"Have you ever had a Chinaman or a Negro?"

"Never."

"Well?"

"I don't know. I can't explain it. But I have that impression."

It was an impression that had come to her slowly with at the same time an astonishment that she had not always known how to hide. The first souvenirs of their idyll consisted only of fine food, of choice fruits and of her worries as a country housewife with refined city tastes. In her mind she could still see Chéri, paler than ever in the sunlight, an exhausted Chéri who dragged about under the Norman hedges and slept on the warm banks of the ponds. Léa waked him to stuff him with strawberries, cream, frothy milk and chicken. As if in a daze he followed with wide empty eyes the flight of moths around the basket of roses on the dinner table, looked at his wrist watch to see if it were not time to go to bed, while Léa, deceived but without resentment, thought of the promises which the kisses at Neuilly had failed to fulfill. Until the end of August if necessary, I'll keep him out to graze. But once in Paris, *ouf!* I'll hand him back to whoever wants him.

She went to bed mercifully early so that Chéri, seeking refuge against her, pushing with his nose and forehead and selfishly hollowing out a fine place to relax, might sleep. Sometimes, the lamp extinguished, her eyes settled on a streak of moonlight glittering on the polished floor. Mixed with the quivering of the aspen tree outside and the shrilling of crickets which ceased neither by night or day, she listened to the breathing, deep like that of a hunting dog, which agitated Chéri's breast.

"What's wrong with me that I don't sleep?" she asked herself vaguely. "It's not his little head on my shoulder—I've held heavier. . . . What marvellous weather we're having. For tomorrow I've ordered some good porridge for him. He already has a little fat on his bones. . . . What's wrong with me that I can't sleep? Oh, yes, I remember, I'm going to send for Patron, the boxer, to train the boy. With me on one side and Patron on the other, we'll show Madame Peloux something in the way of a son that will astonish her."

She fell asleep, a tall woman stretched beneath clean sheets and on the flat of her back, the black head of her disagreeable young charge resting on her right breast. She slept, occasionally wakened —but how rarely—by some desire of Chéri's at daybreak.

The second month of their retreat finally brought Patron, his big valise, his little dumbells of a pound and a half each, and his black tights, his four-ounce gloves and his boxing shoes laced down over his toes—Patron of the gentle voice, long eyelashes and fine tanned skin so much like that of his valise that he did not look naked when he took off his shirt. And Chéri, by turns spiteful, lazy, or jealous of the serene strength of Patron, began the painful and fruitful movements of slow and oft repeated gymnastics.

"One and . . . two and . . . I can't hear you breathing . . . three and . . . Don't think you're fooling me by bending your knee. . . ."

The foliage of the lime trees filtered the August sunlight. A thick red carpet spread on the gravel painted purple the nude bodies of the pupil and his teacher. Léa's eyes followed the lesson attentively. During the fifteen minutes of boxing, Chéri, drunk with his new strength and excited, tried unfair blows and turned red with fury.

Patron stood up under his lunges like a rock and from the height of his glorious sportsmanship let fall on Chéri remarks which carried even more weight than his celebrated fist.

"Careful there. If I hadn't caught myself in time that wandering left eye of yours would have known what my right glove feels like."

"I slipped," said Chéri in a rage.

"It isn't a question of balance," continued Patron. "It's a question of morale. You'll never make a boxer."

"My mother is against it."

"Even if your mother weren't you'd never make a boxer because you're bad-tempered. A mean disposition and boxing don't go together, do they, Madame Léa?"

Léa smiled and tasted the pleasure of feeling warm, of remaining motionless and watching the game between two men, both stripped, both young, whom she compared in silence.—Isn't he a handsome creature, that Patron? He's fine, like a well-built house. And the boy is shaping up beautifully. One doesn't see knees like his every day or I'm no judge. His back is—no, will be—marvellous. How in the devil did Mother Peloux happen to have a child like that? His neck's set on his body like a perfect statue. And how mean he is. When he laughs one would swear it was a greyhound snapping. She felt happy and maternal, bathed in peaceful virtue. "I'd exchange him for almost anyone else," she would say to herself with Chéri at her side in the afternoon under the lime trees, or Chéri in the morning on her ermine rug, or Chéri in the evening by the edges of the tepid pond. "Yes, handsome as he is, I'd willingly exchange him if it weren't a question of principle." She confided her indifference to Patron.

"And yet," Patron objected, "the boy's well-built. Already he has muscles like some of those colored foreigners, though he's as white as milk. Nice little muscles that don't show much. You'll never see Chéri with biceps like cantaloupes."

"I should hope not, Patron. But personally, I didn't take him on for boxing, you know."

"Oh, naturally," acquiesced Patron, dropping his long lashes.

"There's the heart interest that has to be considered." He was always embarrassed by Léa's unveiled sensual allusions and her smile; that insistent smile which she turned on him whenever she spoke of love. "Naturally," Patron started again, "if he isn't perfectly satisfactory. . . ."

Léa laughed. "Perfectly? Hardly. My sole pleasure comes from my impersonal interest in him. In this case I'm like you, Patron."

"Oh, I." He feared and hoped for the question which did not fail to follow.

"Still the same, Patron? You still stick to your point?"

"I still stick to it, Madame Léa. I just had a letter from Liane by the noon post. She says that she's alone, that I have no reason for being so obstinate, that her two friends have left."

"Well?"

"Well, I don't think it's true. And I'm obstinate only because she's obstinate. She's ashamed, she says, of a man who works for his living, above all a living which forces him to get up early in the morning, to train every day, to give boxing lessons and high class gymnastics. The moment we meet there's always a scene. 'You might think,' she says, 'that I'm not glad to support the man I love.' It's handsome of her, I don't deny it, but it isn't included in my set of ideas. I suppose I'm odd. As you so well put it, Madame Léa, it's an affair of principle."

They talked in low tones beneath the trees, he modest and half-naked, she dressed in white, her cheeks a vigorous pink. They savored the pleasure of their mutual friendliness born from similar tastes that led them toward simplicity, health and a sort of gentility of their low world. And yet Léa would not have been shocked had Patron received from the beautiful Liane who was having a great vogue, suitably magnificent presents. Give and take. And she attempted to break down what Patron called his oddness by antique arguments about justice. Their slow conversations which revealed each time the presence of their same gods—love and money—would drift away from both to come back to Chéri, to his faulty upbringing, to his extraordinary beauty which was "inoffensive on the whole," said Léa, and to his character which she had decided was absolutely non-existent. Long conversations which expressed their need for assurance and their horror of new words or ideas, speeches troubled by the unexpected appearance of Chéri whom they thought either asleep or motoring down some hot road—Chéri who loomed in sight half-naked but equipped with an account book and a pencil behind his ear.

"Here comes the chief clerk," Patron said cheerfully. "He's got the entire office force with him."

"What does this mean?" Chéri cried from afar. "This three hundred and twenty francs for gasoline? Somebody must be drinking it. We've been out four times in fifteen days. And seventy francs more for oil."

"The car goes over to the market every day," responded Léa. "And by the way, it seems that your chauffeur ate three helpings of mutton yesterday for lunch. Don't you think he's straining our contract a little? When the high cost of something sticks in your gullet you look just like your mother."

Devoid of reply, he rested a moment uncertain, oscillating on his slender feet, balancing with that flying grace of a young Mercury which always made Madame Peloux swoon with pride and squeal: "Me when I was eighteen! Feet with wings on 'em, feet with wings!" He hunted for some impudent reply and his face quivered, his mouth opened, his forehead dropped in a strained expression which made obvious the peculiar diabolic twist of his eyebrows.

"There, there, don't try to think of anything," said Léa simply. "Yes, yes, you loathe me. Come here and give me a kiss. Handsome devil. Good-looking imp. Little fool."

He came, conquered by her voice and offended by her words. Before this astonishing couple Patron once again let the truth flower from his wise lips.

"For a good physique, Monsieur Chéri, you have a good physique. But whenever I look at you, it seems to me that if I were a woman I'd say, 'I'll come back again ten years from now.'"

"You hear, Léa? He says in another ten years," insinuated Chéri, evading the head of his mistress bent toward him. "What do you think of that?"

But she did not deign to hear and tapped her hand all over the young body which owed her its renewed vigor, touching it anywhere, on the cheek, the leg, the hip, with the irreverent pleasure of a child's nurse.

"What satisfaction does it give you to be unkind?" Patron demanded of Chéri.

Chéri slowly enveloped the Hercules in an impenetrable barbarous glance before replying: "It consoles me. You wouldn't understand."

Truth to tell, neither had Léa managed to understand Chéri even at the end of three months of intimacy. If she still talked to Patron who only came now on Sundays, or to Berthellemy-le-Desséché who arrived without being invited but left two hours later, about "giving Chéri back to whoever wanted him," it was because the phrase had become a sort of tradition and to excuse herself for having kept him so long. She continued delaying the day for his departure and delayed each delay. She was waiting.

"The weather is so fine. . . . And then his trip to Paris last week tired him. . . . And besides it's better that I really get fed up with him."

For the first time in her life she waited in vain for what had never before failed to arrive: the trust, the relaxation, confessions, truthfulness, the indiscreet expansiveness of a young lover—those hours all through the night when the quasi-filial gratitude of an adolescent unrestrainedly poured young tears, secrets and troubles on the warm breast of the ripe sure friend.

—I always had it before, she thought obstinately. So I always knew what they were worth, what they thought and what they wanted. But this brat, this boy—it's really too much.

Robust now, proud of his nineteen years, gay at table and impatient in bed, he gave nothing of himself except himself and so remained mysterious to Léa. He was tender if tenderness could be proved by his involuntary cries, the involuntary tightening of his arms. But his unkindness always returned to him with speech and the constant fear of being transparent to another human being. How many times at dawn Léa held in her arms a lover contented, assuaged, the eyes half-closed like his mouth into which life seemed to flow back each morning, each embrace making it handsomer than the night before: how many times, herself defeated in such an hour by her instinct to conquer and the voluptuous desire to hear a confession, had she pressed her forehead against his, murmuring: "Talk, say something. Speak to me."

But no avowals ever moved his curved lips and few words except sulky or wild apostrophes built about the name "Nounoune," which, though he had given it to her when he was a child, he now fell back on at the height of his pleasure like a cry for help.

"Really, I assure you he's like a Chinaman or a Negro," she declared to Anthime de Berthellemy and added, "I can't explain." She was nonchalant and awkward at defining her impression, strong but confused that she and Chéri did not speak the same language.

September had ended when they returned to Paris. The first evening Chéri went directly to Neuilly on purpose to astonish Madame Peloux. He tossed the chairs into the air, cracked nuts with a blow of his fist, jumped over the billiard table and played cowboy in the garden at the heels of the terrified watch dogs.

"*Ouf!*" sighed Léa on entering alone into her house in the Avenue Bugeaud. "How nice an empty bed is."

But the next night while she was sipping her coffe at ten o'clock and forbidding herself to find the evening long and the dining-room too big, the sudden apparition of Chéri, upright in the frame of the door, Chéri arrived on quiet winged feet, pulled from her a nervous outcry. Sulky, silent, he ran toward her.

"Are you mad?"

He shrugged his shoulders, disdainful of explanations, and merely ran toward her. He asked her no questions such as, "Do you love me? Have you already forgotten me?" He ran toward her.

Later in Léa's great metal bed, Chéri feigned sleep, weariness, the better to grit his teeth and batten down his eyes, a prey to his fury of speechlessness. But still she heard him, lying next to him, listened with delight to the delicate vibration, the distant and defeated tumult throbbing in a body that denied its agony, its gratitude and its love.

"Why didn't your mother tell me this herself last night at dinner?"

"She thought it better that I should mention it."

"No!"

"That's what she said."

"And you?"

"What about me?"

"You think it's better too?"

Chéri lifted an uncertain glance toward Léa. "Yes." He seemed to think a moment and repeated, "Yes, yes, of course, can't you see it is?"

In order not to embarrass him, Léa turned her eyes toward the window. A tepid rain blackened the August morning and fell in straight lines on the three plantain trees, already turning rust-color, in the gardened court. "It's like autumn," she said and sighed.

"What's the matter?" demanded Chéri.

She regarded him with astonishment. "Nothing. I simply don't like the rain."

"Oh, good. I thought that . . ."

"What?"

"I thought you were unhappy."

She was unable to check her frank laughter. "Unhappy because you're going to get married? Oh, no, listen, you're . . . you're absurd." She rarely laughed outright and her good-nature vexed Chéri. He shrugged his shoulders and lit a cigarette with his customary grimaces, his chin thrust out, his under lip protruding.

"You shouldn't smoke before lunch," said Léa.

He answered impertinently but she did not hear him, occupied as she was at listening to the sound of her own voice and the echo of her daily mechanical advice coming back in repercussion over a distance of the last five years. —It's like seeing oneself in a series of mirrors, she mused. Then with a slight effort she tried to come back to reality and good humor. "I'm in luck, passing on to someone else the job of keeping you from smoking on an empty stomach."

"She's not going to have a word to say about anything," declared Chéri. "I'll marry her, you see? She'll have the privilege of worshipping at my feet and blessing the day she was born. And that's the way it's going to be managed."

He exaggerated the thrust of his chin, tightened his teeth on his cigarette holder, opened his lips and only succeeded in looking like an Asiatic prince in white pyjamas and with skin paled from the impenetrable darkness of the palace.

Léa, nonchalant in her dressing robe of a pink she called "chronic" with her, brought together the ideas which were tiring her and which, one after the other, she decided to throw against the feigned calm of Chéri. "Well, why are you marrying the little girl, then?"

His elbows on the table, he unconsciously imitated the set face of his mother. "Oh, you understand, dearie . . ."

"Call me Madame or Léa. I'm neither one of your housemaids nor a playmate of your own age." She lifted herself in her divan and spoke dryly without raising her voice. He wanted to make a quick reply, brave the beautiful face a little bruised under its powder, and the eyes which covered him with their frank blue light, but he softened and conceded in a tone which was not habitual to him:

"Nounoune, you asked me to explain to you. . . . It would have to happen some day anyhow. And besides there are big interests at stake."

"Whose?"

"Mine," he said without a trace of humor. "The girl has a large personal fortune."

"From her father?"

He rocked in his chair, his feet aloft. "Oh, how do I know? You ask too much. I suppose it's from her father, though. You wouldn't expect her highness Marie-Laure to draw fifteen hundred thousand out of her own bank account, would you? Fifteen hundred thousand and some high class jewels besides."

"And how much have you?"

33

"Oh, I've more than that of my own," he said with pride.

"Then why do you need any more money?"

He shook his smooth head where the daylight ran in waves. "Need . . . need . . . ? You know we haven't the same ideas about money. So there's no point in our talking about it."

"I'll do you the justice to say that you've spared me from any references to it during the past five years." She leaned toward him and put her hand on his knee:—"Tell me, my dear, how much have you put by from your income in these five years?"

He jumped like a clown, laughed and rolled at Léa's ankles, but she pushed him aside with her foot. "No, tell me the truth. Fifty thousand a year? Sixty? Tell me. Seventy thousand?"

He settled on the carpet, leaned his head on her knees. "Wouldn't I be worth that much?"

He stretched himself at full length, turned his head, opened wide his eyes which seemed black but whose true color Léa knew to be a heavy rusted brown. As if to point out and choose what was finest among all his charms, she touched her forefinger to his lashes, his eyelids, the corner of his mouth. At moments the outward form of this lover whom she slightly despised inspired her with a kind of respect. To be as handsome as that amounts to a sort of nobility, she thought. "Tell me, darling—and the young lady in the case—how does she feel toward you?"

"She loves me. She admires me. And she never says anything."

"And you—how do you feel toward her?"

"I don't feel at all," he answered simply.

"What charming tender moments you must pass together," said Léa dreamily.

He reared himself and sat tailor-fashion. "It seems to me that you think entirely too much about her," he said severely. "Can't you consider yourself at all in this tragedy?"

She gazed at Chéri with an astonishment which made her look young, her eyebrows lifted, her lips apart.

"Yes, you, Léa. You, the victim. You should have the sympathy in all this because I'm deserting you." He had become a little pale and in his attack on her seemed also to wound himself.

Léa smiled. "But, darling, I have no intention of changing my life. For a week from time to time I'll find a pair of socks, a cravat, a handkerchief, on my shelves. A week? Not even that. You know how often I tidy my shelves. Oh, yes, and I'll have the bathroom redone. I've a notion to use encrusted glass. . . ."

She fell silent and took on a ruminative air, her finger tracing a vague plan in space. Still Chéri would not soften his vindictive manner. "But what is it you want?" she said. "Do you expect me to go to Normandy to hide my grief? To get thin? To stop dyeing my hair? To have your mother running to my bedside?" She imitated Madame Peloux's trumpet tones and flapped her arms.—'She's just a shadow of her former self, just a shadow of her former self. The poor thing has aged a hundred years, a hundred years.' Is that what you want?"

He listened with a brusque laugh and a trembling of his nostrils which might have been emotion. "Yes," he cried.

Léa placed on Chéri's shoulders her heavy, bare, polished arms. "My poor boy. But at that rate I would already have been dead four or five times. To lose a little lover. . . . To exchange one disagreeable youngster. . . ." She added in a lower, lighter voice: "I'm used to it."

"It's a well-known fact," he said harshly. "I don't give a damn,— you hear me?—I don't care a God damn that I wasn't your first lover. What I would have liked to be, or rather what I wished, what would be fitting, decent, is that I should be your last." With a turn of his shoulders he made her superb arms fall. "After all, what I am saying you now is for your own good."

"I understand perfectly. You think only of me, I think only of your fiancée. It's marvellous, just what one might expect. It's plain to be seen that we're all noble, self-sacrificing souls." She rose, waiting for him to give her some blackguardly response but he said nothing and she suffered at seeing for the first time on Chéri's face a sort of discouragement. She bent and put her hands under his arms. "Now, now, come along, finish dressing. I have only to put on my frock, I'm ready underneath and what on earth can we do on a rainy day like this except to go to Schwab and pick out a pearl for you? After all I must certainly give you a wedding present."

35

He jumped up, his face shining. "Wonderful! Oh, yes, a pearl for my shirt front, a pale pink pearl, I know which one."

"Never in the world, a white one, something masculine, for pity's sake. Don't tell me, I know which one just as well as you. It'll ruin me as usual. However, think of all the money I'm going to save once you're out of the house."

Chéri took on his reticent air. "Oh, that . . . that depends on my successor."

Léa turned at the threshold of the boudoir and showed her gayest smile, her strong sybaritic teeth, her eyes with their easily deepened blue. "Your successor? Forty sous and his pipe tobacco. Oh, and a glass of blackberry cordial on Sundays—that's all the job will be worth. And I'll settle money on all your offspring."

They both became very gay during the weeks which followed. The official betrothal of Chéri separated them for a few hours each day and occasionally for a night or so. "We mustn't make them lose heart," Chéri declared. Léa, whom Madame Peloux kept at a safe distance from Neuilly, satisfied her curiosity by plying Chéri with hundreds of questions, he being heavy with secrets which he scattered the moment he crossed her door sill, burlesquing everything as soon as he had Léa in sight.

"My friends," he cried one day, clapping his hat on Léa's portrait bust. "My friends, wait till you hear what's been going on at the Peloux's palace since last night."

"Take your hat off of that in the first place. And secondly don't mention your lousy friends around here. Well, what is it now?" she scolded, already laughing in anticipation.

"A riot, Nounoune. A riot between the ladies. Marie-Laure and Ma'me Peloux have taken to pulling out each other's hair over my marriage contract—you know—whether the girl's money is to be put in my care or not. A riot, I tell you."

"No!"

"Yes! It was a superb sight. Be careful of the hors-d'oeuvres while I give you an imitation of Ma'me Peloux's arms. 'Separate bank accounts? Why not put a sheriff to over-see what my son does with the family cash? It's a personal insult, a personal insult. After all my son is monied in his own right, I want you to know, madame. . . .' "

"She called her madame?"

"Large as life. 'I want you to know, madame, that my son is used to money, that my son has never had a sou of debts since he came of age and the list of his investments bought since 1910 is worth . . .' is worth this, that, the other, including the end of my nose, plus the meat on my backsides. In brief, she was Catherine de Medici all over, only slightly more diplomatic."

Léa's blue eyes shone with tears of mirth. "Chéri, you've never been so funny since I've known you. And the other, her highness Marie-Laure—what was she like?"

"She? Oh, terrible, Nounoune. That woman must have left a trail of twenty-five dead men in her wake. Dressed up all in jade green, red hair as usual, marvellous complexion—in a word eighteen years old but with her smile. All my venerated parent's trumpetings failed to budge her an inch. She waited to the end of the solo to say, 'It would perhaps be better, my dear madame, not to talk too much about all the money your son saved in 1910 and the following years. . . .' "

"Bang! Right in the eye. Right in yours, I mean. Where were you when all this was going on?"

"I? In the big armchair."

"You were present?" She ceased laughing and eating. "You were there? What did you do?"

"Said something witty naturally. Ma'me Peloux had already picked up one of her most valuable pieces of bric-a-brac to throw at Marie-Laure's head to avenge my honor when I stopped her without even leaving my seat. 'Dear, darling mother, calm yourself,' I said. 'Copy me, copy my charming mother-in-law who's as sweet as honey —or sugar.' And that's where I won the day. The marriage contract will be made out so that any money the girl may possibly—mind you, possibly—inherit after the wedding, will belong equally to both of us."

"But I don't understand."

"The famous sugar plantations which the poor little old Prince Ceste willed to Marie-Laure. . . ."

"Yes?"

"The will's illegal. The Ceste family's up in arms. There'll probably be a lawsuit. Now do you follow?" he crowed.

"I follow, but how did you know all that?"

"Ah-ha! The old Lili has just thrown herself at the head of the old prince's son who is seventeen years old and a good little boy."

"The old Lili? How awful!"

"And the Ceste boy murmured the family secrets while lying in Lili's arms. . . ."

"Chéri! You're making me sick."

"And the old Lili gave me the tip at mama's at-home last Sunday. She adores me, that old Lili. She's very appreciative of me because I never tried to make love to her."

"I should hope not," sighed Léa. "And yet—" As she began reflecting Chéri felt she lacked enthusiasm.

"Well, aren't I smart? Aren't I?" He leaned over the table. The sunshine on its silver dishes was like a footlight brightening his face. "Don't you think so?"

"Yes." She thought: He doesn't resent it. That poisonous Marie-Laure treated him flatly like a renter—a sponger—a . . .

"Is there some *fromage à la crème,* Nounoune?"

"Yes." She thought: And he was no more offended than if she'd presented him with a flower for his button-hole.

"Nounoune, will you give me that address? The address of the place where you get your *fromage à la crème* for my new cook I've engaged for October?"

"What are you thinking of? My chef makes them here in the house. Your cook won't be capable of much more than mussel stew and custards." And she continued to herself: I suppose it's true that for five years I've practically kept the boy. But just the same he has an income from three hundred thousand francs. Can a man be called a sponger who has three hundred thousand francs? Though why not, it doesn't depend on the money but on the man. There are men I could have given a half million to but they wouldn't have been spongers. But how about Chéri? After all I've never actually given him money. Just the same though . . . "Just the same," she burst into speech, "she treated you as if you were a disgusting little gigolo."

"Who did?"

"Marie-Laure."

He brightened up like a child. "Didn't she? Didn't she now? Nounoune, that's what she meant, didn't she?"

"I have that impression."

Chéri lifted his glass filled with Château-Chalon which was the color of brandy. "Then here's to Marie-Laure. Quite a compliment, she paid me, eh? And if they can still say it about me when I'm your age, I won't ask anything better."

"If that's what will make you happy—"

She listened distractedly through the end of the luncheon. Accustomed to the half-silences of his reliable friend, he was satisfied with her constant maternal phrases: "Take the brownest crusts of bread. . . . Don't eat so rapidly. . . . You never know how to choose the best peach. . . ." All the while, secretly smoldering, she tried to calm herself by thinking:—At any rate I must make up my mind what it is I wanted. What did I expect him to do? Draw himself up and hiss, "Madame, you have insulted me. Madame, I am not the vile creature you think." After all, I'm the one who's really responsible. I've brought him up on a silver platter, I gave him everything he wanted. Who would ever have thought that one day he would want to play at being married? Certainly I never had such an idea. As Patron said, "Blood will tell." If Patron had ever accepted the propositions of his Liane and anyone had called him a gigolo, his blood would have boiled. But Chéri has Peloux blood. He's just straight Chéri. He's . . .

"What were you saying, my dear?" she interrupted herself to ask. "I wasn't listening."

"I said that nothing, absolutely nothing, will ever give me a bigger laugh than my tiff with Marie-Laure."

—There you are, Léa managed to tell herself, he only thought it was funny. She rose with a weary movement. Chéri put his arm about her waist but she evaded. "What day is your marriage?"

"A week from Monday."

He seemed so innocent and detached that she was bewildered. "But it's fantastic."

"Why fantastic, Nounoune?"

"You don't look as if you thought about it at all."

"I don't," he said tranquilly. "I don't have to. Everything's arranged. Ceremony at two o'clock which lets us out of inviting everyone to an expensive lunch. Tea at five at Ma'me Peloux's. And then the night train, private compartment, Italy, the lakes . . ."

"Are the lakes still being done?"

"They are. Then there'll be villas, and there'll be hotels, limousines and restaurants, and then there'll even be Monte Carlo, eh?"

"And the girl," she protested. "You've forgotten her."

"And the girl, of course. There's not much of her but she'll be with me."

"And I won't be, ever again."

Chéri did not expect her words and showed it. A sickened twist of his eyes and a sudden discoloration of his mouth disfigured him. He caught his breath with caution so she should not hear it and became himself again. "Nounoune, there'll always be you."

"Monsieur overwhelms me."

"There'll always be you, Nounoune. . . ." He laughed awkwardly. "As long as you can do anything for me."

She did not answer. Humming, she bent to pick up a pin of tortoise shell that had fallen and inserted it again in her hair. She prolonged her song complacently before the mirror, proud of having conquered herself so easily, of having successfully hidden the only emotional moment of their separation, proud of having held back the words which must not be said: "Speak, ask for whatever you want, demand it, put your arms about my throat, you have just made me happy."

Madame Peloux must have been talking a great deal and for a long time before Léa's entry. The fire in her cheeks added to the sparkle of her big eyes which ordinarily never expressed anything except indiscreet and impervious watchfulness. This Sunday she was wearing a black afternoon gown with an exaggeratedly tight skirt and no one could fail to see either that her feet were tiny or that she was corseted too high. She stopped talking, took a little swallow from the goblet which was becoming tepid in her hand and bent her head toward Léa with happy languor. "Isn't it a beautiful day? Such weather! Such weather! Could anyone believe it was October?"

"Yes, could they? Oh, certainly not," two servile voices murmured.

A stream of red sage flowed down the length of the path between rivers of asters whose lilac was almost gray. Yellow butterflies flickered through the air as in summer but the smell of seasonal chrysanthemums over-heated in the sun, entered the open hall. A yellowing birch tree trembled in the wind above a rose arbor which captivated the last of the bees.

"But," suddenly declaimed Madame Peloux with a lyric throat, "what's this weather compared to what *they* are having in Italy?"

"Just what I was thinking. Of course, of course," the servile voices piped up.

Léa turned her head toward them, frowning.—If only they would keep quiet, she thought.

Seated at a card table the Baroness de la Berche and Madame Aldonza were playing piquet. Madame Aldonza, an antiquated dancer with swaddled legs, suffered from rheumatism and wore her shiny black wig a little askew. Across from her and dominating her by a head and a half, the baroness squared her shoulders, broad as a country parson's, beneath a huge face which age had masculinized to an alarming degree. Her physiognomy consisted entirely of hairs in her ears, tufts in her nostrils, and on her lip a hirsute horde.

"Baroness, don't forget I made a run of ninety," bleated Madame Aldonza.

"Mark it up, mark it up, my friend. All on earth that I want is to

41

see everyone happy." It was her habit to bestow ceaseless benedictions on all around her and thus hide her savage cruelty.

Léa looked at her with disgust as if seeing her for the first time and then back at Madame Peloux.—At any rate, Charlotte looks human, she thought. She . . .

"But what's the matter with you, Léa? Aren't you feeling quite up to your usual self?" Madame Peloux inquired tenderly.

Léa stretched her handsome torso and answered: "Of course I am, Lolotte dear; it's so comfortable here that I was merely enjoying myself." She thought:—Careful. She's ferocious like all the rest. At once she spread over her face a look of complacent content, of greedy revery, which she accentuated by sighing: "I lunched too well. I ought to lose weight. Tomorrow I'm going to start on a diet."

Madame Peloux beat the air with her hands and simpered: "A broken heart isn't enough to make you thin, eh?"

"Oh! Ho-ho! Ha-ha," guffawed Madame Aldonza and the Baroness de la Berche. "Ha-ha-ha!"

Léa rose, impressive in her gown of toneless autumn green, handsome beneath her satin hat bordered with fur, youthful among all these relicts over whom she cast a sweet eye: "Oh, la-la, my dears! Give me a dozen heart-breaks like that if you think it would help me to lose one pound."

"Léa, you're superb," the old baroness tossed her in a puff of smoke.

"Madame Léa, think of me please, when you decide to throw away that hat," begged the old Aldonza. "Madame Charlotte, you remember your blue one? It lasted me two years. Baroness, when you've finished ogling Madame Léa will you please hand me the cards?"

"There they are, my sweetheart, and here's hoping they'll bring you luck."

Léa waited a moment on the threshold of the hall, then descended into the garden. She plucked a rose whose petals fell off in her hand, listened to the wind in the birch tree, to the tramways, to the sounds from the avenue, to the whistle of the local train. The bench on which she sat was warm and she closed her eyes, letting the sun heat her shoulders. When she opened her eyes she hurriedly turned her head toward the house with the certainty that she would see Chéri standing in the entry to the hall, leaning against the door.—What can be the matter with me? she asked herself.

Outbursts of shrill laughter, a little chorus of greeting in the hall brought her to her feet trembling slightly.—Am I developing nerves?

"Ah, there they are, there they are," trumpeted Madame Peloux. And the heavy bass voice of the baroness chanted: "Here comes the happy pair."

Léa shook, ran to the entry of the hall and stopped herself. Before her was the old Lili and her young lover, the Prince of Ceste, who were making their entry.

Perhaps seventy years old and with the fleshiness of a corseted eunuch, it was usually said of the old Lili that she was beyond the pale without making clear of what the pale consisted. An eternal childish gaiety lighted her round pink painted face where the circular eyes and the tiny mouth, fine and shrunken, coquetted shamelessly. The old Lili followed the fashions without restraint. A striped skirt of war-like blue held in the lower part of her body, a little blue jacket yawned around her bare chest whose skin was wattled like a tough turkey-cock's. A silver fox failed to hide her naked neck, shaped like a flower-pot—a neck as thick as a stomach and which had already swallowed up her chin.

"She's frightening," thought Léa. She was unable to tear her eyes from certain particularly sinister details—the white felt sailor hat, for instance, childishly cocked on the wig of short hennaed hair, and the necklace of pearls, one moment visible and the next lost to sight in the gully of wrinkles which had once been a girdle of Venus.

"Léa, Léa, duckie, dear," cried the old Lili, hurrying toward Léa. She moved with difficulty on her bloated round feet, cluttered with leather straps and paste buckles and herself was the first to remark on the fact. "I waddle something awful, it's a little way I have. Guido, sweetie, you remember Madame de Lonval? Don't remember her too well or I'll scratch your eyes out."

43

A slim youth with a tapering Italian figure, huge empty eyes, a weak sloping chin, hastily kissed Léa's hand and moved to step back into the shadows without having said a word. Lili caught him in flight, pulled his head down to her horny chest, calling the ring of onlookers as witness: "Do you know what this is, Léa? Ladies, this is the love of my life."

"Pull yourself together, Lili," advised Madame de la Berche in her bass voice.

"Why? But why?" cried Charlotte Peloux.

"Out of decency," said the baroness.

"Baroness, that's not nice of you. I think they're sweet. Ah," the mother sighed, "they remind me of my own two children."

"I thought of them," said Lili with a happy smile. "It's our honeymoon too. Speak up, Guido. Indeed we've come just to ask news about the other happy young couple. We've come to hear every single little thing. Everything!"

Madame Peloux became stern: "Lili you don't expect me to give you spicy details, do you?"

"Oh, yes, yes," cried Lili clapping her hands. She tried to skip but only succeeded in rotating her shoulders and hips a little. "That's always been my besetting sin and always will be. Curiosity. Nobody can cure me. Ask that big scoundrel there, he knows already."

The silent youth, put to the test, refused to open his mouth. His black eyes rolled round in his white face like frightened insects. Stunned, Léa watched him.

"Madame Charlotte told us all about the wedding ceremony," bellowed Madame Aldonza. "It seems that in her wreath of orange blossoms the bride looked a perfect dream."

"Like a madonna, like a madonna," rectified Charlotte Peloux at the top of her lungs and with a burst of religious fervor. "Never, never did anyone look so divine. My son was walking on clouds, on clouds, I tell you. What a couple they make, what a couple!"

"You hear that, sweetie—all about the orange blossoms?" murmured Lili. "And, tell me, Charlotte, how about our mother-in-law, Marie-Laure?"

"Oh, her! Out of place, absolutely out of place. She looked like an eel, dressed in skin-tight black and I swear you could see her breasts, her stomach—everything, everything!"

"The hussy!" roared the Baroness de la Berche with the delighted gusto of an old soldier.

"And that air she always has of being better than everybody else, of having poison in one pocket and a knife in the other all ready to slit you up the back. As I said, out of place completely. She acted as if she could only waste five minutes on us, she hardly wiped her mouth off with her napkin before she said, 'Au revoir, Edmée, au revoir, Fred,' and away she went."

The old Lili was breathing hard, sitting on the edge of her chair, her little ancestral mouth with its puckered corners hanging half open. "And who gave them the little talk?"

"What little talk?"

"The little talk—sweetie, hold my hand while I say it—the little talk that somebody always gives young people who've just been married. You know. Who told them?"

Charlotte Peloux measured her with an angry glance. "Maybe they used to do that when you were young but it's not done any more."

The old girl settled her fists on her thighs and said coarsely: "Isn't done any more? How would you know anything about the style in marriages? There's precious little marrying done in your family!"

"Oh! Ha-ha!" the two helots imprudently guffawed. But a single glance from Madame Peloux silenced them.

"Peace, peace, little birds in their nests should agree. Everybody here lives in a perfect paradise on earth and we should be full of love for our fellow-men." And Madame de la Berche stretched out a peaceful policeman-like arm between the lowering heads of the ladies.

But Charlotte Peloux was like a war-horse that had smelled the smoke of battle. "If you're looking for trouble, Lili, you won't have any trouble finding it. Considering your age, I ought to treat you with respect but if it weren't for that—"

Lili shook with laughter from head to foot. "If it weren't for that, you'd get married just to call me a liar, eh? Ho-ho, it's not hard to get married. I could marry Guido in a minute if he was only of age."

"No!" gasped Charlotte, forgetting the fight.

"I'm telling you. Princess Ceste, my dear, the *piccola principessa. Piccola principessa,* that's what my little prince always calls me." She pulled at her skirt in turning and displayed a gold bracelet strapped around the place where her ankle should have been. "Only," she continued mysteriously, "his father . . ." By now out of breath, she made a sign to the silent young man who continued in a low rapid voice as if it were a recitation learned by heart:

"My father, the Duke of Parese, will put me in a convent if I marry Lili."

"In a convent?" squealed Charlotte Peloux. "A man in a convent?"

"A man in a convent, did you say?" whinnied Madame de la Berche in an agitated bass. "Well, I'll be damned if that isn't exciting!"

"They probably don't know any better where he comes from," Aldonza lamented, joining her misshapen hands together piously.

Léa arose so suddenly that she upset a glass of wine.

"It's white glass," said Madame Peloux in satisfaction. "To break white glass brings good luck. You'll bring good luck on my happy young couple. But where are you running off to? Are you afraid your house is on fire?"

Léa managed a sly smile. "On fire? Well, in a way. . . . Ssh, no questions. It's a secret."

"What? Already? It's not possible!" Charlotte Peloux cackled with eagerness. "I was just saying to myself that you looked as if—"

"Tell us, tell us everything," the three oldest girls clamored.

The quilted fists of Lili the deformed stumps of Aldonza, the hard fingers of Charlotte Peloux had seized on her wrists, her sleeves, her gold mesh-bag. She pulled herself away from all these claws and managed to laugh again teasingly. "No, no. It's too soon, it would spoil everything, it's my secret. . . ." And she rushed into the vestibule.

But the door opened before her and a dried old gaffer, a sort of playful mummy, took her into his arms. "Léa, lovely creature, give your dear old Berthellemy a kiss or he won't let you pass."

She cried out with fright and impatience, struck off the gloved bones which restrained her and fled.

Neither in the avenues of Neuilly nor in the wooded alleyways of the Bois, blue under a hasty twilight, did she give herself a moment to think. She shivered slightly and closed the door of her car. The sight of her well-ordered house, of her pink bedroom and boudoir, over-crowded with furniture and flowers, comforted her. "Quick, Rose, light the fire in my room."

"But the house is warm, madame, the heat is turned on full as if it were already winter. Madame was foolish to go out with only that little furpiece around her neck. The evening air is treacherous."

"Put the hot-water bottle in my bed at once and for dinner bring me a big cup of thin hot chocolate beaten up with the yolk of an egg, a roast and some grapes. Hurry, my friend, I'm freezing. I caught cold in that junk shop at Neuilly."

In bed she gritted her teeth to prevent their chattering. The warmth of the bed relaxed her stiffened muscles but she still refused to give up and concentrated on the expense book of Philibert, the chauffeur, until she received her chocolate which she drank boiling. She chose her hot-house grapes one by one, balancing the cluster still attached to its stem, a long cluster of greenish amber when held toward the light. Then she turned out the lamp on her night table, stretched herself in her favorite pose, flat on her back, and relaxed.

"What's the matter with me?"

She was seized again by anxiety, by a trembling. The vision of an empty door obsessed her—the door of the hall flanked by two tufts of red sage.

—It's unhealthy, she thought. One doesn't get into a state like this for a door.

She also saw again the three oldest girls as well as Lili's neck and the beige coat that Madame Aldonza had trailed about in for the last decade.

—Which one of them am I going to look like ten years from now? she wondered.

But this prospect did not frighten her. Still her anxiety grew. She wandered from one incident to another of her past, from this scene to that, in an effort to free herself from the picture of the empty door framed in scarlet flowers. She felt lonely in her bed and trembled slightly. Suddenly a pain so keen that at first she thought it was physical stirred her, twisted her mouth and pulled from her in a raucous breath a sob and a name:

"Chéri."

This was followed by tears which she could not control at once. As soon as she could dominate herself, she sat up, dried her face and lit the lamp. —Good, she thought. Now I understand.

She took a thermometer from her night table and placed it in the pit of her arm. —My temperature's perfectly normal. So whatever I have is not physical. I know. I'm suffering, that's it. We'll have to do something about this.

She took a drink; rose, washed her inflamed eyes, powdered herself, poked the fire and lay down again. She felt cautious and full of defiance against an enemy she had never known—grief. Thirty years which had been spent living easily, pleasantly, often in love, occasionally avaricious, had just fallen away from her and left her at almost fifty, young and unused. She jeered at herself, no longer felt her pain and smiled. —I must have been out of my mind a moment ago. I'm quite all right now.

But a movement of her left arm, involuntarily opened and curved to hold and shelter a sleeping head, brought back all her agony and she sat up with a jerk. "Well, that's going to be nice," she said in a loud severe voice.

She looked at the clock and saw that it barely marked eleven. Above her head the slippered tread of old Rose passed, reached the staircase leading to the servants' quarters beneath the roof and was heard no more. Léa resisted her impulse to call this deferential old spinster to her aid. —Careful, don't give the servants anything to gossip about. We don't want that.

She left her bed, wrapped herself warmly in a quilted silk bathrobe and warmed her feet by the fire. Then she opened her window and leaned out to listen for she did not know what. A softer and humid wind had brought clouds with it and what leaves were left on the trees in the Bois close at hand rustled beneath the attacks of the breeze. Léa closed the window, picked up a newspaper and read the date:—The twenty-sixth of October. Just a month ago today Chéri was married.

She never said, "since Edmée was married."

In imitation of Chéri, she had not yet counted as among the living his young shadow of a wife. Chestnut eyes, ashy-blond hair which was beautiful and a little too curly—everything else about her melted when recalled, like the contours of a face one has seen in a dream.

"They're in each other's arms in Italy at this time of night, of course. And that—all that—makes no difference to me." She was not boasting. The picture she made of the young couple, the familiar embraces it brought to her mind, even the face of Chéri, fainting for a moment, a line of white showing between his eyelids sapped of strength—none of these aroused either curiosity or jealousy in her. But instead the animal-like convulsion seized her again, brought her low as her eyes fell on a nick in the gray enamel of her wood-work —a mark of some brutality of Chéri's.

—"The lovely hand which here left its trace is now turned from you forever," she quoted. How well I recite! At this rate grief is going to make me positively poetic.

She walked, she sat down, she went to bed and waited for day. At eight o'clock Rose found her writing at her desk, a sight which upset the old maid.

"Madame's not ill?"

"Not ill, not well. I'm not so young as I was, Rose. The doctor thinks I ought to have a change of air. You'll come with me, eh? It's going to be a cold winter here. We'll go south and eat in the sun."

"But just where are we going?"

"You want to know too much. Simply have my trunks brought up. Get out my fur rugs and give them a good beating."

"Madame is taking her car with her?"

"I think so. In fact I'm sure of it. I'll want everything to make me comfortable. For once, Rose, I'm going alone. It's going to be a pleasure trip."

For five days Léa rushed about Paris, wrote, telegraphed and received telegrams and letters from the south of France. And she departed from Paris, leaving for Madame Peloux a letter which was brief but which she had started three different times.

"My dear Charlotte,

Don't be angry if I leave without saying good-bye to you and without telling you my little secret. I'll always be a lunatic for the sake of love! And why not? It's a short life, let's make it a merry one. I send you my best. Remember me to the boy when he returns.

Your incorrigible,

LÉA.

P.S. Don't take the trouble to come interviewing my butler or the concierge. No one at my house knows anything at all."

"Do you know, dear heart, that I don't think you're looking very well?"

"It's having spent all night in the train," Chéri answered briefly.

Madame Peloux did not dare say all she thought. She had found her son greatly changed. —He's—yes, now he's positively irresistible-looking, she decided, and said loudly with enthusiasm: "It's the effect Italy had on you."

"If you want to put it that way," conceded Chéri.

Mother and son had just finished breakfasting together and Chéri with a few well-chosen blasphemies had deigned to praise the Peloux Palace coffee—a sugared coffee, pale with cream which, once boiled, had been placed to simmer again on a slow fire after having been covered with morsels of buttery toast which browned at leisure and hid the rich beverage under their succulent crusts.

He was cold even in his white woolen pyjamas, and clasped his knees in his arms for warmth. Charlotte Peloux, hoping to find favor in her son's eyes, had put on a new yellow bathrobe and worn a breakfast cap fitted tight around her temples which gave her face a look of sinister importance.

While her son stared at her, she simpered: "You see? I've decided to become old-fashioned. Do you like this cap? It's regular eighteenth century, don't you think? Something like DuBarry or Pompadour. How do I look in it?"

"Like an old convict," Chéri snapped. "You oughtn't to put on a thing like that without giving people warning."

She moaned, then guffawed. "Ha-ha-ha! Darling, you certainly have a poisonous tongue."

But he did not join her in her laughter and stared out into the garden where the light snow from the night before still lay on the grass. The spasmodic twitching of muscles along his jaw was the only sign he gave of his nervousness. Madame Peloux, intimidated, copied his silence. The trill of a distant bell sounded.

"That's Edmée, ringing for her breakfast," said Madame Peloux.

Chéri did not answer. "What's the matter with the heat? It's cold here," he said a moment later.

"That's what Italy's done for you," repeated Madame Peloux lyrically. "You come back from there with sun in your heart and in your eyes. And here you land at the North Pole. Positively at the North Pole. The dahlias didn't have a chance to bloom for even a week. But don't worry, sweetheart—precious. Your little love-nest will soon be done. If the architect hadn't come down with typhoid, it would be ready to step into now. I warned him; I said to him twenty times if I said to him once, "Monsieur Savaron—"

Chéri who was at the window turned suddenly: "Was that letter dated?"

Madame Peloux opened her large infant-like eyes: "What letter?"

"That letter from Léa which you just showed me."

"It wasn't dated, my love, but I remember I received it Saturday before my last Sunday at home in October."

"I see. And you don't know who it is?"

"Who what is, sweetheart?"

"Who that fellow is, you know—whoever she went away with?"

The naked face of Madame Peloux became malicious: "No. Just imagine it, nobody has any idea. The old Lili is in Sicily and none of the ladies who come here has the slightest clue. A mystery, a deep mystery. However, you know me, I've picked up a few bits of reliable information here and there. . . ."

Chéri's dark eyes swelled. "Well? What's the gossip?"

"It seems it's a young man," whispered Madame Peloux. "A young man and not particularly nice, you understand what I mean —But very good-looking, of course." She made up what she could, careful to assume the worst.

Chéri finally shrugged his shoulders. "Good-looking, did you say? Don't make me laugh. Poor Léa, I can see him from here—probably a little thug like Patron with black hair on his fists and wet hands. . . . Well, I'm going back to bed. You make me sleepy."

His feet trailing in his mules, he started for his room, dawdling in the long corridors and on the large landings of the house which he seemed to be discovering for the first time. He ran into an enormous pot-bellied wardrobe and was astonished. —Damned if I knew that thing was there. Oh, yes, I remember vaguely. And who in the devil can this old freak be? He peered at an enlarged photograph, funereally hung in its black frame near some object in polychrome faïence which Chéri was equally unfamiliar with. Madame Peloux had been installed in this house for twenty-five years and kept *in situ* each unfortunate example of her ridiculous collective instinct. "Your house looks like the nest of a magpie that's gone off its head," she had been reproached by the old Lili who had a hearty appetite for the paintings, and above all the painters, of the modern school.

To which Madame Peloux replied: "I believe in letting well enough alone." Did one of her corridors of sickening green—a hospital green, Léa called it—need renovating, Charlotte Peloux ordered it painted again in the same sickening green and to re-upholster one of her ruby plush sofas, hunted all over town for the same ruby plush.

Chéri paused by the open door of a dressing-room. The red marble of the washstand was fitted with white wash basins with engraved initials and ornamented with electric lights molded in the shape of lilies trimmed with beads. Chéri lifted his shoulders to his ears as if a current of cold air had reached him:—Good God, it looks like an auction room.

He lengthened his steps. The end of the corridor through which he strode finished off in a window bordered with red and yellow stained glass. "I only needed that," he grumbled. He turned to the left and noiselessly opened a door—the door of his old room—without even knocking. A small outcry rose from the bed where Edmée had just finished breakfasting. Chéri closed the door and looked at his young wife without coming any closer.

"Good morning," she smiled. "You seemed surprised to see me here."

The reflections from the snow outside shed on her a blue steady light. Her hair was hanging. Its crinky ashy-brown locks fell over but failed to cover her beautiful sloping shoulders. With her cheeks, pink and white as her nightgown, her pink mouth which fatigue made pale, she was like a new picture, not quite finished and seen from too far away.

"Aren't you going to say good morning to me, Fred?" she insisted.

He sat down beside his wife and took her in his arms. She fell back softly, carrying him with her. He leaned on his elbows the better to see close at hand this creature who was still so new that weariness could not fade her. Her lower lid, padded, full and without a line, seemed particularly to amaze him—that and the suavity of her golden cheek.

"How old are you?" he asked suddenly. Edmée opened her eyes which she had tenderly closed. Chéri saw the chestnut color of her eyes and her small square teeth which her laughter uncovered.

"Oh, come now. I'll be nineteen the fifth of January and I hope you'll try to remember it."

53

He brusquely withdrew his arm and the young woman slipped into the hollow of the bed like a scarf thrown aside.

"Nineteen years old—as much as that, eh? Do you know that I'm more than twenty-five?"

"But of course, Fred, I know it."

He took from the night table a blond tortoise shell mirror and gazed at himself. "Twenty-five years old."

Twenty-five and with a face of white marble that seemed indestructible. Twenty-five but at the outer corner of the eye and directly beneath, delicately repeating the design with which antique sculptors once treated the lid, were two lines, visible only in full light, two incisions made by the most relentless and light of hands. He replaced the mirror. "You're younger than I am. That seems strange to me."

"Not to me," she answered in a biting voice filled with hidden meaning.

But he did not stop there. "Do you know why I have beautiful eyes?" he asked her in all seriousness.

"No," said Edmée. "Perhaps because I love them?"

"That's just being poetic," said Chéri, shrugging his shoulders. "The real reason is because I have an eye shaped like a sole."

"Like a what?" she exclaimed.

"Like a sole." He sat down near her in order to make his demonstration. "Look, it's like this, the corner close to the nose, that's the head of the sole. And the upper curve, that's the back of the fish; while the under line is perfectly straight,—that's his belly. And then the corner of the eye which slopes toward my temple, that's the sole's tail."

"Ah?"

"Yes, but if I had an eye shaped like a flounder, that is to say, as much curved at the bottom as on the top, then I'd look stupid. See? You've been to college. Well, did you know all that? Did you?"

"No, I admit that I . . ." She stopped, feeling guilty because he had spoken sententiously and with exaggerated force as is the habit of certain extravagant natures.—At moments he looks like a savage, she thought. Like someone from the jungle. But he doesn't know anything about plants or animals and sometimes he doesn't even seem to know anything about people.

Chéri, seated against her, held one arm about her shoulder and with the other hand played with the small, round but flawless and perfectly matched pearls of her necklace. She breathed in the scent which Chéri used to excess and, intoxicated, drooped like a rose in an over-heated room. "Fred, come back to bed. We're both tired."

He seemed not to hear. He stared at the pearls with an obstinate and frightened look.

"Fred."

He started, leaped to his feet, tore off his pyjamas in a fury and threw himself naked into the bed, seeking a place for his head on a shoulder where the delicate bones were still sharp with youth. Edmée obediently received him with open arms. Chéri, motionless, closed his eyes. Cautiously she remained awake, a little smothered by his weight and thinking him asleep. But after a moment he turned from her with a bound, imitated the snoring of a heavy sleeper and rolled himself in the sheet at the other side of the bed.

"He always does that," Edmée declared.

She was to awaken during the entire winter in this square room with its four windows. Inclement weather delayed the completion of the new mansion in the Avenue Henri Martin and also the caprices of Chéri who wanted a black bathroom, a Chinese drawing-room, a swimming pool and a gymnasium in the basement. To the architect's objections he said: "I don't give a damn. I'm paying and I'm going to have what I want. I don't care what it costs." But now and then he went through the estimates furnished him with an eagle eye, warning that "no one was going to trim the young Peloux." Indeed he discoursed on factory prices, fibro-cement and colored stucco with unexpected glibness and a memory for figures which demanded the contractor's respect.

He rarely consulted his young wife though for her benefit he paraded his authority over the workmen and took care to hide his occasional mistakes by giving sharp orders. She discovered that he knew by instinct how to use colors but that he despised beauty of form and all the characteristics of styles.

"You simply clutter up your head with all that stuff, dearie—er, Edmée. An idea for the smoking-room? All right, here's one. A blue for the walls, a blue that isn't afraid of anything. And a violet carpet that knows the blue isn't afraid. Then, to go with all that, don't stint on black or gold either for the ornaments and furniture."

"Yes, you're probably right, Fred. But all these strong colors will be a little harsh. The room ought to have grace, have a light note in it, a white statue or vase. . . ."

"Nonsense," he interrupted rather rudely. "The white vase'll be me with nothing on. And don't forget a cushion or pillow, some kind of pumpkin yellow thingamajig for me to loll on, on those occasions."

By turns secretly revolted or excited, her mind was filled with these pictures which transformed their future dwelling place into a sort of questionable palace, a temple to the glory of her husband. But she did not oppose his wishes, merely begging gently for a little corner of her own in which to hang her minute and precious furnishings of tapestry woven on white, a present from Marie-Laure.

This gentleness that hid a determination which, though young, was already practiced, allowed her to camp out for four months at her mother-in-law's and to evade traps laid fresh every day of the visit—traps for her happiness, her gaiety which was still susceptible, for her tact. Charlotte Peloux, excited by the proximity of so tender a victim, lost her head a little and wasted her poison, striking right and left.

"Control yourself, Madame Peloux," Chéri advised her from time to time. "There's won't even be any bones left for you to pick by next winter if you don't call a halt now."

Edmée looked at her husband with eyes in which fear and gratitude trembled together and tried not to think too much about Madame Peloux nor to look at her too often. One evening at dinner Charlotte, as if at the height of her heedlessness, three times tossed across the chrysanthemum centerpiece the name of Léa instead of Edmée.

Chéri lowered his devilish eyebrows: "Madame Peloux, I gather that your memory is breaking down. Do you think anything short of solitary confinement will cure it?"

Charlotte Peloux did not say a word for a week but Edmée never dared to ask her husband: "Was it because of me that you were angry? It was I you defended, wasn't it? It wasn't the other woman —the one before me?"

Her childhood, then her adolescence, had taught her patience, hope, silence and the easy manipulations of the weapons and virtues of all prisoners. Her highness Marie-Laure had never scolded her child; she merely punished her. Never a hard word and never a tender one. Solitude, then boarding school, then the loneliness again of summer holidays and her frequent relegations to her own pretty room; finally the threat of a marriage, any kind of marriage, as soon as the eye of the too beautiful mother noted in her child the unclosing of another beauty, a timid beauty like that of the oppressed and therefore all the more moving . . . In comparison with this mother of hard ivory and gold, the moon-faced malice of Charlotte Peloux seemed like a bed of roses.

"Are you afraid of my venerated parent?" Chéri demanded one evening.

Edmée smiled, made a small grimace. "Afraid? No. A door slamming can make one jump but it doesn't make one afraid. What I'm afraid of are snakes in the grass."

"Marie-Laure is a pretty perfect snake, eh?"

"Pretty perfect."

He waited for further confidences which did not come and with a comradely gesture threw his arm over his wife's slender shoulders. "You and I are orphans in a way, eh?"

"Yes, we're orphans. We're nice little orphans." She clung to him. They were alone in the big hall. Madame Peloux, as her son said, was upstairs mixing her poisons for the next day. The night, already cold behind the windows, mirrored the furniture and the lamps as in a pond. Edmée felt warm and protected, confident in the arms of this unknown. She tilted her head and cried out with shock, for he lifted toward the light overhead a face which was magnificent and desperate, closing his eyes over two tears, captured and glistening between his lashes.

"Chéri, Chéri, what's the matter?" In spite of herself she had used this tender nickname which she had hoped never to pronounce. He answered its call with bewilderment and turned his gaze on her. "Chéri, oh God, I'm frightened. What is wrong with you?"

He held her before him at arm's length. "Poor child, poor little thing. What is it you're afraid of?" He turned toward her his eyes of velvet, handsomer for their tears and peaceful, wide-open, inscrutable. She desired only that he would not talk, but he continued: "How silly we are . . . that idea that we are orphans . . . it's idiotic—it's so true."

He immediately resumed his air of comical importance and she breathed with relief, knowing that now he would speak no more. He began snuffing out the candles with his usual care and then said to Edmée with a vanity which was either naïve or very shrewd: "After all why shouldn't I be sentimental like everyone else?"

"What are you doing there?"

Though his question came quietly, the sound of Chéri's voice thrust Edmée forward as if she had been pushed. Still standing close to the desk which opened wide, she spread her two hands on some scattered papers.

"I'm putting these in order," she said feebly. She lifted one hand which stopped in midair as if it had become numb. Then she seemed to come out of her torpor and ceased lying: "Listen, Fred. You told me you hated getting ready to move to our new house and looking after all your things—all your belongings in this room, the furniture . . . I only wanted to help, to put your possessions in order, sort them out . . . And then the temptation came, and bad impulses . . . a bad impulse . . . I ask your forgiveness. I touched things which didn't belong to me." She trembled bravely and waited.

His head was bent, his hands knotted in a menacing gesture but he seemed not to see his wife. His expression was so veiled that she always saved out of this hour the impression of once having held a conversation with a man who had white eyes.

"Ah, yes," he said finally. "You were hunting—you were hunting for love letters." She did not deny it. "You were looking for my love letters."

He laughed his awkward strained laugh.

She blushed, wounded. "Obviously you think I'm stupid. I should have known that you'd be the kind of man who would have decently put them in a safe place or burned them. And anyhow, they're none of my business. I've got just what I deserved. You won't hold it too much against me, Fred?" Her petition cost her a certain effort and she tried to look appealing, her lips drooping, the upper half of her face secreted in the shadow of her frothy hair. But Chéri's attitude did not change and she noted for the first time that his skin which was ordinarily only without shadow had taken on the waxiness of the white winter rose and the oval of his cheeks had thinned.

"Love letters," he repeated. "It's too killing."

He took one step and grasped a fistful of the papers which he scattered. Postal cards, checks from restaurants, announcements from shop-keepers, telegrams from dancing girls met one night and never seen again, *pneumatiques* from hangers-on hunting a free meal, three lines, five lines; several narrow pages armed with the saber-like script of Madame Peloux.

Chéri turned again toward his wife. "I haven't any love letters."

"Oh," she protested. "Why do you—?"

"I'm telling you the truth," he interrupted. "It's nothing you'll understand. I never noticed it myself until now. It's not possible for me to have any love letters because—" He checked himself. "Oh. Wait. Wait. There's just a chance that once . . . I remember now when I didn't want to go to La Bouboule and . . . Wait a minute, wait." He jerked open drawers, feverishly tossed the papers on the floor. "That's too much. What have I done with it? I could have sworn it was in the upper left hand corner. . . . No."

He slammed back the empty drawers and fixed his wife with a heavy stare. "You didn't find anything? You didn't take a letter which began, 'But of course I'm not lonely. I regard a separation of one week out of every four as an excellent plan,' and then went on to something else, I don't remember what, in connection with a honeysuckle vine which bloomed outside a window. . . ." He stopped merely because his memory carried him no farther, leaving him gesturing with impatience.

Edmée, hardened and thin before him, did not falter: "No, no, I took nothing, mind you," she insisted with dry irritability. "Since when have I been apt to take things? But how do you happen not to know exactly where it is, this particularly precious letter that you can't find? A letter like that—I don't need to ask if it was from Léa."

He winced slightly but not as Edmée had expected. An errant half-smile wandered over his handsome detached face and with head tilted, eyes attentive, the arch of his mouth beautifully stretched, he listened perhaps to the echo of a name . . . All the young and undisciplined amorous force of Edmée's nature burst open in cries, in tears, in gestures of her hands, first knotted then extended to scratch: "Go away, I hate you. You've never loved me. You don't pay any more attention to me than if I didn't exist. You wound me, you despise me, you're coarse, you're . . . you . . . You only think of that old woman. It's unhealthy, it's degenerate, it's . . . You don't love me. Often I ask myself why you married me. You're . . . You . . ."

She shook her head like an animal that had been seized by the throat and when, suffocating, she lifted her head to breathe, there became visible the shining, milky little pearls of her necklace. Chéri contemplated with stupor the incoherent stretchings of her charming graceful throat, the appeal of her hands knitted one to the other, and above all, her tears, her tears. . . . He had never seen so many tears. . . . Who had ever cried before him or because of him? No one. Madame Peloux?—But the tears shed by Madame Peloux wouldn't count, he thought. Léa? No. . . . In the most hidden depths of his memories he consulted, as if for authority, two honest, blue, sincere eyes which had never sparkled except for pleasure, malice and a tenderness that was always a little mocking. What a quantity of tears she shed, this young woman who was struggling before him! What did one do in the presence of so many tears? He did not know. Still he stretched out his arms and as Edmée drew back, perhaps fearing some brutality, he placed his hand—beautiful, soft, scented—on her frantic head and patted it while trying to imitate a voice and words whose power he knew well: "There, there . . . Now what's all this? . . . What's it all about, eh? . . . There, there."

At once Edmée collapsed and fell on a sofa where she rolled in a heap and began to sob with a passion, a frenzy, that rose in swells like laughter or the jerky rhythms of joy. Her pretty body shook, exalted by grief, jealousy, anger and a servility of which she was unaware; and yet like a wrestler fighting for his life, like a swimmer in the hollow of a wave, she felt bathed in an element which was new, natural and bitter.

She cried for a long time and came to herself slowly over moments of calm still crossed by shudders and gasps for breath. Chéri had seated himself near her and continued to caress her hair. He had passed the high point of his own emotion and was tiring. He glanced at Edmée, thrown at an angle across the straight couch, dissatisfied that her straggling body with its lifted skirt its trailing scarf, should augment the disorder in the room.

As soft as his sigh of boredom was, she heard it and sat up. "Yes," she said, "I'm more than you can stand. . . . It would be better to . . ."

He interrupted her, fearful of a torrent of words. "It's not that. It's simply that I don't know what you want."

"What I want?" she echoed. "What I—" She lifted her face, still sick with tears.

"Now listen to me."

He took her hands. She tried to free herself. "No, no, I know that tone of voice. You're going to treat me to some long harangue that I won't understand. When you start to talk and look like that I know you're going to prove that your eye is shaped like a super-brook-trout or that your mouth looks like the figure three upside down. No, no, I don't want any of that."

Her recriminations were childish and Chéri relaxed on realizing that they were both very young. He shook her warm hands which he still held. "But listen to me," he insisted. "Good God, I'd like to know what you have to reproach me with? Do I ever go out at night without you? No. Do I leave you often during the day? Do I keep up a secret correspondence?"

"I don't know if you do—I don't think that you do."

He turned her from side to side like a doll held in his hands. "Have I a separate room from yours? Don't I make love well?"

She hesitated, smiled, delicately suspicious. "Do you call that love, Fred?"

"There are other words for it but you wouldn't appreciate them."

"What you call love . . . isn't it possible that it is . . . is perhaps only a sort of alibi on your part?" She added hurriedly: "I'm just generalizing, Fred, you understand. I say 'perhaps' . . . in certain cases . . ."

He dropped Edmée's hands. "That," he remarked coldly, "was perfectly the wrong thing to say."

"Why?" she demanded in a feeble voice.

His chin in the air, he whistled, removing himself from her by several steps. Then he came toward her again, looking her over as if she were a stranger. A wild beast has no need to leap in order to promote fear. Edmée saw that his nostrils were flaring and the tip of his nose was white.

"Ugh," he breathed contemptuously, looking at his wife. He lifted his shoulders and walked away. At the end of the room he turned and came back. "Ugh," he repeated, "look what's talking."

"What?"

"Look what's talking and what it says. What cheek, my word!"

She rose in a rage. "Fred," she cried, "don't dare to speak to me again in that tone. For whom do you take me?"

"For a woman who knows the perfectly wrong thing to say— and says it, as I just had the honor of informing you." He touched her shoulder with a hard finger. She suffered as if it had made a bruise. "You, who've had a college education, isn't there some kind of proverb that says 'Don't play with fire?'"

"Yes," she said mechanically.

"Well, my child, don't play with fire. In other words don't wound a man . . . in his favors, if I may so express it. You wounded me in my gifts of love to you. . . . You wounded me in the favors I bestowed on you."

"You—you talk like a cocotte," she gasped. She blushed and became weak. She hated him for remaining pale, for retaining a superiority of which the entire secret lay in the carriage of his head, the steadiness of his limbs, the easy gait of his shoulders and arms.

The hard forefinger once more indented Edmée's shoulder. "Pardon. Pardon me. I'll probably astonish you in stating that on the contrary it's you who think like a whore. In estimating such little matters as the pretty ladies there's no one who's more an authority than the young Peloux. I'm fairly well informed about 'cocottes' as you call them. I know them inside out. A 'cocotte' is a lady who usually arranges to receive more than she gives. You hear me?"

What she actually heard was the distant formal tone in his voice.

"Nineteen years old, white skin, hair which smells like vanilla; and in bed, closed eyes, dangling arms. All of it very pretty but has it anything that's so unusual? Do you really think it's so rare?"

She shook at each word and each stab roused her for the duel of the female against male. "It's barely possible it's quite rare," she said in a firm voice. "Though how would you know?"

He did not reply and she hastened to take her advantage: "Personally, I saw men in Italy who were handsomer than you. The streets are full of them. My nineteen years are worth what any other girl's are worth, just as one handsome young man is no better than another. Come, come, everything can be arranged. . . . Nowadays marriage is simply a yardstick that doesn't measure anything. Instead of embittering ourselves with silly scenes . . ."

He stopped her with a shake of the head that was almost merciful. "My dear child, it's not so simple as that. . . ."

"Why not? There's such a thing as quick divorce if one's willing to pay." She spoke in the pathetic peremptory voice of a runaway school girl. Her hair, pushed back from her forehead, the soft and enfolding slope of her cheek made all the more somber her anxious and intelligent eyes—unhappy woman's eyes, matured and definite in a still unripened face.

"That wouldn't help anything," said Chéri.

"Why?"

"Because"— He bent his forehead, his eyelashes seemed revelled out into two winged points: he closed his eyes and then opened them as if he had swallowed a bitter dose. "Because you love me."

She only noticed the intimate tone again and above all the sound of his voice, full, a little stifled, the voice of their happiest hours. She acquiesced in the very center of her being:—It's true, I love him. For the moment there is no help for us.

The bell for dinner sounded in the garden, a bell which was too small and which ante-dated Madame Peloux—a bell, sad and clear like that of a provincial orphan asylum. Edmée shivered. "Oh, I don't like that bell."

"No?" said Chéri, absentmindedly.

"In our home dinner will be announced. There'll be no bell. In our home there are not going to be any boarding-house manners. You'll see, in our home—"

She talked while hurrying down the hospital-green corridors, without turning or seeing behind her the savage attentiveness Chéri bestowed on her last words or his sneering smile.

He walked along lightly, stimulated by the dull spring which could be verified only in the irregular humid wind or in the scent cast up from the parks and private gardens. A mirror recalled to him from time to time in his progress that he was wearing a becoming felt hat pulled over his right eye, a light loose overcoat, pale heavy gloves and a terra-cotta colored cravat. The silent homage of women followed him, the most candid among them offering him that stupefaction that they could no more feign than hide. But Chéri ignored women in the streets. He had just left his mansion in the Avenue Henri-Martin where for the benefit of the decorators he had left orders which were contradictory but delivered in the sure tone of authority.

At the end of the Avenue he breathed deep of the herbaceous smells which came from the Bois on the wet heavy wing of the west wind, and hurried his steps toward the Porte Dauphine. In a few minutes he gained the lower end of the Avenue Bugeaud and there stopped short. For the first time in six months his feet were treading a familiar path. He unbuttoned his coat.

—I walked too rapidly, he thought. He took a few steps then stopped once more and this time his glance was settled on a precise point. Fifty feet away, bareheaded and his chamois-skin in his hand, the concierge, Ernest—Léa's concierge—was polishing the brass on the gate in front of Léa's house. Chéri began to hum as he walked until he noticed by the sound of his voice that he had never known how to hum, so he stopped.

"Everything all right, Ernest? Hard at work as usual?"

The concierge brightened respectfully. "Monsieur Peloux. It's a pleasure to see monsieur again, monsieur hasn't changed a hair."

"Nor you either, Ernest. Madame is well, I trust?" He spoke only in profile, his eyes attentively observing the closed shutters on the second floor.

"I suppose so, monsieur, all we've had has been a few postal cards."

"Where from? From Biarritz, I believe?"

"I—I don't think so, monsieur."

"Where is madame?"

"It would be difficult to tell monsieur that. We send her mail— and there mostly isn't any—to madame's solicitor."

Chéri pulled out his wallet, affixing Ernest meantime with an affectionate eye.

"Oh, Monsieur Peloux, money between us? Oh, you wouldn't do that. Anyhow, even a thousand francs couldn't make a man tell something he doesn't know. But if monsieur would like to have the address of madame's solicitor?"

"No, thanks, it's of no consequence. And when is she coming back?"

Ernest lifted his arms. "Another question that's beyond me. Maybe tomorrow and maybe next month. But still I keep everything clean as a pin for we never can be sure of madame. If you said to me now, 'There she comes around the corner of the avenue,' I wouldn't be any more surprised than you."

Chéri turned and looked at the corner of the avenue.

"That's all Monsieur Peloux wants of me? Monsieur just happened to be walking by? It's a fine day. . . ."

"Yes, thanks, Ernest. Au revoir, Ernest."

"Always at monsieur's service."

Chéri walked as far as the Place Victo-Hugo, swinging his stick. He stumbled twice and almost fell down, like people who fancy they are being spied on. At the balustrade which framed the entry to the Metro he stopped, leaned his elbows on the railing, stared into the rose and black shadows of the pit and felt crushed with fatigue. When he finally lifted himself he saw that the lamps had been lighted in the square and that night had colored everything blue.

"No, it's not possible. . . . I must be ill."

He had been at the bottom of a deep revery and came back to life painfully. The necessary words finally emerged. "Come, come now, for the love of God. Young Peloux, are you off your track, my boy? Don't you know it's time to go home?"

This final phrase brought back to him a picture which the last hour had been capable of extinguishing: a square room, the big room Chéri had had ever since he was a child, a worried young woman waiting by the window and Charlotte Peloux, sweetened by a Martini cocktail.

"Oh, no," he said aloud. "No. That's finished."

With his lifted stick he stopped a taxi.

"Take me to—er—to the Restaurant du Dragon Bleu."

He crossed the grill room to the sound of violins, bathed in a ferocious glare of electricity which he found stimulating. The maître d'hôtel remembered him and Chéri shook his hand. Before him rose a hollow tall young man and Chéri sighed affectionately: "Well, Desmond. The very person I wanted to see. What luck!"

The table they selected was garnished with pink carnations. A small hand and an enormous aigrette trembled in Chéri's direction, launched from the next table.

"It's Loupiote," Desmond warned him.

Chéri did not recall the lady who was known under this title but he smiled at her enormous aigrette and without rising touched her little hand, located at the end of a cheap paper fan. Then with his air of solemn conqueror, he eyed an unknown couple near by because the woman had forgotten to eat ever since Chéri had sat down in her vicinity.

"The man with her looks like a deceived husband, eh? Poor old thing." To murmur these words he leaned toward his friend's ear and the pleasure in his eyes twinkled like an inundation of tears.

"What do you drink since you're married?" demanded Desmond. "Camomille tea?"

"I drink Pommery," said Chéri.

"And before the Pommery?"

"Pommery—before and after." And, flaring his nostrils, he inhaled in memory the sparkling roselike odor of some old champagne of 1889 which Léa had reserved for him alone.

He ordered his dinner like a milliner on a spree—cold fish *au porto*, roasted birds and hot soufflé whose inner cave was filled with a sour red ice.

"Heigh-ho," cried Loupiote, waving a pink carnation in Chéri's direction.

"Heigh-ho," responded Chéri, lifting his glass.

The chime of an English time-piece on the wall struck eight. "Oh, damnation," grumbled Chéri. "Desmond, ring up someone for me on the telephone."

Desmond's pale eyes brightened with the expectation of interesting revelations.

"Ask for Wagram 17-08 which is my mother's house, and tell her that you and I are dining together."

"And if it's the young Madame Peloux who comes to the telephone?"

"Say the same thing. I'm a free man, don't forget. I've got her well trained."

He drank and ate a great deal, careful to appear serious and blasé. But the slightest outburst of laughter, the tinkling of a glass, the slimiest waltz, augmented his pleasure. The hard blue of the mirrored walls made him think of the Riviera at the hours when the sea, too blue, blackened at noonday beneath the melting disk of the sun. He forgot the habitual coldness which was a part of his rôle and began sweeping his most professional glances over the dark lady across from him, a creature on whom each glance left its mark.

"And Léa?" Desmond suddenly demanded.

Chéri did not tremble: he was already thinking of Léa. "Léa? She's in the Midi."

"It's all over between you?"

"Oh, naturally, you understand. We separated in good style, the best of friends. It couldn't go on forever. But what a charming, what an intelligent woman, my boy. However, you knew her yourself. Broadminded. Truly remarkable. I don't mind admitting to you, old man, that if there hadn't been the question of age between us. . . . But there was a question of age, and of course, you understand. . . ."

"Oh, perfectly," Desmond interrupted.

The young man with discolored eyes who knew from the bottom up his hard and difficult job of being a perfect parasite, had indiscreetly yielded to his curiosity and scolded himself for it. Chéri, however, perfectly circumspect and completely drunk, continued to talk about Léa. He said all the correct things redolent of domestic good sense. He praised marriage while giving Léa's virtues their due. He vaunted the submissive sweetness of his young wife in order to find an opportunity to criticize Léa's independent character. "Oh, that old war-horse. I don't mind telling you that she had ideas of her own."

He went farther with his confidences, he went so far in the matter of Léa as to treat her with severity, with impertinence. And all the while he talked, sheltered behind his ridiculous words which fanned in him that defiance peculiar to a persecuted lover, he savored the subtle happiness of being able to talk of her without danger. A little more and, in celebrating within his heart all the memories he had of her, he would have sullied her sweet and soft name which he had not been free to speak for six months, and the whole merciful vision he retained of her, bent over him with her two or three irreparable deep wrinkles, her beauty, lost for him but, alas, always present.

About eleven o'clock they rose to go, chilled by the emptiness of the restaurant. However, at the next table Loupiote was dashing off a few letters and called for more paper. She lifted her inoffensive sheep-like face toward the two friends as they passed.

"Well," she said, "and don't you even say good night?"

"Good night," Chéri conceded.

Loupiote called her girl friend to witness what a fine young man Chéri was. "Pretty as a picture and plenty of cash to boot. Some people have everything in this world." But when Chéri offered her nothing more than a cigarette from his case she became embittered. "Some people have everything except the gift of knowing what to do with what they've got. . . . Run home to mama, duckie."

"Which reminds me," said Chéri to Desmond when they reached the street, "which reminds me that I wanted to ask you, Desmond. . . . But wait till we're out of this mob."

The soft and tepid evening had collected sidewalk strollers but the boulevard, after the Rue Caumartin, was still awaiting the rush from the closing theaters. Chéri took his friend's arm. "Listen, Desmond. . . . I want you to telephone for me."

Desmond stopped in his tracks. "Again?"

"Call Wagram—"

"17-08."

"You're the man of my dreams. Telephone and say I've been taken ill at your house—where do you live, by the way?"

"At the Hotel Morris."

"Perfect. Say I'll be home tomorrow morning—say you're making me a hot grog. Here. Either give this to the telephone girl or keep it yourself. Don't make me wait. I'll be on the terrace of Weber's café."

The tall, useful and haughty young man departed, crumpling the banknotes in his pocket and without making any reply. He returned to Chéri who was bent over an orangeade still intact and in which he seemed to be reading his fortune.

"Ah, Desmond. Who came to the telephone?"

"A woman," his messenger answered laconically.

"Which?"

"I don't know."

"What did she say?"

"That it was quite all right."

"In what tone of voice?"

"The same as I used just now."

"Ah. Good. Thanks."

It was Edmée, Chéri thought. They walked toward the Place de la Concorde and Chéri hung on Desmond's arm. He did not dare admit that he felt weary.

"Where do you want to go?" Desmond demanded.

"Listen, old man," Chéri said with gratitude, "let's go to the Morris at once. I'm dead."

Desmond forgot his customary impassibility. "What? Honestly? We're going to the Morris at this time of night? But what for? You're joking. Do you mean you want to—"

"Sleep," said Chéri. And he closed his eyes as if ready to collapse, then opened them. "Sleep, sleep, you understand?"

He clung without strength to his friend's arm.

70

"Right. Come along, then," said Desmond.

In ten minutes they were at the Morris. The sky-blue and ivory of the bedroom; the sham Empire of the little salon smiled at Chéri like old friends. He took a bath, borrowed from Desmond a silk night shirt that was too small, lay down and, wedged between two large soft pillows, sank into happiness without dreams, a sleep which was black and thick and which guarded him on all sides.

He counted the shameful days which then began. Sixteen, seventeen. . . . When three weeks are up I'll go back to Neuilly. But he did not go home. Lucidly he took the measure of a situation which he no longer had the strength to remedy. At night or sometimes in the morning he would flatter himself that his cowardice would have ended within a few hours. You haven't got the courage? Oh, excuse me, excuse me. . . . You haven't got the courage *yet.* . . . But it will come. When the clock strikes twelve what won't I bet that I'll be in the dining-room in the Boulevard d'Inkermann? One, two. . . . The stroke of twelve found him in the bathtub or driving his automobile with Desmond at his side.

Meal-time always gave him a moment of domestic optimism as punctual as a recurrent fever. Sitting down like a bachelor with Desmond, he always saw Edmée and thought in silence of the inconceivable deference his young wife always showed him. She's too nice, really, that sweet child. No one ever heard of a little wife as perfect as she. Never a word, never a complaint. I'm going to take her one of those big bracelets when I go home. Ah, training, that's it. Show me anyone who's the equal of Marie-Laure when it comes to bringing up a young girl. But one day in the grill room of the Morris the appearance of a green gown with a chinchilla collar, a costume something like one of Edmée's, turned him pale with fright.

Desmond found life wonderful and grew a little fat. He regained his old-time haughtiness only during the moments when Chéri, solicited by him to visit some English charmer, extraordinarily full of vice, or some Indian prince in his opium den, refused flatly or consented with unconcealed contempt. Desmond no longer understood Chéri but at any rate Chéri paid and better than he had during the days of their adolescence. One night they ran into the blond Loupiote at the house of her friend whose real name no one could ever remember: "What's-her-name—you know—the pal, the *copine* of Loupiote."

La Copine, thus called, smoked opium and helped others to do the same. Even in the entry way her modest flat started to smell of escaping gas and the drug which had been allowed to cool, but she conquered her guests by a tearful cordiality and a constant encouragement to be sad which was not entirely inoffensive. Desmond was received by her as a "great big desperately heartbroken boy," and Chéri as a "spoiled beauty who has everything, including all that can make him unhappy." But Chéri did not smoke, looked at the box of cocaine with the repugnance of a cat looking at a bottle of castor oil and sat up almost all night on the matting, his back against the wall between Desmond who was asleep and La Copine who never stopped smoking. Almost all night, wise and defiant, he smelled the odor of that which satisfies both hunger and thirst and seemed perfectly contented except when he regarded with a painful and questioning intensity the faded throat of La Copine—a throat which was red and rough and about which shimmered a string of artificial pearls.

Once Chéri stretched his hand and with the tip of his fingers caressed the henna-tinted hair on the back of her neck: he weighed her large, empty, light pearls, then pulled back his hand with the nervous shiver of someone who has caught his finger-nail on worn silk. Shortly after he arose and departed.

"Haven't you had enough?" Desmond demanded of Chéri. "Enough of these infernal holes where you eat, where you drink, where you never touch a woman, and this hotel where they're always slamming doors? Enough of cabarets in the evening and of eternally driving your sixty horse power from Paris to Rouen, from Paris to Compiègne, from Paris to Ville-d'Avray. Why not the Riviera? It's not December or January that's the chic season down there, it's March, it's April, it's . . ."

"No," said Chéri.

"Well?"

"Well, nothing."

He became affable without becoming sincere and took on what Léa formerly called his air of worldly superiority.

"My boy, you seem not to appreciate the beauty of Paris at the moment. This . . . this indecision, this springtime without sun, this soft gray light . . . whereas the banal brilliant Riviera. . . . No, you might as well know it, I like it here."

Desmond almost lost his servant-like patience. "Yes, and maybe the divorce of the young Peloux. . . ."

Chéri's sensitive nostrils faded white. "If you've made your usual private arrangement with some lawyer, both you and he can give up hope. There'll be no divorcing for the young Peloux."

"My dear fellow," protested Desmond trying to look hurt. "You have a curious way of speaking to a childhood friend, one who on every occasion has always—"

Chéri did not listen. He turned in Desmond's direction a pointed chin, a mouth which he pinched into that of a miser. For the first time he had heard a stranger disposing of his own worldly possessions.

He reflected. A divorce for the young Peloux? He had considered it many hours of the day and night and the very words had come to represent freedom, a sort of recovered youth, and perhaps something better still. . . . But the voice, purposely nasal, of the Vicomte Desmond had aroused in him the necessary picture: Edmée leaving the house at Neuilly, resolute in her little automobile hat and her long veil, departing toward some unknown man. Obviously that would settle everything, admitted Chéri, bohemian even in his thoughts. Yet at the same time another Chéri who was singularly timorous, resisted recalcitrantly: No. That's not the thing to do. The picture became more precise, gained in colors and movement. . . . Chéri heard the solemn musical sound of the clos-

73

ing gate and on the other side of the grill saw a white naked hand, a gray pearl, a white diamond. . . .

"Farewell," the small hand waved.

Chéri rose, pushing back his chair.—They're mine, he thought. All of them. The woman, the house, the rings, they all belong to me.

He had not spoken aloud but his face expressed such savage violence that Desmond thought the end of his days in clover had arrived. Chéri was moved to pity without becoming benevolent. "Poor pussy-cat, I frightened you, eh? Ah, the worn-out old aristocracy. Come along. I'll buy you some underdrawers as good as my shirts and some shirts as good as your underdrawers. Desmond, is it the seventeenth of the month today?"

"Yes, why?"

"The seventeenth of March. In other words, spring. Desmond, smart people, but I mean the really chic lot, women or men, won't be able to wait much longer before ordering their new spring wardrobes, will they?"

"Hardly."

"The seventeenth, Desmond. Come along then, everything's going to be all right. We're going to buy a big bracelet for my wife, an enormous cigarette holder for Ma'me Peloux and a little wee scarf-pin for you."

In this fashion, two or three different times, he had the overwhelming presentment that Léa was going to return, that she had already arrived, that the shutters on the second floor, now opened, gave a glimpse of the pink ruffles at the window sills, the network of the huge lace curtains, the gold of the mirrors. The fifteenth of April passed and Léa had not yet appeared. Irritating events illumined the somber flow of his life. There had been the visit from Madame Peloux who thought she was breathing her last before a Chéri thin as a greyhound, his mouth closed and his eyes wandering. There had been the letter from Edmée, a letter entirely, surprisingly calm, in which she explained that she would remain at Neuilly "until further orders" and added that Madame de la Berche sent her best regards. He thought she was making fun of him, didn't know

74

what to reply and finished by throwing the incomprehensible letter away. But he did not go to Neuilly. In proportion as April, green and cold, flowering with pawlonia, tulips, with hyacinths in pots and laburnum in yellow clusters, perfumed Paris, Chéri buried himself alone in austere seclusion. Desmond, ill-treated, galled, discontented but well-paid, was alternately commissioned to protect Chéri from familiar young females and indiscreet young men or to go out and fetch both to make up a small regiment which ate, drank and screamed between Montmartre, the restaurants in the Bois and the cabarets of the Left Bank.

One night La Copine who was smoking alone and bewailing all evening a grave infidelity on the part of her friend Loupiote, saw enter her rooms the young man with the satanic eyebrows. He demanded cold water for his handsome and changed mouth which some secret heat had made dry. He did not show the slightest interest in the misfortunes of La Copine which she narrated at length while pushing toward him the lacquer tray and the pipe. He accepted only his place on the matting, the silence and the half-obscurity, and rested there until dawn, economical of his movements like someone who fears if he moves to reveal a wound. At daybreak he demanded of La Copine: "Why weren't you wearing your pearls today, you know, your big pearls?" and politely took himself off.

He formed the unconscious habit of walking at night alone. His rapid, lengthy stride led him toward some goal which was distinct but inaccessible. Past midnight he would escape Desmond who would find him toward dawn on his bed in the hotel, sleeping flat on his stomach, his head between his folded arms, in the position of a child with a sorrow.

Oh, there he is—all right, then, thought Desmond with relief. With a lunatic like that one never knows. . . .

One night when the solitary Chéri was walking wide-eyed in the dark, he turned up the Avenue Bugeaud because he had not yet given in all day to his superstition which took him back there once every forty-eight hours. Like those eccentrics who cannot go to sleep without having first touched the door knob three times, he invariably rubbed along the gate, put his finger on the bell and called under his breath, as if it were a joke, "Hello, there," and then went away.

But one night, a certain night while he stood before the grill, a lump rose in his throat, then sank to strike at his heart. The electric globe in the court glimmered like a mauve moon above the portal, the door of the service entry, wide open, brightened the pavement and on the second floor the light from the room inside sifted through the shutters in the form of a golden comb.

Chéri leaned his back against the closest tree and hung his head. "It's not true," he said. "I'll close my eyes and when I open them again everything will be black as usual."

He straightened at the sound of the voice of Ernest, the concierge, who called in the corridor: "Tomorrow morning at nine o'clock, exact, Marcel and I will bring up the big black trunk, madame."

Chéri turned precipitately and ran as far as the Avenue du Bois where he sat down. The electric globe which he had looked at in the court danced before his eyes, a dark purple ball edged with gold and now suspended between him and the black of the still meager spring trees. He pressed his hand to his heart and took a deep breath. The night smelled of lilacs in bloom. He tossed his hat to one side, opened his coat and sprawled against the back of the bench, stretched his legs and his opened hands drooped weakly. A suave and suffocating weight had just settled over him.

"Ah," he said in a low voice. "Is this happiness? I didn't know."

He took time to regard himself with pity and then with contempt for all that he had missed in his miserable life—the life of a rich young man with a small heart—then he ceased thinking for a moment or perhaps an hour. At the end of that time he was able to believe that he wished for nothing else on earth, not even to go to see Léa.

When he shook with cold and the blackbirds cried the dawn he rose, stumbling, light, and took the direction of the Hotel Morris without even passing by the Avenue Bugeaud. He stretched himself, swelled his lungs and overflowed with a feeling of forbearance for all mankind.

Now, he thought, exorcised, now how nice I'll be to Edmée.

Up at eight, shaved, dressed, feverish, Chéri shook Desmond who slept lividly and looked revolting, swollen by slumber like a drowned man.

"Desmond, hey, Desmond. . . . Stop it. You're too hideous when you sleep."

The sleeper sat up and turned on Chéri eyes which were the color of muddy water. He pretended stupor to prolong his cautious examination of Chéri—Chéri dressed in blue, pathetic and superb, pale under a velvet coating of powder perfectly applied. There were still hours when Desmond with his affected ugliness suffered because of Chéri's handsomeness. He yawned on purpose and at length. What's he done now, he wondered while gaping:—That idiot is better-looking than he was yesterday. Especially his lashes, his lashes are—he stared at Chéri's lashes, lustrous and thick, and at the shadow they shed over the brown-black and blue-white of his eye. Desmond also remarked this morning that the contemptuous arched lips were open, moist, refreshed and panting a little as if after some hasty voluptuous moment.

Then he relegated his jealousy to the far plane of sentimental cares and questioned Chéri in a tone of weary condescension: "May one inquire if you're going out at this hour of the morning or just coming in?"

"I'm going out," said Chéri. "Don't bother about me. I have errands to do. I'm going to the florist's. I'm going to the jeweler's, to see my mother, to see my wife, to see—"

"Don't forget the Pope."

"Why not?" answered Chéri. "I'll take him some solid gold collar buttons and a bunch of orchids."

Chéri rarely responded to a pleasantry, ordinarily receiving them in icy silence. The importance of his facetious reply therefore informed Desmond of the unwonted condition his friend was in. He considered the reflection of Chéri in the mirror, noted the pallor of his dilated nostrils, the wandering motion of his glance and attempted only the most discreet inquiry: "Are you coming back to lunch? . . . Hey, Chéri, I'm talking to you. Are we lunching together?"

Chéri shook his head. He whistled lightly on seeing his reflection in the oblong mirror, exactly waist length like the one in Léa's room between the two large windows. Soon that mirror's heavy gold frame would serve as a mounting for his reflection on a background of sun-strewn pink, his image naked or draped in loose silk, his portrait as a handsome beloved young man, happy, pampered, playing with the rings and necklaces of his mistress. . . . Perhaps it's already there in Léa's mirror—the reflection of a young man? This thought cut across his exaltation with such virulence that, thinking he had seen it, he gasped.

"What did you say?" Desmond demanded.

"I didn't say anything," his easy-going friend of a moment ago answered formally. "It's someone talking in the court."

Chéri left Desmond's room, slammed the door and closed himself in his own rooms. The Rue de Rivoli, awakened, filled them with a soft ceaseless tumult and Chéri could see through the opened window the spring foliage, stiff and transparent like jade knives in the sun. He closed the window and sat down on a useless little chair which filled a melancholy corner between the wall, his bed and the bathroom door.

"How does it happen," he began in a low voice and then fell silent. He did not understand why in the space of six and a half months he had never thought about the lover of Léa. "I'll always be a lunatic for the sake of love," said Léa's letter which Charlotte had piously saved.

A lunatic for love? Chéri shook his head. It's curious but I don't see her as that. What kind of man could she be in love with? Something like Patron? More that than one like Desmond, naturally. A little Argentine with waxed hair? Hardly. . . . But still. . . . He smiled with naïveté. Outside of me who could really please her? A

78

cloud passed over the sun and the room became dark. Chéri leaned his head against the wall. Nounoune, my Nounoune. . . . Have you deceived me? Have you disgustingly deceived me with someone else? . . . Have you done that to me?

He whipped his unhappiness with words and pictures which he constructed painfully, astonished and without rage. He tried to bring to mind morning pastimes with Léa, the delicious sleepiness of winter in the warm bed and the cool room with Léa. But either in the pink daylight which glowed within her curtains or in the afternoon, he always saw in Léa's arms one lover, only one lover: Chéri. He rose as if brought to life again in an impulse of spontaneous faith.

It's quite simple. If I'm not able to see anyone else near her, it's simply that there isn't anyone else to see.

He seized the telephone, almost called her and hung up the receiver softly. None of that, now.

He walked out, erect and squaring his shoulders. His open motor took him to the jeweler's where he grew tender over a slender little bandeau of burning blue sapphires mounted in invisible blue metal, just the thing for Edmée's hair, which he took with him. He bought flowers which were a little stupid and ceremonious. Eleven o'clock had barely struck and he spent another half hour here and there, in his bank where he drew money, at a kiosk where he ran through the English magazines, at a tobacconist's who specialized in Oriental blends, at his perfumer's. Finally he stepped into his motor again, seated himself between his bouquet of flowers and his parcels tied with ribbons.

"Home."

The chauffeur turned around on his seat. "Monsieur? What did monsieur say?"

"I said to go home, Boulevard d'Inkermann. Do you need a map of Paris?"

The car shot for the Champs-Elysées. The chauffeur speeded zealously and his back, in which his thoughts could be read, seemed to curve uneasily over the gulf which separated the feckless young man of the months past, the young man with his, "As you choose," and "Have a glass, Antonin?" from young Monsieur Peloux, strict with his servants and watchful of the gasoline.

Young Monsieur Peloux, leaning against morocco leather, his hat on his knees, drank in the spring wind and used all his concentration in an effort not to think. He closed his eyes like a coward between the Avenue Malakoff and the Porte Dauphine in order not to see passing the Avenue Bugeaud and congratulated himself: I have courage.

The chauffeur sounded his horn at the Boulevard d'Inkermann for the opening of the gate which sang on its hinges with a long note, solemn and harmonious. The concierge in his cap bowed, the watchdogs raised their voices to salute the familiar smell of someone they recognized. Perfectly at ease, sniffing the verdant odor of the clipped lawn, Chéri entered the house and mounted with a master's step toward the young woman whom he had left three months before as a European sailor on the other side of the world deserts his little savage bride.

Léa cast far from her, to the distant open desk, the photographs which she had taken from the last trunk. Good God, how ugly people are. How dared those women give these to me? Do they think I'm going to put them on the mantelpiece in a nickel frame, perhaps, or in a little folding case? The waste basket's where they're going and in four pieces.

She took up the photographs again and before destroying them fixed them with the hardest expression of which her blue eyes were capable. Against the background of a postcard a fat woman without a waist draped her hair and the lower part of her cheeks with a veil which the wind lifted. "To my dear Léa in memory of the exquisite hours passed at Guéthary. Anita." In the center of a square of pasteboard, rough as dried mud, another photograph displayed a large mournful family, a sort of penitentiary colony governed by a painted grandam on squat feet who waved a cotillion favor in one hand and posed one foot on the bended knee of a butcher-faced youth, sly and strong.

"Such things shouldn't be allowed," said Léa, crumpling the mud-like card.

An unmounted print which she unrolled spread before her an aged pair of provincial spinisters, eccentric, noisy, quarrelsome, who every morning used to be seated on a bench in the Mediterranean promenade and every evening were to be found between a glass of blackberry cordial and their silk sewing frames on which they embroidered a black cat, a toad, a spider. "To our lovely sprite: from her little friends at Trayas, Miquette and Riquette."

Léa destroyed this souvenir of her recent voyage and lifted her hand to her forehead: It's horrible. And after these just as before these, others—others who look like the same thing. Nothing can be done about it. Life's like that. Perhaps everywhere there's a Léa there pops out of the earth some kind of Charlotte Peloux, de la Berche or Aldonza; all those old horrors who have been lovely when young—people, in other words, just people—impossible, impossible, impossible.

She heard as part of these recent souvenirs the voices which were always lifted in hail from the steps of the hotel, which called from afar "hoo-hoo" over the blond beach, and she dropped her head with a hostile bullish movement.

She had come back after six months a little thinner and mollified, less serene. Now a censorious and habitual gesture lowered her chin over her collar and casual barbers had lighted in her tinted hair a too bright flame. But her amber skin, whipped by the sun and the sea, flowered like that of a beautiful farm wench and could still dispense with paint. However, it was necessary to drape prudently if not indeed entirely to hide her ruined throat, girdled with great wrinkles which the sunshine had not penetrated.

Seated, she halted in the midst of her small occupations and hunted about her as if for a lost piece of furniture, her old-time energy, her promptness in ordering her upholstered domain.

"Ah, that journey," she sighed. "What possessed me? How tiring it was."

She knitted her eyebrows and drew down her mouth in her new dissatisfied habit on noting that the glass was broken on a little portrait by Chaplin, a head of a young girl, pink and silver, which Léa found ravishing.

"And a rent as big as my two hands in the lace curtain. And that's only the beginning. . . . What was I thinking of to stay away for so long? And in honor of whom? . . . As if I couldn't have indulged my grief here in comfort."

She rose to ring, pulled about her the muslin of her tea-gown and apostrophized herself crudely: "Get along with you, you old sentimentalist."

Her maid entered, burdened with lingerie and silk stockings.

"Eleven o'clock, Rose. And my face hasn't been massaged. I'm late."

"Madame has nothing to hurry for. Madame hasn't those Demoiselles Mégret to drag madame off on picnics and to pick all her roses every morning. There's no longer Monsieur Roland to drive madame mad tossing pebbles against the window of her room."

"Rose, there's plenty to keep us busy here in this house. I don't know if moving the proverbial three times is as bad as one fire, but I do know that being away from home for six months is as bad as one deluge. Have you seen the lace curtain?"

"That's nothing. Madame hasn't seen the linen room yet. Mouse tracks everywhere and the carpet in holes. And just the same, it's queer that I left Emérancie twenty-eight dish cloths and I can find only twenty-two."

"No!"

"Just as I'm telling madame."

They looked at each other with equal indignation, mutually attached to this comfortable house of silent carpets and silks, of full cupboards and shining basements. Léa slapped her knee with her strong hand.

"All that's going to change, my friend. If Ernest and Emérancie don't want to be given their eight days notice they'll find those six dish cloths. And that donkey of a Marcel, did you write him to come back?"

"He's already here, madame."

Dressing promptly, Léa opened the window and leaned out to contemplate complacently her avenue of renaissant trees. No more obsequious spinsters, no more Monsieur Roland, that heavy and athletic young man from Cambo.

"The idiot," she mused.

But she pardoned this passing creature his silliness, holding against him only the fact that he had failed to please. In her memory, that of a healthy woman with a forgetful body, Monsieur Roland was nothing more than a strong animal, a little ridiculous and at times unusually awkward. . . . Léa would have denied now that a blinding flood of tears—one certain rainy night when the torrent rolled, perfumed, among rose geraniums—had for an instant hidden Monsieur Roland behind the image of Chéri. . . .

The brief adventure had left Léa neither regret nor embarrassment. Afterwards, as before, the idiot and his foolish old mother would have continued to find in Léa's rented villa at Cambo the well-served teas, the rocking chairs on the balcony, the delicious comfort that Léa knew how to dispense and in which she took great pride. But the idiot, mortified, departed, leaving Léa to the mercies of a stiff and handsome officer, already turning gray, who aspired to marriage with Madame de Lonval.

"Our age, our fortune, our taste for independence and society, don't all these things point to our being destined for each other?" murmured the colonel who still kept his slim waist.

She laughed, she enjoyed the company of this rather dry man who ate well and drank without becoming drunk. He erred, read in the beautiful blue eyes and in the confident continued smile of his hostess the consent that she deferred giving. An unfortunate gesture marked the end of their dawning friendship which Léa regretted, honestly blaming herself before her own conscience.

It was my fault. One shouldn't treat a Colonel Ypoustègue of a good old Basque family like a Monsieur Roland. I set him down a little too hard. Still he ought to have been a good sport and a man of spirit and come the next morning as usual in his dog cart to smoke his cigar and tease the two old maids.

She did not perceive that a man of mature years could accept his refusal but not certain glances which gauged him physically, which clearly compared him to another, to the unknown, to the invisible. . . .

Unexpectedly kissed, Léa had not hidden that terrible and prolonged ocular investigation of a woman who knows where to look for the withering that age imposes on a man; from the hands, dry and manicured, ribbed with tendons and with veins, her eyes mounted to the sagging jaw, to the forehead barred with wrinkles; came back cruelly to the mouth, set in crow's feet like commas. And all the elegance of the so-called Baroness de Lonval exploded in a "Hoh, là, là!" so outrageous, so explicit, so common, that the handsome Colonel Ypoustègue retreated over her doorstep for the last time.

My last loves, thought Léa, leaning out of her window. But the bright Parisian weather, the aspect of her clean and sonorous court with its clipped round laurels set in their green tubs, the scented warmth which escaped from her room and caressed her neck, little by little filled her again with malice and good humor. Women passed in silhouette, strolling toward the Bois.

"Skirts are changing again," Léa stated, "and hats are higher." She outlined a visit to her dressmaker, to Lewis; a sudden desire to be lovely seized her.

Lovely? For whom? For myself. And also to annoy the Mother Peloux.

Léa was not ignorant of Chéri's flight but the mere flight was all she knew. Severe with what she always called Charlotte's private detective system, still she permitted a young milliner whom she pampered to discharge her debt of gratitude by way of gossip poured into Léa's ears while the fitting was going on or received it with "a thousand thanks for those delicious chocolates," scrawled across a large sheet of paper embossed with the firm's letterhead. A postal card from the old Lili had reached Léa at Cambo, a postal card on which the ridiculous old harridan, without periods or punctuation and in a trembling script, recounted an incomprehensible story of love, of flight, of a young wife emprisoned at Neuilly.

It was fine weather just like today, Léa recalled, the morning at Cambo when I read the card from old Lili in my bath.

She recalled the yellow bathroom, the sunlight dancing on the water and on the ceiling. She heard again the echoes of that thin noisy villa throw back a great burst of laughter, rather ferocious and forced—her laughter—and then the cry that followed: "Rose. Rose."

Shoulders and breasts out of water, dripping, robust, with her magnificent arm still stretched and resembling more than ever a figure from a fountain, she shook the moist card between the tips of her fingers. "Rose. Rose. Chéri—Monsieur Peloux has jumped the traces. He's left his wife."

"Madame doesn't surprise me," said Rose, "and the divorce will be happier than the marriage which looked like a first class funeral to me."

All that day an importunate hilarity possessed Léa. Ah, my poisonous young lad. Oh, the wicked brat. Fancy.

And she shook her head, laughing quietly to herself like a mother whose son has stayed out all night for the first time.

A varnished phaéton filed before her gate, shone and disappeared, almost noiseless on its rubber tires and the fine feet of its trotting pair.

"Well, well, there goes Spéleïeff," Léa declared. "A fine chap. And here comes Merguilier on his spotted horse. It must be eleven o'clock. Berthellemy-le-Desséché will be next, en route to thaw his bones on the Sentier de la Vertu. It's curious how people can go on doing the same thing all their lives. I could believe that I had never left Paris if Chéri were here. My poor Chéri, it's all over with him for the present. Out all night, women, eating no matter when, drinking too much. . . . It's too bad. Who knows but what he might have made a fine man if he'd only had a red face like a butcher and flat feet."

She left the window, rubbing her numbed elbows, and shrugged her shoulders. One can rescue Chéri once but not twice. She polished her nails, breathed on a tarnished ring, inspected at close range the unsuccessful red of her hair and the whitening roots and made some notes in her engagement book. She did everything quickly and with less composure than usual in order to fight off one of those subtle attacks of anxiety which she knew well and which she called—denying even the memory of her former pain—her moral indigestion. She wanted by fits and starts a well-swung victoria drawn by a regular dowager's cob, then a high-powered automobile, then directoire furniture for her salon. She even thought of changing the style of her coiffure which for twenty years she had worn high, revealing the nape of her neck. A little knot, low down, like Lavallière? That would allow me to cope with those loose-belted dresses they're wearing this year. In short with a strict diet and my henna decently done I can pretend to ten—no, let's say five years more of. . . .

An effort restored to her her common sense, filled her with lucid pride. A woman like me and not enough courage to know when to call a halt? Come, come, my fine friend, we've had our money's worth in our time. In her mirror she surveyed the tall Léa standing erect, her hands on her hips, smiling at herself.

A woman like that doesn't finish off in the arms of old men. A woman like that who's had the luck never to soil her hands or mouth on a wrinkled human being. Yes, there she is, the perfect vampire, if you wish, who only wants fresh flesh.

She recalled in her memories the passing faces and lovers of her youth which had been unpolluted by old men and to herself she seemed clean, proud, devoted for thirty years to radiant striplings or to fragile adolescents.

After all, the fresh flesh has been indebted to me. How many of them have me to thank for their good health, their beauty, their little worries which were never questionable, egg-nogs when they had colds and the habit of making love without selfishness or monotony. And I could dream now, merely in order not to have an empty bed, of some old gentleman in his—in his—

She cast about and decided with majestic unconsciousness: an old gentleman in his forties.

She pressed one of her beautifully made hands against the other in disgust, made a right-about face.

Pah. Goodbye to everything, that's cleaner. Let's buy a pack of cards, good wine, bridge scores, knitting needles, all the paraphernalia needed as a stop-gap for life, everything needed to hide that horror—the old woman.

As a substitute for knitting needles she had numerous new gowns and a bed jacket that was like the clouds at dawn. The Chinese pedicurist came once a week, the manicurist twice and the masseuse every day. Léa was seen at the theater and before the theater in restaurants which she had never frequented in Chéri's time.

She permitted that young women and their friends, that Kühn, her former tailor and now retired, invite her to their loges or to their tables. But the young women treated her with a deference she did not require and Kühn called her "my dear friend," to which she responded at the beginning of their first feast: "Kühn, no question about it, being a client is not becoming to you."

She hunted out Patron again like one seeking a refuge, Patron, now umpire and promotor in some boxing scheme. But Patron was married to a young creature who ran a bar and was slight, terrible and jealous as a rat terrier. In order to find this sensible athlete, Léa had even risked going to the Place d'Italie, wrapped in her sapphire blue gown heavy with gold, her bird of paradise feathers, her imposing jewels and her hair the color of new mahogany. She had breathed the odors of sweat, of vinegar and turpentine, cast off by the "white hopes" Patron was training, and left, sure of never again setting foot in the enormous low hall where the gas whistled in green flames.

The effort she made to enter into the unsettled life of idle people cost her a weariness that she could not understand.

What's the matter with me?

She rubbed her ankles a little swollen by the time evening came, scanned her strong teeth below which the gums were only ever so slightly receding, tapped with her fist, as if sounding a cask, on her large-lying lungs, on her jovial stomach. Something indefinable in her, deprived of its absent support, was bending and carried her in its decline. The Baroness de la Berche, met in a cheap bar where she was washing down two dozen snails with a glass of wine fit for a cab driver, was the one who finally informed Léa of the return of the prodigal to the fold and of the rising of a new honeymoon in the Boulevard d'Inkermann's sky. Léa listened to this moral tale with indifference. But she turned pale with painful emotion the day after on recognizing the blue limousine before her gate and Charlotte Peloux who crossed the court.

"At last, at last. I've found you again, Léa, sweetheart. Handsomer than ever. Thinner than last year. Take care, dearie, don't risk getting too thin at our age. As you are now, but no more. And even at that. . . . However, what bliss to see you again."

Never had the grating voice sounded so sweet to Léa. She let Madame Peloux talk, grateful for this acid flow which gave her time to collect herself. She had seated Charlotte Peloux in a low armchair on small feet beneath the soft light of the little salon with the painted silk walls, as in other days. She herself mechanically took the stiff backed chair which compelled her to throw back her shoulders and lift her chin, as in other days. Between them the table spread with wrinkled old embroidery supported, as in other days the tall cut crystal carafe half full of aged brandy, the quivering chalice-shaped glasses, thin as a sheet of mica, cold water and dry biscuits.

"Well, sweetheart, now we're going to be able to see each other again freely, freely," sniveled Charlotte. "You know my motto—cut your friends dead when you're in trouble; only make them part of the happy moments of your life. All the while that Chéri was playing truant and I didn't give you any sign of life, it was on purpose, you understand? But now that my two children are happy once more, and I'm telling it to you, I throw myself in your arms and we start our good old life again," . . . she interrupted herself, lit a cigarette, as clever in creating suspense as an actress, "without Chéri, naturally."

"Without Chéri, naturally," acquiesced Léa, smiling.

She watched and listened to her old enemy with dumbfounded satisfaction. Those large inhuman eyes, that garrulous mouth, that short body, obese and restless—everything facing her had come only to put her strength to a test, to humiliate her as in other days, always as in other days. But as in other days, Léa knew how to respond, to despise, to smile, to assemble her forces. Already the sad weight which had been oppressing her yesterday and the days before seemed to have melted. A light which was normal and customary bathed the salon and played among the curtains.

Here we all are, thought Léa briskly. Two women a little older than last year, habitual malice and stock phrases, mild battles and our meals together; the financial page in the mornings, scandal-mongering in the afternoons—all that must be taken up because it's life, because it's my life. The Aldonzas and the de la Berches, the Lilis and a few old gentlemen without homes, all that lot squeezed around a gaming table where the brandy glasses and the cards will lie side by side maybe with a pair of little socks begun for a baby who'll soon be born. . . . Let's start it all again since it's in the order of things. And let's do it in good style since anyhow I fall into it as easily as slipping into a pair of old shoes.

And she settled herself, eyes clear and mouth parted, to listen to Charlotte Peloux who talked avidly about her daughter-in-law.

"You ought to know, Léa dear, if the ambition of my life hasn't always been peace and quiet? Well, I have it at last. Chéri's flight after all was just like breaking out in a rash. Far be it from me, my dear, to reproach you, but admit that from his nineteenth to his twenty-fifth year he really didn't have a chance to lead the life of a young bachelor. Well, he's led it now for three months, he has sowed his wild oats once and for all. And a good thing it was."

"It's better than that," said Léa without losing her gravity. "It's a pledge he gives to his young wife."

"Just it, just the word I was hunting for," squealed Madame

Peloux radiantly. "A pledge for their future. And ever since that day their life has been a dream. For you know when a Peloux once comes home after having really painted the town red, he doesn't go out again."

"Ah, a family tradition, I suppose?" demanded Léa.

But Charlotte was in no mood to listen. "Furthermore, he was well received when he came home. His little wife—ah, there's one worth having, I'll say. You know if I haven't seen a few little wives in my day—well, I never saw one who could even hold a candle to Edmée."

"Her mother is so remarkable," said Léa.

"Think, only think, sweetheart, Chéri left her on my hands for almost three months and between us I don't mind stating she was lucky that I was there."

"That's exactly what I was saying to myself," said Léa.

"Well, my dear, not one complaint; not a scene, not one stupid thing did she do, nothing, nothing. Patience itself, she was, and sweetness, with the face of a saint, a saint."

"It's terrifying," said Léa.

"And do you think when our young rapscallion walked in one morning, serene as if he'd just finished a stroll in the Bois, do you think she allowed herself to comment? Nothing. She didn't say that much. Also he, who in his heart ought to have felt a little ashamed—"

"Oh, why?" said Léa.

"Oh, really now, after all—As I was saying, he found a perfect reception and they made their peace in their bedroom, bang! just like that and without losing any time. Ah, I assure you, during that hour there wasn't a happier woman in the world than me."

"Except Edmée, perhaps," suggested Léa.

But Madame Peloux had an ear only for the soul and made a superb soaring movement with her fins. "I don't know what you're thinking of. Personally I thought of nothing but the home that was once more united."

She changed her tone, curled her eye and her lip. "In any case

I don't see that little girl in any delirium or crying out loud with ecstasy. Twenty years old and skinny. . . . Pah. At that age they yawn. And anyhow, between us, I think her mother's cold."

"Your theories of family solidarity lead you astray," said Léa.

Charlotte Peloux candidly displayed the depth of her enormous eyes in which nothing could be read.

"Oh, no—oh, no. Heredity. Heredity. I'm a firm believer in it. Therefore my son who is fantasy itself. . . . What? You didn't know he was fantasy itself?"

"It must have slipped my mind," Léa apologized.

"Well, as I started to say, I have high hopes for my son's future. He is going to love his home as I loved mine, he'll look after his fortune, he'll love his children as I loved him."

"Don't prophesy so many sad things at once," Léa begged. "What's it like, the home of the young people?"

"Sinister," cackled Madame Peloux. "Positively sinister. Violet carpets. Violet, mind you. A black and gold bathroom. A salon without any furniture in it and full of Chinese vases as big as I am. The result is they're always at Neuilly. Anyhow, without being conceited, the little wife adores me."

"Hasn't she ever had some strong nervous disorders?" demanded Léa with solicitude.

Charlotte Peloux's eye brightened. "She? No danger of that, we're up against a will of iron there."

"We? Who's we?"

"Pardon, sweetheart, habit, just habit. We are up against what I call a brain, a real brain. She has such a way of giving orders without raising her voice, of accepting Chéri's sallies, of swallowing poison as if it were condensed milk. . . . I ask myself sometimes, I really wonder if some day there mightn't be a danger in her for Chéri. I'm afraid, I'm really afraid that she'll put a damper on his originality, his—"

"What? He's toned down?" interrupted Léa. "Take some more of my brandy, Charlotte, it was Spéleïeff's, it's seventy-four years old and could be given to a new-born babe."

"Toned down's not the word exactly, but he's—inter—imperturb
—er—"

"Imperturbable?"

"You said it. For instance when he knew I was coming to see
you—"

"What? He knew it?"

The blood impetuously bounded to Léa's cheek and she damned
her hot emotions and the bright daylight of the little salon.

Madame Peloux with a suave eye fattened on Léa's distress. "But
of course he knew it. No point in blushing about that, sweetheart.
Aren't you a baby."

"In the first place how did you know I had come back?"

"Oh, for heaven's sake, Léa, don't ask questions like that. Everybody saw you everywhere."

"Yes, but Chéri—you told him I was back?"

"No, sweetheart, he was the one who told me."

"Oh, it was he who— Curious." She heard her heart beating in
her voice and dared not risk long sentences.

"He even added, 'Madame Peloux, you'll please me by going to
get news of Nounoune.' He's still so fond of you, the dear boy."

"How nice of him."

Madame Peloux, red in the face, seemed to abandon herself to
the influences of the brandy bottle and talked as in a dream, nodding
her head. But her russet eyes remained firm, steely, and kept watch
on Léa who sat stiffly, armed against herself and waiting for she did
not know what blow.

"It's nice but it's natural. A man doesn't forget a woman like
you, Léa mine. And do you want to know what I really think?
You've only to make a sign and—"

Léa put her hand on the arm of Charlotte Peloux. "I don't want
to know what you really think," she said kindly.

Madame Peloux let the corners of her mouth fall. "Oh, I understand you, I approve," she sighed in a wan voice. "When one's made
other arrangements in one's life like you have— Of course I haven't
said a word to you about yourself yet."

"But it seems to me you have."

"Happy?"

"Happy."

"A great love, eh? Marvelous voyage? Is he sweet? Where's his photograph?"

Léa, relieved, shook her head and sharpened her smile. "No, no, you'll not find out a thing. Hunt. Has your private detective system broken down, Charlotte?"

"I don't rely on any private detective system," replied Charlotte. "It wasn't because this one or that one told me that . . . that you'd been deserted again . . . that you'd had awful money troubles. . . . No, no, not I, you know how little attention I pay to twaddle like that."

"No one knows it better than I. My Lolotte, you can leave here without a worry on my behalf. Tell your friends the same. And I only hope they made half the killing I made on Oil Preferred between December and February."

The alcoholic cloud which had softened the features of Madame Peloux lifted. She showed a face, clear, dry, aroused. "You were on oil? I might have known it. And you didn't tell me."

"You didn't ask. Your mind was on your family only, quite naturally."

"Fortunately my mind was also on Pressed Bricks Common at the same time," the stifled trumpet fluted.

"Ah? And you didn't tell me either."

"Intrude on love's young dream? Not likely. Léa mine, I'm going now, but I'll come back."

"You'll come on Thursday because at present, Lolotte, dear, your Sundays at Neuilly . . . they're finished for me. Would you like it if we had little Thursdays here? No one except old friends. Mother Aldonza, our Right Reverend Father, the Baroness—your poker, my knitting—Well?"

"You knit?"

"Not yet, but it will come soon. Well?"

"I skip with joy at the thought. Look if I'm not skipping with joy. And you know I won't say a word about it at the house. The boy would be capable of coming here and asking for a glass of porto on Thursday. Just one more little kiss, sweetheart. God, how good you smell. Have you noticed that as the skin gets less firm, perfume lasts better? It's such a pleasure. . . ."

Hurry, hurry . . . Trembling, Léa's glance followed Madame Peloux as she crossed the court. Hurry on your evil way. Nothing will stop you. You turned your ankle? Yes, but you won't fall down. Your chauffeur is careful and doesn't skid, so he won't wreck you on a tree. You'll arrive safe enough at Neuilly and you'll choose your moment—today, tomorrow, next week—to say all the things you never should say. You'll try to upset those who perhaps are at peace. The least you'll do is to make them tremble momentarily like me.

Her limbs quivered like those of a horse that has climbed a hill but she did not suffer. The guard she had maintained over herself and over her replies rejoiced her. A pleased vivacity illumined her skin and her eyes and she kneaded her handkerchief into a ball because she still had force to expend. She was unable to take her thoughts off Charlotte Peloux.

We've found each other again, she thought. Like two dogs finding the slipper they're in the habit of chewing. How curious. That woman is my enemy and it's from her my comfort comes. How bound together we are, she and I.

She dreamed for a long time, by fits and starts fearful and then accepting her fate. The relaxation of her nerves afforded her a brief sleep. Seated and with her cheek on her hand in dream she penetrated into her immediate old age, imaged her days one after the other and all the same; saw herself across from Charlotte Peloux, and prevented by a lively rivalry which shortened the hours from sinking into the ripe woman's degrading indifference first to her corsets, then to the tinting of her hair and finally to fine underclothes. She tasted in advance the shameful pleasures of the senile which are nothing but secret struggles, murderous wishes and hot hopes constantly refreshed in imagined catastrophes which spare but one human being, but one spot on earth—and woke astonished in twilight pink and comparable to the dawn.

"Ah, Chéri," she sighed.

But it was no longer the raucous hungry outcry of the year past nor the tears nor the revolt of the whole body which suffers and mutinies against the inorganic grief that tries to destroy it. . . . Léa rose, rubbed her cheek, tooled by the cushion's embroidery.

My poor Chéri. . . . It's curious to think that in losing your old mistress, I my scandalous young lover—we both lost the most honorable thing we had on earth.

Two days passed after the visit of Charlotte. Two gray days which were long to Léa and which she patiently endured with the soul of an apprentice. "Since we are going to have to live like this, let's start," she stated. But she applied herself with awkwardness and an exaggerated industry that augured ill for her novitiate. The second day she wanted to go out, to walk as far as the Lakes just before noon.

I'll buy a dog, she decided. He'll keep me company and force me to walk. And Rose had to hunt in the bottom of the cedar closet for a pair of yellow boots with thick soles and a rough-looking suit which smelled of the Alps and the forest. Léa started out with that swing which certain types of shoes and wool clothing impose upon their wearer.

Ten years ago I would have risked carrying a cane, she thought. Still close to her house she heard behind her a rapid light step which she thought she recognized. A stupefying fear which she had no time to combat enervated her and despite herself she was overtaken, then outdistanced by an unknown hurried young man who did not glance at her.

Relieved, she breathed; "I'm too absurd."

She bought a dark carnation for her button-hole and started off again. But before her, thirty paces away, firmly planted in the diaphanous fog which covered the lawns and the avenue, a masculine silhouette awaited her.

This time I know I recognize that cut of the waistcoat and the fashion of swinging the stick. No, thanks, I don't want him to see me wearing shoes like a postman's and a thick jacket that makes me look fat. If I must meet him, I'd rather he saw me in something other than this, since he never could stand brown anyhow. No, no, I'm going home, I'm . . .

At this moment the man who was waiting hailed an empty taxi, stepped in and passed in front of Léa; he was a blond young man with a small mustache. But Léa did not smile and no longer felt at ease. She turned on her heel and went home.

"One of my bad days, Rose. Tired. Give me my peachblow tea gown, the new one, and the big robe, the embroidered one without sleeves. I'm smothering in all this wool."

There's no point in forcing my luck, thought Léa. Two times in succession it wasn't Chéri; the third time it would have been. I know these little tricks of fate. There's nothing to be done against them and today I have no fight in me. I'm weak.

She occupied herself all day with her patient efforts at solitude. Cigarettes and her newspapers amused her after luncheon and she welcomed with brief joy a telephone call from the Baroness de la Berche, then one from Spéleïeff, her former lover, the handsome horse-dealer who had seen her the night before and who wanted to sell her a fine pair.

Then there followed a long hour of total silence which was frightening. Her arms bare, her hands on her hips, she walked up and down, followed by a magnificent train of her heavy robe broidered in gold and roses.

Come, come, let's try to see the facts as they are. The moment that the boy no longer cares anything about me is not the time for me to become demoralized. I've lived alone now for six months. In the Midi I managed very well. For one thing, I went from place to place. And those creatures in the Riviera and the Pyrénées did me good, each time one of them went away forever I felt quite revived. . . . Poultices on a burn won't cure but they relieve on condition that one changes them all the time. My six months of changing are the life story of that horrible Sarah Cohen who married the ugliest man on earth. "Each time I look at him," she said, "I think I'm pretty."

But before those last six months; I knew what it was to live alone. How did I live after I left Spéleïeff, for instance? Oh, yes, I did all the bars and night places with Patron and right after that I had Chéri. But before Spéleïeff, the little Lequellec whose family dragged him away so they could carry him off, poor lad, with his beautiful eyes full of tears. . . . After him I was alone four months, I remember. The first month I cried a lot. No, it was for Bacciocchi that I cried so much. But when I finished crying no one could hold me I was so delighted to find myself alone. Yes, but during the Bacciocchi period I was twenty-eight years old and after Lequellec I was thirty and between them I had known. . . . Well, it doesn't much matter. . . . After Spéleïeff I was disgusted with so much money badly spent. Whereas after Chéri, I'm . . . I'm fifty years old and I committed the imprudence of holding him for seven years.

She wrinkled her forehead, made herself ugly in a bad-humored grimace.

It serves me right. At my age one doesn't keep a lover for seven years. Seven years. He ruined what was left of me. In those seven years I might have had two or three little happinesses quite comfortably instead of one enormous regret. . . . A liaison of seven years is like following a husband out to the colonies; when you come back no one recognizes you and you've forgotten how to wear your clothes properly.

To strengthen her resistance she rang for Rose and they rearranged Léa's laces in the small armoire devoted to their care. Night settled down, hatching the lights beneath it. Rose was called below to her other duties in the house.

"Tomorrow," Léa said, "I'll take the car and motor to the Norman stud farm of Spéleïeff. I'll take old La Berche if she wishes—it will recall to her mind the carriages of her former glory. And my word, if the younger Spéleïeff casts his eye my way, I don't say that I wouldn't . . ."

She took the trouble to smile with a tempting mysterious air in order to deceive whatever phantoms might be strolling around her dressing table and her formidable bed which scintillated in the shadow. But she felt cold all over and contemptuous of the voluptuous pleasures of others.

Her dinner of fine fish and pastries provided a recreation. She replaced Bordeaux with dry champagne and hummed on leaving the table. Eleven o'clock surprised her as she was measuring with a cane the width of the panels between the windows of her room where she considered replacing all the big mirrors with old canvases painted with flowers and balustrades. She yawned, scratched her head and rang to be made ready for the night. While Rose removed her long silk stockings, Léa considered the conquered day already shed into the past, which gratified her like a penance performed. Sheltered for the night from the danger of idleness, she discounted the hours of sleep against those of wakefulness, since restlessness recovers along with night the privilege of yawning out loud, of sighing, of cursing the sound of the milk carts, the street sweepers and the first sparrows.

During her preparations for the night she turned over her mind mild projects which she would never realize.

Aline Mesmacker has taken a restaurant-bar which has turned into a perfect gold mine. Obviously it's something to do as well as an investment. . . . But I can't see myself behind a cashier's desk and if one hires a manager it's not worth while. Dora and that fat Fifi are running a night club together, old La Berche told me. Everyone's doing it. And they wear boiled shirts and smoking jackets to attract a special clientèle. Fat Fifi has three children to bring up— well, they're her excuse. . . . Then there's Kühn who is bored and would be delighted to take some of my capital to open a new tailoring business.

Naked and tinted bright pink by the reflections in her Pompeian bathroom, she scented herself with her sandalwood and with unconscious pleasure unfolded a long nightgown of silk.

All those are idle words. I know perfectly well that I don't like to work. To bed, madame. You'll never have any other place of business and all the clients are fled.

She wrapped herself in a white gandourah whose colored lining lent it an indefinite pink light and returned to her dressing table. Her two lifted arms combed and clasped her hair, hardened by dye, and framed her tired face. They remained so magnificent, these arms, full and muscled from the arm-pit down to the rounded elbow, that she contemplated them a long moment.

What lovely handles for such an old urn.

With negligent fingers she planted a pale comb at the nape of her neck and without much hope chose a detective story from the shelf of a dark closet. She had no taste for fine bindings and could not break herself of her habit of relegating books to the bottom of closets in company with empty boxes and bottles from the pharmacy.

As she stood bent over her big open bed, stroking the fine cold linen, the deep bell of the court vibrated. The solemn, round, unwonted sound shocked the midnight hour.

"What on earth—?" she said aloud.   66791

She listened, lips apart, holding her breath. A second peal was even louder than the first and Léa in a gesture of self-preservation and modesty ran to powder her face. She was going to ring for Rose when she heard the front door slam, the noise of steps in the vestibule and staircase, two voices mingled, her maid's and someone's else. She had no time to make a decision, the door opened under a brutal hand; Chéri was before her, his coat wide over his evening clothes, his hat still on his head, pale and menacing.

He leaned against the closed door and did not move. He looked not so much at Léa as at the entire room, in an errant fashion, like a man about to be attacked.

Léa who had that morning trembled before a silhouette guessed at in the fog, so far felt nothing more than the displeasure of a woman surprised in her undressing. She closed her tea gown, settled her comb, hunted with one foot for her fallen slipper. She blushed but when the blood left her cheeks she had already gained the appearance of calm. She lifted her head and seemed taller than the young man leaning in black against the white door.

"That's a nice way to enter," she said rather loudly. "You might at least take off your hat and say good evening."

"Good evening," said Chéri in a haughty voice.

Its sound seemed to astonish him; he looked about him more humanly. A sort of smile descended from his eyes to his mouth and he repeated gently: "Good evening." He removed his hat and took two or three steps. "May I sit down?"

"If you wish," said Léa.

He sat down on an ottoman and saw that she remained standing. "Are you dressing? Aren't you going out?"

She made a sign of denial, seated herself far from him, took up her nail buffer and said nothing. He lit a cigarette and asked permission to smoke after it was lighted.

"If you wish," said Léa indifferently.

He said nothing more and lowered his eyes. The hand holding his cigarette trembled slightly which he noted and braced it against the edge of the table. Léa applied herself to her nails with slow movements and from time to time passed a brief glance over Chéri's face, above all over his lowered lids and the somber fringe of his lashes.

"It's Ernest as usual who opened the door for me," said Chéri at last.

"Why shouldn't it be Ernest? Should I change my staff of servants just because you are married?"

"No. . . . I mean, I simply remarked that . . ."

Silence fell again. Léa broke it. "May I ask if you have the intention of staying much longer? I haven't even asked you yet why you permit yourself to come to my house at midnight—"

"You may ask me," he said quickly.

She shook her head. "It doesn't interest me."

He lifted himself forcibly, spinning the ottoman behind him, and walked toward Léa. She felt him bend over her as if he were going to strike her but she did not draw back. She thought: What should I be afraid of in this world?

"You don't know why I've come back here? You don't want to know why I've come back?"

He tore off his coat, threw it wing-like toward the chaise longue, crossed his arms and cried close to Léa's face in a tone of stifled triumph: "I've come home."

She was manipulating a delicate manicure instrument which she closed unhurriedly before drying her fingers. Chéri fell back on a chair as if he had no more strength.

"Good," said Léa. "You've come back. That's very pretty. Whom did you consult about that?"

"Myself," said Chéri.

She lifted herself now in her turn the better to dominate. The beating of her calmed heart allowed her to breathe freely and she wished to play her scene without a fault.

"Why didn't you ask my advice? I'm an old friend who knows all about such tricks. How did you happen not to think that in coming here you might not embarrass—someone?"

With bent head he inspected the room horizontally; its closed doors, the bed girded in metal and its embankment of precious pillows. He saw nothing unwonted, nothing new, and shrugged his shoulders.

Léa expected more than that and insisted: "You understand what I mean to say?"

"Perfectly," he answered. "The gentleman of the house hasn't come in yet? The gentleman is passing the night somewhere else?"

"Those things are none of your business, my dear," she said tranquilly.

He bit his lip and nervously shook the ash from his cigarette into an old-fashioned carved jewel cup.

"Not in there, I always tell you that," cried Léa. "How many times must I—"

She broke off, reproaching herself for having taken on without noticing the voice of their familiar quarrels. But he seemed not to have heard, examining a ring, an emerald bought by Léa on her voyage.

"What's . . . what's this?" he stammered.

"That? It's an emerald."

"I'm not blind. I mean to say, who gave it to you?"

"No one you know."

"Charming," said Chéri bitterly.

His accent returned to Léa all her authority and she gave herself the pleasure of pushing her advantage farther.

"Isn't it charming? Everywhere I go I'm complimented on it. And the setting. Did you notice the filigree of diamonds which—"

"Enough!" bawled Chéri with rage, striking his fist on the fragile table.

Some roses shed their leaves at the impact, a porcelain cup slipped without breaking to the thick carpet. Léa stretched toward the telephone a hand which Chéri stopped with a rough arm.

"What are you going to do with that telephone?"

"Call the police," said Léa.

He took her two arms, feigned boyishness in pushing her far from the transmitter. "Oh, listen, don't be silly. One can't say a word without your becoming melodramatic."

She sat down and turned her back on him. He remained standing, his hands empty; his mouth, open and swollen, was that of a sulky child. One black lock hung down over his eyebrow. In a mirror Léa spied on him clandestinely but he seated himself and his face disappeared from the glass. In turn Léa, embarrassed, felt that he was looking at her back, enlarged by the fullness of her robe. She returned to her dressing table, stroked her hair, replanted her comb and, as if for want of something better to do, opened a vial of her perfume. Chéri turned his head toward this odor.

"Nounoune," he called.

She did not answer.

"Nounoune."

"Beg my pardon," she said without turning.

"Not jolly likely."

"I'll not force you. But you'll have to leave. And at once."

"Pardon," he said promptly and in a snarling voice.

"Better than that."

"Pardon," he repeated in a low voice.

"Good." She came to him and passed her hand over his bent head. "Now tell us all about it."

He trembled and shook under the caress. "What do you want me to tell you? It's not complicated. I've come home here, that's all."

"Talk, go on, talk to me."

He balanced on the edge of her chair, pressing his hands between his knees, and lifted his head toward Léa but without looking at her. She saw his white nostrils flare, she heard his rapid breath which he sought to discipline. She only had to say once more; "Go on; talk," and push him with her finger as if to make him fall over.

"Nounoune, darling," he called. "Nounoune, darling," and threw himself against her with all his force, embracing her long limbs which suddenly bent.

Forced to her chair, she let him slip to the floor and roll against her with tears, with incoherent words, with groping fingers which caught at her laces, at her necklace, seeking beneath her robe the form of her shoulder and the place for his ear beneath her hair.

"Nounoune, darling, I've found you again, my Nounoune, oh, my Nounoune, your shoulder and your perfume and your necklace, my Nounoune. Oh, it's wonderful. . . . And that little burnt taste always in your hair—ah, it's wonderful."

Fallen back, he exhaled the childish word like the last breath from his lungs. From his knees he clasped Léa in his arms and offered her his forehead shadowed with hair, his trembling wet mouth and his eyes where joy poured out in luminous tears. She observed him so deeply, with so perfect a forgetfulness of all that was not himself that she did not think to kiss him. She tied her arms around Chéri's throat and pressed him to her in a tender synchrony with the rhythm of murmured words: "My dearest, my bad little thing. . . . You're here. . . . You've come back again. . . . What is it you've done now? You're so naughty. . . . My beauty."

Behind closed lips he commiserated with himself softly and hardly spoke. He listened to Léa and placed his cheek on her breast.

He begged "Again" when she suspended her tender litany and Léa, who feared crying with him, scolded him with the same voice.

"Wicked little beast. . . . Heartless little devil. . . . My good-for-nothing."

He gave her a look of gratitude. "Yes, yes. Abuse me, Nounoune."

She held him at arm's length the better to enjoy him. "You love me then?"

He lowered his eyes in childish confusion. "Yes, Nounoune."

A little outburst of strangled laughter which she could not imprison warned Léa that she was close to giving herself over to the most terrible joy of her life. An embrace, the collapse, the open bed, two bodies joining like the two living halves of an animal which had just been sundered. No, no, she thought. Not yet, not yet.

"I'm thirsty," sighed Chéri. "Nounoune, I'm thirsty."

She rose in haste, felt of the tepid carafe and disappeared to return in the same breath. Chéri, rolled in a ball on the floor, was resting his head on the couch.

"Rose will fetch you some lemonade," said Léa. "Don't stay there. Sit on the chaise longue. Does the lamp annoy you?"

She trembled with joy at serving and giving orders. She seated herself on the divan and Chéri half reclined against her.

"Perhaps you'll tell me a little now about—"

The entry of Rose interrupted her. Without rising Chéri turned his head languidly toward Rose. "Evening, Rose."

"Good evening, monsieur," said Rose discreetly.

"Rose, tomorrow at nine I want—"

"Brioches and chocolate," Rose finished for him.

Chéri closed his eyes with a sigh of well-being. "How right you are. . . . Rose, where am I going to dress in the morning?"

"In the boudoir," said Rose complacently. "Only I'd better take the couch out and shouldn't I bring in the dressing table as it used to be?"

She looked for consultation toward Léa, proudly in evidence and holding up her spoiled charge while he drank.

"If you wish, Rose," said Léa. "We'll see. That'll be all now."

Rose retired and during the moment of silence which followed nothing could be heard except the uncertain sound of the wind and the cry of a bird that mistook the moon for dawn.

"Chéri, are you asleep?"

He drew one of his long hunting-dog sighs. "No, no, Nounoune. I'm too happy to sleep."

"Tell me, darling. . . . You didn't make trouble for anyone—over there—did you?"

"At home? No, Nounoune. Not at all, I assure you."

"Was there a scene?"

He looked up at her without lifting his trusting head. "Honestly. I left because I left, that's all. The child's very nice, there was no trouble."

"Ah."

"However, I wouldn't take my oath that she had no suspicions. This evening she had what I always call her orphan expression; you know, sad eyes beneath her lovely hair . . . you know what pretty hair she has?"

"Yes." She offered monosyllables only in a low voice as if she answered one who talked in his sleep.

"I suspect," continued Chéri, "that she must have seen me cross the garden."

"Ah."

"Yes. She was on the balcony in a white beaded dress, a sort of frozen white—oh, I don't like that frock . . . that dress had made me want to cut and run ever since dinner."

"Yes?"

"Yes, it did, Nounoune. Still I'm not really sure she saw me. The moon wasn't up. It rose while I was waiting."

"Where were you waiting?"

Chéri vaguely waved his hand toward the avenue. "There. I was waiting; you understand. I wanted to see. I waited a long time."

"But what for?"

He moved away from her brusquely, sat down on another chair. He resumed his expression of savage suspicion. "I wanted to be sure there was nobody here."

"Ah, yes, you thought that . . ." She could not resist a laugh of

105

contempt. A lover in her house? A lover as long as Chéri was alive? It was grotesque. How stupid he is, she thought with enthusiasm.

"You're laughing?"

He stood up before her, put his hand on her forehead and pushed back her hair. "You can laugh? You're making fun of me. You've . . . you have a lover—you? You have someone?"

He bent over her as he spoke, forcing her neck against the chaise longue. She felt on her eyelids the breath from his malevolent mouth and made no effort to free herself from the hand that strained at her forehead and hair.

"Dare to say it, that you have a lover."

Her eyelids wavered, she was dazed by the bursting visage which bore down on her and she said finally in a toneless voice: "No, I have no lover. I love you."

He released her and began pulling off his dinner jacket, his waist-coat; his cravat whistled through the air and settled around the throat of the bust of Léa on the mantelpiece. He did not move away from her, however, and still kept her, knee to knee, seated on the chaise longue. When she saw him half naked, she asked him almost sadly: "Ah, why, Chéri. . . . Yes?"

He did not answer, absorbed by the idea of his approaching pleas-ure and his eagerness to possess her again. She submitted and served her young lover as a good mistress, attentive and grave. Only with a sort of terror she saw approaching the moment of her own defeat; she endured Chéri like a form of torture, pushed him with her weak hands, but kept him between her powerful knees. Finally she seized him by the arm, cried out feebly and sank into that abyss from which love remounts pale, taciturn and full of regret for its death.

They did not leave each other's embrace and no word troubled the long silence in which they came back to life. Chéri's body had slipped against Léa's side and with eyes closed he lay with his head hanging on the sheet as if he had been stabbed upon his mistress. She, turned from him a little, bore almost all his weight which spared her nothing. She panted quietly; her left arm, crushed, hurt her and Chéri felt his neck growing numb, but both waited in respectful immobility until the decreasing bolt of pleasure should pass farther away from them.

He's sleeping, thought Léa. Her free hand still held Chéri's wrist which she pressed softly. A knee whose beautiful curve she knew well, was bruising her knee. At the height of her own heart she felt the equal stifled beating of another heart. Tenacious, violent, a mixture of oily flowers and exotic woods, Chéri's perfume wandered through the room. He is here, she thought. Leaving his house, his silly little, pretty little wife, he has come back, he's come back to me. Who could take him away? Now, now I can organize our lives. . . . He doesn't always know what he wants, but me, I know. Doubtless we'll have to go away. We won't hide but we'll need quiet. . . . And then I have to have time to look at him. I couldn't have looked at him enough all the years I didn't know I loved him. I'll have to find some spot where there'll be enough room for his caprices and my will. . . . I'll think for both of us. . . . Let him do the sleeping.

As with precaution she withdrew her left arm, prickling and painful, and her shoulder which immobility had paralyzed, she glanced at Chéri's tilted face and saw that he was not asleep. The white of his eyes was gleaming and the short black wing of his long lashes beat irregularly.

"What? Aren't you asleep?"

She felt him tremble against her and he turned over in one complete movement. "But you're not asleep either, Nounoune." He stretched his hand toward the night table and touched the lamp; a curtain of pink light covered the bed, heightened the pattern of the lace, dug dark hollows between the padded hills of the down quilt. Chéri, extended at full length, saluted this scene of his peace and of his passionate pleasures. Léa, leaning on her elbow at her side, caressed the long lashes which she loved and lifted Chéri's hair from his forehead. Lying thus and with his hair scattered over his temples, he looked as if he had been blown down by some furious wind.

The enamel clock struck. Chéri brusquely sat up in bed. "What time is it?"

"I don't know; what difference can it make to us?"

"Oh, I just asked. . . ."

He laughed briefly and did not lie down at once. The bottles of the first milk-cart rang out their noisy chimes and he made a slight movement in the direction of the avenue. Between the strawberry-colored curtains the cold blade of dawning day insinuated itself. Chéri brought his glance back to Léa and contemplated her with that force and fixity which make the attention of a perplexed child or an incredulous dog so formidable. An unreadable thought rose in the depths of his eyes whose form, whose gilliflower color, whose alternating severe or sad brilliance only aided him in conquering rather than in revealing his mind. His nude torso, large through the shoulders, slim about the waist, emerged from the mussed sheets as from foam and all his being breathed forth the melancholy of perfect things.

"Ah, Chéri . . ." breathed Léa drunkenly.

He did not smile, accustomed to receiving praise simply. "Tell me, Nounoune. . . ."

"What, my beauty?"

He hesitated, winked his eyes, trembled. "I'm tired. . . . And tomorrow, how will you manage about . . ."

With tender force Léa thrust the naked arms, the heavy head back among the pillows. "Don't worry about all that. Lie down. Isn't Nounoune here? Don't think of anything. Sleep. You're cold, I wager. . . . Here, take this, it's warm."

She rolled him in the silk and wool of some small feminine garment plucked from the bed and extinguished the light. In the shadow she lent him her shoulder, bent herself about him happily, listened to the breathing which echoed her own. No desire tormented her but still she did not hope for sleep. Let him sleep, it's for me to think, she repeated to herself. I'll manage so that our departure will be painless, discreet; what I wish is to cause the least amount of scandal and suffering. . . . It'll be the Midi again which would please us most, it being Spring. If I consulted only myself, I'd rather stay here, peacefully. But the old Madame Peloux and the young Madame Peloux. . . . The image of a young woman in a nightgown, anxious and standing by a window, checked Léa only long enough for her to shrug her shoulders with cold impartiality. I can do nothing about that. What makes one person's happiness. . . .

The black silk head moved on her breast and the sleeping lover moaned in a dream. With a savage arm, Léa protected him from his nightmare and rocked him so that he finally rested—without eyes, without memory, without plans,—resembling some spoiled child she had never given birth to in her youth.

Awake for some time, he refrained from moving. Cheek on folded arm, he tried to guess the hour. A pure sky must have been shedding its precocious heat on the avenue since no shadow of a cloud mitigated the ardent pink of the curtains. Ten o'clock, perhaps? Hunger gnawed him, he had eaten little the night before. A year ago he would have bounded out of bed, disturbed Léa's rest and furiously called at the top of his lungs for creamy chocolate and iced butter. . . . He did not move. He feared by moving to crumble the last of his joy, the occular pleasure he tasted in the ember-pink of the curtains, the steel and copper spirals of the bed shimmering in the colored light of the room. His great happiness of the night before seemed to have taken refuge, melted and small, in the reflection of a rainbow that flickered on the side of a crystal cup.

The circumspect footsteps of Rose grazed the carpet of the landing. A discreet broom was sweeping the court. Chéri heard a distant tinkling of china in the butler's pantry. . . . How long this morning is, he thought. I'll get up. But he remained motionless because behind him, Léa yawned, stretched her legs. A soft hand touched his back but he closed his eyes and all his body enacted a falsehood by feigning the softness of sleep. He sensed that Léa left the bed and he saw her pass in black silhouette before the curtain which she half opened. She turned toward him, glanced and shook her head with a smile which was not victorious but resolute and equal to all dangers. She was in no haste to leave the room and Chéri, opening his eyes by a hair's-breadth of light, spied on her. He saw that she opened a time table and moved her finger down its column of figures. Then she seemed to calculate, her face lifted toward the sky and her brows knitted. As yet unpowdered, a meager twist of hair on the nape of her neck, with double chin and ruined throat, she imprudently offered herself to the invisible eye.

She moved away to the window, took her checkbook from the drawer and inscribed and detached several checks. Then she spread some white pyjamas on the foot of the bed and left the room without a sound.

In taking a long breath, Chéri realized he had not breathed since Léa left the bed. He rose, put on the pyjamas and opened the window. "It's stifling in here," he gasped.

He had the vague and uncomfortable impression of having done something which was rather ugly. Because I pretended to be asleep? But after all, I've seen Léa hundreds of times just after she got out of bed. Only this time, I pretended to be asleep. . . .

The bursting bright day restored its floral tint to the pink room and to the blond and silver Chaplin portrait smiling from the wall, gave back all its sentimental nuances. Chéri bent his head and closed his eyes so that his memory might restore to him the room of the night before; mysterious and tinged like the inside of a water-melon, an unearthly lighted dome for a lamp and an exultation which carried him, reeling, through his delights. . . .

"Are you up? The chocolate's coming at once."

He noted with gratitude that within a few minutes, Léa had dressed her hair, was rouged slightly and impregnated with the familiar perfume. The sound of her fine cordial voice expanded in the room along with the odor of buttered toast and cocoa. Chéri sat down by two steaming cups and received from Léa's hands the heavily buttered toast. He hunted for something to say and Léa never suspected it since she had known him to be taciturn at best and contemplative in the presence of food. She ate with good appetite, with the preoccupied haste and gayety of a woman whose trunks are strapped, breakfasting before the train leaves.

"Your second piece of toast, Chéri?"

"No thanks, Nounoune."

"Not hungry any more?"

"Not hungry."

Laughing, she shook her finger at him. "What you need is probably a couple of rhubarb pills, they'd fix you, eh?"

He wrinkled his nose, shocked. "Listen, Nounoune, really you have a passion for occupying yourself with details which are. . . ."

"Tchk, tchk. That's my affair if I choose to. Stick out your tongue. You won't? Then wipe off your chocolate whiskers and let's talk briefly but to the point. The quicker disagreeable things are finished, the better."

Across the table she took one of Chéri's hands in both of hers. "You've come back. It was our fate. You trust yourself to me? I'll take entire care of you."

Without wishing to, she interrupted herself and closed her eyes, docile before her victory. Chéri saw the impetuous blood flood the face of his mistress.

"Ah," she continued in a lower voice, "when I think of all that I never gave you; of all that I never said to you! When I think that I believed you were merely a young transient in my life like all the others; a little more precious than all the others. How stupid I was not to understand that you were my love, the love, the great love which only comes once."

She opened her eyes which seemed to have become more blue, a blue re-dipped in the shadow of her eyelids. She breathed unevenly.

"Oh," Chéri prayed to himself, "if only she doesn't ask me a question; if only she doesn't expect an answer now; I couldn't speak a word."

She wrung his hand. "Come now, we'll be serious. As I said, we'll go away, we are going, we are gone. Very good. What preparations will you make . . . over there . . . at Neuilly? Let Charlotte arrange the necessary money settlements for that house, it's wiser—and make her be generous, I beg of you. How will you let them know, at Neuilly?—by letter, I suppose. It's not convenient but the less ink spilled the better. We'll see about that together. There's also the question of luggage, none of your things are here any more. . . .

All these details are more aggravating than any big problem but don't worry about them. . . . Will you kindly stop pulling at your toe like that? It's with such pretty little habits that one gets infections."

Mechanically he let his foot drop. His native speechlessness crushed him and he was obliged to focus his jaded attention in order to listen. He scrutinized the animated, the joyous imperious face of his friend and asked himself vaguely. Why does she look so happy?

His stupidity became so evident that Léa, who by now was monologuing on the desirability of buying old Berthellemy's yacht, stopped short.

"Could anyone believe that you haven't a word of advice to give? Ah, you'll never be anything else but twelve years old."

Chéri, torn from his stupor, passed his hand over his forehead and enveloped Léa with a melancholic gaze. "To you, Nounoune, I'll probably seem twelve years old for another half century."

She winked her eyes several times, as if he had blown on the lids, and let the silence settle between them.

"What are you trying to say?" she finally demanded.

"Nothing except what I did say, Nounoune. Nothing but the truth. Can you deny it, you who are the most honest person alive?"

She decided to laugh with a carelessness which already hid a great fear.

"But your childishness is half your charm, stupid. Later it will be the secret of your eternal youth. And you complain of it! . . . You have the cheek to complain of it to me."

"Yes, Nounoune. Who would you rather I'd complain to?"

He took her hand which she had withdrawn. "My Nounoune, darling, my dearest Nounoune; I'm not only complaining of myself, I'm accusing you."

She felt her hand gripped in a firm hand. And the large dark eyes with shiny lashes, instead of evading hers, clung to her eyes miserably. She did not wish to tremble yet. It's nothing; it's nothing, she thought. It'll only need two or three sharp words, then he'll become insulting and then I'll forgive him. . . . It's nothing more than that. . . . But she failed to find the rebuke necessary to alter the face watching hers.

"Come, come, my dear. . . . You know there are certain jokes which I won't put up with for long."

But at the same time, she adjudged the sound of her voice to be both feeble and false. How badly I said that, she thought. It was like bad theater. The ten o'clock sun reached the table which separated them and Léa's polished nails glittered. But the sunshine also lighted on her large, well-made hands, and in the soft, loose skin, on the backs, around the wrists, carved a complicated network, concentric grooves, minute parallelograms like those which a drought engraves, after the rains, on banks of clay. Léa rubbed her hands with a distracted air, turning her head to lead Chéri's gaze toward the street, but he persisted in his wretched, dog-like contemplation. Brusquely he reconquered the two ashamed hands which pretended to play with a loop of her belt, kissed them and re-kissed them, then couched his cheek upon them, murmuring, "My Nounoune. . . . O, my poor Nounoune."

"Let me alone," she cried with inexplicable anger, jerking her hands from him.

She took a moment to control herself, frightened at her weakness. She had almost burst into sobs. As soon as she was able, she spoke and smiled.

"So now it's me you're sorry for? Why did you accuse me just now?"

"I was wrong," he said humbly. "For me you have always been—"

" 'Have been?' " she underlined in a biting voice. "Is this a funeral oration, my young lad?"

"You see?" he reproached her.

He shook his head and she saw clearly that she could not anger him. She tightened all her muscles and restrained her thoughts for the benefit of two or three words, always the same, and which she repeated in the center of her being; He is there, before my eyes.

... You see, he's still there.... He's not out of reach.... But is he really still there before my eyes?

Her thoughts escaped from this disciplinary rhythm and a great inner lamentation replaced the hypnotic syllables; Oh, if someone could only give back to me the moment when I was saying, "Chéri, your second piece of toast?" That moment is still close to us, it's not lost forever, it hasn't yet disappeared into the past. Let's start from there, the little that's happened since won't count, I'll wipe it out, I'll wipe it out.... I'll talk to him about trains, our luggage....

She spoke to him, in truth, but she said, "I see.... I see that I can't regard as a man a creature who's capable, by weakness, of upsetting the lives of two women at the same time. Do you think I don't understand? As far as voyages are concerned, you like them short, eh? Yesterday at Neuilly; today here, but tomorrow . . . Where tomorrow? Here? No, no, my dear; it's not worth lying about, that guilty face wouldn't fool somebody even stupider than I, if there is one over there . . ."

Her violent gesture which indicated the direction of Neuilly, upset a plate of biscuit which Chéri straightened. In proportion as she spoke, she developed her pain, changed it into a burn-chagrin, aggressive and jealous, the garrulous chagrin of a young woman. The rouge on her cheeks turned to wine lees; a lock of her hair, crimped by the curling-iron, trailed down her neck like a small dry snake.

"And even that one—even your wife—you won't find her there every time that it pleases you to go home. Wives, my dear, one doesn't know how one gets them and still less how one loses them. . . . You're going to have your wife kept under lock and key by Charlotte, eh? Marvelous idea.... Oh, how I'll laugh the day that—"

Chéri rose, pale and grave. "Nounoune."

"Why Nounoune? Why that? Do you think you frighten me? You want to lead your own life, do you? Lead it, then. And pretty sights you'll see by the way with a daughter of Marie-Laure. No arms, a flat behind, but that won't prevent her from—"

"I forbid you, Nounoune."

He seized her arm but she rose, freed herself vigorously and broke into hoarse laughter.

"Oh, of course, of course. 'I forbid you to say a word against my wife.' Isn't that it?"

He walked around the table and shivering with indignation, came close to her. "No. I forbid you,—you hear me?—I forbid you to spoil my Nounoune."

She retreated to the end of the room, stammering, "What's that? . . . What. . . ."

He followed her as if to punish her. "You heard me. Is that the way for Nounoune to talk? Dirty little insults, something in the style of Madame Peloux! To think they could come from you, Nounoune."

He tilted his head arrogantly. "I know how Nounoune should talk. I know how she ought to think. I had time to learn. I haven't forgotten the day you said to me, just before I married, 'At least don't be cruel. Try not to make her suffer. . . . I have a feeling that they're throwing a fawn to the dogs.' Those were your words. That's really you. And the night before I married, when I ran away to come here and see you, I remember you said to me . . ."

His voice stopped but his face continued to gleam with a bright memory. "Oh, my darling, you were marvelous."

He put his hands on her shoulders. "And even last night," he went on, "the first thing you were afraid of was that I'd made trouble . . . at home. My Nounoune, I knew you as grand, I loved you as grand when we first started. If we have to finish now, must you start being like all other women?"

Confusedly she sensed the guile beneath the praise and seated herself, her face hidden in her hands. "How hard you are, how hard," she stammered. "Why did you come back? I was so calm, so alone, so used to . . ."

She heard herself lying and stopped short.

"Well, I wasn't," said Chéri. "I came back because . . . because . . ."

He lifted his arms, dropped them, lifted them again. "Because I couldn't do without you, there's no point in hunting any other explanation."

They said nothing for a moment.

Overwhelmed, she contemplated this young man, white, impatient as a seagull, his light feet and opened arms already seeming prepared for flight.

Chéri's dark eyes roved over her. "You can be proud of yourself," he said suddenly. "You can be proud. For three months you made me lead a life . . . a life that . . ."

"Me?"

"Who was it if it wasn't you? If a door opened, it was Nounoune; the telephone rang,—Nounoune; a letter in the mailbox in the garden,—Nounoune. . . . I hunted for you in everything even down to the wine I drank without so much as finding the fine Pommery I'd had at your house. . . . And as for the nights. . . . Oh, là, là. . . ."

He marched rapidly and without any noise up and down the carpet. "I can say that I know what it is to suffer for a woman, oh believe me. At present, I'm waiting for all those that'll come after you—dust, that's all they'll be like. Oh, yes, you've perfectly poisoned me."

She sat up slowly, turning first one way, then another, to follow the coming and going of Chéri. Her cheeks were dry and shining with a febrile red which rendered the blue of her eyes almost intolerable.

His head bent, he walked and talked without ceasing. "Imagine Neuilly without you, the first days after my return. As far as that's concerned, everything without you! . . . I almost went crazy. One night, the child—you know—she was ill; I don't remember with what, headache, neuralgia, something. I felt sorry for her but I had to leave the room, for nothing on earth would have kept me from saying to her, 'Wait, don't cry, I'll go fetch Nounoune and she'll cure you.' And you'd have come too, wouldn't you, Nounoune? . . . Oh, là, là, what a life it was. . . . At the Hôtel Morris, I hired Desmond and paid him well so sometimes at night I could say to him as if he didn't know you, 'Old man, a skin as soft as hers doesn't exist. . . . And your sapphire cabochon, well, hide it, because the blue of her eyes doesn't turn gray in the light like that stone.' I used to tell him how you could hold your own and no mistake, how nobody ever had the last word with you, not even me. . . . I used to say to him, 'Old man, when that woman has the right hat on'— you know, your blue one of last year, Nounoune, with the wings— 'plus her way of wearing her clothes, bring any woman you choose up beside her and she'd put them all in the shade.' . . . And then the grand way you always walked, talked, your smile, the chic way you carried yourself. . . . I always said to Desmond, 'Ah, what a woman, that Léa.' "

He snapped his fingers with the pride of ownership. I never said all that to Desmond, he thought. And yet it's no lie I'm telling now. Desmond understood it just the same.

He wanted to continue and looked at Léa. She was still waiting to listen to him. Sitting erect now, she showed him in the full light her noble and ruined face, waxed by burning tears which had dried. An invisible weight pulled down her chin and cheeks, saddened the trembling corners of her mouth. Amidst this wreck of beauty, Chéri could still find intact only the lovely dominating nose, the eyes the color of blue bloom.

"And so, you see, Nounoune, after months of a life like that, I came here and . . ." He halted, frightened at what he had almost said.

"You came here and found an old woman," said Léa in a weak tranquil voice.

"Nounoune, listen, Nounoune . . ." He threw himself on his knees against her, letting be seen on his face the cowardice of a child who can find no words to hide his mistake.

"And you find an old woman," repeated Léa. "What are you afraid of, darling?"

She put her arms about his shoulders, felt the stiffness, the defense of his body which suffered because she had been wounded. "Come, come, my Chéri. . . . What are you afraid of,—of having hurt me? Don't cry, my beauty. . . . If you knew how I really thank you. . . ."

He sobbed in protestation and struggled without force.

She bent her cheek to the mussed black hair. "Did you say all that, did you think all that about me? Was I really so lovely in your eyes, really? And so good? At the age when most women have stopped living, for you I was still the handsomest, the best of women and you loved me? Oh my darling, how I thank you. The finest, you said? Poor child."

He collapsed and she supported him between her arms. "If I'd really been so fine, I'd have made a man of you instead of thinking merely of the pleasure of your body and mine. The finest? Oh no, my darling one, I wasn't that since I wouldn't let you go and now it's almost too late. . . ."

He seemed to sleep in Léa's arms but his eyelids, obstinately closed, trembled without cease and with a motionless closed hand, he clung to her robe which slowly tore.

"It's too late, it's almost too late . . . and yet . . ." She bent over him. "My darling, listen to me. Wake up, my beauty, listen to me with your eyes open. Don't be afraid to look at me. After all, I'm the woman you loved, you know,—the finest woman . . ."

He opened his eyes and his first moist glance was already full of a pleading egotistical hope. Léa turned her head. Oh, his eyes. . . . Let's get it over with quickly. . . . She placed her hand on Chéri's forehead. "It was me, dearest, the woman who said to you, 'Don't make any unnecessary pain, spare the fawn' . . . it really was me? I don't recall it any more. Fortunately you remembered. You're breaking away from me very late, my darling, my bad little boy, I've carried you next my heart for too long and now you have heavy burdens of your own—a young wife and maybe a baby. . . . I'm responsible for everything you lack. Yes, yes, my beauty, owing to me, here you are at twenty-five, so light, so spoiled and so sad. . . . I have a great deal to suffer for. You'll give pain, you'll get pain. You who loved me. . . ."

The hand which slowly riddled her silken robe clenched and Léa felt on her breast the painful nails of a bad child.

". . . you who loved me," she went on after a pause, "could you. . . . I don't know if I can make myself clear. . . ."

He leaned away from her the better to listen and she almost cried out, "Place your hand again on my breast and your nails in their marks, my strength leaves me when your flesh leaves mine."

But she bent over him in her turn, on his knees before her and continued, "You who loved me, who will miss me." . . . She smiled at him and at the look in his eyes. . . . "What vanity, eh? . . . You who'll miss me, I hope that when you feel yourself close to frightening away the fawn that is your own, who is in your care, that you'll hold her, that you'll invent in that moment all that I never taught you. . . . I never talked to you about the future. Forgive me, Chéri; I loved you as if we would both of us die within an hour of each other. Because I was born twenty-four years before you, I was doomed and I carried you along with me. . . ."

He listened with a concentration that made him look hard. She passed her hand over his troubled forehead to smooth its furrow. "Can you see us, Chéri, going to lunch at Armenonville? . . . Can you see us inviting Monsieur and Madame Lili? . . ."

She laughed sadly and shivered. "I'm just as finished as that old creature. . . . Quick, child, quick, go hunt your youth, it's only just caught on the bones of old women, you still have it and she has it, the girl who's waiting for you. You've tasted youth. You know it doesn't satisfy but that one always goes back for more. . . . Oh it wasn't just last night that you started making comparisons. And what was I doing, giving good advice and showing off my noble soul? What do I know of you two? She loves you, now it's her turn to tremble, she'll suffer like a lover and not like a mother gone astray. You can talk to her as a master and not as a capricious gigolo. . . . Go. Go quickly."

She spoke in a voice of hasty supplication. He listened, standing, planted before her, his chest bare, his hair stormy, so tempting that she knotted her hands together to prevent them seizing him. He guessed it perhaps and did not undress. A hope, crazy as that which might come during their fall to people dropping off a tower, flashed between them and went out.

"Go," she said in a low voice. "I love you. It's too late. Go away. But go at once. Dress yourself."

She rose and fetched him his shoes, spread out his socks and his crumpled shirt. He stood in place, moving his fingers awkwardly as if they were numb and she had to find his braces, his cravat; but she refrained from coming close to him and did not help him. While he dressed she glanced frequently into the court as if she were expecting something.

Dressed, he looked more pale with eyes which augmented their halo of fatigue.

"You don't feel ill?" she asked him. And she added timidly, her eyes lowered, "You could . . . could rest a moment." But at once she mastered herself and came back to him as if he were in great danger; "No, no, you'll be better at home. . . . Hurry, it's not yet noon, a good hot bath will refresh you and the open air. . . . Here, your gloves. . . . Oh yes and your hat on the floor. . . . Put your coat on, you might catch cold. . . . Au revoir, my Chéri, au revoir. . . . Yes, that's it, give Charlotte my . . ." She closed the door behind him and silence put an end to her desperate, vain words. She heard Chéri stumble in the staircase and she ran to the window. He descended the steps and stopped in the middle of the court.

"He's coming back, he's coming back," she cried, lifting her arms.

A gasping, old woman repeated her gestures in the long oblong mirror and Léa asked herself what she could have in common with this old lunatic.

Chéri continued his path toward the street, opened the gate and passed through. On the sidewalk he buttoned his topcoat to hide his evening clothes of the night before. Léa let the curtain fall. But she still had time to see that Chéri lifted his head toward the spring sky and the flowering chestnut trees and that in walking he filled his lungs with air like a man escaping from prison.

The Last of Chéri

Part One

CHÉRI closed the iron gate of the small garden behind him and breathed the night air deeply. "Ah, but that's good—" But at once he corrected himself. "No. I don't like it."

The chestnut trees bore down; the heat was imprisoned by their branches. Above the nearest street light quivered a parched green mass of leaves. The Avenue Henri-Martin, smothered by trees, must wait for dawn to bring a faint breath of fresh air from the Bois.

Standing bareheaded, Chéri looked at his cheerless, brightly lighted house. He heard windows being slammed down, and then Edmée's voice, clear, edged with reproof. He saw his wife come to the hall window on the first floor and lean out. Her white gown, trimmed with pearls, lost its snowy tint in the greenish reflection of the street light, and gleamed yellow against the golden silk of the curtain beside her.

"Is that you out there, Fred?"

"Who do you suppose it would be?"

"Didn't you go home with Filipesco?"

"No. He'd gone when I came out."

"Oh! I really wish, though— Oh, well, it doesn't matter. Are you coming in?"

123

"Not right away. It's too hot. I'm going for a walk."

"But—oh, well, do as you please!"

She was still for a moment, and she must have laughed; he saw the beaded front of her dress quiver.

"All I can see of you from here is your white shirt front and your white face, standing out in the dark. You look like a poster for a night club. It's irresistible."

"You do love to talk like my mother," he said, thoughtfully. "You might as well let the servants go to bed. I have my key."

She waved her hand, and one by one the windows grew dark. A single light, deep blue, told him that Edmée was making her way to the bedroom, which looked out on the garden at the back of the house, through her boudoir.

"Boudoir!" he said to himself. "No—let's have it straight! The boudoir is her study these days."

Janson-de-Sailly struck the hour and Chéri, head lifted, felt the strokes of the chimes as if they had been drops of rain.

"Midnight. She's in a great hurry to get to bed. Oh, of course, she has to be at her hospital at nine in the morning."

He walked away, with nervous steps, shrugged his shoulders, and then quieted down.

"The truth is, I might as well have married some classical dancer. A lesson at nine o'clock—that's sacred. That comes before everything."

He walked to the entrance of the Bois. In a sky dulled by the dust that hung in suspension in the still air the brilliance of the stars was dimmed. He heard regular footsteps, matching his own. Chéri, who disliked having any one walk behind him, stopped.

"Good evening, M. Peloux," said the watchman, touching his cap.

Chéri acknowledged the greeting by raising a finger to his temple, with an officer's condescension—a trick he had learned in the war from association with his fellow sergeants. He walked on, passing the watchman, who was trying the locks of the small garden gates.

In the entrance of the Bois a pair of lovers, seated on a bench, were exchanging whispers. Chéri listened for a moment to the sound, so like that of a ship's prow cleaving still waters, coming from bodies closely embraced and from lips he could not see.

"The man's a soldier," he said to himself. "I heard his belt buckle."

Unburdened by thought, all his senses were alert. There had been quiet nights during the war when his hearing, as keen as that of a savage, had brought him curious and subtle delight and salutary fears. As a soldier his fingers, black with mud and his own grime, had still been able to distinguish, by a single sure touch, medals and coins, to recognize by stem or leaf plants the very names of which he had not known.

"Hey, Peloux—tell me what I've got hold of here?"

He evoked the image of the red-headed boy, in the dark, slipping a dead mole, a tiny snake, a toad, part of a bit of fruit, a lump of filth, into his fingers, and exclaiming: "He's right again!"

He smiled, without pity, at that memory, at the picture of that red-headed corpse. He often saw him in his thoughts, Pierquin, his old comrade, lying on his back, asleep forever, a look of scorn in his staring eyes. He often talked of him. Even this evening, after dinner, Edmée had easily drawn out the short tale, told with a deliberate awkwardness, which Chéri knew by heart. Always it ended the same way. Pierquin was talking.

" 'Listen, old man, I snoozed for a minute, and I dreamed again about the river, and of how disgustingly dirty it was at home. That won't do—' That was when he was hit—and just by a bit of shrapnel. I tried to carry him—and they found us a hundred yards away, with him on top of me. He was a splendid chap. I like to remember him." Then a pause. And then: "It was partly because of him that I got this."

Again the modest pause. And then Chéri would let his eyes drop to his bit of green and red ribbon and crush out the glowing tip of his cigarette as if to give himself something to do. He considered that it was no one's business that the pure, fortuitous chance of an exploding shell had tossed the two of them, Chéri alive and Pierquin dead, so that one was flung across the other's shoulders. As it happened the truth, far more ambiguous than a lie, had left the living

Chéri, furious and revolted, half crushed under the appalling weight of a Pierquin suddenly powerless to move. Chéri still held that against Pierquin. And, besides, he had despised the truth ever since a day when it had burst from him like a hiccup, involuntarily, to soil and to spoil.

This evening, though, at his house, the American Majors, Atkins and Marsh-Meyer, and Wood, a Lieutenant, also an American, apparently hadn't listened to him. Looking like athletic children awaiting their first communion, with clear, vacuous eyes, they had only been waiting, with an almost painful anxiety, for it to be time to go off to dance. As for Filipesco. . . . "He'll bear watching," Chéri decided, laconically.

A moist fragrance, proceeding rather from the newly cut lawns sloping away from it than from the stagnant water, pervaded the shores of the lake. As Chéri leaned against a tree a shadowy female figure accosted him.

"Hello, there, kid—"

He shuddered at the last word. It had been uttered in a deep, worn voice, the voice of thirst, of the parched night, of the dusty road. He did not answer, and the woman took a step toward him, furtively. He was conscious of the odor of hot cloth, of soiled linen, of damp hair, and immediately he turned away and set out at a swift pace toward home.

The deep blue light was still burning; Edmée had not yet left the boudoir-study. Undoubtedly she was writing, signing orders for drugs and dressings, reading the records of the day and a secretary's terse reports. Her curly hair gleaming red in the light, she bent over her papers, with her pretty, school-teacher's, head. Chéri reached into his pocket for his flat key, attached to a slender gold chain.

"Here goes! Before she's done she'll have to have a prescription to make love to me!"

2

HE ENTERED his wife's room without knocking, as he usually did, but Edmée neither started nor broke off the telephone conversation she was carrying on. Chéri listened.

"No, not tomorrow. But you don't need me for that. The General knows you very well. And at the Board of Trade there's— What— I have Lémery where I want him? Not at all. He's charming, but— hello—hello—"

She laughed, showing her small teeth.

"Oh, come, you exaggerate. Lémery makes himself agreeable to every woman who hasn't lost an eye or a leg. What? Yes, he's just come in, this very moment. No, no, I shall be most discreet. Good-by —till tomorrow."

Edmée's white negligée, of shiny material that matched her pearl necklace in color, left one shoulder bare. Her fine chestnut hair, curly because of the dry heat, had been let down.

"Who was that?" asked Chéri.

She asked a question of her own as he spoke, while she was replacing the receiver on the telephone.

"Fred, will you leave the Rolls for me tomorrow morning? I want it to bring the General here for lunch."

"What General?"

"General Haar."

"A Boche?"

Edmée lifted her eyebrows.

"My dear Fred, I must say your jokes are a little young for your age. General Haar is inspecting my hospital tomorrow. He'll be able to tell them, in America, when he goes home, that it needn't fear comparison with anything they have over there. Colonel Beybert is bringing him, and they will both have lunch here afterward."

Chéri tossed his dinner jacket on a chair across the room.

"All right—but I shall lunch in town."

"What—what did you say?"

For a moment Edmée looked angry, but then she smiled, picked up his dinner jacket carefully, and spoke in an altered voice.

"You asked who was on the telephone? Your mother."

Chéri, leaning back in a deep chair, said nothing. He had assumed his handsomest and most impenetrable mask. Upon his forehead rested a disapproving serenity, as upon his lowered eyelids, beginning to grow darker as his thirtieth year drew near. His mouth was closed without perceptible contraction, as if he were asleep.

"You know," Edmée went on, "she wants to get in touch with Lémery, at the Board of Trade, on account of her three shiploads of hides. Three ships, full of hides, that are in the harbor of Valparaiso. It's an idea—don't you think so? Only Lémery has nothing to do with giving importation permits—at least, he says he hasn't. Do you know the minimum commission the Sounabis have offered your mother?"

Chéri swept ships, hides and commission away with a wave of his hand.

"Rubbish," he said.

Edmée let the matter drop.

"You will have lunch here tomorrow, won't you?" she said, her voice tenderly reproachful. "I might have Gibbs, the *Excelsior* reporter who took the photographs of the hospital, and your mother."

Chéri shook his head, but without impatience.

"No," he said. "General Hagenbeck—"

"Haar—"

"A colonel—and my mother—in uniform! Her tunic—what do you call it? Her jacket? Little leather buttons—elastic belt—shoulder straps. Her officer's collar—and her chin over it! And her cane. No—really—look here, I'm as game as the next fellow but there are limits! I prefer to go out."

He laughed, very quietly, and there was no mirth in his laughter. Edmée laid a hand already trembling with irritation on his arm, but her tone was light.

"You aren't talking seriously?"

"I certainly am! I shall lunch at the *Brekekekex*—or some place."

"With whom?"

"Any one I please."

He sat down, kicked off his pumps and stretched his feet. Edmée, leaning against a black lacquer chest, sought for words to bring Chéri to his senses. The white satin of her negligée moved in time with her swift breathing; she crossed her hands behind her back with the air of a martyr. Chéri looked at her with a pretence of deference.

"She really looks like a lady," he thought. "With her hair down, even in a chemise or a bath wrap, she does look well-bred."

She lowered her eyes, met Chéri's, and smiled.

"You're teasing me," she said, plaintively.

"No," Chéri replied. "I shall not lunch here, and that's flat."

"But—why not?"

He got up, walked to the open door of their dark bedroom, heavy with the nocturnal scent of the garden, and then came back to her.

"Just because. If you make me explain myself, I'll talk badly and I'll lose my temper. You'll cry—you'll let your wrap fall from your shoulders 'in your deep distress'—and, unhappily, I shan't be moved a bit."

Once more, for a second, anger showed in her face. But her patience was not exhausted yet. She laughed, and lifted a round shoulder, bare under her hair.

"You can always say that doesn't affect you—"

He wandered about the room, clad now only in short white silk drawers. As he moved he tried the strength of leg and instep; with one hand he rubbed two tiny twin scars under his right breast, seeking to keep them livid, since their color was fading. Slender, a little fleshier than he had been when he was twenty, but harder and more finely molded, he was showing off, deliberately before his wife, her rival rather than her lover. He knew he was handsomer than she, but he appreciated, as a connoisseur, in a fashion quite abstract, the skill with which Edmée clothed flat hips, breasts not quite rounded enough, graceful, almost overlong lines, in sweeping straight gowns and clinging tunics.

"Have you been losing weight?" he would ask her, sometimes, for the sheer pleasure of hurting her a little and seeing her fly into a passion.

Her answer had displeased him. He wanted her to be aloof and distinguished, to be mute, if not insensible, in his embrace. He paused, frowned, and considered her.

"A nice way to talk!" he said. "Do you learn such tricks from your head surgeon? The war, Madame!"

Again she shrugged her bare shoulder.

"What a child you are, Fred! It's lucky we're alone. Scolding me for a joke—which happens to be a compliment! Reminding me of the conventions—you—you—after seven years of marriage!"

"How do you make out that it's seven years?"

He sat down, as if for a long argument, naked, his legs thrust out.

"Good Lord— Nineteen thirteen—nineteen nineteen—!"

"Forgive me—we're not using the same calendar. I reckon—"

Edmée flexed her knee, stood on one leg, admitting her weariness. Chéri interrupted her.

"What in the world are we trying to get at? Come, let's go to bed. You have your dancing lesson at nine o'clock in the morning, haven't you?"

"Oh, Fred!"

She twisted a rose that was set in a black vase, and then threw it away. Deliberately Chéri stirred the fire he had kindled in Edmée, evidenced by the tears that stood in her eyes.

"That's what I call your work with the wounded when I forget myself."

Without looking at him, her lips trembling:

"A savage—a savage—an abominable being," she murmured.

He was by no means put out. He laughed.

"What do you expect me to say to you? Oh, as for you, of course, and for yourself, you are performing a sacred task. But how about me? You'd have to be at the Opéra every day, in the Rotunda up-stairs—and I can't see the difference. In either case it's just the same for me— I'm left to my own devices. And your pay—it's your wounded—wounded fellows a little luckier than the rest, perhaps. But I've nothing to do with them, either. I'm pushed to one side there, too."

She turned to him so swiftly that her hair streamed out behind her.

"Darling! But you mustn't feel so! You're not pushed to one side, you are foremost always—"

He got up, attracted by a pitcher of ice water upon which the cold vapor condensed slowly in blue drops. Edmée hurried to get it.

"With lemon or without, Fred?"

"Plain. Thanks."

He drank; she took the glass from him when it was empty, and he went toward the bathroom.

"By the way," he said, "that crack in the cement in the pool. We ought—"

"I've attended to that. The man who does mosaics in glass tile is a cousin of Chuche, one of my wounded. I shan't have to speak to him twice, depend on that."

"Good." As he stepped into the bathroom he turned back. "Listen, about this *Ranch* business we were talking about yesterday morning. Ought we to sell or not? Suppose I mention it to old Deutsch tomorrow morning?"

Edmée burst out laughing like a school-girl.

"Did you think I'd waited on you? Your mother had a brain wave this morning, while we were taking the Baroness home from the hospital."

"Old Berche?"

"Yes, yes, the Baroness. Your mother dropped a hint to her— she's been a shareholder from the very first, and she's always in touch with the Chairman of the Board—"

"Except when she's plastering herself with powder!"

"If you won't stop interrupting me! Well, at two o'clock, every share was sold—every share! There was a little flurry on the Bourse in the afternoon—oh, it was momentary—and it put 216,000 francs in our pockets, Fred! That will pay for some medicine and some dressings, won't it? I wasn't going to tell you till tomorrow—with one of those stunning new wallets. Do I get a kiss?"

He stood, white and naked, under a lifted drapery, looking attentively at his wife's face.

"Fine," he said, at last. "And just where do I come in?"

Edmée shook her head maliciously.

"Your power of attorney is still good, my love. 'The right to sell, buy, and sign leases in my name . . .' That reminds me, I must send the Baroness a little souvenir."

"A pipe," Chéri suggested, thoughtfully.

"Don't laugh. That worthy soul is worth a great deal to us."

"Us?"

"Your mother and me. The Baroness can talk to our men in their own language. She tells them stories—well, they're a little thick, but they are amusing. They adore them!"

Smiling oddly, Chéri let the curtain fall behind him, so that he was blotted out as sudden sleep obliterates a thought. He moved along a passage, dimly lighted by a blue radiance, like a disembodied spirit; he had insisted that every floor in the house, from top to bottom, be thickly carpeted. He loved silence and the appearance of stealth; he never knocked at the door of the small room that his wife, ever since the war, had called her study. That never troubled her; she always felt his approach and he did not startle her.

Chéri bathed now, spending little time in the cool water, perfumed himself, absent-mindedly, and went back to the small room.

In the neighboring bedroom he heard a sound that marked the movement of a body among the sheets, and a tinkle as a paper knife struck a cup on the bedside table. He sat down, his chin in his hand. He read the next day's menu, lying beside him on a small table; Edmée prepared it every day for the butler.

"Lobster Thermidor, cutlets Fulbert-Dumonteil, cold duck in aspic, salad Charlotte, a Curaçao soufflé, cheese straws." Very good—nothing to correct. "Six places." Yes. There was a correction to make, after all. He altered the number, and cupped his chin in his hand once more.

"Fred, do you know what time it is?"

He did not answer the soft-voiced question, but went into the bedroom and sat down by the great bed. One shoulder bare, the other veiled by a wisp of white linen, Edmée smiled, despite her weariness. She knew she looked better in bed than when she was up and about. But once more Chéri, when he was seated, rested his chin upon his hand.

"'The Thinker,'" said Edmée, hoping either to force him to speak or abandon his pose.

"You don't know how right you are," Chéri said, sententiously.

He drew his Chinese robe about his legs and crossed his arms with a dramatic gesture.

"What am I doing here?"

Edmée either failed to understand him or refused to do so.

"That's exactly what I'd like to know, Fred," she said. "It's two o'clock, and I have to be up at eight. And tomorrow is another of those trying days. It's unkind of you to keep me awake. Come— here's a breeze! We can sleep in a draft, and pretend we've gone to bed in the garden."

He gave up, then, and a moment later he threw off his silk robe, while Edmée put out the one remaining light. In the darkness she drew close to him, but he made her turn over, adroitly, slipped a firm arm about her waist, and whispered, sleepily: "Like this—as if we were riding in a bobsled." He fell asleep at once.

3

HE WATCHED them in the morning, from the small window in the linen closet, where he had hidden himself. His car, painted in a yellow like the yolk of eggs, and the other motor, a long American machine, slipped almost noiselessly along the avenue, under the thick, low-hanging chestnuts. The newly sprinkled pavement and the green shade lent a deceptive freshness to the air, but Chéri knew that on this June morning, in Paris's hottest month, the sun was scorching the bed of blue forget-me-nots in the garden on the other side of the house—that bed like a little pond bordered with rosy pinks.

He was shaken by something like fear when he saw two men in khaki uniform, with gold stars and kepis braided with crimson velvet, approaching the door of the house.

"He would be in uniform, the swine!"

That was Chéri's name for the head surgeon of Edmée's hospital, and, without quite admitting the fact to himself, he loathed this sandy-haired man who talked to Edmée of medical technicalities in a caressing voice. He indulged himself in vague but heartfelt abuse of the medical corps, and of all those who persisted in wearing uniform in times of peace. But he grew silent when Edmée, brisk and alert, dressed and shod in white, appeared, holding out a white gloved hand. Her voice was high pitched; she spoke quickly and gayly. Chéri did not miss a single word that fell from the laughing red lips. She went as far as the cars, and then turned back to get a forgotten note book from a footman; she laughed and joked as she waited for him to bring it to her. She spoke in English to the American colonel, and lowered her voice, as if in involuntary deference, when she replied to some remark of Dr. Arnaud's.

Behind the curtain Chéri stood still, frozen. So accustomed was he to defy and to deceive the world that his features were trained; he was on guard against any display of his real feelings even when he was alone. His glance flew back and forth from Edmée to the doctor, from the American colonel to Edmée, and more than once she looked up, as if she sensed his watching presence.

"What are they waiting for?" he muttered to himself. "Oh—of course! For Christ's sake—!"

Charlotte Peloux, in a sports roadster driven by a young and eminently correct chauffeur, had just come up. In a tight fitting uniform of gabardine, she carried her head high, in its tiny military bonnet, under which her short, red hair was to be seen. She stayed in her car, while the men greeted her, received a kiss from Edmée, and, obviously, asked about her son, since she raised her head to look at the first floor windows. So she unveiled her magnificent eyes, which revealed, like the great eyes of an octopus, a mysterious and more than human thought.

"She's wearing her little bonnet," Chéri muttered.

Shuddering, to his own disgust, he smiled as the three cars drove off. He waited patiently until his own motor was brought to the house, at eleven, and even then he left it there for some minutes. Twice he reached for the telephone, and then pushed it away again. His vague idea of picking up Filipesco was short-lived; then it occurred to him that it might be pleasant to get hold of young Maudru and his girl.

"Or—Jean de Touzac might be more fun. But at this hour he wouldn't be shaved—he's probably still snoring. All that lot—Desmond's worth all of them put together, to tell the truth. Poor old chap!"

He thought of Desmond as of some one killed in the war, but with a regret he never felt for the dead. Desmond, alive and lost to him, inspired him with an almost tender melancholy, as well as with the respect due to a man who had a job. Desmond managed a night club and sold antiques to Americans. Pallid and without vigor during a war in which he had carried everything but arms—dispatches, mess tins, filthy hospital vessels—Desmond had attacked peace with a warlike ferocity the rapid rewards of which had amazed Chéri.

"Desmond's," established on a shoe-string in a private house in the Avenue de l'Alma, was a place of heavy stone arches, ceilings adorned with swallows and wild roses, windows of stained glass portraying lush reeds and vivid flamingos, where frenetic couples danced in silence. At Desmond's they danced by day as well as by night, as people did just after the war. The men were free at last from the need of thought, from the constant fear of death; they had had a sort of rebirth of innocence, young and old alike. The women were votaries of pleasure—of a pleasure transcending mere voluptuousness. For them there was, once more, the companionship of men, contact with the bodies of men, the perception of the very odor and heat of masculinity, the certainty, that they felt from head to foot, in every recess of their beings, that they must become the victims, the prey, of men wholly alive at last, the supreme ecstasy of yielding, in the arms of men, to a rhythm as close, as intimate, as that of sleep.

"Desmond—" thought Chéri. "Oh, he turned in at three o'clock—half past, maybe. He's slept long enough."

But once more he dropped the telephone. He went downstairs quickly, treading the deep, yielding pile that carpeted every floor in his house. As he passed the dining room he gave a tolerant glance at the five white plates, set like a crown about a shallow bowl of black crystal in which there floated pink water roses, of the same tint as the linen on the table. He paused only at the mirror that reflected the massive door of the sitting room, on the ground floor. He always sought, yet always half feared, this glass, which was lighted by a transom, cloudy and blue, and shaded, moreover, by the foliage outside. His own reflection always shocked Chéri a little. It troubled him that what he saw was not the exact reproduction of a young man of twenty-four. Nor was he ever able to see by just what imperceptible strokes, laid upon a handsome face in the very hour of perfection, other stages of a beauty even more obvious, that nevertheless were those that presaged the decline of that beauty, had been traced by time.

There could be no question in Chéri's mind of a falling off that he had in vain endeavored to see in his features. Encountering this thirty-year-old Chéri, failing to recognize him, he often asked himself: "What's the matter with me?" It was as if he felt a little faint, or as if his mirror conveyed a vague suggestion that he had put on some unbecoming garment. Then he went on and thought no more about it.

"Desmond's," the more serious establishment, by no means slept at noon, in spite of its late hours. A concierge was washing down the paved court with a hose; a boy was clearing the steps of the trashy but still distinguished accumulation of the night—fine dust, silver paper, champagne corks, gold-tipped cigarettes, bent straws. All these things bore witness daily to the prosperity of "Desmond's." Chéri stepped lightly over these relics of the previous night, but the smell inside stopped him as a stretched rope might have done.

Forty couples, crowded together, had left that odor there, that impression of linen soaked in perspiration, grown cool and dry, and impregnated with cigarette smoke. Chéri rallied his forces, however, and attacked the stairs, guarded by banisters of heavy oak, with posts like caryatids. Desmond had squandered no money in modernizing the stuffy magnificence of the eighties. He had torn out a couple of partitions, put in an icebox in the basement and provided the best of jazz bands; he would need nothing more for another year.

"I'll turn modernistic when I must to draw the crowds—when the craze for dancing dies down a bit," Desmond was in the habit of saying. He slept on the second floor, in a room adorned with painted bindweed and swan patterned glass. He bathed in an enameled zinc tub beside a frieze of water plants painted on the tiles, and the decrepit water heater snored and wheezed like an old bull dog. But the telephone shone like some cherished weapon in daily use, and Chéri, taking four steps at a time, found his friend, lips buried in the transmitter, as if it had been a chalice from which he was drinking some dark and mysterious fluid. He let a wandering glance rest on Chéri for a moment. His yellow pajamas were hardly kind to his face, haggard from want of sleep, but Desmond, grown fat in his new prosperity, had stopped letting his ugliness worry him.

"Hello, there!" said Chéri. "Here I am. Your staircase stinks. It's worse than a dog."

"You'll not get 'Desmond's' for twelve francs," Desmond was saying into the void beyond the telephone. "I shan't put myself out to lay in Pommery at that price. As for my own cellar, Pommery ought to be eleven without labels—hello—yes, the labels were lost in the shuffle—and that's my point. Hello—"

"You're coming out to lunch—my car's outside," said Chéri.

"Not by a damned sight," said Desmond.

"What?"

"No. Meaning no. Hello? Sherry? Are you joking? I don't keep a wine shop. Champagne or nothing. Don't waste your time—or mine, either. Hello! You may be right. Only—just now I'm in fashion, you see. Hello. Two o'clock sharp, then. I wish you a very good day, sir."

Desmond yawned and stretched, then held out a limp hand. He still looked like Alphonso XIII, but between the war and the attainment of his thirtieth year, there had come this puffy growth that had altered him. He had escaped death, he no longer had to fight, he could eat every day. He had a new confidence in himself, fruit of such victories as that he had just won over the telephone; he could boast, he could insult people with impunity. Self-assurance and a well-lined purse made him seem less ugly, and one could feel sure that by the time he was sixty he would pass for a man who had been handsome in his day, with a big nose and a well-turned leg. He looked at Chéri now as if he felt a little ashamed of his brusqueness, but Chéri avoided his eyes.

"What ails you?" he said. "Come along. It's noon, and you're getting up."

"To begin with, I'm dressed already," Desmond said, half opening his pajama jacket to reveal a white silk shirt and a rust-colored bow tie. "And, besides, I'm not going out to lunch."

"You're— What's that? I—words fail me!"

"But, if you like, I can give you a couple of eggs, half my ham, half my salad, a share of my stout and my strawberries. And coffee."

Chéri looked at him in helpless anger.

"But why?"

"Business," Desmond said, with an assumed nasal twang. "You heard, didn't you? Champagne. These damned wine merchants! If you don't put on the screws—but I know my way about!"

He rubbed his hands together like a shopkeeper.

"Eh? Don't I make a fine business man?"

"You certainly do, you fathead!"

Chéri flung his soft hat at him, but Desmond picked it up and smoothed it, by way of showing he was in no joking mood. They had cold eggs, ham and tongue, and excellent stout. They had little to say, and Chéri, growing bored, looked at the paved court.

"What am I doing here?" he asked himself. "Well, I'm here so that I won't be at home, eating cutlets Fulbert-Dumonteil."

He pictured Edmée, all in white, the popinjay American colonel, and Dr. Arnaud, before whom Edmée posed as a docile young girl. He thought of Charlotte Peloux's shoulder straps, and turned to his host with a renewed affection, just as Desmond asked him, sharply:

"Do you know how many bottles of champagne they drank here last night—I mean from four o'clock yesterday afternoon until this morning at four?"

"No," said Chéri.

"And have you any idea of how many bottles that came in full went out empty between the first of May and the fifteenth of June?"

"Not the slightest," said Chéri.

"Well, guess—pick out some number!"

"Oh, Lord—I don't know!" Chéri said, wearily.

"You can guess, can't you? Take a number—make a stab at it! Come—a number!"

Chéri plucked at the cloth, like a schoolboy taking an examination. He was bored, and the heat was wearing on him.

"Five hundred," he said, making an effort.

"Five hundred! That's good!"

Desmond turned sharply in his chair and his monocle, catching the light, was reflected in Chéri's eye so that it hurt. He was triumphant. He never could laugh, anyway, except by heaving his shoulders. He picked up his cup and took a sip of coffee, delaying his revelation to make sure that Chéri should be properly impressed. Then he put down his cup.

"Thirty-three hundred and eighty-two—that's all! And do you know what I make out of that—"

"No!" Chéri interrupted him. "And what's more, I don't give a damn. You and your figures! I get enough of that from my mother. And besides—"

He got up.

"Besides—money—I don't care about money—" He spoke with a curious hesitation.

"How odd!" said Desmond, somewhat hurt. "Very odd, indeed. Amusing, one might say."

"Perhaps it is," said Chéri. "There it is. Money doesn't interest me—not any more."

What Chéri said was plain enough, but he spoke with an effort; he did not look at his friend. His foot, groping on the floor, found a crust and played with it. His assertion embarrassed him, and his oddly furtive glance at Desmond gave him, for a moment, a resemblance to himself in the days of his marvelous adolescence.

Desmond was concerned; for the first time he took Chéri seriously; he looked at him almost as a doctor studies a patient. Was he dealing with a hypochondriac, he wondered? And, like a doctor, he sought for meaningless and soothing phrases.

"Don't let it worry you—it's just a passing mood. Every one is out of sorts just now—now that the strain is relaxed. We're not ourselves. Work—that's the thing that gets you back on an even keel. Take my case—"

"I know," Chéri interrupted. "You're going to tell me I need something to keep me busy."

"It's what you really want yourself," said Desmond, with a certain condescension. "Ah, what a happy time—"

About to begin boasting of his success in business, he caught himself just in time.

"But it's a matter of education, too. Obviously Léa taught you nothing about life. You don't understand how to handle your affairs or to deal with people."

"Is that so?" Chéri said, crossly. "Léa didn't think so. She never trusted me—but she never bought or sold a share without asking my advice."

He threw out his chest, proud of his memories of a time when distrust had been a tribute.

"You can make money, if you go at it again seriously," said Desmond. "After all, that's a game that's never out of fashion."

"Yes," said Chéri, absent-mindedly. "Yes, you're right. Only, I'm waiting—"

"What are you waiting for?"

"Why—I—an opportunity—a better opportunity—"

"Better? What do you mean, better?"

"Oh, for Heaven's sake—this bores me! I'm waiting for a good excuse to take over control of all the affairs I had to let go during the war. Put it that way, if you like. After all, there is my capital—"

"Which is quite a fair sum," Desmond suggested. Before the war he would have called it enormous, and in an altogether different tone. Chéri flushed; he felt a momentary humiliation.

"Yes—my capital, my fortune. Well—the little woman is taking care of that now!"

"The devil you say!" said Desmond, surprised.

"Precisely—but you can take my word for it! She made 216,000 francs in a flurry on the Bourse just the day before yesterday. Well— how am I to interfere, with that sort of thing going on? Where do I come in the picture, anyway? If I do venture to say a word they tell me—"

"They? Who are they?"

"My wife and my mother! 'Now, don't trouble your head with such things,' they say. 'Rest—take it easy. You're a soldier. Wouldn't you like a nice glass of orangeade? You'd better drop in and see your shirtmaker—he'll be ashamed of having you for a customer. And, on your way, pick up the clasp of my necklace—I sent it to be mended.' And so on—"

He laughed, doing his best to hide the real anger and resentment behind his words. But his nostrils gave him away.

"Well—ought I to try selling motors, or breeding angora rabbits, or go in for some luxury trade? Perhaps I'd better go to work as an orderly or a clerk in my wife's hospital?"

He strode over to the window, and then turned back to Desmond.

"Then I'd be under the orders of Dr. Arnaud, the head surgeon—I might hand him his instruments when he operates! Or ought I to take over a night club? You see the connection—?"

He laughed to make Desmond laugh, but Desmond, who was obviously disturbed, remained grave.

"How long have you been letting your mind run on this way?" he asked. "You had no such ideas this spring, or last winter—or before you were married."

"I didn't have time," said Chéri, with an engaging frankness. "We were traveling, we had the house to furnish, we bought cars only to have them requisitioned. And the war. . . . Before the war—oh, before the war—I was nothing but a rich kid—I had money, that was all."

"Well, that's still true."

"Yes, that's still true," repeated Chéri.

He hesitated, trying to find the right words to express what was really in his mind.

"Yes—but nowadays it's not the same. Every one seems to have St. Vitus's dance. Everything's the same—work, avocations, public service—and these women serving their country! They're all hysterical. They're such go-getters that they make you sick of the very word business. They go to work—and they manage to disgust you with the very idea of working." He looked at Desmond with troubled eyes. "Is there anything wrong about having money and liking to live comfortably?"

Desmond, reveling in his new part, was getting back some of his own for those old days when he had been under Chéri's heel. He laid a comforting hand on Chéri's shoulder.

"Listen, old man," he said, "go right on being rich and getting all you can out of life. Put it to yourself that you are a reincarnation of a dead aristocracy. Let the feudal barons be your models. You are a soldier."

"Piffle," said Chéri.

"That's in character. But, my dear chap, let the workers go ahead and work."

"You, for example?"

"Yes. By all means."

"But you don't let women clutter up your life, do you?"

"I do not," Desmond said, dryly.

He had managed to conceal from all his friends a perverse liking for his cashier, a brunette, a little hairy, a little masculine in looks, who wore her hair drawn back and always carried a locket at her throat. She had a habit of remarking, with an agreeable smile: "I'd kill any one for a sou. I'm like that."

"No," Desmond went on. "I should say not! But you can't talk about anything without dragging in your wife or women in general or harking back to 'When I was living with Léa—' Good Lord—is there nothing else to talk about in 1919?"

It seemed to Chéri that over Desmond's voice he could hear another, far away but still distinct.

"Nothing else to talk about?" he repeated to himself. "Why should there be anything else?" He sat, musing, his mind stilled by the sunlight and the heat, growing worse as the sun neared its zenith. Desmond talked on, unaffected by the temperature; his face always looked like bleached winter endive. Chéri caught a word. "Little tarts—" He listened.

"Yes, a whole series of amusing situations, which I can put you in the way of enjoying, naturally. And when I talk of tarts I'm using a loose word for a group of girls that's unique—I give you my word, unique. The lot that come here every night make fine game—and the last four years have made them better than ever. Oh, when I've once turned over my capital a couple of times I'll have a restaurant worth talking about! Not more than ten tables—with people fighting to get them. I shall roof over the court—I have a lease long enough to make it worth my while to do some work on the place, you see. I'll put down a special dance floor—I'll have colored lights —oh, there's a future in this place!"

143

This dealer in tangos declaimed like a founder of cities. He flung out his arm toward the window. The word "future" struck Chéri and he turned to look at the spot at which Desmond was staring, above the court. He saw nothing; he felt tired. The two o'clock sun beat down with a fierce glare on the slate roof of the former stable in which the concièrge of "Desmond's" now lodged, and was reflected pitilessly into the room.

"What a hall it will make!" Desmond said ecstatically, pointing to the paved court. "I shall have it—and soon!"

Chéri looked with absorbed interest at Desmond, who confidently expected a fall of manna from Heaven each day—and was not disappointed.

"Yes—but how about me?" he thought, with the despair of frustration.

"Hello—here's my seller of wine-dregs!" Desmond exclaimed. "Get out, will you? I'm going to give him beans."

He shook Chéri's hand. Desmond's hand, Chéri realized, had altered. Once narrow and soft, it had grown large and forceful, and by some miracle of camouflage Desmond had made it significant, even hard.

"The war again," Chéri thought, with an inward chuckle.

"Will you get out?" Desmond said.

But he held Chéri at the head of the stairs long enough to show off an impressive looking customer to the champagne dealer.

"Like that," said Chéri, with a wave of his hand.

"I want to mystify him," whispered Desmond. "On your way, mighty Sultan. Enjoy your afternoon."

"Oh, no," said Chéri. "You're mistaken."

He visualized some woman, with a soft and yielding body, naked, her lips parted . . . For no reason, he shuddered with distaste. Repeating, in a low tone, "You're mistaken," he stepped into his car.

He was troubled by a restlessness he knew only too well. He was irritated by the knowledge that he could never make himself clear, that he never met the one person to whom he could make a vague and indefinite but frank avowal of his thoughts, reveal a secret that might well alter everything, and, for example, take the curse, the evil spell, even from this afternoon of sun-baked pavements, of asphalt melting in the heat. . . .

"It's only two o'clock," he said, with a sigh. "And it stays light until after nine, this month."

The wind made by the speed of his car struck him in the face like the blow of a hot, dry towel. He longed for the cool darkness blue curtains gave, creating an illusion of night, and for the little air of three notes that the fountain in his garden played.

"If I slip into the house quickly perhaps I won't be seen," he thought. "They'll still be at coffee—"

He evoked the aroma of luncheon at its end, the lingering odor of a melon, of the dessert wine Edmée served after fruit; he saw, prophetically, a faintly green Chéri closing the door and reflected in the mirror as he did so.

"Oh, well—I might as well try!"

Two cars, his wife's and the American machine, rested under the heavy foliage before the garden gate, in the care of a single sleeping chauffeur—an American. Chéri drove as far as the Rue de Franqueville, which lay deserted in the heat, to leave his car and walk back to the house. He opened the door, noiselessly, glanced at himself in the green mirror and went lightly upstairs to his bedroom. It was all he had longed for, blue, filled with the perfume of flowers, a place dedicated to rest. Everything the altered trend of his thoughts had made him yearn to find was there.

Indeed, there was more, for a young woman in a white dress was powdering her face and arranging her hair in front of a long mirror. Her back was turned, and she did not hear Chéri come into the room. So he had ample time in which to study in the glass features animated by the heat and the effort of eating, and singularly transformed by emotions that suggested triumph, a sort of outraged victory. Just as he completed his appraisal Edmée saw him. She did not cry out in surprise; she turned to him at once, and looked at him, waiting for him to break the silence.

From below, through the open window that overlooked the garden, Dr. Arnaud's baritone came up to them. He was singing "Ay, Mari, ay, Mari—"

It was as if Edmée's whole body responded to the song. But she refrained, by an effort, from turning her head toward the window.

In her eyes a courage inspired a little by wine hinted at unsaid things that might become serious. But, whether he was contemptuous or afraid, Chéri preferred silence, and enjoined it with a finger lifted to his lips. Then, with the same imperative finger, he pointed to the stairs. Edmée was obedient; she passed before him with a resolute bearing. But she could not resist, when the interval between them was narrowest, a movement that accentuated all the charm, all the allure, of her body and that awoke in Chéri, for the fraction of a moment, a half formed wish to hurt her. He leaned over the rail, like a cat perched high in a tree; he still thought of punishment, of a blow, of flight. He waited for a surge of jealousy to sweep him on. Nothing came, except a little pang of shame, which was easy enough to dismiss. But to himself he said only: "Punish her? Smash everything? I can do better than that. Yes— I can do better than that."

Only—he did not know just what it was he could do that would be better.

4

EVERY morning, whether he woke early or late, Chéri began another day of waiting, of expectancy. At first this had not troubled him, for he had supposed it simply the persistence of a morbid habit of thought acquired in the war.

In December, 1918, he had been prolonging, as a civilian, a short convalescence from a minor injury, a twisted kneecap. He would stretch himself every morning at daybreak, and smile.

"I'm well," he would say to himself. "I'm going to be better. Christmas ought to amount to something this year!"

Christmas had come. Truffles had been eaten, a sprig of holly, soaked in brandy, had blazed on a silver dish. There had been Edmée, ethereal and affectionate, his mother, Madame de La Berche and a whole motley crew of invalided officers, Roumanians, athletic, half-baked American colonels, uniting in praise of him. And, eagerly, he had thought: "I wish they'd go, these people! I want to sleep in my own fine bed, with my feet warm and my head in the cold, fresh air!" Two hours later he had lain flat in bed, longing for sleep, waiting for sleep, mocked by the tiny winter birds twittering in the branches of the trees outside.

In the end he had fallen asleep, but seized again as soon as morning came by that endless and insatiable expectancy of something, of anything, he had begun to wait for breakfast, seeking to cloak his impatience with good humor as he asked Edmée what in the world they could be about, down in the kitchen.

"What's happened to the chow?" he had asked.

He had not realized that the use of the slang word, of a poilu's speech, betrayed, as always with him, a mind full of bitterness, an odd evasiveness. Then he had had his breakfast, duly served by Edmée, but her very promptness made him suspicious, made him feel she was thinking of the time, that she was in a hurry to be off to her duty. He asked her for another bit of toast, for a roll he no longer wanted, only to gratify his own spleen, to delay her departure, to postpone the moment when his eternal waiting must begin again.

A Roumanian lieutenant, of whom Edmée sometimes made use in those days, had been a peculiar source of irritation to Chéri. Edmée would send him in search of ambergris or cotton wool— still scarce in those days before normal trade had been resumed— or, on occasion, to make a plea to some minister. "Things the government refuses out of hand when a Frenchman wants them a foreigner gets for the asking!" she used to say. The Roumanian drove Chéri mad with his talk of a soldier's duty and his endless tributes to the Edenic purity of the hospital.

Once Chéri went there with Edmée and drew into his nostrils the hateful antiseptic smell that, for him, always evoked the thought of masked corruption. He recognized a former comrade among those suffering with trench feet, and sat down on the side of his bed, making an effort to treat him with that warm cordiality of which the war novels and the patriotic plays always made so much. But in his heart he knew perfectly well that a whole man who had escaped from the war was not in the least like these mutilated fellows, that he had nothing in common with them and could find no peers among them.

He looked at the white caps and veils of the nurses and the leathery hands and faces spread against the white sheets around him. He was conscious of an odious sense of impotence, weighing him down. He caught himself bending one arm, limping a little, in sympathy. Yet the next moment, in spite of himself, he was swelling out his chest and stepping out among those bedridden mummies like a dancer. When he came across Edmée he eyed her with impatience, resenting her rank as a non-commissioned angel of mercy and her offensive whiteness. She passed through a ward, and laid her hand on Chéri's shoulder as she went by, but he understood perfectly that by that tender and delicately possessive gesture she meant only to arouse envy and anger in a young, dark nurse who had been looking at Chéri with the frankly amorous eyes of a savage.

The place bored him; he was like a man, taken against his will to a museum, who yawns as he comes face to face with masterpieces crowded in rows. The ceilings were too white; the dazzling whiteness was reflected from the floors. The very angles of the walls were abolished; Chéri pitied the poor devils in their beds, to whom no one thought of giving the blessed alms of a little shade.

The noon hour sends wild beasts into retreat to rest, it silences birds perched on the branches of trees, but civilized man no longer lives by the laws of the stars. Chéri moved toward his wife. It was in his mind to say to her: "Draw the curtains, put in a punkah, take that dish of macaroni away from that poor devil who's blinking and sniffling over there—you can feed him at dusk. Let them have some shade, let them have any color but this everlasting white—" But Dr. Arnaud's coming had made an end of his impulse to give advice, to be of some real service to the wounded.

The doctor, with his sandy hair and his white linen garb, had no sooner entered the room than Edmée, the soaring angel of mercy, fluttered down to fulfill the humbler destiny of serving as his satellite, flushed with faith and zeal. Then Chéri had turned to Filipesco, who was handing out American cigarettes.

"Are you coming?" he said, disdainfully, and took him away, after saluting his wife, Dr. Arnaud, the nurses and the orderlies with the affable haughtiness of an official inspector. He crossed the graveled court, got into his car, and allowed himself only the briefest of comments.

"It's the usual thing," he said to himself. "Naturally the Head Surgeon gets his effects!"

He never went to the hospital again, and thereafter Edmée invited him to go only as a perfunctory gesture, such as one makes when one offers game to a vegetarian guest.

5

HE GREW thoughtful now, prey to an idleness that, before the war, had been agreeable, varied, as full of meaning as the resonant note of an empty, uncracked cup. During the war, too, he had submitted to the military rule of sloth, an inertia relieved, however, by cold, mud, danger, sentry duty, even occasionally by a little fighting. Inured to idleness, to vast leisure, by his life as a young man given to voluptuousness, he had seen companions fresher, and so more easily its prey, wasting away from enforced silence, from loneliness, from a sense of their own impotence. He had seen what the inability to get hold of reading matter could do—it had been like the sudden cutting off of a drug, once the habit had been acquired, for the intellectuals the war had swallowed. While he, satisfied with a note, a postcard, a cleverly packed parcel from home, had basked like a cat in a garden at night, content to remain quiet and reflective, others, superior beings as they were called, had suffered as from starvation. So he had learned to bolster his patience with a new pride. He had been content to dwell on two or three ideas, two or three memories, tenaciously held, as keen and vivid as the memories of children—and on his utter inability to grasp the idea that he himself might die.

Often, during the war, waking, sometimes from a long, dreamless sleep, sometimes from sleep caught in snatches broken every minute or two, he had found himself far from the moment in which he was living. He had been a child again, with all the more recent past wiped out. He had been with Léa again. Then, a little later always, there would be Edmée, immaculate, with her lovely figure, and his evocation of her, coupled with his momentary forgetfulness of the filthy present, had always put him in good humor.

"That's two for me," he would say.

He never heard from Léa, nor did he ever write to her. But there were postcards signed by Mother Aldonza's twisted fingers, and cigars chosen for him by the Baroness de La Berche. Sometimes he had slept upon a long, soft, woolen scarf, because it was of the blue of a pair of remembered blue eyes and because of the indefinable perfume that had come from it in long hours of warmth and rest. He had loved that scarf, pressing it to him in the darkness. Then it had lost its faint scent and its fresh color, and he had thought of it no more.

For four years he had not been troubled by memories of Léa. Old lookouts in his mind, in case of need, would have sensed and apprised him of things the possibility of which he could hardly imagine. What had Léa to do with illness, with change?

In 1918, incredulously, he heard the Baroness de La Berche make some casual reference to Léa's new apartment.

"Has she moved?" he asked.

"Where have you been?" the Baroness rejoined. "Why, every one's talking about that. She was in luck when she sold her house—to some Americans, of course. I've seen her new place—it's small, but it's charming. Once you're settled down you stay."

"Small, but charming." Chéri dwelt on that description. With an effort he imagined a pink scheme of decoration, into which he fitted that vast ship model of gold and steel, the great bed with its lace coverings. He hung the painting, with its mother of pearl breasts, in a cloud of flowing draperies.

Desmond had been looking for some one to supply capital for his night club. The knowledge had worried Chéri, put him on guard.

"Damn him—he'll get hold of Léa, he'll get her mixed up in his racket and lose her money for her. I'm going to call her up and warn her."

But in the end he had done nothing. For it is more daring to telephone to a discarded mistress than to offer your hand, in the street, to an intimidated enemy who is trying to catch your eye.

6

CHÉRI was still expectant, after the day when he had surprised Edmée at her mirror, when he had come upon her flushed, disordered, exalted. He let time pass, doing nothing, by putting the matter into words, to accentuate what he regarded as certain, an understanding, still almost innocent, between his wife and the man who had sung "Ay, Mari . . ."

He was more at his ease, and for several days he never thought of glancing at his wrist watch as twilight approached. He formed the habit of sitting in the garden, in a wicker chair, as if, on some trip, he had just settled down in a hotel garden. He would sit, watching the gathering darkness blot out the blue of monkshood, substituting for it another shade of blue in which the outline of the flowers vanished, even while the green leaves remained clear, in color and in outline. The border of rose pinks turned to the color of dying violets and then grew swiftly black and the yellow stars of July gleamed among the branches of the plumed ash tree.

In his own garden Chéri's pleasure in all he saw was that of a passer-by sitting down for a moment in a square. He lost all sense of the passage of time as he sat back, his hands hanging beside his chair. Sometimes he thought of what he called the scene at the mirror, of the tension in the blue room, secretly troubled by that gesture of hers as she passed him. He said to himself, under his breath, with a methodical and deliberate stupidity: "After all, that's something accomplished."

Early in July he tried out a new open car. He called it his seaside motor. He drove Filipesco and Desmond over roads white with dust, but every evening he turned back toward Paris, rushing through air packed in alternate layers of heat and freshness, that grew staler and more odorous as Paris approached.

One day he took with him the Baroness de La Berche, mannish in her uniform, who lifted a finger to her tiny felt hat to salute the guards as they passed the *octrois*. He found her an agreeable companion, sparing of words, alert to spy out little inns covered with wistaria and village markets, with their fine smells of old cellars and sand damp with wine. Silent, impassive, they drove for something like three hundred kilometers without opening their mouths except to smoke or eat. Next day Chéri delivered his invitation to Camille de La Berche with a "How about it, Baroness?" and took her off with him again.

The car plunged into the green countryside; in the evening it returned to Paris like a ball at the end of a string. That particular evening Chéri, without taking his eyes from the road, saw on his right the profile of an old woman with the face of a man; she had the fine presence of some old coachman of a great house. It surprised him to find that her simplicity compelled his respect, and he realized, though still vaguely, that a woman burdened with a sexual abnormality could not sustain it at all without bravery and a certain grandeur of spirit such as men sometimes display under sentence of death. It had taken this experience, alone with her, away from the city, to give him a truer estimate of her.

She had ceased to indulge in her perversion since the coming of the war. The hospital had put her back in her proper place, among men. And among men, moreover, just young enough, just sufficiently afflicted, to let her dwell among them in serenity, forgetting her aborted womanhood.

Chéri, unobserved by her, regarded with intentness his companion's big nose, her graying, hairy lip, her little peasant's eyes, straying indifferently over ripening wheat and new-mown meadows. For the first time Chéri was drawn to the old woman by a feeling akin to friendship.

"She's all alone," he said to himself. "When she is away from the soldiers and my mother she is utterly alone—she, too. In spite of her pipe and her glass she is all alone."

On the way back to Paris they stopped at an inn where there was no ice, where shriveled roses were dying on the pillars and around vessels of stone, once used as baptismal fonts, scattered about the lawn. A wood close by kept the breeze from reaching this dusty spot; overhead a small hot cloud, red with heat, hung in the sky. The Baroness knocked out her short briar pipe on a marble faun.

"It's going to be hot in Paris tonight," she said.

Chéri nodded his agreement and looked up at the ruddy cloud. A pink light descended on his dimpled chin and his white cheeks, until he looked as if he had been made up.

"Yes, it'll be hot," he said.

"Well, if the country tempts you, why go back until morning? All I need is time to buy a cake of soap and a toothbrush. You can telephone to your wife. In the morning we can start at four o'clock, while it's still cool and fresh."

Chéri started to his feet.

"No—oh, no—I can't!"

"You can't? Oh, nonsense!"

Looking down he saw her small, mannish eyes laughing at him; her great shoulders shook.

"I didn't suppose you were still so firmly bound," she said. "Still, as soon as that's in question—"

"What are you talking about?"

She had risen too, and now she clapped him on the shoulder, heartily.

"Yes, yes. You circulate all day, but you go home every evening. Oh, you're nicely caught."

He looked at her coldly. Already he liked her less.

"There's no hiding anything from you, Baroness. Let me take you to the car—in two hours or less we shall be at your house."

Chéri never forgot their return that evening, the melancholy glow lingering in the west, the scent of hay, the feathery moths held captives in the beams of the headlights. A black shape, made darker still by the night, the Baroness sat beside him. He drove carefully; when he slowed down at the turns the fresh air that met them when they were going at full speed grew warm. He was proud of his keen eyes, his sure, powerful muscles, but he found his thoughts dwelling, in spite of himself, on the strange, massive old woman at his side, so still, so motionless. He came to feel a sort of fretfulness, an irritable nervousness, that caused him to come within a hand's breadth of hitting a wagon without lights. At that moment a great hand touched his arm.

"Watch your driving, youngster."

He had looked for neither the gesture nor the tenderness in her voice. But it seemed to him that neither surprise nor anything else could account for the emotion they stirred in him, the lump in his throat.

"I'm an idiot—I'm a damned fool!" he told himself.

He drove more slowly. He found himself, for a few moments, trying to laugh at the queer, dancing patterns of light that were formed by the tears that stood in his eyes.

7

"S HE told me that it holds me—that I can't get away! If she could see us—Edmée and me! How long is it since we slept together?" He tried to reckon the time. Three weeks? Longer, perhaps. "And the queer thing is that Edmée makes no demands—that she's always smiling when she wakes up." He always said queer, when he was talking to himself, when what he meant was sad. "A settled household—oh, the devil—yes, a settled household. The wife and her head surgeon—the husband and his—his car. And old Camille said I was held fast. If ever I take her with me again!"

He did take her again, for July was doing its best to consume Paris. But neither Chéri nor Edmée complained of the dog-days. Chéri came back each evening, polite, absent-minded, the backs of his hands and the lower part of his face deeply sunburnt. He wandered, naked, between the bathroom and Edmée's boudoir.

"You people in the hospital must have been broiled today," Chéri said, teasingly.

A little pale and spent, Edmée straightened her pretty back and disclaimed her weariness.

"Oh, it wasn't so bad! There was more air than yesterday. And my office over there is cool, you know. Besides, there isn't time to think of the heat. My little 22 who was doing so well—"

"Yes?"

"Yes. Dr. Arnaud doesn't like the way he looks."

She never hesitated to throw out Arnaud's name; she used it as one might a major piece in chess. But Chéri did not frown. Edmée let her eyes follow him, his nudity faintly touched with green by the reflection of the blue curtains. He passed her again and again, exposed, white, perfumed. His very assurance, his superb confidence in his incomparable body, condemned Edmée to a silence that was faintly hostile. At this moment she could only have claimed that beautiful, nude body in a voice lacking in passion, a voice that would only have been that of a tender and fond companion. An arm downy with tiny gold hair, a passionate mouth beneath a golden mustache, held her now, and she looked at Chéri, wise, avid, with the assurance of a lover who has marked for his own a virgin inaccessible to all.

They talked of holidays, of getting away, conventionally, lightly.

"The war hasn't changed Deauville enough," said Chéri, with a sigh. "And the crowd—!"

"There's no decent place to eat," Edmée insisted. "And it's something of a task to reorganize the whole hotel business!"

8

J u s t before Bastille Day Charlotte Peloux came to lunch and made announcement, at the table, of the successful outcome of a new flyer on the Bourse. Her only regret, and she voiced it freely, was that Léa had shared the profits. Chéri, amazed, stared at her.

"Are you seeing her?" he asked.

Charlotte Peloux gave her son an affectionate look, inspired chiefly by old port, and appealed to her daughter-in-law.

"Such talk—the way he goes on! Like one of those poor fellows that was gassed—yes, that's the way he sounds. He really upsets me sometimes. I've never stopped seeing Léa, darling. Why shouldn't I see her?"

"Yes—why on earth shouldn't she see her?" Edmée repeated.

He looked at the two women. There was something puzzling about their attitude.

"Well, you've never mentioned her to me," he said, lamely enough.

"I've never mentioned her—!" Charlotte was outraged. "Oh, listen

—really— Do you hear that, Edmée? Oh, well, it's his passion for you. He forgets everything that doesn't concern you."

Edmée smiled, but had nothing to say. She bent her head and pulled up the lace that edged the neck of her frock, twisting it between her fingers. Her movement attracted Chéri's glance, and he saw her breasts under the yellow linen of her gown, and the two little mauve points, like twin scars, that revealed her nipples. His involuntary movement of aversion made him realize how utterly estranged he had become from that lovely body, so frankly revealed; that this woman, young, beautiful, easy and disloyal, stirred no feeling in him now except one of definite and fastidious repugnance.

"Oh, come, come!" he said to himself. But he was whipping an insensitive animal. Charlotte was still talking, volubly, nasally.

"Only the day before yesterday I was saying—and you were there—that, taking them both as cars, I preferred a taxi—a taxi, I tell you!—to that old wreck of a Rénault of Léa's, and it wasn't the day before yesterday, it was yesterday, that I was talking about Léa, and I said that if one was a woman living alone and felt one must keep a man servant one might just as well have a good looking one. And what about Camille, just the other evening—you were here—going on because she'd had that second piece of Quart-de-Chaume sent to Léa instead of keeping it for herself? Darling, I think I ought to scold you for being ungrateful instead of praising your fidelity. Léa deserves better of you. Edmée will be the first to admit that."

"The second," Edmée amended, drily.

"I heard none of all this," said Chéri.

He sat there, stuffing himself with hard, July cherries, tossing the pits, when he was done, to the sparrows in the garden, through the space left under the lowered blinds. The garden had been too freely watered, and now it was steaming like a hot spring. Edmée, sitting very quiet, was still thinking of Chéri's remark. He had told the truth, she knew; he really had not heard a word. None the less, his lack of interest, his pretense of boyishness as he gripped a cherry stone to aim it at a sparrow, with his left eye closed to sight his mark the better, told Edmée a good deal. "What was he thinking about?" she asked herself. "Why didn't he hear?"

Before the war, she would have sought to learn the name of his latest mistress. A month ago, the day after the scene of the mirror, she would have feared reprisals, a blow, some act of barbaric cruelty. But no—nothing of the sort. Nothing at all. He went about innocently, taking his long drives, peaceful in his freedom, like some prisoner in the confines of his gaol. He was as chaste as some animal brought from the antipodes, that does not even trouble to seek a mate in a new hemisphere.

Was he ill? He slept well enough, ate as much as he ever did, and according to his appetite, which was delicate; as always he scarcely touched meat, but loved fruit and new laid eggs. No nervous tic marred his handsome features; he drank more water than champagne.

"No," she decided, "he's not ill. And still—there's something wrong. Something I'd probably find out soon enough if I were still in love with him. But—"

Again she played with the lace about her bosom, and she was aware of the warmth of her body and its subtle scent. Looking down, she too, now, saw the twin mauve and pink mounds of her breasts. She flushed at a sensuous thought; she silently dedicated that scent, those mauve shadows, to the red haired, clever, condescending man she would be seeing again within the next hour.

9

"So they talked about Léa before me every day, and I didn't hear? Does that mean that I've forgotten her? I suppose I have. But what does it mean, to forget some one? If I think of Léa I see her clearly, I remember the intonation of her voice, the perfume she used, the way she wet her hands with it and rubbed them together."

He breathed in the air through his nostrils, he drew his upper lip toward his nose, in the familiar grimace of a gourmand in the presence of a favorite odor.

"Fred, you just made the most abominable face! You looked exactly like that fox Angot brought back from the trenches."

They were passing through the least trying hour of their whole day, after their awakening and their coffee and rolls. Refreshed by their baths, they listened gratefully to the sound of a heavy rain. It was three months ahead of time, loosening the leaves of the sham autumn of Paris and beating down the petunias. This morning they did not take the trouble to find an excuse for the way they persisted in staying in town. Charlotte had relieved them of that task the day before, when she had stated their case.

"We're the real cockneys!" she had said. "The genuine article—we and the concièrges. They can say of us that we really enjoyed the first post-war summer in Paris!"

"Fred—have you fallen in love with that suit? You wear nothing else—and it needs pressing, to say the least!"

Chéri waved his hand toward Edmée's voice, in a gesture seeking silence and pleading with her not to distract his attention, devoted just then to an effort that made exceptional demands upon his mentality.

"If I've forgotten," he thought, "I want to know it. But what do people mean by forgetting some one? I haven't seen her for a year—" He was startled as he realized that his memory had passed over the war altogether. Then he reckoned up the true tale of the years, and for a moment he was too stunned to go on thinking.

"Fred, I never can persuade you to leave your razor in the bath-room instead of bringing it back here."

He turned to her, peaceably enough. He was all but nude, still damp from his bath, and talcum powder stuck to his body, here and there, in patches.

"What did you say?"

Her voice, which seemed so far away to him, burst into laughter.

"Fred, you look like a badly iced cake! A rather sickly cake. Next year we won't be as stupid as we have been this summer. We'll have a country place."

"You want an estate in the country?"

"Yes. Hardly this morning, of course."

As she pinned up her hair she pointed to the sheets of rain that were pouring down from a leaden sky, though there was neither thunder nor wind.

"Next year, though—don't you think we might?"

"It's an idea—yes, it's worth thinking about."

He disposed of her politely. He wanted to dwell upon his astonished realization of the truth.

"It seemed to me I hadn't seen her for a year," he thought. "Just one year—I didn't think of the war at all! But—then it's one—two—three—four—five years since I've seen her! One—two—three—four—But had I forgotten her then? No, because those women talked about her in my hearing and I didn't jump and exclaim: 'What—do you mean to say that's true? And Léa?' Five years— How old was she in 1914?"

Once more he reckoned up the years and came again to an incredible sum.

"Why—that would make her nearly sixty now! Nonsense!"

"We must be careful," Edmée went on, "to make no mistake in choosing a place. Now, there's lovely country in—"

"Normandy!" Chéri suggested distractedly.

"Yes. Normandy. Do you know Normandy?"

"No—I mean—not very well. It's green. There are lindens—lakes—"

He shut his eyes as though he were dazed.

"Whereabouts? In what part of Normandy?"

"Lakes and ponds, cream, strawberries—and—oh, yes—peacocks—"

"You seem to know a lot about Normandy! Quite a place! What else is there?"

He looked as if he were reading what he was declaiming, leaning toward the round mirror in which he always made sure, after he had shaved, that cheeks and chin were smooth. He went on, stammering a little.

"Peacocks. Moonlight, shining on polished floors, and a great, an enormous red carpet laid down in a drive—"

He did not finish. He swayed for a moment, and then fell to the floor. The side of the bed checked his fall; his face, lying against the sheets, always pale, had been weathered by the sun until now, in his swoon, it had the tint of old ivory.

Edmée, without a word, flung herself down beside him, supporting his head, holding a bottle of smelling salts to his nostrils. But he pushed her away, feebly.

"Let me alone—can't you see I'm dying?"

But he did not die, and his hand, clasped in Edmée's, was still warm. He had spoken in a whisper, with the suave emphasis of those who, seeking in extreme youth to kill themselves, seek death and struggle to escape it in the same moment.

His lips parted, showing his gleaming teeth. He was breathing regularly. But he was in no hurry to come to his senses altogether. He took refuge, behind his closed eyelids, in the heart of that green domain he had evoked in his memory at the moment of his swoon —a level countryside of strawberry plants and bees, of springs set about with colored stones. As his strength returned he kept his eyes closed.

"If I open my eyes," he thought, "Edmée will see everything I am looking at."

She still leaned over him, one knee bent. She was giving him an efficient, professional care. With her free hand she waved a newspaper, using it as a fan to cool his forehead. She murmured meaningless, perfunctory words.

"It's the storm. Stretch out. No—don't lift yourself. Wait while I slip the pillow under your head."

He sat up, smiled, thanked her with a squeeze of the hand. His mouth was parched; he felt a craving for lemon juice, for something acid. The telephone called Edmée from him.

"Yes. Yes. I know very well that it's ten o'clock. Yes. What?"

Chéri understood, from the imperative, curt answers she made, that they had called up from the hospital.

"Yes, of course I'm coming. What? In—" She glanced at Chéri, saw that he was better. "In twenty-five minutes. Thanks. Yes—very soon."

She opened the windows wide, letting a few drops of rain come in, bringing with them a faint breath of the river.

"Are you better, Fred? How did it feel? No pain at the heart, was there? You're run down. That's what comes of the absurd way we've spent this summer. But, after all—"

She gave the telephone an almost furtive look, as if it could overhear her. Chéri stood up, with no apparent effort.

"Run along, my dear," he said. "You'll be late at your shop. I'll be all right."

"Would you like a drink—a mild one? How about some hot tea?"

"Don't bother about me. You've been very sweet. Yes—you might ask them to send up some tea as you go out."

Five minutes later she went off, after a look in which she tried to let only solicitude appear, but which was a vain attempt to learn the truth, to arrive at some explanation of things utterly inexplicable. As if the sound of the closing door had broken the chains that held him bound, Chéri stretched his arms. He felt free, cold, empty. He hurried to the window, and watched his wife making her way to the gate, her head bent under the rain.

"Her back looks guilty," he told himself. "It always has. Seen from the front, she's charming, all she should be. But her back gives her away. My faint made her lose a good half hour. But let's get back to our muttons, as my mother says. Léa was fifty-one when I was married—at the very least, Madame Peloux insists. She must be fifty-eight now—even sixty, perhaps. As old as General Courbat? Come, that's simply ridiculous!"

Fantastically, he tried to give Léa, at sixty, General Courbat's bristling white mustache, his furrowed cheeks, his pompous air, so like that of an old cab horse.

"Simply ridiculous!" he told himself, again.

Madame Peloux arrived while he was still trying to amuse himself with his feeble joke. Pale, very still, he was looking out at the garden and the pouring rain, biting a cigarette that had gone out. He took her coming calmly.

"You're out early this morning, Mother," he said.

"I should say you had got out of bed on the wrong side," she rejoined.

"An illusion, pure and simple. Are there extenuating circumstances to explain your unseemly energy?"

She raised her eyes and her shoulders. A cheeky little leather sports hat covered her whole forehead like a visor.

"My dear boy, if you only knew what I have in hand this very moment! If you guessed what a great enterprise—"

He looked intently at his mother's face, with its deep wrinkles, that were like inverted commas about her mouth. He considered, attentively, the soft roll of her fleshy double chin, the ebb and flow of which first hid, then revealed, the collar of her raincoat. He studied the moving pouches her lower lids had become, saying to himself, over and over: "Fifty-eight— Sixty—"

"Do you know what this job is I've undertaken? Do you?"

She paused, and opened her great eyes, heavily penciled in black, wider than ever.

"I'm reviving the hot springs of Passy. The Passy springs. That means nothing to you, naturally. The springs are there, under the Rue Raynouard, two feet down. They're dormant, all they need is to be tapped once more. The waters are most active—highly charged. If we go about it properly it means the end of Uriage—perhaps even the finish of Mont-Doré. But that's too much to hope for! I've made sure of twenty-seven Swiss doctors already. And Edmée and I are working together on the Paris Municipal Council. That's why I'm here—I missed your wife by five minutes, I hear. What's the matter with you? Aren't you listening to me?"

He was trying persistently to light his soaked cigarette. He gave it up, tossed it out on the balcony, where great rain drops were leaping up and down like grasshoppers, and turned to look gravely at his mother.

"I'm listening," he said. "As far as that goes, I know in advance what you're going to tell me. It's all about combines, trickery, bonuses, founders' shares, American underwritings, dried beans and what not. Do you suppose I've been both blind and deaf this last year? You're a pair of designing wenches, that's all. I don't hold it against you."

He stopped talking and sat down, rubbing away, as was his habit, at the tiny twin scars under his right breast. His eyes dwelt on the green, rain beaten garden. Weariness and youth struggled for mastery in his features, beginning now to relax, the former furrowing his cheeks, darkening his eyes, the latter still intact in the charming bow of his mouth, the downy flare of his nostrils, the luxuriant abundance of his black hair.

"Oh, well—that's just your line!" said Charlotte Peloux, finally. "Morality can take care of itself. As for me, I've given my censor a vacation."

He remained silent and motionless.

"And from just what heights do you judge this poor, corrupt world? From those of your own integrity, I suppose?"

Armored in leather, like some medieval reiter, she was a match for herself; she asked nothing better than a fight. But Chéri seemed unwilling to oblige her; he had done with battles.

"My integrity? Perhaps. Though, if I had been seeking a word, I wouldn't have chosen that. You supply it yourself. Call it integrity, if you like."

She did not answer, letting her assault wait till later. She was silent, so that she might give all her attention to her son's strange aspect. His legs were spread out, his elbows rested on his knees, his fists were clenched. He stared persistently at the garden, swept by the driving rain, and after a moment he sighed, without turning his head.

"Do you call this living?"

"Do I call what living?" she asked him, impatiently.

He lifted one arm and let it fall again.

"Oh—my life, yours. All this. Everything we see?"

She hesitated for a moment. Then she took off her leather coat, lit a cigarette, and sat down.

"Are you growing bored?"

He was touched by the unaccustomed softness of her voice, usually so detached and wary. He grew natural, almost confident.

"Bored? No, I'm not bored. Why should I be bored? I'm a little— I don't know—a little anxious, that's all."

"What about?"

"Oh, everything! Myself—you, too."

"You surprise me."

"I surprise myself. All this rabble—this year—the peace—"

He spread his fingers, as if they felt sticky, or had been caught in a long hair.

"You say that the way people used to say 'the war.'"

She laid her hand on his shoulder and lowered her voice, under-standingly.

"Tell me what's the matter?"

He couldn't bear the weight of that questioning hand. He got up, he moved about, distractedly.

"Oh, the trouble with me is that the world's full of shoddy people! No—" His voice grew pleading as he saw the look of haughty indignation in her eyes. "Don't start all over again. Present company is *not* excepted. I do *not* believe we are living in glorious times— the dawn of this, the resurrection of that! No—I'm not in a temper. I don't love you any the less, my liver's perfectly all right. But I'm at the end of my tether."

He walked up and down, snapping his fingers, breathing in the odorous mist that the rain drove in from the balcony. Charlotte Peloux threw down her hat and her leather gloves, giving her gesture, somehow, an appeasing air.

"Explain all this, child," she said. "We're all alone."

She pushed back her red hair, cut short like a boy's. Her dress clung to her figure as a hoop circles a cask.

"Quite a woman—she was something to look at in her day. Fifty-eight—sixty—" Chéri's thoughts ran on.

She turned her lovely, melting eyes toward him; they were full of a maternal tenderness the power of which to move him he had long since forgotten. Now, in his sudden surrender to the charm of her regard, he realized the dangerous ground he would be treading in giving her the explanation she was seeking. But he felt lonely and abandoned; he had an intolerable longing to replenish the emptiness of his life. And, paradoxically, the very thought that he might shock her spurred him.

"You!" he said. "You have your shares, your legion of honor, your diet. You go to the sessions of the Chamber—you're all worked up about young Lenoir's accident. You're absorbed in Madame Caillaux and your Passy springs. Edmée has her hospital and her doctor. Desmond runs his night club and sells champagne—when he doesn't try his hand at being a pimp. Filipesco cadges cigars from Americans and at the hospitals so that he can sell them at night. Jean de Pouzac is a broker—that's enough about him. What a crew! And—"

"Aren't you forgetting Landru?" suggested Charlotte. "Our very nicest murderer!"

His eye was brighter as he paid her the tribute of an admiring glance. She was fun, with her malignant humor; it kept her young.

"Oh, leave Landru out—he's pre-war. Landru's normal enough. But the rest of you—! In a word—well—oh, I mean you're all such rotters and—and—I don't like it. That's all."

"You're commendably brief, but I can't say you make it very clear," Charlotte said, after a moment. "You don't flatter us, do you? Mind you, I don't say you're wrong. For myself, I like to think I have the virtues of my defects, and at least I'm not afraid of anything. But I don't see what you're driving at, my dear."

Chéri balanced himself awkwardly on his chair. He frowned, and wrinkled his forehead, as if he were trying to keep the wind from blowing his hat away.

"What I'm driving at—well, I'm not so clear about that myself. I wish people weren't so rotten—at least, I wish there were some who weren't always rotten. I suppose I'd be satisfied if I didn't see it so clearly."

Charlotte was amused by that. The boy was so uncertain, he was so obviously troubled, so plainly in need of getting something out of his system.

"Why do you insist on seeing so much, then?" she said, with a laugh.

"Ah, that's it—that's precisely the trouble—"

He smiled disarmingly, and she saw how much older he looked when he smiled.

"We ought either to give him something real to worry about or find some way to distract him," she thought. "Simple diversion does him no good." Then, aloud, she permitted herself a remark as artless as some of Chéri's. "You never used to notice such things, before—" she began.

"Before—?" He raised his head abruptly. "Before what?"

"Oh—before the war."

"Oh—that's what you mean," he said, flatly. "No, I suppose not—before the war. But in those days my point of view was quite different."

"Why?"

The simple question left him without an answer.

"My dear boy, it's as I told you—you've acquired integrity," Charlotte said, mockingly.

"I suppose it wouldn't occur to you, by any chance, that it would be truer to say that I've simply retained it?"

"No—not a bit of it! Let's not confuse the issue."

She was flushed; she was filled with all the polemic zeal and fervor of a good fortune teller.

"After all, you know, my dear—the way you lived before the war. . . . Understand me, I'm talking now like the narrow minded people who call a spade a spade, for whom black is always black and white can never be anything but white—but, after all, that sort of thing—well, there's a name for it, you know."

"Ye-es." Chéri admitted it. "What of it?"

"Well—doesn't that affect one's point of view? You saw life as a gigolo does."

"That's entirely possible," Chéri said, indifferently. "And again—what of it? Are you criticizing me for that?"

"Not at all," Charlotte protested, with her childish simplicity. "It's only—you must admit that there's a time for everything."

"By all means."

He sighed deeply, looking up to the sky, heavy with clouds from which rain was still pouring down.

"There is a time to be young and a time to put youth away. There is a time for happiness. . . . Do you think I need you to tell me that?"

All at once she was disturbed. She walked around the room, and in her tight fitting dress her rump, as round as that of a fat and pampered little dog, shook and quivered. She came back and sat down face to face with her son.

"Darling, you worry me. It seems to me that you're on the point of doing something foolish."

"What?"

"Oh, after all, you haven't such a wide choice. You might go into a monastery—or retire to a desert island—or fall in love."

Chéri smiled in surprise.

"Fall in love?" he said. "Do you want me to—in love with—?"

He nodded his head toward Edmée's boudoir. Charlotte's eyes gleamed.

"Who's been talking to you about her?"

He laughed. In self-defense he fell back upon the weapon that sometimes served him well with Edmée, his peculiar coarseness.

"You'll be offering me an American wench next!"

She disclaimed the suggestion with a theatrical gesture.

"An American! Really! Why not a Negress?"

He had to admire her chauvinistic mind. He had known since childhood that a Frenchwoman never condescended to live with a foreigner except to exploit him—unless, of course, he had seduced and ruined her. He knew by heart the long list of insulting characterizations Parisan courtesans applied to the licentious and dissolute foreigners who sought their pleasure there in the capital of gayety. But, smilingly, without irony, he declined her bid. Charlotte, baffled, looked at him, her lip protruding helplessly. Her expression was that of a puzzled diagnostician.

"I don't suggest that you go to work," she said, rather timidly.

Chéri disposed of that idea with a shrug.

"Work," he echoed. "Work. That means to be with the riff-raff all the time. After all, one doesn't work alone—unless one colors postcards or does sewing at home. Darling mother, what you can't seem to get through your head is that if the men I know disgust me the women don't suit me any better. The truth is that I'm done with women," he admitted, finally, with a certain heroism.

"Good heavens!" Charlotte exclaimed. She was really distressed at last.

She clasped her hands, as if to go to his help, but he checked her, silenced her, with a gesture. She could not help admiring the virility, the authority, of this handsome son of hers who had finally confessed his impotence.

"Chéri! My darling boy—"

He looked at her, gently, absent-mindedly, with eyes vaguely deceptive.

Charlotte looked at him closely. The purity of the whites of his eyes, his long lashes, the hidden emotions that lay in their depths, gave them, perhaps, a deceptive brilliance. She longed, through the portals those eyes represented, to penetrate the mysterious depths of this strange and obscure being whose life had begun within her womb. Chéri seemed to have given up the effort to guard his secrets from her, to be submitting willingly to an hypnotic probe. More than once, in the past, Charlotte had seen her son when he was ill, sullen, out of humor. But never before had she seen him unhappy. The experience exalted her in an extraordinary way, she knew something of that intoxication of the spirit that brings a woman to a man's feet in that moment when she dreams of turning the mysterious, the despairing stranger who is her hopeless lover into a lesser being by putting an end to his despair.

"Listen, Chéri," she whispered. "Listen— You should. . . . Darling, let me talk to you, at least—"

But he checked her with a savage toss of his head, and she did not insist. It was she who broke off their long exchange of silent contemplation, the one of the other. She put on her coat and her little leather hat and walked toward the door. But as she passed the stand she stopped and picked up the telephone, carelessly.

"May I, Chéri?"

He nodded, and at once she began talking, nasally; she sounded like a clarinet.

"Hello—hello—hello. Passy, 2929. No—2929, Mademoiselle. Hello —is that you, Léa? Of course it's me. Charming weather, isn't it? My dear, don't speak of it! Yes, I'm very well. Oh, yes—every one's well. What are you doing with yourself today? You won't stir out? Oh, I know you, you sybarite! I? You know I can't call my soul my own, these days. That? Heavens, no—not any more. I've something else under way now. Something magnificent. No—no—not on the telephone. Then I'll find you at home whenever I come? That's splendid. Thanks. Good-by, Léa darling."

She replaced the receiver. Now he could see only her convex back. As she went out she inhaled and then exhaled blue smoke, and she disappeared in a cloud, like some genie who has come and fulfilled his task.

Part Two

CHÉRI was in no hurry as he climbed the one flight of stairs to Léa's apartment. At six o'clock it had stopped raining, and outside the Rue Raynouard was noisy with the song of birds and the din of playing children; it was like the garden of a boarding school. He missed nothing. Refusing to be either surprised or impressed he took in the heavy mirrors, the gray staircase, the blue carpet, the lift cage, as liberally adorned with gold leaf as a sedan chair. On the landing he was conscious of the same agony of hesitation that is the common lot of all who have forced themselves as far as a dentist's door. He was on the point of turning away. But then he reflected that he might find himself under the compulsion to return another time. The thought vexed him, and he pressed the bell button with a resolute finger. A young maid took her time to open the door; she faced him inquiringly, dark, a butterfly cap of fine lawn on her bobbed head. Chéri, face to face with a stranger, was denied his last chance to indulge in dramatics.

"Is Madame in?"

The girl hesitated. But, plainly, she liked his looks.

"I am not sure, sir. Are you expected?"

"Of course," he said, with a touch of his old sternness.

She left him to wait and disappeared. It was dark; between that and his momentary flash of temper he saw little, as his eyes darted about. Here there was no trace of a familiar scent, but some commonplace aromatic gum was being consumed in an electric incense burner. Chéri felt as if he had stopped at the wrong floor. But through a curtained door he heard, all at once, a hearty, unaffected laugh, deep-toned, rippling down a descending scale. Instantly a flock of memories rose to torment him.

"Will you come into the drawing room—?"

He followed the white butterfly. "Léa isn't alone," he said to himself. "She was laughing. She must have some one with her. If only it isn't my mother—!"

Through a doorway he saw daylight, tinged with pink. It was like a dawn, he thought. What new world awaited him?

A woman was seated at a desk, writing, her back turned to him. Chéri saw a great back, thick gray hair, cut short, like his mother's, a fat, bulging neck.

"Well, I knew she wasn't alone. Who's that good soul at the desk, I wonder?"

"Do you mind writing down the address, too, Léa, and the masseur's name? You know how I am about names—"

He had never heard the speaker's voice before. It was a woman, dressed in black, who had spoken from a chair. As he saw her Chéri had an appalling premonition. Where was Léa? The gray-haired woman at the desk turned. Chéri was looking straight at her; her blue eyes met his with the force of a blow.

"Good heavens—is that really you, Chéri?"

He approached her like a man in a dream, bowed, kised her hand.

"Princess Cheniaguine—M. Frédéric Peloux."

Chéri saluted another hand, sat down.

"Is he—?" The woman in black spoke as if he had been deaf, pointing to him as she did so.

Once more that vast, hearty, carefree laugh filled the room. Chéri sought its source anywhere except in the throat of the gray-haired woman.

"Not a bit of it!" Léa said. "At least—not any longer. Look here, Valérie, what are you after?"

She was not monstrous, but she was huge; everything about her had grown enormous. Her arms stood out, away from her body, like rounded thighs; they were too fat to touch her body at any point. Her clothes implied a renunciation of feminine allurement, the long, plain skirt, the severe coat, half open over her linen blouse, gave her a sort of sexless dignity.

Léa was standing between Chéri and the window, and her solid, her almost cubic bulk, did not at first greatly impress him. But when she moved toward a chair he saw her features plainly, and he began, in his mind, to supplicate her, as he might have some madman who had armed himself. Her cheeks were glowing, they had, indeed, a slightly over-ripe look, but she was using no powder now and when she laughed her mouth gleamed with gold fillings. She looked like what she was, a healthy and well preserved old woman, with a double chin and a heavy jowl, well able to carry her flesh, as innocent of props as of fetters.

"Well, where in the world did you spring from?" she said. "It seems to me you don't look well."

She held out a box of cigarettes, smiling at him, her blue eyes laughing. They had grown smaller, he thought. It appalled him to find her so changed, so simple, so merry, like an old man. She was treating him like a child, and he resented it, but he strove for patience, in the hope that this first impression must give way to some flashing survival of the past. The two women were looking at him; they spared him neither curiosity nor benevolent good will.

"He reminds me of Hernandez, rather," said Valérie Cheniaguine.

"Oh, no," protested Léa. "Ten years ago, perhaps—but no, Hernandez had much more of a chin."

"Who is this?" Chéri asked, with an effort.

"A Peruvian who was killed in a motor smash, six months or so ago," Léa said. "He was keeping Maximilienne. She was terribly grieved."

"She's managed to find consolation," said Valérie.

"Every one does," said Léa. "You wouldn't expect her to die of grief, would you?"

She laughed again, and her jolly blue eyes disappeared, lost in her fat cheeks. Chéri looked away, toward the other woman. She was a big brunette, commonplace, feline, like thousands of women from the South of France, and so meticulously dressed like a woman of breeding that she seemed to be disguised. Valérie wore what for years had been almost a uniform for foreign princesses and their attendants, a badly cut tailored suit, tight under the arms, a blouse of fine batiste, a little strained by her breasts. Pearl earrings, the traditional necklace, the high collar stiffened with whalebone, all were as royal as the excellent name of Valérie. Just as royally, she displayed cheap stockings, stout walking shoes, and expensive gloves, striped in black and white. She looked at Chéri as if he had been a piece of furniture, attentively and rudely. Then, without lowering her voice, she resumed her comparison.

"Oh, yes, I'm right. He does look like Hernandez. But, do you know, you'd think Hernandez had never lived, to hear Maximilienne now that she's finally landed this Amérigo of hers. And still—really—and, mind you, I know what I'm talking about. I've seen him, this Amérigo, with my own eyes. I saw him, finally, at Deauville. As a matter of fact, I saw them both—together."

"No! Did you? Tell me about that."

Léa sat down, filling a great armchair completely. She had acquired a new mannerism, a trick of throwing back her head to get rid of her short white hair, and every time she did it Chéri had a glimpse of the lower part of her face, quivering like that of Louis XVI. She made a show of listening to Valérie, but two or three times Chéri caught her looking at him intently.

"Why, it was like this," Valérie said. "She'd hidden him away in a villa well away from Deauville—at the other end of nowhere, my dear! But that didn't suit Amérigo at all, and he let her know that wasn't what he'd bargained for. She lost her temper then. 'Oh—that's the way it is, eh?' she said to him. 'You want to be seen, do you? Very well—seen you shall be!' So she telephoned to reserve a table at the Normandy for the next evening. It was all over town within the hour, and I reserved a table too, with Becq d'Ambez and Zahita.

"We were thrilled. We were going to see him, this Paragon of hers. Well, on the stroke of nine, Maximilienne came in, all in white and covered with pearls—and Amérigo with her. My dear, what a blow! Tall—yes, he's tall enough—even too tall. You know what I think of giants—show me one, just one, who's well built. His eyes—well, yes, I grant him good-looking eyes. But for the rest—well, his cheeks are too round—he looks like a baby. His ears are set too low—in a word, he was a wash-out. And as stiff as if he'd swallowed a poker."

"You're exaggerating," said Léa. "As for the cheeks, that's a detail. But for the rest, why, I think he's handsome—his eyebrows, the bridge of his nose, his eyes! I won't argue with you about his chin—that will grow flabby very soon. And his feet are too small—small feet look ridiculous on so tall a chap."

"As to that, I don't agree with you at all. But I did notice that

174

his thighs were too long, in proportion to his legs from the knee down."

They went on with their discussion of his points.

"They're experts in beef on the hoof," thought Chéri. "They'd have done good work in the Commissary Department."

"When it comes to perfect proportions, you'll never touch Chéri," said Léa. "You picked the right time to drop in, my dear. Go ahead and blush! Valérie, if you can remember Chéri as he was only six or seven years ago—"

"Of course I remember him. And he hasn't changed so much, after all. How proud of him you were!"

"No, you're wrong," said Léa.

"Do you mean to tell me you weren't proud of him?"

"No," Léa said quietly, "I loved him."

She turned her great body slightly to give Chéri a look innocent of any hidden meaning.

"Oh, it's true that I loved you! I do still."

He lowered his eyes, stupidly awkward and ashamed before these two women, the fatter of whom had just serenely admitted that they had been lovers. But at the same time Léa's voice, so deep and low that it was almost like a man's, richly voluptuous, assailed him with tormenting memories almost beyond endurance.

"How foolish a man looks when one reminds him of anything at all that has to do with a love affair of the past! Haven't you learned that, Valérie? Stupid, it doesn't upset me to remember those days. I love my past. I like my present very well, too. I'm not in the least ashamed of what I've had, and I'm not a bit sorry not to have it any longer. Tell me—am I wrong?"

"Good heavens, no!" He cried out as if he had been struck. "On the contrary!"

"How nice that you're still friends," remarked Valérie.

Chéri expected Léa to explain that this was the first time he had called on her in five years. But she only laughed and gave him an understanding wink. His agitation increased, but he didn't know what to say, how to protest. He would have liked to shout that he didn't want the friendship of this huge woman, with her hair cut like some old cellist in a female orchestra. He wished he could cry out that had he guessed the truth he would never have climbed her stair, never crossed her doorsill, nor touched her carpet nor, above all, sunk into this chair, with its down pillows, in which he now cowered feebly, stricken dumb.

"Well, I must be going," said Valérie. "I don't want to get caught in the rush hour in the Metro."

She got up, facing the light boldly. But it was kind to her rugged features and her Roman nose. She must be nearly sixty, but she was still vigorous and hale. She clung to old fashions in make-up; cheeks evenly powdered with white, lips touched with a rouge so dark that it was almost black.

"You're going home?" Léa asked.

"Indeed I am. What do you suppose that little baggage of mine could cook by herself?"

"You still like your new apartment?"

"It's a dream! Especially since the windows have been barred. I had the casement window in the pantry covered with a steel grill, too—I hadn't noticed that before. Now, what with my two electric bells and my burglar alarms—well, it's time I felt safe."

"And your house?"

"Cleaned out. It's for sale. My pictures are in storage. Oh, my flat is a gem for the eighteen hundred francs I pay. And I'm not surrounded by greedy cutthroats any more. Heavens—those two footmen! It still gives me the creeps to think of them."

"Oh, you always worried too much—"

"My dear, you have to go through that sort of thing to know what it's like. It's been delightful to see you, M. Peloux. Don't get up, Léa."

2

CHÉRI watched her cross the room and pass through the door, but he dared not follow her example. He remained standing, still borne down by the talk between the two women. They had referred to him casually, as if he had been dead! But Léa was back, laughing.

"Princess Cheniaguine! She has sixty millions—she's a widow. And still she isn't satisfied. If that's the joy of living—really!"

She slapped her thigh as if it had been a horse's crupper.

"What's wrong with her?"

"Funk—pure, abject funk. She has no idea of what to do with money. Cheniaguine left her every penny he had, and you'd think sometimes that he might better have taken her own money from her. You heard her, didn't you?"

She lowered herself into a chair, and Chéri writhed at the soft squashy sound the silken cushions gave out as she settled her vast bulk down upon them. She ran her fingers through a groove in her chair, and lifted it, covered with dust. She frowned.

"Things aren't the way they used to be, are they?" she said. "It's not only servants—"

He knew he was pale, and the skin around his mouth grew taut, as it does in cold weather. He was conscious of an almost irresistible impulse to cry out, bitterly, pleadingly. "Stop! Enough of this! Give up this masquerade. You must be there, somewhere, underneath— I hear your voice! Come out! Show yourself, freshly powdered, your hair dyed red this morning. Put on your corsets again, wear that blue dress I loved, use that old meadow perfume of yours that I've longed for here in vain. Leave all this behind, come along, through Passy still wet from the rain, with its birds and its dogs—come to the Avenue Bugeaud—don't you know Ernest will be there, cleaning the brass on your gate?" He closed his eyes, spent.

Her voice came to him.

"Look here, my dear boy, I'm going to tell you something for your own good. You must have your urine analyzed. I know what your ivory color means, and that tightening of the lips—you've been neglecting your kidneys."

Chéri opened his eyes and let them look upon the serene ruin across the room.

"Do you think so?" he said, heroically. "It's quite likely."

"It's quite certain. And you're too thin. It's all very well to say the best roosters are the thin ones, but you're ten pounds underweight."

"Lend me ten of yours," he said, smiling. But he knew that his very cheeks resented that smile.

Léa burst into her jolly laugh, the same laugh that in the old days had greeted some fantastic and outrageous bit of impertinence from her lover. And her laugh gave Chéri a delight such as he had not known for a long time.

"I certainly wouldn't miss them!" she said. "I have put on weight, haven't I? Oh, well—after all—you know how it is!"

She lit a cigarette, inhaled, and blew the smoke out through her nose. She shrugged her shoulders.

"I'm growing old, that's all."

She said that so lightly, so playfully, that she inspired in Chéri an absurd and extravagant hope. "Of course—she's joking. Soon she'll slip away and come back to surprise me—" He looked at her, and for the first time, for a moment, she seemed to understand what his eyes told her.

"I have changed, haven't I, dear boy? Luckily, it doesn't matter. But as for you, you have a look that puzzles me. What was it we used to say—you're like a bird beating its wings against its cage? Hein?"

He didn't like that, this new way she had of ending every sentence with a jerky "Hein?" But every time he heard it he steeled himself, and checked an impulse the origin and end of which alike he found himself unwilling to consider.

"I won't ask you if you have domestic complications," she said.

"In the first place, it's not my business, and in the second I know your wife as if she were my own child."

He heard what she said without really heeding her words. He was realizing that whenever she stopped smiling or laughing she became sexless. In spite of her huge breasts and her crushing weight, her age gave her serenity, strength, an air of repose.

"I know that your wife is well calculated to make a man happy, too."

He could not quite conceal his amusement. Léa took him up sharply.

"I said a man—not any man. Well, here you are, to see me— without telling me you were coming. And I'm not to assume that my charms brought you, am I?"

Her eyes, her beautiful eyes, rested upon him. They were shrunken; little red veins marred the whites. They mocked him. They were neither kind nor cruel. Wise they were, certainly, and lustrous, but— But what had become of the dewy, healthy moisture that used to tint the whites with azure shades? Their old rounded contour was gone, that had made them like round fruit, like a woman's breasts—and blue, always so blue, like a rich land watered by many streams.

"So—you've turned detective!" he said, with a forced laugh. "Get along with you."

He was amazed to find that he was sitting slumped in his chair, his legs crossed, like some handsome youngster who feels a little out of sorts. For he saw in himself his double, down on his knees, flinging his arms out in a wild appeal, calling upon her incoherently.

"I see as much as the next person, I suppose," Léa said. "But you must admit that you haven't set me a very hard task today."

She bridled a little and her chin became more prominent. And Chéri's double, the kneeling one, bowed his head as if he had been mortally hurt.

"You have all the symptoms of a man afflicted by the fashionable disease of the times. No—let me talk. You're like the rest. You're looking for paradise, aren't you—that paradise the world owed you after the war? Your victory, your youth, your lovely girls. We owed you everything and we promised you everything—my word, why not? And what have you found? A perfectly good, perfectly ordinary, commonplace life. So you're homesick and languid—you're disappointed—you grow neurotic. Am I wrong?"

"No," said Chéri. It seemed to him he would give a finger to have her stop talking!

Léa tapped his shoulder and let her big hand, with its enormous rings, stay on it for a moment; as he bowed his head he was conscious of the heat of her hand against his cheek.

"Look here," Léa went on, raising her voice, "you're not the only one, you know. I've seen any number of lads in your case since the Armistice—"

"You have?" Chéri interrupted her. "Where?"

The sharpness of his interjection, and his aggressive tone, altered Léa's mood. She had been kindly, almost tender. Now she withdrew her hand.

"My dear boy, there are any number of them. Will you persist to the end in that false pride of yours? Can you seriously suppose you're the only one who finds something lacking in the world now that we're at peace? You'd better face the truth."

She laughed her low pitched laugh, tossed her gray head, and smiled complacently.

"You and your pride—you must always fancy yourself the only one to be considered!"

She stepped back, looked at him with a keener eye, and spoke now with something like malice.

"My dear, you were only unique when—oh, for a little while."

That taunt, so feminine, so indirect, and yet so precisely timed and chosen, was what Chéri had needed. He looked up; he felt better already. That was more like Léa.

"But you didn't come here to be lectured like this," Léa said, her voice kinder again. "You came on an impulse?"

"Yes," said Chéri.

He almost wished that might be the last word between them.

Distraught, nervous, his eyes wandered about the room, avoiding Léa. He saw a tiny, dry cake on a plate, shaped like a curved tile, and picked it up. But then he put it down, sure that if he bit into it his mouth would be filled with a powdery red dust of crumbs. Léa saw him, and the effort with which he swallowed.

"Oh—I see—we're suffering from nerves, are we? You have the chin of a starved cat and circles under your eyes. Fine business!"

He closed his eyes, taking a cowardly refuge in the thought that even if he must listen he need not look.

"Listen, my dear, I know a place in the Avenue des Gobelins—"

Once more he looked at her, inspired by the hope that she was going mad, and that so he might forgive both her physical deterioration and her senile preaching.

"Yes, I know a place— Let me speak, will you? Only, you must hurry to get there before it's discovered and made a haunt of fashion or they'll get rid of the cook and put in a chef. It's the owner's wife who does the cooking now, and let me tell you, my dear—"

She put her fingers to her lips and kissed them, and Chéri looked over at the window. Outside, the branch of a tree, swaying rhythmically in the wind, cut off the sunlight periodically, like a reed swinging in a stream.

"What a ridiculous conversation this is!" he ventured, in a voice he could not make sound like his own.

"It's no more ridiculous than your being here at all," Léa replied, acidly.

His gesture showed that he wanted peace, nothing but peace—as few words as possible, and preferably silence. He was conscious that in this old woman there were still elements of vivid strength, appetites still vigorous and hale, that put him to rout. Already Léa's color, always quick to rise, was mounting, staining her neck and her ears. "She has a neck like an old hen," Chéri thought, evoking some semblance of his old savage humor.

"That's true, and you know it," Léa cried, losing her temper. "You

come here looking like a ghost. I try to help you—after all, I know
you fairly well—"

He smiled at her, trying to silence her. How could she think she
knew him?

"My dear boy, half the time this sort of disillusionment, this oppression of the spirit, comes from an upset stomach. Oh, go ahead
and laugh—"

He wasn't laughing, but she might well have thought so.

"Romanticism, neurasthenia, weariness of life—a matter of the
stomach. Every bit of it, I tell you—the stomach. And even love! If
people were only frank they'd admit that there are two sorts of
love—love properly fed and love due to the wrong diet. Everything
else—well, that's what the novelists make up. If I could write, my
dear, I'd have something to say about that! Oh, of course I couldn't
invent anything, but at least I'd know what I was talking about.
Which is more than most writers nowadays do."

Chéri found himself troubled by something worse than this ali-
mentary philosophy of love and neurasthenia. He sensed in Léa an
affectation, a studied gayety, a pretended air of naïveté. He wondered if she had not assumed this new joviality, this epicureanism,
for the same reason that certain actors always played the parts of
men about town—because they had put on weight around the waist.
As though defiantly she rubbed her shiny nose with the back of her
finger and fanned herself with the two revers of her long coat. It
seemed to Chéri that she could not possibly, in reality, be content to
look as she did. But then she even ran her hand through her thick
gray hair.

"Bobbed hair is becoming to me, don't you think?" she said.

He declined to answer except with a faint negative movement of
his head; it seemed to him she had not meant her question to be
taken seriously.

"You were saying you had found a place in the Avenue des
Gobelins—?"

"No," she said, indifferent in her turn, and the quivering of her
nostrils made him realize that at last he had succeeded in upsetting

her a little. At once the sleeping animal in him stirred. He felt better. His instinct, subdued, terrified, until that moment, asserted itself again. Again he dreamed of re-establishing, through the medium of that shameless corpulence, the shock of gray hair, even her appalling joviality, so like a legendary friar's, communication with that deeply buried woman of the past to whom he persisted in trying to return, as a murderer is supposed to revisit the scene of his crime. A peculiar sense in him, like that by which some men divine the presence of water beneath the soil, assured him that he really was not so far from the hidden treasure he sought.

"I wonder how she came to grow old?" he asked himself. "Was it all at once, some morning when she woke? Or did it happen gradually? And this flesh, this massive weight under which the very chairs groan! Did some grief, some tragic blow, change her so, unsex her? And what was it? Was it because of me?"

But he asked his questions only of himself, and silently.

"She's angry. She's beginning to understand me. Now she'll tell me—"

He saw her get up, cross the room to her desk, pick up the papers scattered on the lowered flap. He saw that she was more erect now than when he had come in. Under his eyes she straightened herself still more. He had to admit that she really was enormous, that there was no perceptible curve at all between arm pit and hip. Before she turned back to Chéri she drew a white silk scarf more closely around her neck, in spite of the intense heat. He heard her breathing heavily. Then she turned back to him, smiling, walking with the light tread of some great beast.

"I haven't received you very graciously, I am afraid," she said. "It is rude to greet a visitor with advice—especially worthless advice."

A fold of the white scarf slipped down, and Chéri saw and recognized a pearl cross. Imprisoned beneath the frail shells of the pearls the seven colors of the rainbow flamed mysteriously in each precious gem. Chéri recognized the dented pearl, the one that was slightly oval in shape, the largest one of all, that stood out from the rest by reason of its extraordinary rose tint.

"They have never changed—they and I," he thought. Aloud he said: "I see you still have your pearls?"

The trite phrase seemed to amaze her. It was as if she sought to give it some symbolic meaning.

"Why yes, the war spared those, at least. Did you think I could have sold them—or that I needed to? Why should I have sold them?"

"For whose sake, I might ask," he said, jokingly, in a tired voice.

She could not refrain from a swift glance at the desk, with its scattered papers, and Chéri, in his turn, sought to give that glance a meaning, and decided that it must have been directed at a yellowed picture, on a postcard—the likeness of a beardless boy in uniform. In his mind, disdainfully, he considered it. "It's none of my affair," he thought. And then, a moment later: "What does concern me, here?"

The disturbed spirit he had brought with him to Léa's was spreading beyond him, pointed by the sunset, the cries of predatory swallows, the stripes of light and shadow on the curtains. He remembered how Léa had always borne with her, wherever she went, that incandescent, rosy glow, as the ebbing tide carries out to sea the earthy scent of hay and flocks.

They had nothing to say for a time, relieved of the need of speech by the clear, fresh song of a child outside, to which they pretended to be listening. Léa had not seated herself. Erect, massive, she held her hopeless chin higher; a sort of restlessness was made apparent by the twitching of her eyelids.

"Am I keeping you? Are you going out? Do you want to dress?"

The abrupt question forced Léa to look at Chéri.

"Dress? And what, in heaven's name, would you like me to put on? I am dressed—as fully dressed as I shall ever be."

She laughed her incomparable laugh, beginning on a high note and falling by the scale to that low pitch reserved for sobs and amorous complaints. Chéri, not knowing he had moved, raised an imploring hand.

"I am dressed for life, I tell you! It's convenient, this rig. A few

blouses, fine linen, this uniform over all—and I'm ready for anything. Ready for dinner at Montagne's or at M. Bobette's, ready for
the movies, for bridge, for a walk in the Bois."

"Are you forgetting love?"

"Oh, my dear!"

Under her high color, which never faded, and was due to her
arthritis, she blushed, and Chéri, after a moment of cheap satisfaction in the outrageous thing he had said, was ashamed and sorry
as he saw her reaction, so like that of a young girl.

"I was only teasing," he said, awkwardly. "Did I shock you?"

"Oh, no. But you know very well I never did like smut and a
certain type of funny story that never struck me as being funny."

She was making an effort to speak calmly, but it was plain to be
seen that she was hurt, and she betrayed an emotion that might well
be offended modesty.

"Good lord—if she starts crying!" he thought. What a disaster
that would be! He could fairly see her cheeks bathed in tears—her
cheeks creased now by a single ravine near her mouth. And her
eyelids, inflamed by the salt of tears. . . .

"Why—oh, I didn't mean—" He was frantic. "Really, Léa—you
mustn't think—"

Her sudden start made him realize that it was the first time he
had called her by name. Proud, as always, of her self-control, she
interrupted him, gently.

"It's all right, my dear—I'm not angry with you. Only, don't leave
me with any unpleasant memories of the little time you will be here
with me."

Neither her manner nor her words, which were, it seemed to him,
rather more than the occasion called for, touched him.

"Either she's lying," he thought, "or she has really become the
sort of woman she is showing herself to be. Peace, purity—and what
else? All that suits her about as well as a nose ring. A heart at
rest, all she can eat, a movie. . . . She's lying—she must be—of
course she's lying! She's trying to make me think it's comfortable,
even pleasant, to become an old woman. Let her try that on some

one else. She can get away with her tales of a quiet life and little places where they give you provincial cooking with others—but to try them on me! Me—born among beauties of fifty with their electric vibrators and their reducing creams! I, who have seen them, all my painted fairies, fighting over a wrinkle, ready to do battle for a gigolo!"

"You know," Léa said, "I've grown away from that habit of yours of sitting, lost in thought. Seeing you there I keep thinking you have something to tell me."

Opposite him, with a little table on which stood a decanter of port and some glasses, she made no effort to avoid the scrutiny he applied to her now. But there were evidences, almost imperceptible, of the effort she was making to maintain her pose of indifference.

"I wonder how often she went back to her long corset, gave it up, went back to it again before she finally put it away?" he asked himself. "How many mornings were there when she tried some new powder, experimented with a different rouge for her cheeks, massaged her neck with cold cream and rubbed it with ice wrapped in a handkerchief, before she resigned herself to this varnished leather that is her skin now?"

Perhaps it was only impatience that was making her a little tremulous, but those tremors made him hope for some miraculous blossoming, some metamorphosis.

"Why don't you say something?" Léa insisted.

In spite of her determined pose of calm, she was growing excited by degrees. She played with the pearls in her long necklace, winding them in and out among her withered, manicured fingers.

"Perhaps she's simply afraid of me," thought Chéri. "A man who sits like this, saying nothing, is always a little mad. She's thinking of Valérie Cheniaguine and her terrors. If I held out my arms would she cry for help? My poor Nounoune—"

He was afraid he would utter that name aloud. And so, to avoid what would have been a sincere moment, no matter how fleeting, he broke his silence.

"What will you think of me?" he asked her.

"That depends," she said, craftily. "Just now you make me think of the sort of man who leaves a box of candy in the hall when he comes in. 'There'll always be time enough later to give it to her,' he says to himself. And then—he takes it along when he goes."

The end of the silence had restored her morale. She could parry and thrust now like the Léa of the old days, that old, keenly perceptive Léa, who had had a fine peasant shrewdness of mind. Chéri got up, moved the table that stood between Léa and himself, and so was bathed in the full light from the window, already ruddy with the tints of sunset. Léa, watching him, could take her time to study his features, still almost untouched by time, but threatened from every direction. So she could measure the time that had passed, the days, the years. So secret, so gradual, so almost imperceptibly beginning was the process of decay that pity was stirred in her, and memory awoke, and a word, a gesture, were torn from her that flung Chéri into a frenzy of abasement. Standing there, in the light, he invited a last affront, he ventured a final, silent plea, a last tribute. His eyes were closed, as if he were asleep.

Nothing happened, and he opened his eyes again. Once more the truth demanded his acceptance. He saw only his old friend, seated at a prudent distance from him, according him a calculated kindliness, gazing at him warily with her blue eyes.

Bewildered, baffled, he looked for the Léa he still sought. "Where is she?" he asked himself, desperately. "This other woman is hiding her from me. I am boring this woman. She's waiting for me to go, and she's thinking what a bore all these memories are, and this ghost. . . . But if I appealed to her—if I begged her again to let me see Léa—?" Within him that kneeling double of his stirred again, like a body bleeding to death. With an effort he had not believed himself capable of making Chéri dispelled the illusion that was tormenting him.

"I must go," he said aloud. And, with a mocking banality he added: "And I shall take my box of candy with me."

A sigh of relief shook Léa's vast breast.

"As you please, my dear. But—you know you can always count on me if you are in trouble?"

He was acutely conscious of the bitterness that underlay that protestation. Once more that mass of flesh revealed a feminine quality, for all its thatch of silvery hair; again she had become a complete, a harmonious being. But the ghost, in character again, insisted, in spite of himself, on its own dissolution.

"I'm sure of that," Chéri said. "Many thanks."

From that moment he knew, unerringly, without an effort, how he must proceed, and the right words came, easily, as if they had been part of a ritual.

"You know, I came today—I wonder why it was today, rather than yesterday? I should have come long ago—but you will forgive me—"

"Of course," said Léa.

"I'm even more hare-brained than I used to be before the war, you know, and so—"

"I understand—say no more about it—"

He thought, when she interrupted him, that she was eager for him to go. A few more words passed as he made his way to the door; one of them bumped into a chair; a beam of blue light came through a window open on a court. A great ringed hand was raised to Chéri's lips. Léa laughed, and as the notes rippled down the scale they broke off abruptly, half way, like a jet of water suddenly cut off, so that it falls in scattered drops. . . . Under Chéri's feet the stairs were like the bridge of sleep between two dreams, and he found himself in the street, not knowing how he had reached it.

He saw the sunset sky mirrored in the stream, still swollen by the rain and on the blue backs of the swallows, flying low, and because the dusk was cool and the memory he had brought away with him hid itself, treacherously, in some deep recess of his spirit, there to gather strength and to assume its final shape, he believed that he had forgotten everything, and he was happy.

Part Three

ONLY the hoarse coughing of an old woman, seated with a green mint before her, disturbed the stillness in this place where all the noise of the Place de l'Opéra died away, muted by some atmospheric curtain that accomplished an acoustic absurdity. Chéri ordered a lemonade and dabbed at the back of his head with his handkerchief. In him there still survived childhood memories of women talking to one another, gravely. "If you want any cucumber in your cream of cucumbers make it yourself. . . . Never wipe perspiration from your face—it only drives it into your skin and ruins it."

About the silent, empty bar there was an illusion of coolness. At first Chéri did not notice a couple at a table, their heads close together, talking in inaudible whispers. But the faint murmur of their speech attracted his attention after a moment; they were earnest and impassioned in their talk, so that their voices, hushed though they were, came to him with the stress of sibilant consonants. And when he glanced at them he could see their faces, standing out in the gloom; they looked harassed, unhappy, overworked.

He sipped his iced drink, leaned back against the yellow plush cushion of his bench, and realized, happily, that the queer, exhausting mental daze in which he had lived for a fortnight was passing. For some reason the oppression of his spirit, from which he had so long been unable to escape, had not followed him into this old-fashioned bar, with its garish decorations. He could see a great provincial fireplace, and through the open door of the lavatory he caught a glimpse of the old woman attendant, with her white hair, counting threads as she mended linen by the light of a green shaded lamp.

A passer-by came in, but stopped short of the yellow room and took his drink standing at the bar, as if he were nervous. He went out without saying a word. The smell of the green mint, which reminded him of toothpaste, annoyed Chéri, and he glanced at the old woman with a frown. In the half light she was a vague, indistinct shape. Under a soft black hat stiff with age he saw a weather-beaten old face, deeply wrinkled, marred by swellings here and there, which she had tried to adorn with paint and kohl, dabbed on carelessly. Chéri smiled at the idea that she made up her face as casually as he dropped his keys, his handkerchief, his loose change, into his pockets. It was a common, vulgar old face, apathetic and indifferent. She coughed, opened her handbag, blew her nose, and laid her bag down on the marble table top. Of a rusty black, it was much like her hat—it was made of the same worn taffeta.

Chéri studied her with an absurdly exaggerated repugnance. But he was abnormally sensitive, just then, to anything, both old and feminine; that obsession had haunted him for two weeks. The handbag, lying on the table, almost drove him from the place. He tried to tear his eyes from it, but he could not; they were drawn back by an unexpected gleam that came from a little jeweled ornament. The fascination it had for him surprised him, but he found himself, a moment later, staring at it again, and his mind was blank. The little ornament had all but hypnotized him. But then, abruptly, he regained his senses.

"Of course—I see now!" he said to himself. "A monogram—two L's entwined!"

For a moment he was at peace, he knew something like bliss, he felt like a man at the end of a long journey. He really did succeed in exorcising the memory of short gray hair, the abominable, shapeless coat over a distended stomach, the hearty contralto laugh—all that horde of memories that for two weeks had beset him, depriving him of his appetite, giving him the feeling that he was never by himself.

"But it's too good to last," he told himself. And then, deliberately, with an effort not without heroism, he faced the truth. He looked straight at the outrageous bag.

"Of course," he said to himself. "It's the little jeweled monogram

Léa had made first for her antelope skin purse—then for her tortoiseshell dressing set—then for her note paper!"

Not for a moment would he admit that the monogram on the bag might represent another name.

"Another name!" he said to himself, with an ironic smile. "Don't talk to me of such a coincidence. This evening, quite by chance, I see this bag. Tomorrow, by another coincidence, I'll find that my wife has hired some footman Léa used to have. I'll never be able to drop into a restaurant after this, never look in at the movies, never stop at a tobacconist's for cigarettes without seeing Léa. It's my own fault—all I had to do was stay away from her."

He laid down some change beside his glass and got up; then called to the bartender. He turned his back on the old woman as he passed between the tables, shrank into his clothes, like a cat squeezing itself under a door, and still he managed to knock over the glass of green mint with the edge of his coat as he passed. He muttered an apology and hurried to the door, longing for freedom, for fresh air to fill his lungs. And then, appalled, but not in the least surprised, he heard his own name.

"Chéri."

He yielded and turned. He found himself quite unable to find a name for the old hag, but he made no further effort to escape; he would know soon enough who she was.

"Don't you know me? Really? Oh, well—why should you? The war aged women—just as it killed men! And, after all, I ought not to complain—I ran no risk of losing any one I loved in the war. Well—Chéri!"

She laughed and at last he knew her, and saw that what he had taken for senility was only poverty and a profound apathy. Sitting up, laughing, she looked no more than the sixty she probably was and her hand, as it stroked Chéri's, was no longer that of a palsied grandmother.

"Old Copine!" Chéri said, in a voice almost admiring.

"Are you glad to see me, then—really?"

"Of course I am!"

He told the truth. He felt better, gradually.

"It's only— Poor old Copine! And I was afraid— Won't you have something, Copine?"

"I might take a whisky and soda. You're as good looking as ever, in spite of everything."

He swallowed the bitter compliment, which she tossed him from the serenity of her old age.

"And you were decorated, too!" she said, out of sheer good nature. "Oh, I heard all about that—we heard plenty about you, I can tell you."

That slightly ambiguous plural pronoun left Chéri unsmiling, and Copine was afraid she had offended him.

"When I say we," she said, "I mean those who really were your friends—Camille de La Berche, Léa, Rita, I. You can be sure it wasn't Charlotte who told me—she ignores my very existence. But for that matter, I've cut her off my list, too."

She stretched out a pale hand across the table in a stern gesture.

"For me, mind you, Charlotte will never again be anything but the woman who had poor little Rita arrested and held for twenty-four hours. Poor Rita, who never knew a word of German! Was it Rita's fault that she was born in Switzerland?"

"I know, I know the whole story," Chéri said, interrupting her.

Copine bent her dark, humid eyes upon him. As always they were full of pity and understanding—and they never, by any chance, saw the truth!

"Poor youngster," she said, with a sigh. "As if I didn't know! Forgive me—you've had your bad times, too."

He gave her a puzzled look. He had forgotten her habit of speaking in superlatives, which had always filled her chatter with magnificent irrelevancies. He was afraid she would insist on talking about the war. But she was not thinking of the war. Quite possibly she never had thought of it, for the tragedy of the war affected only two generations.

"What a thing it was for you to have such a mother," she said. "A boy who always lived cleanly, before marriage and after. A fine, well-behaved boy, who was never promiscuous and didn't waste his inheritance."

She nodded and, little by little, he remembered her as she had been. Now he saw her, her face that of a commonplace old prostitute, come to an old age that lacked dignity. But she had escaped sickness at least, and opium, a drug that is merciful to those unworthy of it, had not ravaged her features.

"You don't smoke opium any more?" Chéri asked her, suddenly.

She raised her white, neglected hand.

"What do you think! That sort of thing's all very well in good company. When I had my boy friends—it was fun then. Do you remember, when you used to come, late at night? Ah, you enjoyed it! 'Just one more pipe, Copine, and well filled!' you used to say."

He knew she was lying simply to flatter him, and he let it go. He smiled at her knowingly—and in the shadows under her shabby hat, under the black tulle about her throat, he looked for the gleam of a necklace of great, pale pearls. . . .

Mechanically he took little sips of the whisky they had brought him by mistake. The spirits, which, as a rule, he didn't like, suited his mood that evening. His drink made it easier for him to smile, it made his nerves less sensitive, so that he did not shrink as his fingers touched some rough surface or a bit of cloth. He listened good-humoredly to this old woman, who wasn't living in the present at all. They met in a forgotten, a vanished age, over the bodies of the young, importunate dead, and Copine tossed off a string of names—the names of old people who bore charmed lives, who had been galvanized into a factitious activity in the war, or who had become petrified and would never change again. She spoke of some scandal in 1913, of a fraud that had been a sensation just before August, 1914, and her voice trembled when she recalled some one called Louiote who had died in the very week of Chéri's marriage.

"We're all in the hands of fate, you see!" she said. "After four years of pure and devoted friendship!"

"Oh, we'd quarrel in the evening, sometimes—" She sighed. "But only when there were people around. It made them believe we were living together. If we hadn't had our tiffs, what would outsiders have thought? As it was, they talked about us—how they talked! They teased us— 'A fine pair of lovers,' they'd say. My dear, there's something I'd like to tell you while you're here—you know, the tale of that will they said Massau had made—"

"What Massau was that?" Chéri asked, absent-mindedly.

"Oh, come—you knew him—there was only one. I'm talking about the will he was supposed to have left with Louise MacMillar. That was in 1909. I was one of Gérault's crowd then—do you remember, they called us his kennel? There were five of us—he used to give us dinner every evening at the *Belle-Meunière*, in Nice. No one looked at any one but you on the Promenade—you were all in white, always, like an English boy, and Léa wore white, too. What a couple you made! Gérault used to tease Léa. 'You're too young, my dear,' he'd tell her, 'and, what's worse, you're too haughty. But I'll add you to my list in fifteen or twenty years—just wait!' And a man like that had to die! Real tears were shed at his funeral—every one mourned him—a whole people. But I'm forgetting about the will."

Chéri, sitting there, was deluged with a flood of reminiscences, a disjointed tale of vain regrets and soothing memories, pieced together with the skill of one of those Corsican women who make a living as professional mourners. He leaned toward Copine, and she, in her turn, bent her head closer, lowering her voice when she came to a dramatic incident, interjecting a sob here, a laugh there. He saw in the mirror how like they were, he and this old hag, to the couple that had been whispering when he came in, who had left them to themselves by this time. He got up, for the idea plagued him, and the bartender rose, too, in his place, like a sensible dog when his master is finally ready to go home.

"You must be going, I suppose," said Copine. "Well, I'll tell you the rest another time."

"Yes—after the next war," Chéri said, joking. "Tell me—that monogram— Yes, that monogram in brilliants, on your bag. It's not yours, is it, Copine?"

He pointed to the black bag, putting out his finger and at the same time drawing back, as if the bag had been alive.

"You never miss anything!" Copine said, admiringly. "Yes, it's mine. She gave it to me—really she did. She said it was too feminine for her, these days. She asked me what I thought she wanted of a place to put a mirror and her powder now that she's grown as fat as some old policeman. She made me laugh—"

To silence her Chéri pushed the change from a hundred franc note across to her.

"You'd better take a taxi, Copine," he said.

They passed into the street through the half hidden door, and Chéri realized that it was very late.

"Haven't you your car?" she asked him.

"No. I usually walk. It's good for me."

"Is your wife in the country?"

"No. Her hospital work keeps her in Paris."

Copine's shapeless hat nodded.

"I know about that. She's a fine woman. The Baroness told me they were thinking of giving her the Cross—her name has been proposed."

"What's that?"

"Hold on—stop that cab for me, that little closed car. Charlotte is doing all she can—she knows people who have influence with Clémenceau. That makes up a little for what she tried to do to Rita—a little, not much. She's a wicked woman, Charlotte, my dear."

He put her into the cab, and she melted into the darkness inside and ceased to be. The moment he no longer heard her voice he wondered if he had really seen her at all. He looked around, and breathed deep of the dusty night air. Tomorrow would be another scorching day. He closed his eyes, and it seemed to him that he was dreaming, and that soon he would wake at home, surrounded by gardens watered every evening, with the scent of Spanish honeysuckle in his nostrils, the songs of birds in his ears, his young wife touching him lightly as she lay beside him. . . . But Copine's voice rose shrilly from the depths of the cab.

"Two hundred and fourteen, Avenue de Villiers! Remember my address, Chéri. And if you ever want to find me, remember I often dine at the *Girafe,* in the Avenue de Wagram. You might want to find me, sometime, you know—"

"Find her? Not much chance of that!" Chéri said to himself as he hurried away. "Heavens—next time I'll go around the block, if I see her in time!"

2

COOL and rested, he strode along easily, and stuck to the river as far as the Place de l'Alma. There he picked up a taxi and drove home to the Avenue Henri-Martin. In the east a dull, coppery glow was already coloring the sky; it suggested rather the setting of a planet than a summer dawn. The sky was cloudless, but a smoky haze covered the city. Soon it would blaze with all the color of a great fire, it would take on the look of red hot iron.

For at dawn the dog days bathe great cities and their environs in tints of foamy rose, of violet; an azure dew comes to refresh the open spaces where trees and grass find a little room to grow.

There was no sound in the house when Chéri put his tiny key into the lock. In the flagged hall the odor of dinner still lingered faintly, and boughs of syringa, arranged in vases as tall as a man, filled the air with a heavy fragrance not to be breathed with impunity. A gray cat, a stranger to him, slipped past him and took possession of the hall, looking at him with cold disdain.

"Come here, you imp," said Chéri, in a whisper.

The cat, unmoved, blinked at him insultingly, and Chéri reflected that no animal, no dog, no horse, no cat, had ever taken to him. He could still hear old Aldonza, fifteen years ago, prophesying, in her husky voice: "Look out—there is a curse on people that animals don't like." But as the cat, wide awake now, began worrying a little green burred horse chestnut with its front paws, he smiled and went upstairs.

His bedroom was as dimly blue as a room in a play, and the dawn came no farther than the balcony, where roses and stork's bills, trained on a trellis of raffia, grew in profusion. Edmée was asleep, bare arms and feet free of the light covering. She lay on her side, with her head a little bowed, and one finger was thrust down inside her pearl necklace, so that she looked, somehow, in the faint light, more like a woman lost in thought than one asleep. Her curly hair strayed down across her cheek; Chéri could not hear the sound of her breathing.

"She's at rest," Chéri thought. "She's dreaming of Dr. Arnaud, or of her Legion of Honor—or of the Royal Dutch Shell and the money she hopes to make if its shares go up! She's pretty—how lovely she is! Don't worry, darling—sleep another hour or so—then you can be off to your Dr. Arnaud again. That's not so long to wait, really. You'll be back in the Avenue d'Italie, in that delightful hole that stinks eternally of carbolic. You'll be saying, 'Yes, doctor, no, doctor,' like a little school-girl. You'll be extremely correct, you'll juggle with thermometers, and rattle off your ninety-nine point six and your hundred and one point three and he'll squeeze your pretty little antiseptic hand in his great paw, all covered with coal tar derivatives. How lucky you are to have found romance, my sweet! I'll never be the one to spoil it for you—I envy you—I'd like something of the sort myself!"

Edmée awoke suddenly, with so sharp a start that Chéri caught his breath, like a man rudely interrupted in the middle of a sentence.

"Is that you?" she said. "For heaven's sake—is that really you?"

"If you were expecting some one else, I can only offer my apologies," Chéri said, smiling at her.

"Do you have to try to be clever—?"

She sat up in bed, pushing back her hair.

"What time is it? Are you getting up? Oh—no—I see—you haven't been to bed—you've just come in. Oh, Fred, what on earth have you been up to this time?"

" 'This time' sounds like a compliment. My dear, if you knew what I'd been doing—!"

There had been a time, long ago, when she would have begged him, her hands over her ears, to say nothing, to tell her nothing. But Chéri, always quicker of wit than she, missed that innocent and diverting time when, coming home like this in the small hours, he had been able, quite naturally, to torment a tearful young wife and then sweep her, in his arms, into the sweet sleep of lovers reconciled. No more fancies, no more trifling infidelities. There remained only a chastity he was incapable of avowing.

He kicked off his dusty shoes, and turned a pale face to her, a face skilled in hiding everything except his purpose to hide everything. He sat down on the bed, with its sheer linen and its lace.

"Smell my breath," he said. "Get it? I've been drinking whisky."

Their lovely mouths almost touched as she put her hands on his shoulders.

"Whisky?" she repeated, wonderingly. "Whisky? But why?"

A less astute woman would have asked him with whom he had drunk it, and Chéri did not fail to mark the point to her. He proved that two could play at that game in his answer.

"With Copine," he said. "Do you want to hear all?"

She smiled. He could see her better now, as the light outside grew stronger, reaching the bed first as it came through the window, then the mirror, then one wall, then goldfish circling in a crystal bowl.

"Not all, Fred, please! Not all! Half a truth, perhaps—truth enough for such an hour as this, no more—"

Nevertheless she was thoughtful, being almost sure that neither a love affair nor some vulgar debauch had kept Chéri away. She yielded her body readily enough to his encircling arm, but he was conscious of the slender, hard hand, eloquent in its warning that she held herself, her real self, aloof and inviolate.

"The truth—" he said. "Well, the truth is that I don't know her real name. But I gave her—listen, now—I gave her eighty-three francs."

"Really? Like that? Out of hand? The first time you met her? That was princely."

She pretended to yawn, and snuggled down into the hollow of the bed, as if she did not expect him to answer her. For a few moments he felt a sort of passing pity for her, until a beam of light struck her, outlining more clearly the almost naked body that lay beside him. His pity was dispelled.

"She—oh, she's beautiful! It isn't fair."

Turning again, she lay, eyes half open, lips parted. He saw in her eyes the gleam of that look, not really womanly at all, unmistakable, single in its purpose, that women keep for the man who attracts them, and the chastity he refused to confess was outraged. His answer was the ungracious, strangely confused look of the man who rejects a woman's proffer of herself. He was unwilling actually to pull away from her; he merely jerked his head toward the gilded window, the dewy garden, the vocal arabesque the blackbirds were raising above the chirps of the sparrows.

Edmée could see now how tired he looked, how much thinner his cheeks were. They were faintly blue; he needed a shave. She could see his magnificent, nervous hands, his nails, unwashed since the evening before and the little blue points of shadow under his eyes. It seemed to her that this handsome husband of hers, sitting there, collarless and in his stockinged feet, looked precisely like a man who had been arrested and had spent the night in a cell. He had lost none of his good looks, but he had lost in stature, in some mysterious fashion, so that control of the situation had passed to her. She abandoned all thought of seducing him, sat up in bed, and touched his forehead with her hand.

"Do you feel ill?" she asked him.

Slowly he took his mind from the garden and came back to her. "What's that? Why, no—there's nothing wrong except that I'm sleepy. I'm so tired that I can't get around to going to bed."

He smiled, revealing pallid lips and dry, coral gums. But most of all his smile betrayed a sadness that was incurable, and that he bore as uncomplainingly as the poor do their troubles. It was in Edmée's mind to try to find out what was the matter, but she gave up the idea of questioning him.

"Come, you'd better lie down," she said, making room for him.

"Lie down? But I want a drink. My mouth is dry and—oh, it's like a nightmare—"

He found the strength to seize a carafe and drink from it and to throw off his coat; then he collapsed on the bed and lay still, overcome by sleep.

For a long minute she looked at this half dressed stranger who lay beside her in his drugged sleep. Her eyes wandered from his blue lips to his heavy eyelids, from his dangling hand to his forehead, still creased by some weighty secret. Then she banished all expression from her eyes, as if he might wake and surprise her as she spied upon him. Then, very quietly, she got up, and before she drew the curtains to darken the windows, she laid a silk covering over him. Concealing the disarray of his body, the wrap left his handsome face in full view. Carefully she drew a fold of the silk over his hand, with a little shudder of distaste, much as she might have hidden a weapon that had, perhaps, done its work.

He did not stir; he had slipped away, for the time, into some impregnable retreat of exhaustion. Besides, the hospital had taught Edmée a dexterity, professional in character, so that her hands were not only gentle but sure, skilled in dealing with any part of a patient's body without disturbing him. She did not go back to bed, but sat down, reveling in the heavenly, fresh coolness of the hour when the rising sun stirs the dawn wind to life. The long curtains rose and fell with the breeze, and as they moved blue shadows stirred on Chéri's sleeping cheeks.

Looking at him Edmée was not reminded of the wounded in her hospital, nor of the dead whose peasant hands she had crossed over the coarse white cotton sheets. No wounded man, raving in a nightmare, no corpse that she had seen in the hospital, was in the least like Chéri, endowed by sleep, by rest, by silence, with an unearthly beauty.

His extraordinary beauty lacked sympathetic appeal; there was about it nothing racially characteristic; the passing of time served only to make it more austere. Even his brain, whose duty it was to chasten his pride by degrees as he grew older, was obliged to concede that Chéri represented a superb monument to pure instinct. How could love, with all its intrigue, its calculated unselfishness, its passionate violence, prevail against that messenger of light?

Edmée was willing enough to apply her intelligence to the acquisition of unwelcome and humiliating, but still useful, truths. But there was still instinct within her the deep, omnivorous womanly appetite of those who are destined, by inheritance or vocation, to exploit the art of love. Patient enough, and at times even subtle, she did not sufficiently realize the way the feminine instinct of possessiveness tends to emasculate its victims, and may end by turning a man into something no better than a courtesan. Her parvenu brain was incapable of understanding the wisdom of renouncing conquests so recently achieved—money, leisure, a petty domestic tyranny, the settled prerogatives of marriage. And, after all, the war had made all these new-won pleasures doubly dear.

She looked at the body on the bed, huddled, remote, looking almost as if the spirit had deserted it.

"That's Chéri," she said to herself. "Chéri. How little he amounts to, this Chéri!" Shrugging her shoulders, she went on. "There he is, this Chéri of theirs!" She was spurring herself to a sort of contempt for the sleeping man. She thought of nights of love making, of warm mornings of delight and languorous relaxation. But she could pay this man, sleeping like the dead, under his silken shroud, cooled by the breeze that stirred the curtains, only a cold and vindictive homage, for more and more, as time went on, he had shown his disdain for her body. She touched her small, pointed breasts, low on her slender torso; she seemed to be calling them, the most alluring of her charms, to bear witness to the injustice of his rejection of her young body.

"What he wants—oh, I suppose he'd rather have something else— What he needs—"

But it was in vain that she tried to despise him, to heap insults upon him. Even a woman loses both the desire and the ability to despise a man who suffers uncomplainingly, and her secret inclination is to place the man who has escaped her on a pedestal.

Abruptly, Edmée found herself revolted by the contrast between the effect produced now by the shadow of the curtains, the whiteness of the bed and the pallor of the sleeping man and the romantic and colorful tones in which night and the image of death had painted the scene before her. She sprang up, alert, vigorous, in sudden hot rebellion against any new assault upon her emotions. He was there, in the disordered bed, the man who had betrayed her, who had taken refuge now in sleep, in silence—a silence that outraged her. Yet she was neither angry nor touched by any shadow of regret.

If her blood flowed more swiftly through her veins, if it touched her pale cheeks with color, it was because the thought of another man had come to her, that red-haired, self-confident man whom she called 'Dear Master' or 'Chief' in a jesting tone that served to veil her true feeling. Arnaud's laugh, his firm, delicate hand, the ruddy gleams that the sun or the powerful lights of the operating room struck from his red mustache, sustained her as she thought of them. She seemed to see his white robe, put on and discarded in the hospital, never worn elsewhere—like the most intimate of all garments, that never crosses the threshold of the room where lovers meet. . . . Edmée rose on dancing feet.

"Ah—yes—I can wait!"

She tossed her head, so that her long hair flew back like a horse's mane, and went into the bathroom without a backward look.

Part Four

TRITE in design, poorly proportioned, the dining room owed what little distinction it had to yellow hangings, with contrasting touches of green and purple. The white and gray plaster of the walls flung back far too much light on those at the table, who were obliged to sit under the glare of lights hanging from the ceiling.

A crystal star sparkled with every movement of Edmée's evening dress. Mme. Peloux still wore, for this family dinner, her tailored uniform with its leather buttons, and Camille de La Berche retained her nurse's veil, in which she bore a considerable resemblance to a somewhat shaggier Dante. The women were silent because of the heat, Chéri because it was his habit. A hot bath and a cold shower had rested him, but the merciless light revealed the hollows in his cheeks and he looked down, shading his eyes as well as he could.

"Chéri looks about sixteen this evening," the Baroness said, out of a clear sky, in her deep bass.

No one answered her, but Chéri made a little bow of acknowledgment.

"It's ages since I have seen the oval of his face so thin," she went on.

Edmée frowned faintly.

"I have," she said, "as recently as during the war."

"That's true, you're quite right," Charlotte Peloux agreed, her voice as shrill as a fife. "Heavens, he was as thin as a rail at Vesoul, in 1916. Edmée, my dear—" She changed the subject without modulating her voice. "I saw him today—you know who I mean— and everything is going splendidly."

Edmée blushed, in a manner wholly strange to her, and Chéri stared.

"Who was it you saw, and what goes so well?" he asked.

"The matter of Trousselier's pension. You know—that boy of mine whose right arm had to be amputated. He was discharged from the hospital on the 20th of June. Your mother's been putting in a word for him at the Ministry of War."

Her eyes met his frankly. She had answered promptly and without apparent reflection. But he knew perfectly well she was lying.

"It's her bit of red ribbon they're really after," he said to himself. "Oh, well—why not? She's certainly earned it!"

But she had lied to him, before these two women, who knew she was lying.

"Suppose I picked up the water bottle and smashed it on the table?"

But he made no move. There was no passion in him, none of the leaping emotion that must be translated into violent action.

"Abzac is leaving us in a week," said Mme. de La Berche.

"That's not quite settled yet," Edmée said, with a show of interest. "Dr. Arnaud's not at all sure he ought to be allowed to go off so soon with his new leg. After all, if he's left to his own devices, he may do something silly, and there's always the chance of gangrene. Dr. Arnaud saw too many such cases, all through the war. . . ."

Chéri was looking at her, and she broke off, suddenly, for no reason. She was wielding a long stemmed rose like a fan. She nodded a refusal of the dish that was being passed for the second time, and leaned her elbows on the table. Dressed in white, her shoulders bare, she could not conceal, even in her immobility, a self-satisfaction, a sort of conceit, that placed her very precisely. There was something almost shocking about the smooth contour of her features. An indiscreet gleam in her eyes was eloquent of her determination to attain whatever she wanted, and it bore witness, too, to the unbroken succession of her victories in the past.

"Edmée," Chéri thought, appraising her, "is a woman who should never have grown past her twentieth year. She's beginning to look like her mother."

A moment later the resemblance had vanished. There was nothing about Edmée now, nothing visible, at least, to suggest Marie-Laure. Of the poisonous, auburn loveliness, so flamboyant, so daring, that Marie-Laure had used as a snare throughout her career, Edmée could claim only one attribute: shamelessness. Careful never to offend, she gave offense, none the less, as a necklace too obviously new or a second-rate racehorse may give offense to those who owe either to nature or to lack of training a subtlety of perception akin to that of primitive folk. Servants and Chéri were at one in suspecting Edmée of a fundamental vulgarity.

Encouraged by Edmée, who took a cigarette, the Baroness de La

Berche lit a cigar with great care and smoked it with a truly voluptuous enjoyment. Her white veil, with its red cross, fell about her
sturdy shoulders, and made her look, somehow, like those grave and
serious minded men who, toward the end of a New Year's Eve
party, deck themselves out in paper caps. Charlotte unfastened the
leather buttons of her jacket, reached for the box of Abdullas, and
relaxed. The butler, accustomed to the habits of the family when
it dined informally, rolled up beside Chéri a little table such as con-
jurors use, full of secret recesses, and a well covered by a sliding
top equipped with liqueurs in silver filigreed decanters. Then he left
the room, and the shadow of the old Italian, with his wooden face
and his white hair, no longer played against the wall.

"Giacamo really has the grand manner," said the Baroness. "I
know it when I see it."

Mme. Peloux shrugged her shoulders, a gesture that for a long
time had left her breasts still. Her chest stretched her white silk
blouse; her short dyed hair, still abundant, glowed darkly above
her great dark eyes and her really beautiful forehead.

"All old Italians with white hair have the grand manner," she said.
"To look at them, you'd think they were all Papal chamberlains.
They can write you a menu in Latin—but if you open a door sud-
denly you'll find them trying to rape some seven-year-old child."

Chéri welcomed that virulent outburst like a timely shower. His
mother's malice scattered the clouds, brought a breath of fresh air
into the room. He had delighted, just lately, in finding her more
like the old Charlotte, who had once, standing on her balcony,
called some pretty passer-by a 'three franc woman.' Chéri had asked
her if she knew the girl, and she had answered: "No, but I may
have to make her acquaintance, street walker though she is!"

A little puzzled, he had begun, lately, to relish Charlotte's
superior vitality, to prefer her to either of these other women, but it
did not occur to him that this partiality, this preference, might
represent filial devotion. Inwardly he laughed, and applauded Mme.
Peloux for still being, and unmistakably, the woman he had known
of old and, knowing, had detested, suspected and insulted. For a

moment he saw her as she was, in her true character; he estimated her at her true worth, a creature impetuous, greedy, calculating, reckless, all at the same time, like some great man of affairs; capable of a true humorist's delight in sheer malignity.

"She's a scourge," he said to himself. "A scourge, yes—but nothing more. And, at least, she's not a stranger. She is my mother. No one ever told me that I look like her, but I do."

The woman at that table who really was a stranger in his house, an alien, had the sheen of a lovely pearl, white, misty, remote. Chéri heard the Baroness's deep voice mention the Duchess of Camastra, and he saw a sudden gleam of savage emotion in Edmée's eyes, that passed in a moment, like a tongue of flame appearing suddenly among the embers of a dying fire. But she said nothing, and lent no support to the military epithets the Baroness was applying to a rival hospital.

"There's some scandal down there, it seems," she said. "Two dead in two days from injections of some damned drug. You can't tell me they weren't to blame!" She laughed, genially.

"You're crazy," Edmée said, curtly. "That's an old story about Janson de Sailly that's been dug up again."

"There's usually fire where there's smoke," Charlotte said, mildly enough for once. "Are you sleepy, Chéri?"

He was exhausted. He had to admire the resiliency of the three women who were still full of energy, in spite of their labors, the Parisian summer, their constant activity and their eternal talk.

"It's the heat," he said, briefly. Edmée's eyes met his, but she said nothing and did not give him away.

"The heat? A likely story," said Charlotte. "Nonsense."

Her eyes met Chéri's, mischievous in their hint of understanding, their suggestion that she had him at her mercy. As always, she knew the whole story. Servants' gossip, a hint dropped by a concièrge—quite possibly Léa herself, for sheer feminine delight in a half truth, snatching at a last chance to show her power, had told her. The Baroness chuckled; she sounded like a horse, neighing.

"Oh, the devil!" Chéri swore, in his weary impatience.

He pushed his chair back so abruptly that it fell; Edmée, watchful and alert, was on her feet as soon as he. If she was surprised, her expression gave no hint of such a feeling. Charlotte Peloux and the Baroness jumped up, too, frightened, lifting their skirts like women afraid of a mouse, ready to run. Chéri, his hands on the table, was breathing hard, and turning from side to side like some wild beast caught in a trap.

He shook his fist at Charlotte.

"You first—" he cried. "You—"

She had seen men threaten her so before, but this violence, before others, startled her.

"What? What do you mean?" She spoke jerkily. "Are you threatening me? You miserable little wretch—why, if I told all I knew about you—"

So shrill was her voice that the glass on the table shook, but a voice more piercing than her own silenced her.

"Leave him alone!" cried Edmée.

The abrupt silence, after those three outbursts, was almost deafening. Chéri, recovering his dignity, shook his head, smiled, and bowed to his mother.

"I beg your pardon, Mme. Peloux," he said, mockingly. His face still had its greenish, unhealthy pallor.

But she was reconciled already; she waved his apology away and smiled at him, as a boxer smiles at his opponent when the bell marks the end of a round of furious sparring.

"You were always hot-headed," she said.

"He's always spoiling for a fight," the Baroness said. She squeezed Edmée's hand. "I'm going to say good night, Chéri. My slut of a maid is sitting up for me."

She refused Charlotte's offer of a lift; she wanted to walk home, she said. As she went off along the Avenue Henri-Martin her tall figure, her flowing white veil and her lighted cigar were enough to strike terror into the heart of the most determined footpad. Edmée went to the door with the two old women, a tribute she seldom paid to departing guests; she thus gave Chéri a chance to consider the significance of her intervention in his behalf, her sudden emergence as a peacemaker.

2

He sipped a glass of cold water, slowly, standing in the merciless light in the dining room. He was overcome by a new realization of his utter isolation.

"She took my part," he thought. "Not because she loved me, though. She protected me exactly as she'd chase the blackbirds away from the cherries, or come down on her nurses if they stole the sugar in the hospital, or dismiss a footman who made free with the wine. She must know I went to see Léa, that I came home, and that I've not been there again. She hasn't said a word to me about it—perhaps she doesn't care. She shut my mother up because she knew what she was going to say—not for my sake."

He heard Edmée's voice outside. She sensed his mood without seeing him.

"You're going straight to bed, aren't you, Fred?" she said. "Do you feel ill?"

He saw her now, looking at him around the half opened door. He laughed bitterly, to himself.

"She's so damned cagy!" he thought.

She saw him smiling.

"My dear Fred," she said, asserting herself, "I think I'm almost as done up as you are yourself. Otherwise I wouldn't have gone for your mother that way just now. But I've apologized to her."

She put out some of the lights, dimming the room a little; then gathered up the roses that were spread on the table and put them in water. Body, graceful, slender hands, the becoming roses, the way the humidity had taken some of the tight curl out of her hair, all made her alluring—she might well have appealed irresistibly to a man.

"I said a man—not any man—" Insidiously the thought of what Léa had said came to trouble Chéri.

"I can do as I please with her," he thought, his eyes following her movement about the table. "She never complains, she has no idea of a divorce. I have nothing to fear—not even love. It's entirely in my own hands if I want to be at peace."

But he recoiled, with an invincible repugnance, from the very thought of living with a woman unless love bound them close together. His memories of his illegitimate childhood, his prolonged adolescence spent among strangers, had taught him that in a society that passed as free and lawless there prevailed, actually, a code of behavior as narrow and as strict as that of the most middle class morality. He had learned that love was venal, that it was a business of ready infidelities, of trickery, of base intrigues. But he had worked out for himself a philosophy of life and of love that rejected such standards and made any easy compromise impossible. He let the soft hand that stroked his sleeve slip away. As he made his way at Edmée's side toward the bedroom, where neither kisses nor reproaches were ever heard now, he was ashamed, and he blushed painfully at the thought of their perfect, their monstrous, accord.

Part Five

H E   F O U N D   himself outside, dressed for the street, though he scarcely remembered having slipped on a light raincoat and a soft hat. In the hall behind him smoke hung in a gray cloud, mingled with the perfume of the women, the odor of cut flowers, the acid fragrance of cherries. He had slipped away from Edmée, Dr.

Arnaud, the Filipescos, the Atkinses and the Kelekians. Then there had been two girls, of excellent family, who had driven trucks during the war, and cared for nothing now except cigars, motoring, and the company of mechanics.

He had left Desmond with a stock broker, an under-secretary from the Ministry of Commerce, a mutilated poet and Charlotte Peloux. A fashionable crowd, most of them young, sophisticated, no doubt, in their own way, they had dined with an air of condescension, a certain readiness to be shocked. Seemingly they had half expected Chéri to appear and dance in the nude, or to find Charlotte and the under-secretary making love to one another under the stairs.

Chéri walked along with the consciousness that he had endured the ordeal stoically, and that his only social lapse had been a slight absent-mindedness, a restless indifference to what was set before him. As a matter of fact, though, his moments of forgetfulness of his surroundings had been fleeting, as difficult to measure in terms of time as the events of a dream. Now he was deliberately running away from the alien spirits who crowded his house, and his footsteps echoed lightly on the gravel. The light gray of his coat made him look like a bit of the mist that was hanging low in the Bois; two or three late strollers glanced half enviously at this young man who was in such a hurry to go nowhere.

The memory of the scene in his house was persistent. He could still hear the voices, visualize the faces, see, above all, the shapes of the mouths. An older man had been talking about the war, a woman had discussed politics. He let his mind dwell on the rather sudden cordiality between Edmée and Desmond, and her absorbed interest in Desmond's description of a new issue of shares. "Desmond—she ought to be married to him," he thought. And then, dancing . . . Charlotte Peloux, tangoing. Chéri quickened his pace.

The night was a harbinger of autumn, damp, foggy—the mist veiled the full moon. A great milky radiance, almost like a white rainbow, took the place of the stars, disappearing momentarily from time to time behind scudding clouds. From the leaves that had fallen, withered, during the intense heat there came already a hint of the smell of September.

"It's a pleasant night," Chéri thought.

A bench tempted him, he was so tired, but he remained seated only for a few moments. An invisible companion, with whom he refused to sit, had come to join him. A companion in a long, shapeless coat, with short gray hair, inexorably gay. . . . Chéri looked off toward the Muette, as if he could hear, even so far away, the clamor of its jazz band.

It wasn't time yet to seek refuge in his blue bedroom. For all he knew those two girls—of the very best blood in France, he mustn't let himself forget!—were there, sitting cross-legged on the blue velvet coverlid, amusing the stockbroker with stories of the commissary service during the war.

"I'd like to find a comfortable room in a hotel," he thought. "Pink, and vulgar—oh, very pink!"

But wouldn't even such a room cease to be a refuge when he put out the light and the darkness admitted the long gray coat, the coarse gray hair, that ponderous old woman so full of humor? He could smile at the thought now; he had gained some control over his fear.

"There—anywhere. *She's* faithful enough," he thought. "But I can't stand those people any longer."

Day by day, hour by hour, he found himself growing more critical, more cynical. He was beginning to pass severe judgment on the heroes of this and that great incident of the war and to be scornful of the young war widows who so eagerly strove to acquire new husbands. His disgust extended to the realm of finance, but he was unaware of the significant change in his own point of view.

"Even at dinner—they talked of this shipping trust! Disgusting! They don't even lower their voices any more—"

But not for the world would he have confessed, by any open protest, that he had ceased to be in step with his contemporaries. Wisely, he was as silent about that as about his other cares. Once, when he had accused Charlotte Peloux of some shady deal involving several tons of sugar she had reminded him, in a few extremely plain words, of a time when he had turned to Léa, saying carelessly: "Léa, let me have a hundred francs for cigarettes, will you?"

"Women never understand," he said with a sigh, remembering that thrust. "It wasn't the same thing at all."

So he walked on, lost in thought, carrying his hat, his hair damp from the fog. A woman passed him, almost running. Her swift footsteps, the eagerness, the frantic haste of her movement, were eloquent. It did not surprise him to see the shadow of a man loom up before her in the mist, to see her throw herself into his arms, to watch them strained together in a close embrace.

"A clandestine meeting," thought Chéri. "Each is unfaithful to some one—I wonder who? Every one is cheating these days. But I—" He did not finish, but shrugged, with a gesture that said, plainly: "As for me, I'm pure!" Confusedly, enlightened by a stirring of some bit of his brain—or his body!—hitherto quiescent, he began to see that purity and solitude were complementary burdens.

It was growing late; he felt chilled. From much sleeplessness, he had come to know how the phases of the night differed, and that midnight was an hour of warmth by comparison with that just before dawn.

"Soon it will be winter," he thought, lengthening his stride. "Well, it's time we were done with this interminable summer. This winter I want— Well, what about this winter?"

He stopped, as if his effort to look ahead had been almost too much for him; he stood, his head bowed, like a horse that sees its stable from a distance.

"Next winter there'll still be my wife, my mother, old La Berche. There'll still be business, machines, all the usual rigmarole. There'll be all this mob— There'll never be anything else for me."

He stopped to watch low clouds passing over the Bois, faintly tinged with a reflected glow from the lights of the city. A puff of wind had begun to drive them, to twist them about, to send them, with their accompanying fingers of fog, flying toward the moon and annihilation. Chéri looked with an accustomed eye at all the luminous magic of the night which those who lie asleep think of as simply dark.

The sudden emergence of a vast flat moon, still half veiled by flying clouds which it seemed to be harrying and dissolving, could not turn him from a calculation he had begun. He reckoned up, in years, in months, in days and hours, the tale of a happy time, forever past.

"If only I had stayed with her, that day I went to see her again, before the war, there would have been three—no, four years of happiness! I would have had hundreds, literally hundreds of days and nights to store up, to keep in reserve, for love."

Even that great word did not trip him.

"Hundreds of days—a life—my only life. Like that of old, life with my worst enemy, as she used to say. My worst enemy, who forgave everything and overlooked nothing."

He dwelt upon his past, seeking comfort in it for the barren present, recalling every detail of his superb adolescence, that had been shaped by two great, capable hands, the hands of a matchless mistress, loving, always swift to punish when there was need. That long, oriental adolescence, so deeply sheltered, in which voluptuousness had been a passing phase, like a rest in a bar of music. An infinite luxury, indulgence of every whim, a boy's insensate cruelties that she in her tenderness had ignored. He lifted his head to gaze up at the pearly radiance in the sky and cried: "It's all over— I'm thirty years old!"

Now he walked swiftly toward his house, cursing the precocious haste with which he had lived.

"You fool!" he said to himself. "The worst of it is not her age— it's your own! It's all over for her, probably, but for me—"

He found his house silent at last. He went in quietly. He came upon traces everywhere left by those who had eaten and drunk and danced, and his gorge rose. The mirror in the hall flung back at him the image of a young man grown lean, with high cheek-bones over which the skin was tightly drawn, with a sad, still handsome mouth, a skin that showed his beard blue under the flesh, great, tragic eyes—that young man, in a word, who had inexplicably ceased to be a boy of twenty-four.

"For me," Chéri went on, "I think the last word has been said."

Part Six

"You see, what I want is a place where I can be quiet. I don't care how small—a bachelor flat, just a lighting place—"

"I wasn't born yesterday," said Copine, reproachfully.

She raised her great, mournful eyes to the ceiling.

"A little romance, a few caresses, a place for dreams—something to ease a poor boy's heart—and you think I don't understand! And have you no preference?"

Chéri frowned.

"For whom?"

"You're the one who doesn't understand now! Don't you like one part of town better than another?"

"Oh! No. Just a quiet place."

She nodded, understandingly.

"I see, I see. A place something like mine—like my flat. You know where I live?"

"Yes—"

"No, you don't. I knew you wouldn't write down the address. 214, Avenue de Villiers. It's neither fine nor stately. But, after all, you don't want a flat people will talk about, do you?"

"No."

"I found mine through a little deal with my landlady. A jewel of a woman, by the way—married, or as good as married. A little bird of a woman, with eyes like a periwinkle, but she's marked for tragedy. I've seen in her cards that she takes no care of herself, and—"

"Yes. You told me just now you knew of a flat."

"I do, but it wouldn't be good enough for you."

"Why are you so sure of that?"

"You? Oh, no—"

Copine smothered her laugh in her glass of whisky, the smell of which, like wet leather, offended Chéri. He let her go on talking of imaginary good luck, for he saw that she was wearing a string of large false pearls that he was sure he recognized. Every relic of the past that he came upon silenced him, seemed to shut him from the world by a veil that it evoked, and when such moments came he was at peace.

"Ah!" sighed Copine, "how I'd like to see her. What a couple you must make! I don't know her, but I can see the pair of you! Naturally, you'll want to furnish it yourself?"

"What?" said Chéri.

"Why, your flat, of course!"

Puzzled, he stared at her. Furniture—what furniture? He had been dreaming of just one thing—a retreat whose door should open and close only for him, a place the very existence of which should not be suspected by Edmée, by Charlotte, by any one at all. . . .

"How will you furnish it—with old pieces or modern stuff? Serrano furnished her ground floor entirely in the Spanish style, but that is freakish. Of course, you're old enough to know your own mind."

He scarcely heard her, engrossed in the effort to visualize his future home, well hidden, narrow, pitch dark, warm. He sipped his currant syrup, like some young girl of a past day, in this unfashionable, ornate bar, unchanged for years, and like himself, in a way, since it was here that Chéri, as a little boy, had imbibed his first iced drinks through a straw. Even the bartender was the same, and if the woman opposite him had faded, at least he had never known her when she was young and beautiful.

"My mother, my wife, all the people she frequents, they all change, they live only to change. . . . My mother may turn banker—why shouldn't Edmée become a member of the Municipal Council? But I—"

He fled for refuge to thought of that future shelter of his, that would be he knew not where, but must be hidden, narrow, warm. . . .

"My own place is furnished like an Algerian house," Copine went on. "That sort of thing's gone out, but I don't care—the stuff's all borrowed, anyway. And I have my own things, photographs that remind me of happy days—there are some of people you're sure to remember—and, of course, Loupiote's picture. Come and see me there—I'd love to have you."

"I will. Come—let's go now."

At the door he hailed a taxi.

"Don't you ever drive your car any more? Why not? It seems absurd to me that people who have cars never have their cars with them!"

She gathered her faded black skirts about her, slipped her vanity case into her bag, dropped a glove, and bridled under the stares of those who were passing in the street. A young girl looked at Chéri, standing beside her, smiled insultingly, and offered mocking condolence.

"Good lord, what a waste of good material!" she said.

Patient, long suffering, he let the old woman rattle on in the cab. She told him all sorts of stories, including one of how old La Berche had kidnaped a young bride on her wedding day, in 1893.

"Here we are. Open the door for me, Chéri—the key is hard to turn. I warn you that the hall is dark—like the entry, as you can see. But, after all, when one's on the ground floor! Wait here for a second—"

He waited for her, standing there in the gloom. He heard keys rattling, her heavy breathing, her voice, like that of a bustling servant.

"I'll light up. Then you can find your way about. I have electricity, you see. And here's my sitting room, which is my drawing room, too."

He went in, murmuring polite praise of a room he didn't really see at all, a low ceilinged room with walls painted garnet or some

216

such shade, darkened by the smoke of innumerable cigars and cigarettes. Instinctively he looked for the window, hidden by drapes and
curtains.

"Can't you see? Oh, well, you're not an old owl, like me. I'll light
the ceiling light—"

"Don't bother. I only came in for a second—"

He had turned to the wall that was best lighted. It was covered
with small frames, and with photographs supported by pins at each
corner. He broke off, and Copine burst out laughing.

"Didn't I tell you so?" she cried. "I knew you'd be pleased. You
haven't that one, eh?"

She was pointing to a very large colored photograph, in a blue
frame that had turned almost black from smoke. Blue eyes, a laughing mouth, fair hair, a look of satisfied, wary triumph. She wore a
dress of the first Empire, high waisted; her legs were to be seen,
through transparent gauze, long legs, swelling in the thigh, narrow-
ing at the knee, legs. . . . And a Leghorn hat, with a single feather,
rising like a sail in the wind. . . .

"She never gave you that picture—wasn't I right? A goddess, an
angel come to earth! She walks among the clouds! And how well
she is, even now! I like this picture of her best of all, but I love the
others too. Look at this little one, for instance—it's much more
recent. Isn't it charming?"

A snapshot, fastened by a pin, showed a woman in dark clothes
in a sunny garden.

"That's her navy blue dress, and her hat trimmed with a seagull's
feathers—" Chéri said to himself.

"I'm all for flattering portraits, myself," Copine went on. "When
you look at a picture like that, don't you feel like crossing your
hands and believing in God?"

He was looking now at a retouched photograph, in which a degraded and unworthy hand had improved the throat and the mouth
by cunning distortion. But the nose, just aquiline enough, that
delicious nose, with its slightly flaring nostrils, the lovely mouth,

the velvety upper lip, had been left as they were, unspoiled, respected even by the camera.

"Would you believe that she was going to burn them all, because she insisted that no one cared now what she used to be like? I couldn't bear it, I wept, and she gave them all to me, the same day she gave me her monogrammed bag."

"Who is this fellow, with her—look—"

"What? Don't you know? What's the matter with you? Wait till I put on my hat—"

"I'm asking you who this is—this mutt. Come—tell me—"

"Heavens—you're getting me all confused! That fellow? Why, it's Bacciocchi. You'd hardly recognize him, of course—he was two turns ahead of you."

"Two *what*?"

"After Bacciocchi she had Septfons, and then—no, wait a minute, Septfons came earlier. Septfons, Bacciocchi, Spéleïeff, and then you. Will you look at those trousers? How ridiculous men's fashions were in those days!"

"When was that picture taken?"

He drew back, for Copine had bent her bare head close to him, with her disordered hair, matted like a wig.

"That—let me see—that's her drags costume in—in—1888 or 1889. Yes, I remember now—the year of the Exposition. 1889. You have to take off your hat to that. There are no such beauties nowadays."

"Oh, I don't know— I don't think she's so extraordinary!"

Copine clasped her hands. She looked older, without her hat; her hair was a greenish black, above her yellow forehead.

"You don't! Look at that waist—your two hands would meet around it! Look at that dove's throat! And her dress! Mousseline de soie—sky blue—trimmed with pink pompons—and a hat to match! And the little bag—that matches, too. Oh, what a beauty she was— and to think of how she began—"

"What do you mean? How did she begin?"

She gave Chéri a playful poke.

"Oh, come—are you trying to make me laugh? It must be pleasant to live with you, my dear!"

He turned away, hiding his set face from her. Once more he studied various poses of Léa. In one she was smelling an artificial rose, in another she was bending over a great book with a huge Gothic clasp, revealing her neck, her smooth, lovely throat, round and white.

"Well, I must be going," he said, in the words of Valérie Cheniaguine.

"Going? But you haven't seen my dining room and my bedroom! Just take a peep—see what they're like, so that we can decide about your own flat—"

"Oh, yes— Not today, though, because—"

He glanced at the pictures again.

"I have an appointment, today," he said, lowering his voice. "But I'll come back tomorrow—yes, probably tomorrow, before dinner."

"Very well. And I'm to go ahead?"

"Go ahead—?"

"About your flat—"

"Oh! Yes—by all means. If you will. And thank you."

2

"Heavens and earth—what a time we're living in! Old and young—I wonder which are the worst! Two turns before me! And such beginnings, such dazzling beginnings, says this old procuress! And all this without a blush—what a world!"

He realized that he was rushing along at an absurd pace; he was out of breath. Moreover, a distant storm, that was not going to break over Paris at all, had cut off the breeze, behind a thick bank of violet cloud that rose to the very sky. On the fortifications, along the

Avenue Berthier, a scattering of Parisians in sandals, half naked children in red jerseys, gasped for breath under trees the leaves of which had been withered by the heat, as if they hoped that the sea would come up to them from Levallois-Perret. Chéri sat down on a bench, heedless of the certainty that his strength, mysteriously restored since he had worn himself out the night before, was bound soon to fail him, since he had eaten nothing.

"Two turns! Oh, really, now—that's too much! Two turns ahead of me—and how many came afterward? If you add them all up, including mine, how many were there altogether?"

Once more he saw beside a Léa dressed in blue Spéleïeff, big and tall, all smiles and laughter. He remembered how, when he had been a little boy, Léa had stroked his hair. Her eyes had been red from weeping, she had murmured something about a filthy beast of a man.

Léa's lover. . . . Léa's new flame. Customary, meaningless phrases, as commonplace as the weather predictions in the papers, as the shores of the pond at Auteuil, as the talk of thieving servants.

"Want to come along with me, youngster?" Spéleïeff had said once to Chéri. "I'm going to have a glass of port at Armenonville while I wait for Léa—I can't budge her this morning."

"She has a new one—a man called Bacciocchi—he's simply enchanting!" Mme. Peloux had told her son, when he was fourteen or fifteen.

But in those days, innocent and sophisticated at the same time, familiar with talk of love, blind to what it meant, Chéri had talked of love like a child. Like a child, he had learned all the words of a language, clean and unclean, taking them all alike purely as sounds, regardless of their meaning. For him there had been no suggestion of anything carnal about Spéleïeff, newly risen from Léa's bed. And what difference had there been for him between a 'simply enchanting' Bacciocchi and 'an adorable love of a Pekinese'?

Pictures, letters, remarks falling carelessly from the only truthful lips he knew, nothing had ever been able to spoil the Eden in which, for so many years, Léa and Chéri had lived together. For Chéri there had been nothing of any moment that preceded Léa—how should he have given a thought to all that happened, before he knew her, to harden, to hurt or to enrich her?

A fair haired boy, with big bare knees, came and leaned his arms on the bench, beside Chéri. They looked at one another with the same faintly hostile look, since Chéri regarded all children as aliens. This child looked at Chéri for a long time with pale blue eyes, and Chéri saw him smile, finally, a smile that spread from his anemic little mouth to his eyes, a smile full of contempt. Then he turned away, reclaimed his dusty toys, and began to play around Chéri's feet. Chéri had been appraised and dismissed, and now he got up and walked on.

Half an hour later he lay in a tub full of warm water, aromatic, scented, and he reveled in a luxurious sense of well being. The creamy lather, the distant, muted noises of the house, delighted him, as if he had earned all this comfort by some great and heroic effort—or as if he were enjoying it for the last time. Relaxed, he dried himself and wandered into Edmée's boudoir.

His wife came in, humming. She stopped when she saw him, and failed wholly to conceal her astonishment at seeing him, at coming upon him in his dressing gown.

"Am I in your way?" he asked her, without irony.

"Not at all, Fred."

She took off her street clothes with a youthful freedom, that was neither modest nor immodest, with an impatience to be undressed and in the water that amused Chéri.

"I'd forgotten how lovely her body was," he thought, looking at her arched back, so sinuous in its form, her well-covered ribs, as she stooped to take off her shoes.

She had nothing to say; she was like a woman who feels herself alone and unobserved. He thought of the dirty child who had been playing at his feet a little while ago, ignoring him.

"Tell me—"

Edmée looked up, surprised; nearly undressed, her body was ravishing.

"What should you say to our having a child?"

"Fred! What in the world are you thinking of?"

It was almost a cry of terror. And now Edmée held a bit of lingerie at her throat, while with her other hand she reached for a negligée. Chéri could not help laughing.

"Do you want my revolver to protect yourself? I wasn't thinking of raping you, you know."

"What do you mean by laughing?" she whispered. "You should never laugh—"

"I seldom do. But tell me—we talk so seldom, you know, we two —tell me— Is it so appalling, the idea that we might have had, that we might still have, a child?"

"Yes," she said, brutally, and her utterly unexpected frankness seemed to hurt her.

Her eyes never left her husband, who had dropped into a low chair. And she whispered, but loud enough for him to hear her:

"A child—a child that would look like you? Another of you, an echo of you in the one life a woman has? Oh, no—thank you, no!"

He made a gesture, and she mistook its meaning.

"No, please. I've nothing more to say. That's settled. Let's leave things the way they are. We need only take a little trouble, be a little thoughtful, go on as we are— I ask nothing of you."

"And that suits you, does it?"

She answered him only with a look that seemed to plead her nudity, a look full of hurt impotence and of piteous fear. Her freshly powdered cheeks, her youthful, rouged lips, the light touch of make-up around her brown eyes, the care with which her whole face was made up, served only to accentuate the disorder of her body, veiled now only by the wrinkled garment she had caught up to hold over her breasts.

"I can no longer give her happiness, but I can still make her suffer," thought Chéri. "She hasn't been actually unfaithful to me yet, I think. While, as for me, who have never been unfaithful to her at all, in any degree, I have deserted her."

Turning from him, Edmée slipped on her negligée. She had regained her power to move, her selfcontrol. Now a pale pink robe covered this woman. who had so resolutely clung to her last covering a moment before, hiding her breast as if she were staunching an open wound.

She had mastered her will again, the desire to live and rule, she was full again of a woman's illimitable capacity for happiness. Once more, Chéri despised her. But then the light from the window, striking the pink robe full, outlined under its silk the womanly body that was no longer that of the wounded, stricken, naked creature of a moment before, a body that strained to the very heavens, as supple, as strong, as a coiled snake. . . .

3

"I can still hurt her, but she doesn't take long to get over it," Chéri thought. "I'm not wanted here, I'm no use. She's sucked me dry. She's turning to some one else. I had the first turn, as that old hag would put it. I might pay her back in her own coin. Yes—if I could. But I can't. I wonder if I would, if I could? Edmée's not the sort of woman one puts out of one's mind so easily. I remember that Spéleïeff used to say that there were some hunters that, once they had fallen at a jump, even though they weren't hurt at all, were never any good afterward. You could whip them to death, and still they'd refuse. I tried too high a jump!"

He groped in his mind for other similes drawn from the realm of sport, deliberately broad comparisons; it would have soothed him to be able to feel that the wreck of his life was due to chance, to forces wholly beyond his control. But night was falling too early for him. He found himself dreaming of old pictures of a woman in blue, and harking back to all that he had read, in immortal verse and stately prose, of the constancy of lovers faithful even to death, to tales of worn out courtesans and their young lovers, artless and exalted at the same time.

Part Seven

"AND then she said: 'Oh, I know what's happened—Charlotte's been gossiping about me again. Much I care!' and I told her: 'You're a fool to see so much of Charlotte and to tell her everything, the way you do.' And all she said to that was: 'Oh, I've known Charlotte much longer than Spéleïeff, and better, too. I'd miss Charlotte, and Neuilly, and my games of bezique, and the youngster much more than I will Spéleïeff—he can go hang!' And I said to her: 'Look out —you'll pay through the nose yet for trusting Charlotte!' And she just laughed. 'Oh, well,' she said, 'she's worth whatever she may cost me!' You know how she was—always generous, always ready to forgive an injury—but she wasn't fooled for a minute, not she. Later, when she was dressing to go to the races, she laughed. She said she'd take a gigolo with her."

"She meant she'd take me!" Chéri cried, savagely. "Don't you suppose I know what I'm talking about?"

"I dare say—I won't dispute you," said Copine. "I'm only telling you what I know, what I actually saw or heard. She wore a white silk dress, with a strange, exotic Chinese border in blue—the very dress you see in that picture that was taken at the track. And I've always thought it was your shoulder that one sees, in the corner of the print."

"Let me see it—bring it here," said Chéri.

The old woman got up, took out the rusty pins, releasing the photograph, and handed it to Chéri. Lying on the Algerian couch, he raised his hand, gave the snapshot a quick glance, and then flung it across the room.

"Have you ever seen me wear a collar like that—and a covert coat like a racetrack tout's? For Heaven's sake, think of something better than that! That's absurd!"

She clucked, deprecatingly, stooped to pick up the picture, and then opened the door into the hall.

"Where are you going?" asked Chéri.

"I hear the coffee boiling—I'll pour some."

"All right—but come right back."

She went out, with a rustling of worn silk and a shuffling sound of heel-less slippers. Left alone, Chéri let his head fall back on a gaudy cushion. A new and striking Japanese lounging robe, with a pattern of pink wistaria blossoms on a background of amethyst silk, had replaced coat and waistcoat. He had let a cigarette burn down until it almost blistered his lips; his hair had fallen across his forehead.

The feminine garment he was wearing did not make him look effeminate, but the disorder of his mind was reflected in his face; his features were revealed, startlingly, in their true decay. He was sullen and resentful; the gesture with which he had thrown the photograph across the room had been an index to his mood. His eyes were luminous; he was tense and nervous. But, left to himself, he relaxed, after a moment, and closed his eyes.

"Heavens!" said Copine, coming back. "You won't look handsomer even in the peace of death! I've brought some fresh coffee. Will you have some? It's delicious—its very fragrance is enough to transport you to paradise."

"Thanks. Two lumps of sugar, please."

He spoke brusquely, and she obeyed him with a readiness that bore witness to her essential servility.

"I suppose you scarcely touched your dinner?"

"I had plenty to eat."

He drank his coffee without sitting up, leaning on one elbow. An oriental portière hung above the couch; it cast its shadow over a

Chéri who looked as if he had been carved from ivory, overlaid with enamel. He lay upon an old woolen rug, thick with dust.

Copine put down the coffee on a copper table. She had brought a pipe for smoking opium, a lamp, a little jar of the drug, a silver snuffbox full of cocaine, a flask from which, in spite of its tight stopper, the cool, insidious scent of ether stole out into the air of the close room. To these she added a pack of fortune teller's cards, a case of poker chips, and a pair of spectacles. Then she sat down, with the look of a benevolent nurse.

"Didn't I tell you all that stuff bored me?" growled Chéri.

She held up protesting hands, white and deeply veined in blue. At home, she always said, she dressed like Charlotte Corday, with her hair down, great fichus of white linen, and she did achieve a certain resemblance of the heroine of the Salpêtrière.

"That's all right, Chéri. I just brought them in case you felt like something later. And I enjoy seeing my little outfit all spread out, neatly arranged. Ah—there you see the arsenal of dreams, the weapons that command ecstasy, the golden portal of illusion!"

She looked up with eyes like those of an indulgent grandmother who spends all her money on toys for the children. But Chéri would have none of her trinkets. He retained a very real bodily integrity, and his contempt for drugs matched his feeling of disgust for prostitutes.

He had lost track of the number of times he had visited this dark hole, where this prototype of the Fates presided over her dark rites. Lately he had been coming every day. He gave her money, indifferently, without question, for her food, her coffee, the spirits she drank, and for the cigarettes, the fruit, the syrups and the ice he wanted for himself. He had commissioned her to buy his sumptuous Japanese robe, perfumes, delicate soaps. Not so much moved by greed as intoxicated by the feeling that she was linked with him in some intrigue, she devoted herself to Chéri with an ardor that revived in her her old delight in a degraded service, that reminded her of the days when she had undressed and bathed young girls about to sell themselves for the first time, cooked opium, dispensed ether or alcohol. Yet it was strange, for her eccentric guest brought no women to her flat, drank only grenadine or other syrups, and, stretching himself out on the divan, contented himself with a single order:

"Talk to me."

She obeyed, and she fancied that she was talking as she pleased. But, actually, by means now subtle, now harshly direct, he guided the turgid, slow stream of her reminiscences. She talked as a seamstress comes in to sew by the day, with the soothing monotony of women compelled to devote themselves to prolonged, sedentary labor. But she never sewed; she thus maintained her standing as a member of what had been an aristocracy, the guild of prostitutes. As she talked she shuffled the cards; sometimes she even laid them out, as if to tell a fortune. She put on gloves to grind the coffee the landlady bought for her, but it didn't trouble her at all to handle cards greasy and foul with dirt.

She talked, and Chéri listened to the soothing voice, the soft, shuffling sound of her feet as she moved about the place. He lay, in his magnificent robe, in the filthy and neglected room. She never asked him questions. She was satisfied to take it for granted that he was troubled by some obsession. She was ministering to an obscure illness, but an illness, beyond all doubt. Once, taking a chance, she brought in a young woman, extremely pretty, childish in manner, professionally jolly. Chéri gave her about as much attention as he would have paid to a lapdog. Later he said to Copine:

"Are you through with that sort of foolishness?"

She dared not try anything like that again. Once, coming closer than she guessed to the truth, she asked Chéri if he wouldn't like to see some of his women friends of other days—Léa, for instance. He did not even frown.

"I don't want to see any one," he said, quietly. "Look out, or I'll find another place."

A fortnight passed, as gloomily, as monotonously, as the days in some convent. By day Copine went about her affairs, indulging in the cheap pleasures of an old woman of her sort, drinking whisky, eating lunch in stuffy cabarets kept by provincials, where there was peasant cooking that she liked. Chéri arrived at dusk, sometimes soaked with rain. She would hear the opening of his taxi door, but she no longer asked him why he never drove his car.

He left her some time after midnight, usually a little before daylight. During those long sessions on the Algerian couch Copine saw him fall asleep sometimes and lie like one in a trance for a few moments. She herself never slept until he had gone. One morning, as he was gathering, one by one, the things he had taken from his pockets and put down, his keys, his pocketbook, his little flat revolver, his handkerchief, his green gold cigarette case, she ventured to ask a question.

"Doesn't your wife ever wonder where you stay so late?" she said.

Chéri raised his eyebrows; his eyes were heavy from lack of sleep.

"No. Why should she? She knows very well I won't get into any mischief."

"Well, she's right! Heaven knows a child couldn't pass his time more innocently. Will you be here this evening?"

"I don't know. I'll see. Have everything ready, though, as if you were sure I was coming."

He looked once more at all the blue eyes, all the blonde tresses, that decorated the wall at his side, and went out. Twelve hours later, punctual almost to the minute, he was back.

2

WHEN he had contrived, as he supposed, by the exercise of his wits, to lead old Copine to talk about Léa, he always shut her off, with a show of irritation, when she touched upon some episode of Léa's amorous history. He disliked that.

"Never mind all that, let it go," he would say.

He wanted only anecdotes in which men played no part, or those panegyrics Copine was always ready to deliver. He held her to the most meticulous accuracy in all matters of fact; he overlooked nothing. He made mental notes of the names of materials and dressmakers, of places, especially of dates.

"What's poplin?" he would ask.

"Poplin? Why, that's a material of silk and wool—it's very smooth, it doesn't cling."

"I see. And mohair? You spoke of white mohair?"

"Mohair's something like alpaca, only finer. Léa never liked linen in summer. She said mohair was good for underwear and handkerchiefs. You remember her underwear? No queen ever had any finer. And when that picture was taken—that one that shows her legs— they didn't wear the sort of thing they do nowadays, wisps of stuff that lie flat. There were ruffles upon ruffles, a cloud of petticoats, and drawers—drawers all made of lace, black in the center, white at the sides. Can you imagine the effect?"

"Marvelous!" thought Chéri. "Stunning! Black lace in the middle! A woman doesn't wear such things to look at herself in a glass! Before whom did she wear them? I wonder!"

He remembered Léa's gesture whenever he wandered into her bathroom or her boudoir, the way she would cross her arms over her breasts, shyly. He remembered too how she would lie in her bath, at her ease, trusting to the milkiness of the water, colored by the bath salts she used so freely.

"But for other men she had lace drawers—"

He pushed one of the cushions to one side, and it fell to the floor.

"Are you too warm, Chéri?"

"No. Let me see that photograph for a second—the framed one over there. And turn the lamp on the table this way—more—that's better—"

Abandoning his usual wariness, he studied the picture attentively, marking details that were new to him.

"A high waistline, with cameos—I never saw that, I'm sure. And old fashioned buskins. Did she wear tights? No—her toes are bare. Stunning!"

"Where did she wear that costume?" he asked, aloud.

"I don't remember, exactly— At a reception at the club, I expect— or at Molier's, perhaps."

He held out the picture at arm's length, looking bored and disdainful. He took his leave soon afterward, while it was still dark. The night air smelled of woodsmoke and there was, too, the curious, soapy smell from the great public wash houses.

He was changing sensibly, but he scarcely knew it any longer. Eating little, sleeping scarcely at all, he was losing weight, and he exchanged his strength for a deceptive and treacherous vigor, a meretricious rejuvenation that ceased, by day, to animate him. At home he did as he pleased, avoided guests or met them, according to his humor. They were birds of passage, who knew nothing of him except his name and that he was handsome, though his good looks were becoming unreal, and he looked more and more like a statue of himself carved by a critical and unflattering sculptor. Some of them were struck by his extraordinary ability to ignore their presence in his house.

Until October was nearly over he carried his burden of despair lightly; he still treated it as something inevitable, almost negligible. He was seized with mirth one afternoon when he caught Edmée shrinking away from him uncontrollably. "She thinks I'm crazy now!" he thought, with the gay smile of one hardened to his fate. "I'll never go that way, though!"

But his amusement was short-lived, for it occurred to him that as between a rogue and a lunatic, the rogue had all the best of it. Frightened by the lunatic, Edmée, after all, had held her ground when she thought she was dealing with a rogue, biting her lips, repressing her tears, resolved to outface him.

"She doesn't even think I'm malicious any more," he told himself bitterly. "Well, I'm not. Oh, the woman I deserted has punished me —no doubt about that! After all, I'm not the only man who left her —and she sent a few men about their business herself! How are Bacciocchi and Spéleïeff and Septfons getting along now, I wonder? To say nothing of the rest! But I have nothing in common with the others. She used to call me the little bourgeois because I counted the bottles in her wine cellar. Little bourgeois, trustworthy, faithful man, great lover—those were my titles, my real names. She was bathed in tears when I left her and—she—oh, she's the one who'd rather be old now than have me back—Léa! She sits by the fire, ticking off her memories on her fingers. 'I've had my life, Chéri— and such a life—!' I thought she belonged to me, and I never saw that I was only one of her lovers! Who is there, now, who can't despise me?"

Grown used by now to schooling himself to impassivity, he was at pains to hide the ravages of the emotional storm that had swept him from his moorings for a moment. He was possessed by a devil, but dignity remained. He could at least be worthy of his fate. Haughtily, dry-eyed, his hand steady as he held a match, he glanced sideways at his mother, of whose intent scrutiny he had become aware. Having lighted his cigarette, he managed to become an actor, playing a part before an invisible audience.

Out of countenance for an instant, the factitious strength born of dissimulation and of long wariness came to his aid, rising from the depths of his troubled spirit. He realized, vaguely, that the very anguish that clouded his mind could be turned to account, that it could be used to give an illusion of serenity, that while it robbed him of peace it gave him wisdom. More than once Chérie made use of a sincere anger, a fury of rebellion, to give point to an outburst of pretended anger over some trifle about which he cared nothing, which in turn, served to conceal the real nature of his despair.

3

An October afternoon of gusty winds and flying leaves, an afternoon of sudden showers, of glimpses of blue sky among the clouds, summoned Chéri to his dark refuge, his dark priestess with her touch of white at her chest, like a tabby cat. He was eager to be

231

off, longing to hear tales that were as succulent under his tongue as blackberries, and that, like blackberries, were guarded by thorns. He repeated to himself words, phrases that had a curious fascination for him.

"The masseuse used to pluck out the hairs on her legs, my dear, one by one."

He turned from the window. Charlotte, sitting down, was looking at her son, eying him from head to feet, and he saw a tear form in one eye. Chéri was pleased; he felt gay. "How sweet of her," he thought. "She is crying over me!"

An hour later he found his old accomplice at her post. But she was wearing a hat like a priest's, and she handed Chéri a bit of blue paper.

"What's this? I have no time. Tell me what it says—"

She looked at him, perplexed and troubled.

"It's my mother."

"Your mother? Are you joking?"

She looked hurt.

"Certainly not. You might, at least, show some respect—she's dead." And, as if by way of excuse, she added: "She was eighty-three years old."

"You have my sympathy. Are you going out?"

"No. I'm going away."

"Where?"

"To Tarascon. There I get a train on a small branch line that takes me to—"

"How long will you be away?"

"Four or five days—at the least. I'll have to see the lawyer, about the will, because my younger sister—"

"Good heavens—a sister!" he cried, throwing up his hands. "Why not half a dozen children, too?"

Hearing himself shouting, he controlled himself.

"All right, all right. What can I do about all that? Get along with you. Go."

"I was just going to write you a note—my train goes at half past seven."

"All right—take it at half past seven."

"There's nothing about the time of the funeral in the telegram. My sister only says she's been put in her coffin. It's very hot down there, and they can't delay. There'll only be the legal business to keep me—and that's something no one can hurry."

"Yes, of course."

He strode back and forth between the door and the wall that was covered with photographs. He bumped into a traveling bag. A steaming coffee pot and some cups stood on the table.

"I made coffee for you, in case you came—"

"Thanks."

They both drank, standing, like people at a buffet in a station. Chéri shivered, and in his impatience he gnashed his teeth.

"Well, good-by, my dear," said Copine. "You can be sure I'll get back as soon as I can."

"Good-by. I hope you have a pleasant trip."

They shook hands; she was afraid to kiss him.

"Wouldn't you like to stay here a little while?"

He looked around, startled and disturbed.

"No—no—"

"Do you want the key?"

"Why on earth should I?"

"You're used to coming here. It's come to be a habit. I've told Maria to come in every day at five o'clock and light up and to make coffee. You'd better take my key, really."

Submissively he accepted a key, which seemed enormous. But almost at once he wanted to give it back to her, or leave it with the concièrge. Growing bolder, she talked to him, in the hall, as if he had been a child of twelve.

"The electric light switch is on your left, as you come in. The kettle's always on the gas stove—you need only touch a match to the burner. I've told Maria always to lay out your Japanese robe on a corner of the couch, and to have cigarettes ready."

233

Chéri nodded his understanding, his acquiescence, with the assumed cheerfulness of a boy going back to school after a holiday. And even when he was alone he did not find it in his heart to laugh at his old servant, with her dyed hair, who after all reckoned at their true value the last prerogatives and pleasures of a man all others had cast off.

4

HE AWOKE, the next morning, from a dream in which all of the hurrying people in the street who were going in the same direction as himself played a part. Though he could see only their backs, he knew them all. He saw his mother, Léa—nude, strangely enough, and breathless in her haste—Desmond, Copine, young Maudru. Only Edmée turned and smiled at him, with the pinched, toothy little smile of a sable. "Why, that's the sable Ragut caught in the Vosges!" he exclaimed, in his dream, and the discovery pleased him beyond all reason. He kept on naming over the people who hurried along —but only those, always, who were moving in the same direction as himself.

"But there's one missing," he kept saying to himself. "Some one is missing—" Already half awake, emerging from his dream, he realized that he himself was the one who was missing. "I must go back," he thought. But his effort to move, so like that of a fly caught on a bit of gummed paper, roused him; his eyes opened and he saw the blue light. Reality crowded upon him. He stretched his legs, and found a cool place in the sheets. "Edmée must have got up long ago," he thought.

Looking through the window a new garden, full of yellow camomile and heliotrope, startled him. He remembered only the garden of the summer, all blue and pink. He rang, and in answer there came a maid he had never seen before.

"Where's Henriette?" he asked her.

"I've taken her place, sir."

"Since when?"

"Why—a month ago—"

He said, "Ah!" and it was as if he were saying: "That makes every‐thing clear." And then: "Where is Madame?"

"She is just coming. She is ready to go out."

Edmée came in just then, briskly enough. But in the door she hesitated for a second, and Chéri, noticing her confusion, was a little amused. He indulged his fondness for teasing her by saying: "But it's Ragut's sable!" Her eyes wavered under his steady gaze.

"Fred, I—"

"I know. You're just going out. I didn't hear you get up."

She flushed faintly.

"That's hardly surprising. I've been sleeping so badly lately that I had a bed made up on the couch, in my boudoir. You're not doing anything special today, are you?"

"Yes, I am," he said, gravely.

"Something important?"

"Something very important, indeed." He hesitated for a moment. "I'm going to have my hair cut."

"But you'll be having lunch here?"

"No, I'll have a chop in town. I have an appointment at Gustave's at a quarter past two. The man who usually comes here is ill."

He told the lie easily, amiably, rather childishly. Because he was lying, his mouth looked like a little boy's, pursed up as if he were about to kiss some one. Edmée gave him a friendly glance.

"You look well this morning, Fred. I must be off."

"You're catching the seven thirty train?"

She was startled, and she went out so precipitately that he was still laughing at her when he heard the front door slam behind her.

"That did me good," he said. "How easily one is amused when one has stopped expecting anything!"

He decided, as he was dressing, that he had become an ascetic, and he hummed a little tune that accompanied his thoughts.

He found that he had almost forgotten the look of Paris. The crowd upset his assumed equanimity, which was no more than a pose encouraged by a sort of imaginary crystal gazing and his intense concentration upon his wretchedness. He saw himself, from head to feet, in a plate glass window in the Rue Royale, just as the sun, coming out at noon, scattered the rain clouds, and he found it hard to recognize himself, flanked by jade necklaces and neckpieces of silver fox, among the reflections of shop girls and newsboys. Moreover, he was aware of a slight feeling of vertigo, which seemed to him to suggest that he needed food. He dropped into a restaurant.

Sitting with his back to the light, he lunched on small oysters, fish and fruit. Two young women, sitting nearby, who paid no attention to him, gave him the same sort of pleasure that comes from holding a bunch of chilled violets to one's closed eyelids. But then, all at once, the aroma of coffee drove him to his feet, eager to be off to keep the appointment that odor brought to his mind. Before he went, however, he stopped at his barber's, yielded his hands to the manicure, and knew a moment of ineffable rest and peace while her expert fingers took over, mysteriously, during the petty rite, all of his own responsibility for life and thought.

The great key weighted down his pocket.

"I won't go, I will not. . . ."

To that refrain, blindly, lost to all sense of whither he was moving, he made his way straight to the Avenue de Villers. For a moment his awkwardness in finding the keyhole, the stiffness of the key in the lock, quickened his pulse, but the heavy warmth in the hall quieted his nerves.

He moved warily, master of this empire of a few square feet, so completely his, so strange to him. The landlady had set out the usual daily provision; dying embers of charcoal still glowed under the ashes, around an earthenware coffee pot. Chéri emptied his pockets and laid out his cigarette case, the huge key of the front door, the smaller key of the flat, his flat revolver, his pocketbook, his handkerchief and his watch. But, even after he had put on his Japanese robe, he did not lie down. He opened door after door, looking around with the stealthy curiosity of a cat. A tiny dressing room, uttery feminine, offended his abnormal modesty. In the bedroom, where the chief piece of furniture was a bed, there was a scent of eau de cologne; it was like the room of some old bachelor. Chéri went back to the sitting room and lighted all the lights. He heard distant sounds, faintly, and, alone in the shabby room for the first time, let his mind dwell upon those, dead now, or merely moved on, who had peopled it in the past. It seemed to him that he heard and recognized a familiar footstep, like the tread of slippered feet or of some old dog. Then he shook his head.

"It's not she," he said to himself. "She won't be back for a week. And, when she does come, what difference will anything make to me? I'll be—"

He seemed to hear old Copine's voice, still echoing in the room.

"But let me finish telling you about the row Léa had with old Mortier at the races. The old fool thought that, what with the publicity he could command in *Gil Blas*, he could do as he pleased with Léa. My dear, he soon found out how mistaken he was—the old windbag! She went to Longchamp by herself, looking like a dream, all in blue, in her victoria, drawn by two piebald horses. . . ."

He glanced at the wall, where so many pairs of blue eyes smiled at him, and so many soft white throats rose above rounded, lovely breasts.

"That's what I'll have—only that! To be sure, you might call it a good deal. How lucky I was to find her again, she herself, here on this wall! But, now that I've found her again, I can do nothing but let her go. I'm held up by a few rusty pins, just as she is. How long will they last? Not long. And then—oh, I know myself too well! I'm perfectly capable of exclaiming: 'I want her! I must have her! Now—at once!' And—what would I do then?"

He pushed the couch over toward the wall covered with her pictures, and lay down. Lying thus, so near, the pictures of Léa that showed her with lowered eyes seemed all to be looking at him.

237

"I know though—that's only the way it seems!" he told himself. "What do you expect, then, when you let me be so near you, Nounoune, after sending me away? You knew what you were doing when you made that gesture, you knew what this fellow Chéri amounted to—you weren't taking much of a chance. But we've been punished, haven't we, both of us—you for being born so long before me, me for having loved you above all the women in this world. There you are, done for, and taking comfort in something of which you ought to be ashamed, and I. . . . Oh, as for me, it's as they say: 'There was a war, you know.' There was Léa, too—Léa and the war. I thought I was through with them both, that I needn't think of either of them again—and yet it's they who've brought me to this. Henceforth I shan't take up much room. . . ."

He drew the table closer, so that he might look at his watch.

"Half past five. The old woman won't be back for a week. And this is the first day. Suppose she dies while she's away?"

He stirred, restlessly, on the couch, smoked a cigarette, drank a cup of lukewarm coffee.

"A week. After all, I mustn't expect too much of her. In a week—what will she have to tell me? I know the story of Drags by heart, the quarrel at Longchamp, the account of the break. . . . And when I've heard all she can tell me, what will there be then? Nothing—nothing more. In a week this old woman, for whom I'm waiting already as eagerly as if she were to come to give me a hypodermic—oh, in a week she'll be here, and—she'll have nothing for me."

He glanced once more at his favorite among the pictures. Already it was losing its power to quicken his pulse, to embitter him, to rouse him to ecstasy. He tossed restlessly on the couch; he was reproducing, involuntarily, the movements of a man eager to fling himself from some high building and afraid to make the leap.

He forced himself to groan aloud, to repeat "Nounoune, my Nounoune," in an effort to make himself believe that he was beside himself. But he grew silent, touched by shame, for he knew that he had no need of any exaltation, any stirring of passion, to make him reach for the little revolver on the table. Without sitting up he

238

sought a fitting posture. In the end he stretched himself out, resting on his folded right arm, the muzzle of the pistol in his ear, the gun half smothered by the cushions. His arm began to grow numb, and he knew that unless he hurried his fingers would refuse to do their part. He uttered one or two stifled moans, for his forearm, cramped by the weight of his body, hurt. The last thing he knew in this world was the movement of his index finger against a tiny steel rod.

The Other One

1

"T H E postman brought nothing at eleven o'clock. If Farou did not write last night before going to bed, it's certain he had a late rehearsal."

"You think so, Fanny?"

"I'm sure. 'The House Without Women' is not difficult to stage, but little Asselin isn't at all the type of woman to play Suzanne."

"She's very pretty, though," said Jane.

Fanny shrugged her shoulders.

"My poor Jane, how does it help her to be pretty? No one ever wanted a pretty woman to play Suzanne. It's a part for a Cinderella like Dorilys. Didn't you see the play when it was first produced?"

"No."

"It's true. How stupid I am . . . 1919!"

"The play does not date?" asked Jane.

Fanny turned toward her an eye half hidden under a bandage of black hair.

"But of course, my dear, like all plays—even Farou's. Only Farou himself does not date."

"All the better for you!" said Jane.

"For little Asselin, too, at the moment," Fanny finished.

She laughed good-humoredly and peeled a juicy peach.

Jane tilted her chin in the direction of Little Farou; but Little Farou was busy scooping up crumbs of sugar, pressing them on to his finger and licking them off. He did not appear to have heard.

"You know," Fanny Farou continued, "Asselin got the part on tour, because it was to include Deauville, the seaside places and the casinos. For a tour of the casinos, there's a good deal to be said in favor of Asselin's motorcars, lovers and dresses. Free publicity—in fact the very thing to prevent a summer tour from being a complete fiasco. Do you understand, Jane, little pale Jane?"

"I understand."

She was pale and preoccupied, as happened to her four days out of seven. Excuses for it rushed out:

"I slept badly, you see . . ."

Little Farou raised his blue eyes to her, but she did not notice. And it was to him that she went on, mechanically:

". . . and then, I think there's a rat in the wainscot . . ."

"And a loose blind, and an owl in the plane tree, not to speak of the wind that whistles under the door and the kitchen window that tick-tacks, tick-tacks all night," completed Fanny. "Eh, Jean? Have I forgotten anything?" She laughed, and forced them to laugh too. "Jane, my dear, get it into your head that you're entitled to be sleepless as well as idle. It's hot; we ourselves merely exist, Farou sweats, swears and curses; and only Asselin 'takes.' "

"I do admire—" Jane was beginning. But again she met the blue eyes of Little Farou, drained a little of color by the dazzling noonday glare, and she interrupted herself.

"Little Farou, pass me the gooseberries, please."

He obeyed hastily, and his hand met Jane's under the electroplated basket. His fingers recoiled convulsively almost with a start of disgust, and he blushed so vividly that Fanny burst out laughing.

"There's still the four o'clock," Jane went on, after a moment or two.

"The four o'clock what?" asked Fanny, with a mouth full of juicy peach.

"Post."

"Oh," said Fanny, pushing back her band of hair with one finger. "I wasn't thinking any more about that. The four o'clock post hardly ever brings anything from Paris. Do you want a drink, Little Farou?"

"Yes. Thank you."

"Thank whom?"

"Thank you, Mamie."

He blushed, because he was fair and because he thought his step-mother a little rough. Then he relapsed into one of those remote trances of youth, during which his savage name, Farou, translated itself in turn into a hut of bark and straw trousers. He lost all ex-pression, pulled down his brows, opened his mouth a little, and sheltered a secret eagerness, a sensitive delicacy that a word or a laugh could torture, beneath his usual immobility. . . . He was sixteen years old.

Shade from the veranda allowed the great table, cleared of its papers and some piece of needlework, to be pulled every day as far as the threshold of the hall for luncheon. In the evening, when Big Farou rejoined his own, four places were crowded onto the chipped iron table that never left the terrace.

"I've eaten too much," sighed Fanny Farou, getting up first.

"For a change," said Jane.

"This cream cheese; Oh my dears! . . ."

Lazily she reached the wide divan and stretched herself out on it. . . . Lying down, she looked charmingly pretty. White skin, long black hair, eyes and mouth full and sweet; yet she was proud of nothing but her short, silvery nose with its rounded nostrils.

"Fanny Farou, you will get fat," threatened Jane, standing over her.

They exchanged looks full of mischievous security. The one knew herself beautiful, lying there with her charming nose and tender throat—the throat of a woman too passionate and too good—thrown back. The other held upright a beautiful body, perfectly free from fat, a head crowned with golden hair, if you can call golden that

245

color of delicate ash that barely gilds the nape of the neck, and almost silvers the temples. Seized by a genuine physical solicitude, Jane bent down, slipped a linen cushion under Fanny's head and covered her long lazy arms and bare ankles in stiff net.

"There! Don't move now, or the flies will get in under the net. . . . Sleep, Fanny, idle Fanny, incorrigible Fanny, greedy Fanny . . . but only for half an hour!"

"What are you going to do, Jane, in this heat? . . . Where's Jean? . . . While the sun is so full overhead he oughtn't to . . . I must tell his father . . ."

Subdued by the sudden drowsiness of the well-fed, Fanny murmured a little and was silent. Jane looked a moment at her relaxed features, her southern build and coloring, and went away.

The rapid beating of her heart made Fanny dream, a dream both commonplace and unintelligible. She saw the hall, the terrace, the dry valley, the familiar inhabitants of the villa. But the violet color of a storm hung over them and penetrated beasts and men, even the countryside with the same uneasiness.

A dream Jane, standing on the veranda, questioned the empty pathway below the terrace, and wept. Fanny woke with a shock and sat up, clutching both her hands to her breast. Before her, on the veranda stood a very real Jane, motionless and unoccupied. Reassured, Fanny would have called her. But Jane, drooping her head, passed her brow against the glass; and the little movement shook a tear from her lashes, which rolled down her cheek, shone quivering upon the soft curve of her lip and fell onto her bodice where two fingers gathered it delicately and crumpled it like a crumb of bread.

Fanny lay down again, closed her eyes and relapsed into slumber.

"Mamie, the postman!"

"What! Is it four o'clock? How long have I slept? And, Jane, why, . . . where is Jane?"

"Here, on the ladder," answered the high, muted voice that Farou the Great called voice of an angel.

Astray with sleep and some memory of her dream, Fanny sought

Jane in the air, as if she were seeking a bird, and Jean Farou burst
into a rare laugh.

"What is there to laugh at, little fathead? Do you know, a
moment ago when you wakened me I was dreaming that—"

But suddenly she realized that Jean was holding a large white
letter at arm's length and dancing it in front of her. She snatched it
quickly.

"Be off, errand-boy! At least, no. Stay here, little Jean: this is a
letter from our Farou to us all, children . . ."

She read with one eye, the other still bandaged by her ribbon of
black hair. Her white gown rucking up, strained against her breasts;
and she abandoned this faintly disordered beauty to view with an
unconscious simplicity that gave her an air slightly Creole, slightly,
as Farou said, "George Sand." She raised a hand to enforce attention:

"'After yesterday's rehearsal and the one of the day before,'" she
read, "'I have every reason to think that the touring company will be
excellent and that "The House Without Women" will be better
played than at its first performance. Little Asselin. . . . [Aha, Jane!
. . .] Little Asselin amazes everyone, even me; we work together
perfectly. We have put an end to our scenes, nervous crises, our
swoons, and other lunacies; and it was not too soon. Oh, my poor
Fanny, if women only knew how trying a man can find them when
he has no smallest desire to be the cause either of their tears or of
their happiness! . . .'"

With one finger Fanny pushed back her lock of hair and pulled
a comic and scandalized face:

"Why, tell me, Jane (Jean, go away), tell me, doesn't this look as
if poor Farou, if I dare say so much, has let himself get utterly devoted?"

"It does look like it, to me," repeated Jane. She sat down on the
divan beside her friend and combed her hair with a gentle hand,
tidying the fine bluish parting above the left eyebrow.

"What a state you're in . . . and your skirt, all crushed and
screwed up. . . . I've had enough of this dress; tomorrow I shall

247

bring back from the village a lovely yellow remnant, or a pale blue one, and you shall have a new dress for Farou's return on Saturday."

"Yes?" said Fanny indifferently. "Is it worth while?"

They looked at each other, the thick-lashed, full black eyes questioning the gray eyes of their fair friend. Jane shook her head:

"Oh, how I admire you, Fanny! . . . You really are extraordinary."

"Me? That remains to be seen."

"Yes. Extraordinary. You admit, without contempt, spite, or any trace of snobbery that Farou may be . . . devoted."

"Just as well," said Fanny. "If I didn't admit it, what would happen? Exactly the same thing."

"Yes . . . yes . . . but all the same, I confess . . . yes, I confess—"

"That in my place you would not look forward to the party?"

"That wasn't what I was going to say," said Jane evasively.

She got up and walked as far as the terrace to assure herself that Little Farou, apt to dissolve like a snowflake on a warm pane of glass, was not listening to them.

"It's just this, Fanny. I think a man who was to be my man, who was to make me his woman . . . to learn that this man, at this very minute was applying himself to some actress creature, and to conclude philosophically that 'he's let himself get devoted' that 'it's part of his job'—well, no . . . a thousand times no. . . . I admire you, but . . . I could never do it!"

"All right, Jane. Luckily, no one asks you to be able to do it."

Jane flung herself at Fanny and crouched at her feet.

"Fanny, please, please, don't be vexed with me. I have days when I'm worth nothing, when I'm tactless, naughty, unhappy. You know me well, Fanny . . ."

She rubbed her cheeks and her little curved ears against the white skirts, and her forehead sought her friend's hand.

"You have such lovely hair, little Jane," murmured Fanny.

Jane laughed with some constraint.

"You say that as if it would excuse me!"

"In a certain degree, Jane, in a certain degree. I couldn't be vexed with a Jane who has such lovely hair. I can't scold Jean when his eyes are very blue. As for you, you are all dusted, hair, skin, eyes, and all, with silver ash, with powder of the moon, with . . ."

Jane lifted up to her a face, provoked to sudden tears, and cried:

"There's nothing lovely in me. I'm worthless. I deserve to be hated and shorn and beaten."

She let her head fall back into Fanny's lap and sobbed pitifully, while the first growls of thunder, rolling low and distant, were thrown from summit to summit by the echoes of the little mountains.

"This is her crisis," mused Fanny patiently. "It's the stormy weather."

Jane, already quieter, shrugged her shoulders in mockery of herself, and blew her nose.

"All the same," Fanny considered, "she said 'actress creature' and 'apply himself.' I've never before heard her use a word of slang, or a crude phrase. A difference in language, in her mouth, is equivalent to a violent gesture. A violent gesture in this weather!—it's mad. What shall we do before dinner?"

Jane, who was still crouching like a suppliant at Fanny's feet, raised her head.

"Would you like to go and have tea at the cake shop in the village? We can walk back . . ."

"Oh," moaned Fanny, frightened.

"No? You are getting fat, Fanny."

"I always get fat when it's hot and I have more than ten thousand francs in the bank. You know enough of 'the order of the march' to realize that I never lack opportunities to get thin."

"Yes. . . . Would you like me to wash your hair? No, you wouldn't like it. Shall we squeeze the gooseberries and black currants left over from luncheon? A handful of sugar, a drop of kirsch; we can pour the juice over the day before yesterday's spongecake, and it will swell. If we serve it with a little separate pot of fresh cream, we shall have an entirely fresh sweet for this evening, and it will cost nothing."

"That would be household catering," said Fanny disgustedly. "I don't like rejuvenated sweets."

"As you like, dear Fanny. May God continue to keep from you that household catering in which I learned to use up odds and ends. . . ."

The gentleness of the reproof seemed to weary Fanny, who stood up, using Jane's shoulder as a lever.

"After all," she cried, "fresh cream, gooseberry juice . . . yes; that'll do for me. On one condition, Jane . . ."

"I mistrust you. . . ."

"It's only that you should amuse yourself alone with this culinary treasure. I want to write a word to Farou, and to splash myself with cold water, and . . ."

"And?"

"And that's all. It's plenty!"

Standing up, she looked less big than lying down. She was utterly without any sort of defensive coquetry and swayed her beautiful hips with an assurance that would have become a woman of the people. Jane's glance followed her.

"Fanny, when are you going to decide to wear some sort of belt?"

"It's a matter of temperature, my dear. At five degrees above zero I wear a belt. Consult the thermometer. And don't let the fresh cream turn before evening. I'm so fond of it. . . ."

Jane had reached her, and after smoothing out the hem of her skirt, with a light touch she pinned up the lock of long black hair.

"Go then, naughty Fanny! All shall be perfect this evening. I will even try to call Jean back for dinner by beating a bowl as they do on farms when they throw the grain to the fowls. What a profession you thrust on your friend!"

Laughing unconstrainedly, she was already gathering the fallen petals on the cloth into her hand, blowing away crumbs, emptying an ash tray. . . .

"My friend? . . . Yes, she is my friend. All the same, that's a good deal to say, 'friend' . . ." thought Fanny, step by step up the staircase. "Who has ever shown so much of friendship toward me? No one.

Then she is my friend, a real friend. It's odd I should never think of Jane as my friend. . . ."

She threw off her clothes as soon as she was alone in the room with the two beds. The tall branches of the trees touched the balcony and at night scratched at the closed shutters. For two years, now, the careless owner of the place had neglected all pruning, and bit by bit the great open bay in the leafage was closing up. Undulating, planted with trees, the place breathed the melancholy of waterless land. No river, the sea a hundred leagues off, not a lake to double the wide expanse of sky. The façade of the house and the terrace, bathed in sun in the morning, by two o'clock resumed their real expression crisscrossed with little beams, with hooded windows and chocolate-colored Venetian shutters. And the hill opposite illuminated them, by reflection, with a mock light that sadly imitated the sun. Fanny, barely covered by her chemise, leaned her elbows on the balcony and contemplated the landscape that she had thought, on leaving it last year, never to see again.

"Farou wished it," she thought. "Two summers running in the same country, that hasn't often happened to us. But so long as Farou likes it here . . ."

She turned her head and measured the room behind her. It was as large as a barn, and its size was increased by the half-darkness from the partly closed shutters.

"It's all too big here. What can you do with two servants? . . . If it weren't for Jane, we should be driven to flight." She followed with her ear the lively step crossing the hall on the ground floor.

"She is extraordinary. In this heat! And so nice, when she's not in her crises of sensitiveness. A shade too useful to be a friend . . . yes, that's it: a shade too useful . . ."

She caught sight of her image in the glass, brown and careless, hands on hips, hair tumbling down, and snubbed it:

"What a sight! and to treat Jane as if she were too useful for a friend—I who cannot even tap out Farou's manuscripts on the typewriter!"

She flung herself into cold water as if to make a demonstration of housewifely activity, did her hair, put on a last year's summer dress, blue with mauve flowers, and sat down to write. She found a sheet of white paper, a yellow business envelope, was quite content with them, and began her letter to Farou.

Dear Big Farou—

Leaving to one or two little Asselins the care of conducting your life, I can sum up our existence in two words: nothing new. We wait for you. Jane the active meditates select nourishment; Little Farou still wears his air of a prisoner languishing in the uncomfortable age; and your lazy Fanny—

A little English song drifted up from the terrace.

"Ah," thought Fanny, "it's the day when Jane regrets Davidson." She was ashamed of the gibe, and then took pleasure in her shame.

"Well? It wasn't unkind, what I thought. On the days when Jane remembers Davidson, she sings in English. Days when it's Meyrowicz, she calls Jean Farou: 'Jean, come here, and let me teach you a Polish folk-dance.' And when it's Quéméré, she digs up horsy memories, an old, wistful tenderness for a certain Breton mare—a roan, very saddle-backed . . ."

She powdered her face again, and watched encroach upon the nearest hill the shadow of another.

"How sad it is, this place! What beauty can Farou find here? Never, in the twelve years of our marriage, have I seen him come back two years running to the same place. I hadn't realized how sad it was here. Next summer . . ."

But she lost courage before a future twelve months off.

"First, we must know if the play will be finished and how well Farou does out of his second season at the Vaudeville. But if they put 'Atalanta' on again at the Français in October— Ah, well, after all don't let's think about it; that's wisdom."

She had never learned any other.

"The main thing is for Farou to come back here and work at his third act. We are all so dull, when he's away. . . ."

A silent puff of air lifted the branches touching the balcony, and revealed the white backs of lime-tree leaves. Fanny finished her letter, and went to lean on the balcony again, her hair loose, her shoulder bared. Below her, Jane, arms crossed upon the low wall of the terrace, also leaned over the countryside where there was neither stream, pond, laugh of water, mirrored reflection, nor mist, nor the spongy, flower-sweet smell of a river bank. From above, Fanny threw out a little singing call that floated down toward the round head with its short, charmingly trim hair, ash-colored and veined in gold. Jane threw back her head without turning round, as cats do.

"You've been asleep, I bet?"

"No," said Fanny, "actually not. . . . Do you know I hate this country."

Jane turned quickly and flattened her back against the brick wall.

"No; that's not true? Since when? Have you told Farou? Can't you—"

"Good Lord, Jane, not so much fuss! Can't I have an opinion as simple as that without your turning round and round on yourself with incoherent words, before dashing your head against the wall?"

She laughed, leaning over, and shook out the flag of black hair, fallen down again upon her shoulder.

"My long hair descends even to the foot of the tower," sang Jean Farou, coming up the slope toward the terrace.

"There's someone," cried Fanny, "who already sings as flat as his father."

"But he hasn't Big Farou's voice," said Jane. "Jean, try to speak in Big Farou's voice when he comes in. 'Aha, all my fine women! I have women in my house!' . . ."

Jean went by her without answering, and disappeared into the hall. Jane jerked her head up to the balcony on the first floor:

"My dear, such a look he gave me! My lord doesn't understand a joke?"

"Nobody understands a joke at his age," said Fanny, thoughtfully. "We spend our time flaying that child alive, without meaning to."

She heard a step on the staircase, and called, "Jean!"

253

The boy opened the door of the room and stood on the threshold: "Mamie?"

He wore, with no loss of dignity, summer clothes that were almost in rags; a worn-out tennis shirt, trousers of white linen, green at the knees and too short, a belt and sandals that the caretaker's son would have despised. He waited for Fanny to speak and parted his lips to breathe, patiently presenting to his stepmother the healthy, innocent, mobile, and impenetrable face of a child of sixteen.

"What a state you're in! . . . Where were you?"

He turned his head toward the window, indicating vaguely that he came from the country, from all that country, from the violet of the shadows, from the green of the fields. . . . His blue eyes shone with a nearly uncontrollable animal life, but they surrendered nothing but their blue and their luster.

Jane, below, took up her little English song again and Jean Farou, slamming the door on himself, regained his own room.

"What a madcap!" thought Fanny. "There he goes, in love with Jane. Nothing wrong with that, if only she could be a little kinder to him."

Dinner brought the three of them together again on the terrace. In Farou's absence, Fanny and Jane sparkled with small, fitful gaiety, while Jean Farou, whether his father were there or no, kept a stubborn, intolerant silence, rarely broken.

"It's queer," said Fanny, raising her head toward the pale sky, "how graceless the end of day is, here. The sun sets for others down there, behind . . ."

"The mountain faces are monotonous," Jane broke in.

"Maeterlinck," muttered Jean.

The two women burst out laughing, and Little Farou looked at them insultingly.

"I've had enough of your lame cheerfulness!" he cried, leaving the table.

Fanny shrugged her shoulders and followed him with her eyes.

"He's becoming impossible," said Jane. "How can you allow it, Fanny?"

254

Fanny raised her white hand gently: "Hush, Jane. . . . You know nothing about it."

"Your goodness . . ."

Jane shook her head, and the soft hair stirred on her brow and about her tiny, almost round ears. When she wished to persuade Fanny, she opened wide gray eyes speckled here and there with gold, and raised her upper lip to show four little teeth, short and white. But Fanny paid no attention to what she called Jane's "filial face." She was smoking, and not enjoying it; she put out the cigarette, crushing it under her thumb with veiled animosity.

"No, Jane. Don't tell me all the time that I'm good. But let me tell you again that you don't understand anything about that child."

"And you?" asked Jane.

"Probably I don't, either. All I know is that we often make Little Farou unhappy: you especially. Because, of course, he's in love with you. And you treat him sometimes with a negligence that's rather hard."

"He's beginning early, I must say."

"Good God, Jane, how easily shocked you are! You're pretty, and my stepson is sixteen. I know very well that Jean would never dare, never even wish, perhaps, to make you a 'declaration' . . ."

"That's just as well."

Jane rose and propped her elbows on the low wall of the terrace.

"There we are," thought Fanny. "She answered me, as sharp as a blow. She's going to talk of the education they give youths in England. It's Davidson's day, decidedly."

But Jane, when she turned round, disclosed the laughing face of a child of about thirty years, and cried:

"You can't think, Fanny, how maddening it is not to have a single thing that's cold or even cool to touch near one for weeks. The walls are hot after midnight, the silver's warm, and the pavement. . . . It's exhausting. . . ."

"And whose fault is it? That cursed Farou's. . . . He wanted to finish the play here. . . ."

255

"You will have to protect yourself, Fanny, protect us, all of us. Even the valet-de-chambre who's dying of languor . . ."

She knitted her ash-pale brows, accented by a slender penciling, and looked sternly at the country asleep in the dry evening.

"But you say yes, and again yes . . . as if your slavish yes-my-dearisms would help you at all. . . . Women, really—"

"Kss! . . . Kss . . ." whistled Fanny.

Jane fell silent, blushing in her own way, that is to say, with a deepened tan.

"I'm meddling with what doesn't concern me, I know that. . . ."

"Oh, what does that matter!"

Fanny realized, as an afterthought, that an absolution as ambiguous as this might hurt Jane, and she added:

"Jane, don't mock Little Farou so much. He's sixteen. It's hard for a boy."

"I've had it. No one took pity on me."

"But you were a girl. It's utterly different. And also," said Fanny in response to a pathetic look, "you ended, in very despair, at the same age, or a little more, by throwing a rose over the wall to a passer-by. . . ."

"That's true, that's true," agreed Jane, suddenly moved. "You're right as usual, Fanny. . . . I tell you I'm bad, naughty, illogical. . . ."

She caught Fanny's shoulders to her, pressed her cheek against the black slackly knotted hair and repeated:

"I'm bad . . . bad . . ."

"But why?" demanded Fanny, who rarely bothered with a polite lie.

Jane turned up to the flushed sky a candid and simple face, and showed her four little teeth:

"Do I know? . . . Life hasn't spoiled me. . . . Old grudges show their ugly snouts. . . . Dear, very dear Fanny, take care of me. . . . Don't tell Farou I was so . . . so impossible in his absence. . . ."

They stayed there, until it was time to light the lamps, shoulder to shoulder, speaking little, pointing with a finger to a bat, a star, listening to the faint, fresh wind in the trees, imagining the flaming sunset that they could never see, except by climbing the hill opposite.

On the lower terrace, the gravel creaked. Obedient, Jane called: "Hello, Jean Farou!"

"Yes?" asked a young husky voice.

"Shall we put on the gramophone? Would that be a success?"

"Good . . . yes . . . as you like," said the sulky voice.

But he ran to them so swiftly that Fanny started to find him suddenly beside them, white, save for his face and arms, and illumined by the tragic nimbus that haloes adolescence.

Jane took him fraternally by the elbow and led him to the card-table, whose green motheaten surface smelled of mold and old cigars.

"Hello, boy!"

"Decidedly," thought Fanny, satisfied, "it's Davidson's day."

2

"Are you listening?"

"I'm listening."

"Is it still the scene of the stolen letter?"

"I think so. Yesterday morning he gave me fifteen pages to type. Five minutes later he seized them back, with an air—but with such an air—!"

"I know," said Fanny laughing. "As if you had taken away the bone he was gnawing. But what else do you want? He never goes to bed, even, without lightnings and thunders. How do the two first acts come out?"

"Sublime," said Jane.

"Yes," said Fanny thoughtfully. "It's disturbing."

A murmur of mass, of a crowd at prayer, of a riot in its beginnings, was exhaled from the house. When it stopped, the grave responses, given from high in air by bees at work on the crests of the lime trees and the ivy, were audible. The rasping growl of a wild beast interrupted the indistinct office that was being celebrated behind the half-open shutters; but the two women did not start. Neither did Jean Farou, stretched out on a long wicker chair with a book between idle hands.

"The scene still closes with Branc-Ursine caught in the act of breaking open the drawer," said Fanny. "If there were two Farous writing and pouring out their plays, where could we go for refuge?"

Jean's blue eyes, revealed for a moment, flashed. "I shall never write plays, Mamie."

"Easier to renounce than to attempt them," retorted Jane.

"It's not always so easy to renounce," said Jean.

He blushed at having dared to reply, and Fanny saw the blood beating more rapidly under the boy's ear and down his bare neck.

"Come, Jane; don't torment your little friend."

"I love teasing him, it's true," said Jane good-temperedly. "It suits him so well. I don't know what day it was when he looked so charming with a tear between his lashes. . . ."

She threatened him gaily with a hand on which shone her thimble. Fanny freed her forehead of its black, silky band.

"What! He also?"

"He also?" repeated Jane. "Explain yourself, darling Fanny, explain."

She laughed, sewed, and threw about her a happy gray glance dappled with amber; a badge of the westering sun moved on her bare head, and she seemed to wear joyously this evening of a graceless summer, that smelled only of hot granite.

"The other day," said Fanny—"wait, it was the day of Farou's letter, when we didn't know—nor he for that matter—that he would be able to return so soon—"

"Wednesday," said Jean, without raising his eyes.

"Perhaps. . . . I slept after luncheon, and, waking suddenly, I saw you standing on the veranda, where we are now . . . A tear was hanging on your eyelashes. It flowed down your cheek, and you gathered it up, like this, between two fingers, as if it had been a tiny strawberry, a grain of rice—"

Jane's expression, while she listened, changed from a smile, to the look of a sulky schoolboy, and so to one of coaxing reproach. With her little cleft chin she indicated Jean Farou.

"Fanny, Fanny, pray respect my little secrets, my changes of mind, before an audience so—so—"

She stopped speaking sharply, a look of stupefaction written on her face. Fanny, turning her head, saw her stepson standing up, with his mouth open as if to cry out. He threw his arms into the air, and fled precipitately down the staircase of the terrace.

"What's that? . . . What is it?"

"I don't know," said Jane. "He threw his arms up, didn't you see? And made his escape."

"He frightened me. . . ."

"There's really no need," said Jane.

She undressed her fine needlewoman's finger, and carefully removed the threads of cotton from her dress.

"He's going through what we all go through at his age," she continued, "an irritable romanticism. That will pass."

"You think so? . . ."

Fanny mechanically folded a width of string-colored linen, a cloth she was decorating with red flowers done in large awkward stitches. She went to lean over the breastwork of the wall, and call:

"Jean, are you there?"

A rather mocking voice came back, imitating her own:

"Wolf, is that you?"

"Stupid creature," cried Fanny, "you shall see what sort of person I am. Indulging in the temperamental behaviors of a big first part? Be off then, cock-of-the-north . . . you species of . . ."

Without finishing, she turned round, veering upon her beautiful hips, which dated, in the opinion of Big Farou, from a better period. She had just heard the voice of her husband coming nearer.

"That's it, he's finished," she said quickly to Jane.

"For today. . . ." said Jane, doubtfully.

Leaning one against the shoulder of the other, they watched Farou approach. He walked with a sleepy step, and emerged slowly from his day of work, in the course of which, mumbling, muttering, or roaring his third act aloud, he had removed with an unconscious hand his collar, a shantung coat, his tie, and his waistcoat. At six feet from the earth, he carried a graying head, a fleece of curls that fell over, entangling themselves in his eyebrows, and shadowing his amber eyes. Huge, weary, strong, perhaps ugly, confident of pleasing, he walked habitually as if he were going to battle or to a burning; and when he crossed the village to buy cigarettes, the mothers called their children to them and sheltered them against their skirts.

He looked at the two women without seeing them, and plucked a rose. He dwelt still in the somber and luxurious boudoir, where Branc-Ursine, the advocate-general, was so demeaning himself as to force open a bureau and steal letters that would ruin the beautiful Madame Houcquart, his mistress, whom he no longer loved.

"Beautiful Farou!" cried Fanny tenderly.

Jane's sweeter voice mimicked her, for fun:

"Beautiful Farou!"

And the mimicry was so faithful that Fanny, surprised, heard it as if it were an echo.

Farou, struck by the double voice and by a Spanish honeysuckle whose heavy perfume barred his way, paused and chanted his little ritual song:

"Aha, all my fine women! All my fine women! I have women in my house."

He yawned, and appeared to wake and discover the universe. He hitched up his shantung trousers, which were slipping down, scratched his head. Neither suspicious nor flirtatious, he was happy most of the time, and young at forty-eight like all men who surround themselves, in the course of life, only with women.

"Who called me first?" exclaimed Big Farou.

He did not wait for an answer, but began to dance, singing in a pleasant, flat voice an improvised couplet that abused Monsieur Branc-Ursine, beautiful Madame Houcquart and their affairs in round, military terms. But suddenly noticing his son coming up the steep steps to the terrace, he stopped as if frozen, and clowned for the benefit of Fanny and Jane, who were admiring him:

260

" 'Ware the cops!"

"Have you finished, Farou?"

Fanny showed nothing but a calm uncertainty.

Farou, with a shrug, had already got so many third acts out of the mud . . . He looked at her with an eye fierce but entirely without malice.

"Finished? What a genius you are!"

"But still you've made some progress?"

"Progress? Yes. Of course I've made progress. I've chucked the whole scene into the air."

"Oh!" said Fanny, as if he had broken a vase.

"It's good work, that, my pretty. Jane, get ready to type the authorized version."

He clapped his hands, prowling to and fro with the step of an ogre. "Until today, it went very badly. But today . . ."

"And has Monsieur Branc-Ursine behaved himself today? This pompous old magistrate, has he put his letters into a safe place?"

Fanny, who had been busy combing Big Farou's hair, shut up her little pocket comb and ranged herself alongside him, to make room for the answer.

"I should like it," said Farou nonchalantly, "if Jane would add to her other diverse and numerous accomplishments that of penmanship."

"But I can learn it," exclaimed Jane. "There are copybooks. . . . I know an excellent one. . . . Why?"

"People tell me that the penman, a slave to the signs of writing, to the bars of an 'I,' to the loops of an 'L,' is incapable of reading—in the sense of understanding—the texts that are entrusted to him."

Jane flushed fiercely. "Is that a reproof?"

"A joking one."

"But one I shall take into account."

Farou's yellow eyes sparkled. "Don't put on your expression of a daily sewing woman. It doesn't impress me, Jane."

She bit her lip, holding back two tears. And Fanny took Farou up, with the air of a woman accustomed to such situations:

"Farou! Brute! Aren't you ashamed? All that for this rake of a Branc-Ursine. Tell me, Farou, is he still stealing letters from the furniture?"

"And what else should he be doing?"

She pulled a face and rubbed her charming nose with her finger.

"You don't think it's a bit cinemaish . . . or a bit—a bit melodramatic?"

"A bit melodramatic? Look at that, now!"

He teased her condescendingly, rather ungently.

"Yes," insisted Fanny. "I assure you."

He opened his great arms.

"What would you do if, knowing that there are in a chest, a drawer, a truck, anywhere, letters from a man who was the lover of —Give your nose a good blow, Jane, and come and help us. . . . What would you do, Fanny?"

"Nothing."

"Nothing," repeated Jane's voice on the same note.

"Ah, my poor little darling, you say that, but—"

"Nothing," decided Jean Farou, returning with the evening and reassured by the dusk.

"Insect," growled Farou.

"From the moment that Jean is for doing nothing— Psychologist, come here a minute. . . . You don't look well, these days."

"It's the heat, Mamie."

"The fact is—I know someone," proclaimed Big Farou, "who's going to sleep on the little divan tonight. It's me."

"No, me," said Fanny.

"And me on the terrace," outbid Jane.

"And me not," said Jean.

"Why, Jean?"

"Full moon, Mamie. Cats and boys run by night."

In the falling darkness his hair, eyes, and teeth gleamed phosphorescent, and he trembled like a spring of water. His father measured him with a glance that lacked charity and paternal pride.

"At your age—" began Farou.

"—I had already killed and begotten a man," quoted the child.

Farou gave a flattered laugh.

"That's pretty, I must say," scolded Jane.

"It's only a quotation," Farou condescended to explain.

Youth's wide look rested upon Farou for a moment, a large look, empty or laden with secrets, inscrutable. The evening train screamed and labored sadly along the line that girdled the nearest hill, above the village already lost in the blue dusk. A moon, faintly red, left the horizon and mounted up the sky.

"Where are you going, Jane?"

"Grand inquisitor, I'm going down to the lower terrace, and coming back. I've eaten too much."

"Three spoonfuls of rice and a handful of gooseberries," said Fanny.

"It doesn't matter. Fanny, aren't you coming down?"

"To bring up all that! . . ." said Fanny, terrified.

The white dress, the little English song receded; Fanny, raising the heavy arm of her husband, placed it on her shoulders. He let her do it, and his idle fingers fondled Fanny's breast. Bending her head, she kissed the hand, a little hairy like the leaves of sage. The wrist, whiter, softer, showed green veins. Disarmed and trusting, the hand consented to the almost timid caress.

"How sweet you are," breathed the dreaming voice of Farou above Fanny.

The timid mouth pressed more strongly against the wrist, against a man's hand made for the handle of the plow, the hoe, heavy weapons, but occupied now only with the management of a fountain-pen.

Supported on his wife's shoulder, Farou, upright and open-eyed, seemed to sleep.

"Is he perhaps already asleep?" Fanny asked herself. From the hand and the abandoned arm, she inhaled a healthy odor of warm skin and perfumed spirit. She did not say: "This man who suffers me to bear the weight of his arm was and still is my great love." But there was no line of the palm, no braceleted wrinkle round the wrist, already aging, that did not rouse in her a passionate memory, the fever of service, the certainty of belonging to one man, and of having belonged only to him.

The stealthy sound of a cat parted the leaves, a light body glided against the trunk of the lime tree.

"That's Jean," thought Fanny. "He's watching Jane, below."

She nearly laughed and drew Farou's attention, but thought better of it. The shadow of the trees in front of the moon gathered the gravel into their blue, and in a few moments the sky had become a night sky.

"It wouldn't have been so hot in Brittany," sighed Fanny.

Farou withdrew his arm and seemed to perceive that he was not alone.

"In Brittany? Why, in Brittany? Isn't it all right here?"

"Oh, you! . . . You are a lizard of the sands!"

"One doesn't work badly here. . . . Do you want to go away?"

"Oh! no, not now. . . . I said that for next year. . . . We shan't come back here next year, shall we?"

Two broad shoulders shrugged in sign of ignorance.

"Certain things are awkward here. . . . It's too hot, but there's not enough sun. . . . The boy isn't comfortable in his room, which is really a furnace. We ought to move him."

"But, of course."

"You amaze me! . . . There's not another room for him "

"Nonsense. There's always another room."

"Yes . . . The east room."

"Whose is that?"

"It's the room Jane has."

"If Jane has it, it is in fact not free then."

"But will Jane be with us next year?"

Farou turned an ingenuous countenance toward his wife.

"I don't know at all. How should I know? Why think about it?"

"It was because of Jean . . ."

"What? Is he complaining, then?"

"Sh! Farou . . . That wouldn't be at all like him, to complain, especially, don't you see, if it would inconvenience Jane . . ."

"Ah! Yes? . . ."

Fanny saw Farou's eyebrows join above the yellow eyes where a spark of moonlight shone. The wind rolled some flower-heads and scorched leaves along the ground. A light step imitated the sound of the leaves on the gravel, and Jane's white dress reappeared at the end of the terrace. At the other end, Jean Farou came to earth with a noiseless bound, leaving the strategic branch of his lime tree.

"My children," exclaimed Farou, "I don't know if you are in the same state, but I'm dropping with sleep."

"That is to say that everyone must go to bed," said Jean.

"Exactly. And you, Jane, be off to your eastern room."

"Have I an eastern room?"

She shook her head, to flutter her hair.

"Yes, Dust-of-the-Moon! A room in the east. Cooler than the others. Fanny has just told me."

"Àpropos of what?" demanded Jane involuntarily. "Oh, I'm sorry! How badly brought up I am."

"Sometimes," conceded Farou. "Give me your paw. Good night, Jane. Go ahead, son."

"Oh, papa . . . only a quarter to ten! On a night like this? It's a shame!"

A languid valet-de-chambre dragged himself through the villa, switching on here and there a feeble reddish electric light. Farou had hardly crossed the hall, bellowed a yawn on the staircase, and shaken his son's hand abstractedly, before Jean Farou, behind the closed doors of his stifling room, began to spy on all Jane's movements through the yawning planks.

3

CROSSED though it was by creditors, actors, drafts, and temporary servants, Fanny Farou's life at Paris passed fairly peaceably. Fanny carried her peace with her, at the same time as the plaid rug of soft long-haired vicugna which caught and retained crumbs of cake and kept her chilly body from the cold. The gesturing shadow of Farou had fallen on her in the course of a rehearsal of "The House Without Women," in which Fanny took the part of the piano off-stage, for the act of the evening party.

"You look like a nut half-shelled, between your black bands," Farou threw at her as early as their first encounter.

Habitually ill-dressed, that day he trailed the broken elastic of a suspender across one of his shoes.

"You are as white as a native woman; come with me," he ordered her, eight days later.

"But . . . my parents . . . I am . . . I'm only a girl," Fanny confessed, frightened.

He looked bored.

"Oh, how tiresome! So much the worse. . . . We'll get married if you like! . . ."

At Paris, the Farous—three, if we count little legitimatized Jean —lived sparely. Then Farou's plays, rich in a rather massive beauty, and in brutalities that he found quite simple, descended from the Batignolles to the boulevards, formed the habit of passing the hundredth performance, and the face and personality of the man Farou became very useful to Farou the author. Porto-Riche found him coarse, because, in fact, he was coarse with Porto-Riche. He refused, in terms of some warmth as if it were a degrading piece of forced labor, to collaborate with a member of the Academy. Bataille treated as important the "genial, crude, and disarming follies" of Farou; a "Docklaborer" in three acts, by Flers and Caillavet, resembled Farou, who sometimes posed as tramp or foundling before people who did not know that a father Farou for a long period had taught history to boys of twelve in an obscure school.

With the arrival of fame, the Farous lived like princes and thought nothing of it. Like princes, between reporters, gossip-writers, actors, and the public, they had a house of glass; but nothing is more impenetrable than a house of shining glass. In royal fashion, Farou, ready for brilliant and brief adventure, did not cease for so little to delight in Fanny. During the dead seasons he got into debt royally, but, like a prince, he never lost his appetite for the humblest pleasures. Farou was enraptured at the sight of a large, smoking dish, and rated idleness at its proper worth. Behind a closed door, he would brood in his shirt-sleeves over the illustrated weeklies, while Fanny, one shoe off and one shoe on, her heavy hair undone and hanging down her cheeks, bent her gentle antelope's muzzle over a game of patience, beginning it again twenty times before it would come out.

A young companion shared these joys. Jean Farou leaned his child's forehead against Fanny's shoulder, then, later, his boy's chin, and advised his stepmother:

"You've made a frightful failure, Mamie, with your club sequence!"

The child, whom you would have called amiable because of his beauty, and tender because of his blue eyes, gave Fanny a somewhat vague affection, but he ranged himself on her side every time he divined her to be discontented with Farou, or annoyed; while she displayed toward her stepson a kindness less particular than universal, regarding him as some mysterious emanation of Big Farou.

"You're positive you haven't kept a photograph of his mother?" Fanny asked her husband. "I should so love to have seen that woman's face. . . ."

Farou answered with his open-armed gesture, that sent memories, regrets, and all responsibilities flying.

"Not a hope of finding one of them! . . . But she was a nice creature, not very strong, poor thing. . . ."

"Intelligent?"

Farou's wandering golden eye came to rest astonished, on his wife. "I knew her so little, you see . . ."

"Yes; I believe that," thought Fanny. "Will he say the same of me, if ever . . ."

She would not risk herself further than that "if ever . . . ," for all her conjurer's bravado, so incapable was she of imagining life without Farou, without Farou's presence, his mutterings like the mass, his habit of shutting doors with a kick to punish a refractory third act; his hungers for women, his hours of gentleness, when she murmured tender praises of his mildness in his ear:

"You are kind . . . you are soft as sage . . . smooth as a hoof . . . you are gentle as a sleeping deer. . . ."

He treated her so charmingly as favorite, that she would not dispute with him the right, common to all reigning despots, of scattering a few bastards here and there.

"Beautiful Farou! Naughty Farou! Monstrous Farou!"

In a whisper, or in her heart, she named him without commentary, like one of the faithful for whom the litany is enough.

She had tried, in the first years, to serve her master as well by day as by night. But Farou impatiently discouraged the zeal of his secretary apprentice. So she remained at her post of lover, a fatalist, turning to childish things, to greediness and to goodness, lazy like those whom the weight of a serious attachment overcomes with weariness after the middle of the day.

Since the end of the last rehearsal of "Atalanta" when to Farou's triumphant "Well?" from the back of a box at the Français, Fanny had offered the remark, "The scene between Piérat and Clara Cellerier is obviously too long; if you let someone enter in the middle, to bring in some coffee or a telegram, the scene will move much more briskly after that, and the public will be refreshed," Farou had never asked for an opinion. But all the same, she never failed to give him one. If Farou, dour in the face of criticism, let fall upon his wife a "Do you think so!" weighted with a look as yellow and heavy as gold, Fanny experienced on such an occasion a strange sense of liberty in mind and word. She would explain herself and insist, raising her great eyebrows with an air of detachment and unconcern.

"Me? Yes. But it's all the same to me. You will do as you wish. Only do not oblige me, me the public, to find it natural that a woman should wish to kill herself for such a trifle. . . ."

"A trifle?" Farou exclaimed after her. "A betrayal? And a betrayal as meticulous and considered as this one! A trifle? Well really!"

Fanny lifted her nostrils and looked at Farou between her lashes with unusual impertinence:

"Perhaps it's not a trifle. But shall I tell you what your Denise's action is? It's a man's reflex and nothing else. A man's reflex."

He turned the argument aside, whatever she did, sometimes with a diplomacy that he never employed except in this extremity. But more usually, he broke off the discussion with a sudden appeal:

"My collar-stud; good God! And the letter from Coolus? Where is the letter from Coolus? In yesterday's suit? Does no one empty my pockets, then? No?"

Running, losing a slipper, scattering the tortoise-shell prongs that held up her long, unfashionable hair, Fanny changed color, look, and language. Twelve years of marriage had not cured her of a particular reverence in which, all the same, Farou's talent and his fame counted for less than he could have believed. Sudden in emotion, she was wise enough to adopt the habit of uncertainty.

Between Farou and his creditors, she interposed a patience stripped of invention, the nobility of a faithful servant. But, having exceeded "Bloch's advance" and the transfer of the cinema rights, she never looked farther than the sale of the car and her fur, and the pawning of her ring.

"It's odd how little you belong to our time. You ought to take yourself in hand, by Jove!" Clara Cellerier of the Français advised her.

The large-hearted, aging actress, very well known, though she ran no risk of celebrity, shook her head in pity. Her hair, greenish gold and admirably cut, was always encased in little tight hats. Slender in her youthful black gowns, rather boldly dressed, Clara Cellerier did not at all emphasize her sixty-eight years except in a use of the phrase, "By Jove!" in a certain military boyishness and by her trick of saying of a man, "He's a man who'd look well in the saddle."

"One doesn't quote anyone," Berthe Bovy proclaimed, "whom she has relegated to foot."

Clara treated Fanny as a young cousin from the provinces, with the easy kindness of the theater; with "Come, little one!", recipes for beauty, and addresses of renovating dressmakers. But Fanny never thought enough about clothes to dress well and wore her gowns two years, although she was seen sometimes in furs. She had the beaver of "Atalanta," the mink of "The House Without Women," the blue fox of the "Stolen Grape," which she sold when "The Bargain" met its sensational failure—a rebuke to Farou for having mixed with the war a story of lovers oblivious of the war.

Fanny did not forget that harsh turning point: no money or next to none, Little Farou ill with typhoid fever, the maid flown, afraid of contagion. This was the moment chosen by the police to arrest the valet-de-chambre in the service of the Farous, and accuse him of offenses against decency. Farou, however, withdrawn from the world, labored at the fourth act of his new play, and complained with blows of his fist on table and door that his stenographer, Madame Delvaille, should have allowed herself to be brought to bed before his fourth act had seen daylight.

"Everything's in a muddle!" he shouted in the distance, behind shut doors.

"You may well say so," wept Fanny quietly, squeezing lemons for feverish Little Farou, in a faded dressing-gown, and with lack-luster hair.

One morning, when a light as bleak and uncompromising as a hospital's exposed a litter of dirty clothes, carpets with curling corners, lemon rinds, stray bedroom slippers, the smell of a water-heater not properly regulated and eau-de-Cologne on wet com-presses, Fanny, awaking on a divan-bed whence hoarse appeals had dragged her all night long—"Mamie . . . I'm hot . . . Mamie . . . something to drink"—felt surge up in her the irritation of an animal goaded to the breaking point or of the sort of woman who has a pretty but rather soft chin.

"I've had enough of this. The charwoman comes late, we haven't enough money to pay for a nurse; Farou finds this quite natural, and thinks of nothing but his third act. . . . I shall go and wake him; I shall, and I shall tell him exactly what I think of him and of all this; I shall give him back his son and tell him it's his turn to . . ."

But Little Farou groaned the name of "Mamie," and Fanny heard, as if for the first time, this child who even in delirium looked for help only to a strange woman. . . . She began again to heat water, rinse basins, squeeze lemons, and grind coffee.

On the same morning a pretty young woman rang, asked for "the master," and announced that Madame Delvaille, "happily delivered of a beautiful boy of eight pounds," could certainly not resume her work before three months' time. She offered her temporary services to a silent and ferocious Farou. He accepted them with a sign. In the days following, little Jane Aubaret lent a good and reassuring charm to breakfast with the Farous at the corner of the table. She remade the feverish boy's bed, and quieted Fanny with the help of egg-yolks beaten in port. Little by little, Jane showed what she could do.

Assisted by Fanny, who took heart of grace again, the two of them were worth four servants, each watching the other out of the corner of an eye. By their identical method of polishing brown shoes, of cleaning a bath without having recourse to patent soaps, of breaking eggs into a bowl, and lighting the furnace without dirtying their fingers, they recognized each other mutually as workmen of quality, children of France's sound middle class—those exacting workers who take account neither of their own labors nor of the toil of their race. In the world of the poor but proud and scrupulous middle class, the girls are still taught that, before school, the beds must be made and tucked in, bicycles polished, stockings and cotton gloves soaped and rinsed in the basin.

Such a collaboration bore fruit. A young valet-de-chambre, smitten with the theater, replaced the satyr, the maid servant returned, the smell of apple pie and furniture polish mingled in a fresh and tart incense, and Little Farou's temperature fell to 37.2 degrees centigrade on the thermometer. Big Farou, inspired, laughing at brown Fanny and fair Jane, at his son, frail and transparent as a shell, pulled his third act out of its mud, cut in at the Vaudeville under the nose of Pierre Wolff, received "a fine advance" from Bloch, and tousled Fanny amorously.

"Fanny, if there's one piece of advice I should like to give you, it's this. Go and choose yourself a fur. Don't wait too long, Fanny."

She caressed him with a beautiful, gleaming eye, rubbed her mouth and her soft, velvety nostrils against him, and held herself tight lest she be overwhelmed; she had, imprudent one, paid the doctor.

"Don't forget," said Farou a little later, "the present for Jane, since we no longer need her. A wrist-watch, naturally."

But neither Farou nor Fanny could have foreseen that Jane, when the time came to say good-by, would hurl herself into their arms with tears, and confused prayers in which they discerned sincere grief at leaving "the master," fear of a dangerous loneliness, the need of devoting herself to a friend like Fanny. . . . Fanny dissolved into tears, Farou's eyes filled and sparkled like a cat's in the dark, and Jane explained promptly that a modest income delivered her from the most disagreeable alternatives: to live at the charges of her new friends or to accept a salary from them.

Middle-class bohemians, like other bohemians, are enraptured by disinterested friendship. In private, the Farous hymned the perfections of Jane, and their personal pleasure in having discovered, in having invented her.

"That girl is a treasure," said Farou, "really a treasure."

"I don't know whether she's a 'treasure,'" retorted Fanny, "but at least she's worth more than your compliments in the 'reference' style. Imagine, it was she who cut and sewed this lamé tunic so that I could wear it with my pleated black marocain skirt."

"A pretty way of rehabilitating what I have degraded—to make a day seamstress of her! . . . For the matter of that," added Farou, with a look full of leonine sweetness, "Jane is rather like one of those distinguished persons who go to sew for the rich through dread of contact with the poor. . . ."

Fanny laughed, in spite of herself.

"God save me from any good you might speak of me, Farou."

As she lost her attentions in the rôle of new relative, unknown nurse, undeciphered friend, Jane surrendered none of her virtues. She bore with Farou's mood, his merriments more wounding sometimes than his rages, typed rapidly on the machine, did the telephoning. She remembered numbers of theaters, names of general secretaries, flattered "the ladies" of the box offices. She called Quinson "great friend" and shared, without any appearance of surprise, the financial disorder of a pair who, although trained to deprive themselves of necessities, clamored rudely for luxuries.

Fair Jane—if the most delicate ash, that of poplar wood, is fair— on being made free of the Farous' bathroom, one day learned the scandalous little baptism that the owners' acquaintances had given her.

"With which does the pretty ash-colored girl sleep? With brown Fanny, I believe?"

"But of course not, darling. With that goat-foot of a Farou, who adorns her with the title of secretary and imposes her on his wife. . . ."

Farou, questioned bluntly by Clara Cellerier, put them right in a word:

"Don't allow your imagination too much license, my charming friend. I am, like you, a respecter of the classics. There's nothing between Jane—who is my natural daughter—and myself, but a fine, simple little matter of incest. That's all."

"Where's Jane?" Fanny asked all day, dominated by the habit of encountering an amiable and active young woman wherever she cast her eye.

Jane's presence might have passed for a luxury of Fanny's. Seven years of seniority authorized a certain carelessness in Fanny, while

Jane had the courtesies of a lady-in-waiting or an eager niece. Farou, when he came home, greeted Jane no more than a piece of furniture. But he fussed if she was absent.

"Where's Jane?"

"In her room, I think," answered Fanny. "She's just back from Pérugia's."

"She gets her shoes at Pérugia's now, does she? the bitch!"

"And why shouldn't she get her shoes at Pérugia's if she wants to? As she has a foot a little smaller than mine, and as I'm feeling tired myself, Jane took a pair of woolen stockings with her and tried on my shoes for me. . . . Shall I call her?"

"No. What do you want done about it?"

"But a moment ago you were asking for her. . . ."

"Who? . . . It was for my glass of vittelpipérazine."

"There's the valet-de-chambre for that. Soon you'll be making Jane wash your handkerchiefs."

"Well, and what about you?"

They exchanged a laugh of understanding and mutual reproach. "Where's Jane?" asked Little Farou, with pinched mouth and anxious eye, halting in front of Jane's empty chair as if a rope were stretched there. And Fanny, malicious woman, often answered him out loud before he had spoken.

In July, the Farous were accustomed to leave Paris for a summer holiday, chosen from the advertising columns of "Country Life" or recommended by Clara Cellerier.

Farou had to have solitude, weeks of capricious work without method or proportion, the certainty of never meeting people he called "the jaws." Outside Paris he hid with difficulty his inaptitude for appropriating to himself the large, visible goods of life,—sea, sun, and forest: he infected Fanny with the same restlessness, the arrogant timidity of ordinary people.

"People tell me Pau is so pretty," suggested Fanny. "You know, I've never been to Dinard. Doesn't it amuse you, that I don't know Dinard, at my age?"

"What would not amuse me," growled Farou, "would be to have Max Maurey's nose, for instance, under mine three times a day."

"What has he done? Hasn't Max Maurey been nice to you?"

"But of course he has."

"Well, then?"

"That's nothing to do with it my dear. . . . You don't understand. Maurey likes dressing himself three times a day in summer. I don't. Once and for all I wish to spend my summers alone, without shoes or a stiff collar."

He satisfied his authority as nomadic chieftain in organizing the departures.

Followed by a movable household, the Farous, with two new trunks and twenty badly tied packages, would settle themselves into rather moldy villas, somberly furnished manors, cottages with thin walls, all places left aside by modern travel or places where Clara Cellerier had tasted furtive joys in other days. The typewriter, the season's latest novels, Farou's manuscripts, the dictionary, the wardrobe trunks, and Fanny's plaid rug took their places, and Jean was allowed to run wild.

"What will become of Jane without us, and us without Jane?" a perplexed Fanny asked herself when July threatened the friendly honeymoon.

But she calmed herself when she heard Farou:

"Jane, you will take One and Two with you, and all the notes for Three. You will give the typewriter to the valet-de-chambre, who will bring it to the train."

"Then, it's all settled," sighed Fanny.

She looked amiably again at the present, and once more found room between the windows for cane armchairs, a new book, the angora rug, the box of sweets, and a leather cushion.

A day came, nevertheless, when she had to make room for a past, Jane's past.

"It's right that you should know everything about me, Fanny," Jane began, rather formally.

"Why?" asked Fanny, in whom politeness always yielded to honesty.

"But, Fanny, I should die of shame if I concealed from you . . .

275

after the welcome I've had here. You must know what I am, for better or worse, and judge me . . ."

At this preamble, Fanny's eye, blue-black like that of a blood-horse, fled, and grappled itself, in terror of the storm, to the lamp, to a passer-by in the street, avoiding Jane and her affectionate expression, Jane and her airy head, Jane and her simple gown—so simple that no one could see it without noticing it.

"Why," Fanny pursued within herself, "why is it that I'm as bored already as if I were at an adaptation of an American play? But also, why all this paraphernalia of pedigree, of ins and outs, by a fireside where no one inquires about anyone else? Is it any use? Is it worth while?"

Already Jane had revealed how, as the portionless child of a drawing master in the city— "You can see my father's works at the Lycée Duguay-Trouin, among others a charcoal of the first order, 'Asses at the Drinking Trough'"—she had walked bruised and shaken in the little garden of Saint-Mandé, between bare lilac-trees and laurel-bushes in tubs, a haggard spirit, ready for anything, desperate, a girlish spirit, young, poor, and without a profession.

Jane never spoke in front of Farou. She waited until the end of the meal restored him to his work or his idleness. She waited again until, alone with Fanny, the older woman let her book slip onto her knees, or woke up suddenly, fresh and alert— "What news, Jane?"—from her nap. As Jane never set about it from the beginning, Fanny never knew exactly whether Meyrowicz, a Pole of extreme beauty, and a bit of a collector besides, had run off with Jane from Davidson, or whether he had received her from the thin dangerous hands of that same Davidson, "the" English composer.

"Can they have only one of them in England?" mused Fanny.

But, at least, she knew Jane's first misfortune, Antoine de Quéméré, by heart.

"When I used to wait for my father at the end of the little terrace," recounted Jane, "I began to wait so long ahead of time, leaning over like this, that I had a bar of pain from it, here about the height of the stomach. I used to become giddy from looking and looking and never seeing anything new. . . . I used to balance a flower at the end of my arm. . . . Girls are fiends, you know . . ."

"No, I don't know," Fanny answered, within herself.

". . . and on the worst days, I said to myself: 'If only a man would pass by, I'd drop this flower . . .' In the end, one day I did let the flower slip; it fell between the ears of a horse . . . but there was a rider on the horse."

"Bravo," exclaimed Fanny, to herself again. "What a pretty curtain for a first act! If I were to suggest it to Farou? . . ."

But suddenly, she wrinkled her nose.

"Why does that remind me of an English play? Meyrowicz at least beat Jane. She swears it; besides, she showed me a place on her arm where that disgusting sadist burned her . . . They have no more effect on me, even less, than 'The Broken Lily' at the cinema, these misfortunes of Jane. . . ."

"Farou," she said one day to her husband, "will you tell me why, when an unmarried woman speaks of her lovers, she generally calls them her 'misfortunes'? And why the same men are labeled 'Happiness Number I, Happiness Number II,' and so on, if the lady happens to be married?"

"Leave me in peace," answered the great dreamy voice, "and don't bother me."

"Farou, I shall end by thinking that you know nothing about anything. Can you understand why Jane speaks with contempt and ill will of all men with whom she has slept?"

Farou appeared to reflect.

"Well, yes, I can understand it. It's natural."

"Oh! . . ."

"It's the honorable survival of modesty in the female. It's contrition. It's aspiration toward a better life."

"Farou, you make me laugh!"

He covered her severely with his yellow glance, as if Fanny were his flock, or his kitchen garden, surrounded by walls.

"It's you who understand nothing. You are much too simple. You are a monster. And then you love me, which deprives you of all perspicacity."

She put her arms round his neck, and rubbed her little white nose against him.

"You're making me hot," said Farou, disengaging himself. "You're as logical and consistent as a third act. Let me work. Send Jane to me, and a glass of orangeade, a grape—things that have no weight. . . ."

"A pretty little second act . . . a bedroom scene?" Fanny suggested maliciously.

"Peace, Fanny. No wit! no wit! You are the only ordinary woman whom I know. Watch over your prerogatives."

With a heavy, gentle hand, he stroked his wife's black hair, and she asked him softly and without boldness if he loved her.

"I don't know at all, my dear. . . ."

"How? . . ."

"No. I do not always notice that I love you. But if I stopped loving you I should notice it immediately. And I should become very unhappy. . . ."

She looked up at him with an insistence, calculated, because she knew that an imploring look emphasized the white round the black irises of her eyes.

"Oh! . . . very unhappy? Can you be very unhappy then?"

"I hope not," he said, a little nervously. "I never have been. . . . Have you?"

She shrugged her shoulders to signify no, and shook her head.

"No. . . . No. . . .

"No," she repeated to herself. "Annoyances, a heap of annoyances . . . tricks you play me oftener than I deserve, probably . . . your nasty Farou character—and myself, my useless self. . . . But none of that counts at all. . . . No. . . . No. . . .

"Beautiful Farou— Naughty Farou— Farou who has no manners."

Moved to the heart, she hummed in a whisper, lest he should hear that the thread of her voice shook like a jet of water in the wind. . . .

4

"Very unhappy . . . can he be very unhappy? or even sad? In any case, he's not bad. But no one has ever had occasion to say, or hear it said, that he is good. Nor gay. On the contrary. How little like a man of the theater he is. All the same, he loves the theater. . . . No, he doesn't love the theater, he loves writing plays. Why am I so made that I compare his job, his art to a woman's capricious sort of work? No: not exactly to a woman's work, but to some very easy profession. But if it were an easy profession, numbers of others would have succeeded in it. If Farou has succeeded it's because he has great talent. Has he great talent? . . ."

Brought to this extreme point of conjecture, Fanny experienced the same discomfort as in a too vivid imagination of a bullfight for instance, a hemorrhage, or a sudden fall. She snatched herself back from the terrifying void that beckoned her, tossing familiar little calls about her:

"Jean, where are you? Jane! I've lost my lipstick again. . . . Jane! Where's the big blue vase? I've brought some flowers back from the hollow."

No one answered her. She yawned, tired with having risen so early this morning. Leaning on the brick parapet, she admired the slope, then the path across the fields, then the lane bordered with young plane-trees—

"All along there. What a way I've walked! How impressed they'll be."

The air still held the fragrance of the dawn twilight. The wind, blowing from the northeast, refreshed all the countryside, gathering up resins, wild thyme from the little chain of grassy hills, the crisp scent of oak-bark from the low grove, to shed them again upon the hillside that bore the Villa Déan.

"It's a desert, this house. Where are they all?" A faint clatter of dishes came from the kitchen which gave upon the green and spongy-looking opposite face of the villa. Among the yellow-painted iron furniture, unoccupied and hideous, Fanny saw herself suddenly abandoned in this country little known, little loved. . . . She threw the great bunch of pink hemp and campanulas, already fading, down on the table.

"Farou!" she called.

"Present, as for him!" answered Farou, so near her that she jumped.

"You are there? Are you really there?"

"What's the matter? Are the sheep in the corn again?"

He was not unaware that "Farou" is a name often given to sheep-dogs and condescended to be amused by it.

He blocked the hall door, standing, lightly, negligently, freshly clothed, with head bare, and a knotty cane in his hands. He began to laugh, because Fanny in her amazement opened her mouth wide, like a fish. She was angry.

"What are you laughing at? You certainly weren't there before, because I've just brought the fat red bowl out of there. You've come back from a walk . . . No, because I've just come from the fields down there. Where did you pass? You aren't a pin or a sylph. D'you hear me, Farou? And then your nose is large. I've never noticed before how large your nose is. Why do you play tricks on me? Why don't you say something?"

He laughed, showing his open teeth, teeth predestined to happiness. Fanny lowered her tone because of this mouth lined with sanguine red, and smoothed her face to the expression of a petted handmaid.

"You've finished?" asked Farou.

"Naturally I've finished. You aren't worth more!"

She contemplated the fine weather mirrored in Farou's eyes and began to croon one of her Farouche litanies, which she sometimes invented, both words and music, in the quiet hours after passion, when love was still:

"Color of old amber . . . color of angry gold . . . of burning topaz . . . of the Moret Nuns' barley sugar."

An emotion flickered in the eyes of which she was chanting, and Farou's tired eyelids fluttered.

"Ah! Farou . . ." sighed Fanny, flattered. . . . But she corrected herself at once and cloaked her pleasure under an awkward and conventional shyness. Farou, following Fanny's glance, saw his son disguised and beautified in a blue overall belted at the waist. He fled at once to his traditional joke:

" 'Ware the cops!"

"Ah, there's one of them!" cried Fanny. "Where do you come from, *Vergissmeinnicht?* Where do you come from kingfisher? Where's Jane?"

"I don't know," answered Jean Farou, politely.

"You haven't come from the village dressed like that, I hope?"

"The mechanic's costume is worn a good deal this year," said Jean in the same tone.

Calm as he was, he seemed to vibrate with impatient immobility; his blue linen costume exaggerated the blue of his eyes, and the wind lifted a flame of golden hair from his forehead.

"Admit that he's becoming a delightful boy," Fanny whispered softly to her husband.

"Very," Farou agreed briefly. "But what a way to dress himself! . . ."

"Yes, but listen. Funds are low. I'm waiting as long as possible before overhauling the boy's wardrobe. Truly you know he'll not have a shirt to his back by the end of the holidays."

"Don't wait any longer, Fanny. The 'Atalanta' stuff is sold at last. Buy him silk pants—in moderation."

He held out to her a check and a letter which she could not read.

"Is it English?"

"American, madame. Fifty."

"Thousand? . . ."

"Yep, and that's a good omen for 'The Stolen Grape.' Touch wood."

281

"Jean. Come here, Jean."

"I heard," said Little Farou from the distance. "Bravo, papa. Thank you, papa."

"Was it this morning, my Farou? while I was in the fields? Blessed be the hand that gives me my present."

All warm with contentment, she pushed back the black lock from her right eye, and bent down quickly to kiss the strong perfumed hand that still held the check and the letter from America. On the dry knuckles she saw greasy violet-colored stains, and she cried out, laughing like a child:

"Oh, you've been with Jane, you made her translate the letter. That's the ink of the machine which she keeps in her room. Caught!"

"That—" said Farou, looking at his dirty hands. "That? Good heavens, what an eye!"

"You can put it in your next play. I give it you for your Branc-Ursine."

She pealed with laughter and whipped Big Farou with a long stalk of flowering hemp. She pirouetted round him, a little breathless, agile and plump. She did not stop until she met the eye of Little Farou, hard and charged with scornful innocence.

"Jane was right," she thought, offended. "The child is getting impossible. . . ."

"Jane," she cried in a shrill voice.

"Ja-a-ne!"

"What do you want with her now?" grumbled Farou.

"I want her to come to the village with me. Sign your check Farou; I'm going to the local King's. . . . We'll bring back sweet champagne from the confectioner, and a hot cake. In fact we'll clear out the shop. . . . Ja-a-ne!"

Jane appeared, her hands over her ears. She wore a frock of lilac cotton, shrunk in the wash, but becoming to her tanned skin, and to her hair, which was lighter-hued than her forehead. She tried to insert a word between Fanny's cries.

"How—how money goes to your head, Fanny! . . . How . . . The butcher will hear you. . . ."

"I don't give a damn for him," shrilled Fanny. "I'll throw his eighteen hundred francs at him, like this, in one lump. Jean roll down to the garage and tell Fraisier to get out the car. . . . Oh, children, how good for us this is! Big Farou, you are an ace. Jane, what do you want?"

"Me? But—nothing . . . nothing at all. . . ."

"Do you hear her, Farou? Insist, Farou, insist on her wanting something."

She swung round with a jerk to take him to witness. Removed from this splashing, bubbling joy, he stood with head bent, the heavy brown curled locks interwoven with white, seeming to listen to a softer sound, to contemplate some more tranquil image.

"What is it? . . ." asked Fanny in a small voice.

Farou raised his eyes, bringing them back from a far journey.

"Be off, be off! And come back quickly. Already I'm getting one of those hungers. . . ."

They took down their big hats of white rush and yellow linen, and ran down the slope; Fanny pulled Jane by the hand, and Jane, giving at the shoulder, adapted herself gracefully, careful not to weigh heavy, careful not to stumble, supple and a little absent-minded. Farou watched them descend, his face still subdued to a gentleness that expressed in him the most natural uncultivated innocence. He heard his son's step and changed his expression.

"You aren't going with them?"

"No, papa."

He added:

"If you allow me."

The deferential formula came just late enough for Farou to be able to interpret it as veiled insolence. He raised his eyes toward his son, who sat crosswise on the wall, juggling with round pebbles, and would have spoken as roughly to him as to a woman. But he stopped short on looking more attentively at this stranger, his own issue, scarcely formed, but in build and attitude, as he carelessly

283

leaned over space, altogether virile, endowed indeed with that excess of virility which often emanates from a frail body and triumphs over its delicacy. Farou checked his anger and prudently abandoned it.

"What are you going to do?"

Jean Farou treated this with scorn.

"But . . . well, wait for them. They won't be gone long."

With an effort, Farou took his hand out of his pocket, to refute this. He changed his tone with meaning:

"No . . . I mean: what are you going to do?"

"Ah! . . . Well . . ." He tried the timid request like a weapon: "Will you let me go away . . . a long way? Will you find me . . . something, perhaps with your friends the Secrestats in the Argentine? . . ."

Farou turned his head toward the slope, where the yellow dress and the lilac dress had floated a moment before like two flowers whirling and embracing, and his handsome, mature man's face softened.

"That depends," he answered without enthusiasm. "That depends, naturally, upon the conditions in which I can . . . We may be able to plan and arrange such a distant visit for you."

Jean seized hold of this half-acquiescence.

"Of course! and anyhow there's no hurry. . . . If you'll let me, I'll make an appointment as soon as we return to Paris with the French Secrestats. There's the question of my military service, but I might have almost three years of South America and commercial life, before that."

He forced his young voice to exaggerate the precision, the speed of his words, in order that a certain weakness that had deadened and retarded his father's might be emphasized. Each of them, looking at the other, detested an aspect of humanity different from his own. Farou was offended at this blue metallic son, lit by gold, cut with sharp hard facets, and mysterious refractions. While Jean reddened if he so much as touched the thick softness of Big Farou, yielding, elastic, capricious, and as thoroughly deprived of a sense of the future as if he had been a pleasure-loving woman.

Farou constrained himself easily in silence, less easily in the gesture which raised his heavy arm to his son's shoulder.

"We could walk a little way down to meet them," he said.

"No. . . . No. . . ." protested Jean Farou to himself, revolted by his muscular burden. "No. . . . No. . . ."

Nevertheless he bore the weight of the arm with a confused sort of pain; the hairy finger joints hanging against his cheek, and their smell of brown skin, tobacco, and scented lotion undid his boy's proud heart again, and tormented him with a terrible longing to weep and kiss the pendent hand. . . .

But he denied himself, already knowing bitterly that what is allowable in a child does not outrun childhood. He suited his step to Farou's, and whenever the path grew too narrow, contracted himself, so that they might walk abreast.

5

"IMPOSSIBLE is too much to say. I was unnerved by the check. I exaggerated very much the other day. He's a poor little boy with nothing to do, and none of us pays as much attention to him as he deserves. . . . He's not impossible at all. He's even very nice. . . ."

"Jean, do you hear me?" said Fanny, aloud. "You are very nice."

He turned his head toward her vivaciously, gave a little smile and a nod of recognition, as if to an intruder, and returned to his active immobility.

"Jean, you won't be short, with four . . . no, with three suits from Brennan. I say three, because it's better to have three suits and an overcoat than— Be a love, Jean Farou, and get me my scissors!"

He bounded, fell in a ball on the scissors, gave them to Fanny, and with one leap regained his seat.

"Don't you agree, that it's better to have an overcoat? Without flattery, it was because of the cut of your clothes that Clara Cellerier said of you: 'That boy would look well in the saddle.' I imitate her pretty well, don't I, eh? . . . eh, Jean Farou? What are you looking at? But what are you looking at?"

"A brown caterpillar," said Jean.

He lied. His glance, of a burning blue, rested blindly on the yellow lichen along the wall. All ears, he listened to the expression of two voices talking on the first terrace, fifteen feet below, the words spoken dispersed unintelligibly on the wind. Fanny, sewing in her usual place on the threshold of the hall, could not even hear the murmur of voices. Jean measured the distance—two, three steps —which separated him from the brick parapet, and estimated the thickness of the coarse, scrunching gravel. He calculated also that at the end of the upper terrace an old hibiscus tree straddling the parapet would allow a head to lean down, invisibly wrapped in its foliage, toward the terrace below. Stress of concentration and calculation made his brown, ruddy face, dusted with freckles on the cheek-bones, look drawn; he compressed his lips and did not blink an eyelash. At last he took a deep breath as if about to jump, and exclaimed aloud in a child's voice:

"I'd love to hold your skein, Mamie, but it will cost you still another tie!"

Then he launched himself toward the hibiscus, soundlessly glided his head and shoulders under the leaves, allowing only his forehead and eyes to project over the wall.

Stupefied, her needle in the air, Fanny watched him. Round-eyed, with parted mouth, she betrayed her astonishment with the simplicity that amused Farou.

After a moment she rose, and Jean, hearing her, threw her an order with a gesture of his arm from behind, to stay quiet. Upon which, sticking her needle deliberately into the linen she was embroidering, she advanced on tiptoe, with tiny steps, and rejoined her stepson under the leaves of the tree.

Below, Farou was standing talking to Jane. A cloud, blown from the setting sun, of a false and sour rose, gave some vague color to his slack white clothing. Seating himself sidewise, with one leg cocked on the wall, he carried on a dialogue in staccato phrases, while he looked down on the thirsty valley. With one hand, he pushed back his heavy curls, and whistled, "Phew!" with an air of fatigue.

Fanny thought he was going to say, "This cursed heat!" or perhaps, "I'm still not through with that fourth act, then." She found him as usual, tired, handsome, and very dear to see.

Jane, in a lilac gown, held typewritten sheets in her hand. She approached Farou, and held out a page to him, which he pushed back laughing, no doubt protesting, "Oh no, enough of that!" But Jane insisted, and Farou, standing up, set her aside with a turn of the shoulder so familiar and so lacking in courtesy that Fanny recognized the gesture, a tramp's gesture, that Farou used to reject a tie, a comb, or a caress offered to him by a loving and conjugal hand.

To her great amazement, Jane showed no annoyance but leaned laughing on a ladder propped against the wall. She laughed heartily, her neck shortened, and raised her hands, shaking the fingers in the air; the sound of her laugh came up to the high terrace; and in the exclamation that she managed at last to make— "Oh, là, là, what a fib!"—Fanny recognized an intonation which did not remind her of Jane's voice.

"It's me she's imitating, my expression . . ."

She turned to the boy spying at her side. He was pressing with both hands on the edge of the wall to assure his immobility, and testifying to his power, his experience in watching, keeping silent, and understanding. He seemed neither surprised nor distressed, and he only caught Fanny's eye with the look of a master who teaches silence, and dignity of attitude, if not of act. . . .

Down below, Farou was taking Jane's merriment badly. She stopped laughing and restored to her countenance an expression of the most sincere and unbridled obstinacy. . . . With a nervous hand she pulled a little twig, and bit it, while Farou addressed her in a deep, slow voice, trailing menace, insolence, and studied invective in its wake. Then she cut him short, barked a few brief words in little bursts at him, twisted the twig she had been biting, flung it at Farou's nose, and made her way with a leisurely, somewhat theatrical step toward the staircase.

"Go, go—get back to your place," Jean Farou ordered precipitately in Fanny's ear.

The boy's hard fingers pushed Fanny to the deck-chair. When Farou emerged first from the top of the staircase, Fanny was sitting holding the thread of a hank of coarse red cotton, which Jean Farou at her feet was tangling, like a cat in play.

"Touching family group," rallied Farou.

His eye was yellow, clear, and hard.

"He's badly off his balance," thought Fanny.

She trembled, and groped painfully after her usual composure, bewildered at having possessed the face and heart-beats of a spy beneath the leaves of the hibiscus. At her feet, Jean Farou, his hands held out as a winder, began to sing in a shrill voice. "He exaggerates," thought Fanny, and she felt she ought to take him to task indignantly.— "How dare you?" But the child raised his eyes to her in a look so vigilant— "We're not through yet"—that she said nothing.

"Fanny," pursued Big Farou in a gentler voice, "it was silly, what I said just now. Don't heed it."

With a little pucker of the lips, she mastered the tears which had so far only moistened her beautiful, full eyes. She felt herself overwhelmed in experiencing for Farou only an adoration, a gratitude, untouched and inaccessible; she longed to excuse herself, to confess. . . .

"No, no . . ." she protested, in spite of the kneeling child, whose eyes never left hers.

But Jane in her turn appeared on the terrace, and Fanny's emotion gave place suddenly to an alert attention that imposed silence on the deeps of her being. She recovered her agility of movement and word, and secretly clapped hands at herself.

"Ah, there you are!" she exclaimed.

"What's the matter with me?" demanded Jane. "Were you waiting for me? I wasn't far off."

"Yes . . . yes . . ." said Fanny lightly, shaking her head and her black lock of hair.

She looked curiously at Jane.

"She, too? . . . with Farou? But how? since when? . . . Is it true? . . . I'm not suffering. It's such a trifle. . . . It's true that I'm used to it. . . . Pretty Vivica who danced in the third act of 'The Stolen Grape' . . . and, lately, little Asselin. . . . These things don't last long with Farou. . . . "

But she remembered Jane's pallor, her distracted, unhappy moods, her vehement tears, all that; what then?

"Oh yes, the day when I read her the letter in which it appeared that Farou was 'devoting himself' to little Asselin."

Jane sat down, opened a book that was lying about on the battered iron table, made a pretense of reading, then lifted her face to the gray sky laden with rain.

"My dears, how quickly the end of summer comes! Jean, it would be so kind if you would give me my little sleeveless wrap which I left . . . oh . . . which I left . . ."

"I know," said Jean, letting go of the hank and running.

Fanny, attentive, resounding with new shocks, heard Jane with amazement.

"But it's *my* book that she's got there! . . . But it's *my* stepson she's ordering about, it's in *my* house that . . ."

She felt her blood beating gently and then more quickly under her ears, constricting her collar, and she remembered a time when she was passionate and jealous. Restlessly she fixed her eye on Farou.

"Isn't he going to—oughtn't he to say something?"

But he dreamed, his stomach leaning against the brick wall, large, heavy, simple, and preoccupied. He turned his head a little toward Jane.

"Is it any good, that old book?"

"So so," she answered, without moving.

Jean Farou brought the little sleeveless garment, put it round

289

Jane's shoulders as if he were afraid of being burned, and vanished. The noise of open cupboards and moving spoons heralded the dinner hour; no one spoke, and Fanny could have called for help, could have begged that mistaken ignorance should be restored to her, or that there might be anger, shouts, a sort of battle. . . . Farou yawned, and announced, "I'm going to wash my hands"; and Jane, springing to her feet, assumed her most girlish air.

"Oh, the hothouse peaches in the refrigerator! they'll be too cold."

She ran, enveloping Fanny, as she passed, in a large, light kiss, planted anywhere. Fanny received it without horror and with no displeasure.

6

S H E slept little, though she hardly moved. The first daylight showed her Farou sleeping in the larger of the two beds. In her weariness she looked at him without thinking either of him or of herself. She noticed that he had indeed a large nose separating his eyes widely from each other. "People say it's a sign of memory." A fresh breath of air was enough to make her shiver, and she was just putting her pretty pajama-leg out from the bedclothes to go and nestle in the other bed against a large immovable body, warm and unconscious. But she resisted her mechanical impulse, drew back her leg and lay down again.

"How absurd I am. Truly, you would think Farou was deceiving me for the first time. He's had mistresses since me—mistresses and mistresses!—I should think so!"

She counted them over in a whisper and, though she was still cold, counting them nearly made her feel cheerful. A vague footstep across the ceiling, a stifled feminine cough, told her that someone else was watching or had awakened with the dawn.

"It's she, I'm certain it's she. She hasn't slept, either. She's waiting for the day, she's waiting . . . Besides, she's a girl who does admirable duty in waiting, in spite of her little explosions. What is she waiting for? All the same, we are a reasonable woman. We know perfectly well that Farou . . ."

But her docile mood at that moment underwent a quiet shock that reversed a short period of time and made her relive an August afternoon, a siesta after a heavy meal, the dream of the storm and the tense certainty in her mind that Jane was furtively weeping. After the dream, reality, like the dream, had shown her Jane weeping where she stood, hiding away a tear. One tear, a single tear gathered and extinguished between two fingers like a tiny ember. . . . Among so many vexed or voluptuous tears, the only tear whose pearl-weight Fanny would have wished to ignore all her life, the only tear also which could create Fanny anew, and restore her to youth, revitalized among the lucid and breathable airs of unhappiness.

She got up quietly, dexterous and as full of precautions as if she were moving in the dark. Farou sighed in his sleep and turned over, dragging the bedclothes after him like a huge folded wave.

Twenty times, malicious gossip or Farou's own carelessness had forced Fanny to imagine this man's body wrestling for its pleasure, taming a soft woman's body. . . . Every recess of her memory hid souvenirs of little, bitter tears, of sleeplessness, of letters extracted and then restored in secret to Farou. Christian names, unknown handwritings, pencil drawings half erased . . .

The revelations came quickly, she could discount them, and put a good face on it while she waited for them.

"I don't know anything more worthy of admiration than Fanny Farou's arrogant indulgence of her tom-cat of a husband!" exclaimed Clara Cellerier at the top of her young, sharp voice of an old lady.

"It's scarcely difficult to be arrogant and even indulgent when one reigns alone over something, even if it's a betrayal. . . . Since when am I no longer the only one in my household to suffer for Farou?"

With a turn of her arm she gathered up the rope of black hair, which seemed tiresome to her.

"Oh, this! three snips of the scissors . . ."

She envied the short hair, silver, honey-soft, barley-pale, which the wind fluttered on Jane's brow.

"Well, Fair-Hair must be finding the time long up there. She cries so easily. I must be a nuisance to her. . . ."

She felt her cheeks reddening, pressed a clenched fist against her teeth and shot a furious look at the sleeping man, whom the gray morning flushing little by little to rose, did not disturb. As he lay on his back, his mouth fell roundly open, and his whole face expressed great candor. A scornful gaiety suddenly seized Fanny.

"Couldn't you swear he was going to sing!"

She looked in detail at Farou's large nose, at the flat space cleft by a vertical wrinkle, that separated his eyebrows, at his short, straight lashes. The jaw and throat in relaxation began to show signs of age, but the face itself, strengthened by an enigmatic happiness, the round treelike neck, the tangled nest of hair, a peaceful triviality of expression, reclaimed it from mythology and from the face of a faun. Fanny turned away from the parted mouth.

"He smells of the zoo, when he's fasting, like everyone else. . . ."

Farou's large hand, palm uppermost, held itself out at the end of an arm with twisting veins. It opened toward Fanny as if in a homage of trust, and to her surprise she could have melted in tenderness on this nailed flower.

"Ah, I must beware of everything now! . . . I must hold myself in, to think, to decide . . ."

She went with silent steps toward the bathroom, attentive, stiff, and dully infatuated with her new sorrow.

7

"Don't stay there, Jean. . . . Jean get up. . . . What's the matter? If you weren't ill, I shouldn't have believed that anyone could let go of themselves in such a fashion. Jean! You fell? Did you fall?"

Fanny dared not shake him, but she was indignant that the child should lie there conscious on the bank by the side of the road, stretched out, fair and still, like an assassinated faun. His long slender body lay on the edge of the slope, hair and feet hanging over. The strange greenish color of his face declared a pallor under the brown and the little moons of freckles. A blue moist gaze traveled upward as far as Fanny.

"Fall . . ." he murmured. "You may well say so, Mamie. Yes I fell."

She lifted an inert hand that did not clasp her own. "Where are you hurt?"

"Nowhere, thanks."

He closed his eyes and took a deep breath. Fanny, looking him over doubtfully in search of some trace of his fall, such as a little blood, in spite of herself began to question the inertia, the languor, the very pallor of this child impregnated with secrets.

"You were a very long time in the village, Mamie. . . ."

He spoke with closed eyes and a level voice.

"I like that. . . . With all I had to buy! . . . Anyhow, how do you know I've been a long time? . . . Besides, the post wasn't sorted, I had to wait. . . . I couldn't possibly know I should find you on the road like a flower mown down. . . . And then there's news! I've brought back for Farou— Ah, that wakens you, I see. . . ."

Jean sat up easily, but a sort of violet stain persisted beneath his eyelids.

"A telegram from the Vaudeville. . . . Don't look as if you'd seen it before Farou. . . . 'My dear master, return immediately. Necessity puts The Impossible Innocence' "—

"God, how I hate that title," muttered Jean.

" '—in rehearsal. We open first November. Affectionate admiration. Silvester.' "

"Has he put 'My dear master' and 'affectionate admiration?' Oh, là là!"

"What do you mean? That's right."

"Extremely right. And the first 'novelty' turn promised to Trick and Bavolet by contract? What scamps' juggling has there been this time between them and Silvester? . . ."

"They aren't ready."

"Not ready? As if they were a gang, not to be ready—those two?" He lay back and made his conjectures in a biting tone.

"Everyone knows more about things than I," thought Fanny.

"Well? Are we leaving?" asked Little Farou after a silence.

"Yes. . . . But don't let's talk of leaving— Here's Fraisier. . . . Fraisier, put my parcels in. . . . If the master isn't working, ask him to come so far to meet me; if he is working don't interrupt him."

"He's not working," whispered Jean, behind the chauffeur's back.

"What do you say?"

Fanny stared into her stepson's face so roughly that he lowered his eyes, and got to his feet, as if to avoid a blow. She eyed him as he stood, defeated, ashamed, and newly stained with the opinion he had offered.

"If he's not working he'll come down here. I'll rest on this bank; you know he doesn't like sick people. Since you feel better, go and wash and make yourself tidy. I don't care about his seeing you in that condition."

The boy obeyed, and climbed the slope. He was fighting against the breathlessness that remained from his fainting fit. In his fair hair he brought back sand and lumps of soil like one of the young dead returning to earth.

Fanny felt no kindness toward him until he was out of sight.

"Poor little thing. One is so quickly a cad, a hero, or a desperado, at his age."

Proud of having gaged him, she sat down to rest on the wooden bench on the slope. The sky, washed only half-clean by the morning rain, was just opening to the setting sun; stretched cloud and mountain burned with the same bronze violet, a violet that rivaled clematis and wallflower in depth of color. Farou came down to her, while she still looked at it.

"What is it, my Fanny? You aren't ill? . . . I wasn't working," he added. "So little now is needed to finish it. . . . There are things one can't write; they make themselves, alone like this, written in the air, sung in the train, invented at the same time as a play or scene."

He made hieroglyphics on the sky with his finger, and Fanny recognized in his yellow eyes, in his appeased features, as much as in the healthy and luxurious fragrance of the body bending above her own the utter grace that bathed Farou all over after love-making. She steeled herself and did not burst into tears.

"Still, they must be written quickly, my Farou. Here. . . ."

He read the telegram, snorted two little "Well, well's," vindictive and pleased, then knitted his eyebrows.

"I shall not have Charles Boyer, then. Bernstein will never release him."

"But Bernstein is so sweet—"

"That's nothing to do with it. Sweet—sweet—this habit of talking about Bernstein as if he were a bullfinch or a kitten! . . . Sweet! . . . Jane!" he cried, raising his head.

"What do you want with Jane?"

"I want with her, that we go back to Paris, of course. . . . A telegram to Blanchar—telegram to Marsan—oh, and that cursed little Carette . . . to play the barman. Quinson has his address. . . ."

He foraged in his hair with all his talons, and suddenly there was a lull.

"It's going to begin again, that quarreling about parts. . . . Thirty names in all: no one . . . Jane! What on earth does she do, that woman, when one wants her? Still tidying her hair, or making sweets in a little pink apron. . . . Domestic angel . . . good genius of the vacuum-cleaner. . . . Jane!"

He radiated natural ferocity and ingratitude. Fanny listened to him, dumb and overwhelmed for the first time. The yellow eye came to rest on her.

"Well, Fanny, you don't look as if you had any idea that it's our year and perhaps other things that are going to be played with here. . . . Trick and Bavolet moved back. . . . God exists, upon my word! Bestir yourself, my girl! Can we catch a train tonight? Jane!"

"But you don't want to make us take the train at three o'clock in the morning, do you, Big Farou? A train without couchettes and full of Swiss. . . . Isn't that right, Fanny?"

Jane ran up to them quickly but without hurrying herself.

"At a pinch, you could take it alone—"

He burst out naïvely:

"Alone? Since when must I travel alone, when it isn't necessary? And dawn at Paris, the house shut up, the gas to turn on, and all the rubbish. . . . Oh, well, do as you like. . . . Women, really! . . . I'm a very good-tempered man, after all!"

He lost patience as he did every time he gave way, and went up to the house with a large gesture that repudiated both women.

"Let him be," said Jane in a low voice. "I'm going to book seats on the day train tomorrow. Tomorrow evening at eight o'clock we shall be at the house, and from nine o'clock till midnight he will talk with Silvester. What would he do with his afternoon, at Paris? We always have to arrange for his good in spite of himself; he's like all the others. . . . In any event, he won't have Yvonne de Bray. . . . Ah, but he ought to have had Yvonne de Bray!"

She laughed excitedly.

"A little more, with you, Fanny, and he would have pinned us down to leaving tonight. . . . 'Yes, my dear!' . . . Fanny, I must ask for Fraisier again to take the telegrams. I'll type them at once. Altogether, we've each one trunk to pack, and Farou's. If we could get Jean, I should send him to the station. . . . No, I shall go more quickly than he. . . . The washerwoman is late with the laundry. Fraisier can collect it while I'm at the post."

She calmed down and put on a prudent, boyish look:

"Fanny, I want you to have a marvelous dress for the general rehearsal. Clear the decks for action. . . . See my nostrils quiver!"

Fanny, passive, leaned over the valley where the first colchicums were coming out after the rain. The red heather, mown by a ray of sun, soaked up the traveling light.

"It's odd," she said at last, "I thought I hated this country. And now, when I know we shall never come back, I find it endearing."

She tried to summon energy, dissimulation, but found only a degrading lassitude.

"Don't regret it, Fanny. You will have lovelier things than this. You mustn't listen to Farou; next year—next year . . ."

Leaning against Fanny, she lowered her tone with a rancor that did not seem feigned. Fanny detected in Jane's voice a note like that of an accomplice, a malice aimed only at Farou. She accepted the support of the arm which offered itself to her—a sinuous arm, slender as a serpent's neck at the wrist, hollow at the bend, soft, adroit, officious.

"This too serviceable arm . . . But if I had to loathe all the women who have been intimate with Farou, I should shake hands only with men."

She took courage again, in abandoning her scruples and satisfied her self-respect by addressing Jane rather formally:

"Jane, it would be very good of you to find me the inventory of the furniture at the Villa Déan. . . . Old Father Déan is so caviling."

Jane held her by the elbow as they climbed the steepest part of the slope, and answered, "Yes, yes," with an eye on the study door, from which issued a mighty noise of Farou, of cupboards slammed shut, of the table scraping the parquet and the minor complainings of a servant found guilty.

The evening and most of the night passed clamorously. At eleven o'clock Farou took it into his head to alter a scene of his fourth act, and to dictate it in the hall. His voice tossing from one bare wall to another, his resolved air of an inspired fool, his heavy steps hammering a promenade upon the groaning boards of the floor, the pious docility of Jane, who was taking down in shorthand, ousted

297

Fanny, and sent her for refuge to the terrace. The damp, the stillness allowed an odor of reeds and the sickly vanilla of the budleyas
to hang suspended in the motionless night air.

Before the open door giant moths whirled in a gray cloud, and
Jean Farou beat down the largest of them with great sweeps of his
hat. Sometimes he jumped vertically upward, as cats do, and Fanny's
attention wandered from this dance of a graceful child at his task,
impromptu, respected, and difficult. She exhorted herself to feel a
coward's dread, and turned away her face whenever Farou's
countenance, traversing the rectangle of light lying on the terrace,
recalled her to her duty of sorrow.

"Another Farou play . . . Manna, uncertain . . . What shall I do
at Paris? Is this to be a destruction of everything for me, this episode of him and Jane; or is it simply a sickness which will cure
itself, as she came, without my noticing? . . ."

A hot cheek sought her pendent hand. Jean Farou had curled
himself noiselessly on the ground beside her.

"What do you want?" she whispered in a low, irritated voice.

"Nothing," replied an invisible mouth.

"Are you suffering?"

"Naturally I suffer," confessed the shadow discreetly.

"That's good."

"Have I complained?"

"You're nothing but a little malefactor."

"Ah! Mamie, you have no sense of loyalty."

The cheek, damp now, pressed against her hand.

"No," breathed Fanny proudly. She felt in herself a point of firm-
ness, a hard little corn of solitary strength, and she repudiated
lament as much as conspiracy.

"What are all these little nuisances? Get away, get away!"

The jerk of her head undid her hair, and she felt it slide down
over her back, cool and snakelike.

"You are truly lucky, Mamie," sighed the shadow.

She rattled the gravel with her foot.

"We're not talking about my luck. We're not talking about me at all. You won't manage to turn the conversation in my direction. You are sixteen and a half, you are in love, you are unhappy; everything is in order; so set yourself to rights."

"Set yourself to rights! Set yourself to rights! Ah, Mamie, do you really find that a reasonable piece of advice?"

They whispered violently but with extreme caution, insured against indiscretion by the coming and going of Farou, who now and then crossed the threshold, mumbling words into the night: "M'm . . . M'm . . . *Control yourself, my good Didier. . . .* m'm . . . *become again what you were before this abominable day. . . .* No, that's idiotic. . . . *Become again the fine little man who had the courage to tell me yesterday. . . .*"

He took no notice of Jane as he dictated, and marched up to Fanny as if he were going to crush her, without noticing. She did not like these rare crises of work in public. They seemed like a form of exhibitionism.

"*Control yourself, my good Didier, I implore you! It is not yourself speaking, it is she, who by your mouth*—m'm . . . *I implore you* . . . Oh! that's enough then! Why did you let me dictate that, Jane?"

"What? This?"

"'I implore you' and 'Control yourself.' And have you ever called anyone 'my good Didier'? . . . In fact, though, I believe you'd be capable of it. . . . Say a little: 'My good Farou!'"

With strained ear, Fanny and Jean caught Jane's strangled, unhappy little laugh.

"You've no wish, then, to call me 'my good Farou'?"

"None. . . ."

"*Didier, I implore*— Let us remember that the Vaudeville is a sort of theater of the quarter. . . . *I implore you, control yourself. . . .* At three-quarters past eleven, everyone in a theater is full of uplift. . . . *Become again what you were yesterday,* etc., etc. The rest is to follow the manuscript. Good night! Fanny, I'm going up!" cried Farou.

Behind him, Jane arranged the pages, piling them up on their edges, and dusted her typewriter for the journey. She was pale and neutral, like a tired employee, and Fanny could discover no sign in her of secret triumph, or even of a habit of love.

"Shall I never think of anything but her, now?" Fanny asked herself fearfully.

At the same moment an anxious look from Jane came to meet her invisible glance, and she rose, leaving Jean Farou gathered into a disconsolate little heap.

"Are you going up, Fanny?"

"Oh, well, yes. . . . I've had enough already of tomorrow's journey. . . . And those Paris people we shall have to see again. . . . Farou kept you very late."

"It's my job. But it's unbelievable what a fuss he makes about that little end of a scene. . . . It grows childish. . . ."

She defended even while accusing him, but with a bad grace. She slipped her arm through Fanny's.

"Fanny, why is it never you who take my arm, but always I who take yours? I'm tired, Fanny—"

"With good reason! Since morning what a rôle you've filled!"

"A rôle," thought Fanny, further, "of housemaid, postman, secretary, steward, and half an hour of love—I'm liberal—into the bargain. . . . True, I perceive perfectly the burdens of her situation, but the advantages!"

She felt she was being a little coarse, and it cheered her up completely. But her optimism failed when, lying not far from Farou, who slept with the soft whistling breath of a kettle, she had in front of her the bluish screen of the uncurtained window. Empty two days before, flushed with gold at the moment when the eyes between their rebel lids draw slowly backward to the enchantments of the brain, the nocturnal window ornamented itself with a wreathing frost of images, which Fanny watched, lying motionless in a haycock of black hair, and rocked by a sick man's hope:

"Is it only that? Is it nothing but that?"

8

AT THE moment of departure she was the least cheerful, but they were all accustomed to Fanny's sensitive awkwardnesses, a lingering in station entrances, a faint embarrassment with the steps of motorcars. When the time came to hand over the keys of the Villa Déan to the caretaker, Fanny seeming to awake, tied the ends of a scarf under one ear, and buried herself down to the end of her nose in the felt hat, which her great knot of hair pushed out of shape. She came and went with uncertain step on the terrace; she touched the lock of the closed door.

"No, Fanny, no; you haven't forgotten anything," cried Jane to her.

"I should like," said Fanny to herself, "I should like to begin the summer again, fortified by what I know. I should see the house differently, and the country, and people, and myself. Already the empty chairs have different faces; this great building is less ugly; the plan of the rooms and of the two stories grows clear to me, as if the façade of the house had slipped away. . . ."

She heard laughter, and saw Jean Farou, covered amusingly with the coats piled one on top of another, walking away comically like a rick of straw. She copied their laughter, stumbled, and twisted her ankle.

"Always your butter feet!" scolded Farou.

"You would do better to give her your hand," retorted Jane.

She came last, looking very pretty in a girl's pale blue silk waterproof. Farou halted to wait for her, thrust his hand into the white leather belt that held Jane's trim waist, and hurried her:

"Gee-up, gee-up! Kh-kh, little blue horse!" He had an air, as always at the end of his summer holidays, of wearing borrowed clothes, his waistcoat and coat open, his hat pushed on the back of his head. On his forehead curled the thick tuft of hair, that might have adorned a bull's crest. The missing crease in his trousers, his careless tie annoyed Jane; but Farou, his eye clear, laughed, showed his teeth, and succeeded very well in making light of fashion with coquetry.

"Kh-kh, little horse!"

"What innocence!" marveled Fanny. "And what did she say to him, just now? That he would do better to give me a hand. . . . How often in the past three years—no, four years—has she made remarks of that kind? I paid no attention to them. . . . 'You would do better to give her your hand. . . .'"

Spider-webs barred the path; the sun of half past seven, still low and ruddy, had not yet dried the dew. A sere and golden autumn licked the feet of the little mountains like a careless flame. On her way Fanny leaned over the hedge of the kitchen garden and picked purple asters she would have disdained the day before.

In the train Jane, wanting to fit up a "Fanny Corner," unrolled the light kasha rug and slid a paper-knife between the pages of a brand-new novel. But Fanny desired neither care nor slumber.

"I'm all right, thank you, I'm all right," she said in an abstracted voice.

Her beautiful eyes wandered, like some gentle animal's, over the fields. A violet arabesque upon the wings of her scarf combined with the vivid rouge of her lips to blanch her sun-browned pallor still further.

Jean Farou, on the platform, promised to leave the steering wheel in the hands of Fraisier, promised not to wander about after dark, promised with celerity and bad faith whatever anyone asked him to promise.

"What paper do you want, Fanny?"

"None for the moment, thank you. I'm doing very well."

"And the best part of it is that I'm not doing at all badly," she continued to herself.

The first little stations of Franche-Comté flashed past the train, laden with vines and their neat, black grapes. Farou read the papers after his fashion:

"They don't announce it. . . . No, they don't announce it, yet."

"What?" asked Fanny, startled.

"That it's gone into rehearsal, of course. Where are you wandering?"

"Me? You know what happens to me, when I'm made to get up at five o'clock. . . ."

A curve of the line gathered under Fanny's eye, in the distance, the hill she had left and the square villa she would never see again. She leaned out to watch until it disappeared, one of the few houses since their marriage which they had occupied for two summers.

9

"HAs he had luncheon? I'm sure he hasn't lunched!"

"But of course. He said he'd have something brought into the theater. . . . As if Farou were accustomed to let himself starve! . . . You make me laugh."

"It doesn't matter then that he hasn't gone to bed for three nights until four o'clock!"

"Well, that's normal."

"Ah, what a Spartan you are! The Spartan spouse, that's what you ought to be called. One would never think it, to look at you. On the other hand, there's a nobility, a grandeur about this austerity, this scorn of everything material. . . ."

They were not yet so far gone as to beg "a little corner with the dressmakers," but they craned religious faces, anguished, dedicated to Farou, across Fanny, and already exhibited the cynical ecstasy that prowls about dramatic authors and actors with reputations. They did not mention Farou; they said "he," or even better, "the master."

"Well, what about it?" thought Fanny. "He has written a play;

303

yes, he's done another play. If he were a cabinetmaker, or if he had invented an electric brush, a fly-trap, a serum, would they be here, worshiping as if at a Nativity? . . ."

She lifted her rather plump chin, bridling a little, and was silent, so that these importunate beggars might go. But even then their zeal paid no attention to her.

"Is it at all in the same vein as 'Atalanta' or 'The House Without Women'?"

"That would be looking backward, wouldn't it? Mademoiselle Aubaret said to me, the day before yesterday, that . . ."

"Ah, really, Jane, you said the day before yesterday . . ."

Fanny turned toward Jane her Paris smile, rouged and full-lipped, and Jane, who shone golden in the corner of the room, was extinguished instantly.

"Who knows nothing, says nothing, Fanny. The master leaves me, like you, in complete darkness. But Madame Cellerier has ears everywhere!"

Clara Cellerier, smoking like a manly schoolboy, whistled, "Phew." A hat of plaited straw, like a little coal-scuttle, with no brim, the only misfortune in her black and gray costume, gave her a chin which Fanny would not have known as hers. The old actress dressed herself audaciously with the touch of provincial bravura that she had imposed for thirty years upon the public of the Comédie Française. On the day in question she had brought to Fanny's, one of those young women of the theater, expert at telephoning early in the morning to a playwright, at meeting him in a lift, at losing their voice under his regard, at kissing his hand, with a clumsy, brusk kiss, and at dying of shame afterward. Clara Cellerier's protégée hoped ardently in the shadow that Farou would come in to dinner. She confined herself, dumbly, to afflicting her warm golden countenance with a consternation that was near tears when she learned that Farou had hardly slept, eaten, or come home, for a week past.

"You will learn what it is, child, you will see what it is, this fever of last rehearsals," Clara Cellerier promised her.

"Oh, madame! . . . I should be so happy if I might learn. . . . The least occasion for employing me—"

Fanny considered her, with a courtesy, soft, cold, and familiar.

"I know the type. She will probably get her little part; she's so obstinate. . . ."

Jane did not rise to remove an empty port glass from the hands of the candidate.

A few women were waiting until it was time to go and dine.

"They'll go away," thought Fanny, "when they find it convenient to go home or to join their friends at a restaurant. They'll go away saying they've had 'a charming half-hour with the Farous.' . . . I don't like this lawyer, nor this great dressmaker, nor Cousin Farou, who thinks it her duty whenever she comes here to make eyes and plaster herself with rouge which she wipes off again on the Métro stairs afterward. . . . What a bore my house is! And the furniture— one wouldn't want it for a scene from a second act at the Scala! I must . . ."

A sort of bird-woman, metallic green, with nervous, exposed legs, crossed the gloomy square room. A comic star of the music hall, the bird-woman burned to play in drama or in comedy. Her little face—like the face of a child of the poor—seemed, even when powdered and rouged, to be the most negligible accessory of her acrobat's body. She strutted like a feather-legged pigeon, obsessed by her habit of peacocking across a huge stage dragging dappled trains and a foam of plumage, and, by a trick, of making jump at each step a little muscle cultivated in the shape of a heart upon her sailor's calf.

She seized Fanny's hands between her green gloves, gave a sigh, and a distinguished groan; and her condoling exit roused a little gaiety again.

"The old hen," said Clara Cellerier. "And when you think that it's she, very likely, who will create 'New Skin,' Farou's next play!"

"She wants a receipt for it," said Fanny.

"But it isn't signed," said Jane.

The young woman from the theater moved grievously upon her chair.

"Put on your cape, child, I'm going to take you away," Clara Cellerier ordered her. The young woman from the theater took a few steps with head bent as if going into exile, and Clara Cellerier took Fanny's head between her two hands, like an egg, in order to kiss her forehead.

"My dear Fanny, what have you done with your nonchalance?"

"My nonchalance?"

"Yes. Your—what shall I say? Your pliable amiability—what a pretty old-fashioned word—your detachment from everything? . . . I see you now, very much awake? It's evident that these last days are putting you to the rack. . . . But what a relief, after the triumph! Beautiful eyes, full of care . . ."

With her palm, she gently closed Fanny's eyelids, which opened again after the caress.

"The sharp old thing! she sees everything. . . ."

Fanny contemplated the bold face of the old society woman, her precise, hard makeup which severely reprehended flowing lines, her hat of plaited straw, her girlish black dress. . . . She was about to reply at random when Farou entered. As if wounded, the young woman from the theater closed her eyes, parted her lips and put her hand to her throat. Farou's first look was for her. Faint, dusty in patches, his brow damp, his shirt collar twisted, he emerged from his rehearsal as if from a boxing match in a basement, or from a fall down the cellar steps. But at the sight of the young woman from the theater, he lit up with a smile of convalescence, feeble, happy, and rejuvenated in a few minutes by leaps and bounds.

"What a condition!" sighed Clara Cellerier.

Farou snapped his fingers impatiently at her. He stared at the young woman of the theater and fumbled for her name.

"Pour him out some port," breathed Clara Cellerier in Fanny's ear.

Fanny shook her head and with a tilt of the head indicated Jane, who was bruskly crushing sugar into the yokes of raw eggs, and mixing them with marsala.

306

"Rascal," whispered Clara, "she doesn't appear to be amused by what she's doing there, Mademoiselle Aubaret!"

They exchanged a laugh which humiliated Fanny a little, and Farou spoke at last:

"Good day, everyone! . . . I ask your pardon, Clara, I'm dead with fatigue. But this child here, this little one . . . Let me see . . . I only know that she—the little—"

He held the hand of the young woman from the theater by the tip of the little finger and swung a pretty, bare arm without hindrance.

"The little Inès Irrigoyen," breathed Clara Cellerier.

"Pretty name for a blonde!" said Farou.

"But it's mine," confessed the young woman, wavering.

"Good! Good; we'll overlook that. . . . But what are you all doing, standing up like this?"

"We're going, we're going," said Clara. "In another moment."

Her excellent move of a false leave-taking had brought to their feet and then chased away the loiterers, even Cousin Farou. Behind them, Clara repeated, pawing the ground in one place:

"Let us go, let us go. . . . We must run away . . . in another moment. . . ."

"It went well?" demanded Fanny.

An angry memory knotted Farou's eyebrows, and his yellow eyes threatened an absent horde.

"Yes, yes. . . . Ah, the camels! All the same they were admirable . . . they will be admirable . . . especially—"

"Especially who?" asked Clara greedily.

He threw a glance of professional distrust at her. "Nearly all of them were admirable."

"How lucky they are!" risked the fair disciple. "Three lines in a play by you, master, would be a great part."

He laughed maliciously at her, with a little snort that conveyed that he wasn't to be taken in. Fanny knew this smile, rather like a darky's, this candid-looking grimace, with wrinkled nose and bared teeth, which Farou abused in his photographs and in his interesting tête-à-têtes.

"Three lines? Would you like them?"

As if seized with vertigo the young woman called Inès seized hold of Clara's hand and held her breath.

"Three lines—and a naught beside the three? The little part of the secretary? Well? well? . . . What's this horror, Jane?"

He pushed away the glass that Jane's hand was holding out to him.

"Still your muck of raw eggs? Give that to a consumptive, my dear. A little port, if you please."

He drank and changed his tone.

"Mademoiselle . . . Inès, you will please remember that the rehearsal is at one o'clock exactly," he said coldly. "Favier has the part; he'll send it to you. Mademoiselle Biset threw it up this afternoon."

"Threw it up?" repeated Clara briskly. "My dear friend, in what age are we living? Threw it up? Biset throw up a part?"

"Yes. As a matter of fact, I chucked it into the air for her, if you prefer that."

Clara drew herself up like a soldier. "Yes, indeed, I prefer that. For the honor of the art of the theater, I prefer that. . . . Will the general rehearsal be postponed, Farou? No? You come out on the day fixed? That's splendid. Come, child. How happy you've made her, dear master."

She hurried the fair young woman away, the latter paying some attention to her departure, stumbling a little, stammering, and clapping her hands like a child on the threshold of the open door.

"Not bad, not bad," estimated Farou, pulling off his tie and his collar. "She has that deficiency in naturalness which the part needs."

"There is also the concierge's daughter," insinuated Jane from the back of the room.

Fanny sought her with an astounded eye. She found her pale, her eyes dark and brilliant.

"You," answered Farou tranquilly, "you can go and tell the maid to run me a bath, and tell her to put out my shirt and shoes. And keep your theatrical gifts for jobs of that kind."

Jane vanished without a word, but she slammed the door noisily.

"What a way to speak to her! . . ." said Fanny, embarrassed.

"Don't worry yourself about it, Fanny-my-puppet!" He lay down, bare-necked, in the hollow of the divan and closed his eyes. He was exhausted, and sure of himself, and victorious in his repose.

"Are you going to eat?" asked Fanny in a small voice.

"Certainly I'm going to eat."

"Will you dine?"

"No. I shall be too tired if I dine; I should fall asleep. . . . I shall get something to eat, down there."

"Are you pleased?"

"Pleased enough."

He limited himself to the brief phrase, and she did not insist further. What was she wanting to know? She knew certain scenes in the play, a surprising climax at the end of the second act, which she did not much like. Farou had asked her opinion of it, with affected indifference. She felt constrained and more than ever a stranger in her husband's professional life.

"Look at us. . . . Nearly twelve years of marriage, and such an awkwardness between us, such a stiffness in the hinges. . . ."

"You look charming, at this moment."

She started and hurriedly smiled at the beautiful yellow eyes fixed on hers.

"I thought you were asleep, Farou."

"You look charming, but you have a sad little air. Perhaps, at bottom, you are sad."

He raised a hand, and let it fall limp on the divan.

"What an odd moment to choose, Farou—"

"Fanny, my dear, what makes you think we choose? . . . I've come out of a wilderness," he said, getting up and stretching his arms. "Those people, down there . . . There's a man who can only play his chief scene if he shows his right profile. If I make him change sides, he becomes hopeless. There's a woman who plays a

scene of despair with her hair cropped and stuck down with glue.
. . . If you saw her head rolling about on her lover's knees like a
billiard ball—oh, no! . . . And Silvester, above all—what a cage of
animals! . . . Now you have a delightful face, like a human being."

He put his heavy hands on Fanny's shoulders and delighted himself with her white face, and its dark eyelids, smooth and curved
like a Turk's. She let him contemplate her with an emotion profound and agreeable as some luxurious sorrow. The parquet creaked
and told Fanny that Jane had just come in. "I like to learn," said
Farou without turning, "that you sometimes know how to shut a
door quietly, Jane."

He received no answer. Leaving Fanny, he advanced mischie-
vously upon Jane.

"Well, benevolent sprite of the Dundee Marmalade, you are
calmer now, it appears."

Overflowing with fatigue, he laughed a little drunkenly, and
avenged himself for the endless arguments, the stifled outbursts in
the show, and behind the stage. . . .

"It seems to me that you do not appreciate fair actresses—eh,
Jane?"

Fanny ran after him and pulled him back as if he were leaning
over an abyss. "Farou, be quiet!" she begged. She inspected Jane,
Jane exasperated, singularly pale, insulting.

"I'm going to give myself trouble," said Farou, very loud.

And Jane gathered herself up as if fearing a blow, she were trying already to give it back by parrying it with her fair forehead
and cloudy hair. An unrecognizable grimace distorted the childish
curve of her mouth, and her expression became spiteful and
wretched.

"Jane!" cried Fanny, holding out her arms. Her cry, her gesture,
shook the taut body, whose contraction of hostility woke in Fanny
the memory of a young Fanny of other days, bullied by Farou and
resembling this enemy, this valorous woman, blanched with a
leaden pallor.

"Go!" Fanny ordered her husband. "Yes, indeed, go. You've

things to do outside. And another time vent your ill temper on me, if you please, not on others. Not on others, in front of me. . . . You —you are impossible, before a play. In three days you will be—you will be much better."

She stammered slightly and felt her chin trembling. For a long time now she had not known what it was to be angry, and even in fighting against herself she smiled vaguely, as certain animals smile, charmed from their proper anger. Farou was mistaken in this smile, and gave way with the grace of a guilty man.

"Frightful," he sighed, "I know I'm frightful. What a brute!"

He underlined the word and repeated it in a tone of banal complaisance. Fanny drew breath again and compressed her lips to stop her chin's trembling.

"Jane, will you be so good as—" he began in a softened voice.

But Fanny cut short his words.

"No, not this evening. Tomorrow, everything will go better. Be off to your rehearsal and sharpen your claws on Pierre or Paul, on Silvester or the program-girl if you like, but leave us alone!"

"There aren't any program-girls at rehearsals," said Farou, shocked.

"Go, Farou, go to your bath, go. . . ."

He went out, while Fanny busied herself at once in collecting the empty port glasses and talking, so that Jane could stay silent for a little while longer.

"Oh, là! là! . . . No, really, no. . . . How poisonous that profession is. . . . You know, in the condition he was in, the little port he drank was enough to make him lose his self control."

But she thought:

"I've had a narrow escape this time! How could Jane let go of herself like that? She was going to speak, to cry out, to give everything away."

Powdered again, and her hair tidied, Jane was reddening her lips. She bit them, licking off the fresh color, and then reddened them again mechanically.

"Oh, you know," she said suddenly, "I shouldn't have been hard

311

put to it to answer him. He doesn't frighten me for all the Big Farou that he is. I've known others. . . ."

She defied the door that Farou had shut, and which shielded him equally from the reproaches of an angry girl, or of a susceptible workman. The little flat grimace changed her mouth again, and Fanny shivered with discomfort and loneliness.

"Jane, shall we dine? I've a horror of these nervous exhibitions. We are alone; Jean is at his meeting of the Active Youth League."

Jane took her by the arm. Her fingers, still contracted, danced on Fanny's arm, and she gave her a kiss, devoid of any feeling, behind the ear.

"For two months now," thought Fanny, "I might have sat myself down to table quite alone, or even rather smartly snubbed the lady. . . . But I'm so shy since I knew them to be culpable. . . ."

Across from her she had a stoical companion, who drank, ate, and spoke. But at moments Jane kept a transparent silence. Then Fanny read in her the passage of sorrow or of violence, as she might have divined the secret movements of her child on the face of a woman in labor.

A little later in the evening, Jean Farou came back. He smelled of tobacco and the odor of other men. He vibrated still with the cries that a hundred presumptuous mouths had uttered round him, with senseless and vain words that he himself had thrown into the smoke. Dressed in new clothes, his tie ill-chosen, his eyes swollen with grief, and a new shadow upon his lip, he seemed to Fanny like bruised fruit. He broke by his entrance a long silence of sewing and reading, in which the two women, sitting almost neck to neck under the domestic lamp, had taken refuge.

"Were you amused? Did you yell properly? Did you drink disgusting messes? and bandy stories, and overthrow other people? Have you got indigestion?"

Fanny did not wait for the answers; she was interposing herself between Jean Farou and Jane; but Jean, infallible, looked only at Jane's face. He did not turn to Fanny except to ask her with his eyes:

"What's the matter with her? What has happened? What have you done to her?"

Fanny, tired, answered with a turn of her shoulder:

"Oh! shut up and don't bother me!"

Little Farou did not dare to speak to Jane, who held him at a disdainful distance, separated from him above all by a sort of monogamous repugnance.

"Yes," he said at last, paying no attention to the fact that no one had asked him anything, "it was brilliant. We did honor to our fathers. They would not have disowned the stupid things we said. What a pandemonium!"

He had changed since the return, acquiring an assurance that lessened him in some way. Fanny, sometimes maternal, looked at him sadly.

"My father is at the Vaudeville?"

"Of course," said Fanny.

"It's going all right?"

"He says so. Hasn't he taken you down there yet?"

"No more than he has you, Mamie. And you, Jane?"

"No favorable treatment for me," answered Jane, her eyes on her book. "Since they began rehearsing at the Vaudeville, I've only heard scraps of lectures, grinding of teeth, and discussions between Silvester and his decorators. Farou hides his work on the stage, really, like—"

"Like a cat her little affairs in the sand," said Fanny, who wanted to amuse them. "And, after all, I ask myself, why?"

"Through shyness," said Jean.

Jane raised her head at the word, and lowered it again at once with a malign little smile on her lips.

"You aren't going to ask me to believe that you've never noticed, Mamie, that father is shy?"

"I confess," said Fanny, vexed, "that this—characteristic had not exactly struck me until now." She spoke hesitatingly, considering it.

"I believe you, Mamie, I believe you, without difficulty. . . . Jane probably has not remarked it either."

This indirect attack did not ruffle Jane. Jean's glance greedily devoured Jane's shoulders, arms, the knees of Jane, Jane's hair. But Fanny read in the inflamed blue of his eyes, bloodshot now with smoking, nothing but gluttony and a rancor without hope.

"Perhaps he's beginning to hate her," thought Fanny.

Little by little, he was losing the good will of his stepmother, and he took account of it. Free from having to give him material care, she still took him to task rudely, like a nurse: "Have you cut your toe-nails and taken your Eno's Fruit Salts? I know you. Your motto is 'Silk socks and doubtful feet—clean teeth and a dirty tongue.'"

But she would not for anything in the world—sitting opposite those blue eyes overflowing with color, clairvoyant, trained for battle—have asked:

"Tell me how you know that your father is shy. . . . Explain to me, you who do not live with him, who speak so little to him, who are not his ally, explain to me what you pretend to know, what you miraculously do know of him."

The young creature, mysterious and unhappy, shifted his feet, took up the papers, shook an empty cigarette box; but Jane never stirred, nor left her book until they heard a distant clock strike midnight.

"Well? What now? Are you staying here, you two?"

"Farou has enough for the night. Silvester sticks to the dates. Friday a matinée for the dressmakers, Friday evening, the general. . . ."

"Twenty-four thousand in takings on Saturday," pursued Jean.

"If Allah wills!"

"Who came today, Mamie?"

"People," said Fanny laconically. "Clara. Cousin Farou. Other people. . . . No one."

Jane, roused by the names of Clara and Cousin Farou, and dreading that of Inès Irrigoyen, held up an unhappy and quarrelsome face, but Fanny did not even remember the fair young woman at this moment.

"And on that, my children, I'm going to bed."

"Me too," said Jane.

"Striking—striking harmony," mocked Jean. He had not dared to say "loyalty." Jane understood him and took the offensive.

"Oh yes, Mr. Little Farou, oh yes! Striking loyalty. Do you find any fault with that, Mr. Little Farou?"

"Me? No. . . . Not at all. . . ."

Losing all his pride—the pride of a hurt child—Little Farou contemplated his first enemy with terror.

"Hush, hush! Peace, peace!" commanded Fanny gently. "Oh, all these Farous—I've had enough of them. . . ."

She pushed Jean Farou toward his room. "Sleep well, my child."

But she could not prevent Jean, at the moment when he turned back on his threshold, from seeing Jane leaning against Fanny's shoulder with a deliberate air of weakness and defiance.

10

THE days that followed brought Fanny all that was necessary in worry and commonplace accident. Esther Mérya, the principal actress, caught cold; Henri Marsan sprained his ankle; a new setting refused by Farou, imposed by Silvester, in its turn delayed the general rehearsal. At each incident, Fanny stated quietly:

"That's how it was with 'Atalanta.' It's the same setback as we had for 'The Stolen Grape.' . . ."

But Farou, forgetful and sensitive, disgusted with these upsets to his text, became really angry.

"Where could you see such a muddle? Where? Go to Berlin, go to London! . . . What a mess! What carelessness! . . . What—"

"And your little Irrigoyen, what is she doing in all this?" asked Fanny inconsequently.

315

"Who? . . . Oh yes! . . . She's doing nothing, thank God! Biset took up her part again."

"Really!" wondered Fanny. She ceased to wonder when she remarked in Jane, the return, the unfolding of a happiness that brightened her eyes, her skin, and her voice.

At Fanny's smallest request, she came running to her— "What is it you want, my Fanny?"—like a young girl, fair, rosy, winged, and active as a bee. A little restrained song, hardly perceptible, did not stray beyond her closed lips.

If she were spoken to suddenly— "What, Fanny?"—she allowed the candor and hope of an acknowledged sweetheart to be surprised on her face.

At the same time, Farou recovered—from the time that he turned his back on the rehearsals, on the lighting experiments, and on Esther Mérya's pillow—his gentle mood, sometimes soaring, sometimes plunging lower than the earth, his glance of peaceful gold, even the fragrance that he exhaled when he was sensually content.

And Fanny grew gloomy again. Betrayal had left the lower levels and mounted as high as herself. Farou's pleasure ceased to be momentary, a caprice born in the street, of the street, of the theater, and satisfied no matter where. She came to the point of discussing childishly with herself the ranks of a hierarchy of adultery.

"The little Asselins, the Vivicas, the Irrigoyen, and all the small fry, that's Jane's affair. It's for her to be maddened, to weep a little in corners, and to have—if she dare—scenes with Farou. But Jane herself, in my house, my poor woman's domain in which now nothing is my own . . ."

Being sleepless, she longed, and for the first time, for a room where she could have slept or watched alone. The flat had only one spare room, and that Jane occupied. Little Farou slept in a room that would have been called madame's boudoir if he had not been there. At night, Fanny and her husband lay side by side; one frame in English cabinetmaker's work of the Bing period enclosed their twin beds. Their docile bodies had sailed together at night for years. Farou, unfaithful and yet a creature of routine, demanded the presence, the warm immobility of Fanny, her sheaf of black hair spread out, so that he could clutch it in handfuls by stretching out his arm in the darkness. . . . His slumber loved Fanny's, her curving eyes, so closely protected by their large eyelids, her mouth which looked foolish when she was asleep, and her whole exclusively feminine body, undulating, hilly, couched upon its side, with knees drawn up to elbows.

"Nothing is more shut away and secret than you are, when you sleep," he said to her.

"He treats me like a sleeper-out, because of this setter's attitude of mine. In old days, he used to say that I ought to have scoured the roads and lain in ditches."

Now unhappy and fearful, now wise and dissembling, she forbade her face, open and sensitive as children's faces are apt to be, to betray a sign of these tumults in her heart, and went about, straying between an anxious sorrow and a horror of external manifestations of it such as cries, confessions, contortions of the face or body. . . .

Passers-by, seasonable as starling or swallow, distracted her. They went through the house, open-mouthed, announcing that the stormy period of rehearsal was nearing its end, that the play at last was going to open. Fanny caught a glimpse of one of Farou's colleagues, a specialist in recrimination; she heard from behind closed doors, loud and tearful claims:

"No, my friend, if you make it your business to snatch my subjects from under my feet, or to borrow systematically everything that I've given the stage, with more or less success, then there's this to be said: Your 'Impossible Innocence' is my 'Amazon,' you understand, nothing else but my 'Amazon.' . . . What! Love is a theme common to all writers for the theater? I agree, friend, but that doesn't prevent these remarkable similiarities being there! Flers and Croisset have already made a most impudent use of my 'Rosine' . . . Confess that I play with misfortune—"

"You play only with that!" answered Farou, who easily turned, as Fanny said, "nasty with men."

She saw young actresses go in and out, lowering their voices to suggest ideas of complicity to Farou's mind; duennas like thunder; a very pretty young man who went away swollen with tears, like a rose with rain.

"What's the matter with him? What have you done to him, Farou? He's crying!"

Farou roared with laughter.

"I should think he is crying! That's Crescent!"

"Who?"

"Crescent."

"Who is Crescent?"

Farou flung up his arms.

"Oh, it takes you not to know the Crescent story! I haven't time. Ask Jane to tell you."

Fanny never knew what it was, this Crescent story. . . . There came, lastly, special reporters for advance interviews, and photographers. For these and for those, Farou put on his grin of a faun in the sun, standing up, leaning with both fists on his bureau. . . . There came, the one without the other, Henri Marsan and Esther Mérya, the chief actors, complaining bitterly of each other. There came obscure actors with faces like beadles, who, having rehearsed conscientiously and unpretendingly for a month, now declared, four days before the general, that they would not play "under such conditions."

"What conditions, Farou?"

Farou made a gesture of despotic indifference.

"I don't know. . . . 'Under those conditions . . .' 'In the midst of all this . . .' 'In proof of which . . .' Such phrases express indignation, and are obligatory."

"Is it serious?"

"Of course not, Fanny mine. Lord, what a gull you are! It's only normal. They will play, and very well too."

"Well, then, why do they make such a song and dance?"

"Ah, why do they make such a song and dance? . . . And what

about nightmares? And what about the need to increase their importance in my eyes and in their own?"

He changed his tone, and spoke dryly:

"Fanny, on the day after tomorrow, I want you to come to my last rehearsal. If you see my son, it will be very nice of you to tell him he may accompany you."

"And Jane?"

"She is already advised."

"It's a requisition," thought Fanny, "not an invitation. Let us distinguish. Why does he take this tone, when he decides to show me his new piece? 'Through shyness,' says Jean."

"You will doubtless be pleased to learn that I have shortened the scene of the safe . . . Branc-Ursine still steals the letters. But he steals off-stage, in the room at the side."

Fanny suppressed a shriek of laughter, and bit her cheeks inside to keep her face straight. Farou never allowed himself to speak to her of his plays except in the tone of a harsh schoolmaster.

"Through shyness," pondered Fanny again. "That remorseless child is right."

But she began to laugh again inside herself.

"He steals off-stage. . . . That's delicious!"

"In such a way," continued Farou, as if he were at the blackboard, "that the public is sufficiently informed by seeing him with the bundle of letters in his hands. The silent play of action is more impressive than a cry. . . . That is the curtain. . . . Do you understand?" he finished in an easier voice.

"Excellent! Excellent!" approved Fanny. "That's much better! Much less—"

"Yes, yes, I know," interrupted Farou. "Run to your final fitting. Will you look lovely?"

She swayed herself, like an Andalusian, velvet-eyed beneath her black-banded hair.

"Irresistible. Irresistible and discreet. Lace; skin under lace; a coral-red rosette in the middle of the bodice, here. . . . Your grandmother to the life."

"Minx! Am I to make love to my grandmother?"

Long afterward she remembered that he had a distracted look
that day, a nervous twitch in his right eyelid, a terrible longing for
holidays, vulgarity, follies and feasts, visible beneath his mask of
overwork. He smiled at Fanny, like a woman, and lowered his
voice:

"They tell me there's such a good film at Aubert. . . ."

She felt a sudden pity for him, realizing that he lacked sleep and
freedom, leisurely meals and fresh air; and that notwithstanding, he
never shirked a professional responsibility or a job of work.

"You aren't going down this afternoon?"

"Not for my weight in gold! I shall only go this evening. Besides,
they rehearse better without me. I worry them, rather . . . yes, I
worry them," he repeated gloomily. "It's odd, I can never be much
use to them at the end."

"Well, then, go and rest, and make yourself beautiful. . . . Jane, are
you coming to my last fitting?" she cried.

Jane emerged from the dining-room, sleeves rolled up, an apron
tied over her skirt, looking very pretty.

"Fanny, you're mad! And the new maid? What is she to do?
She doesn't even know how to lay a table! You'd think no one
ever ate in her last place. . . . And then, I'm ironing combina-
tions . . ."

She flourished an iron, held captive at the end of its long electric
cord, and Fanny went off alone.

She came back tired out with playing the "author's wife" to
frozen young saleswomen and gushing old saleswomen, nimble,
plumed with white hair or red hair, swollen with false emotion,
bloodthirsty for gossip, burning with an out-of-date passion for the
theater, for actresses and "the plays of the boulevard." These asked
Fanny a hundred questions, stopping themselves miraculously on
the brink of outrageous indiscretions. She loved the sharp old ladies,
bristling with claws, satanic and maternal instruments of a hell for
the convalescent damned.

The house, when Fanny came in, smelled sweet. Even in the

anteroom, an aroma of toilet vinegar announced that Farou was relaxing himself in a bath. He sang in the distance, coming and going between the study and the bathroom, once white, but yellowing now and old-fashioned in its comfort.

The new maid, full of zeal for the first forty-eight hours, followed the valet-de-chambre and gathered up the pieces of instruction that he let fall in a low tone. Both of them revolved round the dinner table, with devout steps, as if they were tiptoeing about a funeral bier; but Fanny was aware that the new employee already smoked in the pantry, and put out cigarette ends with her thumb. . . . Never mind; on such a night the house was like a fireside endowed with a master, adorned with a friend, probably a devoted friend, and certainly rather an innocent one. . . . A need to love in peace, to be unaware, to grow a little older and a little milder, softened Fanny's heart.

> "When crises are over and life looks merry,
> When Rip, Pierre Wolf, and all the Bourdets
> Shall have earned their cherry,
> When Mirande the lofty, his share of the quarry,"

sang Farou, who was not superstitious.

Jane's laugh greeted the improvisation, and Fanny, who, before lighting the gas bracket, was putting her large box on the bed, saw against the light background of the bathroom Farou in his shirtsleeves and Jane covered up in a servant's apron, rinsing a shaving brush.

"What?" said Farou. "That's not a good song perhaps?"

"Stupid," answered Jane's angel voice.

"Oh yes, stupid? . . ."

He pressed Jane against the wall, hiding her entirely behind his tall, solid body. Nothing was left of her but two little feet and a bare elbow on Farou's shoulder.

He put the palm of his hand on her forehead, forced her head back, and kissed her comfortably on the mouth, without delay.

"And that, is that stupid?"

321

The young woman disguised as a servant shook herself with a coquettish air of bravado, looked at herself, and declared in a rather muffled voice:

"It's worse than stupid, it's bungled."

She left the lighted bathroom, and Fanny trembled with fear.

"She'll see me. . . . She's coming in here . . . . She'll know that I saw them. . . ."

She fled into the dining-room, where she was drinking a glass of water to keep herself in countenance when Jane joined her.

"Water before meals? Are you turning sensible, Fanny? You've come back? Where's the dress?"

"I brought it back," said Fanny.

"It's the safest thing to do. But don't drink so fast! What's the matter with you?"

"I'm rather cold," said Fanny.

Jane took the glass, half-full, away from her.

"Cold? Oh no, Fanny! No jokes, please. Not influenza on the eve of the first night. But I don't at all like the look of the face you've brought home. Give me your hands."

Fanny's hands allowed violence to be done to them by two hands that still kept a scent of perfumed vinegar from Farou's bath; two eyes, dark gray, firm and penetrating, searched her own and hunted down in them the possible illness. . . . She choked a sob, and her eyes filled.

"The throat? Of course! Aspirin, quinine, bed, hot drinks . . . Farou!"

"Leave him alone. . . ."

"You think so! . . . Farou!"

He came, his cheeks and ears white with powder, his little improvised song on his lips.

"She's ill," interrupted Jane, bruskly.

"No," protested Fanny, struggling.

"No?" asked Farou.

"She—is—ill!" affirmed Jane. "Big Farou, you are going down there? Then go past the big chemist's shop that's always open and

322

send back in the car English aspirin, a box of plasters and some calomel. I'll write it all down, and you can give the paper to Fraisier."

She went out, while Farou bent over Fanny repeating:

"Well, my Fanny? Well? . . ."

"Ah, now! So much the worse, but it's more convenient this way," thought Fanny.

She smiled a little deprecatory smile at Farou, closed her eyes, and slipped full length upon the carpet.

Her sham faint gave her respite and repose. Entrenched behind her closed eyelids, she heard the sound of voices, and hurried breathing. Farou gathered her up in his arms, with awkward strength; she abandoned herself to those man's arms, designed to ravish and to wound. She knew that he knocked his foot as he went through the door, but that he held her firm. Always this odor of toilet vinegar. . . .

"Hello! Get out of the way, so that I can pass," he said to Jane.

"I was holding the door open for you; it was pulling to. . . . Is that the way you carry a fainting woman? . . . Wait while I turn down the bed. . . . Go and tell Henriette to fill a hot-water bottle. . . ."

"Shall I telephone to Dr. Mareau?"

"If it amuses you. For the moment, I know as much as he. The main thing for her is to get a quick reaction. . . . There's nothing the matter with the lungs; she's breathing properly."

They talked rapidly and quietly. Fanny prolonged this trick, this catch, this alibi. She let herself be arranged so that her head might fall in a position that increased her beauty, and the bedside lamp cast a rosy glow on her lowered eyelids. A hand slipped the flabby, burning bottle beneath her unshod feet.

"It's boiling," said the voice of the maid. "I'll pull madame's stockings off . . ."

"Well, then? . . . Shall I be off?" . . . asked Farou.

"Yes; away with you. Don't forget the chemist."

"What a question! . . . Shall I telephone from the Vaudeville?"

"If you like. My impression is that it's a very fleeting indisposition."

"But she hasn't got the habit of indispositions," said Farou, perplexed.

"And that deprives her of the right ever to have them, I suppose? Go along, quickly. . . ."

Jane's hand, seeking the fastenings of her dress, skinned Fanny's breast, and Fanny could not suppress the tremor of a woman very much awake. She opened her eyes, ashamed.

"Ah, there you are!" said Jane. "Ah, there you are! Really . . ." She wanted to laugh, and burst instead into nervous tears.

Oblivious of the rite that sent her to Fanny's lap, to rest her head and her scattered tears, Jane stood and wept simply, with a handkerchief rolled into a ball, at her eyes. With one hand, she made a sign:

"Wait; this will be over in a minute."

Fanny's great eyes fixed upon her, dark and expressionless, did not discomfort her. She sat down on the bed and lifted the band of black hair that was sliding down the white cheek.

"Now, tell me. What happened?"

Fanny gripped her hands close, and gathered all her strength, to remain silent.

"If I speak, Jane will exclaim: 'What! was it because of that? Because Farou and I . . . ? But that's as old as the hills. You aren't going to attach importance to that. You've said yourself, twenty times—' "

"You aren't pregnant, by any chance?" Jane asked.

The word seemed so absurd to Fanny that she smiled.

"What did I say that was so funny? Do you think yourself protected from every kind of little Farou or Farouette?"

"No," said Fanny, embarrassed.

Everything in her which was most normal and most sensitive pondered for a moment the image that troubles all women: a child, indistinct, small. . . . Fanny put her hand on Jane's fair forehead, and was hesitatingly incautious.

"That would not . . . you would not . . . In short, you wouldn't . . . hate it, if I brought a naughty little Farou into the world?"

Jane's eyelids drooped, all the features of her face—the white dilated nostril, the trembling corners of the mouth, the chin which betrayed the movement of a throat swallowing emptiness—fought and triumphed.

"No," she said, opening her eyes again. "No," she repeated, repudiating some stifled claim—"No."

"I don't believe she's lying," judged Fanny.

She did not withdraw the hand that was smoothing the fair hair. For thus she held at a distance, at arm's length, a head, a body that she might have drawn into her arms, constrained by the leveling confusion of the harem.

A little later she exacted the narrow benefits of her situation. She represented one of the two powers which domestic servants revere: sickness and wealth. She had a cup of consommé, mashed potatoes soaked in gravy from the joint, grapes, and illustrated papers on her bed. Jane stayed in the salon so that she might not tire "the invalid."

"What a fuss they're making over me," thought Fanny. She drilled herself to stay lying on her back, her bare arms flung out on the bedclothes to seek the fresh air.

"Probably I've a touch of fever; no it's the buzzing of the aspirin. . . ."

A volume of sound, ebbing and flowing, approached her, and fell back into the distance, bringing near and removing again a picture whose significance at the moment she could not well estimate: Jane, flattened against the wall, almost crushed by Farou's considerable body. . . . She fell asleep and did not wake until about eleven o'clock; Jean Farou was asking Jane in a low voice whether he might go into Fanny's room. Jane, on the threshold, made him respect her warning manner.

"You would tire her. . . . It's not the place for a boy. . . . Tomorrow, if she has a good night. . . ."

Rested by her short sleep, Fanny no longer wanted to be treated like an invalid, and cried out:

"Yes, yes, you can come in. Sit down there. . . . There's nothing the matter with me, you know."

"Nothing?" protested Jane. "She fell stiff, look, here where I'm standing. She came back from her fitting, I didn't even hear her come in, and we were thinking, as a matter of fact, that she was late—"

Jean, who was already growing bored, as if he were visiting a bed in a hospital, raised his head intelligently:

"We? Who?"

"Your father and I. . . . Your father did not go to the rehearsal. The actresses were all with the dressmakers. He bathed, shaved and turned himself out fit for a bride. . . ."

But Jean was not listening. He stopped listening, ostentatiously, and when Jane left the room he remained dumb.

"I can talk," Fanny said to him, when they were alone. "Besides, there's nothing the matter. I'm staying here resting, because it's so nice in bed and because I don't want to look plain at the dress rehearsal; people will think I've got stage fright."

He did not answer. At the end of a moment of silence, he stared at Fanny, and threw her a "Well?" so crooked, so harsh and inquisitorial, that she reddened at it.

"Well? What? . . . Well nothing!"

She moved restlessly in the bed, and pushed up her pillow.

"Well," repeated Jean, "they were there when you came in?"

She did not answer, and her eyes fled from the metallic blue gaze that was tracking her down.

"And then? . . . Then you are—you felt ill? . . . How?"

At these words she saw again the child lying on the slope, head and feet pendent, fair hair clotted with earth. . . . But today, that child was no more than a stranger enraged with pain egoistically intoxicated with a craving to hurt, and hurt again. No shadow of pity misted the blue eyes, conducting their inquiry without care for her; and upon the pure, half-opened mouth trembled a single shameful question, the same, always the same. . . .

"They were—where?" he stammered.

She had never imagined he could bring himself to that.

No shadow of pity. . . . She turned her cheek upon the pillow to hide her tears.

"When you came in, were they—"

Between her lashes, tangled in tears, she saw the child whom she had tended in sickness and health, who had grown at her side for almost twelve years. Strong in his first grief, he lived only to nourish it.

"How cruel a being is a child without hope," Fanny said to herself.

And easier tears hid from her the fair face, the hard curiosity of the blue eyes.

"Were they here?"

As she was silent, he made a gesture of uncontrolled impatience, in which his contempt of tears was visible.

"If I were you, Mamie—"

A childish look of haughtiness excused the big threatening gesture with which Jean rose from his chair.

"A child . . ." thought Fanny. "A child brought up by me . . . he was so dear."

She increased the tender pull of the shared past to excite herself to further tears. But what was new in her, and recently awakened, would not tolerate this fooling.

"Brought up? . . . That needs discussion. And as for his dearness— he takes pity on nothing, not even at the moment on the woman he loves. . . ."

She froze at contact with this diseased child, and spoke without hesitation.

"You will never be me, my child. Do not expect it. And let me sleep now. Good night, my child, good night."

He did not go. He touched everything round him with a look that summoned to his aid these witnesses, these partisans, a unanimous outcry. He did not rise, with obedient celerity, until Jane's voice:

"It's lasting a long time, this late visit. . . . Isn't he tiring you, Fanny?"

"A little. . . ."

"Jean? Do you hear? Run away quickly, dear."

He crossed the threshold, avoiding contact with Jane; and Fanny, delivered from this child at arms, from his immovable, unbridled, wall-shattering obsession, breathed again.

The solitude and silence were not broken except by noises from the street, and by the coming and going of Jane, tall, luminous, and by a faint wind which seemed to send the flow of her gown and her gentle slave-girl movements even to the bed.

A lamp below in the avenue served as night light. And Farou's bed, its white sheets turned down, gave another light to the room.

Insomnia in its beginnings is almost an oasis where minds that must think and hearts that must suffer find refuge for their needs. Since three o'clock Fanny had been longing for darkness and for exactly this insomnia. She found almost nothing in it but the image, fresh as in the colors of life, of a group pressed against the wall of the bathroom. She examined it in its detail, the bare elbow placed upon the masculine shoulder, Farou's hair like a bunch of mistletoe on the wall, two corners of a fluttering apron. . . . Nothing very terrible, in short, no indecency, no outburst of the flesh that might have justified in Fanny's breast this unequal beating of the heart, this imagined hardening of the heart, nor the trouble, nor the unreasoning fear that the couple might have divined her presence.

"I must speak to Farou. To Farou or to Jane? To Farou and to Jane. . . ."

She no longer knew herself.

"You are really too simple, you are a monster," Farou said of her. Where was this Fanny, this monster?

"Yes, it's Farou I must approach first. Without cries or a scene, to show him kindly that the situation is impossible . . . impossible, you see. . . . We are no longer young lovers, so that I'm not speaking in the name of a physical jealousy, which has no least part in this . . ."

But some impish trick of this least part brought back to her mind Farou's dear, fostering, healthy mouth, and the breath of his nostrils when he prolonged a tenacious kiss. She sat up suddenly, put on the light and seized a mirror from the table by her bed. Her expression of an angry woman superimposed upon a naturally gentle face gave her a double chin and a projecting lower lip, which she corrected. Except for the beautiful eyes and their forlorn gaze, she found herself ugly. But the expression of her wrath did not displease her.

"I can still get angry," she thought, as in times of siege she might have said: "Come! we still have enough sugar for three months!"

She smoothed cheeks and throat with her hand, and pushed the angry expression away.

"In case of need . . . you never know . . ."

She grew quieter, restored to a sort of security because she had seen and touched upon her own face, the native savagery of women, intact and ready for all needs. A movement of loyalty sounded truce:

"Later. In any case, not till after the first night."

Accordingly she sensibly put out the light, and when Farou came in toward three in the morning she lay motionless under her hair and watched him.

In the half-light he turned about aimlessly, coughing with fatigue and nervous exhaustion. Then he abandoned his clothes, like someone beaten in battle. His broad back was bowed when he was not thinking of it; the arms pulled the shoulders forward. At the sight of this physical distress, an inalienable ally of other days, crouched under the great scarf of black hair, would have flown to his help, would have offered him drinks, smiles, words, all the comforts tested during the passage of twelve years. . . . She contented herself with suffering grotesquely and counterfeiting sleep.

11

"There will be nobody there but us, Farou?"

"Of course not. Cellerier is coming too, I couldn't say no to her."

"Why?"

"She has a certain influence—an officious influence—at the Comédie. . . . If the—"

"She puts on airs of gray-haired distinction all over the place," inserted Jane.

"If 'The Stolen Grape' leaves the Gymnase, where it's been bottled up for three years, and comes to the Française . . . I'd just as soon have Cellerier for me as—"

"Ah, yes! . . . And who else?"

"My ladies the dressmakers, my lords the dress-designers . . . Pérugia . . . an American agent, two creatures from the German Theater . . . photographers . . . and Silvester is bringing some people. . . . And Van Dongen, because he's painted Esther Mérya's portrait.

"I see," said Fanny, annoyed. "It's the dressmakers' rehearsal, isn't it? The whole of Paris. You ought to have told me. Oh, this telephone!"

Farou looked at his wife, astonished. He had never before seen her murmuring and losing her temper on the occasion of a new play. The telephone had kept Jane at its elbow, the receiver to her ear, since morning. "The critic of 'L'Echo de la Peripherie' wants a seat for the second performance," Jane transmitted.

Farou did not bother to answer . . . Idle, with nothing to occupy him either out of doors or indoors, he had passed a slow and disagreeable afternoon.

"Why don't you go down today?"

He gave a forced smile.

"Because no one needs me there any more. . . . Jane ask who that was at the door. Ernest is so stupid. . . . Afterward, will you ring up Silvester's office? . . . What have we done about flowers? . . . We've remembered Esther's red roses?"

"Yes," said Jane.

"And Marsan's cigars, and the note-case for Carette?"

"Yes," said Jane.

"And Abel Hermant's box? Have you done what was necessary to—"

"Yes," said Jane. "Changed it for the lower box he prefers."

"What are these papers under the block of crystal?"

"Requests for places, of course."

Farou began to fuss in a meddlesome sort of way.

"But I've never seen them. You must always show them to me, always. What were you waiting for before deciding to show them to me?"

Jane held out the papers to him. He pushed them aside. Fanny listened and said nothing.

"That's rain, that noise I hear?" asked Farou, with a start.

"Yes," said Jane. "But the barometer is going up."

"What time is it?" asked Fanny in the silence.

"Oh, Fanny!" gnashed Farou. "It's always too soon! With Esther's famous change in the second act alone, we shall have an hour of trying on, of tears, and of crises this evening. . . . We're going to eat something beforehand, I suppose? If Jean isn't back yet, I don't wish to wait for him."

"Jean is meeting us at the Vaudeville," said Fanny.

"And where is he dining?"

"With his committee."

"He has a committee?"

"He's seventeen years old."

Farou raised his eyebrows and suppressed a smile, as he did each time Fanny showed temper.

"If I had known there were to be so many people there, I should have dressed," said Fanny. "Will Silvester be in the stalls?"

"Yes," answered Farou. "And he'll be on the stage. And also in his office, as well as in the gallery and the pit."

"What does he say about the play?"

"I don't know."

"What, you don't know!"

"No. We don't speak any more."

"But you never told me that. Why?"

"We are on the eve of a general rehearsal, we've rehearsed for forty days; he is producer, I am author. There's no other reason."

331

He tapped the window-panes, streaked with long tears of rain. He yawned plaintively.

"It's not such fun as it looks, being done with a play."

On the stage the curtain was up, and a discussion was extending into eternity between scene-shifters and scene-decorator. It had lasted for half an hour, and it seemed unlikely ever to terminate, for the chief scene-shifter, opulent in shape and reedy in voice, would not transgress either the tone or the vocabulary of courtesy; while the decorator who looked like Barrès, spurred to rivalry, displayed in his turn a tireless politeness. Jane and Fanny, in a lower box, already knew by heart all the details of the first set, remarkable for genuine old furniture, English silver, and "real" bound books; and they retired into the depth of their box, chins sunk in fur collars, shoulders hunched, as if they were on a railway platform. Toward half past nine, Jean Farou gliding into the box, inquiring, "It hasn't begun, has it?" received nothing but uncertain signs in answer. Breaking off his dialogue the decorator turned toward the audience and hailed the empty blackness with its vague rows of dust covers:

"Is Mr. Silvester in the house?"

At the end of a pause that seemed incredibly long, a sentence fell from some seraphic tenor voice, flying high and invisible:

"Not arrived."

The rain pattered monotonously on the dome.

"What are we doing?" asked Jean.

"Waiting," answered Jane. "Ah, there's Farou."

The stage increased his stature. He exchanged a few words with the impassive decorator, abstracted into a corner the balloonlike and floating first scene-shifter, who went out and collected two other weedy-looking hands. With their aid a blue couch flanked by a lacquer table disappeared; a ministerial writing-desk and two chairs replaced it. Then the decorator brushed his Barrèsian lock from his brow, put on his hat and left the stage. Out of a large basket which the accessory man held out to him, Farou fished a little Louis XIV clock, a Japanese vase, a desk candlestick that looked as if it were made of silver, and a blotter in morocco leather. He distributed these knickknacks among the furniture and ruffled some artificial roses in a vase. He stepped back to judge the effect, altered the angle of a chair, adjusted the equilibrium of a flower. Fanny followed this frivolous business unsympathetically, as if she were watching Farou concocting women's hats or embroidering at a frame. Jane touched her arm.

"You will see, they'll forget to put the stick of sealing-wax in the drawer."

Fanny saw she was serious and attentive, and tried jealously to imitate her.

A white-gloved hand detached itself from the group glued together in the middle of the stalls, around the photographer's apparatus.

"It's Cellerier signaling to you that she's there," said Jane.

"Cellerier, and who?"

"People she's brought with her, probably."

"What cheek!" said Jean.

"The heads of the dressmaking houses are farther back, under the circle. Well, if Mérya is dressed and Dorilys too—then, I ask you, what are we waiting for?"

She gnawed her thumb-nail. Fanny, attacked by a fit of yawns, pulled her coat closer round her shoulders and wrapped it over her legs. Jean Farou left the box and came back with some whitish sweets tasting like old vinegar. With little sidewise dancing steps, the invited glided between the rows of stalls, greeting each other in low voices, as if they were in church.

From the gaping boxes that Fanny had thought empty escaped a cough, a laugh, the click of a bag closing.

On the stage a woman's head shining with all the colors of the rainbow peeped out between two leaves of the folding doors, and withdrew immediately.

"That's Mérya," said Jane in a low, considering voice.

"How fair she is," remarked Jean.

"And a beautiful makeup. Did you have time to see it?"

333

"Yes. Radiant. She looks ten years younger. At least I thought so."

They whispered feverishly. Jean squashed against Jane in the awkward box, touched her with his elbow and knees, and breathed an air saturated with her perfume and her golden warmth. The darkness disarmed him, but he stifled a little mocking laugh when his father crossed the stage gravely carrying a Spanish shawl over his arm.

"Ah, that's Marsan with Farou. . . . Do you like Marsan's coat?"

"You can't like a coat. Nobody can. Why is he wearing it?"

"He's burst something underneath," declared Jean, from the height of his own new suit.

"Fanny, do you remember your wild laugh at the dress rehearsal of 'Atalanta'?"

"My wild laugh?"

"Yes; at Grault's smoking suit, his seducer's suit in beetle-colored Ottoman silk; my dear, you couldn't stop yourself—"

"My wild laugh—I laughed wildly. Yes, and I want to laugh wildly, uncontrollably again. I shall get through this state I'm in, it will pass like an illness. . . . I want . . ."

"Mérya's coming on now," breathed Jane. "Oh, that's a lovely dress! Fanny, look at Mérya's dress . . . isn't it?"

"Black is so distinguished. . . ."

"After the first act, will you go round to Esther Mérya's box, Mamie? I can go with you, can't I?"

"No, no," said Fanny quickly, shrinking into herself and pulling her coat round her. "I'm not going. Go with your father."

"Her real name is Mayer, isn't it, Mamie?"

"Naturally."

From the first appearance of one or two stage figures in their arbitrary coloring, she saw the boy brighten in spite of himself, absorbing the false light of the theater.

He professed an extreme coldness and distaste for Farou's profession; but in the presence of an actress or an actor, powders, stifling boxes, the ceremony and preparation of theatrical ritual, he became a dazzled child again.

"Farou looks green," remarked Jane.

"By contrast," said Fanny. "Marsan has made himself up as brown as a colonial. What an odd notion!"

"It makes him look manly."

"Does it?" asked Jean in an anxious voice.

Fanny smiled to see how naïvely, beneath his passion and his hostility, he attached the greatest weight to Jane's smallest decree. The curtain fell; a cold voice called for silence, and added:

"I must ask all persons not concerned in the play to be so good as to leave the stage."

"Who is speaking?" asked Fanny.

"The box at the back," said Jean. "That one, with the large black mouth. It's Silvester, who has just arrived. It's my father whom he calls 'persons not concerned in the play.'"

The "foreman" struck twelve rapid strokes, then gave three solemn knocks; a little roll of lazy dust rose along the level of the boards under the curtain; the important furniture appeared again, and the rehearsal began. In order to hear, Fanny leaned her temple against the partition and closed her eyes. She opened them again at a muffled exclamation of Jane's.

"Ah, her cry misfired badly! What a mercy it's today and not tomorrow she made such a mess of it. . . . All the same, for a woman with as much technique as she has—it's inexcusable. Farou ought to be in a fine rage. What do you say, Fanny?"

Fanny said nothing. She had emerged stupefied from a profound slumber that had seemed momentary. "Is it possible I've been asleep? . . ." She estimated the isolating thickness of her anxiety. She repeated in imitation, as the curtain fell:

"It really is, inexcusable. . . ."

A dim light showed again in the auditorium. Jane, very pale, was biting her thumb-nail furiously. The door of the box opened under Clara Cellerier's gloved hand.

"That's of no importance, my children!" she exclaimed. "Only she must look out tomorrow. It takes an old-stager like me to know how such accidents come about. They're purely vocal. The heating of the boxes, that's all. And fatigue, I grant you fatigue. . . . If Mérya had pitched her voice a little farther forward, you understand —hin, hin, hin, like that—the break would never have happened. . . . Ouf, it's over now, anyway."

She sat down. The faint, diffused light, robbing her of her fresh coloring, reduced her face to huge shadowy holes of eyes, and a deep ravine of mouth. Fanny thought to herself that the few seconds of her sleep had lasted long enough to age Clara Cellerier twenty years.

"Let's discuss the play. By Jove, what a work! That direct method of attack, eh! Farou's a regular wild boar. What a snout! I must admit Marsan is in the first rank. And he certainly would look well in the saddle today. Between you and me, Fanny, when Mérya, all nerves, answers him, 'Many women have come to you in this office to implore you to save them, but as for me I shall not leave this place without having ruined either you or myself'—don't you find that a little . . . don't you think it rather gives the play away, m'm?"

Fanny blushed in the darkness; these cues had not brushed the surface of her slumber. Before she could speak, Jane flashed:

"Oh, madame, a woman like the beautiful Madame Houcquart could not speak otherwise. She's big enough to unmask her batteries."

"It's not a stuffed bird that Madame Houcquart is meant to be, nor an ingénue," added Jean. "She would not demean herself by playing more subtly with a chap like Branc-Ursine! Don't you agree, Mamie?"

"You're deafening me, all of you! As for me, I shall need to hear the play again, at least twice. . . . I'm not as quick on the uptake as you are," said coward Fanny.

She sensed Farou's approach; the moment after, he came in. He seemed neither irritated, worried, nor even disappointed. Perhaps he tasted already that disgusted boredom which estranged him, once the first night was over, from all theaters where his plays were performed.

"Good day, Clara! . . . It went well, didn't it, except for Mérya's broken voice—and that's a purely material damage."

Clara hung upon his shoulder, giving him the accolade:

"What a work! What a structure! Pure Farou granite."

Farou sought Fanny's eye.

"Oh," he conceded amiably, "it's nothing probably but coke. . . . Fanny, did you like it, or didn't you?"

She took his hands and pressed them, trying to satisfy him by the exultations of silence.

"You shall tell me later. . . . You are my severe little critic; I tremble. . . ."

He joked with an air of constraint, and Fanny thought that he lacked arrogance. She detested in Farou everything approaching humility, and vented her irritation on her stepson.

"Well, Jean, have you nothing to say to Big Farou? All the same you were bold enough a little while ago. I could not hold them in," she said, nodding at Jean and Jane.

"Oh, bravo, papa, bravo!" applauded Jean self-consciously.

"Yes?" said Farou abstractedly. "Let's wait till the end. . . . You are all very kind. . . . And on that, my children, I must return to my muttons."

"If Marsan could hear you!" burst out Clara. Her delighted laugh, in the half-light, scooped a great black hole in her head like the mouth of a skull.

The photographers hoisted their flashlight apparatus toward the orchestra, and Clara yawned:

"It's going to take some time. Why don't we go and smoke a cigarette outside, and drink grog?"

"No, no!" said Fanny sharply.

She corrected herself:

"Not me, at any rate. I'm shivery, on edge. . . . Go along, all three of you. I'll stay quiet here. . . . Yes, yes, do go!"

When she was alone she leaned her temple once more against the partition and exercised patience. Her misfortune disappointed her. She would so much have preferred, sometimes, the uncontrollable grief of a young girl, exclaiming, disheveled, outside the pale of ordinary human behavior; and then sometimes she regretted the careless detachment of a year ago, the bitter little mystery of the absolutions she had granted Farou. She could not forgive her own grief for being bearable, and for taking a place between despair and indifference, in a spiritual region that allowed of distraction, pleasure, scruples, and compensations. She was endlessly amazed that the betrayal should not have changed Farou in her eyes, and even Jane herself. . . .

"Except that I can't bear *that,* I don't wish her ill. . . . At least, I think I don't wish her ill. . . ."

Clara Cellerier returned before Jane did.

"Have you slept well, fair shadow? I'll leave you. . . . No? Shall I tell you the news of the house, child? Marsan has a boil beginning and a touch of fever . . . Dorilys and Biset say—they say they shout out loud—that Chocquart only had them taken on here so that the two of them might be more conveniently at his disposal. . . . If you could have seen Farou keeping the peace! He took Dorilys by one door, and Biset by another; they profited by the situation as you might expect, Dorilys particularly. You would have died laughing. . . ."

"When one has no friends," thought Fanny, "where does one go for counsel? Nowhere. In any case, what use is a friend's counsel? This old Clara would advise so exactly on the lines of tradition, her own tradition, that it makes me sick in advance to think of it. . . . She would give me advice from Francillon or Mimi. . . ."

"It's stopped raining," exclaimed Jane. "I knew the barometer was not lying. It's nice now. . . ."

A fresh damp air entered with her, and the sooty odor of Paris rain. Her cold hand suddenly groped for Fanny's.

"It's beginning, Fanny. Look out, Madame Cellerier! Silvester has given out that he'll have the woman guillotined who opens a door or lowers a seat after the curtain goes up. . . . The second and third acts are played in the same setting, so we may hope in two hours or a little later— I've left Jean Farou with one of the Silvester boys; they're like twins; I can't tell you how like . . ."

She bent over Fanny, seeking her under the brim of her hat.

"I don't know why, but I feel as if something were wrong with you. . . . I'm not easy. I don't like leaving you alone. . . . Look, here's a bunch of violets. They have everything but the proper violet smell. . . ."

Fanny touched without seeing a tight little bunch pearled with rain, still living and exhaling a smell of pools like some small creature of the ditches. She made a sign of gratitude, smiling with closed lips. Beside her sat the only human being to whom she might speak with some chance of being understood.

She wrapped her coat round her again, and made room for Jane.

"They're saying in the café next door that it's talked of as a very powerful work—"

"Yes, yes—for a change."

"For a change?"

"Why, yes, why, yes. . . . 'A powerful work—the third act is powerfully constructed. . . . An irresistible grip draws the persons of the drama toward their fate. . . .' We've had enough of those clichés and you, more than I, since you paste up the cuttings. . . . Farou's 'strength'—it's . . . it's Farou in flesh and bone. It's his physique, his manner. . . . I've always thought that if Farou had been a little scrubby man with glasses we'd have had other phrases to read—'an acute subtlety,'—'a thousand-pointed irony.' Don't you think so? Tell me."

"How does Farou take such a viewpoint? Have you put it to him?"

"It's not so easy to talk to Farou. Haven't you ever noticed that?"

"Yes," said Jane.

The curtain rose. On the stage, Mérya and Dorilys, this one pitching her white, childish voice high, that one playing in a rather threadbare velvety contralto, attacked their big scene. The one intended to keep the lover whom she would not marry, the other fought for the same man to belong to her. Several times, among the fifty odd of the audience, isolated and vigorous applause crackled out here and there, like pods of gorse touched by fire.

"It's good, this," whispered Jane.

The two actresses redoubled their false coolness, their feigned dignity; already they sniffed tomorrow's success. Their acting was subdued to that heightened quality of naturalness and conviction which brings the theater within range even of the least enthusiastic. Fanny heard Clara Cellerier's voice cry, 'Bravo,' during a pause which Farou had designed purposely to allow someone to cry 'Bravo,' and the harsh dialogue went on. This time Fanny listened irreverently.

"Perhaps he really thinks it would happen so in real life. He makes me laugh."

Without turning her head, she slid a veiled look toward Jane. Jane was gnawing her nail, and her eyelashes were fluttering.

"She's moved. . . . Perhaps she, too, thinks it would happen so. . . . What day ought one to choose to teach her, to teach myself, that it does not happen so? . . ."

Tragic cries wounded her ears. Mérya was giving way before Dorilys who stood erect, visionary and valiant as Joan of Arc, and braved her thus:

"You do not know, you no longer know, madame, what it is to be young, chaste, and a woman. . . . All the untapped strength, all the ignorance that I carry within me, the worst act that I am capable of committing, the highest beauty I am capable of realizing—all these I launch against you, I thrust into the battle, for him! . . ."

Inside herself, Fanny was watching two real women, sad, moderate, careful to control any raising of voice in order to escape the kitchen's curiosity, to save appearances . . . She was cold. "It will come soon. . . . It will come soon. . . ." A hand slipped behind her neck, put up her fur collar, glided under her arm, and came to rest in the warm fold of the elbow, as if it were asleep

"Always this hand. . . . What shall I do with this hand? And what if, one day soon, I have to throw off this hand, to prise open the fingers which will cling, perhaps to my arm, to the stuff of my dress? . . ."

This motionless hand occupied her more than the close of the act. On her side Jane hung rigid and vigilant upon the coming and going of the actors, as if she were uncertain of hearing clearly. Jean

340

Farou reentered noiselessly and sat down in the corner seat which Jane, pressed against Fanny, had left empty. Until the end of the act, he thought of nothing but those intertwined arms, cursing them, looking brutally at Fanny, enjoining her to unloose the arm that had sought refuge. Voicelessly, stubbornly, Fanny fought him, and the curtain descended before she had given in.

"Oh! . . . Bravo!" cried Jane, a second behind the frantic applause of the public.

The curtain maneuvered as curtains do at a dress rehearsal. Mérya flaunted already every sign of the emotional exhaustion which would bring her credit on the morrow, and Dorilys, taking her call, again renewed that invincible youth upon which the theater would be able to count for another quarter of a century.

The third act and the fourth, soldered out of two scenes, taxed Fanny's patience and her strength. Half the night went by there. A confusion which respected routine, customary revolts, classical accidents to properties, delayed the hour when a delivered Farou, with the coldness that he showed to each of his works when the time came to let them fall upon the public, could say:

"There's nothing more for me to do here."

Fanny and her two companions found him again on the stage. A stage manager near him was checking off:

"The stick of sealing-wax forgotten in Act I; the pocket electric lamp in Act II did not light; the door bell in Act III to be brought nearer; the coffee did not smoke in the cups, Act III again; the moonlight to be less blue (Julian is seeing to that) and another type of telephone to be used. . . . There was nothing else, Mr. Farou?"

"No . . . no, old man— Ah! the lampshade in the second act—the frill is too short; the audience in the front stalls get the globe in their eyes."

"Mr. Silvester marked that."

"I noticed nothing else. . . . Good night, old man, and thank you!"

He restrained his impatience. But his eyes with an activity devoid of expression wandered from right to left, from left to right, upon the platform cleared now as if by magic.

"Where are they?" asked Fanny. "Where are they all?"

"Who?"

"But—Mérya, Chocquart, Dorilys, Marsan?"

"Gone."

"But how? . . . It's not possible, the curtain is only just down. . . . I wanted to—"

Farou shrugged his shoulders, tying himself in a woolen scarf.

"Gone, I tell you. Ouf! . . . They are admirable, but I can't see them again . . . until tomorrow. They too; they couldn't bear to see me. We're all bored stiff with each other, can't you see? . . ."

He put an arm under the elbows of the two women and drew them away.

"It was a great success," said Fanny in a pensive tone.

She wanted to weigh it dispassionately, and to do justice to Farou for having, as always, worked alone and faithfully. She bent herself, enthusiasm making her weak, to measure the value of the work by the fruits it would bear.

"Yes, it was a great success," she repeated. "I'm certain."

They separated to descend the narrow staircase. Farou went in front, swinging his arms. He cleared the last three steps at a jump, stretching his arms to make them crack. "What a pity! . . ." sighed Fanny to herself.

She sighed with a confused sense of regret, as she always did when she caught a glimpse of the prisoner confined in Farou, of the man who could swing an ax, drive an engine, hold the reins or the oars. . . . Jean Farou followed the group, throwing onto the walls a shadow with drooping head.

Outside, Farou sniffed the rainy air.

"Oh, we might walk home! . . ." But he threw himself in a heap into the car, and did not move.

He kept Fanny on his right, Jane on his left. His indifferent hands rested, for lack of room, one on each feminine shoulder. Jean Farou, on the little seat, obstinately kept his eyes fixed on the empty streets of two o'clock in the morning. At each street-lamp, Farou's hand hanging on Jane's shoulder emerged from the darkness, and Fanny in spite of herself began to watch for this recurring light, the abandoned hand, and Jean's stubborn profile.

"Half past two," announced Farou. "Tomorrow—a nasty day."

"Oh! . . ." protested Jane. "It's already won."

"That doesn't prevent us from being dead for sleep, does it, Jean?"

"Dead," acquiesced a feeble echo.

Fanny found the drive long, and suffered afresh. She was terrified lest her own tension, Jane's anxiety, and Jean's irreconcilable silence should break out in confusion into some sort of disaster before it was time, before they could find cover behind closed doors. . . . Farou yawned, stretched his long legs, let fall two or three insignificant words, patted himself on the back at the sight of the moon threading her veiled way among the clouds, and foretold fine weather. Insensible to other, more subtle omens, he nevertheless charmed into stillness by his gentle human murmurings all that might suddenly threaten his serene and patriarchal immorality.

12

"It's extraordinary how they can never type the figures opposite the printed name, in these author's lists. Look, Fanny. Because of the misspacing of the typewritten column, it's we who look as if we'd made twenty-four hundred and forty the night before last, and the Mathurins twenty-two thousand."

Jane held out the sheet of returns to Fanny.

"Have you the sheets for the first week, Jane? Let me have them. . . . Twenty . . . sixteen, seventeen thousand and four, eighteen thousand and four, twenty thousand and thirty-two . . ." read Fanny softly. "That's good, isn't it?"

Jane nodded her head.

343

"Good? I should think so! It's a fortune, Fanny! . . . And then there are the holidays coming. . . ."

"Holidays?"

"Why, yes. Christmas, of course. Three matinées, two Christmas-eve suppers . . . and the 'House' on again at the Antoine . . . and the tour of the 'Grape' in the suburbs. . . . This Farou! We shall no longer be fit to speak to him," said Jane rather bitterly.

"Then it is . . . it is really a success?" insisted Fanny. "We're sure of it, now?"

"What a question! Why do you harp so on—"

She noticed that Fanny, head bent over the leaflets, was no longer reading them. She noticed, also, that Fanny, grown more slender, was wearing a new dress, dark blue in color, which lent her an air of one making a discreet visit or a departure; further that the papers were trembling between her hands.

"Then—" sighed Fanny, "then—let's get it over."

She raised to Jane a troubled, almost imploring look. The lipstick on her mouth left a tiny margin of lip inside, of a strange whitish mauve, and the low December sun, playing across the trees in the Champ-de-Mars, made her blink her eyelids.

The same sunshine touched almost to a tender green the hair like young wheat on the head of Jane, who slipped out of its light with a swift movement.

"Let's get it over," repeated Fanny in a sad voice. "You see—my poor Jane . . ."

The beating of her heart, the blood drumming in her ears, disordered all her resolutions.

"What have I said? . . . My poor Jane, it's not that; that must . . ."

But she had to do with a rival who would not consent to any inferiority, and who would allow her to pronounce only a very few more words:

"Look . . . Jane . . . I've learned that you—that Farou . . ."

"Wait!" interrupted Jane. "Wait one moment! . . ."

She gathered up her forces gravely. Upon her cheeks a pink

344

powder showed, so delicate in hue as to be invisible generally, defining the outline of the lengthened oval of her face.

"What are we going to do?" she demanded.

Fanny reddened at that "we."

"How do you mean, what are we going to do?"

"Yes. . . . Is it for Farou or for us to make decisions? If you will allow me, I'm going to sit down. I don't feel at ease standing up."

Seated, Jane had to raise toward Fanny's a face that at first seemed peaceful and lighted only by its habitual candor. To fight more freely she seemed to have discarded all but the essentials of her features, which, denoting an age near thirty, disclosed the changing shape of the mouth under a rather long nose, and the beautiful eyes of a jealous woman. She went on:

"Have you spoken to Farou?"

"No. You ought to have known I wouldn't."

"Not necessarily. . . . Thank you for speaking to me about it first."

"First? Were you going to speak to me?"

With her hand, Jane waved far away from her such an initiative.

"No. . . . Good heavens, no! . . . For having first spoken about it to me. Now—what do we decide to do?"

A calm like this, even if it were simulated, took Fanny unprepared. She knew herself capable of improvising, but only in the interests of a movement of passion. She smiled for want of anything better.

"It seems to me that what *we* decide is not the point," she said.

"Good. I understand. Well then it's *your* decision, Fanny, it's for you alone to decide. . . ."

The gray eyes, full of prayer, told Fanny that she ought not to reckon with the assurance of the words, but with the inexplicable thought behind that dictated them. Fanny, however, opened her white nostrils, and the approach of anger cleared the air.

"Don't fly into a rage, Fanny. . . . Good Lord, what attention we have to pay to our words! . . . Are you going to leave Farou outside our—our argument? Is he not to know of today's conversation?"

"No, of course not! What are you looking for? It's impossible!"

345

"Have you considered that, Fanny?"

"Perfectly considered it."

She lied. She had only thought that after a sort of cry, "I know all!" things would arrange themselves or upset themselves irretrievably. But here she had before her only a reasonable young woman—moved, certainly, but already discussing ways and means, already no doubt preparing herself to use all her practical knowledge, and an adaptable resignation.

"It's because she knows," thought Fanny. "She has disputed with more than one woman for more than one man. . . ."

"I fear," said Jane, shaking her head, "that you have not considered it as long as I have. . . ."

"For a smaller period of time than you, very likely."

"If you prefer to put it that way."

But Fanny liked neither this suppleness nor this ease. She lowered her head like a horse putting on a hood, and made a double chin.

"What's she going to do?" asked Jane, more quietly, as if to herself.

Fanny smiled, showing the pale margin of her red lips.

"Are you frightened?"

"Frightened? No—well, perhaps yes."

"Frightened of what?"

Jane leveled a sad look into Fanny's eyes.

"But of all that may happen, Fanny; of all that may change our lives. . . ."

"You can always see things from the outside," said Fanny in a disagreeable voice.

"See whom? . . . Ah, Farou . . . I wasn't thinking of Farou."

"That's rather ungrateful," said the same voice.

"I owe Farou no gratitude," replied Jane, raising her eyebrows.

"It's forbearing of you not to claim him for your own in front of me."

A convulsive cough cut short Fanny's breath. Jane made a gesture of discouragement, and putting her elbows on the table, leaned her head on her hand. The December sun had left the room, and the clear green light of dusk made verdant again Jane's extraordinary hair, which left bare a flat and too broad interval of cheek, between the nose and the tiny ear. A tear shone upon this flat cheek and reached the corner of the mouth, which drank it indifferently.

"Three years and a half, four—nearly four years . . ." corrected Jane to herself.

With the aid of a violent movement Fanny came out of her frozen stiffness.

"I'll give you a dispensation from statistics and details, you know," she cried.

The profile lit by a tear turned sharply, and Jane surveyed her friend.

"What do you think, then, Fanny? Are you thinking that for four years I have been—that Farou is—"

"Don't be afraid of words. And as to the time—we know, that has nothing to do with it, don't we?"

"Oh, well, yes, my dear, if it's a question of Farou. . . ."

She shrugged her shoulders as if she were laughing.

"Fanny, you have before you a perfectly ordinary caprice of Farou's . . . everything in the world that is most ordinary. . . ."

Jane's humility and twisted, bitter expression revolted Fanny as much as certain gestures in low comedy.

"It's not true. Have the heart, at least, not to lie. Have I threatened you? Have I complained? Let us at all events finish decently— properly—what we have embarked on."

She grew hoarse with speaking so loud, and with a bewildered pleasure abandoned to her anger the power of leading her still further. But at the same time, she repeated the word "properly," attaching a moderator's virtue to it. She had the shock of seeing Jane, risen to her feet, advancing upon her with a bold face.

"What? What isn't true? And what am I to be, then? The woman Farou loves, I suppose? Do you think I'm belittling myself to win your kindness? My poor Fanny! You gave me a dispensation from statistics, and without them I make no mystery of the number of weeks that have gone by since Farou has deigned to treat me other- wise than as—"

A door shut with a bang in the flat and cut short her words. Both of them in their attitude of rude quarreling, hands on their hips, stood listening.

"It's not he," said Jane at last. "If it were we should have heard the landing door first. . . ."

"It makes very little noise since they put on the new felt," said Fanny. "But anyway, he never comes in here before dinner. . . ."

Chilled, they separated, one from the other, as if silently renouncing a plan of battle. Fanny went to pull the double curtains across the two windows, and lighted the lamps on the tables. She sat down, poked the embers, and piled up the andirons with logs. She felt the cold of oncoming night, crystal-clear and tingling with the north wind, and she shivered in spite of radiators and a wood fire.

Her furious moment past, she had already less taste for insulting, however "properly," Jane and the truth or Jane and a lie. Sagacious and brief in anger, she told herself already:

"We were better *before*. . . . Neither of us two can extract either profit or happiness from what comes after. . . . If Jane were never to mention it again, that would be best. . . ."

But Jane spoke again.

"Ah, Fanny, if I could only make myself understood . . . You don't know, you don't know . . ."

Fanny freed her white brow from its touching black lock.

"But I'm going to know," she said sadly. "I do not see how I can prevent you, now, from making me know. I beg you, don't let us be carried away into exchanging confidences—the sort that women love to make about their lovers, their periods, and their illnesses, disgusting things. . . ."

She swallowed her saliva with repugnance and, contrariwise, she added:

"Besides, I know enough about it. . . . And then I saw you one day in the bathroom in the middle of an embrace, a day when you had on an apron, and were ironing—"

She stopped, ashamed. But Jane no longer cared either for shame or silence. She pounced upon this memory with a greed for confession and grievance.

"In the bathroom? One day when I was ironing? Oh yes, of course! Oh yes, let's talk about that. You've hit on a good instance."

She began to walk up and down the room, tapping her palm with a flexible paper-knife:

"Yes, yes. That day—perfectly! He embraced me as he would have embraced the maid, do you understand? And when I say like the maid, I'm less than a maid in his eyes, less than all the Asselins and Irrigoyens in the world. After all, you know what Farou's crazes are, Fanny. You've talked enough about them to me; you've demonstrated to me often enough your superior wisdom, your indulgence . . . your complaisance—"

Jane stopped an instant, shook her hair back and sniffed with vexation. Two poor little tears trembled and shone at the corners of her eyes, and she went on clacking the paper-knife. The nearer Jane got to confusion, the more Fanny returned to an inopportune calm, from the vantage of which she came to the conclusion that no paroxysms were becoming to Jane.

"She's made for moderate manifestations; ash-blond sorrows. . . ."

"One would think, to hear you, Fanny, that you did not know what Farou is!"

"He is my husband," said Fanny.

She stamped her reply with a rather pompous simplicity, and was not pleased with it. But she did not withdraw from the effect that she would have discounted, for Jane exclaimed:

"Thank God, Fanny!"

"I had not thought I had any cause for gratitude to whomever there may be. Not even to you."

Jane, for the first time, seemed intimidated, and looked first to one side, then to the other.

"I meant: 'Thank God you were there too—at the same time as he. . . .' One feels so terribly alone with Farou . . ." she finished at a venture.

She added in the same manner, hesitating and precipitate:

"With other men, of course, one felt alone too. . . . But much more

349

so with Farou. . . . I owe no gratitude to Farou; that's the exact truth. But I owe recognition to someone here—"

"A charming manner of showing it to me," burst out Fanny.

At this cry, Jane grew quieter, as if it were her turn for coolness. "I have shown it you, Fanny, in my measure. . . . It was not easy. For four years I have thought so much more of you than of Farou. . . ."

Fanny rose, coldly:

"No," she said. "Not that. At present there's nothing disgraceful between us; everything is even rather banal. But I cannot bear the sentimental complex . . . Oh, Jane! . . ."

She hid her face in her hands and uncovered it again immediately, in case Jane should think she were weeping.

"It's not a sentimental complex," protested Jane. "Why should I have thought as much as that about Farou?"

She read in Fanny's features the astonishment which Farou called "the stupefaction of a pretty fish" and went on impatiently:

"But, yes . . . What you don't understand at once you treat as a lie. You are so innocent, Fanny. . . ."

She softened and stretched out toward Fanny's hot face a hand curved like a cup, as if to enclose in her palm the smooth, heavy contour of the cheek.

"So innocent . . . so fresh. . . . How different from me—"

"Yes, yes," interrupted Fanny, attending to something beyond the phrase, for she was suddenly fearful of seeing Quéméré and Meyrowicz and Davidson enter the conversation, and . . .

"You say yes, yes; but how are you going to understand, in your condition? Yes, this state of innocence, this virginal atmosphere in which you pass your life . . . For you there is Farou, and still Farou and only Farou and no other man but Farou. . . . It's very pretty— and then again, I'm not so sure that it is very pretty—but I, I do not see, I have never at any time seen Farou with the same eyes as you; let us say, with the same heart as you. . . . I did not take long to make a difference between you two, Fanny; and from the moment when I made it, then—oh, then!—"

She grew agitated, and changed her tone as if she had at last touched and almost entered the most painful region of their conversation. She set aside, then gathered to her, with her hand, all that she wanted to express. Sincerity retired into the distance and returned to her as a temptation.

"Then, you understand, that didn't pull! No that didn't pull!"

"Well, what in the end?" asked Fanny.

Jane moved her shoulders under her dress with a provincial and affected awkwardness which Fanny noticed for the first time.

"It hurts me to say it, Fanny. . . . It doesn't hurt at all to talk of Farou to you. Farou is a man, a man who is attractive, a distinguished man with great talent: and, Fanny, I admit to you that it doesn't take much to seduce a girl like me, who has no serious reason for living, for remaining chaste and solitary. . . . There's nothing really very odd in my becoming easily amorous, jealous, unhappy, and indeed all that you've seen of me. . . . But apart from the fact that Farou is Farou, there's nothing so extraordinary about him as a man. . . . While you, Fanny, you—"

She sat down, took out her handkerchief, and began to weep in a manner abundant, easy, and discreet, that seemed new to her, and not unpleasant.

She dried her eyes, and went on quietly:

"You, Fanny, you are much better as a woman, than Farou as a man. Much, much better. . . ."

"Oh," said Fanny haughtily, "you cannot have known him very well."

Jane turned toward her a keen woman's look.

"The token . . ." she said, half-smiling . . . "you failed thoroughly in trying to make me think him incomparable."

"That's it," said Fanny, nodding her head: "it's going to be my fault."

"Yes and no—in a certain sense."

She wanted, without doubt, to explain, to expose to Fanny the position of the new and elegant freed-women—utterly detached and journeying as winged seeds do in the air—their adaptability, their

351

nameless seductiveness, but she abandoned it before the brown, stumbling woman, of sedentary habit, who upheld an older code of living.

"I'm speaking of the first days, naturally. After—"

"After you became my friend," said Fanny, with a sweetness that augured badly.

"No," Jane replied curtly. "I was that before. I could not cease being. . . ."

"For so little," suggested Fanny.

"The fact is, there's nothing of the vamp woman about me at all," pursued Jane. "Nor of the acquisitive dirty kind, nor of the ambitious ones. You can do me that justice. What risk do you run with me? Not much. . . ."

"Yes—you would like to have been the only one to deceive me," detailed Fanny with the same sweetness.

"But against me, against us, I had your indulgence of Farou, your cursed indulgence, your would-be understanding of Farou—your mania for covering him with praise, and then with maledictions a hundred times more flattering than praise. . . . Your 'superiority,' which consisted in putting Farou at the disposal of all women—you find that honorable, Fanny? I don't. Ah no! I don't at all. . . . It's a trait that disfigures you, that lowers the ideal I had made of you. . . . You," she said, looking at Fanny with urgent admiration, "you were my own soul at its fairest."

She drew away, lifted the window curtain for a moment, and let it fall promptly as if to hide again what she had seen in the crystalline night. She came back, put her hand on Fanny's shoulder and shook it lightly.

"And you asked me a moment ago if I was afraid? But I tremble, I freeze with fear, Fanny. As for you, you are thinking to be quit of me, you are thinking that these little affairs of physical love are crimes if I am mixed up in them, you think to snatch Farou from me, as if he had not already ceased to be occupied with me this long while now; you think to make your way clear, to burn resin and benzoin in my room, perhaps. . . . It's incredible that anyone can make as much of love as that. . . . It's not so important. A man? He's not eternity. A man is—he's no more than a man. . . . Do you think any of us meet a man all alone, like that, isolated, free and ready to devote his life to you?

"A man is never alone, Fanny, and it is terrible enough, in fact, that he has always a wife, another mistress, a mother, a maid, a secretary, a relative, some woman, somewhere. If you knew what I have had to meet for women, around a lover! . . . It's horrible. The word is not too strong."

She gripped her forearms with her hands so closely that the ends of her fingers became livid. She abruptly poured out a glass of water for herself, and raised it to her lips. But on second thought she handed it to Fanny.

"Pardon. I'm dying of thirst."

"And I," said Fanny.

They drank in silence, courteous as beasts that call a truce on the brink of a stream. Emotion marked them differently: Jane was flushed on her cheek-bones, and Fanny pale, with dark charcoal-colored circles round her eyes and a mouth without its makeup mauve-colored like a Negro's. Fanny, after she had drunk, gave vent to a long sigh of fatigue, and Jane once again sketched a movement of her hand round the curving cheek, but did not touch it.

"Poor Fanny! . . . What torture I've put you to! . . . Would you—"

She dared go no further. Fanny said shortly, "No, thanks," and sank into an absorption, seeking the exact terms in which Jane had once remonstrated with Farou. "She said to him, 'You would do better to give her your hand' or 'to take her by the hand,' I don't remember more exactly than that. . . . She said to him, too, on the day when they thought I had fainted, 'Don't knock her feet against the door' or something like that, and, 'Is that how you carry a woman?' . . ."

"I ought to know the love of serving you," said Jane gently.

Fanny could contain her agitation no longer; she rose and began to turn around on the same spot, as she sometimes did in hours of gaiety, with the light and agile movements of a plump creature.

353

"No," she said. "No, I cannot bear it. . . . Since all is spoiled, you must change your language, you must stop appealing to our emotion, exploiting this bond, this past, this—"

A door opened behind her.

"A-a-a-ah!" yawned a great cheerful voice. "All my fine women! All my fine women! I have women in my house!"

He entered, untidy and content: his fine yellow eye, languishing and impenetrable, betrayed that he had just left a rapid pleasure or a long spell of work. Easy circumstances for some months, a recrudescent success dressed him in a youth not only unseasonable but unreal. He wore it like a cravat with spots.

"I've just met Pierre Wolff," he exclaimed. "I must look exceedingly well, for he threatened me with arteriosclerosis, shaking paralysis, and—"

He realized that Fanny as well as Jane had not moved at his entry. He consulted the two faces, saw them both changed from what they had been in the morning, and asked in the tone of a master:

"What's the matter?"

"Farou—" began Fanny.

"Fanny, I do assure you—" begged Jane.

"What's the matter?" repeated Farou more loudly and impatiently. "Women's quarrels? Some fuss with the maids?"

Fanny looked at Jane and gave a little laugh. Jane sketched a movement of retreat with her whole body, a sort of mock courtesy as if to say: "I must leave you free, speak . . ." To which Fanny responded by a sign of the head: "I take the responsibility for everything."

"Farou," went on Fanny, "we have been having a serious explanation, Jane and I. You see how calm we are. We intend to remain so."

She spoke with a mouth on which the mauve pallor had now encroached everywhere, and articulated with care. Farou had just time to see this pallor of the lips on his wife's face, these eyes, too large, too beautiful, invaded by dullness, and no longer able to express anything. He must have thought she was going to faint, for he put out an arm. But she explained herself:

354

"Jane is your mistress, I am your wife, we cannot decide anything properly without you. . . ."

Farou, who had seated himself, rose slowly. His eyebrows descended majestically upon his face, and the two women felt no fear for a moment, because they found him beautiful. They waited, the one and the other, for what thunder they knew not. . . .

"Which of you spoke of it?" Farou said at last.

"Me, of course," declared Fanny, offended.

He rested his eye upon her, but without fire, and with a defiance already meditated.

"Have you known about it for a long time?"

She lied, out of a sort of boastfulness:

"Oh, for a very long time. . . ."

"And you hid it so well? My compliments."

She thought this a common counter-offensive and shrugged her shoulder.

"But," continued Farou, "if you have really hidden it for such a long time—which surprises me—yes, which I must say surprises me —why did you not continue to do so?"

Speechless for a moment, she recovered herself and cried:

"You think then that one can keep such a thing to oneself, that one can be silent indefinitely?"

"I'm convinced of it," said Farou.

With a gesture, she left this to Jane, murmuring, "That passes all bounds. That's—"

"Above all, you," added Farou.

"Because I'm habituated to it?"

Up to that point, Farou had been watching Fanny's trembling hands. But he saw her eyes full of tears, and took comfort.

"Because you are habituated to it, if the phrase suits you. Whatever I have done, have I ever withdrawn the least part of my tenderness from you in these twelve years?"

At this, Jane came forward into the light with a gliding softness, and Farou trembled.

"I realize intensely, Jane, that this scene has something peculiarly

355

painful to you in it. . . . But all your words can only make it more painful still; I do implore you to remember that."

"But I don't want to speak," said Jane.

"For the rest," continued Farou, "I'm ready to claim all responsibilities."

A sharp exclamation from Fanny interrupted him.

"Responsibilities? Which responsibilities? Who wants you to be responsible? . . . It's not that, Farou. . . . Say what you want, do something, concern yourself with us, but not in that fashion. . . . Quick, Farou, quick! . . ."

She had a horror that he should know, at such a moment, how to moderate himself, and was already accusing him of subservience to the immemorial ways of men caught between two women. How often had not Farou stormed, flung all human equity to the devil, all the precautions and sensitiveness of Jane and Fanny, and ravished in his arms the object, however temporary, of his splendid choice? "How slow he is, my God, how slow he is. . . . A violence, but a loving violence, and for one of us, no matter which, a despair, but a passionate despair. . . . Are we so old that he must stay thus frozen, and that he will not even curse? . . ."

"We are not idiots," said Farou. "I am only a man, but a man determined to preserve the maximum of balance in a situation in which so many men and women lose theirs. If I have been toward Jane—"

"I am not in question," intervened Jane. "I make no claims, it seems to me. I am not in question unless Fanny wants me to go away . . . which would be very natural."

He agreed with a grave nod of the head. Fanny sought throughout his whole masculine face, hewn out in large features, shadowed by its horse's crest, for some male decision and a trace of that emotion which Jane's words had awakened in her.

"Fanny knows very well . . ." said Farou. He continued, addressing himself to his wife: "You know very well, Fanny, that you are my darling Fanny. And as for me, I've always benefited by your tenderness to me, through everything, for more than ten years now.

It is those ten years that assure me that you will know how to arrange what deserves to be arranged. I am grateful to you for it in advance."

"What deserves to be arranged." Jane received this without disturbing the close of the period or breaking Fanny's stupor. She even indicated, with pursed lips, a whistle of ironical appreciation. Since Farou's entry, she seemed to have lost the faculty of movement and of amazement, and followed the gestures of Fanny and Farou with narrowed eyes.

"What does that mean? Farou, what does that mean? . . ." murmured Fanny in consternation.

She returned to Farou just in time to see him repress a yawn of nervous strain.

"The longing to be away from this is oozing out of his pores!" thought Fanny, beside herself. "He will go away. . . . He'll find a pretext for going away. . . . Is this all he has to say? Is it thus we close or that we begin a new season of life? . . ."

"Farou," she appealed, in furious sorrow.

"Yes, my Fanny? I am here. I hear you. Do you want us to talk alone?"

"Farou! . . ."

She repulsed this gentleness, this kind attention which treated her as if she had a delirious fever. She could have killed Farou to see jet from him something involuntary, something irrepressible, blood, imprecations, laments. . . .

Farou ran the risk of laying one hand on her head and of bending over her, pressing back her brow. In the depths of his great amber pupils, Fanny read the desire to conquer her by sensual means, but, still deeper down, it seemed to her, a spirit of precaution, something cowardly, crouched, lurking and attentive. . . . Her madness fell back into her furthest depths, and by bending her neck she let the weighty hand glide over her hair.

"Listen, Farou . . . I am not capable of discussing this with you. . . . You came in too soon, you see? That's it, you came in too soon."

"All the better," said Farou, very dignified. "My place is here. Let's quit all that."

Fanny considered him, discouraged. She wanted in her turn, to speak to him in that accent of deplorable good-heartedness.

"No, Farou, let be. . . . It simply remains for Jane and me to finish, to talk it over together and to make, this evening, some . . . practical dispositions. Nothing shall be uttered between Jane and me that forces us to raise our voices. . . . Will it, Jane?"

"Naturally not," said Jane.

She was still standing in the same place, a little behind Fanny, with an attentive eye.

"Good . . ." agreed Farou. "Very well. . . . I see nothing difficult in that. You don't expect me to stay beside you in the study? Of course nothing which concerns us all three will be served up as food for the public? Not even for office gossip? I have absolute confidence . . ."

He profited by his suspended phrase to gain the door, slowly walking backward and imposing his yellow gaze from its superior height, now on one woman, now on the other.

"Yes, yes, yes," answered Fanny each time. She assented impatiently with her head, and the black rope of hair came undone at last. With both hands she twisted it hastily together again.

Farou's attention did not stray from the two tired faces, the thick, loose hair, which the white arms twisted. . . . A proposal of peace flickered through his eyes, which Fanny could not see. But it was of such sort that Jane advanced upon Farou with an aggressive movement.

"Yes, you may have confidence. But leave us alone, now, to talk."

Farou obeyed with a little shriveled smile. Jane followed him as far as the door, which she shut again, and then returned to Fanny, who was finishing pinning up her hair.

"That's that," said Jane dryly.

"Yes . . ." sighed Fanny, overwhelmed. "That's that!"

She let her arms fall down, along her sides.

"Rest, Fanny. Nothing is urgent."

Fanny made for her armchair at the corner of the hearth, and squeezed herself close to the fire. The maid going through forced Jane to sit down, and to paste up Farou's letters and the papers from the Authors' Society, which she pretended to be classifying. The maid crossed the room again, bearing Farou's shirt and dinner jacket.

"He's going out," said Fanny in a small voice.

"Yes," said Jane. "It's the dress designers' evening at the Gymnase. Are you going?"

Fanny did not answer. She curled herself into a ball in the armchair, her breasts against her knees, and contemplated the fire. Jane, sitting on the very edge of her chair, appeared to be waiting for someone to relieve her from duty. She took notes on a little pad, seemed to make mental calculations, and looked at the time by her wrist-watch.

About seven o'clock Jean Farou came home. Fanny answered his "Good evening, Mamie," mechanically, and did not move. But a perfume so offensive and so telltale was exhaled from Jean that the two women raised their heads at the same moment.

"Is it you who smell like that?" asked Fanny.

"Like what, Mamie?"

The bruised look of his eyelids, his glazed mouth with lips thickened and feverish, his youth darkened in its fall, the boy dedicated them all to Jane—turning them toward her like a persistent insult. He laughed, but without hardness, and drove himself to breathe the low perfume, the announcement at last of his deliverance, the scent of another woman. . . .

"Go and change," Fanny ordered him. "You make us ill."

He went out, proud of being compromised, proud of being censured.

"Would you believe it?" said Fanny. "What an ugly thing it is when a little boy changes into a man. . . . A little more and he'll bring her back to us. . . . So proud of having a mistress for himself . . ."

"For himself and against me," said Jane.

359

"That's true."

They felt themselves severely alone, and spoke without any reserve.

"He does as best he may; he hurts you so that he may cease loving you. . . ."

"Oh, loving me! . . . Perhaps enough to wish to do me harm. . . . Perhaps he has done me harm already. . . . I don't want to question you, Fanny," added Jane eagerly. "If you would like to, let's talk quickly and be done while we are quiet. . . . Let us admit that I'd better leave tomorrow—"

"No, no," interrupted Fanny. "Later, after dinner. . . . You can hear that they are already laying the dinner."

Jane gave her friend a long look.

"Do you wish me to dine here?"

"But that goes without saying," said Fanny wearily. "Don't let us complicate matters."

"Very well. You are right. I'm going into my room to tidy some things. If you need me . . ."

She found Fanny again, in the same place near a fire that was nearly out. She breathed to her: "Fanny, dinner!" And Fanny after a hasty toilet went into the dining-room, where the perfume brought back by Jean Farou strayed still but more faintly. With unusual courtesy Farou waited standing until his wife was seated.

Fanny noticed that he was newly shaved, his hair brushed, and that he was discreetly dusted with ocher-colored powder. His dinner jacket fitted his loins closely, and he straightened his neck so that his shoulders were less conspicuous.

"Whose mischief is he up to, tonight?" she asked herself, "Perhaps mine . . ."

Seated at table, she felt herself broken, weak, and hungry. She ate heartily, to Farou's great surprise, as he watched her while talking with his son. Jane also talked to Jean, who, not without impertinence, made a marked pause of astonishment before replying. Farou inclined the carafe of champagne ceremoniously toward his wife, and she mocked him:

"You have an air tonight rather like the large junior lead who plays in comedy, I don't know why . . ."

And she began to laugh the easy laugh that escapes from convalescents or from exhausted people. She thought:

"And my grief, what will become of it, in all this? When shall I have time to busy myself with it? There has been room today for reason and unreason, for anger, for everything except that. . . . They'll end by taking it from me. . . ."

Farou left the house cunningly and nimbly, talking, lighting a cigarette, putting on an overcoat. Fanny thought he was in the anteroom, Jane believed him to be in the bathroom, when he was already crossing the street. Fanny, alone, opposite Jane, nodded a head a little light now, with the dry wine:

"That's what I call the charwoman's style of exit."

"How?" Jane broke in.

"Haven't you noticed that one never knows exactly when the charwoman goes? She vanishes like a sylph. It's because she takes off with her some little souvenir, a slice of veal for her husband, coffee grounds in a bottle, the crumbs in the sugar-basin. . . ."

She laughed again. But in the salon where she now sought refuge someone had already made up the fire and folded over the arm of her favorite armchair, the large vicugna shawl; and grief in its most egotistic form seized Fanny by the throat. The idea of being abandoned, the threat of an approaching solitude, dissipated the fleeting warmth that she had derived from the plentiful meal. "One is so alone with Farou . . ." She sat down, tucked the shawl round her legs, and closed her eyes upon two tears.

"Do I worry you?" asked Jane in a low voice.

"No, no," said Fanny without opening her eyes.

"Would you rather we talked now? . . . Yes? . . . Tomorrow morning early I can reach Delvaille by telephone. At bottom she will be delighted to take up her old post—"

"What Delvaille? . . . What post?"

Fanny took combs and hairpins out of her hair and pillowed her head upon the long damp seaweeds of its blackness.

"Why, Farou's old secretary, don't you remember?"

"Not Delvaille, Jane! No, no, not Delvaille."

"What did she do to you?"

Under her loosened hair and her eastern pallor, Fanny opened the wet eyes of a gentle, wild shipwrecked creature. She recovered herself with difficulty, to chase away the image of a Delvaille, old, fat, short, active, and with child. . . . Delvaille at work. . . . "And Jane? And Jane?" Jane, absent, Jane effaced. . . . "Nothing," she admitted. "But really, there are more important things to do than calling Delvaille back. Farou's red tape can't wait any longer? Well, let it go to the devil, Farou's red tape!"

"To the devil, with all my heart, but not to you. . . . Consider—"

"Exactly. I shall take time to consider."

She fell back again on her pillow of hair. When Jean Farou came bursting in, in evening dress, she complained.

"Still feeling rotten, Mamie? It happens rather often now. . . . Why not see a doctor? . . . I just looked in to say good night. . . ."

He kissed the tips of her fingers, and she noticed that he had changed the way of brushing his hair. He had round his wrist a thin gold chain, and in his shirt a jeweled stud that she did not recognize. The two women read as if in clear language the seals stamped on him by a woman.

"Luckily I leave you in good hands. . . . Good night, Jane. . . ."

He went out with a naughty, light-hearted air.

"Look how pleased he is," said Jane. "He went out if I'm not mistaken on a 'barbed allusion.'"

"Poor boy!" said Fanny vaguely.

"Oh, all the same," Jane took up, "you have better things to do than to commiserate with *them*."

The plural made Fanny thoughtful. The crackle of the fire and the regular pricking sound of a needle benumbed her.

"What are you sewing?" she asked suddenly.

"I'm mending my thick gloves," said Jane. "This leather is as solid . . . it won't wear out, and they're so good for a journey. . . ."

"Ah yes . . ."

Fanny shivered at the word "journey." She dreamed of cold, of a whistling wind, of arid white platforms, she saw the hotel room and the electric light bare on the ceiling. She was not among those who take themselves into exile; she could not imagine a solitude greater than that of being pushed on one side, nor any other resolve than to wait.

The valet-de-chambre crossed the room, bearing a bottle of mineral water, oranges and two glasses for the tables beside the bed.

"Oranges and two glasses . . ." said Fanny to herself. "It's true; Farou is coming back."

She feared the night hours, the beds and the twin bodies, Farou and perhaps his strategic sensuality, which was not without its dangers. . . .

"I know him," thought Fanny humbly. "He will shine more than he did this afternoon. . . . Oh, this afternoon! . . ."

"Jane," she exclaimed, "can't you tell me—"

The woman sewing, waited, needle in air. She had not yet concealed her real face behind the mask of a girl nearly thirty, and she smiled with desolating hollows in her cheeks.

"I don't see what there can be that I can't tell you, Fanny, now. . . ."

"Then tell me, didn't you, as well as I, think Farou gave himself away incredibly this afternoon? . . . That he was—"

She could control herself no longer, and rose to her feet, giving herself the comfort of crying out:

"I found him beyond everything, quite beyond everything! Why did he behave so?"

"How would you have had him behave?" retorted Jane sharply. "Did you think he was going to show temper? or beat you? or throw me out of the window? . . . A man in such a situation? . . . But there's not one man in a hundred who'd come out of it to advantage, let alone to his honor."

She shook her head.

"It's too difficult for them," she concluded, without comment, and as if keeping to herself the most enlightening part of her experience.

363

"Why?" asked Fanny weakly.

Jane bit the thread off with her teeth.

"Because. It's like that. They're nervous, you know," she said, still using the same disobliging plural. "And then they are so made that in the middle of the sort of thing we call a scene or a dispute, they suddenly see the possibility of being rid of us forever. . . ."

Fanny did not reply. She saw again old days, passionate days, when she wept and railed with jealousy before a Farou mute, detached, withdrawn upon one of his heights from whence his hostile male regard whirled and plunged her down into the abyss; her, his most cherished possession, his superfluous encumbrance. . . . She walked up and down between the windows to relax the stiffness that was cramping her body. She halted before Jane, and looked long and deeply into her face.

"You have an aim in talking so slightingly of Farou to me?"

"An aim? No."

"A motive, at least? A project? An intention, look, an idea!"

With both hands she flattened her dark, loose, rose-colored gown against her thighs, and shook a fume of hair above Jane.

"Do you suspect me?" asked Jane with quivering lip.

"No. I don't suspect you yet. But why do you speak so ill of Farou?"

Jane narrowed her eyes, as they looked toward the study door. But, as if it would have taken more words to explain the man than to accuse him, she had recourse to her original grievance.

"It's out of spite," she affirmed, sustaining Fanny's stare.

"Out of spite? . . ." repeated Fanny. "As she did for Quémeré and for Davidson, then? . . ."

She could not realize that Jane might treat Big Farou as no more than a plain Meyrowicz, or that Jane might use the single word "spite," to denote the ingratitude, the sardonic nicety, with which the woman in all races pays the man from whom, not without injury, she has escaped.

"Out of spite," insisted Jane, "out of spite. What would you have me say! . . . You don't understand, do you? That's because you are

364

Fanny. . . . You are far too good a human being for that, dear . . .
dear Fanny. . . ."

She had dared at last to make captive the drooping hand, and
pressed it against her cheek The hand fought painfully, wriggled
and made itself limp so that it might get loose, and Jane took up her
needle again.

"It has come," thought Fanny, in front of the dark panes, "it has
come, then, the hour when I must decide whether I am to unclasp,
by main force, this hand that tends me . . . this hand fastened upon
my wrist, soothed in the hollow of mine, crooked under my elbow,
this hand on my shoulder, this companion of my hand during our
holiday walks. . . . I might have been certain I should have to deal
with this hand that brings the vicugna rug, that turns up my coat
collar, that tends my hair, this hand that met my hand under the
damp sheets of little sick Farou. . . . It is the same hand, stained with
copying ink, that dyed the fingers of Farou in violet, and betrayed
him to me. . . ."

"It's icy between those two windows, Fanny. . . ."

"But," pursued Fanny, returning docile to the fire, "where shall
I find, and by what right shall I find a balance that will weigh what
I owe this hand against what it has stolen from me? . . ."

She fell into a long reverie, at times almost like sleep. When she
opened her eyes again, and turned them away from the fire, she
stared slowly round the room, planted with tall lamps and their
large lampshades.

Jane, at one of the tables, was arranging files and documents.
"Farou's red tape. . . ."

"Is it any use, all that?" asked Fanny.

The short hair, brilliant with clear gold and silver, the young,
tired face turned eagerly toward her.

"Not the least. But he likes me to keep everything. It's a mania.
It has to be looked at. I leave nothing untidy, you know. . . ."

The warm silence closed in again, attacked from outside by little
noises, protected from within by the low and even chatter of the fire.

365

Toward eleven o'clock Jane rose and carried the files and papers into the study.

"Tomorrow," mused Fanny, "tomorrow, if she goes away, I shall be like this, alone by the fire, like a woman who has done with a great part of love. Farou will perhaps have the notion of keeping me company. . . . That would be the worst. For he would batter at walls, windows, and chimney, he would break in the paneling, or he would sleep, his head across this chair. Or else he would work beside me, in quest of Jane at every moment, and the two of us would curse each other. At the end of a week, he will have replaced her. . . . But I, I shall not so easily replace her. He will find again his favorite Moslem type of happiness; it is his destiny. He will find again his innocence, his solitude, and his profession. But I—with whom can I now be two again? Two is not too many, to be alone with Farou . . . against Farou. . . ."

She sat up in her armchair, seeking with her eyes for a book or a game; the green table folded against the wall no longer waited for its litter of cards.

"Before Jane, there was here at my side a little boy, fair and charming, who played cards with me. . . . He was there for a long time, almost for a dozen years. I have lost this little boy. He was pretty, and the sound of his voice, his secrets, his delicate health in the old days put something feminine into our house, where there was nothing but Farou. . . . I am no longer young enough, rich enough, brave enough, to stay alone with Farou—nor far from Farou. . . ."

She set herself by will to conjure up a strict vision of Farou stripped of her wifely touching-up. But she wearied of it as she would have wearied of following, with her head thrown back, one of those silent birds that fly in great circles round a nest upon which they hardly ever come to earth. She passed in review certain steadfast couples, endeavoring to estimate the man's part in adapting himself to women.

"Phew! . . . The most certain sign of their possession is that they speak of their man, that they complain of him, that they boast of him, and wait for him. But everything that they set up might be done just as well without the actual presence or existence of the man. ..."

She realized that she was blackening the remains of a pure religion, whose faithful lived only in expectation of the god and in the childishness of the cult. And she retraced her steps on that road, toward a security which could come to her only from loyalty, be it wavering or sometimes treacherous, a woman's loyalty, constantly undermined by the man, constantly built up again at the man's expense. ...

"Where is Jane?"

"Jane!"

Jane came at once. In spite of the weariness that made her face look gray, she was ready to watch, to answer every call, to work meticulously.

"Jane, don't you want to go to bed?"

"Not before you."

"Are you waiting for Farou?"

"Not without you."

She sat down on the side of the fireplace opposite Fanny, and poked the fire anxiously. She strained an ear for the after-midnight sounds, and became motionless as a taxi, going down the street, slowed up.

"If I flayed Jane, with the first blood I should meet Farou again," thought Fanny. "Tomorrow, the day after tomorrow, and later it will be the same to me if she comes into collision with me. ..."

The heavy house door shut downstairs, then the little door of the lift on the landing. Jane consulted Fanny with a nervous look, and got up.

"Where are you going? It's only Farou who has come in," said Fanny, exaggerating her calm.

But Jane, losing color, confessed her nervousness, and muttered:

"A scene ... so painful ..."

"A scene? ... with Farou? My dear," said Fanny, resuming her dignity as the elder, "you mustn't think of it. Why a scene with

Farou? We've mixed Farou up too much already in our affairs. I reproach myself for it," she added, forcing herself a little.

They listened to the long turning of the key. Steps in the anteroom took the direction of the study, halted, and returned meditatively toward the salon. Then they changed their tone, grew very light, and tiptoed away, and ceased.

"He's gone away," said Fanny, very low.

"He saw the light under the door. . . . Perhaps you ought to go and find him?" suggested Jane.

Fanny shrugged her shoulders. With her ten fingers, she lifted the weight of her hair from the nape of her neck to refresh herself, edged her toes near the fire, and peeled an orange.

"There's no hurry," she said at last. "We've all the time in the world. Is he very late?"

"No, no. . . . It's scarcely half past twelve," Jane assured her. "It's so good here," she said, disguising the pain in her voice. "Tomorrow I—"

"Hush, Jane! Who asks you to think about tomorrow? Tomorrow is a day like other days. It will be fine. . . ."

They exchanged nothing more except an occasional ordinary word. Feigning, one of them to read, the other to sew, they wished for nothing better than to be quiet, to let themselves rest and relax the forces which the man had not outfaced, and to set themselves silently to nourish their weak security, as yet hardly born.

Duo

*H*E OPENED the door brusquely and stood for a moment on the threshold. "Good God!" he sighed, as he groped his way to the sofa and, throwing himself on it, reveled in the coolness of the shaded room.

But he wanted to grumble, not rest, so he sat up sharply.

"They put me through the whole program. Chevestre dragged me everywhere—look at those shoes! First it was the barn falling in on the cows, then the river overflowing the willow patch, and the man on the other bank who dynamites the fish. . . . Really, I had to—"

He stopped short.

"You look very well in that setting."

His wife had placed the plain old desk in the deep recess of the window, where the sunlight, scintillating with floating particles of dust, fell full upon it. In front of her stood a low dish of thick glass filled with purple-tinted orchids, mute evidence that she had been down in the damp meadows, among the thickets of alder and willow. Her hand rested on a leather portfolio of the same color as the flowers; it cast a reflection on her face and gave a darker tone to her greenish gray eyes, which Michel said resembled the leaves of the willow tree.

371

Alice listened good-humoredly to her husband's complaints, responding merely with a drowsy smile. It always gave him infinite pleasure to notice how her eyes, when she smiled, assumed almost the same shape and size as her mouth.

"Your hair takes on a reddish tint down here," Michel remarked. "In Paris it is black."

"And white, also," Alice replied. "Ten—twenty white hairs right here, on top."

She leaned forward into the sunlight as she told this coquettish lie, being proud that, at thirty-seven, she still kept her youthful, carefree face and supple figure. She noticed that Michel was getting up to come toward her.

"No, Michel, please! Those shoes of yours! Have mercy on the floor, which was just waxed this morning. Look at all that red mud!"

The sound of her voice always won the day with Michel. It, too, was drowsy, with a slightly plaintive note, and had a way of protesting gently against good and bad alike in the same tone.

Michel spread his legs V-fashion and took care to have only his heels touch the wide, well-worn planks of the flooring.

"That red mud, my dear, came from the banks of the river. The hero who has the honor of addressing you started out from here about nine this morning and never stopped a minute except for a glass of white wine—and what wine! Ugh! Of a deadly, greenish white—stuff fit to scour pots and pans with and put an edge on the kitchen knives."

Michel got up with some effort, rubbing his back.

"My dear, it's the price we have to pay for our Easter vacation here. Who knows whether we shall still be the owners of this place a year from now? That fellow Chevestre looks for all the world as if he would like to get possession of it. And as for me, I don't know how much longer I shall be in the mood to hang on to it."

He walked up and down the room, leaving a trail of dry mud behind him, but Alice was no longer thinking of the floor.

"Are things in such a bad state here, Michel?"

What struck Michel most forcibly in her pleading tone was the need to be reassured, so he replied:

"No, not exactly that, little one. No worse than elsewhere. It's only what one would expect. The roofs have served their time. The farm is limping along with a fifty-year-old equipment. . . . Chevestre takes only the normal amount of graft, I imagine. . . . We would have to make up our minds to devote every penny, all the profits from the Petit Casino, to patching up Cransac and putting it in proper condition. When I think how only a few years ago one picture used to run for months and how we used to fit out a road company in a musical comedy every winter with Jeanne Rasimi's left-over costumes. When I recall—"

Alice raised her hand to check him.

"No, don't recall it. That's just what you should try not to remember. How about the willows?"

"They have branched too much. We shall get very little for them."

"But why did they branch that way?"

Michel, looking down at her affectionately, said with the condescending air of an expert, "Why? My dear child, do you mean to say you don't know?"

"No. Do you?"

He laughed softly.

"No, I don't, either. I don't understand their ways at all. Chevestre claims it was on account of the heat. But Maure, the tenant, maintains that Chevestre ought to have cut them back sharply two years ago and that anyhow the land there is too swampy. All of which means very little to me, as you can well understand."

He said this with a gesture of mock despair. Then he became serious and silent and turned toward the French window. In the first burst of spring foliage the neglected clumps of shrubbery were crowding toward the house their unpruned shoots and long rosebush suckers, reddened with an apoplectic rush of sap. The green of the poplars was not yet visible under the gold and copper of the tender leaves. A wild-apple tree, its white petals lined with carmine, had

373

overgrown a sickly Judas tree, and the syringas, in their effort to escape the deadly shade of the shiny green aucubas, thrust out between the broad, domineering leaves of the latter their own slender branches, dotted with creamy white, star-like flowers.

Michel took in at a glance the overgrown path, unpruned shrubbery and tangled vegetation.

"They are struggling against one another," he said in a low tone. "If you watch them too long, it becomes a depressing sight."

"What does?" Alice asked.

Half turning in her chair, she compared the Michel of today with the Michel of a year ago. Very little changed, she thought. Although he was her height, he seemed rather short of stature and she very tall. He resorted more than she did to conscious use of a certain purely physical charm and to a youthfulness of movement that came from his having been engaged in two or three lines of business in which one must make oneself attractive to women as well as men. As he talked, he showed his well kept teeth and his soft brown eyes. To hide the sagging flesh under his chin, he had recently taken to wearing a little Spanish beard reaching from ear to ear, silken and curly and so short that it looked as if it had been painted on his skin. With his low forehead and its fringe of curly hair, his undistinguished nose and full lips, he resembled some old Roman bust.

Alice glanced at him furtively now and then as she sketched. Her chief dread was that he might confide to her, all at one time, too many worrisome problems. The fine weather and a gentle, tingling bodily lassitude had undermined her morale and made her desire to be left in ignorance of the fact that, each time it rained, the roof lost some of its lichen-gilded tiles and that, down at the cow barn, they had taken to stopping the holes in the walls with straw, instead of sending for a mason. In Paris, at any rate, she did not have to think of such matters.

"Anything else?" she asked in spite of herself.

Michel gave a start and then mumbled, like a man just aroused from sleep, or someone trying to gain time:

"What do you mean, anything else? . . . No, nothing else. As you

374

know, Chevestre never talks to me about anything except annoying matters. Three hours of exasperation when we arrive and three more the day before we leave, one or two disgusting little items during our stay—that's the price I pay for our Easter vacation. Is it worth it or not?"

Passing behind his wife, he leaned his elbows on the worm-eaten window sill and breathed in the fragrance of his birthplace. The soft, purple-tinted earth, the grass already high, the catalpa blossoms over-topping the red hawthorn, the shower of wild-rose petals on the threshold of the French window, the syringas forced into bloom by the warm weather, the laburnum hanging in long yellow clusters —he would have liked never to give up any of these neglected old possessions, so refreshing to the eye, although the only thing he clung to with unreasoning tenacity was Alice herself. In the distance, like the smoke of a brush fire, mist was rising under the sun's heat from the river, hidden from sight and swollen with the cold spring freshets.

"Chevestre would pay the top price," he thought to himself. "He wants the place badly, the crook. He has played his cards well. Capderac, over there, was right when he warned me, 'When your manager takes to wearing riding boots, get rid of him or else he will get rid of you.'"

A slender hand rested on his sleeve.

"It's certainly worth it, Michel," Alice replied to his question.

Without getting up, she had turned her chair around facing the window and the incoming flood of sunlight, insect sounds and cackling of hens and the oft-repeated song of the nightingales. The low, brown-raftered ceiling, the dark tones of the furniture, and the wallpaper, with its flowered pattern on a tan background, absorbed the light and cast only occasional reflections on the round surface of a porcelain vase, a copper jug or the bevel of an Italian mirror. Alice spent virtually all her time in this combination study and living room, but always either at the French window or before the fireplace, avoiding the somber corners and the two huge bookcases, reaching to the ceiling.

"You're very sweet, dear," Michel said abruptly, as he stroked his wife's smooth hair.

He felt himself giving way, about to yield to a wave of emotion, which he tried to hide.

"Getting soft, eh?" he mused. "It must be fatigue, and then the weather! Such heat! I'll wager it's warmer here than in Nice."

From his years as a manager of casinos he had acquired the habit of comparing everything with Nice, Monte Carlo or Cannes, but he no longer dared do this in Alice's presence, lest she frown, wrinkling up her cat-like nose, and complain in a scolding tone of voice, "Don't talk shop all the time, Michel!"

The round, smooth head submitted to the caresses of Michel's skilful hand, for he knew how to stroke it in such a way as not to disarrange Alice's invariable way of doing her hair, perfectly straight and with a thick bang cut parallel to her horizontal eyebrows. She wore daring dresses, but a special timidity kept her from ever changing her coiffure.

"No more, Michel. It tires me."

He leaned over the seductive upturned face—so slow to show the years, despite the absence of cosmetics—and those eyes, so quick to close from either ennui or unbearable bliss.

"If I should sell Cransac," he reflected, "we could begin to put something aside. Even without making any repairs, this place is a heavy load to carry. If I got rid of it, it would be a great relief and I could do more for Alice. I would still be only too glad to go on working myself to death for her—for both of us."

In his silent monologues he liked to use romantic expressions and hunched his shoulders, as if in the struggle for existence.

"You're very warm and friendly this morning, dear—more so than you were last night."

Alice did not protest but took care after that, when she looked at him, to let him see only a slender, bluish white line behind her darkened eyelashes and the smile playing about her mouth. He whispered some caressing, brutally frank words, to which she responded with a quivering of the eyelashes, as if he had shaken a moist bouquet over her. They were both very susceptible to this sudden hunger for one another as a result of some chance incident, or a journey, or some unexpected manifestation of nature's beauty.

They had arrived at Cransac the night before in a spring thunderstorm and had found there rain, the setting sun, a rainbow over the river, lilac bushes weighted down with moisture, the moon rising in a greenish sky, glistening little hoptoads under the steps of the porch. During the night they had listened to the raindrops falling heavily from the trees and to the generous singing of the nightingales.

Now, as her husband pressed her head and warm shoulder close to him, stroking her chin with a hand that forgot to be gentle, she suddenly pushed him away with the whispered warning, "Maria's coming—it's half-past twelve!"

"What of it? Let her come. She's caught us more than once."

"Yes, but I've never liked it. Nor has she. Pull down your sweater and smooth your hair a bit."

"All right," Michel agreed. "Let's look natural. Here comes the policeman."

Alice never laughed when her husband joked in a certain clumsy, obvious way, but she showed no sign of impatience, having learned to distinguish between his intentionally exaggerated vulgarity and his innate delicacy. "I don't like it when you're witty," she was wont to say. "It's a sign you aren't happy."

The billowing wooden floor in the hallway creaked under Maria's footsteps. Noisily opening the door and sticking her head part way in, she asked, "Shall I ring the first bell, ma'am?"

"What about me?" her master called out jestingly. "Don't I count at all, you old grouch?"

Maria somewhat resembled a horse or, more especially, one of those grasshoppers with a horse-shaped head. She laughed, showing her appreciation with a wink of her twinkling little eye, and shut the door with a bang. Alice got up and started putting away her drawing materials.

"You go to a lot of trouble to keep in Maria's good graces," she remarked.

"Jealous, eh?" Michel exclaimed in his best headwaiter manner.

His wife did not deign to reply. With the palm of her hand she felt to make sure that her smooth, oddly dressed hair was in order. She knew very well that Maria, faithful as a watchdog, did not recognize any other authority than Michel's or submit to anyone else's cajoling. Shrewd and angular, at fifty Maria played very well the rôle of "the master's old nurse" and knew how to clasp her hands and sigh, "You ought to have seen him when he was a young man!"—whereas the fact was, she had been only ten years in his employ and, if she sometimes looked Alice squarely in the eye as though they were equals, it was because they had both arrived at Cransac in the same year. Notwithstanding all this, Alice did her full justice for the stern, honest vigilance with which she watched over Cransac, with no one to help her but her husband, a robust, weak-willed Jack-of-all-trades, discouraged by the thirty acres which the estate comprised.

"Well, suppose we go and wash up?" Michel suggested.

"All right, but in the kitchen, because the bathroom has just been cleaned and I forbid you to go in there. I even polished the metal fixtures."

He laughed and called her a "double-barreled fanatic."

"Do you think Maria will like our washing at her sink?"

Alice indolently turned her dark head and looked at him out of her handsome gray eyes, flecked with green by the dazzling light from the window.

"No, but she knows she can't always show it when something displeases her. Where are you taking those flowers?"

Michel was gingerly carrying the little bowl of thick glass, overflowing with wild orchids.

"Why, to the dining room. Their violet reflection in your eyes and on your cheeks was too lovely—like that! But we ought to have that other thing, too—that what-you-may-call-it of the same color—you know what I mean."

"I have no idea what you're talking about. Look out, Michel, you're spilling the water. Are you coming?"

"I never spill anything. I mean that sort of portfolio you had there on your desk. I don't see it any more—did you put it away? What were you using it for? Were you writing some letters?"

"No, I was just sketching some costumes in an aimless sort of way."

"What for?"

Alice looked at him in a faraway manner, as she replied, with an apologetic little smile:

"You know, it's a weakness of mine. I keep thinking, if they should put on *Daffodil* again next winter, the costumes I've designed wouldn't cost any more—and probably less—than to make over the costumes of *Mogador* and, without wishing to brag—"

She completed the sentence with a shrug of the shoulders and a wave of her slender hand.

"Let me see them," Michel commanded impulsively, as he set the little bowl down on the desk. "Where are your drawings? In the purple portfolio?"

Alice snapped her fingers with impatience.

"Do come along, Michel! Why all this fuss? There isn't any purple portfolio. Let's go and have lunch."

Michel looked at his wife with an injured air.

"What an idea! There isn't any purple portfolio? Talking to me as if I were an infant!"

Pointing to the spot on Alice's cheek where the now vanished reflection had been, he added in a low voice:

"There—and there! A color beautiful enough to paint—like the reflection from red and blue footlights—a purplish red—stunning!"

Alice shrugged her shoulders and pouted as though she did not understand what he was driving at.

"Well, I'm going to lunch, Michel. The omelet will be cold."

"Wait a minute!"

It was his tone, rather than the command itself, which made her stop. He had spoken in a sharp tenor voice. She knew the reason for such a sudden change of tone. As she turned back, she noticed a greenish cast over his face and a quickening of his breath. She paused a moment to allow herself the luxury of reflecting that he

379

looked like a smaller edition of Mathô; then she walked calmly forward into the unknown.

"What are you so upset about, Michel?"

He shook his curly head, as if to reject everything she was going to say.

"Don't try to cover up, Alice. There's something going on here. Come now—you say there isn't any purple whatever-you-call-it. I'm not an idiot. Say it again—is there or isn't there?"

Alice looked disconsolately at her husband's distorted features and at the sudden dark lines around the eyes. She cast a quick glance about her to try to find on the walls or among the rafters some stray bit of color, some purplish gleam, some reflection from one crystal to another. Finding nothing, her eyes turned back to Michel.

"No," she said sadly.

She watched him with so much uneasiness that he misunderstood. Sighing deeply with relief, he sank into Alice's chair.

"Good God, I'm all in! What struck me? What's the matter with me?"

He looked up at her like a child. She almost gave way and was on the point of putting her arms about him and crying a little, and trembling in the protection of his embrace. But she yielded only as far as prudence dictated. Assuming a smile of mild surprise, she consciously opened wide her almond-shaped eyes and met squarely Michel's look of entreaty.

"How you scared me, Michel!" she said plaintively.

He studied her with the stern, anxious affection which many a fickle man inwardly bestows on a faithful wife. He sighed with relief to find her so like herself—the very lightly roughed lips, the lower one full and chapped, the upper one small and tightly drawn —the rather squat little pugnose, homely, Asiatic and inimitable— and especially those eyes, long, leaf-shaped, greenish gray, pale under the evening lamp, darker-toned in the morning.

She did not move or look away, but Michel noticed that one of her eyebrows, under the heavy bang, twitched almost imperceptibly

with a slight nervous contraction. At the same time his nostrils
caught the odor that betrays emotion, the smell of perspiration
cruelly drawn from the pores by fear or distress, an odor like an
imitation sandalwood or heated boxwood, an odor peculiar to
moments of love-making and the long days of midsummer. Freeing
himself from the compassionate embrace of her arms, he turned
partly around and opened the drawer of the desk.

The morocco-leather portfolio glistened as the sunlight fell on it.
Michel's first reaction was a childlike cry of triumph, "There!
See?" Because he smiled as he repeated "See? See?" Alice decided to
smile likewise. She was not thinking of anything in particular, her
attention being centered chiefly on remaining motionless. "If I don't
move," she figured to herself, "he won't either."

But the instant Alice smiled, Michel's expression changed and she
saw that his smile had been a meaningless accident. Grasping
piteously at the first straw within her reach, she remarked, "The bell
has rung for luncheon."

Michel turned mechanically toward the window and leaned forward as if to try to see the little black bell half hidden by the yellow
jasmine and the early roses. Alice hoped he would get himself
under control and, uneasy over Maria's keen observation and the delaying of their meal, come with her and postpone further investigation, discussion or action until after luncheon.

"By that time," she said to herself, "I'll have everything fixed up—
or else we'll both be dead."

She ventured to turn slightly toward the door, but Michel held
her by the wrist.

"Wait!" he said. "We're not through with this yet."

Pretending to be in pain, Alice groaned rather loudly and forced
herself to cry.

"You're hurting me! Let go of me!"

He quickly relaxed his grip and she wrenched her wrist free. Her
hope that he might treat her roughly vanished, for he retained his
composure, but more like a shipwrecked man who, half-choked
with the waves, keeps repeating, "Too bad! I had worn these cuff-

links only twice." He looked at her with an attentive, alert expression, for his state of mind had progressed no further than that and he was still inspired by hope as much as she—he was fighting for her, not against her.

For a moment he became "reasonable" again, as she expressed it—his head a little on one side and a slightly embarrassed smile playing about his soft brown eyes. Alice felt herself grow old in the space of a few seconds. "I shall never be able to save him from what he dreads," she thought and, discouraged, she began to detest him. She slumped down, letting all her weight fall on one leg, and realized that this attitude amounted to a sort of surrender.

Still Michel did not open the purple portfolio and Alice had time to read in his manner a cowardly wish quite like her own—that he might close the drawer and endeavor to recapture a moment which was fleeing and, in its flight, leaving them transfixed, forgotten, motionless—the moment when Michel had mentioned the purple reflection on Alice's cheek. "I'm going to tell him it's just a game," Alice said to herself. "I'll seize the portfolio and run away and he'll run after me and—"

Michel, with his head close to Alice's warm breast, asked apprehensively, "What's inside?"

Alice shrugged her shoulders slightly and leaned toward him as though to say farewell.

"Nothing—nothing now."

Michel pounced angrily on those last two words.

"So you've had time to clear out everything, eh?"

Alice started back, breathing deeply through her distended Asiatic nostrils and moistening her chapped lip. Her face seemed suddenly younger. At last she was going to have to argue, defend herself, make diplomatic admissions, hurt Michel deeply in order to divert his attention and prevent him from wounding himself too deeply. "I must patch up the mess I've made," she thought. "What ever got into me to say there was no purple portfolio? Poor Michel!"

The tears she held back gave added luster to her eyes and the blood mounted to her cheeks as she modestly held her elbows close to her body because of the widening damp spot that was darkening her blue dress under each arm.

"Listen, Michel. I can explain it all so easily!"

Michel laughed ironically, raising his hand.

"You don't say so! Well, I beg to differ. I should be extremely surprised, indeed!"

She had many a time seen him put on that light-hearted manner and cynical smile when he believed some business venture was going on the rocks.

"Michel, if you could bring yourself not to open that portfolio, you'd be doing a very wise thing. What's in there is no longer of any importance to either you or me. But if you must open it, bear in mind that the—er—writing you'll find there no longer means anything at all. It's old stuff, the remains of something that is dead and gone—completely wiped out—of no importance now, absolutely none."

Michel listened to her dumbfounded, raising his eyebrows and plucking at his little beard with a skeptical air, but he caught the essential point.

"Of no importance, eh? We'll see about that."

He seized the polished morocco portfolio, which reflected the sunlight like a mirror. A purple spot of light leapt to the ceiling and quivered among the brown rafters. As he opened the portfolio, a small sheet of thin paper fluttered obliquely to the floor between the legs of the desk. Alice laid a hand on his sleeve.

"You really couldn't leave it there?" she pleaded. "I'll throw it away, or burn it, and then—. Michel, for the sake of your own happiness and mine!"

He stooped down with a little effort and, as he sat up again, he cast a quick, angry glance at her. He was vexed with her for having shown so much uneasiness that he had been forced to pick up that thin, metallic sheet of paper, which crackled like a new banknote as he automatically fingered it. "Writing paper for foreign correspondence," he thought to himself. "The kind people use when they write one another letters ten and fifteen pages long."

383

But the sheet bore only a few lines in a very fine handwriting.

"Why, it's Ambrogio's handwriting!" he cried.

Alice caught the naïve note of hope in this exclamation and felt the cruelest moment drawing near. She went over and sat on the couch, not in her usual manner, with her long legs folded under her, but stiffly erect, ready to jump up and run away. This instinctive physical prudence alarmed her; she measured mentally the distance from the couch to the door, which, she remembered, did not open easily, and then from the couch to the window. "Good heavens, hasn't he read it yet?" she said to herself impatiently. "What is he waiting for? We're not going to spend the whole day this way, I hope!"

"Ambrogio!" Michel repeated. "What's the date of this letter?"

"Last November," Alice replied curtly.

"Last November? Why, I was at Saint Raphael then, wasn't I?"

She shrugged her shoulders, annoyed to see him open his eyes wide and hunt about for his round spectacles.

"On the file cabinet," she snapped in the same sharp voice.

"What?"

"On the file cabinet—your spectacles."

She was getting more and more exasperated, keyed up by the prospect of a dispute and a struggle. "My God, how stupid he looks!" she thought to herself. "He knows very well that he can't read Ambrogio's handwriting without his glasses. Am I going to have to read it aloud to him?"

As awkwardly as if he had been stark naked, Michel slowly hooked his spectacles behind his ears. Alice sensed that he felt mortified, on the verge of flying into a rage to hide his embarrassment, so she took care to show no emotion whatsoever. And anyhow, his whole manner changed the minute he glanced at the letter. Alice recalled its contents as he was reading it:

"I don't dare try to thank you, Alice, for such a blissful evening, such a heavenly night. I scarcely dare revive the memory of the

384

great boon you granted me—and plead for more. It is all too sweet,
too beautiful . . . I hold you close in my arms—all of you."

As she waited for Michel to look up, disjointed thoughts passed
through her mind in a strangely objective manner. "This is getting
to be a bore—He certainly takes his time about it—What an idiot
that fellow was to go and mention my name in his very first letter!
—And such a stupid letter!—It's true, the later ones were better—I
should have made up some kind of a story for Michel—It would
have been mere child's play—Just as I was about to tear up that
letter, damn the luck!—This'll teach me a lesson—I swear, if we get
out of this scrape without a catastrophe, I'm going to go to bed to
sleep till tomorrow morning."

When Michel had finished reading the letter, he folded up his
spectacles and looked at his wife. Her first feeling was one of great
relief that he had resumed his normal expression and no longer
showed any sign of embarrassment.

"Well?" he asked sharply.

"Well?" she replied, bridling up.

"I'm waiting for your explanation," he said after a pause.

She refused at first to admit the tone of his questioning. As a
strategic move, she displayed signs of irritation. She dilated her
Asiatic nostrils and puckered her eyebrows, and her thick bang
came down to her eyelashes.

"Does that require an explanation?" she asked in a clear voice.

Michel unconsciously imitated her expression. Frowning darkly,
he returned her wrathful smile, showing his small teeth.

"Well, a little supplementary information might be useful," he
observed ironically. "I am glad to see that you have the good taste
not to attempt to deny anything. . . . I beg you, my dear, not to try
that trick of pouting like a naughty Annamite boy, because that
doesn't go down any more. . . . So it's agreed that, while I was working my fool head off at the Casino at Saint Raphael and Ambrogio
was managing the Avenue Theatre for me, you and he—. Not a
very old affair, eh? In fact, quite recent, it would seem."

385

"Not at all," she replied scornfully. "I told you it ended long ago. I might add that it lasted only a very little while."

"At least, so you say," he retorted insinuatingly.

She made no reply but regretted the unfortunate turn their discussion had taken. She had hoped the matter would be quickly disposed of with a torrent of tears and reproaches, two cruel hands about her throat, the breaking of a vase. . . . She listened for Maria's footsteps and thought of the little black bell. "What's going to happen when the second bell rings?" she wondered. "If only I hadn't held Michel off when he came in, I know very well where we'd be at this moment. What a fool I was!"

She looked toward the door, flanked by the two enormous bookcases, and toward the bedroom, with its twin beds under a fringed canopy, and cursed herself anew. "Too lazy to take off my dress or get it out of the way!" she lamented. "Scared to have Maria notice that we had mussed the bedspread and made a mess in the bathroom. And now look at us!"

She sat there watching Michel's back, as he stood at the window, which the sun's rays were gradually leaving. At last he turned around and looked at her with that kindly expression she knew so well, weary but charming and very poor at registering sadness.

"What have you gone and done to us now, little one?" he remonstrated gently.

Taken unawares, she had to choke back an impulse to cry, check her sobs and gulp down the salty saliva. She struggled against a woman's desire to grovel and beg forgiveness and merely stammered, "Michel, I assure you—Michel, dearest!"

At that very instant the black bell hanging above the window shook off its restraining bonds of rambler rose and wistaria and pealed forth its shrill, insistent note. Alice stood up quickly, smoothed out her dress and arranged her hair. Cursing under his breath, Michel glanced at his wrist watch.

"That's the second bell," Alice remarked.

"And late at that," was Michel's comment. "Ah!" he added, with a gesture of despair which disclosed to Alice that he was thinking of Maria and her husband and Chevestre and the nearby village, with all its keen, inquisitive eyes.

"What are we going to do?" Alice asked softly, looking at Michel searchingly, with the humble expression of a contrite sinner.

"Why, we're going to lunch, of course," he replied, shrugging his shoulders and thrusting his hands deep into his pockets.

He stood aside to let her pass, then stopped her and looked closely at her face.

"You'd better put some powder on. And you have a dark spot under your eye—right there. Not with your finger—you're only spreading it. Do be careful!"

He offered her his handkerchief.

She had imagined that the luncheon would be an involved agony, a mockery of a meal, made stiff and formal by constraint and affected nonchalance, but to her dumbfounded surprise, she saw Michel devote his entire attention to throwing dust in Maria's eyes. Upon entering the dining room, which was always a bit damp and smelled like a cellar, he exclaimed:

"Ah! what do I see? Radishes already? Hothouse, I presume."

Alice stared at him from her chair as if he had made an indecent remark, but, since Maria condescended to laugh, Michel continued to employ the same means to achieve more success of the same sort. He questioned the blunt-spoken servant concerning the vegetable garden and affected intense interest on learning that a swarm of bees was building a hive under the eaves of the old roof. When Maria told him of the death of an old sheep dog that he had seen only twice, he exclaimed with a theatrical sigh, "Poor old chap!"

Meanwhile he poured out foaming cider for his wife, passed her the bread and said, "Beg pardon!" in comic imitation of polite society.

"Really, he's overdoing it," Alice thought to herself, considerably shocked at his behavior. "All these goings-on just for Maria's benefit! He'll arouse her suspicions yet—in fact, he's already done so. She's on to the whole thing."

As though she were reading a book, Maria glanced from one to the other, first at the chattering Michel, then at Alice, who remained a silent spectator, eating busily and husbanding her strength for later on. A damp, rumpled little handkerchief lying beside her plate drew Maria's gaze as if it had been a gold piece.

"Shall I serve the coffee here, ma'am?" Maria asked. "You aren't feeling well. Wouldn't you be more comfortable in the living room?"

Maria always addressed Alice in a respectful manner but with Michel she affected exaggerated familiarity and a peasant manner of speech.

"That's a fine idea!" Michel broke in. "Let's have the coffee in the living room."

"Do you wish brandy with it, sir?"

"Do I want brandy? What a question! Did you hear her, Alice? She's asking if I want brandy with my coffee! . . . After you, my dear. I'll hold the door. Maria, sancta Maria, gratia plena, aren't you ever going to get around to having this door fixed?"

Trembling with displeasure, Alice passed into the living room without uttering a word. "It's disgraceful!" she thought to herself savagely. "All this monkey business just for a servant! He's afraid of her, afraid she may find out his wife has been untrue to him. And to think I was afraid he might do something terrible! Well, I needn't worry on that score. Oh, I'm sick of the whole mess!" She lifted the coffee pot clumsily and nearly burst into tears when a few drops spattered the sugar.

"My dear child, how you're trembling! Come now, I'm not going to murder you!"

As Michel's eyes followed the movements of her unsteady hand, Alice weakened under the caressing tone of his kindly voice and looked up at him gratefully. "He's worn out with it, too," she thought. "The strain is killing. I'm ready to drop."

Michel nodded understandingly.

"I wish you wouldn't look so grateful, dear," he said. "What did you think I was going to do—smash everything and kick you out of the house? Cause a public scandal?"

Half closing her nearsighted eyes in a characteristic far-away manner, she replied, "Oh, no, not exactly that."

Catching the ambiguity of this reply, Michel thrust his chin forward and plunged his clenched fists into his pockets, exclaiming:

"I don't know but it might have been just as well if I had. Don't go and imagine we're not going to have to discuss this matter some more."

"Hmm," he added, with a self-important, pompous air, as he strode toward the window, which the sunlight was quitting. The birds had followed the sunlight and even the bees had abandoned the deep casement. On the desk lay the purple leather portfolio, now lusterless.

"It will soon be evening," Alice thought. Quivering with nervous exhaustion, she half reclined on the couch and threw over her knees the plaid shawl that always stayed behind at Cransac and was now moth-eaten and riddled with cigarette burns from noonday siestas.

"If I ask him for a cigarette, will he take it as a bit of bravado or a sign of callous guilt?" she wondered, her eyes fastened on Michel's back and shoulders as he stood before the window. "He's dilating his nostrils now like a bull and swelling up all over. Maybe he's angry. Or he may be quite cool underneath it all. With these men of part southern blood, you never can tell. . . . Can it be that everything's ruined now and all through my fault? . . . This has been going on for barely an hour and already it seems as if I couldn't stand it a minute longer. If only I could be sure he wasn't unhappy, I'd drop the whole business and go to bed with a hot-water bottle alongside me. But if he's unhappy over it, why that's more than I can stand—it's unfair—too stupid for words. . . . Michel, my poor boy!"

He turned around just as she mentally called to him and this little miracle almost made her hold out her arms to him.

"No, indeed," he said, resuming his threat where he had left off. "Don't get the idea we're through. We've only just begun."

Alice closed her pale eyes and let her head fall back on a faded silk sofa cushion. Raising her hand in a deprecating gesture, she said wearily: "Listen, Michel. That silly thing I did—"

"That shameful thing, you mean," Michel interposed emphatically but without raising his voice.

"All right, have it your way. That shameful thing, then, which merely flitted through my life while you were away, began and ended in less than four weeks—. What's that? Now, see here! You're not going to keep interrupting me all the time!" she suddenly cried out, opening wide her eyes, which seemed almost blue when in shadow. "You let me say what I've got to say!"

With a noiseless bound Michel jumped to the half-open door and closed it, taking care not to make a sound.

"Are you out of your head?" he exclaimed. "They're down there in the kitchen, having lunch. Anybody'd think—really, now!—'on my word! And the postman, too, probably just coming up the hill!"

He stammered and talked excitedly, although he circumspectly kept his wrath under control and did not raise his voice. He gesticulated vehemently toward the window, opening his mouth in a squarish shape, Alice noted, like the masks of classic comedy. Disregarding his warning, she shrugged her shoulders vigorously and resumed her tirade.

"How about the boy who goes after the cows? Aren't you forgetting him? And then there's Chevestre, who is surely lying in ambush somewhere or other. And the girl at the post office? Maybe she put on her Sunday bonnet and is coming to ask your help in getting a promotion. So, that's what you're afraid of—those people! They're the ones who count in your eyes. They're the ones you're concerned about!"

She fell back on the couch and covered her eyes with her forearm. Hearing her breath coming heavily, as if she were sobbing, Michel bent over her.

"My God, Alice, control yourself! . . . Come now, what have I said? Do you realize—?"

Uncovering her red, tearless eyes, she sat up with an angry flounce.

"I haven't the slightest idea what you said! I don't care a damn what you said! But I do know this, that if you're going to poison our existence just because I may have slept for once in my life with

390

somebody else besides you, then I prefer to go away this very minute. . . . Oh, dear, I can't stand this any longer!"

She pummeled the dusty silk cushion with her fists, and her shrill
voice became hoarse.

"Oh, I'm so unhappy, Michel! You see, you've never accustomed
me to being unhappy."

Standing motionless over her, he did not seem to be listening, as
he waited for her to stop talking.

"Once, did you say? You slept just once with—?"

The dread which made him look old, and also the boyish hope
that shone like a half-hidden smile in those eyes she loved, almost
persuaded her to lie, but she remembered just in time that she had
already mentioned three weeks. "He'll remember, too," she thought
quickly. "I know him."

She sat up erect, which forced Michel to straighten up, and she
pushed her black bang aside and mopped her forehead.

"No, Michel," she replied finally. "It wasn't a matter of mere
chance or of being taken by surprise. My physical nature is not so
capricious—nor so insistent."

Michel winced and with a gesture of his hand begged her to stop.
He took one glance at her face, less attractive now because of her
feverish appearance and disheveled hair, and then turned away,
sickened by the thought that she had doubtless looked like that
when she gave herself to the other man.

Alice noticed how crushed he seemed, how utterly without his
customary seductive little mannerisms, and she quickly bethought
herself of a way possibly to heal his wounds.

"Listen, Michel," she said in a low voice. "What is it you're after?
The truth, of course. You're foolishly insisting on having the whole
story. If I don't tell you every last detail, you're going to plague me
to death and make life hell for us."

"You might soften your language a bit, my dear," Michel suggested.

Alice rose to her feet, stretched the stiffness out of her shoulders
and, looking sharply into his face, replied:

"Why should I? That's part of the process of getting at the truth. All right, then—you're going to embitter our lives until you get what you want. Not that it will take long. You shall have your way. This very evening, at the latest, as soon as they leave us alone and I no longer feel someone in the house who—"

She completed the sentence with a glance toward the door and then started to go toward the bedroom.

"Where are you going?" Michel asked from force of habit.

When Alice turned around, he noticed her drawn features and narrow, lusterless eyes, her pale lips and shiny, flat little nose.

"You don't imagine that I'm going to let them see me looking like this, do you?"

"No, of course, not. What I meant to ask was, what are you going to do after that?"

She nodded toward the window and the pure sky beyond, the valley showing through the tender foliage and between the sharp-tipped leafbuds.

"I had thought I might go down there and get some yellow daffodils and see if there's any lily of the valley in the swamp woods, but now—"

Her eyelids began to swell. Michel turned aside. She had a child-like way of crying that unnerved him.

"You wouldn't want me to—I don't suppose you'd care to have me go with you?" he ventured.

Alice put her hands on his shoulders with a quick movement that caused two tears to fall on her blue waist.

"Michel! Why, of course I would! How could you ask? Do come, dear. We'll manage somehow. Come along! We'll cross the river and go to Saint Meix and get some eggs. Will you wait a minute?"

He nodded assent and slumped into an armchair to wait for her, a bit ashamed of his indulgent weakness. When she returned, after putting on some powder and a touch of bistre shadow on her reddened eyelids and arranging her hair tight across her forehead, like a band of silk, he had fallen into a heavy, merciful sleep and did not even hear her come in.

He sat there asleep, all in a heap, his chin buried in his necktie. He looked crushed and misshapen. His hands, lying open, palms up, trembled slightly. In spite of his short nose and Roman chin, which gave strength to his features, he seemed like an oldish child, with hair turning white but still thick and showing a tendency to curl when he did not plaster it down. Alice leaned over him, holding her breath and dreading lest the old floor creak under her weight. She hesitated whether to wake him or let him slumber on. "Only yesterday," she mused, "I'd have put the old shawl over his knees. Or else I'd have called out, 'Michel, it's such lovely weather, come on out! Michel, you're getting middle-aged and stodgy.' But now—" Then, trying to assume a more cheerful manner, she added, "I must confess I don't know just what the books of etiquette recommend for such a situation."

Turning away with a vague feeling of repugnance for that lifeless face, distorted by its cramped posture, she sighed to herself, as if making an admission that was a final explanation and conclusion, "After all, I never did like that new way of trimming his beard Spanish fashion."

She walked softly over to the window, annoyed and impatient, rather than grateful to Michel for involuntarily giving her a respite from suffering and time to think. "To think about what?" she argued with herself. "You don't think before you do something foolish. You do your thinking afterwards."

Suddenly she felt as if a drop of tepid water were trickling down her back between her shoulder blades. With a shudder she turned around and saw Michel sitting there awake and motionless, staring at her.

"What's the matter?" she asked crossly. "Why do you look at me that way?"

At the sound of her voice, Michel roused himself and stirred uneasily.

"I fell asleep," he explained, rubbing his face with his hands and starting to get up reluctantly. "I had forgotten—can you believe it?"

393

His apologetic tone displeased Alice and she cut him short with the retort:

"Well, I hadn't. I've been waiting for you. We were going out."

"Oh, yes. Where to?"

"To Saint Meix, you know very well."

Michel got up and cast threatening glances at imaginary observers hidden behind the syringas and purple lilacs.

"Saint Meix? Of course, I'm coming."

A couple of hours later, tired out, they climbed the hill on which Cransac stood. Their long walk had left them without the slightest desire to exchange another word. They realized that they had spent their strength down in the valley, in the village and beyond it, in the hamlet of Saint Meix.

Alice recalled that, when they came to the little bridge connecting the Cransac driveway with the public road, Michel had offered her his arm so that they might give the inquisitive villagers the impression of a closely united couple. But still, they were well aware that the natives were gifted with a phenomenal flair and hawk-like eyes for anything that concerned the château.

"They noticed that I was wearing my muddy old shoes," Michel thought to himself. "And the druggist's wife advised Alice to try rose water for inflamed eyelids. What an awful lot of gossips!"

Alice recalled also, with a start of indignant protest, that at Espagnat's Michel had put his arm around her waist and squeezed her hand. From there they had followed the sunny lane to Saint Meix, as it wound along beside the swollen river, bordered with primroses and blue veronicas and hedged on both sides with white hawthorn bushes, from which kingfishers and red-breasted bullfinches darted to and fro. From the fertile reddish soil of the farther shore sprang the first vineyards of the mountainside, but it was only higher up on the pebbly slopes that the grapes yielded a sweet-flavored wine. Each year the close-cropped vines around Cransac and the well tilled lanes between them, planted with onions and bush beans, moved Michel to banal observations concerning the lavish productivity of nature, which he emphasized with sweeping gestures taking in the whole horizon.

"This year he doesn't say a word," Alice noted in a spirit of malice for which she hated herself.

"See, the vines are sprouting already!" she exclaimed, in an effort to stimulate her husband's annual burst of enthusiasm.

But he merely let go of her arm and once more assumed the air of a wronged husband whose sense of offended dignity was tempered by a restraining disposition to forgive. "Playing to the gallery—just like the rest of the men," Alice grumbled to herself, as she laboriously climbed the hill leading to Cransac, a gentleman's country place, composed of squat, huddled buildings, of which one saw chiefly tiled roofs and low, massive towers—looking for all the world, as Alice disrespectfully observed, like a fat man with his derby hat pulled too far down over his ears.

Michel and Alice both stopped at the same time, out of breath. As a rule, Alice showed more endurance and also more unconcern than her husband and slowed down as soon as the road became steep, whereas Michel took pride in scrambling up as if attacking a fortress, nimbly and almost on the run, but pale and with his heart beating irregularly—all for the satisfaction of his traditional, triumphant "Well!" when Alice finally caught up with him. But today, their strength sapped by the same preoccupation, they halted to catch their breath when they came to the base of Cransac, where, like intermittent tears, the subterranean water dripped from the clefts of purple rock. While they rested, they made an effort to be friendly.

"You're not too tired?" Michel inquired.

Shaking her head in reply, Alice picked some tender, newly formed fern leaves from the crevices of the rocks, some periwinkles, tinted with the pale mauve of skimmed milk, and a dainty, ill-smelling little pink flower.

"How lovely it is at this hour!" she remarked, pointing to Cransac above them.

"Yes," Michel replied listlessly, and they set out again.

"I wonder what's in store for me up there," Alice thought to herself, as she walked along behind Michel, who was bareheaded. They were uncomfortable in their damp woolen clothing and fatigued from having neither sat down nor had anything to eat or drink since noon.

At the top of the hill, in the long shadow of the lilac bushes before the house, Alice resumed her customary brisk gait, only to be halted at the threshold by a sharp "Where are you going in such a hurry?" Barely turning her head to look over her shoulder, she replied:

"To get a drink. I nearly died of thirst in that oven of a village."

"You could have gotten something to drink there," Michel remonstrated.

"Yes, lemonade full of flies or hard cider—no, thank you! Shall I send some water or cider out to you on the terrace? That's all we have in the house except some sherry, a bottle of port and some cassis. Tomorrow—"

She suddenly stopped and stared vaguely into space. Michel did not comment on the unfinished remark.

"All right," he said. "Some cider, if you please. Are you coming out on the terrace later?"

"Yes—no—not right away. This dress is sticking to my back, the wool is pricking me and I can't stand it any longer."

With an impatient gesture, she disappeared through the low-arched door. As long as his eye could discern her, Michel tried eagerly to follow her figure, as it passed down the dark hall leading to the kitchen. Then he sat down on the wooden bench, leaned against the wall and watched the night come on, breathless, green and soft, like a Provençal twilight. "You can feel the South not very far away," he reflected.

A nightingale, the nearest of the many who, hovering about their well filled nests, spent themselves day and night in unstinted melody, drowned out all the other birds. Michel fell to analyzing the arabesque of the song, watching for the return of the long, identically repeated notes, reinforcing one another. He caught the "tz—tz—tz," which he likened to rings sliding on a brass rod, and the "cotee—cotee—cotee," reiterated as many as twenty times without a pause. Not that this gave him any pleasure, but by holding his breath during the seemingly endless song, he practised a kind of suffocation on himself which checked his thinking and left him merely the sensation of thirst.

"Here's the cider," Maria announced. "Is Madame going to have some, too?"

She dragged over beside the handsome stone bench, with its finely carved legs, a round sheetiron table, purchased at the local store.

"I really don't know," Michel replied. "She's changing her dress. Look out, clumsy! You're spilling the cider."

"You're right, I am," Maria agreed amiably. "That's just like me."

With a lean hand, all bone and sinew, she poured the dark, yellow-foamed cider, while her small, glistening eyes searched her master's face with an ageless coquetry so penetrating that Michel shuddered. "How will we ever be able to hide anything from her?" he thought. He felt so weak and helpless that he greeted Alice with a sense of relief when she rejoined him, tense, restless, her face carelessly powdered, the nose too white and the lips too red. Her pale blue eyes, always more assured as the approach of night gave them a darker hue, looked at him watchfully from beneath the black hair of her low-cut bang.

"I laid out your warm dressing gown on the bed, Michel," she said from a distance. "The evenings here, you know—. You see, I've put on a heavy woolen blouse. Is Maria waiting for something?"

Maria caught the indirect question as she inspected from top to bottom the long blouse of white wool and the red silk pyjamas gathered at the ankle. Meeting her gaze, Alice calmly put her arm on Michel's shoulder.

"Oh, no, I don't need anything," Maria replied. "I'm satisfied as I am."

"Yes, satisfied to have uncorked the cider so clumsily," Michel grumbled. "You're very easily satisfied! What are we having for grub this evening, Mariushka?"

"Why, cabbage soup."

"And what else?"

"Caramel custard. I wanted to make a stew, but Madame said—"

"And she was quite right," Michel interrupted. "Now run along and see that we have dinner on time or I'll cut you off with a shilling."

When they were alone, Alice made a move to withdraw her arm, but Michel's head vigorously pinioned her elbow between his shoulder and his cheek, to the accompaniment of sighs and heavy breathing, and his warm face inhaled the old familiar perfume on her wrist. She brusquely disengaged her arm.

"Do behave, my dear," she insisted. "Aren't you ashamed of yourself? Have a little patience, please! We'll tell Maria we want to go to bed early."

She dared not let him see that his giving way so completely to despair, his spasmodic sobbing and stammering, left her cold and scandalized. Michel repressed his unruly impulse and got up, saying:

"I'll be right back. Is the water fairly hot?"

His restlessly moving eyes, touched with a golden hue by the sunset glow and by the tears he was holding back, looked with envy on Alice's well washed and powdered face and her cool white and red costume.

"Hot enough for these people," she answered, shrugging her shoulders. "What do such folk know about hot and cold water?"

Left alone, she in turn listened to the song of the nearby nightingale, with its continuous accompaniment of other nightingales in the distance. The soloist threw himself into his singing with the full voice of a faultless virtuoso and with a brilliance and precision that precluded emotion. But during his intervals of silence one caught again the softened chorus of distant songsters, singing independently and yet in perfect accord and scorning all thought of rest as they watched beside their nesting mates.

Alice, however, was not in a mood to enjoy the greenish twilight, tinged with red in the west, above the hidden river. But the quiet solitude, her own silence and the coolness of the spring evening, announcing the approach of night, gave her renewed strength and a sort of impatience vaguely resembling the anticipation of sexual pleasure.

When Michel delayed his return, she walked up and down on the open terrace, struggling against a tendency to shiver with cold, against a longing to give up the battle and against all the nameless and formless allies of nervous fear.

She could think of what she had done only as a foolish thing, inexcusable and unimportant. She was not so mortified over her having been caught off her guard and her clumsiness in inventing a lie as she was occupied with trying to obviate the consequences. "I've got to straighten this out somehow," she said to herself. "We never got into a jam like this before. . . . And to think of his taking it so tragically! He's so poorly fitted to play a tragic part." With strategic swiftness she put behind her the disastrous hour of that morning— "the purple portfolio hour," she called it—and threw herself into her predestined rôle, that of remedying a situation without too much scrupulousness, by concealing, effacing, forgetting.

Down in the valley a train whistled, then slowly let off steam and came to a halt at the little station in the distance. When it started up again, it left behind great balloons of white steam, which hung for a long time in the still night air. "Seven-fifteen," Alice remarked to herself. "If I had taken that train, I'd have caught the express at Laures-Lézières and two hours later I'd have been home in Paris. . . . Now, what a silly thing that is to be thinking about! An unpleasant evening comes to an end some time, like any other. We aren't going to discuss the Ambrogio matter forever. We've got to clean this up by tomorrow, or else—"

Michel was calling her. She frowned when she found him tightly buttoned up in his vicuna dressing gown and in a surprisingly good humor. "Not so good," she thought, so she fell in with his mood, put on a gentle manner and jokingly urged Maria to hurry the cabbage soup.

At dinner she played Michel's game quite as skillfully as he. Under the poor center light her hair, which she had dampened and brushed smooth, retained a singularly sharp brilliance, which shifted

399

with the movement of her round head. When she looked up at the old hanging lamp, with its faded cloth shade, her limpid eyes took on a bluish, milky hue and a fixed stare, like that of a blind man. Michel would then stop eating and, resting his spoon on the edge of his bowl of custard, wait for her face to lose its hard expression—"become human again," as he termed it to himself.

"She is biding her time," he thought to himself. "She has plenty of nerve, but she isn't going to get off as easy as that!" The oncoming of night, of the same period when, twenty-four hours before, they had reveled in the joy of all their senses, proud to give and proud to receive, was reviving in him the savage feeling which he had lacked all day, and a curiosity so powerful that it numbed his sense of taste and the pleasure of his wine. He watched Alice help herself twice to custard and heard her say:

"Maria has done herself proud this time. I congratulate you, Maria."

Standing opposite to her, Maria fastened her imperious eye on the back of Michel's neck as she replied, "The custard can't be such a great success when Monsieur doesn't say a word about it."

"I?" exclaimed Michel with a start. "I can't do everything all at once—eat your dinner and weave laurel wreaths for you! The trouble is, you old grouch, your cabbage soup spoiled me for your custard. It was smooth as velvet and flavored to perfection—wasn't it, Alice?"

Having his back to Maria, he dared, while laughing boisterously, to give his wife a sternly disapproving look. She never quailed but, getting up, suggested with a gently impertinent air that they have some coffee. Michel's astonishment rewarded her.

"What! Coffee? At night?"

"You weren't planning to work after dinner, were you?" she inquired. "All right, then how about some linden tea?"

"Very well, if you don't mind."

"Certainly. And I'll have some, too, Maria."

As they entered, a fresh breeze was blowing in the living room. The first little nocturnal moths were flitting in from the serene night and getting caught in the fatal zones around the two lights. Alice tucked up the shade of pleated linen above the pottery vase that had been transformed into an artistic lamp. Michel peered into the surrounding darkness, measuring the height of the two forbidding bookcases, whose cornices touched the ceiling.

"I wonder why Escargnat didn't put in an electric outlet on that side," he remarked. "It's too gloomy. Didn't you tell him to put one there?"

"I can send for him tomorrow," Alice replied.

"Oh, tomorrow," he said dejectedly.

Alice turned around so quickly that she almost upset the lamp.

"Why do you say 'Oh, tomorrow' in that tone? Is life going to come to an end tomorrow and the earth start turning in the opposite direction? Everything's going to crash tomorrow, I suppose—we won't have anything more to do with one another—we'll barely be on speaking terms—we'll get a divorce. That's what you mean by your 'Oh, tomorrow,' eh? Come now, own up to it!"

He half closed his eyes, tempted to run away from her volubility, her terrifying attack, her way of reversing the rôles and anticipating all his plans, even those he had not yet had time to formulate. Alice stopped short and listened intently.

"Maria is bringing the tea very quickly this evening," she muttered. "It generally takes her an hour to make it."

Alice stepped forward to hold the unmanageable door open for Maria. The latter, as she hurried to pass through, turned at the threshold and asked with affected diffidence:

"About the marketing tomorrow, ma'am. You haven't changed your mind?"

"Why, of course not. Have you forgotten? Pigeon pie, with an omelet to begin with. Have you any objection to that menu?"

"Oh no, ma'am. I was just thinking maybe—. Goodnight, ma'am. Goodnight, sir."

She went out with exaggerated haste and embarrassment. Alice shook her fist at the door as it closed behind her.

"Did you see that? Did you notice what she said? And the way she looked all around for damaging evidence? Everything we try to keep to ourselves she ferrets out. That's what you've gotten us into!"

"What do you mean by that?" Michel flared up. "I'll be damned! Did you hear what you just said? I declare, I'd laugh my head off if, like you, I'd lost all sense of—"

He caught himself and sat down.

"You're very clever, Alice," he resumed. "I admit that. But just leave Maria out of this. If I let you have your way, you'd get us all tangled up in a lot of backstairs gossip. But that's not what I'm interested in. You have something else to square up with me this evening."

Alice fixed a pale, angry look on him which he could not face down.

"I don't have to square up anything with you," she retorted. "Nothing of that sort at any rate. Besides, you must be entirely devoid of imagination, like most men, if you still have some questions to ask me."

Once more he recoiled before a woman's frankness of speech. He turned his eyes away and took hold of the handle of the teapot.

"She's broken the cover again," Alice said. "Let me have that. You know the spout pours very badly."

Michel let her fill his cup and put in two lumps of sugar. By force of habit they still went through the motions of reciprocal politeness and little courtesies to one another. But now this made Michel feel uncomfortable because he was hurt that Alice, though caught in a shameful situation and admitting her guilt, should act so brazenly, just as if she were entirely innocent. It was intolerable that she should sit there so little affected by the events of that day, looking her best and ready for any kind of conflict.

Nevertheless, she lost her composure and grew old-looking in an instant and all bent over when a train rushed out from behind the hills, cut across the river, whistled and vanished. She stood at the window and listened to it for a long time, dejected, a cigarette in her hand, her head drooping.

402

"You wish you were far away from here, don't you?" Michel suggested.

She raised her bird-like head at him and realized that she hadn't the courage to answer with a lie. She had sucked some of the rouge from her thick lower lip, and her eyes, turning away from Michel's face, gazed into space with a look of vague entreaty.

"Yes," she answered, "I do—and yet again, I don't. I think, on the whole, I prefer to be here. Where would I go?"

"This is a fine time to be asking that question!" he exclaimed with some restraint. "You should have thought of that before you treated yourself to a night's fun with that—er—that pretty boy. But that's the way you are. When the fit is on, there's no holding you."

Alice shrugged her shoulders.

"You're a fool!" she retorted. "Yes, a fool! As if you didn't know me better than that! A night's fun! At last it's out, what's been eating you. That's just like me, is it? to pick up a man on the fly!"

"Perhaps not on the fly," Michel replied, "but while I was on the road—while I was working like a horse down there—"

"Now see here, Michel," she interrupted condescendingly. "You'll admit you've had jobs that were far more tiring—and more successful, too—than that business of managing a pitiful little pink gingerbread establishment for the Schmil brothers for a couple of months. I told you before you went into it you'd only waste your time, that it would be a winter thrown away, that the Schmil brothers aren't lucky, like Moyses. A woman is always better than a man at picking winners."

Michel listened bewildered. He threw his dressing gown open with an impatient gesture and she recognized the pyjamas he had worn the night before—tobacco brown, to match his eyes. She noticed also his small teeth, which he took such good care of with excusable vanity, and the hands of which he was so proud. Her nostrils dilated at the odor of a perfume which she was accustomed to call "light brown." A fierce desire to assert her rights swept over her. "That's all mine," she protested within herself. "That man belongs to me. Am I going to lose everything stupidly through his fault and my own?"

"Well, let's get down to business," she said brusquely.

Walking over to the window to toss out her cigarette stub with one of those gestures that men call mannish, she came back, lit another cigarette and installed herself comfortably in an armchair beside the desk. She studied her own movements and restrained them consciously, choosing for herself the wicker chair and the corner of the desk to lean on, so that the light should fall on her face. With feigned generosity she left the divan and its shaded corner to Michel. The waxing moon flooded the curtainless window with a powder-blue light, while the lamp tipped with pink the nearest stars of the syringa bush.

"Another cup of tea, Michel?" she asked.

"Kindly cut out the polite attentions, if you don't mind. I've had enough of that sort of thing."

The clear-cut and too honeyed tone of the voice that came from the unlighted part of the room convinced her that she could not put off the moment any longer.

"Don't you remember that I had the grippe while you were at Saint Raphael?" she asked.

"Of course I do," he replied. "I remember it very well. If you hadn't had the grippe, you'd have come with me."

"Exactly. I didn't want to bore you with my illness even in my letters."

"Quite so—besides which, I now know you had something else to keep you occupied."

With an impetuous motion she brushed away the cigarette ashes that had just fallen on the desk.

"Now, none of that, Michel!" she burst out. "Keep your wise-cracks and smart remarks for some other occasion. Just now, either I'm going to be given a chance to talk or I'll shut up for good and all. So, suppose now *you* kindly cut out the sarcasm, if you don't mind."

Into the semi-darkness that shielded him her nearsighted blue eyes, flashing behind their thick lashes, shot a burning glance of insolent, defiant courage. "She never looked so like a pink-complexioned Annamite," he reflected.

"Very well," he replied laconically. "I'm listening."

Apparently embarrassed to have him acquiesce so readily, she made a poor beginning.

"Well, you remember, no doubt, that I wasn't in the best of health. After *Les Dames de Ces Messieurs* had gone on the road, you gave me a number of things to do. I took over a lot of work while you were getting ready for that miserable season at Saint Raphael. So it's no wonder if the grippe—"

Buried in the shadow, he listened only fitfully. While she was talking, the capriciousness of his tired brain and this new, restless sorrow, which he did not know where to lodge, led his thoughts back to the days of their youth, when Alice, a child of chance, was one of a family loaded down with daughters who realized that they were a burden and struggled fiercely to exist. One of her three sisters played the violin evenings in a moving picture theatre. Another was a cloak model at Lelong's and lived on black coffee. Alice designed and cut out gowns and sometimes sold designs for furniture and interior decorating.

"The Four Graces," as they were called, formed a mediocre quartette of piano and strings and played in a large café which went into bankruptcy. When Michel became manager of the summer season at the Théâtre de l'Etoile, the box office window served as a frame for the charming head and shoulders of Hermine, the eldest. But he fell in love with the least attractive of the four vivacious, resourceful sisters, who held their heads high and carried off their poverty with a certain air.

"I wonder if the same thing would have happened to me if I had fallen in love with Colomba or Zizoute," he meditated. Lulled by the sound of Alice's low-pitched voice, he dreamed on, strangely unconcerned, confident that he would come to himself when she reached the really important part of her explanation. "Oh, let's get to the point," he sighed inwardly.

405

"You'll remember, too," she was saying, "that you told Ambrogio not to do anything without consulting me—not even to give out a line of advertising without talking it over with me and letting me phone you long distance at midnight."

"Ambrogio!" Michel thought to himself with a start. "Why, yes, Ambrogio! How does it happen I've thought of him so little since this morning?" He did not want to interrupt Alice but could not help it.

"Consult you? Talk it over with you? Well, what was to hinder his telephoning you?"

Alice had been forcing herself to talk in a calm, precise manner, now looking down at her cigarette stub as she rubbed it out, now trying to distinguish Michel's features in the semi-darkness.

"That's just it!" she said, groping blindly for an opening. "It was the telephone that did it. It happened that one day Ambrogio could hardly recognize my voice over the phone. I had had my throat cauterized that morning. He was worried and that afternoon—"

She was making it up easily, carried along by the calm current of her commonplace invention. "It isn't the truth," she admitted to herself, "but it's the next thing to it."

"And, when he saw the condition I was in, he said to me, 'What! you haven't written Michel that you have such a high fever? You certainly ought to do it at once. Don't bother about the business from now on. There's so little to be done that I can take care of everything. I'll report to you daily concerning the receipts at the Etoile and the rehearsals for *Le Scarabée d'Or*!' Did you say something?"

"No," Michel replied.

"I thought you did," Alice explained. "Do you begin to understand the situation?"

"Oh, yes, very well," said Michel. "Your convalescence—your room, always overheated—pink cambric sheets—your weakened condition—your drowsy manner, like an Oriental woman who has been smoking too much opium—and this fellow from Nice who brings you roses and talks income and expense to the tune of *I Kiss Your Hand, Madame*."

Seized with a spasm of coughing, he had to get up and drink some lukewarm linden tea, after which he went back to his seat on the couch. Alice noticed his bloodshot eyes and vacillating, bewildered expression.

"Go on," he urged. "I'm listening."

But she, too, stopped and took a drink of tea, meanwhile doing some quick, keen thinking. Outdoors, in the silence of the night, the clear-voiced nightingale was beginning again his series of trills and full, flute-like notes, long-sustained variations and single sounds as limpid as the pearl dropped by the lovesick toad of the fairy tale. "Michel hears it, too," Alice thought, "and it is recalling last night to his mind. I must watch my step." Courageously she started in again, like a swimmer tired and on the alert.

"No, indeed!" she said. "It was not that way at all. Not in the least. I'd have imagined just about the same things myself. But that young fellow—"

She stopped an instant to make sure that Michel would not object to her speaking of Ambrogio in that manner.

"As I got to know that young fellow better, I found him quite different from what I had supposed. It was, indeed, a revelation. More cultured than you'd think—interested in things one would never have expected—well informed on a lot of subjects I used to be interested in—a music lover. So that we had many long talks together. . . . Did you say something?"

"No," Michel replied. "I was just laughing."

Alice looked appealingly at Michel, whose features she could barely distinguish.

"Please, Michel, I'm doing my utmost. You should try to be sincere, too, and not make things harder. Don't make it impossible for me to tell you what you want to know. I'm trying my best to satisfy your curiosity. . . . You've been sick yourself and you know what convalescence means—that sort of weakness of the will, a dizziness that comes with the least exertion, the need to confide in someone and get encouragement—"

Noticing his slender hand raised in the darkness, she stopped.

"I'd rather you wouldn't talk about your convalescence," he said, slightly raising his voice. "Skip that and tell me the rest of the story —nothing else."

Alice met the situation adroitly.

"But there's nothing more to tell," she protested. "Do you want to force me to explain, down to the last detail, how a long conversation can very naturally lead to something more intimate, as the culmination of a sort of excitement caused by one's fever and the lateness of the hour and also as a token—unnecessary, I admit, and often unfortunate—of the new-born confidence and friendship, which one would be ashamed not to give generously again and again?"

The great effort she was making inflamed her cheeks and her eyes. She got up and walked about, dropping her hands sharply by her side as she complained aloud:

"It's disgraceful, what you're demanding of me! It's a shame! And it isn't getting us anywhere. It doesn't settle anything—quite the contrary. If you think I'm going to be able to forgive you for this— Well, I suppose you're satisfied now."

Throwing the window wide open, she took a deep breath of the spring night air, so rich and full, so lavishly laden with hovering perfumes, impalpable humidity, bird songs and moonlight, that tears of vexation came to her eyes.

"Oh, it's too stupid!" she cried. "What a heavenly night! And to think of spoiling such a night, when we might have been sitting on the stone bench, warmly wrapped, watching the stars rise and the moon go down!"

Suddenly realizing the priceless value of the aftermath of love, those abashed moments when the bond uniting the lovers lies quietly, buried deep in their hearts, she turned around to make a hurried attempt to save what was in danger of being destroyed. At the same instant she became aware of Michel's long silence. He was still half-reclining, leaning on one elbow.

"Michel!"

"Well?"

"What's the matter?"

"Nothing."

Losing heart, she dropped into a chair.

"Won't you let me know how you feel about it, dear?" she pleaded. "Now that you've made me tell you everything, is there any hope of our living together in peace?"

"Oh, you haven't told me much," he replied scornfully. "Except the worst feature of it all."

"What's that?"

He bounded to his feet. As he came under the light, she noticed his contracted, altered features.

"You don't even understand that the worst thing about it all is precisely that—er—friendship you gave the fellow, those hours you talked together, before sleeping together! By God! you even spoke of 'confidence'! And you said he liked the same things you do—"

"Now, please, Michel! Don't get things wrong. I must have expressed myself very poorly—"

"Keep quiet!" he shouted at the top of his voice, pounding both his fists on the desk right beside her. The outcry and the gesture seemed to relieve his feelings. Alice could scarcely conceal her approval. "It was about time he came out with something real," she commented to herself. "If he'll only follow that track, maybe we'll get somewhere."

Alice recoiled—a bit too late—as if in fear, holding her arms crossed before her face. But Michel was already moving away from her and resumed his moderate tone as he continued:

"My dear child, you'll never understand a man in love and what a betrayal means to him. You'll never understand how a man can forgive and almost forget a mere matter of a woman's night with some other man, a temporary yielding to physical desire—"

"With very good reason," she interrupted sarcastically.

He looked at her squarely and replied with confidence, as a man whose own desires were quickly roused, "Exactly, with very good reason."

His hands in the pockets of his unbuttoned dressing gown, he strode up and down the room, with a rolling motion of the shoulders, as befitted a broad-minded man.

409

"Anyone can lose his head or be swept off his feet by a wave of animal heat," he continued. "We men know what that means, by God! Let him cast the first stone—if he has the heart—who never—"

Alice watched him and listened, silent and once more ready for battle. "Funny, how he thinks he knows all about a woman's sexual desires," she commented to herself, laughing as he disappeared into the darkness between the two bookcases.

He came suddenly back to her and seized both her arms above the elbow.

"Why, my dear child, if you had said, 'Here's how it happened—one evening, at twilight, I lost my head—there was something in the air'—why, my dear child, I'd have been the first to understand and forgive."

She wrenched herself from his grasp.

"If you call me your 'dear child' once more, I'll throw this teapot in your face!" she cried. "No, don't ask me why, or I'll do something we'll both be sorry for."

She felt utterly exhausted and unequal to starting the struggle all over again.

"I'm going to bed," she announced in a lifeless voice. "You can't offer me anything half as inviting. Goodnight."

She left the room, dragging her red scarf behind her like an empty net.

When he finally made up his mind to retire to the bedroom, he found Alice already apparently asleep, her face toward the wall. All he could make out between her black hair and the sheet drawn up to her mouth was the gently curved line of her eyelashes and her oddly formed nostrils, breathing noiselessly. When she closed her eyes of an Occidental greenish gray, everything else about her face suggested the Far East.

The nervous shivering that came over Michel as his body touched the cold sheets showed him how long he had been lying out there alone on the couch, across which a single bar of moonlight fell. He had even thought of passing the night in the living room, notwithstanding the mice and the hard-shelled insect beating against the windowpane.

Once in bed, he made up his mind to lie there and suffer. But his sorrow still lacked rhythm, virtuosity, organization. Every now and then his mental anguish vanished, driven out of his mind by disconnected trifles of everyday life. "I meant to ask Willemetz to let me book Candelaire for a tour of the casinos—I must write Ambrogio to hold up the printing of the Etoile programs." He suddenly recalled with a painful start that the mayor of the village was expecting him for luncheon in a couple of days.

When he put out the light, the moon penetrated the room through the Venetian blinds. Michel turned his head toward Alice's bed. "Is she really asleep?" he wondered. "It's unbelievable." He knew he could not judge by her motionless body, so near him that he could have touched it with his hand. She was lying on her side, with her knees drawn up. An aroma of gentle perfume surrounded her. He knew, through having many times reveled in the joy of it, that she could lie absolutely still throughout an entire night. In the days when their love was seeking every kind of voluptuous self-denial, Michel would hold his young wife's slender body close to him the whole night long and, although her eyes were closed, he was never sure she was asleep. "Can she really sleep after such a day?" he questioned.

He thought he was in great distress, when in reality he was as yet merely disturbed and weary. While feeling between his ribs for the spot where some wandering ailment might lodge and develop, he took care not to move, lest he break the stillness of the night with the sound caused by a naked body turning under its pile of covers. When he finally fell asleep, he carried his perplexity with him and in his dreams continued to imagine he was still awake. He never found out whether Alice had been feigning sleep or not, for, when he opened his eyes, the bed beside him was empty and he heard a fresh, shrill voice over at the window, but not speaking to him.

"Yes, Chevestre, we're taking it easy this morning. Half-past eight and my husband is still asleep—can you believe it? What have you got for us? Good news, as usual?"

Michel woke up with a deadened memory and nothing on his mind except a vaguely outlined uneasiness which seemed to be flying toward him from very far away. At first it seemed to have the shape and name of the manager of his estate.

"She makes a mistake to joke with Chevestre," he thought. "That fellow's sense of humor is limited to playing mean tricks on me, like that matter of the mortgage, for example."

"Alice!" he called softly.

Alice turned from the window and Michel saw that she was all in blue from her shoulders to her feet, wearing a long garment of faded shantung which she called her housemaid's smock. Then he realized his mistake. His distress, his ailment, the cramp in his side which made him catch his breath, was this tall woman in blue, soft blue faded by frequent laundering, the blue of the misty regions where the first star appears after a storm, between two clouds.

"You're awake?" she asked.

She seemed to bring back into the room some of the laughter she had been indulging in at the window and a trace of the mischievous scorn she always visited on Chevestre. Michel did not immediately detect the swelling under her eyes and noticed merely the silky hair and powdered face, the challenging youthfulness of her body and her movements.

"It's Chevestre," she explained in a significant tone, as if to say, "Put something on before you go to the window."

Michel's only reply was an angry motion to close the window. She did nothing of the kind, but continued in the same tone:

"Breakfast is ready, Michel. . . . No, Chevestre, don't wait for my husband. We're half starved. You can see him this afternoon or before lunch. We'll probably stay right here. . . . Very well, Chevestre, come back later."

Getting out of bed, Michel groped about, tied the cords of his pyjamas, looked for his morning glass of water and pushed his hair back out of his eyes, taking care not to turn his face toward the light.

"I had just come to call you, Michel," Alice explained. "It's such a beautiful day, I ordered breakfast served on the terrace, although it almost gave Maria heart failure. There's some honey from the hive they found under the eaves. It's a bit dark but very good. Come soon, dear."

She went away with a quick step, her bare feet in moccasins, and left him weak and vacillating, beset by the need of obeying his wife, as he always did in matters of eating and drinking and taking care of his health. He brushed his hair, pinched up his mouth to pull the wrinkles out of his cheeks, and examined his blood-shot eyes. "Only six years' difference between us—how does she manage to look so young?" he pondered.

He appeared in the doorway with a guilty, unnatural expression which Alice, sitting at the breakfast table, noticed even at that distance with great surprise. But she hid her astonishment and, turning the handles of the coffee pot and cream pitcher toward her husband, she asked, "Did you sleep well?"

"After a fashion," he replied.

A catalpa tree cast on the tablecloth the shadow of its leafless, blossoming branches. A drowsy bee flew clumsily toward the honey jar and Michel waved his napkin to drive it away. But Alice put out her long, slender hand to protect it.

"Leave it alone, dear. It's hungry. It's working."

Michel saw tears suddenly come to her silvery green eyes and tremble on her eyelashes. "What an existence!" he thought bitterly, "if every word, every gesture must bring us up against something hidden, quivering and bleeding! What's she feeling sad over just now? That sleepy bumblebee? Or the idea of hunger? Or work?"

Alice had already shaken off her wave of sadness and was spreading butter and honey on the coarse country bread, exclaiming, "What heavenly weather!" But Michel shiveringly doubled his dressing gown over his chest, likening the cool air to a mint bath. The first mouthful of bread and sip of hot coffee brought a little animal contentment, which, however, he concealed by scowling and refusing to see all about him the bluish dewdrops, the clear, pale blue sky, the periwinkles and the rambler roses, mauve-tinted where the sun did not fall on them. Alice tried to cheer him up by saying softly:

"Look! Everything white seems almost blue. . . . Have you noticed the swallows coming back to their old nests? Just feel how warm the sun is! Take more milk if you want it, dear. I've arranged for us to have three quarts a day—a regular orgy!"

Michel acquiesced with a nod of the head but protested inwardly, calling himself to witness: "Look at the wench! She can enjoy anything—coffee, fresh air, rosebushes—and forget her troubles in anything. If I let her have her way—" Listlessly he dropped the hand that had just carried to his lips the first—always the best—cigarette and, closing his eyes, resumed with a sigh, "If I let her have her way, ah, how happy I might be once more!"

A tinkling bell sounded within the house and Maria, neatly dressed in simple black, with white cap and apron, appeared in the doorway and called out, "A telephone call from Paris, sir."

Michel laid aside his napkin and went in, without looking at his wife. As soon as she was alone, Alice stopped smoothing the butter in the butter dish, covering the sugar bowl and putting a glass over the honey to protect it from ants. She sat as still as a statue, listening intently. But Michel had closed behind him the heavy old door, studded with hand-forged nails. Alice sat there motionless, her mouth open and neck outstretched, looking weirdly like a coolie boy caught in some wrong-doing, until she heard Michel say cordially in a louder tone:

"That's it! You understand? Not a cent less than the amount already agreed upon. Precisely. Goodbye, old man. . . . Thanks. See you soon."

Michel came back and resumed his seat with a nonchalant air and a distant look in his eyes. Alice searched his features for some reassuring sign, but he gave her none.

"What was it?"

"A call from Paris," he replied.

"I know that."

"Then why did you ask?"

"Was it—er—it wasn't Ambrogio, was it? I heard you say 'Good-bye, old man.'"

Unable to lie, Michel answered defiantly:

"Yes, it was Ambrogio. Who did you think it was?"

"Oh! It was! And you didn't—er—! What did you say to him?"

She stammered with astonishment, which he mistook for embarrassment.

"I said what I had to say," Michel replied in a domineering tone. "He had certain business matters to take up with me and I gave him his instructions."

Alice looked at him amazed, fastening her gaze on his lips, his eyes, his curly hair touched with gray, his muffler of golden brown silk, as though he had just come up out of some cellar, all covered with spider webs. With a curt remark he diverted her greenish gray glance.

"Well? Were you expecting something else?"

"I? Oh, no. Of course not. May I take the tray away? Maria must have gone to the village."

She spoke with embarrassment and hurried off with the tray as if a shower had come up. "He thanked him and called him 'old man' and said, 'See you soon'!" she thought to herself. In the pantry she broke a cup and cut her thumb slightly. She sucked her trembling hand, enjoying the warm, salty taste of her own blood, like some cordial that no other creature could supply to her. Leaning her shoulder against the pantry door, she held her hand to her lips, repeating the incantation, "He called him 'old man' and thanked him!"

They got through their second morning fairly well by being considerate of one another's feelings, and sat down to lunch as to an operation at which they had become past masters. Alice persuaded her husband that etiquette required him to call on the mayor before the little banquet the following day, and she talked to him about the community of interests linking the manor of Cransac to the village of the same name and about the wisdom of being a good neighbor. Michel assented, pretending not to recall that usually, the minute he showed any interest in his native town, Alice would exaggerate her bohemian indifference and retire behind a veil of cigarette smoke.

Maria, however, opened wide her dark eyes, sparkling with a golden glint, like hidden mountain springs distilled from their rocky crevices. For the first time in her life she looked at Alice with admiring astonishment, thrusting her head forward in sign of approval, after the fashion of bullocks new to the yoke.

Behind its half-closed shutters the dining room retained its peculiar odor of almost too ripe fruit, combined with that of a well waxed confessional. In the beam of sunlight that fell across the table, the hands of the couple gleamed white as they manipulated the silverware and broke off pieces of bread. Alice watched her husband's wayward little finger, while Michel followed closely the play of her long, agile hand, the hand that had penned letters to Ambrogio and opened for him a door made to turn noiselessly on its hinges—the hand that had dallied in another man's hair, now tightly clenched, now limp and open, following the trend of the whispered, abominable confidences. From his vantage-point in the shadow Michel watched every movement of those glistening hands, but he did not forget a single line of the rôle he wished to play.

"While you're at the mayor's," Alice suggested, "you might also have the car washed at Brouché's garage."

"The idea! So now we're to keep the car clean, are we? You'll ruin us with your extravagance! Maria, couldn't your husband wash the old can?"

The maid lifted her knotted hands to heaven in supplication.

"My husband? Anybody'd think you didn't know him! Whether he's here or away, it's the same as if I was alone."

Michel raised his well kept hand and let it fall again on the table.

"Did you hear that, Alice? She's too funny for words."

"She wasn't trying to be funny," Alice replied. "She understands a man's nature."

Maria dropped a plate and it seemed to Alice that a wave of deep color swept over the woman's face as she explained, apologetically with a southern accent, "My, how you upset me, ma'am!"

"Break forty plates that way and you'll have a fine future on the vaudeville stage," said Michel jokingly.

"It's not a thing to laugh about," Maria rebuked him sternly. "It might have been a very valuable plate, mightn't it, ma'am?"

"We haven't any valuable dishes down here, Maria," Alice reassured her. "You might bring in the coffee right away. I believe my husband is in something of a hurry."

"What's got into her?" Michel inquired as soon as they were alone. "The woman is in a vile temper. She breaks a dish and then calls me down on top of it! And, say, where did you get the notion that I'm in a hurry? I have nothing to do but some tiresome errands down in the village."

Alice listened to her husband as he grumbled and complained like a child who has been arbitrarily punished. "So he, too, has noticed a change in Maria's attitude toward him—a tendency to criticize him," she thought. "I suspect that, at bottom, she sometimes considers him just a bit vulgar."

Alice watched her husband leave the house, waved her hand to him and then chided herself for doing it. "I'm afraid I'm going too far," she reflected. "I'm puzzled as to just how I should behave toward him now. What would I do if I followed my own impulses?"

She looked up and listened intently to the sound of a distant swarm of bees, vibrating in the air like the feverish pulse of spring. Drenched with recent rains, the reddish earth was turning pink as its surface dried. No longer did a white mist mark the bed of the river, hidden behind a narrow strip of woods beyond the meadow.

"What would I do? . . . Tomorrow he'll telephone Ambrogio and the next day and the next. Should I therefore warn Ambrogio? No, indeed—by no means!" Her face unconsciously took on a prudish expression. "It's not I that am keeping up relations with Ambrogio now. And besides, while I may not think very highly of Michel, I wouldn't for the world let that other idiot know how lenient he's been!"

A wave of intolerant feeling carried her to the edge of the terrace, where she buried her face in the syringa blossoms. But the shrub was awaiting the coming of night to give off its full fragrance. Turning up her sleeve and baring her white arm to the hot April sun, Alice reached up into the boughs of the wild-apple tree, with its pink and red blossoms. "This beautiful branch in the gray vase," she thought. Then, losing interest, she released her hold and let the flowers live.

"And this is only the second day!" she mused. "I had more courage yesterday. But yesterday he hadn't yet telephoned to Ambrogio and called him 'old man'." She tried to get a grip on herself and reason fairly. "Still, I wouldn't want to see them come to blows or fight a duel for such a silly reason."

She searched for a better word, but "silly" was the only one she could think of. Without even an inclination to smile, she let it go at that and quit attempting to be fair. She gave up successively the idea of polishing the faucets in the bathroom or figuring out the number of yards needed for curtains in the dining room. More as a precaution than through idolence, she stopped on the threshold and calculated the time of day by the shadow cast in the vestibule by the midday sun. Then she went out on the terrace again without wishing to admit to herself that today that wide band of shadow, parallel to the stone doorsill and advancing into the flagged hallway, frightened her somewhat.

"I never used to be afraid of it," she thought. "Other times I'd have taken the short cut and waited for Michel at the crossing. Then I'd have gotten into the car and we'd have driven to Sarzat-le-Haut to see the view. But today—"

She picked up the purple leather portfolio without any feeling of resentment and carried it over to the iron table in front of the handsome carved stone bench. "I've a mind to write to Bizoute," she said to herself—not that she preferred that sister to Hermine, or Hermine to Colomba, but Bizoute made a practice of sharing with the others the occasional letters Alice wrote her—four, six or even ten pages of random bits of news, and jokes that went back to the days of their girlhood.

"Dear Bizoute:
Just picture to yourself—all three of you—that, as I write this,
I am sitting outdoors, barefooted, just as if it were August."

A tiny Vaugirard studio, poorly furnished, almost poverty-stricken, but cheerful, blotted out Cransac in her thoughts. As she wrote, she felt as if she could almost touch the baby grand piano, which partly blocked the entrance, and the drafting table, strewn with music paper. She smelt the invariable odor of tobacco and cheap jasmine perfume. Was that black-enameled dish, full of cigarette stubs, still wandering about from piano to table and from the table to the arm of the Morris chair? From the hills of Cransac she sent a smile to the old home in Paris and lost herself in indescribably sweet memories of the close comradeship, the physical and mental resemblances, the innocent, unabashed intimacy that formerly bound together the four daughters of old Mr. Eudes, professor of piano and singing. A devotion as close as that of twin sisters, mutual affection such as doubtless is felt by animals born the same day and in the same litter, the joy of the common struggle, a fierce determination not to die of either hunger or disease, the sharing of everything they owned, as well as the privations they suffered—two hats among the four of them, dresses without slips, scanty meals, which Bizoute baptized "the Hollywood diet."

Alice looked back on her youth with discrimination and regret, mingled with deep seriousness. Was she now in danger of having to resume her life between the walls of that crowded, hot studio, yellowed by sunlight and tobacco, amid the sounds of the piano on which Hermine and Bizoute, eternally obscure composers, with a cigarette between their lips, their heads cocked on one side and one eye half closed, tried to work out songs and orchestral themes for some film?

A catalpa blossom fluttered down on the letter she had started and fell across the vivid picture of the disproportionate piano and its adjustable stool.

"just as if it were August. While Michel is down in the village, doing his duty as lord of the manor, I am taking advantage of his absence to reminisce with you girls over our native dovecote. How's the old monkey?"

She stopped, ashamed of herself. "Is that all I can think of to say to them?" she reproached herself. "Nothing but schoolgirl nonsense?" But she knew that Bizoute would laugh as a matter of habit and would welcome with a secret feeling of compunction those veiled allusions to a period of their past life which they had kept closed to the outer world. Hermine would feel about in the air with the tips of her invisible antennae, cough out her cigarette smoke and reply across the intervening space, like the shepherds who sing to one another from hill to hill the chant of their loneliness:

"The agency has cut its rates again—thirty francs for a song entitled Hovering Above You, *one of those exquisite productions which elevate the soul and which we have made a specialty of. As for the old monkey, I've got to admit he's a regular guy—or, to make myself perfectly clear, a firstclass gink. . . . Don't worry about the Queen of Joinville.*

"The studios have started work again and she is still editing films. You know this black dove doesn't mind piling up the jobs. If you should happen to go to see Her Majesty Mimi—*a little gem of humor and sentiment—take a good look at the scene where Mimi reviews her army. The third creature on the right is our beloved sister."*

The freshening breeze which was coming up out of the east played with the sheets of the pad which Alice was covering with her changeable, elastic handwriting, large at the start of a blank page and smaller as the space grew less. Now and then she would stop

420

and watch the blue shadows of evening appear, spread softly and rise between the hill slopes. But her gaze looked beyond the cherry trees and pear trees, still white with blossoms and seeming to float along the lower edge of the vineyards—looked beyond them and saw only the hot little studio and two tall, slim girls, somewhat faded, somewhat weary of laughing and working together, each making a discreet little place in her life for love, one of them faithful to a married orchestra leader, the other mysteriously taken up with a person whose name she never mentioned and whom her sisters had dubbed "Mr. Weekend." "What if it should turn out to be Mrs. Weekend?" Alice thought with a laugh. "That would be a joke!"

Then the Dauphiné landscape once more blotted out the Vaugirard home, and a shadow came over her face. "When I think about my family so much, that's a sign I'm sick and tired of Michel. I know myself. . . . There! I hear the car coming. Already?"

An instant later Michel jumped out of the automobile and came toward her, walking erect, with a quick step. "A good-looking man, I declare," Alice said to herself. "I always did love those nut-brown eyes of his. Notwithstanding which, I don't feel the slightest pleasure at seeing him again." As she watched him approaching, she felt herself in the grip of one of those merciless feminine crises of icy indifference. But Michel spoke to her from a distance and her mood melted at the sound of his voice.

"Can you tell me, dear, whether this is what Maria asked me to get? It was something ending in *-ol*. Ah, you've been writing to someone?"

"Yes, to Bizoute. I haven't finished the letter, but that doesn't matter. It can go tomorrow."

"Good heavens!" she thought to herself. "I'll bet he thinks I've been sending a warning to my mad admirer of last year! Go ahead and examine the purple portfolio, my dear Michel. What a face! Yes, the portfolio's infected, it smells to heaven." Saying nothing, she put her hand reassuringly on Michel's shoulder.

"You're laughing at something?" he asked in a low tone.

"No. I'm not laughing."

"But you'd like to."

Alice raised her hands and let them fall sharply to her side.

"Good heavens! Have I taken a vow never to laugh again? Come, Michel, don't be such a wet blanket! You've come back sooner than I had expected and I'm glad to see you. Even in the depths of my shame, let me be in good spirits once in a while and turn somersaults and blow soap bubbles now and then as I wallow in my sin."

"Don't go too far, Alice," Michel interrupted in the same low, urgent tone. "You need to learn to watch your step. Yes, I've gotten back early. I saw my man."

"Your man?"

"Ferreyrou, the mayor. It's all settled."

"What's settled?"

"I'm not going to lunch there tomorrow, after all. I explained to them I had come down from Paris in rotten shape and that one can hardly drink mineral water at a banquet and so we'd have to put it off. . . . Anybody'd think you were annoyed. . . . Anyhow, I told them I was sick."

He leaned on the table with both hands and closed his eyes. All expression went out of his face and Alice saw merely wrinkles, unhealthy pallor, a mouth and forehead that had aged visibly in twenty-four hours.

"Good!" she responded quickly. "We'll both play sick. Suits me fine! Dressing gowns at all hours of the day, an eggnog at six, and we won't stir beyond the ruins of the old wall."

"But you'll be bored to death," Michel objected.

"I hope so. It's fine for the health. Have you any more packages, dear? Let me take them while you put up the car. No, wait. I'll run the car into the garage myself. . . . We're off! Here's where you're going to see some swell driving!"

"No, no!" Michel called out. "For God's sake, come out of that car! You can have anything you want if you'll only quit. I'll give you an unlimited power of attorney—or my cross of the Order of Isabella. Look out! Your right mudguard is scraping. Put on the emergency brake quick!"

He jumped on the running board while she steered like a novice and swore like a truck driver.

They came back from the garage in a lively, happy mood. Michel did not fall into a gloomy fit again until he caught sight of Chevestre's lank figure coming slowly toward the terrace, dressed in black as a mark of respect, his legs encased in patent-leather leggings which at a distance gave the effect of riding boots.

"There he comes!" Michel groaned. "I'll give him a pair of riding boots—in his rear!"

"But you were expecting him, weren't you?"

"Oh, yes. But even when I'm expecting him, I keep hoping he won't come. He gets on my nerves, walking around here as if he was going to inherit the place."

Michel admitted only his feeling of annoyance and tried his best to conceal the fear he also felt in the presence of his manager. Having risen from farmhand to superintendent, Chevestre had exchanged the limp, shapeless cap of the former for an old felt hat and gave himself airs by wearing a coat and vest. Intimidated by his swinging stride and self-assured bearing, Michel would vainly resort, in their dealings, to the engaging manner he used in his business and a bluntness he had adopted from realistic plays.

Tall and lean, his close-trimmed, white and blond mustache making a tow-colored line across his face, Chevestre drew near. "I'll bet he's the one who put up the money for the mortgage on this place," Michel thought. "Seysset is only a dummy. If Alice knew! But she'll find out when I have to sell."

Alice was likewise watching Chevestre as he came up the slope.

"There's no denying it, Michel," she said, "your manager has a certain air about him. He may be a louse, but he certainly has style!"

"Strange that in all these years she's never gotten into the habit of saying 'our manager'," Michel remarked to himself. "She isn't at home here and never will be. If she should find out about the mortgage—! But what does she care? Now she's going to irritate Chevestre with a lot of exasperating questions, pitch her voice too high as she expresses surprise that the willows should branch low down, or advise him to try quince jelly for chickens with diarrhea. She has no idea how she gets herself disliked with her theatrical manners." He got up and went forward to meet the manager.

"Would you like me to stay here?" Alice offered. "You know Chevestre can't put anything over on me."

"Nor on me, either," Michel replied curtly. "I'll join you later in the living room. But don't you let him get the impression you're running away without saying 'How do you do?' to him. Here he is now. I say, Chevestre," he called out, "I almost thought we'd have to go and take you by the ear and make you come and have a glass of port."

"No, indeed, sir! No, indeed! Only one's work is like a beautiful woman. It doesn't like to be kept waiting."

Chevestre bared his close-cropped head and respectfully waited for Alice to take a step toward him. This she did in a leisurely manner and held out her slender hand, then offered him a pack of cigarettes and, looking into his eyes from between her half-closed lids, inquired as to what the weather was likely to be the following day. Meanwhile Michel, with a smile on his lips as befitted the lord of the manor, grew annoyed that the meeting between his wife and his manager should resemble that of a pretty woman and a well bred man.

"Well, what did he have to tell you?"

"Nothing—nothing new, at any rate. His trick is to slip over suggestions in such a slick, elusive manner that, when you try to sum them up and state clearly just what he advises, he opens his eyes and exclaims, 'Why! I never said that, sir—I'd never think of— You know very well, sir, that I could never afford to'—"

"Afford to what?"

Michel shrugged his shoulders and lied.

"How do I know? You don't imagine, do you, that Chevestre is the person to disclose his schemes if he has any? And besides, I confess I'm not in a frame of mind right now to pay much attention to anything he might have to say."

"How so?" she asked thoughtlessly. "Oh, yes."

"Why, Alice!" he exclaimed.

She checked an impertinent retort and made another attempt to draw Michel out of his depressed mood.

"Why does he address you with such deference?"

"His father," Michel replied, "was valet to our neighbors, the Capdenacs."

"So? Well, that spoils for me that lordly bearing of his which suggests some fair-haired knight of olden France. I can feel my conviction tottering that he was born of the clandestine love of an officer of hussars for a golden sheaf of wheat."

She talked along at random, making an effort to be witty and walking up and down to escape her husband's attention.

"The weather's going to change," she announced. "The wind's from the east. As someone I know would say, at Nice they'll have the mistral tonight. . . . Oh, I've got an idea! Wait a minute."

She ran to the woodbox and came back laden with kindling wood, pine cones and beech chips, with which she made a bright fire.

"Just because we have two lovely days, we think it's summer and then, all of a sudden— There, wasn't that a good idea?"

Pleased with herself, she turned to look at Michel. The golden flame danced in his eyes as he gazed steadily into the fire.

"Wasn't it, Michel?" she insisted.

Seated on the hearthstone, she purposely put a youthful, plaintive expression into her voice, that voice that Michael loved, in order to try its power over him.

"What was it I said a few minutes ago we'd do? Oh, yes, have an eggnog."

As Michel got up to go and fasten the door, which kept opening a little, Alice followed on the wall the slow-moving shadow of a broad-shouldered man with a curly, round head. It seemed as if she were looking at that shadow for the first time in her life.

"Don't close the door, dear. I'm going to the kitchen to get the eggnog. You aren't feeling well, are you?"

"Not very," he replied with an abstracted manner.

He studied the sky, the swift-moving clouds, the tender foliage

425

bending low in parallel lines before the wind, like water-grass in a flowing stream.

"I think we're in for some very bad weather," he remarked. "Let's see how the barometer stands. . . . Good Lord! The barometer—"

The slamming of the door made him turn around. Alice was hurrying to the kitchen to get away from him, from talk about the weather and from the generally leaden scene. In the warm kitchen, brightened by the reddish copper vessels, she gave a sigh of relief.

"My, how good that smells! What is it, Maria?"

"The guinea hen, ma'am. I put it in early so as to have it thoroughly cooked. Do you want the eggnog now, ma'am? . . . Get up there, you rude fellow! Go quick and get me a bottle of red wine."

A pair of shuffling wooden sabots and a peasant's blouse of coarse, dun-colored velvet, stretched tight over a powerful, discouraged-looking back, left the kitchen, aroused and driven out by a witch's mighty arm. Alice sat down for a moment on the chair that Maria's husband had been occupying.

"How comfortable it is here!" she said to herself. "The food slowly cooking on the fire, the red glow of the stove, the welcome heat that goes to your head a little—and that skinny grasshopper bossing her spineless male around. How human and normal and pleasant it all is! What if the cook doesn't like me? That, too, is quite normal. I wish I could stay right here."

But Maria's silence forced her to get up.

"You won't forget to put some cinnamon in the eggnog, will you, Maria? And plenty of sugar."

She walked straight through the living room, where Michel was writing, and dallied a while in the bathroom. With the help of the eggnog, the dinner that followed it and the well-cooked guinea hen, they kept things going fairly well. Shortly after nine-thirty Alice called Maria twice, first for a hot-water bottle, then for a quilted comforter for her bed. Left alone, Michel and Alice listened to the smothered notes of a little wall clock as it struck ten, perched away up near the ceiling on its arbor-vitae bracket. Michel was smoking and dispatching his correspondence, while Alice, seated in the least uncomfortable chair, opened the newspapers of the day before in order not to look as if she were reading her present and future in the flames of the open fire.

"Ten o'clock," she mused. "If we were in Paris now—"

"Do you want to sit here, Alice, to draw or write?" Michel asked.

"No, thanks," she answered, while she thought to herself, "These polite attentions are unbearable. Until now, if I was using the desk, he wouldn't think anything of saying to me, 'Away with you, young lady, and be quick about it.' Ah, here's the rain. If we were in Paris now—"

A door banged shut and Maria's loud, imperious voice could be heard in the distance. Wooden sabots hurried clumsily away in the rain. After they had gone, Alice listened intently. "That's all for tonight," she said to herself. "They've gone off to bed." A burnt log crumbled into embers and made her start with fright.

"How nervous you are, dear," Michel said gently.

Alice made no answer but rubbed her back against her chair in order to get rid of the creepy feeling, like a drop of tepid water, which ran down her spine whenever she felt her husband's eyes on her back. "He's watching me. I know very well I shall never be able to stand eleven—no, twelve evenings like this one. Nor twelve—no, eleven nights such as the one we have ahead of us. What kind of a night is it going to be, anyhow? Oh, I can't stand that drop of warm water another minute!" She turned sharply around and immediately recovered her poise. "That's fine!" she said to herself. "I'm never afraid of anything unless it's behind my back."

"A cigarette, please, Michel."

He brought her the box of cigarettes and the lighter. The flame from the lighter, held between their two faces, cast a light on Alice's well rounded eyelids and her full mouth, puckered to hold the cigarette, which made her face look puffed up like a stone mask spouting water for a fountain. Peering through her lashes, she appraised the barely perceptible change for the worse in Michel's face, a sort of general contraction which made his handsome, bistre-

427

bordered eyes look smaller and seemed to have made his cheeks shrink. "Not so good," was her laconic verdict.

"What are you thinking about, Michel?" she asked. "I can't bear to see this—and this."

She put her finger on a lower eyelid and on the smooth part of his cheek, between the nose and the strip of beard. He shrugged his shoulders.

"I'm thinking about your having been untrue to me," he replied very simply. "What else could I be thinking about?"

It seemed for a moment as if she had not heard him. She looked at him in an absent-minded way, her face so close to his that he could distinguish the slate-blue specks in her eyes and the grayish green lines running out like spokes from a hub.

"How soon, dear, are you going to be able to stop thinking about that?" she finally said.

"I have no idea," he answered.

"But, Michel, we can't go on this way!" she exclaimed, wearily turning her head toward the rain-lashed window.

"It's good of you to realize that," Michel remarked.

Alice turned on him impulsively.

"We can't either of us go on this way, Michel—I no more than you. I simply can't stand unhappiness. To get along on a shoestring, live from hand to mouth while waiting for a check to come in, change from one job to another or make a job out of nothing—you and I are used to that. Besides, I was hardened to it from my earliest childhood. But just to sit down in an unhappy state of mind and make a spectacle of oneself—'Get away from here, everybody, and leave me alone, I'm unhappy'—no, that's too much. All this fuss over a bit of ancient history that isn't of the slightest importance—"

She gave free play to her voice, which so readily took on a plaintive tone, and, as she spoke, shook her head vehemently and rhythmically, with the characteristic gesture of a captive.

"My dear girl, have a little patience," Michel protested. "Bear in mind that for me that bit of ancient history is barely twenty-four hours old."

Alice suddenly lapsed into silence and her face took on the blank stare of a somnambulist, her lower lip sagging and showing the dazzling white of her teeth. Michel took advantage of this stupor to ask, "Why did you keep that letter?"

"I—er—I hadn't meant to keep it. I left it in the portfolio and forgot it."

"Down here?" Michel exclaimed, dumbfounded.

"Oh, no, not down here. That purple portfolio is part of my traveling kit."

Michel breathed more easily.

"Ah! Good!"

"Are you feeling a little better now?" she asked maliciously.

Deeply hurt, he made no reply but sat dreaming, his eyes fastened on the fire.

"If only," he ventured after a long silence, "if only the—er—affair between you and that fellow had been of a different sort from what you told me—"

"Yes," she broke in. "That sounds like the guy who got run over by a bus and woke up in the next world saying, 'If only it had been a Rolls Royce!'"

"I'm not dead, my dear," Michel remonstrated.

"No, thank heaven," she replied bluntly. "I'd never forgive you for that."

She sat down, crossed her knees and bent over to pull on one of her moccasins. As she stooped over, her long arm hanging down across her long thigh and her breasts crushed against her knees, she seemed even taller than usual. In bed Michel used to tell her she was "interminable"—"as endless as a river," he would say, laughing to hide his madly devoted admiration.

While Alice was forcing on the fur-lined moccasin with her hand and her bare foot, Michel covertly studied the freedom of her movements, the suppleness of her knees, her superb back, with the straight groove down the center, her breasts, a little flat—"a bit like jellyfish," she used to say, "but not too big." "I declare! will she never grow old?" he asked himself with resentment. He felt no desire for her and was glad of that. "She even disgusts me a little," he meditated, "which is only natural. The idea of giving that fellow her interest—advice—affection—her dependence as an invalid! Why, she even had the nerve to speak of coming to have confidence in him! And, as if that wasn't enough, she went the whole way and gave him her body, her feverish body and full, chapped lips and all the fragrance of her—! She's—they're all far worse than one would ever suspect."

"Tell me," he suddenly exclaimed. "Did you used to call him 'dearest'?"

Alice stopped rubbing her bare heel. It took her a moment to get his meaning. Then she half closed her eyes, trying to remember.

"'Dearest'? Why, no—unless possibly—"

"Unless possibly—," he repeated. "I catch the significance of that exception. It—er—calls up quite a picture to my mind. Indeed!"

The insolent look came over her face again as she looked at him with half-shut eyes.

"You only got what was coming to you, my dear," she retorted. "Maybe that will teach you not to ask me any more questions."

He sat there without stirring, like a man who has bumped into something in the dark and does not dare take another step.

"Do you know what we're headed for if this keeps up?" he asked finally.

She seated herself in front of the dying embers, her arms about her knees.

"Haven't the slightest idea," she replied indifferently.

"We're headed straight for the rock so many marriages get wrecked on—lukewarmness—I'm speaking only for myself, of course—semi-indifference. And kindly note that I am facing this prospect coolly and not taking it like a crazy fool, thank God."

"Hurry up and come to the point," Alice interrupted disdainfully.

The crash that followed brought her to her feet with a bound. Michel had hurled against the wall the jug that had held the eggnog. After that one violent gesture he leaned over and mechanically picked up the largest piece of pottery, to which the S-shaped handle still remained attached, unbroken.

Relieved that he had at the same time justified and dispelled the fear which she had felt like an imaginary warm drop gliding down her back, Alice almost approved of Michel's act.

"That was rather stupid," she remarked, but not with any severity.

"I admit it," Michel assented, "but I couldn't help it."

He was examining the piece of pottery, hanging from his little finger by the handle.

"That's strange! The jug is in pieces, but the handle didn't budge. . . . Yes, it was stupid of me. . . . Now, why does a reaction as unintelligent as that give one a certain sense of relief? . . . Look, the handle had been glued on once and yet the shock didn't loosen it. That's strange."

"Very strange," Alice repeated, in order to be polite, as she shoved the broken pieces of pottery to one side with her foot.

"Lucky it was empty," was her banal comment.

But she was already withdrawing into hidden recesses in her mind and there weighing the incident coolly. "Oh, yes," she meditated, "it's all very well to say it gives one a certain sense of relief, but so would a blow on my head with a hammer, or even two hands a bit too tight about my throat. I know somebody who is going to slip out here very quietly tonight and sleep on the couch."

She did not do so, however. For Michel quickly fell into a troubled sleep, talking to himself and calling out Alice's name in a loud, thick voice. She reached over, touched a warm hand hanging out of the other bed and turned on the light. Michel woke and lay there silently, his eyes fastened on his wife. He brought back with him from the depths of his dreams a feeling of mildly delirious gratitude. Alice handed him the glass of water, got up and opened the oldfashioned inner blinds and threw the window open a little way. A blanket of damp air, laden with the verdant perfumes that the night and the rain had driven down to the level of the soil, glided over the twin beds. Michel started up, but Alice said "s-s-sh, s-s-sh," lifted his hand back on the bed and drew the covers up over his shoulder. He obeyed her and became yielding, submissive, childlike, while she struggled against the yearning to heal his wounds, bend over the sleeping man, over the warm, familiar odor of his body, and hold him close between her shoulder and her cheek, in that spot where a woman cradles the most precious and at the same time the heaviest burden of her love.

She kept repeating "s-s-sh, s-s-sh" and the last hours of that spring night passed lightly as she listened to the gusts of wind and the recurrent showers.

"Such a fine jug! It's too bad!"

"It wasn't very handsome, Maria."

"Too bad, just the same. Did you notice, ma'am, that the wallpaper is loose here? That's something new."

"Maybe so, but the wallpaper isn't. Too feeble to hang on any longer, I guess."

With gloves on her hands and a silk kerchief tied about her head, Alice was polishing a copper candlestick, while Maria moved the desk, chairs and couch from their accustomed places.

"That's just like Michel, what I said there," Alice thought to herself. "I, too, seem to be going out of my way to be pleasant with her."

All in black except for the white cloth wrapped around her head, Maria was working with her characteristic activity, her powerful, insect-like energy, and trying all the while to make out the story back of the broken jug. From behind a cloud the sun was drawing up the night's rainfall from the warming soil. From the drenched ground about the house there came a strong smell of grass beaten down and of sprouting tubers and mushrooms.

"What do you think's the matter with your husband, ma'am?"

Alice slowly shook her yellow dustcloth over the viburnum bush before she replied, "Overwork—something he caught in Paris—a touch of the grippe."

Maria nodded her grasshopper-like head in approval of these suggestions.

"She seems to feel like talking this morning," Alice meditated. "She hovers over that broken jug like a dragonfly over a puddle of water. And Michel asleep in the next room, with his high temperature!"

"Aren't you going to send for the doctor, ma'am?"

Crouching down, Alice finished rubbing the dustcloth over the rungs of a chair and then stood up and turned toward Maria.

"No. If his temperature goes up this evening, I'll telephone Dr. Puymaigre in the morning. But—"

She seemed to be studying the fragments of the jug which Maria had gathered up in the wastepaper basket.

"But I've a notion it won't go up. It's more of a nervous fever."

With her wiry, wrinkled hand Maria grasped the basket and shook the pieces of broken pottery as if she were taking up the collection in church.

"Was it you dropped the jug, ma'am?"

"No," Alice said sharply. "It was my husband. But whoever it was, that doesn't change the result in the least."

The maid studied the loose bit of wallpaper and the floor thoughtfully, measuring with her eye the distance from the desk to the spot where the jug had landed. Then she announced:

"Oh, your husband? Well, he had no right to do it."

For the second time Alice thought she sensed, under Maria's impenetrable shell, a warm wave of human feeling, an impulse which she likened to the solidarity that unites wife and concubine. She blushed up to her swollen, sleepless eyelids. "Fine conquest I've made!" she thought to herself. "A treacherous peasant woman, devoured with curiosity, who has never liked my presence. Still, even if she hasn't accepted my being here, I have no right to call her treacherous. I don't know of her doing anything underhand. And what a keen insight! ... After all, what have I got against her? Her fierce honesty? Her other virtues?"

Forgetting her household tasks, Alice leaned out of the window and looked down on the riotous vegetation, glistening with rain and dotted with short-lived blooms, half-opened foliage and leafbuds still tinged with the red of their painful effort.

"How beautiful it all was two days ago!" she thought.

An overgrown path led away to the darkest part of the woods, to the wild strawberry blossoms, the tall, slender stalks of Solomon's seal and the ferns, with their freshly opened fronds. "I have no desire to go exploring alone in those woods today," she thought to herself. "Nor with Michel, either."

To reassure herself, she stood and listened to Maria, who, with felt slippers over her shoes, was busily polishing the floors. Her scrawny brown arms swinging rhythmically and her sinewy legs executing a scissor-like dance, she was performing evolutions over the waxed oak floor like a water spider skimming over the metallic scum of a stagnant pond. Alice found a simple delight in the sound of those felt-clad feet. She would have enjoyed quite as much the noise of the chopping bowl, the broom in the vestibule, the meat-grinder—any of the indications of Maria's presence.

"I'd like to pick over lentils in the kitchen," she sighed to herself, "or pull weeds from the garden path. Or go to the fair at Sarzat-le-Haut. . . . But I'm not at all anxious to take some lemonade and fruit salts in to that man in there with the fever. I'm perfectly willing to take care of him but not when he's sick."

As she passed through the living room, she ventured to warn Maria, "You know it's very bad for your internal organs to polish the floor with your feet that way."

Without waiting for a reply, she left the room, a little embarrassed. "I'm almost making advances to her now!" she thought. Behind her the dance of the felt slippers ceased for a moment, then resumed with a sort of joyful abandon.

A small tray tinkling on the flat palm of her hand, Alice entered the dimly lighted bedroom.

"You aren't asleep?" she asked. "Are you feeling any better? Here's some hot lemonade. Let me see your tongue. More. . . . It's terrible! How are your bowels? . . . Since when? What's that?"

Michel turned restlessly between his sheets.

"Oh, do let me alone!" he pleaded. "I have a special horror of this sort of cross-examination."

"Why, Michel, how can you act that way? You've got to—. Come, this is too childish!"

He curled up in a ball, his knees in the air, and pushed the tray away with a hostile, peevish expression on his face.

"Michel, I'm not for one minute going to let you neglect yourself! Here, drink this right down. I put a large spoonful of salts in it. Then lie there quietly till you begin to feel cramps. And you're not to get up till tea-time, about five o'clock."

She patiently watched him as he drank. But after that she started to walk away gladly and too quickly.

"Where are you going now?" he asked.

She stopped abruptly, as if jerked by a halter around her neck.

"Now?" she faltered. "Why—er—I was going—er—out there— just for a turn around the place—I don't know—nowhere."

She looked down and added, "Nowhere in particular."

As she was about to close the door, she turned and came back.

"By the way, Michel, if there should be a telephone call from Paris?"

"Well, I'm here, am I not?" he said with the voice of a man in good health.

"Yes, but if you're asleep, shall I take the call?"

Turning his head on the pillow, Michel looked sharply at her as she stood there in her morning gown, framed in silver by the light coming in from the garden, and gave her a rather disagreeable smile as he replied:

"No, you shall not. That's precisely what you're not to do. You're to call me—that's all."

Alice went out without replying, congratulating herself on her self-control. She regarded her loneliness in the light of a reward, as she strolled musingly from the terrace to the garden and from the garden back to the house, walking with silent steps in the white sunlight, which was intercepted once in a while by idling clouds that now promised, now withheld rain and imposed a temporary silence on the nightingales. At noon Maria brought out to her on the terrace a luncheon of chopped meat and rice, wrapped in cabbage leaves and browned over a slow fire.

435

"Leftovers," the maid said by way of awkward apology. "Because nobody went to the village this morning."

"I only wish I could have leftovers like that in Paris, Maria."

Alice ate greedily, with little jabs of her fork. The soft, melancholy sunlight fell on her pale, half-closed eyes and glossy hair, in which the cloud-flecked sky was mirrored. Listening intently as she ate for any sound from the house, she finally caught Michel's hurried step, the closing of an inner door, and the throwing of a certain bolt. "There, everything's all right now," she said to herself. "By this evening he won't have any more fever."

"What's that you're bringing me now, Maria?"

"Some cantaloup jelly I made, ma'am. Just taste it. I put four lemons in this time to give it more flavor."

As Maria stood beside her chair, it came to both of them that this was the first time they had been alone together. The thought moved them strangely. "How odd it is," Alice reflected. "The first time! Heretofore Michel has always come between us, or Maria's husband, or the laundress, or a ladder for washing the windows, or a kettle of preserves."

"Four lemons!" she said aloud. "That's the secret! I never would have guessed it. I was wondering—"

The telephone bell cut short her remark, altered the kindly gray of the sky and cast a shadow over the reddish hawthorn bushes. Alice laid her spoon down on her plate.

"Oh, that bell!" she exclaimed. "We ought to have it changed."

"Will you answer it, ma'am?"

Alice shook her head, having already heard her husband's voice, his "Hello! Hello there!" in the impatient tone he reserved for underlings when they were out of his sight. As soon as the conversation got under way, his voice dropped and Alice could make out nothing but a polite murmur.

"I'll take my coffee out here, Maria. You can pour it out yourself and just bring me a full cup. Two pieces of sugar, as usual."

She listened again, stretching her head forward, absorbed in the effort to hear. She thought she made out a good-natured chuckle

and pursed her lips with resentment. But after a long silence there
came a distressed exclamation, "Don't cut us off!" Then Michel's
voice became louder, breathlessly expressing astonishment and indignation.

"There's no discussion possible on that point!" he exclaimed.
"No, I could never consent to that. There are no two ways of looking at certain things. ... What! Can it be I've trusted a man who—"

"Now they're at it!" Alice thought to herself. "Hot and heavy!"

She continued to listen but in vain. Her cigarette shook so that it
touched the bit of jelly left on her plate and went out. She did not
realize that she had turned pale, but Maria, bringing the steaming
cup of coffee, stopped a moment and looked at her. At the same
instant Michel appeared on the threshold, slamming the door behind
him. Alice instinctively got up to run away and stumbled into
Maria's outstretched arm, her shoulder, hard as a plank, and all
Maria's firm and sinewy leanness.

"Please, madame! Please!" Maria whispered.

"Did you hear that?" Michel called out from a distance.

Alice shook her head and sat down again. She bit her pale,
chapped lip as Michel came striding toward her.

"Is there any coffee left, Maria?" he asked. "Do go and get me a
swallow or two, will you?"

He sat down beside his wife on the bench. Seeing the bright look
in his eye and his generally toned-up appearance, she relaxed and
took a deep breath to quiet her heart action.

"Here's the situation," he began. "Do you feel equal to turning
out the greater part of the designs for the costumes for *Daffodil*
within the next four or five days—with a reduced cast and stage
setting, of course? It's always the undertakings you think are dead
and buried which come to life and are taken up again. Didn't you
think this one was done for? I wouldn't have given a nickel for it.
Only, now that they want my theater, I refuse to consider using
the old costumes, faded with benzine and bedraggled after a couple
of hundred performances. They're going to use yours—I told them
so. Let's see to it that at least you make a little money furnishing

the designs. A promise is a promise, after all. I laid down the law to them."

"To whom?" Alice asked.

Michel's good spirits fell immediately. He took a full cup of coffee from Maria's hands and waited till she had gone before replying.

"The same old group headed by Bordat and Hirsch. Let me add that I have no confidence in this proposition. But since I have the hall to rent—. As long as they were merely writing letters about the matter, it didn't mean anything. With that crowd you can't count on anything until they get someone to telephone you about it."

"Who did they get this time?" Alice inquired.

Michel took a drink of coffee, made out as if he had burnt his lips, waited a moment, then looked his wife squarely in the eye and, since he could not avoid replying, turned his answer in an insulting manner:

"Why, Ambrogio, of course. Who else would they have gotten to telephone me? Isn't he my partner—if I may use that term?"

He got up, walked away a few steps, then came back.

"Well, have you nothing to say?" he asked.

She turned on him her drowsiest look as she replied:

"About what? Oh, yes. Why, of course I'll do it."

"Do what?"

"Make the designs for them."

"In four days?"

"I already have forty-four sketches done. As for the ballet costumes—"

Michel indulged in a quiet, cynical laugh as he remarked, "I don't believe you'll have to sit up very late over them."

"How so?"

"Pshaw! Four little dancers twirling around on the tips of their toes—"

"In tarlatan," Alice interjected.

"Yes. And a pair of good acrobatic male dancers—"

"And plenty of bare flesh, pinking and rhinestones," Alice added.

"Rhinestones!" Michel protested. "You must think this is before the war. No such extravagance! Spangles, yes, but nothing expensive, not even for the leading actors. They'll squawk like the devil."

Alice appeared to wake up and enter into the spirit of the thing.

"The leading actors? We'll give them artificial flowers instead of feathers, ribbons in place of embroidery, cellophane to produce the effect of silk, and fringe to make it look expensive. I get the idea!"

"Have you got your sketches here?" Michel asked.

"Yes, all of them. In my purple portfolio," she added without thinking.

"That's the time I made a bad break," she thought as she watched Michel, with a bitter look around the corners of his mouth, empty his cup of coffee with a gulp. "I've simply got to cut the words 'portfolio' and 'purple' out of my vocabulary if I don't want to see that sensitive plant curl up its injured leaves every time. And yet this same sensitive plant talks with Ambrogio cordially over the telephone. It's not only strange but also very peculiar, as my late lamented father used to say."

She rubbed her chilly hands together and shuddered with a sort of shame. "It's terrible when you think how much has changed between us," she said to herself. "It takes only two words and there he is all shriveled up, looking weazened and old, and that right eye of his actually shrunken in size. And then the way I never let pass an opportunity to find fault with him, just as if he were to blame for my having slept with Ambrogio!"

"Michel, I'm going to slip on a dress and run down to the village."

"To the village?"

"You see, I haven't anything to sketch with—no paper, paint or tracing paper."

"Are you going to do some sketching?"

"Why, Michel! My sketches for the costumes!"

"That's so. I'm sorry."

"Do you need anything?"

He looked at her with an expression of long-suffering resignation.

"Yes, but what I need you can't give me," he replied, blushing like a young man and striding hurriedly into the house.

When he had gone, she bit her lip, called him a sentimental fool, threw down her napkin angrily and tossed her head back so as to hold two tears behind her eyelashes. Half an hour later she was walking down the hill, turning up her face to catch the occasional drops of rain. On the way she thought out plans for costumes, calculated their cost and picked some early blueberries. "I'll make a hat like this little blue, pointed helmet for the Fairy in *Daffodil*," she said to herself.

In the village she purchased some school pencils, red and violet ink and cakes of children's water colors.

"You can put these in your mouth without any danger," the woman in the store assured her.

Alice climbed the hill again in a cheerful mood and brimming over with goodwill. She sat down by the roadside to sketch a costume for the Snail on the package of paper she had just bought. A fine rain, as impalpable as salty fog from off the sea, attached itself to her powdered cheeks and bare head.

"There's nothing like an hour by oneself and a little work," she mused, "to clear up your complexion and also your bad humor."

When she reached the terrace, there was only a strip of golden sky along the horizon which had escaped invasion by the rainclouds.

"Michel, dear, where are you?" she called out.

It was Maria who came out on the doorstep, her hands in white mitts of flour.

"Has my husband gone out, Maria?"

"No, ma'am. He's in the living room. He hasn't budged from the house."

"Did you take him some camomile tea?"

"Yes, ma'am, but he hurt my feelings by not drinking it," the maid replied, lowering her eloquent eyes and shaking her dark brown arms, with their white mittens. "He was at the telephone and maybe I disturbed him."

She glanced at Alice with a new expression of respectful friendliness and then walked hurriedly away.

"Another telephone call!" Alice thought to herself. "And he never left the house and wouldn't drink anything." She hesitated a

440

moment and then crossed the threshold briskly, having decided to adopt a breezy manner.

"Are you there, dear?" she asked. "Good Lord, how dark it is in here! . . . You'd never guess what they have in this neck of the woods in the way of painting supplies. You can't get any tracing paper for love or money. Well, when in Rome, do as the Romans do. This isn't the first time I've been stranded on a desert island. . . . I got you the newspapers. . . . Anything new here?"

Michel stirred heavily in the semi-darkness but did not get up.

"Nothing much. I've got one of my headaches. . . . Oh, yes, there was a telephone call."

"Who was it?"

"Those people again—I mean the Hirsch and Bordat outfit. I'm terribly sorry, my dear girl, but the deal is off."

"What deal?"

"Why, the *Daffodil* proposition."

"You don't mean it!"

"Yes, they've given up the idea of putting it on at the Etoile." He stirred uneasily again and turned over on the couch.

"Well! Well, I declare!" Alice stammered. "That's—er—that's pretty raw!"

She sat down, untied her little packages mechanically and turned on the desk light.

"Now tell me all about it, dear."

"I tell you I have one of my headaches," Michel complained.

"You can take some aspirin later, but just now, tell me what happened."

"What is there to tell?" he answered with ill humor, his face still turned toward the wall. "When a deal is off, it's off."

"Question of money?"

"Well, yes—that and other things. Hirsch can't afford to let his name appear in connection with the affair, neither as manager nor as silent partner."

"Well, how about yourself?"

"They don't want to let me have sole control. I'm not sufficiently under their thumb."

Alice looked hungrily at the curly head and the body turned away from her and talking to the wall.

"Why not jointly with Ambrogio then?"

Michel did not answer.

"Did you hear me? Why not with Ambrogio? He's one of their crowd, isn't he?"

She saw Michel's back shaking with little jerks.

"You make me laugh," he said condescendingly.

Alice meditated for a moment, nibbling the stem of the now useless blueberry.

"It was you who called Paris," she announced finally.

Michel moved a little and showed his profile.

"Why do you ask me that?"

"I'm not asking you—I'm telling you. It was you who called Paris."

Shrugging his shoulders by way of reply, Michel turned again toward the wall.

"I know what happened," Alice went on after a while. "You lost your head and threw up the whole thing."

He sat up and smoothed his hair with his hand.

"Yes, I threw up the whole damned business, and do you want me to tell you why I did it?"

"No," she replied, deep in thought. "I can guess pretty well. In the last analysis, you could have been only a sort of assistant manager under Ambrogio, who stands in with the Hirsch crowd. . . . Then, too, my working with him on the costumes and stage setting. . . . I see it all now. . . . You preferred to have us lose the contract, so you chucked the whole thing out the window. Wasn't that about it?"

"More or less."

His hands held tight between his knees, Michel rocked back and forth.

"Was it again Ambrogio you talked to?"

"Why, of course."

"And what does he think of your backing out?"

Michel started to laugh, without looking at his wife.

"He? Why, he thinks that, on the whole, I did the right thing—can you beat that? Says it's a clever move—that Hirsch and Bordat will come back with a better propostiion at the very first opportunity. He's as optimistic as they make 'em, you see."

"Yes, I see."

Michel stopped rocking back and forth and, with an ill-disguised effort, asked Alice, "And you—what do you think of my pulling out?"

"I? Why, I think we're losing a fine chance to make some money. But, after all, that's your business. You've never been in the habit of attaching much importance to my opinions—at least, as far as business matters are concerned."

"Please don't get sarcastic, Alice. I'm not in the mood for that today. Try to look at the matter from a different angle. To make a man take such a jealous step—put you ahead of any question of making money, ahead of reasonable considerations, ahead of every-thing—why, in my opinion, in my very humble opinion, there's many a woman would be proud of that."

"Michel, you should never try to decide what makes a woman proud and what doesn't."

"Oh, of course I understand that—"

Alice leaned over him and the light fell full on her bold mouth and squat nostrils.

"No, you don't understand," she interrupted. "Any more than I understand what you think of me since I told you that I—. But I'm beginning to believe that a man and woman can do anything to-gether—anything—with perfect safety, except talk frankly. Ever since the other day, when one of us talks, the other listens with the polite manner of a dead person, or else answers as if a million miles away—God knows where—on some desert island, where he stands all alone, gesticulating. . . . No, please don't try to explain. We'll only get on one another's nerves again. *Daffodil* is dead—let's bury it."

443

She stirred the dying fire, pressed her moist bang against her fore-head and sat down in her favorite spot to sketch in blue pencil the pointed, flowered helmet of some little fairy character. Behind her, in the darkness, there was a tremulous sigh of gratitude. She made an effort to appear very much engrossed in her drawing, holding it out at arm's length to examine it, cocking her head on one side and squinting her eyes. She heard the very fine rain, the crackling of the fire and the little owl-faced clock, perched away up near the ceiling. "Only six o'clock!" she exclaimed to herself. "And here it is only Saturday! Ten whole days yet to go!"

She gave up the costume of the Fairy and took up that of the Dragon Fly. "Cellophane wings. The whole body covered with jointed plates of some light metal, coated with duco—I can just see some lovely greens and blues! And the eyes—ah, the eyes! Two iridescent balloons, one on each side of the head. . . . There! Swell! . . . Only it suggests a musical review, rather than an operetta." She crossed out her sketch and, under the spell of the musical dropping of the rain on the balcony below the leaky gutter, let her pencil wander at random.

"And besides," Michel's voice suddenly broke in, "they wanted us to leave for Paris this evening or, at the latest, tomorrow morning."

Without replying, she tore up her drawing and, on a blank sheet of paper, began to design some doorknobs and radiator covers.

"But to have to face that—er—those people again just now," the voice continued, "well, I'm not proud of it and perhaps it isn't a very fine trait, but I admit—"

"That the task would be quite beyond my strength," Alice added to herself. "When Michel starts a sentence, he could always send it out to be finished. Stock phrase and banal remark, banal remark and stock phrase. . . . Poor Michel, how I treat him! . . . I wonder how I would treat him if I didn't love him. . . . This is simply hideous, what I'm drawing—looks like a pre-war subway poster. I'd never dare offer such an atrocity to the Eschenbach Studios." She crumpled the paper up into a ball and then tried sketching in colored crayons a necklace, belt and bracelet set, with which she was rather well

444

pleased at first. "Squares of heavy glass," she planned. "And here some balls of metal and tropical wood. . . . Or else lacquered plum pits. . . . Bah! net result: a disgusting bit of African trash. Oh, I'm not in the mood today!" She shoved the crayons and the sheet of paper away from her and sat listening to the raindrops falling with musical rhythm into a puddle of water—*mi, sol, sol, mi, sol, mi do.*

"Now if only I had the consolation—," the voice began again hesitatingly, "No, what am I saying? . . . Yes, after all, it would be a consolation. . . . If I could tell myself it was only an outbreak of your physical nature—"

Alice gritted her teeth. "He's at it again," she groaned inwardly.

"In the life of a woman—," the voice went on, "a normal woman, I mean—a sudden onrush of animal passion represents an exceptional crisis, a morbid phase. . . . Do you get my idea, Alice?"

"Perfectly," she replied, adding to herself: "And, what's more to the point, I manage to keep my face straight—though it's true that for some time past I've lost the ability to laugh heartily. But why is it that a man can never talk about a woman's sexual nature without making a lot of silly statements?"

Feeling encouraged, Michel got up and walked about with heavy steps, holding out his arms as though to indicate that he was on his way to greet Fairness, hurrying to welcome Leniency. But, when he came to the farther end of the room, between the two bookcases, he turned on his heel each time with a violence that gave the lie to his laboriously assumed air of kindly indulgence.

"A passing whim—now I could easily understand that. . . . If only. . . . I can't help it, that's the way I'm built."

Alice went on drawing nonchalantly, sometimes casting a furtive glance at Michel, sometimes listening attentively. She caught a stray phrase now and then, variations on a persistent motif which she had dubbed "the If-only theme." Michel stopped at the table to use the cigarette lighter. The havoc wrought in his features startled her and took complete possession of her thoughts. "What a terrible change in such a little while!" she commented to herself. "He looks as if he had made up his face for an old man's part. He's a deadly

445

bore, I admit, but the poor fellow's dying by inches. Eats hardly any-thing—merely nibbles at his food. I'll put up with anything, but I can't stand it to have him wasting away before my very eyes. Look at that face shriveling up, that right eye getting smaller all the time and that wry little smile. . . . Poor Michel! he looks just the way he did when the Spéleïeff failure left us stranded—and that ended in an attack of paratyphoid."

She frowned, deeply moved by an affectionate feeling of hostility which did not yet understand itself clearly but which endeavored to step in between Michel and any illness, Michel and danger, Michel and the hurts that came to him at her own hands. . . . She watched him closely as he paced up and down like a monomaniac, and then she lowered her eyes because she had looked at him ardently.

". . . and you'll admit I'm not altogether wrong, won't you, Alice? . . . Isn't that so, Alice?"

"Beg pardon?"

"I'll be damned! She doesn't even listen to me!"

Laying the palm of his hand on her head with an expression of outraged kindliness, he said, "You dear little monster!"

With a forced smile she endeavored to apologize.

"Don't be mad at me, Michel. I'm trying my best to patch things up. Are you going to smash something every day? Let's have a little peace, or at any rate not talk for a while, will you?"

She pushed the desk light over toward him.

"Here, let's share the newspaper. I'll take the picture section."

"He's making a softy of me," she mused. "It's terrible, the way I'm getting used to this situation! Two days ago, if he had called me a dear little monster, he'd have seen some fireworks! . . . How many hours is it now since we said mean things to one another? . . . If I let him have things his way, he'd get quite accustomed to getting along like this—unhappy every day, more If-only's every day, every day one year older. And on special holidays, so to speak, an intimate embrace, filled with shame and followed by remorse and by the tor-ment of an erotic evocation of the famous Ambrogio. . . . Ambrogio! He's always thinking about Ambrogio."

She pictured to herself quite coolly the features of that handsome young man and his black hair, which glistened like a bird's plumage. "It was pretty, that strange color of his lips," she meditated. "Hardly red at all, more of a reddish beige. And what adorable teeth! ... And all the other admirable qualities he had!" She used the past tense, as if for a dead man. "Always thinking about Ambrogio—when I never give him a thought myself!"

She quietly put down the picture section, of which she had been idly turning the pages. The nervous rustling of a newspaper held in Michel's hands marked the quick, irregular beating of a tired heart.

"You bet he's thinking about him! I'll wait two or three days longer and then I'll take a chance."

She waited, but she made the mistake of letting it be evident she was waiting. The strain of it all, the slight throbbing of blood in her ears, the daily ringing of the telephone, the tinkling of the bell on the letter-carrier's bicycle, the invisible trains which crossed the river, leaving a white, horizontal cloud hanging over the valley— all the daily sights and sounds brought Alice back to keeping track of the passage of time. She had the tense look of a person under a spell.

"What are you listening to?" Michel would ask her, and she would lie with equanimity.

"A mouse in the walls." Or, "It seemed to me the kitchen shutter was banging."

He came upon her one evening, pretending to be reading but with her gaze lost in the dark region between the two bookcases.

"What can there be over there that's so interesting?" he asked.

"Nothing. Just the darkness," she replied.

"Oh! So you, too, like to look on the dark side of things?" he said with a wan smile.

"Yes, I do, too," she said gloomily. "You see, our life is so entertaining just now!"

She turned her full, still supple neck and faced him.

"Michel, would you mind if we went back to Paris tomorrow?"

447

A frown spread over his face as he put himself on the defensive. "To Paris? Are you crazy? When we still have nine days' vacation before I have to relieve Ambrogio! And just as I'm trying to get my nerves under control! And—"

"Don't shout so," Alice broke in. "The windows are open."

"Go ahead—you go back to Paris! I'm not forcing anyone to stay here and be bored. I don't expect anybody to help me, or to understand, or—"

"All right, all right. I'll take it all back. Let's forget I ever suggested it. I'm not unhappy here."

Michel put on his glasses and looked his wife squarely in the face. "That's not true," he said sternly. "You are unhappy here. But I don't particularly see why you should be happy anyhow. Why should you be happy when you don't deserve it?"

"Because I want to be."

"That's a fine reason!"

"Best in the world. The idea of your talking to me about whether I deserve to be happy! What's that got to do with a person's desire to breathe freely and look well and not punish oneself needlessly every morning?"

"My dear girl, you'd do well to stick to subjects you know something about. Punish oneself! When did you ever deny yourself anything you wanted?"

"Include yourself in the picture, my dear Michel. Except that you have more than once bitten your lip to keep from smashing some business man in the face and except that I know how to deprive myself of unnecessary things—wear my old clothes and work hard all the time—so as to hang on to what's indispensable—except for that, as far as self-denial is concerned, we're about on the same footing."

"Indispensable? What, for instance?"

Alice shrugged her shoulders in a way she had, as though she wanted to shake off her dress and step out of it stark naked.

"Love, for instance," she answered. "Our love. A taxi whenever I want one. The right to tell certain people to go to hell. An old tailored suit, if necessary, but a fine chemise under it. I'm willing to drink water the whole year round, but I've got to have a Frigilux to keep it cold. In short, a whole lot of little things—that's what I mean by 'indispensable'."

Alice left the room in order not to see her husband upset, but she swore to herself, "Tomorrow—not a day later!"

She did not sleep much that night. She was always uneasy the first part of the night; she could feel herself trembling and losing her determination. It would be somewhere between midnight and dawn before she got a grip on herself again. With her forehead and knees touching the wall, she kept as far as possible from the other bed, where Michel lay motionless, breathing silently, under the influence of a double dose of aspirin. It was Alice who had advised him to double the dose.

"One gram is a lot," she thought to herself. "When he takes that much, I don't hear his breathing. . . . What a barbarous custom, these twin beds side by side. And how indecent! There's some excuse for a double bed, but these twin beds, like two observation posts! . . . When we come down for our summer vacation, I'm going to change this unsatisfactory arrangement. . . . I wonder what our summer vacation will be like, anyway."

The scattered elements of a dream jumbled together the picture of the squat towers of Cransac, a swarm of many-colored papers and Chevestre's tall, black silhouette ("Just like a priest, just like a priest," Alice kept mumbling to herself) and submerged all of this in the black darkness that hung heavily between the two gigantic, impassive bookcases. It seemed to Alice in her dream as if she got up, gathered the papers together and fled. But the song of the first blackbird suddenly crowded out the monotonous brilliance of the nightingales, forced its way across the threshold of her dream and announced the dawn. She straightened out her knees, unclasped her arms and, reassured, slipped off into restful sleep.

In the morning her preoccupation woke before she did and kept reiterating in the last moments of her sleep, "Tomorrow's the day, tomorrow's the day."

"No, it's today," she reminded herself as she opened her eyes.

449

Michel, his face white and calm, was sleeping as if his soul had left his body. Alice let him sleep and looked at him pityingly. "How young he looks when he's asleep," she said to herself. "Today's the day. With so much to be done, we'll need some hearty nourishment." She put on her moccasins and a white woolen dress and went to look for Maria, whom she found taking the ashes out from under the kitchen range, faced with tiles of blue faience, and at the same time keeping an eye on the milk and coffee as they heated.

"Maria, I'm determined my husband shall get back his appetite."

"So am I, ma'am," Maria responded, wrinkling her high forehead as she took in at a glance Alice's paleness and lassitude. "That is, if it depends on my cooking," she added. "Kindly step one side, ma'am. My milk's beginning to boil."

She stuck a spoon in the milk and took the saucepan off the fire. She had a white cap and a black dress—her invariable costume.

"Does she ever happen to take her clothes off?" Alice wondered. "What's the matter with your arm, Maria—a cut or a burn?"

"It's not worth mentioning, ma'am," Maria replied.

"Not worth mentioning, under a bandage that's worth even less," Alice remarked.

"Is butter good for a burn, ma'am?"

"Not bad, but there are better things. And that bandage of yours might be improved also."

"For a one-handed job it isn't so bad. Here's how you do it, ma'am. You put it on with one hand and tie it with your teeth."

"What's the matter with your husband helping you?"

Maria's eyes gleamed and laughed amidst their wrinkles.

"He did lend a hand, ma'am, but not to put the bandage on."

Standing there, of about the same height, they chatted in lowered tones, Alice breaking off and munching the corners of a piece of toast as she talked. The bitter aroma of the coffee made her mouth water and she stopped once to drink some. "How clean and orderly and feminine everything is here," she thought as there suddenly came before her a vivid picture of the Vaugirard studio, with its appearance of disorder and its involved system of neatness.

"Undo that bandage, Maria, and I'll put on a splendid liniment."

"Right here in my kitchen!" Maria protested.

"Yes, right here in your kitchen."

Out of modesty, the maid put a cover over the milk. Then with her free hand she unrolled her bandage with solemn deliberation and held out her forearm to Alice as if she had been tendering her the keys of a conquered city.

"My!" exclaimed Alice. "Was it boiling water, or the edge of the stove?"

"Neither, ma'am. It was the poker."

"The poker? How was that?"

The two women looked at one another and Maria broke into a laugh.

"It's a riddle, ma'am. Can't you guess who gave me that big blister?"

She nodded with her chin in the direction of the orchard and the vegetable garden.

"It was the big fellow out there—the idiot—that clumsy lout."

"Your husband? Why, what got into him?"

"Revenge."

"Revenge for what?"

"For being my husband and for my being his wife. That's enough, don't you think?"

She laughed scornfully and picked at the blister, full of water, and at the inflamed flesh around it.

"Don't touch that burn!" Alice cried out. "First I'm going to drain the blister."

"Don't I think so?" she repeated to herself. "Indeed, I do!" Being busy, she avoided replying and Maria was subtle enough to take her silence as an answer.

"So you want to have something extra good for dinner tonight? It's rather late to be telling me that. I guess we'll have to be satisfied with a barnyard pheasant. What do you say to my dressing up a couple of pigeons to look like partridges? Or I might have Escudière

451

shoot some blackbirds. Or how about a duck? Only duck gives you dreams."

While Maria was talking, Alice dressed her scrawny, light-boned forearm, reading in the wrinkled skin, the old scars and amber-colored callouses the story of a hand that once was beautiful. She manipulated the long-jointed fingers and the roughened palm, warm as a sunny garden wall.

"Am I hurting you?" she asked.

Maria shook her head and by way of thanks merely said, "That's a fine job, ma'am, very fine." But, before pulling down her sleeve, she laid her cheek against the white bandage as if it had been a new-born babe in its swaddling clothes.

"I have three cards," Alice announced.

"Which are no good," Michel replied.

They were trying to play piquet, Alice with a cigarette between her lips, her head cocked on one side and her eyes half closed to avoid the thin thread of smoke.

"Do put down that cigarette," Michel pleaded.

"Why?"

"It doesn't look well. It isn't chic to smoke that way."

"I can't play cards or smoke any other way. . . . I've got a triplet, too."

She coughed.

"There, you see? That cigarette butt stings your eyes and makes you cough. It's funny, the way, when women adopt a mannish custom, they take over every possible careless and even disgusting feature. That's the way with your smoking."

"All right, mama," Alice retorted. "Anyhow, I've got a triplet and I'll let you know it's to the ace of clubs. Your turn now."

As Michel delayed his play, she glanced up and read in his face an angry wave of sexual desire, an urge to give free rein to himself and enjoy possession. "Well, well!" she thought to herself. "I reckon that's going to complicate the situation for me." When he had counted up the points she had noted on a pad, she deliberately put a fresh cigarette in one corner of her mouth and exaggerated the slovenly way of holding her head. She felt happy that their dispute and all its risks were finally leading him onto dangerous and familiar ground.

The day before, she had put before Michel a dinner long and carefully prepared and abounding in tempting dishes, but he had scorned it, contenting himself with drinking some wine and calling out "Brava, bravi, bravo" to the rather cool and silent Maria. "That shrewd woman," Alice thought to herself, "is like animals with normal instincts, who keep away from men or beasts that are sick or wounded. I'm going to wait another twenty-four hours."

Since the day before, she had been seeking to gain time, putting off the evil moment through cowardice quite as much as diplomacy. A terrific rainstorm had been deluging the region, closing Cransac in with a curtain through which she and Michel, shut in like hermits and watching the raindrops rebounding in cup-like form from the inundated terrace, could just make out the red hawthorn and the mist-enveloped clumps of currant bushes, with their pink clusters. For two days now they had had no other diversion than reading and looking at the fire or the violence of the rain—"a regular movie rain," Michel remarked. Maria would put an apron over her head when she ran out to the woodpile. Her husband carefully turned up the scanty collar of his coat and opened a leaky umbrella when he had to go to the village. But Alice and Michel soon wearied of the news about the rain and Maria's doleful reports of the swift damage caused by the river.

"The water is coming up into the vegetable garden, sir! And the road is flooded! You never saw anything like it."

"Oh, yes, I have," Michel replied. "Approximately ten times in the past ten years. You've got no more memory than a new-born infant."

The day before, Alice, standing idle and restless at the window, had looked beseechingly at Michel as she pointed outside at the silver bars of their watery prison.

"Have patience a little longer," Michel urged. "One can't travel by auto in such a downpour. Just as soon as there's a letup, we'll see about going home. I have a notion spring is done for, anyhow."

For a whole day neither of them had said anything to hurt the other. "Hostilities suspended during the rainy season," Alice thought to herself. She shuffled the cards, dealt and fanned out her hand, her head on one side and a cigarette between her lips.

"Which of Lautrec's portraits is it you resemble?" Michel said.

Glancing at him surreptitiously, Alice saw that he was admiring her with animosity.

"One of his studies of low life, probably," she suggested. "Look out, Michel! Do you realize that I need only twenty-two points more? You're playing like a moron."

By the symptoms of smouldering heat and a restlessness akin to desire, Alice became aware of her husband's agitated state of mind. She pictured to herself their close embrace, a certain favorite intimate practice of his and the regulation gratitude that would follow. "And afterwards I wouldn't any longer have the courage—nor even the desire—to do what I am determined to do. Afterwards he might attach too much importance to me. . . . No, no, none of that!" She put on an expressionless countenance, laid down her cigarette and added up the scores with a businesslike air which Michel was in the habit of calling her "European manner."

"You owe me an enormous sum, Michel," she announced. "Thirty-two francs! You seemed determined to lose."

She refrained from indulging in the hackneyed remark about being "lucky at cards, unlucky in love."

"Will you give me a chance to get even with you?" Michel asked.

"No, Michel, I'm going to have the gall to quit while I'm ahead. And I'm even going to treat myself to a thimble of anisette."

She detested whiskey, brandy and such drinks, esteeming only syrupy liqueurs flavored with fennel, vanilla or orange. The flask tinkled as she held it against the glass. "How absurd that my hand should shake like that," she thought to herself.

"What's the matter with you?" Michel inquired.

Alice was familiar with that loud tone of voice, which became exceptionally clear under stress of anger or suspicion. As she walked back toward him, she gulped down half her glass at one swallow and her nerves became steadier.

"His ears are as keen as a fox's," she said to herself. "If he didn't know me so well, I might tell him it was just a touch of malaria and I would then become an interesting person. But he knows I've never had a bit of malaria—or indigestion—or anything. Except hunger now and then from the time I was fifteen till I was twenty-five. . . . Oh, for the days when he and I were just beginning to get acquainted, when everybody was saying to him, referring to me, 'Why! she's the least attractive of the four sisters.' How new it all was then! He used to look me over from head to foot and exclaim with surprise. And I would listen to him and protest in my embarrassment. It was all so wonderful! He cut quite a figure as manager of La Cancanière, which didn't net three francs a night, while his disgusting little beer garden and concert hall was making big profits."

She sighed silently and deeply. The steady, heavy rain was beating a mad dance on the tiles above the reëchoing attic. With huge, gulping sobs, the leaky gutter was belching its contents on the balcony below. Occasional drops of rain, coming down the uncapped chimney, fell on the fire and made the embers hiss, after the fashion of damp wood. Michel, feeling chilly, spread over his lap the shawl riddled by moths and cigarette sparks.

"Are you trembling, too, Michel? In your case it must be a bit of fever. As for me, I have a very different reason."

"There!" she thought to herself. "In that way I burn my bridges and force myself to speak." Nevertheless, she came near not speaking, after all, for Michel immediately looked at her sharply, as though he understood without asking any questions.

"Michel, I simply must tell you—"

He quietly put his hand over his liver, then withdrew it and started to remove his silk muffler from around his neck.

"Don't be afraid, Michel. I don't want to hurt you—quite the contrary."

Alice reached out her long, slender, unsteady hand but, with a quick motion of his body, Michel drew back just enough so that she did not touch him.

"Afraid?" he retorted. "Can you beat that—afraid! I'm not afraid. Who do you think you are, anyhow?"

She regretted having used that unfortunate word, offensive to his manly pride, and proceeded to make her blunder still worse by explaining:

"I express myself so poorly! I—er—just wanted you to—er—know that what I have to say to you isn't so terribly serious."

She stammered and her chin trembled.

"You're very much upset over it, it seems to me," Michel remarked. "You want to tell me something which you say is not so very serious. If I can judge by your expression, it can't be so very pleasant, either. . . . But take your time about it, my dear. Don't let anybody rush you."

He listened for a while to the small cataract from the gutter, then turned around to look at his wife, with a facetious glint in his brown eyes.

"I'm not planning to go out this evening," he added.

Alice shrugged her shoulders.

"Humor isn't going to help either of us—especially that kind of humor. There's nothing simple about the situation we're in, Michel."

She sat down, dizzied by the small amount of anisette she had drunk. With the tips of her fingers she toyed with some small folded pieces of paper in the pocket of her white blouse.

"Michel," she said finally, "I want to tell you the truth."

Instead of meeting her half-way, Michel burst out laughing.

"Again?" he exclaimed. "You again want to tell me the truth? In the first place, which truth? I know one truth and I admit it's quite enough—I'll even confess it's a bit too much for me. Is there still another truth? Come on, girls, hold out your aprons—we're going to shake the tree of truth again! Well, what is it you want to say?"

"I? Nothing. I'm waiting for you to get through. Is it then so difficult for us to be simple and straightforward with one another?"

Michel lowered his eyes and his tone of voice, and the expression on his face changed as he replied:

"Yes, my dear child, it is very difficult, I assure you. When a man is going through what I'm going through, he has just barely strength enough not to be simple and straightforward—that is, just enough strength to keep up appearances more or less and not take to drink or dope or throw himself into the river or something."

He sat down heavily not far from her.

"It's strange, just the same, that one can be so greatly influenced by the particular kind of suffering, by a special type of betrayal, for instance. I'd never have believed it possible. I've told you once, twice, twenty times, if only it had been a case of—"

Alice jumped up and ran over to his side.

"That's just it! Oh, Michel, do listen to me! It's my fault. I ought to have told you sooner. Luckily, it happens that—"

She suddenly realized that she was showing too much elation. "See here!" she reminded herself. "After all, this isn't his birthday." She would have liked to see him curious by this time and anxious. But he rather held her off, turning his shoulder a bit to one side and half closing his eyes. She then brought into play her fascinatingly plaintive voice.

"Do help me a little, Michel! Can't you see how hard it is for me?"

"I can see more especially, my dear, that you remind me of a gale of wind, with your preambles and your arm-waving. What a hulla-baloo! The truth certainly seems to make a lot of noise!"

She blushed, humiliated in her attempt to make peace with him.

"Very well, I'll cut it short and save words. You see, it's this way—you've told me quite often that you would have much preferred that—"

She tried again.

"That you would have considered the matter of much less importance if only—"

Michel waved aside the words she was about to utter.

"All right, all right. Kindly skip all that."

"And that you could have forgiven—or at any rate understood—"

"Of course, of course."

"If it had only been a case of—"

He closed his fist and pressed it against his teeth.

"For God's sake, get to the point!"

At that, Alice broke out, driven beyond all restraint:

"Very well—I slept with Ambrogio because I wanted to and for no other reason! And I quit sleeping with him because I didn't want to any longer—so there! And the idiot never had the slightest attraction for me in any other way whatsoever. That's what I wanted to tell you!"

She flung the window open violently and turned up her over-heated face to receive a lashing of cold rain and a blast of wind, laden with the odor of drenched humus. Then she closed the window. Michel had not stirred. She felt contrite when she saw him sitting there, motionless.

"There! You forced me to tell it to you all at once like that. I was determined to—"

"Reassure me," Michel suggested.

"Yes," she assented naïvely. "I wanted you to be happier. Are you?"

"Well, that isn't exactly the word," he answered with a smile. His gaze wandered aimlessly and he was deadly pale but showed no other sign of emotion.

"You see, you come and announce to me that you've been lying, that the fellow isn't, after all, the congenial young man, the cultured, attractive friend you said he was, and that it was merely a—how shall I say it?—a chance to—er—have a good time. Is that about it?"

Alice could not find a word to say in reply and felt herself blushing up to the roots of her hair.

"That's all very well, my dear," he went on, "but what proof have I that you haven't changed your tune solely, as you say, to make me happier?"

She was secretly fingering in her pocket some sheets of paper, through the folds of which her memory read several short sentences. "It might be a way out of this," she thought, "but what a nasty one!"

Michel was looking at her in an unbearable manner, with the penetrating gaze of a detective.

"I won't try to hide the fact," he went on, "that I long to believe in you, but don't ask too much of my good will. It likes to have something solid to build on. It's up to you to show that you, too, have based your statements on—er—something firm and hard—if I may so express myself."

Alice could not endure his smile or his insinuations any longer. Closing her hand tight around the crumpled papers in her pockets, she brandished her fist in the air. As though he had been waiting for this gesture, Michel seized her wrist and opened her fingers one by one.

"Give that back to me—it's mine!" she pleaded in consternation, but without making any attempt to recover her property as she heard the paper rustle under Michel's handling, with a slight noise like that of burning straw.

Michel paid no attention to her. Once more face to face with reality, with concrete evidence of just what had happened to him, he was completely engrossed in the seizure of the papers and the gentle, crackling sound they made in his hands, like brand-new banknotes. "It's that same foreign correspondence paper," he remarked to himself. "Here's where I get to the bottom of this." He was breathing vigorously and no longer felt that bar of pain across his chest in the midst of a breath, nor did any "If only" come in between him and the joy of triumph. "Poor Alice," he thought exultingly, "I've caught her this time!"

"This is first-rate," he said aloud mechanically as he intrenched himself behind his desk at some distance from Alice, now sitting there helpless.

He began to unfold the letters carefully, without tearing them, sometimes blowing on the edge of the thin paper the way a hunter will blow up the still warm feathers of a bird he has brought down. Finally he held the sheets all flattened out under the palm of one hand, while with the other, cupped like a shell, he seemed to be shielding a flame from the wind.

At first his face and eyes seemed almost joyful with eagerness. His chin, tautly drawn back, forced forward his throat and the fine, young growth of beard. At the first words he had to reach for his eyeglass. Alice thereupon rested her forehead in her hands and fixed her attention on the sound of the falling rain, but it was coming down in such a monotonous sheet that she soon ceased to hear it. Her heart and the odd little owl clock were beating unequal measures and this furnished her amusement for a while. "My heart is making triolets on the eighth notes of the clock," she thought to herself. "Now, there's a good idea for Bizoute! She would call that *A Song of Sorrow,* like everybody else, or maybe *The Fatal Hour.*" She raised her head and saw that Michel was not reading any longer.

"You've finished?" she asked.

"Yes, I'm through," he replied, looking at her with eyes clouded by the thick lenses.

"Well, I guess you got the proofs you wanted, eh?"

"I—er—yes. But tell me—you answered his letters?"

Alice looked at him with sincere surprise.

"I? No, indeed!"

"Why not?"

"Why, I hadn't anything to say to him. What would I have written him? Why should I write?"

"I don't know—spirit of competition—gratitude—enthusiasm—a little sparring match by mail. If the rest of the letters are up to these samples—"

Alice jumped to her feet and, passing behind Michel, leaned over the desk.

"No, Michel, no! You have the whole miserable story right there in your hands. One, two, three letters—one, two, three weeks. A wretched business but it didn't last long. A dirty little affair like that doesn't taper off gradually, thank God! Besides, you'll find a date in one of the letters—in this one, I think it is—"

As she pointed to the letter, her finger happened to rest on a brutally frank word and, before she had time to draw her hand away, Michel seized it, wrenched it and flung it aside. She needed no explanation as she silently massaged her bruised fingers. While

460

Michel tore the transparent sheet into small pieces, she sat there musing, indulging in the gloomy reflections of a disillusioned philanthropist. "What a fool I was to try," she thought. "You go to all kinds of trouble to try to fix things up, and look at the reward you get! You won't catch me trying that again."

As the pain in her twisted hand lessened, Alice became more severe with herself. "I did something there that I suppose a woman should never do—I let him know about my most intimate reactions and desires—the ones he didn't know anything about. . . . But it's all out now. I wonder if he'll get over this more quickly than when it was only his sentimental pride that was hurt. He certainly gave me reason to think so, with all his If-only's."

She shook her numbed hand and then went and sat down opposite her husband. He had taken off his glasses and was tearing up the last pieces of the other two sheets, closely covered with a fine handwriting in purple ink.

"Well, Michel?"

"Well, my dear. . . . I hope I didn't hurt your hand too much."

Alice smiled and, remembering Maria's laughing remark, answered, "It's not worth mentioning—but how about you?"

"I'm all right, my dear. I think this little shock will have only— yes, only beneficial results."

"Throw them there," she suggested, pointing to the fire.

"Gladly."

He burned the bits of paper and then fell to brooding again.

"Listen!" exclaimed Alice, jumping to her feet. "Did you see that the rain has stopped?"

"You're right, I declare," he agreed politely.

"Michel, aren't you wondering how I happened to have those letters here?"

Michel looked at his wife with an expression which seemed to her not to show the slightest trace of blame or of elementary, vindictive curiosity.

"Yes," he answered. "I was just thinking about that. But it seemed to me it wasn't worth while—now—to question you about it."

"You're quite right. Oh, Michel," she ventured to add with affectionate humility. "We're going to get over this without too much suffering, aren't we, dear?"

She slipped down onto the floor beside him with a flowing ease of movement which he called her "serpentine glide." But he recalled a concise expression of Ambrogio's which described her suppleness in different terms, and he began to read the three letters over again in his too trustworthy memory, without error or omission.

They sat there, deep in thought, gazing into the dying fire and watching the embers slowly change to white ashes. The gutter still choked and gurgled, but the drumming of the rain on the tiled roof had ceased. Coming down from the mountains and borne along by the cold, rushing waters of the river, the wind murmured through the trees and roused the imperturbable nightingales again to song.

"Chevestre says—," Alice remarked, raising a warning finger. "Are you surprised to hear me quote Chevestre? He says, when it stops raining during the night, that means morning is near. Why not let's go now and get some sleep, Michel?"

Beneath the satin-like visor of her hair, her swollen lids and her eyes, so pale under the light and now streaked with red lines gave her the appearance of a woman who has been crying in her cups. But even in that state Michel saw in her the same Alice whom he used to hold in his arms, blissfully happy, limp and speechless, the Alice of her early twenties, who could not get over her surprise at discovering the joys of love. He had the courage to say to her gently:

"Go right to bed, dear. You don't mind, do you, if I stay here a little while longer?"

Alice became uneasy.

"But, Michel, I'd so much rather—if it disturbs you to have me in the bedroom—you know I can sleep anywhere—the couch and my comforter, and I'm all right."

Michel interrupted her patiently.

"That isn't the difficulty, dear. . . . I'm away behind with my correspondence, and the labor of writing, which I detest, will quiet my nerves and makes me sleepy. I assure you it will. Now you run along."

Alice got up reluctantly, separated the last pieces of burning wood and pushed them far back into the fireplace.

"Shall I bring you some fresh water, Michel?" she asked, feeling of the lukewarm carafe.

"This will do very well, thank you."

She drank some water, making a wry face, and tarried a while longer gathering up the scattered newspapers, then slipped a book under her arm and, with her hand on the doorknob, turned back.

"Michel, you don't say anything."

She felt timid and strangely embarrassed.

"Why—goodnight, little one, since you're going to bed."

Seated at the desk, with a blue pencil between his teeth, he was running through the filing cabinet with an important air.

"I hope tomorrow, Michel—"

Michel suddenly looked up at her from behind his eyeglasses with such a keen, enigmatic expression that she stopped short.

"Tomorrow everything will be all right, little girl."

"All right, Michel? Do you really think so?"

A clouded look came over his eyes behind their convex lenses as he replied, "Better, anyhow—much better."

"I'll be so glad of that! Goodnight, Michel."

"Goodnight, little one."

She shut the door behind her and he listened closely for the creaking of the hinges and the shutting of a door in the distance. Not until he heard those sounds did he quit pencil, filing cabinet and scattered papers and take to walking up and down the room with cautious footsteps. He held himself very straight, his jaws set tight, and enjoyed deliberately the pleasure of being able at last, with nobody looking on, to enter into a strange, almost tangible element, of a dark, reddish-brown tonality, where he felt sure of meeting no one. This aberration lasted only a short while. When it was gone, he wished he could call it back. Then he noticed that he could revive it by repeating certain passages from the three letters from Ambrogio, and he realized that an illusion of that sort was nothing else than madness.

"Downright madness," he declared to himself. "But my God, that's better than unhappiness. How little we know about ourselves!"

He stopped to drink some water, then resumed his walking back and forth. "My legs are as strong tonight as when I was twenty," he remarked. When he tried to stop and sit down and calm himself, he was forced to get up and start out again, head held high and fists tightly clenched. As he walked, he automatically made gestures with his arms in unison with the rhythm of his steps. "Nothing better than this to relax the nervous tension," he assured himself.

Nevertheless, he caught himself taking aim at the light as he walked past, and also at the bottle of mineral water, and wishing they would fall and make a loud crash. At the same time, he noticed that his last cigarette, having fallen off the ashtray, was scorching the top of the desk. "That worm-eaten wood is treacherous," he reminded himself. "And Cransac is worm-eaten from garret to cellar." The words "fire", "flames", "finish" fascinated his imagination with their F's, which suggested the rush and smoke of a conflagration.

When the red and brown images and the many-colored flashes of shattered glass which he pictured to himself had all faded out, he sat down, disappointed to have lost the illusion. "Poor little woman," he thought. "If she had been within my reach, I'd have been quite capable of handling her roughly. . . . But now, what am I going to do with myself?"

He rested his elbows on the desk and stared vacantly at his own image in a small pocket mirror which Alice had a way of leaving around the house. He pushed back from his forehead his hair, made curly by the damp weather.

"I don't look so badly," he said to himself. "Except that my complexion has a funny tinge, I think I look younger and handsomer than I did yesterday. Ah, but yesterday I hadn't read Ambrogio's letters. I wasn't very happy, it's true, but still, I hadn't read those letters. It's the whole of the past week we'd have to be able to wipe out."

He turned the pages of the calendar pad with a serious air. "Let's see—today's Tuesday. Therefore the day after our arrival must have been Monday. Yes, that Monday morning I made a tour of inspection with Chevestre in my official capacity as—well, let's say mortgagor. I was in such a hurry to get rid of him that I left him cold, on the plea that I had to telephone Paris. He wanted to make some more suggestions—let's see—oh, yes, that I have some sort of dike or embankment built at the end of the vegetable garden to put a stop to the practical jokes the river plays on us every year."

With the point of his pencil he was poking holes in the thin paper of the calendar pad.

"So that," he calculated, "if I had stuck with Chevestre and pretended to be interested in the matter of the soil that was being washed down into the valley, if I had come back to the house half an hour later, none of all this would have happened? It's simply incredible—incredible. Think of all I'd be enjoying now! I in my straw hat, Alice bareheaded—I at the wheel, Alice beside me—Alice busy designing the costumes for *Daffodil*, her lips blue from chewing on her pencil, her homely little nose all screwed up and a funny expression on her face, the way she does when she draws—I'd have all that now if only I had stuck it out with Chevestre? It's incredible. It's just too much to believe—too much!"

Tears streamed down his face and he made the most of this to work himself up into a frenzy again.

"Yes, it's too much!" he cried out in a loud voice, which shattered the fragile silence of the dead of night. One of the twin bookcases across the room creaked and a glass tinkled against the bottle of mineral water.

A semi-circle of rouge on the edge of the glass was a reminder that Alice had drunk there. "If she were dead, I'd keep that glass," Michel thought. "Yes, but there's the trouble, she's alive, with that large mouth of hers that's so skillful at making a circle. . . . So skillful at making a circle," he repeated to himself. Three or four words came obligingly into his memory to complete a sentence he had read an hour before, and he looked about him in dismay.

"How am I ever going to be able to keep away from words like that and all they now bring up before me? And yet I ought to be

465

able to do it. I'm not the first man—nor the last by far!" He calmed down again and felt ashamed of himself. "That's true," he reminded himself. "But I'm the only one—just like each of the others. And yet the others aren't married to Alice. They didn't put all their eggs in one basket, as I have done for the past ten years. . . . Ten years! What a childish performance, to get so upset after ten years just because—well, because of what, precisely? Yesterday it was because of an idyllic affair—mutual confidences, cozy talks by the fire, rather mushy sentimentalism and all that."

He made a face and laughed mockingly at the darkness, saying "cht-cht-cht" to mimic the sound of silly talk.

"Today it's something else again. Today—"

"You damn fool!" he said aloud.

"Yes, damn fool!" he repeated to himself. "I've made life hell for her and also for myself, because she claimed she had given that fellow a—what was it she called it?—a somewhat voluptuous friendship and her confidence. Was it the idea of confidence or friendship I found intolerable? It's enough to make one laugh. If only I could go back twenty-four hours, I'd say to her: 'Why, that was perfectly all right. It didn't mean anything, what you gave him. Give him your friendship as much as you like, my dear little woman, and your confidence, too—you women don't attach much importance to that, anyhow. And, even if it is a bit voluptuous, go to it, little one—go right ahead'."

He smothered his sobs in his sleeve, his head resting on his arm.

"But today I'm licked. If only I hadn't taken those letters from her! But I took them and read them—yes, I certainly did read them!"

As if to prove to him that he had, indeed, read them, a little phrase raised its purple head in the form of a capital M. It curtsied for a moment and then dashed off, trailing behind it a whole string of obscene words. At the end of the letter the lover had placed, like a flower tossed on the train of a dress, a very detailed little drawing.

Michel raised his head and mopped his face. He knew that the second letter and the third—the former offering allurements, the latter full of gratitude—were quite up to the first, and that the second contained, like a huge blot, a racy quatrain which linked "Alice" with "chalice" in a scabulous rhyme. "It can never be patched up now," he said with a restrained gesture of despair. "Is there anything worse than no longer to have any uncertainty? And besides, if she should now take it into her head to remove her dress in front of me, or turn her back to me and put her leg over the edge of the bathtub, or get down on all fours to hunt for her ring or her lipstick—"

He got up as if forced out of his seat.

"It's unbelievable," he went on, "how much filth can be packed into three letters. It was all written out plainly, described in detail. Upon my word, they had thought of everything possible."

"Every single thing!" he cried out. "Even what I liked best."

The sound of his own voice alarmed him and he looked about. Between the partly closed inner shutters he saw the dawn coming, almost as blue as a moonlit night.

"Daybreak!" he exclaimed. "Already! How quickly the time goes! Already morning! I was so peaceful—no, that's not exactly the word, but anyhow, I was alone. . . . When she gets up—what in heaven's name can I do when she opens the bedroom door? There'll be a lot of questions and then exclamations and well meant anxiety. And then she'll come over to me and put her hands on my shoulders, raising her beautiful arms—the untouchable woman! What can I do now about those beautiful arms when she lifts them up, and the dark little armpits? And then her birthmark—there, beside her navel—as big as a dime."

Unconsciously, in describing Alice's beauty, he reverted to language he used to employ, frank, passionate language which she allowed him to use and which would often make her start at the sound of a word, close her eyes and draw in her breath between her teeth, as one does in bitter cold weather.

"Just one birthmark," he continued. "The size of a cherry. And she could make it move when she wanted to! I used to tell her I had seen many women in my time but she was the only one who had winked at me with her belly. Many women! They're not worth talking about. Alongside of her, they—"

He dozed off into unconsciousness in the middle of a sentence, but the time for rest had not yet come for him and the weight of his head woke him suddenly. He shook himself, stood up and; seeing that the blue strip at the window was turning to white, he opened the shutters. Instead of the bright light he had dreaded and the horizontal rays of the sun along the edge of a sky washed clean by the storm, he saw before him the gray dawn and the heavy sleep of plants bowed down under their rain-soaked foliage. A cock in some henhouse crowed in a muffled tone. The smell of the barnyard floated on the air, rousing a painful sense of hunger in Michel's empty stomach. "If I eat, I'll never go through with it—I know myself," he thought. He put out the desk light but did not open the drawer where he kept his revolver. "What! Do such a thing in my own house! Oblige Alice to see such a sight! Besides, what would Maria say?"

He buttoned up his coat and felt for his wallet in the pocket. "Come to think of it," he decided, "I'll keep it, since the money is in the drawer. Now, let's see—what else? Handkerchief? Yes, I have one. My notebook? I have that. I don't think I've forgotten anything."

To avoid the creaking of the doors, he climbed over the balcony rail, though with some difficulty. "Just like a lover, madame—a lover a bit stiff in the joints, however." As he brushed against the yellow jasmine and the climbing rose, they dropped a shower of rain water down his neck, so cold that he could not stifle an imprudent exclamation. At the edge of the terrace he turned to look back at Cransac, compact and gloomy, its two squat towers capped by low-hanging tiled roofs. "Ah, Cransac, my beloved Cransac!" he exclaimed. But, although he tried to whip up his feelings, no real tenderness came over him and he shrugged his shoulders. "No," he admitted to himself. "There's nothing I really care for except Alice—nothing. Cransac is only a bit of synthetic sentiment—plus a good dose of vanity, I must admit. . . . Nevertheless, I'm leaving them both in a very precarious position, Alice and Cransac."

He experienced the spiteful satisfaction a man feels who has gotten under shelter in time and sees others running past in the rain.

"Oh, she'll make out all right," he reassured himself. "When she wants to she— I can see her now locking horns with Chevestre! And with the life insurance people, who always begin right away to try to upset the theory of an accident. Ah, that will be a fine sight! And there's my contract with Ambrogio—that fellow is going to meet his match this time! By God, she'll be magnificent, with her head tossed back, a cigarette in her mouth, her hand on that fold of flesh just above the hip—"

Not even a wave of dizziness caused by hunger could dim his vision of those hips and the fold of flesh that formed whenever Alice, surreptitiously attacked from the rear, twisted her body at the waist without trying to break away from her attacker.

Michel plunged down the slope, passed through the clump of woods where night still reigned, and found the river at his feet, flowing sluggishly, retarded by its load of iron-streaked silt, its ripples silently lapping the broken-down wall of the estate.

The Cat

1

AT TEN O'CLOCK the poker players around the sitting-room table were beginning to nod over their game. Camille was fighting off fatigue as one does at nineteen—that is, she would rouse by fits and starts and look alert, wide-awake. Then she would yawn behind her closed fingers, and look pale again, her chin white, tired little lines under her ochre-tinted powder and two tiny teardrops in the corners of her eyes.

"Camille, it's time to go to bed."

"At ten o'clock, mama? Who ever heard of going to bed at ten o'clock?" She appealed to her fiancé, who sat exhausted in an armchair.

"Leave them alone," said the other mother. "They still have seven days to wait. They're a little silly just now. That's easy to understand."

"Of course . . . an hour more or less. Camille, you ought to go to bed . . . and so should we all."

"Seven days!" Camille cried. "But today's Saturday. I haven't realized it. Come, Alain."

She threw her cigarette into the garden, lit a fresh one, sorted and stacked the scattered cards and laid them out on the table preparatory to asking them about the future.

"Tell me," she said, "if we two are going to have the car, the darling little roadster, before the ceremony. . . . Look, Alain, I'm not making it up. It's going on the wedding journey, and with the bride . . ."

"Who's going?"

"The roadster, of course."

Alain turned his head toward the wide-open French window through which came a delicious odour of spinach, and of fresh grass from the lawn that had been mowed that very morning. The honeysuckle hanging from an old dead tree sent in the sweetness of its first blossoms. A crystal tinkling announced that old Emile's unsteady arms were bringing in the ten-o'clock tray of cool beverages and fresh water. Camille rose to fill the glasses.

She served her fiancé last, offering him a full glass with a meaningful smile. She watched him drink and was suddenly piqued as she saw him press his mouth against the rim of the glass. But he was so conscious of his fatigue that he refused to notice her annoyance, and merely pressed lightly her white fingers and lacquered nails as she took back his emptied glass.

"You're coming to lunch tomorrow?" she asked him in a low tone.

"Ask the cards."

Camille drew back and playfully imitated a magician's gestures.

"Don't make fun of Twenty-four Hours. . . . Make fun of crossed knives, bad pennies and talking pictures—for God's sake."

"Camille!"

"Excuse me, mama. But don't play any tricks on Twenty-four Hours. Him good little fellow, nice black messenger boy, Jack of Spades, always in a hurry."

"Hurry for what?"

"To talk, of course. Just think, he tells me what's going to happen in the next twenty-four hours and even in the next two days. And if you give him two more cards—one on the right and one on the left—he'll tell you what's going to happen within the next two weeks!"

She was talking fast, and at the same time wiping with her pointed nail two little clots of red saliva from the corners of her mouth. Alain listened, neither bored nor interested. He had known her for several years and rated her at her own price, a modern girl. He knew how she drove a car—a little too fast, a little too well, her scarlet lips ever ready with a coarse oath to be hurled at taxi-drivers. He realized that she lied unblushingly, as do children or very young people. And that she was capable of deceiving her parents if she wanted to meet him after dinner in the night clubs where they danced together and drank nothing but orange juice. Alain never took alcohol.

Before their engagement had been announced, she had yielded him her lips, discreetly dried; her impersonal breasts, imprisoned always in their double pockets of lace and chiffon; and her beautifully shaped legs, in the sheer silk stockings she bought surreptitiously—"the kind Mistinguett wears, you know. . . . Be careful of my stockings, Alain." Her stockings and her legs were her pride.

"She's pretty," reflected Alain, "because she hasn't a single ugly feature, because she's a real brunette, and because her eyes match her hair—which is washed often, brilliantined, and the color of a new piano." Nor was he unaware that she could act impulsively and was as changeable as a mountain stream.

She went on talking about the roadster.

"No, papa, no. You needn't worry, I'll not let Alain touch the steering-wheel while we're in Switzerland. He's too dreamy. And the truth of the matter is he really doesn't like to drive—I know him."

"She knows me," Alain repeated to himself. "She probably thinks she does. Just as I've said twenty times to her, 'I understand you, my girl.' Saha understands her too . . . By the way, where is Saha?"

He scanned the deep corners of the room. Then he drew himself from the depths of his armchair, first one shoulder, then the other, then his hips, then his whole body. And he slipped quietly down the five veranda steps.

Up from the night shadows in the deep garden, surrounded on

all sides by other gardens, came the thick perfume of flower-beds ceaselessly tended, stimulated to fertility. Since Alain's boyhood, the place had changed little. "The house of an only son," thought Camille, who did not conceal her scorn for the cupola perched on the roof like a honeycomb, for the top-storey windows sunk in slate, and for the coy trimmings on the French window panels on the ground floor that reminded her of five-o'clock tea cakes.

Like Camille, the garden seemed to scorn the house.

Large trees, dropping the black burnt twigs that fall from all aging elms, shielded it from neighbors and passers-by. A little farther along, on a building lot for sale and in the playgrounds of a school, similar venerable trees were to be seen straying off in pairs, vestiges of a magnificent avenue—all that remained of a park which a modern Neuilly was despoiling.

"Where are you, Alain?"

He heard Camille calling from the top step. Seized by a sudden impulse, he did not answer, but sought safer refuge in the shadows near the edge of the smooth lawn. In the high heavens rode a veiled moon, magnified by the mist of an early spring day. A single poplar gathered up the white moonlight in her young, shimmering leaves and trickled it down like a waterfall. A single ray glowed like a fish around Alain's legs.

"Ah, there you are, my Saha! I've been looking for you. Why didn't you come to the table tonight?"

"Me-rrouin," answered the cat. "Me-rrouin."

"What do you mean, me-rrouin? And why me-rrouin? What are you trying to say?"

"Me-rrouin," she insisted. "Me-rrouin."

Lovingly he stroked her long spine, softer than the hare's fur. His fingers touched the cool, moist little nostrils, dilated by nervous purring. "She's my cat, my very own."

"Me-rrouin," Saha kept murmuring low. "Me-rrouin."

Again Camille's call from the porch, and Saha darted under the clipped hedge, black-green like the night.

"Alain, we're going now."

476

He ran in the direction of Camille's voice.

"I can see your hair run," she laughed. "Foolish to be as blond as that."

He ran faster, took the five steps at a bound, and found Camille alone in the dining-room.

"The others?" he asked.

"Getting ready to leave. And looking over the new work on the house. Dissatisfaction on all sides: 'It will never be finished . . . I can't see that they ever work.' Which we two don't care a hang about. If one were shrewd, one would keep Patrick's studio for ourselves. Patrick will remodel another for himself. I'll see if I can manage it, if you want me to."

"But Patrick will never leave his apartment except as a favor to you."

"Naturally. That's just what one would take advantage of."

She seemed pleased with a code of morals exclusively feminine— a code that Alain could never get used to. But he made no comment, except on her using "one" instead of "we." She understood it was his love reproaching her, and answered:

"I'll get the habit of saying 'we' in time."

In order to tease him into kissing her, she snapped off the ceiling lights. The lamp from the centre table threw a long, sharp shadow behind the girl.

Her arms lifted and clasped at the back of her neck, Camille tried to lure him with her body. But he had eyes only for the shadow. "How beautiful she is on the wall! Just slim enough, just as I should love her to be!"

He sat down, deliberately to compare girl and shadow. Flattered, Camille leaned back, threw out her breasts, imitated an East Indian dancing girl. But the shadow told her she was not wise. Unclasping her hands, the girl turned; now the exemplary shadow was in front of her. Arrived at the open French window, it bounded out and fled into the garden over the pinkish pebbles in the path, embracing as it flew the young poplar dripping with moonlight. "Too bad," Alain sighed. Then he reproached himself mildly for his tendency

477

to love in Camille a Camille fixed, brought to perfection in a conformation such as that shadow, for instance, or a picture, or the sharp memory he had of her in certain hours, certain costumes . . .

"What's the matter with you tonight? Come, help me on with my wrap, at least."

He noted that "at least," and also the way she shrugged her shoulders as she passed in front of him from cloak-room to butler's pantry. "She oughtn't to shrug her shoulders. Nature and habit look after that for her. When she doesn't take thought her neck and shoulders make her look a little thick-set . . . just a trifle, a trifle squat."

In the cloak-room they came upon Alain's mother and Camille's parents tapping their feet on the hempen carpet and leaving tracks the color of muddy snow. The cat, seated on the outside windowsill, looked at them with neither hospitality nor hostility in her eye. Alain imitated her patience and endured the ritualistic expression of their pessimisms.

"The more they do . . ."

"But they haven't done a thing in the last week . . ."

"If you want to know what I think, my dear friend, it won't be two weeks, it will be a month—what am I talking about?—two months, and still their little nest . . ."

At the word "nest," Camille threw herself so brusquely into the placid squabble that Alain and Saha both shut their eyes hard.

"But if we don't mind it ourselves . . . and if it amuses us to stay in Patrick's studio . . . and it suits Patrick, who hasn't any dough— oh, excuse me, mama—hasn't any money, I mean . . . just our suitcases and, hoop-la, away we fly to the ninth floor! Isn't it so, Alain?"

He opened his eyes again, smiled vaguely as though into space, and laid her light evening wrap across her shoulders. In the mirror facing them he caught Camille's dark look reproaching him, but it did not stir him. "I didn't kiss her on the mouth while we were alone. No, I didn't kiss her on the mouth. She's not had her quota of kisses-on-the-mouth today. She had the quarter of twelve one in

478

a path in the Bois, the one at two o'clock after the coffee, the half past six one in the garden. But she's not had one tonight. Oh well, if she doesn't like it she'll have to charge it up to my account. . . . What's the matter with me this evening anyway? I'm dead for sleep. This life is idiotic; we're seeing too much of each other, getting on each other's nerves. Monday I'll just go back to the store and . . ."

In his imagination he could smell the chemical acids of new silk. And M. Veuillet's inscrutable smile came before him, as he imagined he heard those words which, even at twenty-four, he had not learned not to fear: "No, no, my young man, a new adding-machine at seventeen thousand francs! Will it pay for itself in a year? That's the point. Allow your poor father's oldest colleague . . ." And realizing again the vengeful expression and the beautiful black eyes watching him in the mirror, he took Camille in his arms.

"Well, Alain?"

"Oh, my dear, let him alone. These poor children . . ."

Camille blushed and drew away. Then she offered him a cheek so tomboyish and so brotherly that he almost dropped his head on her shoulder.

"Only let me go to bed . . . just let me sleep . . . good heavens, to bed and to sleep!"

The cat called from the garden.

"Me-rrouin . . . rrrouin."

"Listen to the cat," Camille said casually. "She must be on one of her hunts. Saha, Saha!"

The cat stopped abruptly.

"Hunting?" Alain protested. "Why do you say that? In the first place, it's only May, and then she's saying, 'Me-rrouin.'"

"Well, what of it?"

"That's not Saha's hunting call. What she's saying now—and it's rather strange—is a warning, almost a cry of calling her kittens together."

"My God," cried Camille, impatiently throwing up her arms, "if Alain starts in to explain that cat we'll be here all night."

She sprang down the steps two at a time, and old Emile, standing near, lighted up the garden with two big old-fashioned bluish reflectors.

Alain walked on ahead of Camille. At the wrought-iron gate he kissed her and under the cape pressed her bare arms and elbows. When he saw her take her seat at the steering-wheel, in front of her parents, he began to feel wide-awake, light-hearted.

"Saha . . . Saha . . ."

Out from the darkness sprang the cat, ran when he ran, jumped on ahead of him in long leaps. She dashed on into the hallway, and came back to wait for him at the top of the steps. Her throat distended, her ears flat against her head, she watched him run, lured him with her yellow eyes, deep-set, proud, suspicious, steady.

"Saha . . . Saha."

Hearing her name spoken just that way, softly, with the *h* strongly accented, sent the cat into a wild frenzy. She tapped the floor with her tail, leapt onto the middle of the poker table and with her two cat hands wide apart she sent the cards flying right and left.

"Oh, that cat, that cat," his mother said. "She has no idea of hospitality. See how happy she is now that our friends have gone!"

Alain burst into childish laughter, the laughter that he kept for the strictest intimacy of the home, never allowed to pass beyond the elm walls or the iron gateway. Then he yawned ecstatically.

"Dear me, you look all tired out. How anyone can look like that and still be happy! . . . There's some orangeade left. No? Well, we might as well go up. Leave the lights. Emile will lock up."

"Mama talks to me as though I was getting over a sickness or falling into a fever," he said to himself.

"Saha, Saha, what a little imp! Alain, can't you get that cat?"

By a much-used vertical route along a strip of worn brocade the cat had almost reached the ceiling. For a moment she looked like a grey lizard as she clung to the wall, her paws wide apart. Then she feigned dizziness and ventured a little well-bred cry. Docilely Alain drew near and placed himself below her, offering her his shoulder. Still clinging, the cat slid down as smoothly as a raindrop

480

slides down the windowpane. She landed on Alain's shoulder and together they went to their bedroom.

A long drooping cluster of laburnum, black in front of the open window, became bright yellow when Alain switched on the ceiling light and the lamp at the head of his bed. By tipping his shoulder he turned the cat onto the bed and walked aimlessly about from bed to bathroom like a man too tired to get himself ready for sleep.

He leaned out above the garden; looked hostilely at the pile of white cement being used for the uncompleted renovations; drew out bureau drawers; shut them again. Finally he opened a box where lay some of his real secrets: a gold dollar; a signet ring; an agate charm from his father's chain; a few red seeds from a rare East Indian plant; a mother-of-pearl rosary; a broken bracelet, souvenir of a young, hot-tempered mistress who had remained in his life briefly and left it tempestuously. Some letters, photographs, books, bound and paper-covered.

Dreamily he fingered these small relics, shining and worthless like the bits of broken stones found in the nests of plundering birds. "I must throw away all this . . . or leave it here. I don't care about it . . . or can it be that I do?" An only child, he had never had to fight for nor share what he owned, hence possessions were all the more his.

He saw his face in the mirror and it exasperated him. "But get to bed . . . you're all to pieces . . . it's disgraceful," he said to the beautiful blond young man. "They think I'm beautiful just because I'm blond; dark, I'd be hideous." Once again his nose irritated him, and his long cheek—"too much like a horse." But he smiled so that he might admire his teeth again; affectionately stroked the natural part in his too-thick blond hair; and was pleased with the tints in his eyes, grey, shading into green near the dark lashes; the eye itself surrounded by a purplish circle. Two wrinkles deepened in his cheeks. A short, blond mustache, shaved that morning, already enlarged his lip. "What a mouth! Makes me sorry for myself . . .

no, disgusted. That . . . that the face for a bridal night?" In the depths of the mirror, Saha eyed him gravely from a distance.

"I'm coming . . . coming."

He threw himself down on the fresh sheets. After he had arranged Saha just as he wanted her, he began a ceremony of adulation appropriate to the graces and virtues of a cat known as a Chartreuse, a thoroughbred, small, perfect specimen of her race.

"My little cub has fat cheeks. Lovely, lovely pussy. My sapphire dove . . . my pearl-colored enchantress."

He put out the light and the cat began to step daintily across her friend's chest, using a single claw to penetrate beneath the silk pyjamas. She touched the skin just lightly enough to arouse in Alain a disquieting pleasure.

"Seven more days, Saha," he sighed.

Seven more days and seven more nights, and then a new life under a new roof with an amorous and unconquered young woman. Again and again he drew his hand over the cat's fur, soft and warm, smelling of pine bark, and new-sawn wood, and the fresh lawn. She purred heavily; and under cover of the darkness she gave him a cat's kiss, laying the moist tip of her nose just for a second on Alain's lip—a sudden, incorporeal kiss, rarely granted.

"Ah, Saha, our nights."

Two automobile head-lights pierced the foliage with moving, incandescent rays. Across the bedroom wall passed the lengthened shadows of the laburnum, of a tulip tree islanded in the centre of the lawn. Alain saw Saha's hard eye on the bed, and her face glisten, then darken.

"Don't frighten me," he begged.

For under the protection of sleep, he felt himself become listless again, unreal, stayed in the net of an unended and beloved adolescence.

He shut his eyes; and Saha, keeping vigil, followed the shimmering portents that pirouette about us when we sleep.

He dreamed lavishly, plunged, stage by stage, down into his dreams. Once awake, he never referred to his nightly adventures, for he was not willing to share a world which a delicate and badly-disciplined childhood had prolonged; nor did he want to share the beloved memory of long days passed in bed during his abrupt development into a tall, lank youth.

He loved his dreams, encouraged them, and would not for anything in the world have disappointed the halting-places waiting for him. At the first stage, where he could still hear the horns of the automobiles passing on the avenue outside his bedroom window, he would encounter familiar faces whirling about, distorted ones capable of lengthening and contracting themselves. He passed them by as he would have passed through any good-natured crowd, bowing first to this one and then to that. Moving, convex, they came up nearer and nearer to Alain, getting bigger as they came. Clear against a background, they became clearer still as though they might be receiving light from the sleeper himself. Armed with one huge eye, they progressed in easy gyration. But an underground thrust jerked them back from a distance the moment they had touched an invisible wall. In the watery face of a round monster, in the eye of a fat moon, or in the look of a wandering archangel bearded with beams of light, Alain recognized the same expression, the same purpose that no one of them had yet made clear and which the Alain of the dream noted confidently, "They will explain it to me tomorrow."

At times they would disappear, wisp off into nothingness, scattering themselves in shreds, faintly luminous. Then again they did not seem to exist except as a hand, arm, forehead, very thoughtful eyeball, nose of starry dust, some chins, and always that immense bulging eye, which, just at the moment of explaining itself, turned away and would show nothing more except its other, black face. . . .

Alain, now deep in sleep, pursued, under Saha's protection, his customary plunge, passed on beyond a universe of convex faces and bulging eyes, descended through a black space which admitted nothing but powerful blackness, unspeakably varied and as if formed of immerged colors, on whose borders he halted. Here was the mature dream, complete, well-formed.

He hurled himself against a boundary line which gave back a

great sound like the tinkling reverberation of a cymbal. And he came into the City of Dreams, amid passers-by, citizens standing up on their doorsteps, guardians of the square crowned with gold, and wordless figures posted along Alain's route. He was wholly naked, extremely lucid and cautious, and armed with a walking stick. "If I walk quickly, after I've knotted my tie in a certain way, there'll be every chance that no one will notice that I'm naked." So he knotted his tie in the shape of a heart, and whistled. "That's not whistling, that thing I'm doing now. Whistling's like this . . ." But he was still purring. "I'm not at the end of my resources. The whole thing is to get into that place flooded with sunlight, to encircle the bandstand, to play military music. It's childish. I rush forth making dangerous leaps so as to distract attention, and I get off in the region of ghosts."

But he felt himself paralyzed by the warm and perilous look of a brown figure with a Greek profile, bored through with the huge eye of a fish. "The spirit region . . . the place of ghosts . . ." Two long arms of a ghost, graceful and all rippling with poplar leaves, ran at the word "ghost" and carried Alain off so that he might get some sleep during the most ambiguous hour of the brief night in that temporary tomb where the living, banished, sighs; weeps; is born again with the coming of another day.

2

T H E sun was creeping along the edges of the window-panes when Alain awoke. Yellow clusters of translucent laburnum hung above Saha's head, the daytime Saha, blameless, blue, and now engaged in making her toilet.

"Saha!"

"Me-rrong," burst from the cat.

"Is it my fault that you are hungry? If you are in a hurry, all you have to do is go downstairs and ask for your milk."

She melted at the sound of her friend's voice, repeated the same cry more gently, showed her pink mouth sown with white teeth. Her expression of devoted and possessive love disquieted Alain.

"Heavens! That cat . . . what to do about that cat? I had forgotten that I'm being married. And that I've got to go and live in Patrick's house."

He turned toward a portrait in its chromium frame—Camille encircled in a halo of lustrous hair glistening as though bathed in oil; her mouth hard as though enamelled in black ink; her big eyes set wide apart between two walls of eyelashes.

"Fine professional job, that," he muttered.

He no longer remembered that he himself had chosen it for his bedroom, that photograph which resembled neither Camille nor anyone else. "That eye . . . I've seen that eye."

He took up a pencil, made the eyes narrower, thinned out the excess of white eyeball, and merely succeeded in spoiling the picture.

"Mouek mouek mouek . . . Ma-a-a-a . . . Ma-a-a," said Saha, addressing a little moth between the window and the lace curtain. Her lion-shaped chin trembled and she yapped lustily for her prey. Alain plucked the butterfly between his two fingers and presented it to Saha.

"Hors-d'oeuvre, Saha."

A rake was listlessly combing the garden path. Alain could visualize the hand guiding the rake, a woman's aging hand, working mechanically, persistently, and softly under a loose white glove like a policeman's.

"Good morning, mama," he said.

A voice from the distance answered, a voice whose words he did not hear, only an affirmative murmur, unimportant, dutiful. He ran down the steps, the cat at his heels. In the bright light of day Saha was able to change herself into a kind of excited dog, tumble down the staircase noisily and, quite divested of any catlike charm, arrive in the garden by boisterous leaps and bounds. In the middle of

485

medallions of sunlight, she sat down on the small breakfast table beside Alain's place. The rake, which had stopped momentarily, quietly went on with its work.

Alain poured some milk for Saha, put in a pinch of salt, one of sugar, then served himself, seriously. When he breakfasted alone he didn't feel he had to blush for certain amusing habits, compulsions left from the foolish age, that of a child between four and seven. He felt free to stop up with butter all the "eyes" in the bread, pout when the coffee in his cup passed beyond a certain level marked by golden arabesques decorating the inside. The first thick piece of bread might be followed by a thin piece, while the second cup of coffee cried out for an extra piece of sugar. . . . Finally a very small Alain, buried under a tall, beautiful, fair-haired boy, waited impatiently for the moment when, the breakfast over, he might take the spoon out of the honey jar—an old ivory spoon, discolored and tough—and lick it to his heart's content.

"At this very moment, Camille is eating her breakfast, but never sitting down to it. As she walks around the room, she nibbles at a thin slice of ham between two small pieces of dry toast. Next she eats an apple. Then she sips a cup of tea—no sugar—puts it down first on one piece of furniture, then another. And forgets where she's put it."

He lifted his eyes to the kingdom of his indulged childhood—the garden he loved and thought he knew. Above his head the venerable elms were motionless except where the tips of their young leaves stirred. A blanket of pink catchfly, bordered by forget-me-nots, lorded it over the lawn. From the scraggy crutch of a dead tree, intertwined with four-petal purple clematis, hung a clump of knotgrass trembling at each breath. A sprinkling hose, upright on its single foot, was spraying water on the grass and spreading out its white peacock's tail all barred with the shimmering colors of the rainbow.

"Such a beautiful garden . . . a beautiful garden," Alain mused. Hostilely he eyed the silent piles of rubbish, beams and bags of plaster defacing the west side of the house. "Ah yes, it's Sunday; they're not working. . . . Every day of the week has been Sunday for me." Though he was young and pampered and controlled by caprices, he lived according to the six-day commercial rhythm and something inside him told when Sunday came round.

A shy white pigeon stirred behind the red and white honeysuckle and the dewy clusters of white syringas. "It's not a pigeon; it's mama's gloved hand." The loose white glove was picking up tiny twigs, nipping the lawless blades of grass that shot up overnight. Two sparrows on the gravel pathway came near to peck the breakfast crumbs, and Saha watched them with a passive eye. But a titmouse hanging head down from an elm tree above the table screeched defiance to the cat. Seated, her paws crossed, her ruff—her fine-lady ruff—distended, and her head back, Saha tried to restrain herself; but her cheeks swelled with rage and the small nostrils burned with fiery moisture.

"As beautiful as a demon. More beautiful than a demon," Alain told her.

He put out his hand to caress the wide forehead, filled with one burning thought, and the cat bit him sharply as one way of discharging her wrath. He looked down at two small drops of blood on the palm of his hand, and felt the angry emotion of a man whose mate has bitten him in the midst of passion.

"Bad . . . bad. Look what you've done."

She dropped her head, sniffed the blood, and scanned her friend's face questioningly. She knew very well how to divert him, to win him back: she gathered up a piece of brioche from the traycloth and began to nibble it as squirrels do.

The May breeze blew over them, bent a yellow rose-bush as richly odorous as blossoming furze. Between the cat, the rose-bush, the titmouse family, and the last beetles, Alain was enjoying the moments which escape time, and tasting the pain and the illusion of wandering back into his childhood. The elms grew immeasurably taller, the widened path disappeared under the arches of a dying trellis, and like the haunted sleeper who feels himself falling from a tower, Alain realized again that he was in his twenty-fourth year.

"I might have slept another hour. It's only half past nine. It's

Sunday. Yesterday was Sunday for me. Too many Sundays. But tomorrow . . ."

He smiled at Saha as though she were an accomplice. "Tomorrow, Saha, it's the final fitting of the wedding-dress. I'm not to be there. It's a surprise. Camille is so dark that the white veil will make her beautiful. While she's doing that, I shall see the car. It's a little cheap, a 'half portion' as Camille would say, a roadster. What we get, I suppose, for being 'such young married people.' "

With one upward leap, rising in the air as a fish rises to the surface of the water, the cat caught a small black-and-white butterfly. She swallowed it, choked, spat up one of its wings, licked herself showily. The sun played across her Chartreuse coat, grey and bluish like the throat of doves.

"Saha!"

She turned her head and smiled at him steadily.

"My little puma, beloved cat, creature of lofty peaks! However will you live if we are to be separated one from the other? Would you like it if both of us were to take orders . . . to go to a monastery? Would you like it? For my part I'm not sure."

She listened to him, watched him with a loving, wistful expression; but at a more tremulous note in the beloved voice she turned her eyes away from him.

"To begin with, you will come with us—you don't dislike the car. If we have the sedan instead of a roadster, there's a ledge behind the seats . . ."

He became thoughtful at the recent memory of a girl's voice, strong, with an out-of-doors ring to it, coming down hard on the open vowels *a* and *o*, a voice reciting the numerous virtues of a roadster. "And then when you put down the windshield, Alain, it's marvelous! With all the power on, you feel the skin on your cheeks pull way back to your ears!"

"Way back to your ears, Saha! Imagine that! What a horrible idea!"

He pressed his lips together tightly and, clever at imitation, he made the long face of a petulant child.

488

"It's not all decided yet. Suppose I like the sedan better? All the same, I've got some say in the matter."

He scrutinized the yellow rose-bush as though it were the girl with the beautiful voice. Once again the path widened, the elm grew taller, the dead trellis came to life. Nestling up against the skirts of two or three relatives, tall, their foreheads in the clouds, the child Alain was inspecting another closely united family between whom shone a very dark little girl whose big eyes competed in hostile and shining lustre with her black braided hair. "Say 'how-do-you-do.' Why won't you say 'how-do-you-do'?" It was a voice of another epoch, weakened, treasured through the years of childhood, of adolescence, of schooldays, of army boredom, of false seriousness, of false business success. Camille would not say 'how-do-you-do.' She sucked the inside of her cheek and sketched, briefly and stiffly, the curtsy little girls make. "Now she calls it the 'twist-your-toes curtsy.' But when she's crossed, she still bites the inside of her cheek. And, curiously enough, when she does it she's not bad-looking."

He smiled and became sincerely ardent about his fiancée, pleased on the whole that she was healthy, a little commonplace in sensual passion. Influenced by the purity of the morning, he called forth decent pictures which sometimes aroused his vanity and his impatience, and sometimes gave birth to uneasiness and even confusion. Shaking off his anxiety, he found the sun too glaring, the breeze dry. The cat had disappeared, but the moment Alain stirred to get up she was at his heels and, avoiding the round pebbles in the pink gravel, walked along beside him with the long stride of a stag. Together they went off to the alterations, inspected with equal hostility the piles of plaster debris, a new French window still without glass cut into a wall, squares of faïence tiles, bathroom fittings.

Equally offended, they computed the shame being done to their past and to their present. An old yew tree, uprooted, sprawling, was slowly dying. "Never, never ought I to have allowed it," Alain murmured. "It's sacrilege. You, Saha, you've known that yew tree for only three years, but I . . ."

At the bottom of the hole left empty by the uprooted yew, Saha smelled a mouse whose image if not his odor rose to her cat's brain. For a moment she was beside herself with frenzy. She dug her claws into the earth after the manner of a fox-terrier; slid along the ground in a circular motion like a lizard; jumped up on her four feet like a toad; hid a ball of earth between her thighs as a barn rat does the eggs she has stolen; jumped wildly out from the hole and found herself seated on the grass—cold, demure, controlling her hot panting.

Alain, thoughtful, had not stirred. He knew how to be calm when Saha's devils got control over her. Admiration and understanding of the cat were instinctive with him, fundamental reasons which gave him power to explain her so readily. He read her like a book since that day when, after visiting a Cat Show, he had deposited on the smooth Neuilly lawn a little five months' old kitten, bought because of her perfectly formed face, her precocious self-possession, her hopeless timidity behind the bars of a cage.

"But why didn't you buy an Angora?" Camille asked.

"It wasn't just a little cat I was carrying at that moment," Alain mused. "It was the incarnate nobility of the whole cat race, her limitless indifference, her tact, her bond of union with the human aristocrat." He flushed, and mentally excused himself. "Saha, the aristocrat—that's the one who understands you best . . ."

Still he had not advanced so far as to say "resembles" instead of "understands," for he belonged to a class which forbade itself to recognize and even to have any conception of its kinship with animals. But in the age given to coveting a limousine, a world cruise, a rare binding, several pairs of skis, Alain did not cease any the less to be known as "the young-man-who-had-bought-a-kitten." His narrow world resounded with the news; the employes of the House of Amparat and Son, rue des Petits-Champs, were astonished; and M. Veuillet made some inquiries about "the little beast."

"Before having chosen you, Saha, perhaps I had never known that one could choose. As for the rest, my marriage pleases everyone, and there are moments when it satisfies me, too, but . . ."

He rose from the green bench, assumed the important smile of the Amparat son who was condescending to marry the daughter of the Malmert family, Washing-Machines, "a girl not quite our sort," as Madame Amparat said. But Alain was aware that the Washing-Machine Malmerts, speaking among themselves of the Amparats-of-the-Silks, did not forget to call attention to the fact, raising their chins as they said it, "The Amparats are no longer really in silks. Mother and son have merely retained a share in the business and the son does not figure as the head of the firm."

Calmed from her recent wild conduct, her eyes soft and golden, the cat seemed to be expecting a continuation of the spiritual confidences, the telepathic murmur toward which she extended her silver-tipped ear.

"And you're not just an innocent and glittering spirit of a cat, even you," said Alain. "Your first seducer, the white tom-cat without a tail, you remember? Oh, my ugly one! Oh, my wanderer-in-the-rain! Oh, my shameless one!"

"What a bad mother she is, your cat," Camille used to say, indignant. "She never even thinks any more of the kittens they took away from her."

"But that was only young girl talk," Alain went on defiantly. "Girls are always good mothers—beforehand!"

A steady, full voice fell on the quiet air, and Alain rose with a start, like a guilty man, at the sound of pebbles crushed under tires.

"Camille! It's half past eleven . . . good heavens!"

He drew together his pyjama coat, tied the girdle with so nervous a hand that he rebuked himself. "Well, now, what's the matter with me? I shall see plenty of other things in a week. . . . Saha, you're going to meet her?"

But Saha had disappeared and already Camille was pressing the grass with her hard heels. "Ah, she's really very nice." An agreeable leap of the blood tightened his throat and made him blush. It was the sight of Camille all in white, a lock of black hair effectively drawn on her forehead like a little paint brush, a thin red scarf about her neck, the same shade of rouge on her lips. Made up artistically, discreetly, her youth did not become evident at once. It needed a moment to reveal the white cheek under the ochre, the smooth eyelid beneath a little beige powder put on around the wide, almost-black eyes. The very new diamond on her left hand cut the light into a thousand colored rays.

"Oh," she said, "you're not ready yet! At this hour!"

But she stopped short at the thick, blond hair, uncombed, at the naked breast under the pyjamas, and at Alain's confusion. All her young girl expression confessed so clearly a woman's warm leniency that Alain did not now dare to give her the quarter-to-twelve-kiss, the kiss-in-the-garden, the kiss-in-the-Bois.

"Kiss me," she pleaded softly, as if she were asking for help. Awkward, troubled, ill-covered in thin pyjamas, he indicated the shrubbery, the clusters of roses from behind which came the sound of a clipper and rake. Camille did not dare throw her arms around his neck. She lowered her eyes, picked a leaf, pushed back the glossy lock of hair from across her cheek. But by the movement of her uplifted chin, and the quivering of her nostrils, Alain knew that she was seeking wildly in the air for the fragrance of a blond body, scarcely covered, and in the presence of which, he secretly decided, she did not have quite enough fear.

3

When he awoke he did not sit bolt upright in his bed. Haunted in his sleep by the unfamiliar room, he half-opened his lids and found that the pretence and restraint had not completely left him even while he slept; for his left arm, outstretched to the edge of the wide linen sheet, lay ready to recognize, ready also to repulse. . . . But all the wide bed at his left side was empty and cool. Had there not been facing his bed on the scarcely rounded corner of the three-walled room, the unwonted green darkness, the shaft of bright light, yellow like an amber cane, which separated two stiff dark curtains, Alain would have fallen back to sleep, lulled moreover by a little negro song hummed in his closed mouth.

Cautiously he turned his head, half-opened his eyes and saw now white, now light blue according to whether she was bathing in the narrow stream of sunlight or whether she stood in the shadow, a young naked woman, a comb in her hand, cigarette on her lips, humming. "That's pretty cheeky," he thought. "Perfectly naked! Where does she think she is?"

He recognized the beautiful legs, already familiar to him; but the belly, shortened by the navel placed a little low, surprised him. An impersonal youthfulness redeemed the strongly muscled buttocks, and the breasts were soft, small above the visible ribs. "So she has lost weight?" The prominence of her back quite as broad as her chest startled him. "Hers is a lower class back." At that moment Camille leaned out the window on her elbows, threw her back into prominence and lifted up her shoulders. "She's got a back like a scrubwoman." But she stood up again, danced two steps, made a charming gesture, clasping the air. "No, that's not true. She's beautiful. But what: what cheek! Does she think I'm a dead man? Or does she think it's perfectly natural to gallivant around absolutely naked? Oh, but that will change!"

As she turned toward the bed he closed his eyes again. When he reopened them Camille had sat down in front of what they called their "invisible dressing-table," a translucent slab of beautiful, thick glass resting on a framework of black steel. She powdered her face, touched her cheeks and her chin lightly with the tips of her fingers. Suddenly she smiled and turned her glance away with an expression of seriousness and fatigue that disarmed Alain. "So she is happy then? . . . Happy about what? I don't deserve it. But why is she naked?"

"Camille!" he cried.

He thought she was going to flee into the bathroom, cover her nakedness, veil her breasts with some bit of lingerie. But she gave one leap, threw herself upon the young man in the bed, and brought to him the strong, brown fragrance lurking under her arms, and hidden in the dark down which adorned her little belly.

"Darling, did you sleep well?"

"Quite naked," he said reproachfully.

She spread wide her big eyes, drolly.

"Well, and you?"

Bare down to the waist, he did not know what to answer. So boldly, so far removed from modesty, she strutted up and down in front of him that he tossed her a trifle brusquely the crumpled pyjama lying on the bed.

"Quick! Put that on. I'm hungry, I am."

"Old Mother Buque is in the kitchen, and all the gadgets work."

She disappeared and Alain wanted to get up, dress, comb his tangled hair, but Camille came back tied up in a big new bathrobe, much too long. She was gaily carrying a heaped-up breakfast tray.

"What a mess, my children! There's a kitchen bowl, a pyrex coffee cup, sugar in the lid of a tin box. Everything all piled on together. . . . My ham is dry. These sickly green peaches, they're left over from yesterday's feast. Buque is a trifle lost in her electric kitchen. . . . I'll show her how to get the hang of the plugs. . . . And then I poured the water into the compartments to make the ice-cubes in the frigidaire. Ah, if I wasn't here! My lord's coffee is very hot and his milk scalding, his butter ice-cold. No, that's my tea. Don't touch it. . . . What are you looking for?"

"No, nothing."

The smell of the coffee made him think of Saha. He was looking around for her.

"What time is it?"

"At last one little word of love!" Camille cried. "Very early, my husband. The kitchen clock said quarter past eight."

They laughed a great deal as they ate, and they talked but little.

The odor from the glazed green chintz curtains grew stronger.

Alain could guess the power of the sun beating upon them. He could not keep himself from thinking of the sun outside, of the unfamiliar skyline, the nine dizzying stories of the fantastic architecture of "The Quartered Cheese," which for the time being was to shelter them.

He made every effort to listen to Camille, touched that she was pretending to forget what had passed between them in the night, that she liked this experiment in the temporary dwelling place, and had the easy off-handedness of an old married woman of at least eight days. Since she had put on some clothes, he was trying to find a way of showing her his gratitude. "She has no hard feeling towards me either for what I've done or for what I've not done, the poor dear. Well, the worst part is over and done with. Is a first night often so wounding? A partial success, a partial disaster?"

Warmly he passed his arm about her neck and kissed her.

"Oh, you're so nice," she said.

She had spoken so loud, so warmly from her heart that she blushed and he saw her eyes full of tears. But courageously she fled from emotion and leapt out of the bed under pretext of carrying out the tray. She rushed toward the window, caught her foot in the too-long bathrobe, let out a coarse oath and pulled herself up by the heavy drapery cord. The glazed linen curtain rolled up. Paris with its suburbs bluish and limitless as a desert, spotted with still-fresh green, the big panes of glass like blue insects, entered at one bound into the triangular sleeping room, with its single plaster wall, the other two being of glass halfway to the ceiling.

"It's beautiful," said Alain in a low tone.

But he was uttering a half-falsehood, and his forehead sought the support of a young shoulder from which the bathrobe was slipping. "It's not a human dwelling-place. All that horizon in one's home, in one's bed. And on stormy days? Lost in the top of a lighthouse, amid the albatrosses. . . ."

Camille's arm—she had rejoined him in the bed—was around his neck and, fearless, she looked alternately at the dizzying horizon of Paris and at the blond, tousled head.

Her new pride, which seemed to make her sure of the following night and all the nights thereafter, was content no doubt with the liberties of the present hour; to sleep in the conjugal bed, to press from shoulder to hip against a young naked male body, to accustom herself to its color, its curves, its effronteries; to sustain boldly the sight of the little dry nipples, the hips which she coveted, the strange, compelling power of capricious sex. . . .

They nibbled the same insipid peach and laughed, showing each other their beautiful, moist teeth and their gums a little pale like those of tired children.

"What a day yesterday!" Camille sighed. "And when you think that there are people who marry so often!"

Vanity touched her again and she added,

"However, it went off all right . . . not a hitch. True?"

"Yes," said Alain listlessly.

"Oh, you. That's like your mother. I mean that so long as one doesn't tread down the grass in your garden or throw cigarette butts on your path, you think everything's all right, don't you? Yet for all that, our wedding would have been prettier in Neuilly. Only that would have inconvenienced the sacrosanct cat. . . . Speak, naughty boy; say something. What are you looking around for?"

"Nothing," he said quite truthfully, "since there's nothing to see. I've already seen the dressing-table, I've seen the chairs—we've seen the bed . . ."

"You wouldn't live here? For my part, I'm very pleased with it. Just think, three rooms, three balconies! Suppose one were to remain here?"

"One says, 'supposing *we* were to remain here.'"

"Well, then, why do you say '*one* says'? Yes, suppose one were to remain here, as we were saying?"

"But Patrick will be back from his cruise in three months."

"That's no great matter. He comes back. One explains to him that one wants to stay on. And one sends him packing."

"Oh . . . you would do that?"

She shook her thick black hair affirmatively, radiant at her feminine facility in dishonesty. Alain was tempted to look at her severely, but under his glance Camille changed. She seemed to become apprehensive, as he, too, felt himself afraid. So he kissed her quickly on the mouth.

Without a word, eagerly, she gave him back the kiss, as she sought with a sliding movement of her hips the hollow of the bed. At the same time her free hand in which she clutched a peach stone, was feeling around in the air trying to find an empty cup or an ashtray.

Bent over her, he waited, caressing her with his hand until the woman by his side should open her eyes again.

She tightened her lids on two little shining tears that she did not want to let flow, and he respected that discretion and that pride. They had done their best, she and he, silently, aided by the morning's heat and by their two fresh-smelling pliant bodies.

Alain remembered Camille's swift breathing, and the proof she had given of an eager docility in passion, a little excessive, even though agreeable. She didn't make him think of any other woman: in possessing her for the second time, he had thought of nothing but the consideration she deserved. She lay against his arm, her hands half-closed after the manner of a cat. "Where is Saha?"

Unconsciously he outlined on Camille a caress, "for Saha," his finger-tips wandering delicately over her body. . . . She cried out with shock and stiffened her arms, with one of which she struck Alain, who very nearly slapped her back. Sitting up, her eye hostile under the thick loose hair, she covered him with her portentous look.

"Are you by any chance . . . is it possible that you are one of those . . . unnatural men? Are you a vicious young man?"

He wasn't expecting anything like that, and he burst into a laugh.

"That's nothing to laugh at," Camille cried. "I've always been told that men who tickle women are depraved, even sadistic."

He got out of the bed so that he could laugh more heartily, forgetting that he was not covered. Camille stopped talking so abruptly that he turned around and caught her expression, surprised, dumb-

497

founded, appraising everything about this young man whom a bridal night had just given her.

"I'm using the bathroom for about ten minutes. May I?"

He opened the mirrored door leading to the end of the longest partition wall, the one they called "the hypotenuse."

"And then I'll drop in a moment to see my mother."

"Yes. You don't want to have me go along with you?"

He looked shocked, and she blushed for the first time that morning.

"I'll see if the alterations . . ."

"Oh, those alterations! Are you interested in those alterations? Confess"—she crossed her arms like a tragedy queen—"confess that you're going to see my rival!"

"Saha isn't your rival," Alain said simply.

"How could she be your rival?" he went on to himself. "You can't compete with the pure; your rivals have to be among the impure."

"I didn't need such a serious assurance as that, my dear. Go on quickly. Don't forget that we are lunching informally at old M. Leopold's house. At last informally! You'll come back soon? And you're not forgetting that we're going for a little airing in the car? You hear me?"

He heard particularly that the words "come back" took on a new significance, preposterous, inacceptable perhaps, and he looked askance at Camille. She confessed to a bride's fatigue, exposed the slight swelling of her lower lid in the open corner of the big eye. "No matter at what moment you come from sleep, will you always have such a big eye? Don't you know how to half-close your eyes? It makes my head ache to see eyes so wide open."

He found a dishonest pleasure, an equivocal comfort, in putting these questions to himself. "It's less offensive on the whole than sincerity." He made haste to reach the square bath-tub, the hot water—solitude favorable to meditation. But as the mirrored door arranged in the "hypotenuse" reflected him from head to foot, Alain opened it slowly, complacently, and did not hasten to close it.

An hour later, intending to leave the apartment, he made a mistake and instead went out on one of the terraces which encircled "The Quartered Cheese." He felt on his face the dry stroke of the east wind which gives Paris that blue look, carries off the smoke, and makes Sacré-Coeur, from a distance, glisten as though it had been scoured. Upon the cement balcony six vases, brought there by some well-meaning hand, contained white roses, hydrangeas, and lilies soiled with their own pollen. "That's never pretty, last night's leftovers." Nevertheless, before going down to the street, he set the ill-treated flowers in a corner where they would be protected from the wind.

4

He made his way deep into the garden like a lad just out of bed. The intoxicating odor of the earth being sprinkled; the unseen moisture rising from the fertilizer nourishing the lush, costly plants; the dewdrops chased by the breeze—he drew them all in in one long breath, and discovered that he needed to be comforted.

"Saha!"

A moment or two passed before she came and he didn't at once recognize that bewildered, incredulous expression, as though she were looking through the veil of a bad dream.

"Saha, dear."

He took her in his arms, pressed her against his breast, stroking her soft ribs which seemed to him a little hollow; and from her neglected coat he plucked bits of spider-webs, twigs of pine and elm. She revived quickly. A familiar expression spread over her features; her cat dignity shone again in the pure gold eyes. . . . Under the tips of his thumbs, Alain could feel the little heart beating irregularly and with difficulty; and an abortive purring. . . . He put her down on the iron table and caressed her. But just as she went to drop her head ecstatically and forever into Alain's hand, as she had a trick of doing, she smelled that hand and drew back.

He looked all around for "the white pigeon," as he called his mother's gloved hand, behind the hedges of dewy clusters, behind the rhododendrons aflame with blossoms. He was delighted that yesterday's ceremony, sparing the beautiful garden, had done its damage only to Camille's house.

"Those people, here! And those four bridesmaids in pink! . . . And the flowers they would have picked! And the honeysuckle withering on the bosoms of big, fat women! And Saha!"

He called out in the direction of the house.

"Has Saha had something to eat and drink? She's acting very strangely. I'm here, mama!"

On the threshold in the hall appeared a heavy white silhouette and answered from a distance.

"No. Just think. No dinner last night and she wouldn't drink her milk this morning. I think she was waiting for you. Are you all right, my boy?"

He stood deferentially in front of his mother at the foot of the porch steps. He noticed that she did not offer him her cheek as was her habit and that she held her hands folded one over the other across her belt. He understood, and shared with embarrassment and gratitude that maternal modesty. "Saha didn't kiss me, either."

"For really . . . the cat . . . well, she's seen you go away very often. She's resigned herself to your absences."

"But I didn't go so far," he thought.

Near him on the little iron table, Saha was greedily drinking like a creature who has walked a long, long way and slept little.

"You don't want a cup of hot milk too, Alain? A slice of bread and butter?"

"I've already had my breakfast, mama. We had our breakfast."

"Breakfast . . . not too good, I imagine."

Alain smiled. With the eyes of an exile, he gazed at the cup trimmed with golden arabesques beside Saha's saucer. Then at his mother's face, grown heavy, lovable beneath the thick, wavy hair, prematurely white.

"I haven't asked you if my daughter is happy . . ."

She was afraid he would misunderstand her, and hastened to add: ". . . that is, if she is well."

"Very well, mama. We are lunching in Rambouillet forest. We're going to stroll about . . ."

He corrected himself:

"We're going to drive around in the car, you know."

They remained alone, he and Saha, in the garden, both of them numb with fatigue, with silence, summoned by sleep.

The cat dozed off immediately. Lying on her side, her chin lifted, her teeth exposed, she looked like a dead stag. Clematis petals rained down lightly upon her; but, deep in a dream where perhaps she felt the bliss of security and the inalienable presence of her friend, she did not stir. Her vanquished posture, the drawn and pallid corners of her periwinkle-grey lip bespoke a night of wretched wakefulness.

At the top of an old rotting wooden shaft mantled with climbing vines, a bevy of bees, lighted on the blossoming ivy, buzzed with the sound of a low-toned drum, the same sound Alain had heard for so many summers. "To sleep here on the grass between the yellow rose-bush and the cat. . . . Camille would not be home until time for dinner; that would be lovely . . . and the cat, oh, the cat . . ." Over near the new work a carpenter's plane had been smoothing a scantling; a hammer pounding a metallic beam, and already Alain was building a rustic dream peopled with mysterious blacksmiths. As the clock on the schoolhouse tower struck eleven, he rose and fled without daring to wake up the cat.

5

June came and brought the longest days. Her evening skies were devoid of mystery. But June is cruel only to man pressed against man, hemmed in narrowly between hot bricks, town-dwellers without cars. Around "The Quartered Cheese" a strong, tireless breeze whipped the yellow awnings, crossed the three-cornered bedroom and the studio, struck against the prow of the apartment house and dried up the little privet hedges in boxes on the balconies. Helped out by the daily drive in the car, Alain and Camille lived quietly, calmed down and stupefied by the heat and their own voluptuousness.

"Why have I been calling her an untamed girl?" Alain asked himself, surprised. Camille uttered fewer oaths in the car, shed many of her rough expressions, and lost her passion for night clubs where gipsy girls sang through horse-shaped noses.

She ate and slept a great deal, opened her softened eyes wide, gave up a score of summer plans, and interested herself in the alterations, which she visited every day. Occasionally she would linger a long time in the Neuilly garden, where Alain, leaving the dull office of Amparat and Son, rue des Petits-Champs, would find her idle, ready to enjoy the long afternoon, ready to drive over the hot pavements.

Then a gloom fell upon him. He heard her give orders to the singing painters, to the electricians some distance away. She asked him questions in a general and perfunctory way, as though she was doing it from a sense of duty, and from the moment he arrived she was covered with her new sweetness:

"Business going all right? Hard times still with us? Are you selling some of your polka dot silks to those dressmaker princes?"

She did not even respect old Emile whom she shook until she

made him drop those forms of speech stereotyped to a sickly imbecility.

"What do you think of our new roost, Emile? Have you ever seen the house so beautiful?"

The old valet mumbled in his whiskers, answers that somehow resembled himself—they had neither form nor color.

"You'd never know it any more . . . If anyone had told me that it would be a house cut up into little compartments . . . It's different, all right . . . Everybody will be together; that will be fun."

Either this kind of talk, or he poured into Alain's ear, drop by drop, blessings secretly burdened with hostile meaning; shot through with hidden animosity.

"Monsieur Alain's young wife is getting to look very well. And she has a fine voice too. You can hear her voice all the way from our neighbor's house—it's so clear. And a tone you'd better not disagree with. The young woman has a way of saying things. She swore to the gardener that every night old man honeysuckle creeps into bed with the forget-me-nots. I've laughed about that ever since."

And he gazed at the cloudless sky with his faded eyes—eyes the color of a grey oyster—eyes that had never laughed. Alain didn't laugh either. Saha worried him. She was growing thin; she seemed to be giving up a hope, doubtless the hope of seeing Alain again every day and by himself. She no longer ran away when Camille arrived. But she did not escort Alain to the iron gate and when she sat near him she would look up at him with a deep and bitter wisdom. "Her expression of a little kitten behind the bars, that same look—the very same." In a low voice he would speak to her: "Saha . . . Saha . . ." dwelling distinctly on the h. But she did not jump up, nor lay back her ears; and a great many days had now passed since she had cried out her ringing "Me-rraing!" or the "Mouek-mouek-mouek" of contentment and desire.

One day when Camille and Alain had been summoned to Neuilly to learn that the new square, thick bath-tub as huge as a swimming pool would sink through the foundation, the husband heard his wife sigh:

"Will it never be ready?"

"But," he answered, surprised, "I thought, as a matter of fact, you liked 'The Quartered Cheese' better, with its eagles and its stormy petrels . . ."

"Yes . . . but still . . . And then this is your house, here, your real home . . . our home . . ."

She was leaning on his arm, a little listless, unusually yielding. The solid blue of her eyes, almost as blue as her light summer dress, the perfect and superfluous make-up on her cheek, her mouth and her eyelids left him untouched.

And yet it seemed to him that for the first time she was consulting him, even though without words. "Camille here with me . . . Already! . . . Camille in her pyjamas under the rose arbors." One of the oldest rose-bushes, nearly as tall as himself, bore its burden of flowers which faded the moment they blossomed; and in the evening its Oriental odor pervaded the air even up to the porch. "Camille in a bathrobe under the elm hedge!" . . . Was it not better, everything considered, to keep on housing her in the little lookout of "The Quartered Cheese"? "Not here, not here—not yet . . ."

The June evening, saturated with light, died away slowly as it veered toward the side of night. Some empty glasses on the wicket table contained fat, russet bees, but under the trees, except the pines, a slight dampness spread a promise of cooler hours. Neither the pink geraniums, which scattered their warm odor, nor the fiery poppies languished as yet under the heat of approaching summer. "Not here . . . not here . . ." pounded in Alain's mind to the rhythm of his step. He looked around for Saha; he did not want to call out for her. But he came upon her stretched out beside the little low fence which propped up a bed of blue lobelias. She was sleeping or she seemed to be sleeping, rolled up like a turban. "Like a turban? At this hour of the day and in this kind of weather? That's a winter position, sleeping all rolled up."

"Saha, Saha deary."

She did not tremble when he lifted her up in his arms; and she opened her hollow eyes, very beautiful, almost insensible.

"Heavens, how light you are! But you're sick, my little puma!"

Carrying her in his arms, he hastened to join his mother and Camille.

"But, mama, Saha is very sick. Her coat shows it; she weighs nothing at all and you did not tell me."

"It's because she scarcely touches food these days," said Mme. Amparat. "She won't eat."

"She won't eat? And what else?"

He cuddled the cat against his breast, and Saha yielded, her breath coming nervously, her nose dry. Mme. Amparat's eye, under the thick white curls, shot knowingly in Camille's direction.

"Oh, nothing," she said.

"She's lonely without you," said Camille. "She's your cat, isn't she?"

He thought she was sneering at him and he looked up at her defiantly. But Camille had not changed her expression and was looking inquiringly at Saha, who closed her eyes again, under the girl's stroke.

"Feel her ears," Alain said excitedly. "They're burning up."

It took him only a minute to think.

"This is what I'll do. I'll take her with me. Mama, have someone bring me her basket, will you? And a bag of sand for her dish. We have everything else we need. You understand that I absolutely will not . . . That cat thinks that . . ."

He stopped short and turned slowly toward his wife.

"You will not mind, Camille, if I take Saha with us until we come back here again?"

"What a question! But where do you think you can keep her at night?" she added so innocently that Alain blushed because his mother was there; and he answered dryly:

"She'll pick out a place for herself."

They looked like a little procession as they left, Alain bearing the passive Saha in her travelling-basket; old Emile bent under the bag of sand; Camille in the rear carrying an old fringed cashmere blanket which Alain always called the "Casha-Saha."

6

"No, I didn't think a cat could accustom itself so quickly . . ."

"A cat's only a cat. But Saha is Saha."

Alain boasted proudly of Saha. He had never kept her so restricted. Now she was imprisoned in twenty-five square yards; on view every moment, and reduced for her feline meditation, her passion for shadow and quiet, to borrowing the undersides of vast armchairs which wandered all over the studio with no permanent abiding-place; or a corner in the diminutive hallway; or under one of the wall closets hidden behind mirrors.

But Saha tried to triumph over all these snares. She suited her life to the irregular hours of meals, of going to bed, of getting up; chose for her nocturnal home the bathroom and the rubber bathstool; explored "The Quartered Cheese" with no show of disgust or of resentment. She condescended to listen in the kitchen to Buque's silly talk inviting "pretty pussy" to eat her raw liver. When Alain and Camille went out, she installed herself on the dizzying balcony railing and plumbed the depths of air, following with a steady eye the backs of swallows and sparrows flying below her. Her unconcern on the brink of nine stories, the habit she had fallen into of washing herself slowly, deliberately, on the railing, frightened Camille.

"Don't let her do it," she cried to Alain. "It makes me dizzy to see her there, and gives me pains in my ankles."

Alain smiled at the thought of his influence, and admired his cat, won back to a taste for living and for nourishing herself.

Not that she looked flourishing nor even very happy. She did not get back her iridescent fur shot through with beautiful shades, like the pearl-tinted plumage of a dove. But she passed her days more contentedly, listened for the dull "poum-poum" of the elevator and accepted a few unexpected favors from Camille. For instance, a tiny saucerful of milk at five o'clock, a small chicken bone held a trifle high as we hold it for a dog when we want him to jump for it.

"Not like that . . . like this," Alain said, checking his wife sharply.

And he placed the bone on the bath-mat or simply on the thick, tan wool rug.

"What will that do to Patrick's rug?" Camille objected.

"But a cat won't eat a bone or any meat on a polished surface. When a cat takes a bone from a plate and puts it on a rug before he begins to eat, people tell him that he's dirty. The cat has got to hold his prey under his claws while he crunches it or tears it apart; and he can do that only on bare ground or on a carpet. But people don't know."

Surprised, Camille interrupted him.

"And you . . . how did you know that?"

He had never asked himself how he knew; and got out of his embarrassment by saying facetiously:

"Don't tell anyone, but it's because I'm so intelligent. Don't let on. Monsieur Veuillet doesn't know anything about it."

From time to time he explained to her a cat's ways and habits. It was like leading her into a foreign language overrich in refinements. As he went on, he would put in too much feeling in spite of himself. Camille looked at him with narrowed eyes and asked him scores of questions to which he replied unreservedly.

"Why does the cat play with a piece of string if she is afraid of the heavy curtain cord?"

"Because to her the curtain cord is so thick she mistakes it for a snake. She's afraid of snakes."

"Has she ever seen a snake?"

Alain levelled upon his wife the grey-green eyes shadowed with black, the eyes she found so beautiful, "so faithless," she always said.

"No, certainly not. Where would she have seen one?"

"Well, then?"

"Well, she imagines one. She creates him. . . . You, too, you're afraid of snakes, even if you never have seen one."

"Yes, but I've been told about them. I've seen pictures of them. I know there is such a thing."

"So does Saha."

"How?"

He covered her with a haughty smile.

"How? Why, by instinct, of course. Like all sensitive persons."

"So then I'm not a sensitive person?"

His manner softened, but only out of sympathy for her.

"Heavens, no. Console yourself; I'm not either. You don't believe what I'm telling you?"

Camille, seated at her husband's feet, looked at him thoughtfully with her wide-set eyes, the eyes of that little girl who did not want to say "how-do-you-do."

"I have to believe it," she said seriously.

They got into the habit of dining at home almost every night, on account, Alain said, of the heat; and on "Saha's account," Camille gently suggested. One night after dinner Saha sat astride her friend's knee.

"And I?" said Camille.

"I've two knees," Alain answered quickly.

However, the cat did not take advantage of her privilege for long. Warned somehow or other, she jumped up on the polished ebony table, sat down on her own bluish reflection immersed in shadowy water and nothing about her would have seemed unusual save the fixed attention she gave to unseen things swimming about in the air right in front of her eyes.

"What is she looking at?" Camille asked.

Every evening at the same hour she was pretty in white pyjamas, her hair slightly oiled and waving on her forehead; her cheeks very brown under the powder she kept putting on all day. Sometimes Alain kept on his summer suit, without a waistcoat; but Camille's impatient hands took off his coat, his tie; unbuttoned his collar; rolled up his shirt sleeves; sought his bare skin. He thought it rather bold of her, but let her go on. She laughed a little regretfully, as she curbed her longing. And it was he who lowered his eyes, the better to hide a misgiving not wholly voluptuous. "What burning desire in that expression! It shows in the lines around the mouth . . . In so young a girl! Who taught her to outstrip me like this?"

The round table, flanked by a small, rubber-wheeled service

wagon, brought them together on the threshold of the studio, near the open window. Three tall old poplars, derelicts from a beautiful despoiled garden, swayed parallel with the terrace, and the wide-stretching Paris sun, copperred, subdued by vapor, went down behind their scraggly tops from which the sap was ebbing.

Buque's dinner—she cooked well and served badly—brightened the hour, and, refreshed, Alain forgot his day and the Amparat office and M. Veuillet's guardianship. His two captives in the penthouse received him with open arms. "You were waiting for me?" he whispered in Saha's ear.

"I heard you come," Camille cried, "you can hear everything here."

"You have not been bored?" he asked her one night, fearful lest she be discontented. But she shook her heavy black hair in sign of denial.

"Not a speck. I went to see mother. She said I might have the pearl."

"What pearl?"

"The nice little woman who will be my maid down in the other place. Heaven send that old Emile doesn't get her in the family way. She's all right."

She laughed and rolled back the wide sleeves of white crêpe de chine on her bare arms, preparatory to cutting the pink-fleshed melon around which Saha was turning. But, horrified at the thought of a new servant in his house, Alain did not laugh.

"Yes? Just think," he said, "my mother has never changed her servants since I was a child."

"That's easy to see," Camille cut in. "What a collection of antiques!"

She bit into a crescent-shaped slice of melon and laughed as she looked into the setting sun. Alain admired, without especial pleasure, the brilliance of Camille's eyes, her narrow mouth, the somewhat Italian regularity of her features, and a certain striking primitive glow in her face. But he still went on making an effort to be indifferent.

"You seldom see your girl friends any more, it seems to me. Perhaps you should . . ."

"And which friends?" she answered fiercely. "Is that to make me understand that I'm in your way? That I should take the air oftener? Yes?"

He lifted his eyebrows, made his tongue say, "tt . . . tt . . ." against his teeth and she gave in promptly, with a middle-class respect for the scornful man.

"That's true. I had hardly any friends when I was a little girl. So now . . . Can you see me with a girl friend? I'd have to treat her like a child, or else answer all her filthy questions: 'And what does one do then?' and 'how does he do that to you?' Girls," she explained somewhat acidly, "girls . . . they don't pull together very loyally, you know . . . no confidence in each other. It's not like you men."

"Excuse me. I'm not what you call 'you men'."

"Oh, indeed, I know it," she said soberly. "And I sometimes wonder if I wouldn't rather . . ."

Sadness rarely encompassed Camille; it came to her only from some secret-reticence, or from a doubt that she could not articulate.

"You," she went on, "you hardly have any friends excepting Patrick, who's not here now. And even Patrick, you don't really care a rap about."

At a sign from Alain she stopped.

"Let's not talk about things like that," she said wisely, "or we shall begin to quarrel."

The long screams of children playing below rose from the street, reached the air above and mingled with the sharp cries of the swallows. Saha's beautiful yellow eye, little by little transformed into the big pupil of night-time, followed in empty space some specks, moving, floating, invisible.

"What is that cat staring at? Tell me. There's nothing there where she's looking."

"Nothing . . . for us . . ."

Alain recalled the nights his cat friend used to pass on his breast.

He missed the soft trembling, the bewitching fear which she lavished upon him then.

"You're not afraid of her, at least?" he said condescendingly.

Camille burst into a laugh as if she had been waiting for just that insulting word.

"Afraid? There's not much I'm afraid of, I'll have you know."

"That's the remark of a stupid little woman," Alain said, irritated.

"Have it your own way," Camille answered, shrugging her shoulders. "There's your storm."

She pointed to the lavender-clouded wall which seemed to rise higher as night came on.

"And you are like Saha," she added. "You don't like thunder storms either."

"Nobody does."

"I don't hate them," said Camille in the superior tone of the initiated. "At all events, I'm not afraid of them much."

"Everybody in the world is afraid of storms," said Alain belligerently.

"Well, then, I'm not everybody in the world, that's all."

"Yes, you are, for me," he said, with an impulsive and artificial gallantry, by which she was not taken in.

"Oh," she scolded in a low tone, "I'll beat you . . ."

Across the table he showed his glittering teeth and he bent his blond head toward her.

"Beat me."

But she resisted the pleasure of running her hand through his golden hair, of offering her bare arm to that glistening mouth.

"You've got a humpy nose," she threw at him fiercely.

"It's the storm," he said, laughing.

That subtlety was not to Camille's taste, but the first low rumblings of thunder distracted her attention. She threw down her napkin and rushed out onto the balcony.

"Come on out. We're going to see some beautiful lightning."

"No," said Alain, without stirring. "Come, you."

"Where?"

With a motion of his chin, he indicated their bedroom. Across Camille's face passed the determined expression of dull lust that he knew so well. Yet she hesitated.

"But can't we watch the lightning first?"

He shook his head in refusal.

"Why, bad boy?"

"Because I . . . I'm afraid of the lightning. Choose . . . the storm or me."

"Oh, that's easy!"

She rushed to their bedroom with a wild leap which made Alain proud. But on joining her he saw that she had purposely switched on the light under the slab of bright glass beside the wide bed, and purposely he turned it off.

As they settled down, the warm rain, fragrant with fresh air, beat against the windows and on the balcony. In Alain's arms, Camille made him understand that during the raging storm, being with her, she wanted him to forget his fear. But, nervously, he counted the vast flashes of sheet lightning and the tall trees gleaming against the clouds and he drew away from Camille. She raised herself on her elbow, and with one hand combed her husband's thick, bristling hair. In the irregular quivering flashes their faces of blue plaster now rose out of the darkness, and now were swallowed up in it.

"Let's watch the end of the storm," she said.

"Ah, there you have it," Alain said to himself. "That's all she can find to say after a meeting which, I must admit, was worth while. She might at least have kept silent. It certainly is as old Emile says: 'The young woman has a way of saying things.'"

A sharp lightning flash as long as a dream was reflected like a blade of fire in the thick crystal slab on the invisible dressing table. Camille pressed her bare leg against Alain.

"Is that to reassure me? It's understood that you're not afraid of thunder."

He raised his voice so as to drown the peals of thunder and the noise of the rain pelting on the flat roof. He felt exhausted and peevish, sensitive to injury, dismayed at having to admit that he was never alone any more. Sharply his mind turned back to his old bedroom, papered with cold flowers on a white background, the room which no hand had ever made an attempt either to beautify or to mar. His desire was so keen that the sighing of the old, badly regulated stove followed the vision of the flat, bright bouquets in the wallpaper, the sighing and the breath of the dry cellar coming out of a register set in the floor. A breathing which mingled with that of the whole house, and the whispering of the old servants rubbed smooth by long years of habit, half-buried in their basement and whom even the garden itself no longer tempted. "They used to say 'She' in speaking of my mother, but from the moment I first wore trousers I was 'Mister Alain'."

A dry thunder clap called him back from the brief doze into which he had slipped after his enjoyment of Camille. Leaning over his body on her elbows, his young wife did not stir.

"I love you very much when you sleep," she said. "The storm is passing."

He took that for a hint and he sat up.

"I'll do likewise," he said. "How stifling it is! I'm going to sleep on the waiting-room bench." That's what they called the narrow divan, the single piece of furniture in a small nondescript room, a passageway with glass walls which Patrick intended for his sun-baths.

"Oh no, oh no," Camille pleaded. "Stay here . . ."

But he was already slipping out of the bed. Great lights from the clouds revealed Camille's hard, offended expression.

"Pooh! Silly boy!"

As she said this, she tweaked his nose. With the back of his arm, which he could not control and did not in the least regret, he struck aside the disrespectful hand. A sudden cessation of wind and rain found them in the midst of silence, and as though they were deaf. Camille rubbed her numb hand.

"But," Camille said at last, "but you're cruel . . ."

"That may be," he answered. "I don't like to have anyone touch my face. Isn't the rest of me enough for you? Don't ever touch my face."

"But it's true," Camille repeated slowly, "you're cruel."

"Don't insist upon it too much. Except for that, I've nothing against you. But just remember."

He drew his bare leg back into the bed.

"You see that great grey square on the rug. That's dawn coming. Shall we sleep a little?"

"Yes . . . I want to so much," said the same baffled voice.

"Well, then, come!"

He stretched out his left arm for her to put her head on and she came obediently and cautiously. Pleased with her, Alain lifted her gently, drew her by the shoulders but kept her at a distance by slightly bending his knees; and quickly he fell asleep. Lying awake, Camille breathed carefully and turned her head toward the whitening patch in the carpet. In the three poplars, whose swishing imitated the sound of the rain, she heard the sparrows celebrating the passing of the storm. When in changing his position Alain drew his arm away from her, his hand, gliding three times over her head in an unconscious caress, seemed used to smoothing fur much softer than her soft black hair.

7

TOWARD the end of June incompatibility definitely settled down between them just as though it were a new season; and indeed, it had at times all the surprises and pleasures of one. Alain breathed it in as he would have a harsh spring which had fallen in the middle of summer. He carried about with him his unwillingness to provide a place for the young outsider in the house in which he was born.

514

He concealed the feeling without effort, secretly nourished it by talking about it to himself when he was alone, and kept it brewing by covertly watching the progress on the new bridal apartment.

One sultry day Camille, excited, cried out from the end of their terrace on which not a breath of air was stirring:

"Oh, let's leave all this, take the little wagon and go soak ourselves somewhere. What do you say, Alain?"

"All right. I'm with you," he answered with cautious promptness. "Where'll we go?"

Peace reigned while Camille listed the beaches and some of the hotels.

His eyes upon Saha—thin, lifeless—he was taking plenty of time to think.

"I don't want to travel with her. I . . . I don't dare. I like very much going off by the day as we do and coming back for dinner late. But that's enough. I don't like spending the night in hotels— all the evenings in the casinos." He shuddered. "I know I'm slow at getting used to anything new, that I've a very difficult disposition, that . . . But I don't want to go away with her." He felt ashamed to admit that he was saying "She" just as Emile and Adele had done when they spoke in low tones of "Madame."

Camille got out some road maps and they played at travelling across a France laid out in sections on the polished ebony table, which reflected two inverted, elongated faces.

They added up the miles, found fault with their car, insulted each other warmly, and felt refreshed, almost revived, by a forgotten comradeship. But sultry, sudden downpours drowned the last days of June and the terraces of "The Quartered Cheese." Saha, behind the closed glass, watched the flat brooks wind in and out on the tiles, and saw Camille soak them up by stamping on some dry towels. The horizon, the city, the sudden shower took on the color of clouds bursting with inexhaustible water.

"Would you rather go by train?" Alain ventured to ask in a smooth tone.

He expected that Camille would jump at that abhorred word. Jump she did, and reviled the idea.

"I'm afraid," he added, "that you may be bored. All those trips we promised ourselves . . ."

"All those summer hotels . . . all those intimate little eating-places . . . all those gay bathing beaches . . ." she went on wistfully. "Do you know, we two have the habit of driving a good deal; but what we know is only the highway, not the pleasure of seeing new places."

He saw that she was a little melancholy, and he gave her a brotherly kiss. But she faced about, bit him on the mouth and under the ear; and once again they resorted to the diversion which passes the time away and inflames human bodies to amorous indulgence. Alain wore himself out. If, when he and Camille were dining at his mother's house, he tried to hide his yawns, Mme. Amparat lowered her eyes and Camille did not miss the chance of laughing a little laugh of vainglory. For she noted with pride that Alain was falling into the habit of making use of her—body to body—a habit which was becoming hasty, almost churlish. The indulgence over, he would cast her aside, panting, and slip into the cool side of the uncovered bed. Ingenuously she would join him there; he did not forgive her this pursuit, even though silently he did yield to her further desire. At that price he was able afterward to seek in peace for the sources of what he called their incompatibility.

He had the intelligence to locate them outside frequent intercourse. Clear-minded, aided by fatigue, he went back to the fastnesses where inevitable hostility between Man and Woman keeps itself fresh, never grows old. Sometimes she disclosed herself to him in a banal way when she lay sleeping like a child in the bright sunlight. For instance, he was amazed, even repelled, to learn how dark Camille's skin was. Lying back of her on the bed he could see on her shaven neck short hairs like the spines of sea-urchins, outlined on the skin like parallel shadings on a map, the shortest ones blue under the skin and each one visible before it should grow out of a small blackish pore.

"Haven't I ever had a brunette mistress?" he asked himself. "Two

516

or three little ones never left me with the memory that they were so dark." And he held his own arm up to the light, the normally white arm of a blond, downy with soft fine hair, greenish-gold, and streaked with veins the color of jade. He likened his own hair to forests with purple shadows, shadows which on Camille revealed a peculiar whiteness of skin between the crinkly down and the richly abundant hair.

The sight of very fine black hair growing from the armpit nauseated him. Then the slight giddiness changed; and it wasn't color but form that disturbed him. Holding quietly in his arms the young body whose exact outlines the darkness modified, Alain began to reproach a Creator as grudging as the English nurse of his child-hood—"no more prunes than rice, no more rice than chicken"—for having molded a Camille adequate, but with nothing about the body to stir the imagination, nothing lavish. He carried his reproach and his regret into the entrance to his dreams at that vague moment during which the black landscape became alive with bulging eyes, Greek-nosed fishes, moons, chins. There he prayed for nineteenth century buttocks, fully developed below a slim waist, that would make up to him for the acid insignificance of Camille's breasts. At other times he compromised and, half-asleep, preferred a full throat, a moving, twofold enormity of flesh with exciting breasts. . . . Such longings, engendered by the embrace and persisting after it, did not confront the light of day nor complete consciousness. They existed only in that narrow margin between nightmare and sensuous dream.

Warmed, the strange woman of his dream smelled of wood gnawed by flame, of birch, of violet—a whole bouquet of blended sweet odors, haunting, persistent, which clung a long time to the palms of his hands. These perfumes affected Alain peculiarly: they excited him, but they did not always give birth to desire.

"You are like the smell of roses," he said one day to Camille. "You take away the desire for food."

She looked at him dubiously and fell into that awkward, stooped pose with which she received ambiguous praise.

"You're the spirit of 1830."

"Less than you," Alain retorted. "Yes, less than you. I know whom you resemble."

"That actress, Marie Dubas. I've already been told so lots of times."

"Great mistake, my girl. Barring the braids, you're like those maidens up in high towers who wept over Loïsa Puget's heroines. They dropped their tears on the first page of the novel, from big prominent Greek eyes just like yours, and from those same thick-edged lids which send tears streaming down the cheeks . . ."

His senses one after the other betrayed Alain and they doomed Camille. He had to admit that, at least, she could take in good part certain brief comments which burst from him point-blank—words less of gratitude than of challenge—at moments when, stretched flat on his back, he appraised her with a look from narrowed lids, and rated neither with indulgence nor with reservation the new virtues of such a young bride: Camille's passion a little monotonous but already cleverly possessive, and her own special aptitudes. These were the moments of pure enlightenment, of certainty, whose box-ing-match breathlessness, tight-rope suspense, perilous balancing Camille yearned to prolong.

Being without deep malice herself, she never suspected that, a partial dupe of selfish conflicts, of pathetic needs, and even of a cold, primitive cynicism, each time Alain possessed his wife it was as though for the last time. He made himself master of her as he would have clapped his hands over her mouth to keep her from screaming, or as he would have felled her to the ground.

And yet, fully clothed and sitting upright beside her in their road-ster, he could not make out, looking at her closely, what had tran-spired to make her his worst enemy; for, getting his breath again, feeling his heart-beats decrease, he himself was no longer the dra-matic young man who undressed before overmastering his mate. And the short, sensuous preliminary, the awareness of being nude, the gratitude, feigned or sincere, receded to the region of that which is done, of that which, no doubt, will never come back again. Then was born again that idea which absorbed him most completely, and which to him seemed natural and honorable: that question which, having earned it by priority, took its place—the first place—in his thoughts:

"How can I keep Camille from coming to live in *my* house?"

The period of hostility against the alterations passed. He had in good faith put his hope in returning to the house in which he was born; in the soothing arrangement of a life close to the soil, a life dependent upon the earth, upon everything the earth produces. "Here I ache for the out-of-doors! Ah," he would sigh, "the undersides of branches . . . the bellies of birds . . ." Yet he admitted sternly, "The country is not the solution." And he fell back on his indispensable support, the lie.

On an afternoon of blazing heat which melted the asphalt pavement, he went to his home. Neuilly was nothing but deserted streets, empty trolleys, gardens where dogs lay yawning. Before leaving Camille, he had made Saha comfortable on the coolest balcony of "The Quartered Cheese," vaguely apprehensive each time he left his two females alone together.

The garden and the house dozed in the bright sunlight and the little iron gate did not creak. Full-blown roses, red poppies, the first canna plants with their ruby throats, dark snapdragons were burning up on the lawns. In the side of the house gaped the new door, and two more windows in a little new first-floor construction. "Everything is done," Alain affirmed. He walked carefully, as he did in his dreams, and he stepped only on the grass. At the low sound of a voice which came up from the basement he stopped and listened, absent-mindedly. They were only the old familiar voices— grumblings like incantations, tones of servility—the same old voices that used to say "She" and "Master Alain" and flattered the little blond head, the slender boyish form, his dark eyes. . . . "I was king," Alain said to himself. And he smiled wistfully.

"So then soon she'll be sleeping here?" one of the old voices asked distinctly.

"That's Adele," Alain murmured. Propped up against the wall, he listened unscrupulously.

"That's the idea," Emile bleated, "of that apartment. It's pretty badly laid out."

The chambermaid, a girl from the Basque country, getting grey, mustached, broke in:

"I should say so. From their bathroom, you can hear everything that's happening in the toilet. Monsieur Alain won't like that idea much."

"*She* said, the last time she was here, that she didn't need any curtains in her little sitting-room, since there weren't any neighbors in the garden."

"No neighbors? Well, what about us, if any of us should be going to the wash-house? What will we see when she'll be with Monsieur Alain?"

Alain could imagine the snickers at this remark and old Emile answered.

"Oh, perhaps we won't see so much as all that. She'll find herself put in her place oftener than she expects. Monsieur Alain is not one to let himself go like that on the divans at every hour of the day or the night."

During the silence Alain heard only the sound of a blade on the knife-sharpener, but he stood listening quietly against the warm wall and vaguely looking between a flaming geranium and the vivid green grass for Saha's moonstone fur.

"If you want my opinion," said Adele, "I find her perfume too strong."

"And her clothes," Juliette the Basque went on. "Her way of dressing. Not in the style of the best dressmakers. More like an actress, that brazen way of hers. And what's she going to bring with her for her maid? A creature from an orphanage, it seems, or something worse . . ."

A casement window opened and shut and the voices died down. Alain realized that he was trembling; he felt limp; and he was breathing like a man spared by murderers. He was neither shocked nor angered. Between his own manner of judging Camille and the harshness of the basement critics, the difference was slight. But his

520

heart beat to listen in this scurvy manner. Not to be punished for it, and to gather testimony of partisans, of accomplices, without having any agreement with them. He wiped his face, took in deep breaths of air, as if that outburst of universal woman-hatred, that pagan incense dedicated to the single Male Principle must be making him dizzy. His mother, waking from her afternoon nap, rolled up the shades of her bedroom, saw her son upright, his cheek still leaning against the wall. Loving mother that she was, she said softly, "Ah, my boy . . . you're not ill?"

He laid his hands over hers on the window-sill, like a lover.

"Not at all, mama. I was out for a walk. I came in."

"That's a good idea."

They smiled at each other, but neither believed the other's lies.

"May I ask a little help of you, mama?"

"A little money help, I'll wager. You're not oversupplied this year, my poor children, it's true."

"No, mama. If you please, I would like you not to tell Camille that I came today. As I have come without any reason. I mean, with no other motive than to kiss you, I prefer . . . That's not all. I would like you to give me some advice. Between ourselves, you understand?"

Mme. Amparat lowered her eyes, rumpled up her white curly hair, tried to stave off the secret.

"I'm not a chatterbox, you know. You take me by surprise, all in disorder like this . . . I look like an old hag. Don't you want to come in where it's cool?"

"No, mama. Do you think there is a way—it's an idea I can't shake off—a kind way, naturally—which might be agreeable to everyone—a way to keep Camille from coming here to live?"

He pressed his mother's hands, expecting they would tremble or be withdrawn. But they lay cool and soft between his own.

"Those are the ideas of a bridegroom," she said, troubled.

"You mean?"

"Yes. With a newly-married couple either things go too well or

521

else they go too badly. And I can't say which is best. But it's never an easy matter."

"But, mama, that's not what I'm asking you. I'm asking you if there's not some way . . ."

For the first time he was losing confidence in his mother.

"You are talking like a child. You go out for a walk in these hot streets and you come to me after a quarrel to ask me questions . . . I do not know . . . questions which have no answer except in divorce, or in separation, or God knows what."

She breathed with difficulty from the moment she started to speak and Alain reproached himself when he saw her flushed, breathless after so few words. "Enough for today," he decided prudently.

"We did not quarrel, mama. It's only I that cannot get used to the idea . . . I would not want to see . . ."

With a sweeping, embarrassed gesture he indicated the garden surrounding them, the green pond on the lawn, the bed of petals under the rose bower, a film of bees under the flowering ivy, the ugly, beloved house . . .

The sensitive hand he had held in one of his own closed, stiffened into a little fist and he quickly kissed it. "Enough, enough for today . . ."

"I'm going now, mama. Monsieur Veuillet will telephone you tomorrow at eight o'clock about that matter of the lowered stocks. Do I look better, mama?"

He lifted to her his eyes, greened by reflections from the tulip tree, and he changed his expression—which he restrained by habit, by affection, by discretion—to make himself look as he had when he was a boy. A wink of the lids to beautify the eye, a seductive smile, pouting lips . . . The mother's hand opened again, moved along the window-sill, reached out for and stroked on Alain the sensitive spots she knew so well—the shoulder blades, the Adam's apple, the top of the arm. And her answer did not come until after the gesture:

"A little better. Yes, quite a little better."

"That pleased her, my asking her to keep something from Camille." Remembering that last maternal kiss, he drew in the belt under his waistcoat. "I'm getting thinner, I'm thinner. . . . No more physical culture—no other exercise but love."

He stepped lightly, clad for the hot weather, and the freshening breeze dried him, blowing in front of him as he walked the sharp odor of his blond perspiration, akin to black cypress. He was leaving his native stronghold inviolate, his basement cohorts intact; the rest of the day would run smoothly. Up to midnight no doubt, seated in the car at the side of the unoffending Camille, he would drink in the evening air, now leafy from the oaks bordering the muddy creeks, now dry, smelling of the harvested grain. "And I'll bring back some fresh catnip for Saha . . ."

He reproached himself violently for the fate of the cat, living so passively at the top of the apartment house. "She's like her own chrysalis, and it's all my fault." At the hour when man and wife were enjoying each other, she would exile herself so completely that Alain had never seen her in the three-cornered bedroom. She ate just enough, forgot her varied languages, her demands, and more than anything else she preferred to pass her days in one long expectation. "Once again, she's waiting behind the bars. Waiting, and for me . . ."

As he reached the landing, Camille's piercing voice penetrated through the closed door.

"It's that damned pig of an animal. If she'd only die, good God! What? No, Buque, when you say . . . I'm fed up with her? Fed up!"

He made out some more blasphemous words. Guiltily he turned the key in the lock, but once past his own threshold he could not bring himself to listen without being seen. "'A damned little pig of an animal'? But what animal? An animal in the house?"

In the studio, Camille, in a little sleeveless sweater, a knitted beret stuck miraculously over one eye, was furiously drawing on her funnel-shaped gloves. She started, dumbfounded, at the sight of her husband.

"You! . . . Where are you going?"

"I'm not going. I'm just coming back. And you? Who's making you so angry?"

She avoided the direct thrust, attacked Alain by a clever parry.

"There you are, all on edge, for once in your life when you're on time. I'm ready. I'm waiting for you."

"You're not waiting for me, since I'm on time. But who is it you're so angry with? I heard 'damned little pig of an animal.' What animal?"

She turned her glance away slightly, but she did not flinch under Alain's stare.

"The dog," she cried. "That wretched dog, downstairs, that dog from morning till night. He keeps it up. Don't you hear him barking? Listen!"

Her finger raised, she commanded attention and Alain had time to notice that the gloved hand was trembling. He yielded to the simple need of being sure.

"I thought it was Saha you were talking about, imagine . . ."

"I?" cried Camille. "Speak of Saha in that tone of voice? I wouldn't do such a thing! Why should I do that? But are you coming, are you coming?"

"Get out the car. I'll join you below. I'll get a handkerchief and my sweater."

But first he looked for the cat; and all he saw on the coolest terrace near the chintz-covered armchair where Camille sometimes took her afternoon nap were bits of broken glass. He wondered about them, vaguely.

"The cat is here with me, sir," said Buque in her smooth voice. "She likes my straw stool very much. She sharpens her claws on it."

"In the kitchen," Alain thought sadly. "My little puma, my cat that loves gardens, my cat of lilies and spiders. In the kitchen! Ah, all that's going to change."

He patted Saha on the head, chanted very low a few ritualistic phrases and promised her catnip, and some sweet acacia buds. But he sensed that there was something unnatural about the cat and Buque, especially about Buque.

"We shall be back for dinner, or rather we shall not, Buque. Has the cat everything she needs?"

"Yes, sir, yes, sir," she answered hastily. "I certainly do everything I can, I assure you, sir."

The big woman reddened and seemed on the verge of tears; she rubbed a kindly and awkward hand along the cat's spine. Saha curved her back and offered a little "m'hain," the word of an unhappy, shrinking cat which made her friend's heart overflow with sorrow.

The drive was more peaceful than he dared hope. Seated at the wheel, her eye alert, hand and foot in accord, Camille drove him past the little hill at Montfort-l'Amaury.

"Shall we dine outside, Alain? . . . My dear?"

He saw the smile on her profile, beautiful as always in the twilight, the cheek dark and transparent, the corner of the eye and the teeth of the same gleaming white. In the forest of Rambouillet she lowered the wind-shield and the wind brought to Alain's ears the sound of leaves and running water.

"A little rabbit!" Camille cried. "A pheasant!"

"Another rabbit! . . . A little more and . . ."

"He doesn't know his good luck, that little fellow."

"You have a dimple in your cheek, just like those in your baby pictures," said Alain, feeling a little more cheerful.

"Don't talk to me about it. I'm getting enormous," she answered, shrugging her shoulders.

He watched the smile and the dimple come back, and looked down at the robust neck, guiltless of any necklace and as solid and full as that of a beautiful, light-colored Negress. "But it's true; she has grown fat. And in the most alluring way, too . . . for her breasts, even they . . ." He dropped back to his former mood and hit morosely against the age-old male grievance. "She is getting fat on love. She is battening on me." He slid a jealous hand under his waistcoat, tapped his ribs and ceased admiring the dimple and the childish cheek.

But as he sat down a little later at a table in a famous open-air restaurant, his vanity was stirred when he became aware that all the guests ceased their talking and dining, and stared at Camille. He and his wife exchanged smiles; they resorted to all the little coquetries of eyes and chin so becoming to what is called "a handsome couple."

But it was for him alone that Camille lowered her voice, became a little wistful; and showered him with soft and engaging attentions that were not for the public. In return, Alain took away from her the plate of sliced tomatoes and the small basket of wood strawberries, insisted that she eat some creamed chicken; and he poured her out a wine she did not care for, but which she drank quickly.

"You know very well that I don't like that wine," she repeated each time she emptied her glass.

The setting sun did not steal the light from a sky almost white with little clouds spotted with deep pink. But from the straight thick forest behind the tables of the restaurant night and freshness seemed to vanish at the same time. Camille laid her hand on Alain's.

"What? What? What is it?" he said, alarmed.

Surprised, she withdrew her hand. The little wine she had drunk laughed in her moist eyes where were reflected, small and trembling, the pink balloons hanging in the pergola.

"Oh, nothing! Nervous as a cat. Is it forbidden to put my hand on yours?"

"I thought," he answered feebly, "I thought you wanted to tell me something . . . serious. I thought," he went on in one breath, "that you were going to tell me you were pregnant."

Camille's sharp little laugh drew to her the attention of the men seated at nearby tables.

"And did that upset you so much? With pleasure . . . or with annoyance?"

"I really don't know exactly. And you? How would you feel about it? Glad or not? We've given it so little thought . . . I, at least . . . But why are you laughing?"

"It's your face. All of a sudden the expression of a condemned man. It's too funny. You're going to make me take off my artificial eyelashes . . ."

With her first two fingers she lifted off the lashes from both her lids.

"That's not funny, that's serious," said Alain, happy to change the subject. "But why was I so frightened?" he asked himself.

"It's not serious," Camille answered, "except for the people who have no home or who have only two rooms. But we . . ."

Calm, her optimistic mood steadied by the traitorous wine, she smoked and talked as though she were alone. She was sitting sideways at the table, her legs crossed.

"Put down your skirt, Camille."

She did not hear him, and she went on.

"We, one has all a child needs . . . a garden and what a garden! And a dream of a bedroom with its own bathroom."

"A bedroom?"

"Your old bedroom, which they are repainting—by the way, you will be very kind and not have them put a border of little ducks and Swiss pines on a sky background. That would distort our progeny's taste."

He took care not to stop her. Her cheeks flushed, she was putting into words thoughts that came to her from a distance. He had never seen her so beautiful. The base of her neck, an unwrinkled column, a sheaf of muscle, allured him and also the nostrils from which puffed the cigarette smoke. "When I give her pleasure and she draws in her lips tight, she breathes by opening her nostrils like a little horse."

From her rouged and disdainful lips fell prophecies so mad they ceased to frighten him. Camille was quietly going forward in her woman's life amid the ruins of Alain's past. "Good gracious," he thought, "how it is all planned out. I'm learning about it!" A tennis court would later replace the wide, unused lawn . . . The kitchen and the pantry . . .

"Have you never thought how inconvenient they are, and all that lost space? It's like the garage . . . I'm saying all this about it, my dear, so that you will know I'm thinking a great deal about our really settling down. Before everything else we must think of your mother who is so kind, and never do anything without her approval. You agree with me?"

He signified yes, then he signified no—irresponsibly, as he gathered up the tiny wood strawberries scattered over the table-cloth. A temporary calm, a foretaste of unconcern, had freed him, from the moment she used the words, "your old bedroom."

"Just one thing may hurry us," Camille went on. "Patrick's last postal card is postmarked the Balearic Islands, notice. It takes less time for Patrick to come from the Balearic Islands, provided he doesn't lag on the beaches, than for our decorator to finish up everything—may he pass out all purple, that bastard of Penelope covered by a male tortoise! But I'll use my siren's voice: 'My little Patrick' . . . and you know that makes a great impression . . . my siren's voice . . . on Patrick."

"The Balearic Islands," Alain broke in dreamily. "The Balearic . . ."

"Right next door, might as well say. . . . Where are you going? Must we leave here now? It was so comfortable here."

On her feet, sobered, she yawned sleepily and shivered.

"I'll take the wheel," Alain said. "Put on that old coat, under the cushion there, and doze off."

Moths, vivid silver butterflies, beetles as hard as stones, raced like grape-shot in front of the head-lights, and the automobile pressed back like a wave the atmosphere thick with wings. As a matter of fact, Camille did go to sleep, sitting straight up, admonished never to burden, even if she fell asleep, the shoulder and the arm of the driver. Only with slight noddings of her head did she acknowledge the little ruts in the road.

"The Balearic Islands . . ." Alain repeated to himself. Under the favor of the black air, and the white lights which attracted, pressed back, destroyed the flying creatures, he restored the waiting-room overcrowded with his dreams, the dusty firmament of shining faces, of big, hostile eyes which were always putting off till tomorrow a code, a countersign, a password. So absorbed was he in his dream that he failed to take a short cut between Pontchartrain and the Versailles toll-gate, and Camille grumbled in her sleep. "Bravo," Alain applauded. "Good reaction! Nice little reliable, careful sense of direction! Ah, how agreeable I find you, how well we get on when you sleep and I keep watch!"

Their uncovered hair, their sleeves, were dripping with dew when they got out in the new street, deserted in the moonlight. Alain raised his head; right in the middle of the nearly full moon, nine stories up, a little horned shadow of a cat leaned over, waiting. He pointed it out to Camille.

"Look! She's waiting for us!"

"You've got good eyes," Camille answered, still drowsy.

"If she should fall! Careful not to call her."

"Don't worry; even if I should call, she wouldn't come."

"There's a reason," answered Alain with a little sneer.

The moment he had let out those two words he reproached himself. "Too soon, too soon. And what a badly chosen moment!" The hand that Camille extended toward the doorbell never reached its destination.

"A reason? What reason? Look here, have I been lacking in respect to your hallowed animal again? Has the cat been complaining of me?"

"It certainly was too soon," Alain reflected as he shut the car in the garage. He went back across the street, joined his wife, waiting, posed like a warrior ready for attack. "Either I knuckle under and have a peaceful night—or I put an end to discussion with one good blow—or . . . I spoke too soon."

"Well, I'm talking to you."

"First of all, let's get upstairs," said Alain.

Pressed one against the other in the tiny elevator, they did not speak. Once in the studio, Camille hurled off her beret and her gloves as though to indicate that she had not given up the quarrel. Alain was busy with Saha, pleading with her to leave her perilous post. Patient, careful not to displease him, the cat followed him into the bathroom.

"If it's because of what you heard before dinner, when you came in . . ." Camille began violently, when he reappeared.

Alain had made up his mind, and he broke in with a tired air.

"My dear, what is there to say to each other? Nothing that we do not already know. That you do not love the cat at all, that you were abusing Buque because the cat broke a vase—or a glass; I saw the pieces. My answer would be that I care very greatly for Saha, that you would be almost as jealous if I had retained a warm affection for a childhood friend. And thus we should pass the whole night quarrelling. No, thank you. I'd rather sleep. Listen. My advice to you is to get a head start next time, and have a little dog."

Furious, confused by her futile anger, Camille looked at him, her eyebrows lifted.

"The next time? What next time? What are you talking about? What head start?"

As Alain shrugged his shoulders, she flushed, a youthful expression passed over her face and the unusual brilliance of her eyes foretold tears. "Oh, I'm tired." Alain sighed to himself. "She's going to confess. She's going to give me a reason. I'm worn out . . ."

"Listen, Alain."

He tried to show his authority, to seem stern.

"No, child, no. No and no. You're not going to get me to end this charming evening by useless discussion. No, you will not dramatize a childish incident any more than you will keep me from loving animals."

A kind of bitter amusement passed across Camille's eyes, but she did not speak. "I was perhaps a little too severe. Childishness is too strong a word. And as for loving animals, what do I know about that?" A little outline of shadowy blue, encircled like a cloud with a border of silver, sitting on the dizzying edge of night, filled his thoughts and carried him away from a spiritless place where step by step he justified his fate of loneliness, his selfishness, his poetry . . .

"Come now, my little enemy," he said with a treacherous show of kindness, "we're going to get some sleep."

She opened the bathroom door where Saha, settled for the night on the small rubber-top table, seemed to give her the least possible attention.

"But why, but why, why did you say 'the next time'?"

The noise of the water drowned Camille's voice and Alain did not answer. When she joined him in the wide bed, he bade her good night, found in the dark her powderless nose and lightly touched it with his lips; while Camille kissed him on the chin with a greedy little smack.

Waking early, he quietly slipped out into the "waiting-room" and lay on a narrow cot crowded close between two glass partitions.

It was here he came the following nights to finish out his sleep. He drew together on both sides of the bed the dark, glazed chintz curtains, so recently new and already nearly destroyed by the hot sun. His body exhaled the very aroma of its peace, the sharp, feline perfume of blossoming boxwood. One arm extended, the other bent across his chest, he fell back into the relaxed, imperial position of his childhood sleep. Stayed on the narrow peak of the triangular apartment house, he did all in his power to lure back the former dreams which amorous fatigue had disintegrated.

He slid away more easily than Camille would have wished, obliged as he was to flee in the same place, merely by withdrawing, now that escape no longer meant stealthily descending a staircase, slamming a taxi door, a hasty note . . . No mistress had helped him to anticipate Camille and her young-girl readiness of approach; Camille and her immoderate hunger; but also Camille and the point of honor she could urge of a mate outraged.

Fled, stretched on the cot in the "waiting-room" and trying to find the soft little pillow he liked for the back of his neck, Alain turned an anxious ear toward the bedroom he had just left. But Camille never opened the door. Lying there alone, she pulled up over her the crumpled sheet, the down coverlet of padded silk. With ill-humor and disappointment she bent her first finger and snapped off the long bar of metal chromium which threw a narrow bridge of white light across the bed. Alain never knew whether she had slept, in the empty bed where, so young, she was learning that a night passed alone prescribes an armored awaking; for she reappeared

531

bright, slightly made up, the bathrobe and the pyjamas of the night before discarded. She could not understand that man's sensual mood is fleeting and its uncertain return is never a repetition.

Lying in bed alone, bathed in night air, measuring the silence and the height of the building by the muffled screechings of the boats in the nearby Seine, the faithless man staved off sleep until Saha appeared. A shadow bluer than a shadow, she came to him along the sill of the open glass window. There she stopped, staring at him, and did not jump down on Alain's chest until he continued to plead with her in words she knew well.

"Come, my little puma, come . . . my cat of high places, my lover of lilies. Saha, Saha, Saha . . ."

She resisted, seated above him on the window-sill. He could make out nothing about her but her cat outline against the sky, her dropped chin, her ears passionately turned in his direction; he was never able to catch unawares the expression in her eyes.

Sometimes the dry dawn, the dawn before the stirring of the wind, saw them seated on the terrace, cheek to cheek, watching night fade from the eastern sky, and the soaring of white pigeons as, one by one, they left the beautiful cedars in the Folie-Saint-Jammes. They were both surprised to be so far up above the earth, so alone and so little happy. With the burning, undulating movement of a huntress, Saha followed the winging pigeons and breathed out something like ". . . ek . . . ek . . ." a feeble echo of her "mouek . . . mouek . . ." formerly her words for excitement, lust, wild sport.

"Our room," Alain would whisper in her ear, "our garden, our house . . ."

She grew emaciated again and Alain found her slim and alluring but it made him unhappy to see her so gentle and meek, like all those buoyed up and worn out by promises . . .

Sleep crept over Alain in proportion as day, dawning, shortened the shadows. First revealed and expanded by the mists of Paris, then contracted, released, and already blistering, the sun rose, lighting up the twittering sparrows in the small garden. The strengthening light showed up on terraces, on balcony railings, in the little courts where imprisoned shrubbery was languishing, the chaos of a sweltering night—a piece of wearing apparel forgotten on a rattan chaise-longue; empty glasses on a wicker table; a pair of sandals. Alain loathed this immodesty of small dwellings oppressed by summer; and making one leap through the yawning panel of a glass door, he went back to his bed. Nine stories below, in a little patch of wan vegetables, a gardener looked up and saw that young man in white bound like a thief through the transparent wall.

Saha did not follow him. Sometimes she leaned one ear toward the triangular bedroom, sometimes she watched listlessly the awakening of a distant world on a level with the ground. From a decrepit little house a dog, unleashed, shot out, ran around the garden quietly, not recovering his voice until after an aimless chase. Women appeared at the windows; an ill-tempered servant banged doors, shook orange-colored cushions on a flat roof, as servants do in Italy. Men, to their regret, awoke, lighted the first bitter cigarette. . . . Finally, in the fireless kitchen of "The Quartered Cheese" the automatic drip coffee-pot shared space with the electric tea-pot. Through the bathroom porthole floated Camille's perfume and her loud, full yawning. . . . Saha, resigned, folded her paws under the breast and pretended to sleep.

8

ONE July evening, as they were both waiting for Alain to come home, Camille and the cat sat quietly at the same railing, the cat sitting on her elbows, the girl leaning over, her arms crossed. Camille did not like this balcony, reserved for the cat, and shut in by two cement walls which protected it from the wind and from all communication with the front terrace.

Each gave the other a quick, searching glance and Camille said no word to Saha. On her elbows, she leaned out as though to count the flights of yellow awnings, slackened, from the top to the bottom of the dizzying façade of the apartment house; and stroked the cat, who got up, drew away, and lay down again a little farther along on the railing.

The moment Camille was alone she always looked very much like the little girl who would not say "how-do-you-do." Her face took on its childhood expression of merciless innocence, that hard perfection which gives children's faces the look of angels. With an expression impartially severe, which could have no reproach in it, she was gazing on Paris, from whose sky the light was dying earlier each day. She yawned nervously, got up, took several aimless steps and leaned over the railing again, obliging the cat to jump down to the floor. Saha drew off with dignity, and preferred to go back into the bedroom. But the door of the three-cornered room had been closed and Saha sat down in front of it, patiently. A moment later she had to yield the entrance to Camille, who began to walk back and forth from one wall to the other with long, quick strides; and the cat jumped up on the railing. As though teasing her, Camille dislodged her again as she leaned on her elbows and gazed across Paris. Once again Saha drew back and took up her station against the closed door.

Her eye on the horizon, her back to the cat, Camille stood motionless as a statue. But as Saha stared at that back, her breath came faster and faster. She got up, turned around two or three times, sniffed inquiringly at the closed door. . . . Camille had not stirred. The cat swelled her nostrils; had that distressed look which comes with nausea. A long-drawn-out, desolate "meow," pitiful reaction to a design, menacing and unexpressed, escaped her; and Camille wheeled squarely around.

She was a little pale; that is, her rouge outlined two oval moons on her cheeks. She feigned the preoccupied air she would have had under the glance of a human being. At the same time she began to hum, her mouth tightly closed. Then she resumed her walk from one wall to the opposite one, back and forth, moving to the rhythm of the tune after her voice could no longer carry it. She drove the cat first to regain with one leap her narrow place of observation on the railing, and next to sit tightly pressed against the door.

Saha did not lose her composure; she would have died rather than have uttered a second cry. Closing in on the cat but pretending not to see her, Camille walked back and forth in complete silence. Saha did not jump onto the railing until she saw Camille's feet coming near her; and when she jumped down on the balcony floor, it was to avoid the arm which, if extended, would have thrown her down from a height of nine stories.

She was not confused; she fled with design; jumped carefully; kept her eyes fixed on the enemy; and she stooped neither to anger nor to pleading. Extreme emotion, the fear of death, wetted her sensitive paws with sweat: they stamped the imprints of flowers on the cement balcony floor.

Camille seemed to be the first to weaken, to dissipate her murderous power. She made the mistake of noticing that the sun was setting; glanced at her wristwatch; listened to the tinkling of the glasses inside the apartment. A few seconds more, and her resolution, slipping from her as sleep from a sleep-walker, would have left her guiltless and exhausted. . . . Sensing her enemy's strength of purpose waver, Saha hesitated a second on the railing; Camille, spreading her arms wide apart, pushed the cat off into space.

She had time to hear the scratching of the claws on the cement, to see Saha's blue body, curved into an "S," clutch at the air with the upward leap of a trout. Then the girl drew back and leaned against the wall.

She showed no temptation to look below into the little garden outlined in fresh pebbles. Returned to the room, she put her hands over her ears, withdrew them, shook her head as though troubled by the buzzing of mosquitoes, sat down and nearly fell asleep. But the oncoming night put her on her feet and she chased away the twilight by lighting squares of glass, shining grooves, blinding crystals mushroom in shape, and also the chromium bar which threw an opaline light across the bed.

She moved from place to place elastically, and as she passed them, she touched the objects lightly, dexterously, dreamily.

"I feel as though I had grown thin," she said aloud.

She changed her clothes, dressed herself all in white.

"My fly in the milk," she said, imitating the voice in which Alain had said it. Color came into her cheeks again at a sensual memory which brought her back to reality, and she looked forward to Alain's home-coming.

She bent her head toward the buzzing elevator, and she trembled at every sound—deafening squeaks of a spring-board, metallic slaps, scrapings of a ship at anchor, strangled music—all the discordant life which a new house breathes off. But an expression of fright came into her face only when the sepulchral trembling of the bell in the entrance hall followed the fumbling of a key in the door. She ran, and opened it herself.

"Shut the door," Alain ordered. "If only I were sure that she's not hurt! Come, you can give me some light."

He was carrying the breathing Saha in his arms. He went straight to the bedroom, pushed aside the trinkets on the disguised dressing-table, and carefully put the cat down on the glass top. She held herself up on her feet and kept her balance, but she turned her deeply-set eyes about the room as she would in some unfamiliar house.

"Saha!" Alain called to her in a low tone. "If she's not hurt it's a miracle . . . Saha!"

She lifted her head as though to reassure her friend, and she leaned her cheek against his hand.

"Take a step or two for me, Saha . . . She's walking! Ah, good . . . A fall of five flights! . . . It was the awnings like those on the second floor that deadened . . . From that she swerved off onto the care-taker's little grass patch. He saw her dropping. He said to me, 'I thought it was an umbrella falling! . . . What's that in her ear? . . . No, it's something white from the wall. Wait a moment till I listen to her heart."

He laid the cat down on her side and examined the beating ribs;

the irregular, faint movement of the machinery. His fair hair pushed back, his eyes shut, he seemed to be sleeping on Saha's fur. Then—he opened his eyes and noticed only Camille standing by, silent, looking down on the closed-in group.

"Can you believe it? She hasn't any . . . at least, I can't find anything but a heart terribly excited; still, a cat's heart is normally excited. But how could this have happened to her? I'm asking you that question as though you could know, my poor little Camille. She fell from this side here," he said, looking at the wide-open French window. "Jump down, Saha, if you can."

She held back, then jumped, but lay down again on the rug. She was breathing quickly and she still had that lost expression in her eyes as she looked around the room.

"I've a mind to telephone Chéron . . . And still, look . . . she's cleaning herself up. She wouldn't be stirring as much as that if she had wounded herself inside, somewhere . . . Ah, thank Heaven . . ."

He drew away, threw his waistcoat on the bed, and went up to Camille.

"What a fright! . . . There you are, very pretty all in white . . . Kiss me, my little fly in the milk."

She gave herself to the arms which had at last become aware of her; and she could not hold back the sobs that shook her.

"No! . . . You're crying?"

He in his turn became nervous and he buried his face in her thick black hair.

"I did not realize you were so soft-hearted . . . imagine . . ."

She had the courage not to release herself at that word. Alain, moreover, turned quickly back to Saha, whom he wanted to take out into the cool air of the balcony. But the cat resisted; she was content to lie down near the door-sill and look into the sky as blue as herself. From time to time she shivered slightly and turned to question the depths of the triangular bedroom.

"It's the shock," Alain explained. "I would like to make her comfortable outside."

"Let her alone," answered Camille feebly, "if she doesn't want to."

"Her whims are commands. Especially today. Can there possibly be anything left fit to eat at this hour? Half past nine!"

Buque rolled the table out onto the terrace and they dined looking out on East Paris, the Paris most thickly dotted with lights. Alain talked a good deal, drank reddened water, accused Saha of awkwardness, of imprudences, of what he called "cat mistakes."

"Cat mistakes are the kind of 'accidental' errors, biological 'setbacks' chargeable to civilization and to domestication. They have nothing in common with clumsy, blunt actions that are almost intentional . . ."

But this time Camille did not ask "How do you know that?"

The dinner over, he carried Saha and led Camille into the studio where the cat consented to drink the milk she had refused. As she drank she shivered all through her body as cats do when they are drenched with too cold water.

"The shock," Alain said again. "Even so, I'll ask Chéron to look at her tomorrow morning. Oh, I'm forgetting everything," he said gaily. "Just telephone to the superintendent's flat. I forgot to bring up the roll that Massart, our accursed decorator, left for me there."

Camille obeyed while Alain, exhausted, fell into one of those wandering armchairs, relaxed, and closed his eyes.

"Hello," Camille said into the telephone. "Yes, that must be it . . . a large roll . . . Thank you."

His eyes closed, he laughed. She had come back near him and she saw him smiling.

"That tiny voice of yours! What's this new little voice? 'A large roll . . . Thank you'," he mimicked. "Do you keep such a thin small voice just for the superintendent? Come on; the two of us are not too many to tackle Massart's latest creations."

He spread out on the ebony table a large sheet of water-color paper. Immediately Saha, enamored of everything made of paper, leapt onto the design.

"Isn't she good?" Alain exclaimed. "She wants to show me that she isn't hurt anywhere. Oh, my rescued one! . . . Isn't that a swelling on her head? Camille, feel her head . . . No, she hasn't any bump. Still, just feel her head all the same, Camille."

A miserable little murderess, obedient, tried to draw herself out of the exile into which she was sinking. She put out her hand with a meek sort of hatred, and gently touched the cat's forehead.

The most savage scream, a snarl, an epileptic start responded to her touch; and Camille said "ha," as if she had been burned. Upright on the spread-out print, the cat covered the young woman with flaming accusation, stiffened the fur on her back, showed her teeth and the dry red of her jaw.

Alain had risen, ready to protect the one from the other—Saha and Camille.

"Careful. She is . . . perhaps she's mad. Saha!"

She stared at him fiercely, yet the lucid look in her eye proved that she had her reason.

"What was the matter with her? Where did you touch her?"

"I didn't touch her."

They spoke in low, sharp-edged tones.

"Now that," Alain said, "I don't understand. Put out your hand again."

"No, I don't want to," Camille protested. "Perhaps she's mad," she added.

Alain took the risk of caressing Saha, who stopped bristling and shaped herself to her friend's palm, but brought the glare in her eyes to bear on Camille.

"So, that's it," Alain repeated slowly. "Wait a moment. She has a scratch on her nose; I hadn't seen that. And that's dried blood. Quiet, Saha, quiet," he said, noticing the fury gathering in her yellow eyes. The puffing out of her cheeks, the huntress-like stiffness of the whiskers thrown forward, made the infuriated cat look as though she was laughing. The conflicts within her, coming one after the other in such quick succession, drew down the mauve corners of her jaw, stiffened the palpitating, muscled chin; and all her feline face was straining itself toward a universal language, toward a word forgotten of men . . .

539

"What's that?" asked Alain sharply.

"That what?"

The cat's glare brought back Camille's bravado and her instinct of defense. Bending over the drawing, Alain deciphered some moist pink spots in groups of four around a central irregular spot.

"Her paws . . . moist?" he said, very low.

He turned toward his wife.

"She must have stepped in some water," Camille said. "You exaggerate every little thing so."

Alain lifted up his head toward the dry, blue night.

"In water? In what water?"

His round, staring eyes made him look singularly ugly as he turned toward his wife.

"Don't you know what those marks are?" he said bitterly. "No, you don't know anything about it. That's fear, you understand, the sweat that comes from fright—a cat's sweat, the only moisture a cat has. That means she's been through some terrible fright . . ."

Delicately he took one of Saha's front paws and with his fingers he wiped off the fleshy sole of the foot. Then he pushed back the living white tissue where lay her retractive claws.

"All her claws are broken . . ." he said, talking to himself. "She caught herself . . . tried to stop herself . . . tried to cling to the stone. She—"

He stopped suddenly, took the cat under his arm, and carried her into the kitchen.

Alone, perfectly still, Camille listened. She clasped her hands tightly together, and free, looked as though bound by shackles.

"Buque," said Alain, "have you any milk?"

"Yes, sir, in the ice-box."

"Then it's cold?"

"But I can heat it on the stove . . . I can heat it in a jiffy. It's for the cat? Nothing the matter with her?"

"No, she's . . ."

Alain stopped himself, and changed to: "Some food must have disagreed with her in this hot weather. Thank you, Buque. Yes, you may leave now. Tomorrow morning."

Camille heard her husband turning on a faucet, and knew that he was giving the cat food and fresh water. A diffused shadow above a metal lamp-shade rose to her face and showed the slow moving of her big eyeballs.

Alain came back, automatically tightened his leather belt and sat down at the black table. But he was oblivious of Camille's presence, and it was she who had to speak first.

"You told Buque she could go?"

"Yes. Shouldn't I have?"

He lighted a cigarette and blinked above the flames of the lighter.

"I was going to ask her if she would bring, tomorrow morning . . . Oh, it's not important; don't excuse yourself."

"But I'm not excusing myself. True, I should have."

Lured by the blue depth of the night, he went to the open French window. He noted in himself an agitation which did not have its birth in this recent emotion, a trembling comparable to the quavering of an orchestra, deafening, prophetic. A skyrocket shot up from the Folie-Sainte-Jammes, burst into shimmering petals which faded out, one by one, as they fell, and peace came back into the powdery depth of the blue night. In the park of the Folie, a rocky grotto, a colonnade, and a cascade were illuminated with incandescent white. Camille drew near.

"Is this a gala night? Let's watch the fireworks. Do you hear the guitars?"

Absorbed in his own nervous trembling, he did not answer her. His wrists, his tingling hands, his tired backbone pricked with a thousand torments. His condition brought back to him a hated feeling of fatigue, the fatigue of the athletic competitions of his high school days—running races, boat races—from which he emerged vindictive, despising both his victory and his defeat, palpitating and stumbling with exhaustion. He was not at peace, except about one thing: he no longer felt anxious about Saha. A long moment ago—or a very short moment ago—since the discovery of the broken claws, since Saha's burning fright, he had not exactly been aware of time.

"It's not fireworks," he said. "More likely dancing."

By the movement which Camille made near him in the shadow, he gathered that she wasn't expecting him to answer. But she grew bolder and came nearer still; he felt no dread at her coming. With the corner of his eye he took in the white dress; one bare arm; one half of her face lighted with yellow from the lamps indoors; the other half blue, absorbed from the clear night; two half-faces divided by the same straight nose, each one endowed with a big eye which opened and closed very little.

"Yes, dancing, of course," she agreed. "Those are mandolins, not guitars. Listen. 'Les donneurs . . . de . . sé-é-réna . . des. Et les bel-les é-écou-teu . . .'"

Her voice stumbled on the highest note and fell, and she coughed to cover her defeat.

"But what a thin voice," Alain marvelled. "What has she done with her voice, as big as her eyes? She sings like a little girl and she's hoarse."

The mandolins stopped playing, the breeze brought a faint human murmur of pleasure and applause. In a moment a rocket went up, and broke like an umbrella of violet rays from which dropped tears of living fire.

"Oh!" Camille exclaimed.

Both of them had come forth out of the darkness like two statues: Camille like lilac marble; Alain white, his hair, greenish, his pupils faded. When the rocket burst, Camille sighed.

"They never last long enough," she said plaintively.

The distant music started up again. But the capricious wind transformed the sound of the instruments to a sharp resonance and the lingering pause of one of the accompanying brasses, on two notes, rose discordantly up to the balcony where the two were watching.

"That's too bad," Camille said. "Probably they play the best jazz . . . That's 'Love in the Night' they're playing . . ."

She tried to hum the tune but her voice—it seemed to come in the wake of tears—was too high and trembling to make the sound. This new voice redoubled Alain's uneasiness; it engendered in him a necessity for revelation, a desire to break through the thing which—a long moment ago or a very short moment?—was being built up between Camille and himself; a thing which as yet had no name, but was growing quickly; the thing which kept him from taking Camille by the neck as though she were a small boy; the thing which held him immovable, vigilant, leaning against the wall, warm still with the day's heat. He became impatient, and said:

"Sing some more . . ."

A long, three-colored shower drooping in sprays like boughs of weeping willow lighted up the sky above the park, and revealed to Alain a Camille surprised, already defiant.

"Sing what?"

" 'Love in the Night' or . . . anything."

She hesitated a moment; then refused.

"Let me listen to the jazz . . . even from where we are you can hear how mellow it is."

He did not urge, but restrained his impatience and tried to control the tingling that shook his entire body.

A swarm of gay little suns circling lightly across the night sky took flight while Alain was comparing them secretly with the constellations in his favorite dreams.

"Those are to be kept. I shall try to take them there," he decided seriously. "I have been neglecting my dreams too much."

Finally above the Folie was born and spread out across the sky a kind of vagrant aurora borealis, yellow and pink, which burst forth into bright red medallions, into blazing crystals, into blinding silver streamers. Children on the balconies below screamed and shouted at the miracle by the light of which Alain saw Camille preoccupied, called back into herself by glimmerings of another kind.

When night closed down, he hesitated no longer, and he slipped his bare arm under Camille's. In touching it he seemed to see it quite white, hardly tinted by the summer sun, covered with fine soft hairs lying on the skin, reddish brown on the forearm, paler near the shoulder . . .

"You're cold," he murmured. "You're not ill?"

She wept softly, but so immediately that Alain suspected her of having had her tears in readiness.

"No . . . it's you. It's you who . . . who do not love me."

He backed up to the wall and took Camille against his hip. He could feel her shaking and cold from her shoulder to her knees, bare above the rolled stockings. She did not hold back; she yielded up her whole body to him, faithfully.

"Ah, ah! I don't love you. So that's it! Another jealous scene on account of Saha?"

He could feel that whole body, pressed against his, stiffen— Camille recapturing her self-defense, her resistance; and he went on, encouraged by the moment and the opportunity.

"Instead of, like me, loving that charming animal . . . Are we the only young married couple to bring up a cat or a dog? Would you like a parrot, a marmoset, a pair of love-birds to make me jealous?"

She shook her shoulders and protested by a peevish sound in her closed mouth. His head high, Alain controlled his own voice and spurred himself on. "Come now, come on. One or two more childish bickerings, refillings, and we get somewhere. She's like a jar I have to turn upside down in order to empty it completely. But come on . . ."

"Would you like a little lion, a baby crocodile of, say, fifty years old or so? No? You'd do better to adopt Saha. If you'll just take the trouble, you'll see . . ."

Camille wrenched herself from his arms so furiously that he tottered.

"No," she cried. "That? Never! You hear what I say? Never!"

She drew a long sigh of rage and repeated in a lower tone:

"Ah, no . . . never!"

"That's that," he said to himself delightedly.

He pushed her into the bedroom, lowered the blinds, turned on the square ceiling lights, closed the window. With a quick movement Camille went up to the window, which Alain reopened.

"On the condition that you don't scream," he said.

He rolled up for Camille the single armchair; he himself straddled the one small chair at the foot of the wide, turned-down bed, freshly sheeted. The glazed chintz curtains, drawn for the night, cast a shade of green over Camille's pallor and her crumpled white dress.

"So?" Alain began. "Impossible to settle? Horrible situation? Either she or you?"

An abrupt shake of the head was her answer and Alain was made to realize that he had to drop his bantering manner.

"What do you want me to tell you?" he began, after a silence. "The only thing I don't want to say? You know very well I will not give up that cat. I'd be ashamed to. Ashamed for my own sake, ashamed for hers . . ."

"I know," Camille said.

"And ashamed in your eyes," he finished.

"Oh, as for me . . ." Camille said, raising her hand.

"You count too," he went on severely. "When all is said and done, I'm the one you're really angry with. The only grudge you've got against Saha is that she loves me."

Her sole answer was a troubled and hesitant expression and it annoyed him to have to go on putting questions to her. He had thought that one short, decisive scene would force the entire issue; he was relying on that easy disposal of the matter. Not at all. After the first cry had been uttered, Camille recoiled: she did nothing to feed the flames. He resorted to patience.

"Tell me, my dear . . . What's that? I may not call you 'my dear'? Tell me . . . if it were a matter of another cat than Saha, would you be less intolerant?"

"Naturally; of course I would," she replied very quickly. "You wouldn't love it as you do this one."

"That's true," he agreed, with studied loyalty.

"Even a woman," Camille went on, warming herself up, "even a woman, you would probably not love so much."

"That's true."

"You're not like people who love animals . . . you . . . Take Pat, now, he loves animals. He grabs big dogs by the neck, tumbles them over; imitates cats to see the faces they'll make; whistles to birds . . ."

"Yes, but he's not hard to please," Alain answered.

"But with you, it's not the same thing. You love Saha . . ."

"I've never hidden it from you, but neither did I lie when I told you that Saha is not your rival."

He stopped and lowered his lids upon his secret, that secret concerning purity.

"There are rivals and rivals," Camille said sarcastically.

She reddened suddenly, inflamed with sharp rage.

"I've seen you," she cried. "In the morning after you had spent the night on your little cot. Before daybreak, I've seen you both . . ."

She stretched her trembling arm out toward the balcony.

"Sitting there, both of you. You didn't even hear me. . . . You were like this, your cheeks against each other . . ."

She went to the window, took a breath of air and came back to Alain.

"It's for you to say, honestly, if I'm wrong in disliking that cat . . . wrong in suffering . . ."

He kept silent so long that she was angry again.

"But speak. Say something. At this point, what are you waiting for?"

"The sequel," Alain said. "The end of the story."

He got up deliberately, bent over his wife and lowered his voice as he indicated the French window.

"It was you, wasn't it? You pushed her off?"

She made a swift movement and put the bed between them, but she denied nothing.

With a kind of indulgent smile, he watched her flee.

"You threw her," he said dreamily. "I felt that you had changed everything between us. You pushed her. She broke her claws trying to catch hold of the wall . . ."

He lowered his head, seeming to picture the crime. "But how did you throw her? By clutching her by the skin of her neck? By taking advantage of her sleeping on the balcony? Have you been planning the attack for a long time? Did you two quarrel before-hand?"

He raised his head, looked at Camille's hands and arms.

"No; you haven't any marks. It was she who accused you when I asked you to touch her. She was magnificent."

His glance, leaving Camille, took in the night, the burnt-out stars, the tops of the three poplars with the bedroom lights shining upon them.

"Well," he said simply, "I'm going."

"Oh, listen . . . listen . . ." Camille begged in a low tone.

But she did not hinder him from leaving the bedroom. He opened closet doors, talked to the cat in the bathroom, and from the sound of his footsteps Camille knew that he had just put on his street shoes. Mechanically she looked at the clock. He came back into the room, carrying Saha in a wide basket which Buque used when she went to market. Hastily dressed, his hair hardly combed, a handker-chief around his neck, he had the look of a lover after a quarrel. Wide-eyed, Camille stared at him. But she heard Saha move in the basket and her lips tightened.

"There you are; I'm off now," Alain said again.

He dropped his eyes, raised the basket slightly and, with designed cruelty, corrected himself:

"We're leaving."

He fastened the wicker cover securely and explained as he did so: "That's all I could find in the kitchen."

"You're going to your home?" Camille asked, forcing herself to imitate Alain's calm manner.

"Yes, of course."

"Do you . . . May I count on seeing you one of these days?"

"Surely."

Surprised, she softened again, was on the verge of pleading, of tears, but she made every effort not to give in.

"And you," Alain said, "you will stay here alone tonight? You won't be afraid? If you want me to, I'll stay with you but . . ."

He looked toward the balcony.

". . . but frankly I'd rather not. What do you plan to say to your family?"

Hurt that, by his words, he was sending her back to her parents, Camille drew herself up.

"I have nothing to say to them. That is my business, I think. Family councils are not to my taste."

"I think you're quite right—for the time being."

"Moreover, after tomorrow we shall be able to decide . . ."

He raised his free hand as though to ward off that threat of the future.

"No. Not tomorrow. Today has nothing to do with tomorrow."

On the threshold of the bedroom he turned around.

"I left my key in the bathroom, and the money we have here—"

She cut in sarcastically.

"Why not leave a case of preserves and a compass?"

She was putting up a front, as she eyed him from top to toe, one hand on her hip, her head held straight and steady on her beautiful neck.

"She's giving me a fine send-off," Alain thought. He was tempted to respond by a counterplay; to toss his hair back on his forehead, make use of a look between narrowed lids as though disdaining to alight on her. But he renounced a pantomime so incongruous with Buque's market basket, and he confined himself to a vague nod toward Camille. She did not change her expression, nor shed her theatrical pose. But as he reached the door on his way out he turned, and it was then he saw the deep circles under her eyes, the moisture on her forehead and her smooth neck.

Reaching the street, he crossed over automatically, his garage key in his hand. "No, I can't do that," he said, and he turned back toward the avenue, a few steps away, where taxis cruise all night. Saha whined two or three times and he reassured her with a word. "I can't do it but it would be much more convenient to go in the car. Neuilly is impossible at night." Having counted on a happy re-action, he was surprised that he was losing his composure now that he was alone. The walk did not soothe him. Finally he picked up a wandering cab and found the five-minute ride long.

As he stood in the damp night under the gas jet waiting for the gate to be opened, he felt himself trembling. Saha, who had recognized the smell of the garden, made little meowing sounds in the basket deposited on the sidewalk.

The odor of wistaria in its second blooming filled the air, and Alain began to tremble even more as he stood first on one foot and then on the other as though he was very cold. He rang again, for nobody had been aroused in the house in spite of the deep, imperative sound of the big bell. Finally a light appeared in one of the little outbuildings near the garage; and he heard the sound of old Emile's feet shuffling along the gravel path.

"It's Alain, Emile," he said as the old butler's colorless face peered through the bars of the gate.

"Monsieur Alain?" Emile said, exaggerating his tremulous voice. "Monsieur Alain's young wife is not ill? Summertime is so dangerous. Monsieur Alain has a suitcase, I see?"

"No, it's Saha . . . No, I'll carry it . . . No, don't light the big lamp; it will wake up Madame . . . Just open the outside door for me, and go back to bed."

"Madame is awake; she's the one who woke me up. I hadn't heard the big bell at the gate. In my first heavy sleep, you know . . ."

Alain hurried, wishing to get away from talk, and the unsteady footsteps he heard behind him. He didn't stumble at the turning in the paths although there was no moon.

The dead, vine-covered tree in the middle of the lawn looked like an immense man standing up, his cloak over his arm. The odor of sprayed geraniums made Alain halt, and his throat tightened. He bent down and, groping in the dark, opened the basket and released the cat.

"Saha, our garden . . ."

He felt her jump out of the basket and tenderly he let her go wherever she wanted to. He consecrated the night to her, gave her

549

back the freedom, the soft, spongy earth she loved, the wide-awake insects, the sleeping birds.

Behind the blinds of the second floor a lamp was waiting and Alain's expression sobered. "To talk, and talk some more, to explain to my mother . . . Explain what? It's so simple. It's so difficult."

What he longed for was silence, the bedroom papered with flowers in flat colors, his bed, and more than anything else, violent tears, rough sobs like a cough, compensation guilty and concealed.

"Come in, my dear, come in."

It had not been his habit to go often to his mother's room. His selfish distaste for bottles with medicine droppers, boxes of digitalis, and all kinds of homeopathic pills, dated from his childhood and still continued. But he gave in at the sight of a narrow, unattractive bed and of the woman with the thick, white hair who raised herself up on her wrists.

"You understand, mama, there's nothing unusual . . ."

He uttered those stupid words with a smile of which he was ashamed, a stiff-cheeked, horizontal smile. His fatigue had at just that moment overpowered him with one blow and inflicted upon him the lie which he accepted. He sat down at his mother's bedside and unloosened his neckerchief.

"I beg your pardon for my appearance. I came just as I was. I've come at an unseasonable hour, without warning . . ."

"But you did give me warning," his mother answered quietly.

She glanced at Alain's dusty shoes.

"Your shoes look like tramps' shoes."

"I've only come from our house, mama. But I had to hunt for a taxi for quite a long time. I was carrying the cat."

"Ah," the mother answered understandingly, "you brought the cat back?"

"Oh, naturally. If you knew . . ."

He stopped, held back by a strange reserve. "These are things one doesn't tell. They are not stories for parents," he was thinking.

"Camille doesn't like Saha very much, mama," he said.

"I know."

She shook back her curly hair and forced herself to smile.

"That's very serious, that is."

"Yes, for Camille," Alain said ill-naturedly.

He got up, walked about among the furniture, covered with white for the summer as in country houses. Since he had made up his mind not to accuse Camille, he could find nothing else to say.

"You understand, mama, there were no screams, no dish-smashing. The glass dressing-table did not suffer, and the neighbors didn't rush up to learn what was the trouble. Only, I've got to have a little . . . solitude . . . a little peace . . . I'm not hiding from you that I'm at the end of my strength," he said, sitting down on the edge of her bed.

"No, you're not hiding it from me," she answered.

She laid a hand on Alain's brow, and she turned toward the light the young man's face where a pale moustache was growing. He sighed, turned away his unsteady eyes and succeeded in postponing the tumult of tears he was promising himself.

"If there aren't any sheets on my bed, mama, I'll cover myself up with anything . . ."

"There are sheets on your bed, my dear."

As she said that, he took his mother in his arms, kissed her blindly on her eyes, her cheeks, and her hair, buried his nose in her neck, stammered good night, and went out sniffling.

In the corridor he got hold of himself. He did not go immediately up the staircase; for the dying night and Saha were calling him outside. But he did not go far: the porch was enough. He sat down on a step in the shadow; and the hand he extended could feel Saha's fur, the fine hair of the whiskers, her cool nostrils.

She turned round and round on the same spot, according to the code of the caressing animal. She seemed very small to him, as light as a kitten and, because he was hungry, he thought she needed some food.

"We'll eat tomorrow . . . in a little while . . . dawn will soon be here."

Already she gave off the odor of mint, geranium, boxwood. He

551

was holding in his arms something trustful, perishable, something to be his for perhaps ten years more; and it hurt him when he thought of the brevity of such a great love.

"After you, I shall be at the mercy of anyone who wants me. . . . A woman . . . women. But never, never another cat."

A blackbird whistled four notes to which all the garden re-echoed, and then was silent again. But the sparrows had heard him and they answered. Over the lawn and the gay flower-beds ghosts of colors were being born. Alain made out a sullen white, a feeble red more sombre than black, a yellow ensnared in the surrounding green, a round yellow flower which presently turned more yellow; then showed its eyes and its full round face. . . . Overpowered by sleep, Alain stumbled to his room, threw off his clothes, turned down the made-up bed, and gave himself up completely to the fresh, fragrant sheets.

Lying on his back, one arm thrown out, the cat, motionless and absorbed against his shoulder, he was falling into the depths of sleep, when toward dawn a start brought him back to the swaying of awakened trees and the blessed scraping of the distant trolley cars.

"What's the matter with me? I want . . . oh yes . . . I would like to cry." He smiled as he fell back to sleep.

He slept feverishly, glutted with dreams. Two or three times he thought he was awake, and he was aware of the room where he was sleeping; but watching a winged eye fluttering about, each time he was deceived by the expression of the surly walls of his bedroom. "But, look here. I'm asleep! I'm asleep . . ."

"I'm asleep," he answered again to the crunching on the gravel. "Since I tell you that I'm asleep," he cried to two lagging steps which brushed by his door . . . The feet withdrew and the sleeper in his dream rejoiced. But under repeated solicitations the dream had come to an end, and Alain opened his eyes.

The sun which, according to the window-sill, was a May sun when he had gone away, had become an August sun and it was now no higher than the satin trunk of the tulip tree facing his room.

"How quickly summer has passed!" he said to himself. He got up, naked, looked around for something to cover him and found some pyjamas, too short, with tight sleeves, and an old faded bathrobe. It made him happy to put them on again. The window called him; but he came upon Camille's photograph, left behind on the bed-table. Carefully he examined the little unfaithful picture, lustrous, lighted up here, toned down there. "It's a better likeness than I had thought," he mused. "Why didn't I realize it? Four months ago I said, 'Oh, she's very different from that . . . not so hard.' But I was mistaken."

The long, smooth breeze blew through the trees like a murmuring brook. Dazzled, an aching hunger in the pit of his stomach, Alain let himself go. "How sweet it is! Like recovering from a sickness." As if to complete the illusion, there was a knock at the door and the moustached Basque maid entered, carrying a tray.

"But I might have eaten in the garden, Juliette." She shaped a kind of smile on her sallow lips.

"If I had thought . . . If Monsieur Alain would like me to take the tray downstairs . . ."

"No, no, I'm too hungry. Leave it there. Saha will come in through the window."

He called the cat, who leapt from some invisible retreat as though she had come to life at his call. She climbed along the vertical route of some vines and fell—she had forgotten her broken claws.

"Wait. I'm coming."

He took her in his arms and they ate heartily, she of milk and biscuits, he of bread and butter, honey and steaming coffee. A single rose adorned the handle of the honey-jar on one corner of the tray.

"That's not one of my mother's roses," Alain thought. It was a little, badly-shaped flower, stunted, such as grows hidden under low branches, and it had the pungent odor of a yellow rose. "That, that's a gift from the Basque girl."

Saha, happy, seemed to have grown fat since last night. Her ruff fluffed out, the four shimmering stripes between her ears well-marked, she sat and gazed at the garden with the eyes of a contented monarch.

"How easy it is, isn't it, Saha? At least for you . . ."

It was old Emile's turn now to come in. He was looking for Alain's shoes.

"There's one of the laces quite worn out. Monsieur Alain hasn't any other? That doesn't matter; I'll put in one of my own," he bleated affectionately.

"Decidedly, it's my gala day," Alain said to himself. That word jerked his mind back by contrast to everything that yesterday was mere daily routine—the morning dressing, getting off to the Amparat office; coming back; lunch with Camille . . .

"But I've nothing to put on," he cried.

The razor a little rusted, the egg-shaped cake of pink-tinted soap, the old tooth-brush—he recognized them in the bathroom and used them with the joy of a man who has been shipwrecked. But he was obliged to go downstairs in the too-short pyjamas, the Basque having carried off his clothes.

"Come, Saha . . . Saha . . ."

She walked ahead of him; he shuffled along awkwardly in his raffia sandals. He offered his shoulder to the soothing sun and partially closed the eyelids that had half-forgotten the green reflections on the lawn, the warm color which mounted from a mass of fleshy-headed amaranthus, from a clump of salvia bordered with heliotrope.

"Oh, the same, the same salvia!"

Alain had never seen that little heart-shaped bed anything but red, always bordered with heliotrope, and protected by an old cherry tree, which from time to time bore a few cherries in September.

"I've seen six . . . seven . . . seven green cherries!"

He was talking to the cat who, her eye vacant and golden, affected by the strong smell of the heliotrope, half-opened her mouth and showed the nauseous ecstasy of a wild animal under the power of violent perfumes.

She tasted a blade of grass in order to restore herself, listened to

554

voices, scraped her jaw on the tough stalks of clipped privets. But she did not give in to any exuberance, any irresponsible sport, and she walked augustly within that little silver halo which encircled her completely.

"Pushed off from a height of nine stories," Alain said as he looked at her. "Flung—or pushed . . . Perhaps she tried to defend herself —perhaps she ran away, only to be caught again, and thrown . . . murdered!"

By means of such conjecturing he was trying to keep his righteous anger burning within him and he did not succeed in doing it. "If I loved Camille really, deeply, what anger . . ." Around him shone his kingdom, like every kingdom, threatening. "My mother says that twenty years from now, no one will be able to keep homes, gardens like these. It's possible. I am willing to give them up. I don't want to permit in here the . . ."

The telephone ringing in the house stirred him. "What's the matter with me? Am I afraid? Camille's not so stupid as to telephone me. Give her credit for that; I've never seen any woman use the instrument more discreetly."

But he couldn't resist, and he ran as well as he could, dropping his sandals off, stumbling on the round pebbles, and calling out:

"Mama, who's telephoning?"

The heavy white bathrobe appeared on the veranda, and Alain was mortified that he had called.

"How I do love that big white bathrobe of yours, mama! Always the same, always just the same."

"My bathrobe thanks you very much," Mme. Amparat answered, smiling.

She prolonged Alain's expectation a moment or two.

"It was Monsieur Veuillet. It's half past nine. Have you forgotten the ways of the house?"

She ran her fingers through her son's hair, and buttoned up his outgrown pyjamas.

"There you are now—very pretty. You're not going to spend the rest of your life looking like a tramp, I suppose?"

Alain was grateful to her for putting these clever questions to him.

"You don't need to worry about that, mama. In a few moments I'm going to be busy about everything that . . ."

Very gently, Madame Amparat broke in upon the wide, vague gesture.

"This evening, where will you be?"

"Here," he said, and the tears rose to his eyes.

"Heavens, what a child!" she said, and he took up the word with the literalness of a Boy Scout.

"Perhaps you are right, mama. And so I would really like to come to a decision as to what I should do in order to put that childhood behind me."

"How? By a divorce? That's a door that makes a noise."

"But which lets in the air," he dared to reply, firmly.

"Wouldn't a separation . . . temporarily, a period of quiet . . . or a trip . . . wouldn't that have just as good results?"

He raised offended arms.

"But, my poor mama, you don't know . . . You're a hundred miles from imagining . . ."

He was going to tell everything, to reproduce the whole outrageous attack . . .

"Oh well . . . let me remain a hundred miles. These things do not concern me. Have a little . . . a little reserve, why don't you?" Mme. Amparat said quickly, and Alain took advantage of his error in discretion.

"Now, mama, there is still the annoying side, I mean the point of view of the family which is involved with the business side of the matter. In the eyes of the Malmert family my divorce would have not the slightest excuse, whatever Camille's responsibility may be . . . 'A bride of three months and a half?' . . . I can hear them from here."

"Where do you get the idea that there is a commercial side to the matter? You're not a business firm, are you, you and the little Malmert girl? A man and wife aren't a pair of business partners."

"I know that very well, mama. But still, if matters take the turn

I expect, it's an unpleasant period, that of formalities, interviews and . . . It's never so easy as they say it is—a divorce."

She listened quietly to her son, aware that certain events bear strange fruits and that, in the course of his life, a man has to be born again several times succored only by stumblings, bruises, dangers. . . .

"It's never simple to give up what one wishes to attach oneself to," Mme. Amparat said. "She's not so bad, that little Malmert . . . A little . . . coarse . . . a little lacking in good taste . . . No, not so bad. At least, that's the way I look at it. I don't impose it on you. We have time to think it over."

"I have taken that care," Alain said with peevish politeness. "And although for the moment I prefer to keep to myself a certain incident . . ."

Suddenly his face lit up with a smile, as with a childhood recaptured. Sitting up on her haunches, a spoon-shaped paw above a full watering-pot, Saha was fishing for drowning insects.

"Look at her, mama. Isn't she a wonder of a cat?"

"Yes," Mme. Amparat sighed. "And she's your delusion . . . your chimera."

He was always surprised when his mother used an unusual word. He greeted this one with a kiss, pressed on a hand early-aged, with coarse veins, and spotted with little brown moons which Juliette the Basque called dismally "spots of soil." When he heard the ringing of the bell at the wrought-iron gate, he straightened up.

"Hide," said Mme. Amparat. "We're right in the path of the tradespeople. Go get dressed . . . Don't you see that the little butcher boy will catch you decked out the way you are?"

But they both knew that the butcher's boy did not ring at the visitors' gate. And already Mme. Amparat turned her back, gathered up her bathrobe in her two hands and hastened up to the veranda. Behind the clipped wistaria Alain saw Juliette running in confusion, her black silk apron in the wind; and a shuffling of bedroom slippers over the gravel announced old Emile's flight. Alain cut across his path.

"But at least you opened the gate?"

"Yes, Monsieur Alain; the young woman is there in her car."

He lifted a frightened eye to the sky, squared his shoulders as if under the shock, and disappeared.

"Well, that's my idea of a panic. I would have liked to get dressed. . . . So, she has a new tailored suit . . ."

Camille had seen him and came directly toward him, without too much speed. In one of those difficult, almost ridiculous moments, bred of drama, he thought confusedly, "Perhaps she's coming to lunch."

Carefully and sparingly made up, armed with black artificial eyelashes, with beautiful parted lips, with sparkling teeth, she seemed, however, to lose her assurance when Alain advanced to meet her. For he approached without detaching himself from his protective atmosphere, walked on his native lawn under the magnificent coalition of the trees, and Camille looked at him with mendicant eyes.

"I beg your pardon. I look like a schoolboy shot up too fast. We didn't make an engagement for this morning, did we?"

"No. I brought you your big suitcase . . . full."

"But that wasn't necessary!" he cried. "I could have sent Emile for it today."

"Don't speak to me of Emile. I wanted to have him bring the suitcase to you but the old fool ran away as though I had a contagious disease. The suitcase is out there near the gate."

Blushing with humiliation, she bit the inside of her cheek.

"This begins well," Alain thought.

"I'm sorry. You know how Emile is. Listen," he decided, "let's go to the wistaria-covered summer-house. We'll be quieter there than indoors."

He regretted his choice immediately, for the summer-house, made of logs and furnished with wicker, had formerly protected them in their clandestine love-making.

"Wait a moment till I brush the twigs out of the way. You must be careful of that pretty costume . . . which I don't remember . . ."

"It's new," Camille said, in a tone of deep sorrow, as if she had said "It is dead."

She sat half-turned on her chair, and looked around her. Two rounded arches, one facing the other, were cut in the leafy summer-house. Alain recalled one of Camille's confessions: "You have no idea how your beautiful garden frightened me. I used to come here like the little girl from the village who comes to play in the park with the lord of the manor's son. And still . . ." With one word she had spoiled everything, the last word that "and still," which re-called the prosperity of the Malmets—Washing Machines—com-pared to the waning house of Amparat . . .

He noticed that Camille kept her gloves on. "That, that is a precaution that works to her disadvantage. Without those gloves perhaps I would not have thought of her hands, of what they have done. . . . Ah, there at last comes a little bit of anger," he said to himself, aware of the beating of his heart. "I certainly took my time about it."

"Well," said Camille, in a melancholy tone, "well, what are we going to do? Perhaps you've not yet thought it out . . ."

"Yes," he answered.

"Ah!"

"Yes. I cannot go back."

"I understand, of course, that there's no question today . . ."

"I do not wish to go back."

"At all? Never?"

He shrugged his shoulders.

"What does that mean, never? I do not want to go back. Not now. I do not want to."

Trying to discern the false from the true, she watched carefully to detect purposed irritation from genuine emotion. He gave her back suspicion for suspicion. "She's pretty this morning. She is a little bit the pretty shopgirl. She's at a disadvantage in all this green background. We've already exchanged not a few useless words . . ."

In the distance, through one of the rounded openings, Camille

could see, on one of the façades of the house, evidences of the alterations: a new window, blinds freshly painted. Bravely she hurled
herself in front of the danger.

"And if I had said nothing yesterday," she suggested abruptly,
"if I had known nothing?"

"Fine female notion," he sneered. "It does you honor."

"Oh," she said, shaking her head, "honor, honor . . . That
wouldn't be the first time the happiness of a couple depended on
something that couldn't be acknowledged, or something not acknowledged. But I have the idea that in covering up that affair I
would only have stepped back in order to leap further. I did not
think you . . . How shall I say it?"

She was searching for the word, trying to express it by gestures,
knotting her hands one into the other. "She's making a mistake to
draw attention to her hands," Alain thought mercilessly, "those
hands that have murdered . . ."

"I mean, that you are so little on my side," Camille said. "Isn't
that true?"

Surprised, he mentally decided that she was not wrong. He did
not answer, and Camille insisted in a plaintive tone he knew very
well:

"Speak. Don't be hard; say something."

"But, good God," he burst out, "that's not the point. The only
thing that can possibly interest me about you is to know if you
are sorry for what you have done; if it is impossible for you not to
think of it . . . if you are sick with thinking about it. Remorse, in
other words, remorse! There is such a thing as *remorse*."

He rose, excited, walked about the summer-house, wiping his
forehead on his sleeve as he talked.

"Ah," said Camille, in a penitent, conciliatory tone, "but of course.
I have wished a thousand times that I had not done it. I must have
been out of my mind . . ."

"You lie," he cried, muffling his voice. "The only thing you
regret is that your attempt failed. One has only to listen to you talk,
to see you there with your little hat one side of your head, your

gloves, your new tailored suit—everything you have put on in order to attract me. . . . If it were genuine, your remorse, I would see it in your face, I would feel it . . ."

He cried low, grating out his words, and was no longer quite master of the anger he had incited in himself. The worn material of his pyjamas slit at the elbow; he tore out what remained of the sleeve and tossed it on the hedge.

At first Camille had eyes only for the gesticulating bare arm, extraordinarily white against the dark mass of the wistaria.

He put his hand over his eyes as if to force himself to speak lower.

"A little, innocent animal as blue as the best dreams, a little soul . . . Faithful, capable of dying exquisitely if she loses what she loves . . . That is what you held in your hands, above empty space, and you opened your hands . . . You are a monster! I do not want to live with a monster!"

He uncovered his moist face, bent nearer to Camille, trying as he did so to find words strong enough to crush her. Her breath came short, her glance went from his naked arm to his face not less white, in which no blood seemed to flow.

"An animal," she cried angrily. "You are sacrificing me for an animal! After all, I'm your wife. You are leaving me for the sake of an animal!"

"An animal? Yes, an animal!"

Apparently calm, he withdrew behind a mysterious and initiated smile. "I am happy to say that Saha is an animal . . . If she really is one, what is there superior to that animal and how could I make Camille understand it? She makes me laugh—that little, thorough-going criminal, quite angry and smug, who claims to know what an animal is . . ." He did not go on with his sneering; Camille's voice called him back.

"You're the one that's the monster."

"I beg your pardon?"

"Yes, you're the monster. Unfortunately, I don't know how to explain why. But I assure you I'm not mistaken. I wanted to make away with Saha. It is not a very admirable story. But to kill what troubles her, or makes her suffer, is a woman's first thought, especially if she's a jealous woman. That's normal. What's unnatural, what's monstrous is you, it's . . ."

She was trying make herself understood and at the same time point out to Alain the incidental symptoms of a slight disorder: the torn-out sleeve; the trembling, cruel mouth; the cheek where the blood no longer flowed; the wild tuft of tempestuous blond hair. . . . He did not protest, scorning any self-defense; he looked like a man who has lost his way in a fruitless search.

"If out of jealousy I had killed or wanted to kill a woman, you would probably forgive me. But it is against the cat I lifted my hand; so that is what I pay for. And you want me not to think that you are a monster!"

"Did I say that's what I want?" he broke in arrogantly.

She looked at him with eyes aghast and made a gesture of utter helplessness. And his own eyes, forbidding and aloof, followed every slightest stir of the young hand, gloved and condemned.

"Now, as for the future, what's to be done? What's going to happen to us, Alain?"

Unable to endure more, he almost groaned, and cried:

"We separate, we keep quiet, we sleep, we breathe, one without the other. I go away, very far away. Under this cherry tree, for instance. Under the wings of the black and white magpies or in the peacock's tail of the sprinkling hose . . . Or maybe in my cold bedroom. Under the protection of a little gold dollar, of a handful of souvenirs, and of a Chartreuse cat . . ."

He got hold of himself, and he lied without a quiver.

"But nothing for the moment. It's too early to come to a decision . . . We shall see later on . . ."

This last attempt at restraint and friendliness used him up. He stumbled for the first few steps when he rose to accompany Camille, who consented with an eager hope to that shadowy reconciliation.

"That's true; yes, it is too soon. A little later on . . . Stay here. I don't want to have you come with me to the gate. With your torn sleeve, one would think we had been beating each other. . . . Listen, I may go to Ploumanach to get a little swimming with Patrick's brother and sister-in-law . . . because the idea of living with my family at this time . . ."

"Go in the roadster," Alain suggested.

She flushed, as she thanked him too profusely.

"I'll give it back to you, you know, when I come back to Paris. You may need it. Don't hesitate to ask me for it . . . But I'll let you know when I go and when I return . . ."

"Already she's beginning to make plans; already she casts on the thread of the woof; already she decides on another pattern, new stiches; starts in to weave again. It's terrible. Is that what my mother esteems in her? Perhaps, as a matter of fact, it is very fine. I no longer feel myself capable of understanding her any more than making amends to her. How easily she takes everything that to me is unendurable! If only she goes away now, goes away now . . ."

She left, taking care not to offer him her hand. But under an arch of clipped vines she risked, to no purpose, brushing him lightly with her now beautiful breasts. Alone, he sank into a wide armchair; and miraculously the cat sprang up on the wicker table besides him.

A bend in the path, a breach in the shrubbery allowed Camille to catch one more glimpse of Alain and the cat. She stopped short, made a sudden turn as though to retrace her steps. But she hesitated only a moment; then went on more quickly. For if Saha, on the watch, was following Camille's departure with the expression of a human being, Alain, half-reclining, was listlessly toying in the deep hollow of his hand with the rough green chestnuts of early August.

The Indulgent Husband

1

THERE certainly is something wrong with our marriage. Renaud doesn't realize it yet—how could he?

We've been home six weeks. It's all over now, that indolent, feverish roaming about which for more than a year led us aimlessly from Rue de Bassano to Montigny, from Montigny to Bayreuth and from there to a village in Baden which—to Renaud's great delight—I at first thought was called Forellen-Fischerei because of a huge sign on the river bank advertising the trout-fishing—also because I don't know German.

Last winter, clinging to Renaud's arm, I gazed with a hostile eye at the Mediterranean ruffled by a chilly breeze and gleaming under its harsh sun. That artificial southland was spoiled for me by the swarms of parasols and hats and faces, and especially by our constantly running into some friend of Renaud's—a dozen friends—whole families of them, for whom he obtained free passes, and ladies who invited him to dinner. That incorrigible man goes out of his way to please everybody and particularly the people he knows the least—"because," he explains with irresistible impertinence, "it isn't worth while ruining your disposition for your real friends, since you know you can count on them anyway."

My naïve and restless nature never could see anything in this wintering on the Riviera—lace gowns shivering under fur wraps.

Then, too, my excessive demands on Renaud—and his on me—set my nerves on edge and made it hard for me to accept calmly the rough spots along the road. So at last, after being tossed about and swept along in a half-painful, half-delicious state of physical intoxication and semi-delirium, I pleaded for mercy and rest and for some place to settle down for awhile.

So here I am, home again. What more do I want? Why is it I am not satisfied?

Let me try to straighten out this jumble of recollections, still very recent and yet already so far in the past.

2

WHAT a bizarre spectacle my wedding was! A three weeks' engagement, Renaud constantly near me—and I madly in love with him!—his disturbing glances and the still more disturbing, and yet restrained, caresses of his hands, and those lips of his always seeking out some part of me—well, by the time that Thursday arrived, I had the strained look of a lovesick cat.

I never could understand how Renaud was able to hold himself in check and show such self-control during those weeks! I would gladly have given myself to him, had he been willing—and he knew it. But he safeguarded his happiness—and mine, too, perhaps—

with the finesse of an epicure and held us to a line of conduct that was exhaustingly proper.

Many a time, aroused by a kiss that he broke off sooner than was even decent, I would look at him with an exasperated air, as if to say, "Honestly, what's the difference whether it's now or a week from now? What's the use getting me all worked up and tiring me out this way?"

But Renaud had no mercy on either of us and forced me to stay as I was till the day of our slapdash wedding.

Thoroughly disgusted with the idea of having to inform His Honor the Mayor and His Reverence the priest that I had decided to live with Renaud, I refused to help my father or anybody in any way whatsoever. Renaud tried with patient tact to persuade me, and Papa was unusually attentive, exasperated and blustering.

Only Mélie, blissfully happy to witness the successful termination of a love affair, sang and daydreamed as she looked out on the gloomy little courtyard. Fanchette, with Snail, "more beautiful than a son of Phtah," toddling after her, sniffed at the open packages, the new dressgoods and the long gloves and kneaded my veil of white tulle with her forepaws.

Renaud brought me this pear-shaped ruby hanging about my neck on its slender golden thread, two days before our marriage. How well I remember! Fascinated by its wine-like transparency, I held it up to the light, my free hand on Renaud's shoulder as he knelt before me.

"You squint just like Fanchette when she is watching a fly," he said with a laugh.

Without replying, I quickly slipped the jewel into my mouth—"because I'm sure it will melt with a sharp, raspberry-like flavor," I explained.

Renaud was nonplussed by this peculiar conception of a precious stone. The next day he brought me a box of candy and I must confess that I got just as much pleasure out of that.

On the morning of the great day, I woke cross and grumbling, vexed at the thought of the town hall and the church, at my scalding hot cup of chocolate and the weight of my long-trained wedding gown, at Mélie, already in violet cashmere at seven o'clock in the morning ("Ah, my dear, such a grand time as you're going to have!") and at the invited guests—Renaud's witnesses, Maugis and Robert Parville, Aunt Cœur in her gown of Chantilly lace, Marcel—whom his father had forgiven, just to tease him and poke fun at him, I think—and my witnesses, Monsieur Maria and a muchly decorated and very untidy malacologist whose name I never knew. Papa, absentminded and unperturbed, regarded this strange ending to my passionate martyrdom as the most natural thing in the world.

And I, ready long ahead of time, with my bridal veil awry—bobbed hair isn't always convenient—and my complexion a bit yellowish against my white dress, watched Fanchette in her basket, having her belly kneaded by her tiger-striped offspring, and thought to myself:

"This wedding is a disgusting nuisance! The ideal way would have been to have him come here and we'd have dinner together, just the two of us, and shut ourselves up in this little room where I have dreamed of him in my sleep—and also when I couldn't sleep. And then we'd—only my single bed would be too small."

The arrival of Renaud, with a slight touch of nervousness in his manner, only plunged me deeper into these reflections. However, at the earnest insistence of Monsieur Maria, who was worried sick, I had to go and scold Papa and hurry him up.

My estimable parent, with an absent-mindedness worthy of himself and of the unusual occasion, had completely forgotten that I was to be married that day. We found him in his dressing-gown, solemnly smoking his pipe—at a quarter of twelve! His reception of poor distracted Maria was a classic:

"Come on, Maria, let's get down to work! You're devilish late, considering what a tough chapter we have to tackle today. Hello! what struck you to climb into a dress suit? You look like a waiter."

"But, my dear man—Mademoiselle Claudine's wedding—we're all waiting for you."

"I'll be damned!" ejaculated Papa, looking at his watch as if it were a calendar. "Are you sure it's today? You go on ahead and tell them to begin without me."

It seemed to me as if at least fifty people were crowded into that small room, although there were only Robert Parville, as flustered as a lost poodle because he wasn't trotting along at the heels of that Lizery woman; Maugis, with a roguish air of affected solemnity; Monsieur Maria, as pale as a ghost; Aunt Cœur, stiff and sour-faced; Marcel, looking as solemn as an owl. Hidden behind my veil, I could almost feel my rasped nerves giving way.

From that point on, it seemed to me like one of those indistinct, jumbled dreams in which your feet seem to be tied together. I remember a pink and violet streak of light from the stained glass falling across my white gloves, and my nervous laugh in the vestry when Papa wanted to sign a second time because his first signature wasn't "vigorous" enough to suit him. I had a suffocating impression of unreality. Even Renaud seemed to be far off and without substance.

When we got back to the house, Renaud was troubled by my drawn, unhappy face and questioned me anxiously. I shook my head and replied, "I don't feel any more married than I did this morning. Do you?"

His moustache twitched. I blushed and shrugged my shoulders.

I wanted to get out of my ridiculous wedding gown, so they all left the room except my darling Fanchette, who recognized me more easily in a pink lawn blouse and white serge skirt.

"How can I leave you behind, Fanchette? It's the first time I've done it. But I've got to. I can't drag you around in railroad trains with that family of yours."

I felt a slight desire to cry, an indefinable unhappiness, a cramped soreness around the ribs. Oh, why doesn't my sweetheart come and take me quickly and put an end to this silly uneasiness, which is neither fear nor modesty? How late it gets dark in July! This dazzling white sun is making my head burst.

Early in the evening my husband—my husband!—took me away. The sound of the rubber-tired wheels did not drown the beating of my heart. I clenched my teeth so tight that even his kiss could not pry them apart. . . .

Under the shaded electric light of the reading lamps at this Rue de Bassano apartment (which he had never allowed me to visit), I was barely conscious of what he calls its too close resemblance to some eighteenth-century engraving. I breathed deep, intoxicating draughts of that odor of pale tobacco and lily of the valley—with a suggestion of Russia leather, too—which pervades Renaud's clothing and his long moustache.

It seems as if it were only a few minutes ago. I can see it all before me.

So the time has now come, has it? What do we do? The thought of Luce flashed through my mind. I automatically took off my hat.

I clasped my beloved's hand to give myself courage and looked at him. He removed his hat and gloves pell-mell and stretched his arms, leaning backward a little and drawing a deep, quivering breath.

(I love his handsome dark eyes, his aquiline nose and his once golden hair, combed by a skilful breeze.)

I went over to him, but he teasingly slipped away to the other side of the room and stood there looking at me.

Losing the last vestige of my fine courage, I clasped my hands and pleaded, "Please don't keep me waiting so!"

Little did I realize how comical this sounded. Renaud sat down. "Come here, Claudine."

As I sat on his lap, he noticed my rapid breathing and asked tenderly, "Are you all mine, dear?"

"I was yours long ago. You know it."

"And you aren't afraid, dearest?"

"Not at all. And anyhow, I know all about it."

"All about what?"

I lay back in his arms and he leaned over my mouth. Defenseless, I let him drink in my kisses. I felt like crying—or at least it seemed as if I did.

"You know all about it, you dear little girl, and still you're not afraid?"

"No!" I cried out, as I clung desperately to him, my arms about his neck.

With one hand he started unhooking my blouse. I leaped to my feet,

"No, no! I'll do it myself!"

Why did I say that? I had no reason—just a last outburst of my impulsive nature, I suppose. I would have walked right into his arms completely nude, but I did not want him to undress me.

With clumsy haste I undid my clothes and scattered them right and left, kicking off my shoes, picking up my slip with my toes and tossing my girdle aside without looking at Renaud, who was sitting right in front of me.

Finally I had nothing on but my chemise. "There now!" I boldly exclaimed as I instinctively rubbed the marks left by the girdle around my waist.

Renaud never budged. He merely leaned forward, grasping the arms of his chair and watching me closely. Becoming panicstricken under his gaze, I lost all my courage and ran and threw myself on the bed without stopping to turn down the covers.

Renaud quickly joined me there and seized me so ardently that I could feel his muscles quiver. With all his clothes on—good God, why is he so slow about undressing!—he clasped me firmly, his body not touching mine, and held me with his hands and his kisses from my first spasm of resistance until my desperate yielding, the final shameless moan of voluptuous delight which my pride sought in in vain to repress.

It was not until afterwards that he, too, stripped off his clothes, enjoying mercilessly my amazement over myself and my mortification. But he asked nothing further of me except to be allowed to

573

caress me sufficiently to make me fall asleep toward morning on the bed which we had not stopped to turn down.

Later on I was grateful to him—very grateful, indeed—for his resolute self-denial, his long-sustained patience. I made it up to him as soon as I became less reserved and more curious to learn, and even eager to see that swooning expression come over his eyes, just as he, tense with desire, had often watched for it in mine.

For a long time I was afraid (to tell the truth, I still am somewhat) of—how can I express it?—I think it is called "marital relations." Renaud is so robust.

Except for that, everything is all right—too much so, in fact. It is delicious at first not to know and then gradually to discover so many reasons for laughing nervously, even crying out and uttering inarticulate, ecstatic sounds, your whole body tense even to the tips of your toes.

The only proof of affection I have never been able to give my husband has been to call him endearing names. I never do at any time, neither when I entreat his embrace nor when I yield to his advances, nor even when the exquisite torture of waiting for him to come to me makes me talk brokenly in a voice unlike my own.

Indeed, is there not proof of affection in the very fact that I do not address him with the easy familiarity I use with other people?

He is strikingly beautiful—take my word for it! His smooth, tawny skin rubs so softly against mine! His strong arms have an almost womanly roundness at the shoulder where I love to rest my head night and morning for hours at a time.

And his silvery white hair, his finely shaped knees, his dear chest, rising and falling slowly as he breathes, all that huge body of his where I have made so many rapturous discoveries!

I often say to him in all sincerity, "How beautiful you are!" And he clasps me close to him and answers, "But Claudine, Claudine, I am old!" And a shadow of regret comes over his eyes, so poignant that I look at him in puzzled astonishment.

"Ah, Claudine, had I known you ten years ago!"

"You would have known also the inside of a prison cell. And

besides, at that time you were only a lad, a wicked young rascal making women cry, while I was a—"

"But you would never have met Luce."

"Have you an idea I miss her?"

"Well, no, not just at this moment. Don't close your eyes, please! I won't let you! Their every shade of expression belongs to me!"

"As does all of me!"

All of me? No, and that's just where the trouble lies.

I have shut my eyes to this as long as I could, hoping with all my heart that Renaud would bend my will to his, that his persistence would curb my rebellious reactions—in short, that he would prove to have a soul as domineering as his glances, accustomed to give orders and win compliance.

But as for Renaud's will, Renaud's persistence—. He is like a flame, hot, supple and unsubstantial, which envelops me but does not overpower me. Alas, is Claudine doomed forever to remain mistress of herself?

And yet he has skilfully won control over my slender, golden-tinted body, this skin of mine which clings to the muscles underneath and is so firm to the touch, my girlish head with its bobbed hair. Oh, why did they have to deceive me with false hopes, those masterful eyes, that determined nose, that fine, close-shaven chin of which he is as vain as a woman?

I am gentle and submissive with him. I docilely bend my head to let him kiss the back of my neck. I ask for nothing and avoid any dispute, wisely fearing that he may give in to me at once and lean over to kiss me in too ready acquiescence.

Alas, it is only in love-making that he acts with determination.

(I admit that even that is a good deal.)

I told him all about Luce—yes, every last detail—almost hoping he would frown and become exasperated and press me with angry questions. But no, nothing of the kind! In fact, quite the contrary. He did press me with questions, but not angry ones.

I cut the story short because the thought of Renaud's son Marcel came to me and the irritating recollection of the cross-questioning with which that young fellow used to harass me. But this was not because of any uneasiness as to the effect on Renaud for, even if I have not found a master in him, I have found a true friend and ally.

To all this fine-spun web of emotions Papa, scornful of the psychological melodramatics of his hairsplitting, analytical daughter who likes to pretend she is a very complex personality, would reply, "What of it? A flea can ride a horse and not fall off."

That wonderful father of mine! Since my marriage I have not thought of him often enough, nor of Fanchette. But Renaud has been making love to me too actively during all these months, taking me here and there, intoxicating me with scenery, bewildering me with ceaseless moving about, with strange skies and unknown cities. Little understanding his Claudine, he often smiled with surprise to see me more absorbed in a landscape than in a painting, more enthusiastic over a tree than a museum, more thrilled by a brook than a precious jewel.

He had much to teach me and I have learned much.

The ecstasy of love came upon me suddenly, like a blinding, almost sombre miracle. When Renaud, troubled at seeing me grave and motionless, plied me with questions, I blushed and answered, without looking at him, "I couldn't explain it to you."

And I had to try without words to make it clear to that redoubtable questioner who never tires of studying me closely and takes delight in watching the various shades of embarrassment come over my face.

Renaud's interest in the physical side of love—and this, I realize, is what prevents our complete union—seems to be a compound of normal desire, sexual perversity, light-hearted curiosity and libertine insistence. The climax comes to him joyously, easily and mercifully, whereas it prostrates me, plunges me into a mysterious abyss of despair which I seek and dread at the same time. Renaud is already smiling again, a little out of breath and his grasp of me relaxed, while I am still—despite his efforts—hiding my face in my hands, my eyes big with fright and my mouth quivering in ecstasy. It is only some time later that I seek refuge on his comforting shoulder and complain to my friend of the too precious suffering my lover caused me.

Sometimes I try to tell myself that love is perhaps too new and strange to me, while it has lost some of its bitterness for Renaud. But I doubt if this explains it. We shall never agree on this subject—aside from the deep affection which holds us together.

At a restaurant the other evening Renaud smiled at a woman dining there alone who seemed only too glad to turn her slender, dark face and heavily made up eyes in his direction.

"Do you know her?" I asked.

"Who? Oh, that woman? No, dear. But what a handsome profile she has! Don't you think so?"

"Is that the only reason you are staring at her?"

"Most assuredly, little girl. I hope that doesn't shock you."

"No-o. But—I don't like to have her smile at you."

"Please, Claudine," he entreated, his swarthy face inclined toward me, "let me still believe that people can look at your old husband without repugnance. You don't know how much he is in need of self-confidence! When the day comes that the women no longer pay any attention to me at all," he added, with a toss of his head, "there'll be nothing left for me but to—"

"But why do you care about the other women since I shall love you forever?"

"Ssh! Claudine," he adroitly broke in, "may Heaven preserve me from seeing you turn into an exceptional and abnormal freak."

There you have it! He lumps me in with women in general. Do I say "men" when referring to him? Oh, I know, the habit of living openly in adulterous or illegitimate unions leaves its mark on a man's character and causes him to worry about things a nineteen-year-old bride knows nothing about.

I could not refrain from saying spitefully, "So it's from you that Marcel inherited his character of a flirtatious young girl?"

"Then you don't love my weaknesses, Claudine?" he asked somewhat sadly. "To tell the truth, I don't see whom else he could resemble. But you will admit that this flirtatiousness is not as perverted in me as it is in him."

How quickly he was once more gay and lighthearted! If he had answered sharply, knitting his handsome eyebrows, soft as the velvety lining of a ripe chestnut burr, "That will do, Claudine— leave Marcel out of this," it seems to me a great joy would have come over me, a beginning of that timid respect for Renaud which will not—cannot—come to me.

Whether rightly or wrongly, I need to respect and even somewhat to fear the man I love. Until my marriage, I was as ignorant of fear as I was of love and I should have liked the former to come to me at the same time as the latter.

Memories of the past fifteen months float about in my mind like particles of dust in a ray of sunlight falling across a dark room. One after the other, they come within the streak of light, glitter there for an instant—while I smile or pout at them—and then disappear into the darkness again.

On our return to France three months ago, I had a desire to see Montigny once more. But to tell that story properly, I must get hold of it at the beginning, as Luce puts it.

A year and a half ago, Mélie made haste to spread abroad in Montigny the news of my approaching marriage to "a very fine man, somewhat advanced in years but still all there."

Papa sent out some wedding announcements at random, one of them to the carpenter Danjeau (!) "because he tied up my boxes of books so well." And I sent two, addressed in my most carefully formed handwriting, to Mademoiselle Sergent and her disgusting little Aimée. Which resulted in my receiving a rather surprising letter.

"My dear child," Mademoiselle Sergent wrote, "I am sincerely pleased" (steady now, Claudine, there's something coming) "that you are making a marriage based on friendship rather than love" (how brutally frank one can be in French!) "which will offer you a safe shelter from your somewhat dangerous spirit of independence. Do not forget that the school expects you to pay us a visit if, as I hope, you come back to see once more a region which may well have a hold on your heart because of past memories."

This closing touch of sarcasm fell flat against the all-embracing indulgent mood which I was in at the time. I felt only amused surprise and a desire to see Montigny again—oh, woods which so enchanted me!—this time through more melancholy and less rebellious eyes.

So last September, as we were returning from Germany by way of Switzerland, I begged Renaud to do me the favor to stop off with me just for one day in the heart of the Fresnois country at the mediocre Montigny inn kept by Lange in Clocktower Square.

He consented at once, as he always does.

I can live those days all over again by merely closing my eyes for a minute.

3

As the local train ambled hesitatingly across the green, rolling country, I thrilled at the familiar names of the deserted little railway stations. Good heavens! Blégeau and Saint-Farcy and then we'll be at Montigny. I'll see the crumbling tower once more!

All excited, my legs a-tingle with nervous tension, I stood looking out of the car window, holding tight to the cloth strap on each side. Renaud watched me for a while, his travelling cap pulled down over his eyes, and then came over beside me.

"You dear little bird! Are you feeling a thrill as you get near the old, familiar nest? . . . Come, answer me, Claudine! I'm jealous. I forbid you to be tense and silent anywhere except in my arms."

Reassuring him with a smile, I continued to scan closely the sky-line of the shifting, disappearing hills, with their dense cloak of woods.

"Ah!"

With outstretched hand I point to the tower, its weather-worn, reddish stone thickly covered with ivy, and to the village, which seems to be gradually slipping down from the tower into the valley below. The scene grips my heart so strongly and so tenderly that I lean my head on Renaud's shoulder.

Oh, how was I ever able to tear myself away from that crumbling tower and the clumps of roundtopped trees? And am I to feast my eyes on them only to leave them once again?

Clasping my arms around my sweetheart's neck, I seek to find in him now my inspiration and my reason for living. He must enthrall and absorb me. This is what I hope—what I demand.

The crossing-tender's pink cottage passed by quickly, then the freight station—I recognized the freight-handler. We jumped out on the platform, but long after Renaud had put our luggage into the only bus, I was still standing there, silently counting the humps and hollows and other familiar details of the beloved horizon, which looked smaller than I had remembered it.

Yes! away up there is the forest of Fredonnes which adjoins the Vallées woods. And the road to Vrimes, winding like a serpent of yellow sand, how narrow it is! No longer will it lead me to the home of my darling Claire, my foster sister.

Oh! they've cut down the Corbeaux woods without asking my consent! Its flesh stands out raw and bare. But what a joy to see Quail Mountain again, which wraps itself in an iridescent bluish haze on sunny days but stands out clear-cut and close at hand in rainy weather! It abounds in fossil shells, purplish thistles and un-gracious, sap-less flowers, and is the haunt of tiny butterflies with pearl-blue wings and others spotted orchid-like with orange-colored crescents and slow-flying moths of a dull, velvety gold.

"Hello there, Claudine! Isn't it about time we climbed aboard this sea-going hack?" Renaud called out, amused at my enraptured obliviousness.

I joined him in the omnibus. Nothing had been changed. Papa Racalin, as drunk as ever—immutably drunk—drove his creaking vehicle zigzag up the street, sure of himself and scornful of everyone else.

I scanned the hedges and every turn in the road, prepared to make a protest if they had touched "my country." I said nothing, not a word, until we reached the hovels at the beginning of the steep climb. There I exclaimed, "Why, the cats can't go and sleep in Bardin's hay-loft any longer—there's a new door on the barn!"

"Upon my word, you're right!" Renaud echoed, as if deeply moved. "That brute of a Bardin has gone and had a new door put on."

My silent mood gave way to merriment and a flood of foolish prattle.

"Look, Renaud, look quick! We're coming to the gate of the château. Nobody lives there any more. We'll go and visit the tower . . . Oh, there's Granny Sainte-Albe on her doorstep! I'm sure she caught sight of me. Now she'll go and tell all the neighbors . . . Quick! turn around this way! Those two trees sticking up over Mother Adolphe's roof—those are the big pine-trees in my garden— my pine-trees. They haven't grown a bit—that's fine! Who's that girl? I never saw her before."

The stern tone in which I said that was so comical, it seems, that Renaud broke into a hearty laugh, showing his square, white teeth. But it isn't all going to be so funny! We shall have to spend the night at Lange's and it may well be that my husband won't laugh so loud when we get up to the gloomy inn . . .

Nothing of the kind! The room seemed to him endurable, in spite of the tent-like bed curtains, the microscopic wash-basin and the coarse, grayish sheets—very clean, however, thank Heaven!

581

Stimulated by the humble surroundings and also by the many suggestions of my childhood at Montigny, Renaud seized me from behind and started to draw me over toward the—but no, the time would fly by too quickly!

"Renaud, dear, please don't! It's six o'clock. I beg you, let's go to the school and surprise Mademoiselle before dinner."

"Alas," he sighed reluctantly. "Here I succeed in marrying this proud little creature and she throws me over for a village of 1,847 inhabitants!"

After a hasty brushing of my short hair, made light and fluffy by the dry air, and an anxious look in the mirror to see if I had aged much in a year and a half, we were outside in Clocktower Square, which slopes so steeply that on market days many a huckster's stall, unable to keep its balance, capsizes and goes tumbling down hill with a big clatter.

Thanks to my companion and to my short hair (with an envious twinge I recall the long, reddish-chestnut ringlets that used to dangle down my back) no one recognizes me and I can stare as much as I like.

"Oh, Renaud, just fancy! That woman with a baby in her arms is Célénie Nauphely!"

"The girl who used to relieve her sister's breasts of surplus milk?"

"Precisely. And now it's her turn to be relieved. Can you beat it? It's disgusting!"

"Why disgusting?"

"Oh, I don't know . . . Say, they still have the same peppermint candies in little Chou's shop. Perhaps she doesn't sell any more since Luce left."

Grand Street—three yards wide—is so steep that Renaud asks me where one can buy an alpenstock. But Claudine dances down it, her hat over one eye, pulling Renaud along by his little finger. As these two strangers go by, familiar and none-too-friendly faces appear in the doorways. I can call the name of each one and check off the list of its wrinkles and blemishes.

"I feel as if I were living in a picture by Huard," Renaud declares.

And an exaggerated Huard, at that. I did not remember that the whole village was on such a steep incline, or that the streets were so roughly paved and Papa Sandrée's hunting jacket so warlike. Old Grandpa Lourd was already senile, it is true, but was he quite so grinning and gelatinous? At Bel-Air corner I stopped and laughed out loud.

"Good Lord! there's Madame Armand with her hair still done up in curl papers! She puts them on at night on going to bed and forgets to take them off in the morning, so why should she bother? —it's so late now, she keeps them on for the next night, too, and it's the same thing all over again the following day. I've never seen her without them, twisted like worms across her oily forehead.

"And here, Renaud, where these three streets come together, I marvelled for ten years at a remarkable man named Hébert, who was mayor of Montigny although it was only with difficulty he could write his name. He used to attend faithfully the sessions of the municipal council, where, shaking his handsome head—the red face beneath its white, hemp-like locks suggesting some historic figure of the French Revolution—he would deliver orations that have become famous. For example: 'Be we goin' ter curb and gutter Rue des Fours-Banaux, or be we not? Das ist die Frage, as they say in German.'

"When the council was not in session, he would stand at the cross-roads, purple-faced in winter, red in summer, and watch—what? Nothing at all. That was his sole occupation. He died of it.

"Look! See that carriage-house with the two doors? They keep the fire engine and the hearse in there. Now admit that, even if you are a specialist in diplomacy, you couldn't have thought up a more appropriate combination."

My sweetheart's indulgent laugh sounds a bit weary. Am I too much of a chatterbox for him? No, it is merely that he is wistfully jealous at seeing me so absorbed in the past.

At the foot of the incline the street suddenly widens out into an unevenly paved square. Thirty paces in front of us, behind its iron-gray gates, the huge, slate-capped school rises, its white walls only the least bit soiled by three winters and four summers.

"Is that the military barracks, Claudine?"

"Why no! that's the school!"

"The poor kids!"

"Why 'poor kids'? I assure you we had a good time there."

"You would, of course, you limb of Satan! But how about the others? . . . Are we going in? May the prisoners receive visitors at any hour of the day?"

"Where did you grow up, Renaud? Don't you know this is the summer vacation?"

"Really! And so you brought me here to see an empty jail? Is that the bait you've been jumping for like a hungry trout?"

"You're a poor fish yourself," I retorted, a year of travel having enriched my vocabulary with an assortment of thoroughly up-to-date invectives.

"Look out or I won't yet you have any dessert!"

"Look out yourself or I won't let you have something else you like even better."

I suddenly became serious and stopped talking as I felt the latch of the gate resist my hand just as it used to do in days gone by.

At the pump in the courtyard the same rusty little cup hangs on its chain. The walls, white and chalky a couple of years ago, have been scratched up to shoulder-height as if by thousands of finger-nails exasperated by restraint. During the vacation sickly tufts of grass had pushed their way between the bricks of the gutter.

Not a soul in sight.

With Renaud meekly following me, I go up the six steps of the little stairway, open a glass door and walk down the echoing, stone-paved hallway connecting the upper grades with the three lower classes. A strange emotion comes over me as I catch the cool rank odor of superficial cleaning, ink, chalk dust, blackboards washed with dirty sponges. I half expect to see Luce's little figure in black pinafore come nimbly around the corner of the hall in noiseless slippers and cling to my skirts, pleading and affectionate . . .

584

Starting suddenly, I feel my cheeks quiver. A black-aproned little figure in nimble, noiseless slippers opens part way the door of the upper classroom . . . But no, it isn't Luce. An unfamiliar little face with limpid eyes stares at me without embarrassment.

Recovering my composure and feeling somewhat at home there, I walk toward her and ask where "Mmmzelle" is.

"I don't know, madame—mademoiselle, I mean. Upstairs, I suppose."

"All right. Many thanks. But—aren't you having any vacation?"

"Some of us stay at Montigny all summer."

She is very, very pretty, this little pupil who is spending her summer vacation at Montigny. Her chestnut-brown braid falling down over her black pinafore, she hangs her head and hides an adorable rosebud mouth and golden-brown eyes, beautiful but tranquil, with the expression of a young doe gazing at a passing automobile.

A harsh voice (how familiar it sounds!) bursts upon us from the stairway.

"Apple, whom are you talking to?"

"There's somebody here, mmmzelle," the naïve little girl calls out as she goes running up the stairs leading to the dormitories and the individual rooms.

As I turned to smile significantly at Renaud, I could see by his expression that he was getting interested.

"Did you hear that, Claudine? 'Apple'! One could eat her up with a name like that! It's lucky I'm an old man past the age for such things!"

"Keep quiet, you hardened criminal! Somebody's coming!"

A few hurried whispered words, a firm step on the stairway, and Mademoiselle Sergent appeared, dressed in black, her red hair aflame in the setting sun—so like her old self that I felt a desire to bite her and fall on her neck at the same time, because of all the past that came back to me in her dark, penetrating glance.

She hesitated for two seconds—that was enough—she took it all in, saw that I was Claudine, that I had bobbed my hair and my eyes were larger (which made my face look smaller), that Renaud

585

was my husband and that he was still a fine specimen of a man. (You bet your life he is, Mmmzelle!)

"Claudine! You haven't changed a bit! Why didn't you let me know you were coming? How do you do, sir? What shall we do to this child for failing to notify me of your coming? Don't you think she ought to be given two hundred lines to copy? Tell me, is she just as young and incorrigible as ever? Are you quite sure she was old enough to marry?'

"No, mademoiselle, not at all sure of it. But I hadn't any time to investigate, as I did not want to be married on my death-bed."

(That's fine! They're going to be good friends and get on well together. Mademoiselle likes handsome, virile men—although she doesn't do much about it. Well, let them work it out between them.)

While they were talking, I went ferreting around in the upper class room, hunting for my desk and Luce's right near it. At last I deciphered, under the ink spots and the fresh or discolored scars, the remains of an inscription cut into the wood:—*uce* and *Claudi—Feb. 15, 19—*.

Did I stoop and kiss the spot? I will not admit that I did. It may be that my mouth just grazed the wood as I examined the carved letters closely.

Now that I understand better, if I wanted to be honest, I would confess that I misjudged harshly poor little Luce's slavish devotion and that two years and a husband and a visit to the old school were necessary before I was able to apppreciate the value of her humility, her fresh, young nature and the gently depraved affection she so freely offered me.

My reverie was broken off by Mademoiselle Sergent's voice calling, "Claudine, have you gone completely crazy? Your husband tells me your luggage is up at Lange's!"

"Why, naturally! I couldn't check my nightgown at the railway station!"

"But it's too ridiculous! I have a lot of empty beds upstairs—not to mention Mademoiselle Lanthenay's room."

"What! Mademoiselle Aimée isn't here?" I exclaimed with too noticeable astonishment.

"My dear child, where are your wits?" she replied, coming near and passing her hand over my hair with ill-concealed sarcasm, "the teachers always go home during the summer vacation, Madame Claudine."

(So that's that! And there I had been looking forward to edifying and entertaining Renaud with the spectacle of the Sergent-Lanthenay *ménage!* I supposed that not even a summer vacation could separate this united couple. Well, I'll bet that sly puss Aimée won't hang around her own home very long! Now I understand why Mademoiselle received us with such surprising cordiality. It was because we were not interrupting any little affair. Too bad we weren't!)

"Many thanks, mmmzelle, I shall be only too glad to recapture my youth a bit by spending a night at the old school. And who is that little unripe Apple we met as we came in?"

"She's a young idiot who failed to pass her oral examination after having specially asked to be allowed to take it ahead of time. Fifteen years old! It's too silly for words! She is spending the summer here as a punishment but that doesn't bother her very much. I have two others like her upstairs, two girls from Paris who are to stay out here till October. But you'll meet them all later. First come and pick your room."

Looking at me sideways, she asked in the most natural tone of voice, "Would you mind sleeping in Mademoiselle Aimée's room?"

"There's nothing I'd like better," I replied.

Renaud followed us, hugely entertained and taking in everything. The crude crayon drawings stuck up on the walls with thumb tacks made his nostrils dilate with amusement and his ironic mustache twitch with delight.

Ah, the favorite's bedroom! It has been done over since my time. The white three-quarter bed, the silk draperies at the windows and the mantel set of alabaster and copper (ugh!), the dazzling cleanliness of everything and the subtle perfume fascinated me.

"I say, little one," remarked Renaud after Mademoiselle Sergent had gone out, closing the door behind her, "this teacher's room is pretty grand! It makes me feel more friendly toward the public school idea."

I roared.

"Come now, do you think this is the standard official equipment? Have you forgotten all I told you about Aimée and her position here as Her Majesty's publicly avowed favorite? The other teacher has to be satisfied with a narrow iron cot, a white pine table and a washbowl in which I wouldn't even drown one of Fanchette's kittens."

"You don't mean it! Then it's right here in this room that—er—"

"Why! of course it's here in this very room that—er—"

"Claudine, you have no idea what an effect these spicy recollections have on me!"

I can very well imagine, however! But I remain steadfastly blind and deaf and look at the scandalous bed disapprovingly. It may be wide enough for those two women, but not for us. I shall be very uncomfortable. Renaud will pester me. I shall be too warm and I won't be able to sprawl at my ease. And then that sagging hollow in the middle of the bed—ugh!

Only the wide-open window and the dear, familiar landscape, like a picture in its frame—the woods, poor, close-cropped, scanty fields, pottery kilns reddening the evening sky—were able to restore my good humor.

"Oh, Renaud, see that tiled roof? That's where they make little brown glazed pots and two-handled jugs with a naughty, tubular little navel."

"That's a fine idea!"

"Years ago, when I was just a kid and used to go and watch the potters work, they would give me little brown pots and flat water-bottles and tell me proudly, as they shook the moist clay from their hands, 'We're the guys who made the crockery for the Hôtel des Adrets in Paris.'"

"Did they really, my curly-headed little shepherd-boy? I am old enough to have drunk once or twice out of those mugs but I never guessed that your dainty fingers had passed lightly over their round flanks. How adorable you are!"

An outburst of fresh young voices and the patter of footsteps in the hall made us draw apart. As the footsteps halted and the voices dropped to a whisper, there came two timid knocks at our door.

"Come in!"

Apple appeared, red-faced and feeling very important.

"It's us. Here's your bags. Papa Racalin brought them over from Lange's."

Girls in black pinafores crowded close behind her—one red-haired ten-year-old, quaint and full of fun, and a brunette of fourteen or fifteen, dark-skinned, with big black eyes, liquid and luminous. Embarrassed by my glance, she drew back and disclosed another brunette of about the same age, likewise dark-skinned and with the same eyes. Highly amused, I plucked at her sleeve and asked, "How many of you did they cut out of the same piece of cloth?"

"Just us two. She's my sister."

"I had a faint suspicion of that," I replied. "You weren't born here. I can tell that by the way you talk."

"Oh, no! We used to live in Paris."

With her condescending tone and her half-suppressed little smile of scornful superiority, she was sweet enough to eat.

Renaud hastened gallantly to relieve Apple of the heavy bag she was lugging.

"How old are you, Apple?" he asked.

"Fifteen years and two months, sir."

"And not married yet?"

How they all laughed at this! Apple was naïvely convulsed. The two sisters were more coquettish. As for the ten-year-old little carrot-top, I thought she would die of laughing. It was great—just like the old days!

"Apple," continued Renaud calmly, "I am sure you like candy."

The young girl looked at him with her golden-brown eyes as if she were surrendering her soul to him.

"Oh yes, sir!"

"That's fine! I'll go and get some . . . Don't trouble, dearest, I can find the place alone."

I stayed behind with the little girls. They kept looking down the hall, afraid of being caught in the guests' room. I wanted them to be intimate and unrestrained with me.

"What's your name?" I asked the little brunettes.

"Helen Jousserand, madame," said one.

"Isabelle Jousserand, madame," replied the other.

"Don't call me 'madame,' you little idiots. I'm Claudine. Don't you know who Claudine is?"

"Oh yes!" exclaimed Helen, the prettier and younger of the two. "When we do something naughty, Mademoiselle always says—"

Her sister nudged her and she stopped short.

"Go on, go on! You mustn't keep me on tenterhooks this way. Don't pay any attention to your sister."

"Well, she says, 'Good Lord, this school is getting unbearable! You'd think we were back in the days when Claudine was here.' Or, 'Only Claudine would have done such a thing.'"

I danced with joy.

"What luck! So I am the bugaboo, the monster, the bogeyman! Tell me, am I as terrible-looking as you had expected?"

"Oh, no!" protested little Helen, timid and affectionate, quickly veiling her lovely eyes behind a double row of lashes.

It is evident that Luce's demonstrative ways still pervade this building. And it may well be that a certain other example . . . I am going to make the two little girls talk. But we must get the little redhead out of the way.

"I say, little girl, go out in the hall and see if I'm there."

Her curiosity piqued, she balked at the idea and refused to budge.

"Nana, do as the lady tells you," commanded Helen, flushed and angry. "If you don't you'll see! I'll tell Mademoiselle that the girl who sits next to you at table gives you chocolate drops for carrying letters to the boys' playground for her!"

The youngster did not wait to hear the end of this threat.

I put my hands on the girls' shoulders and looked at them closely. Helen is the prettier. Isabelle appears more serious-minded, with a scarcely perceptible down on her upper lip which will be unfortunate later on.

"Has Mademoiselle Aimée been gone a long time, girls?"

"Twelve days," Helen replied.

"Thirteen," interjected Isabelle.

"Tell me confidentially, is she as—er—friendly as ever with Mademoiselle?"

Isabelle blushed. Helen smiled.

"Never mind. You've answered my question. It was the same way when I was here. This friendship has been going on now for three years—would you believe it?"

"No!" they exclaimed in unison.

"Absolutely. I left the school about two years ago and I had been watching their intimacy for a whole year—a year I shall never forget. By the way, is Mademoiselle Lanthenay still good-looking?"

"Oh yes," replied Isabelle.

"Not as pretty as you," Helen murmured, drawing closer to me.

I pressed my nails into her neck caressingly, just as I used to do with Luce. She never winced. I felt the old familiar school atmosphere getting the better of me.

Apple was listening good-naturedly but uninterested, her hands hanging by her side, her mouth half open and her thoughts far away. Every now and then she would lean out of the window to see if the candy was coming.

I wanted to find out still more about the school.

"Come, Helen and Isabelle, give me some of the gossip. Who are the older girls in the upper class now?"

"Well, there's Liline and Mathilda—"

"You don't mean it! Already? You're right, though—it's two

591

years now. Is Liline still as handsome as ever? I nicknamed her Mona Lisa because of her green and grey eyes, her silent, tight-lipped mouth."

"Oh!" interrupted Helen, pursing her moist, red lips in a pout, "she isn't as pretty as all that—at least, not this year."

"Don't believe a word she says!" broke in Isabelle of the Downy Lip. "Liline is the prettiest of all the girls."

"Pooh! everybody knows why you say that—and also why Mademoiselle won't let you and Liline work at the same desk in the evening. When you two study from the same book—"

The older sister's handsome eyes filled with glistening tears.

"Stop tormenting your sister, you little beast. You don't look any too much like a saint yourself. After all, this child is only following the example of Mademoiselle and Aimée."

(Deep down in my heart I am wild with joy. This is fine! The old school is coming along! In my time Luce was the only one who sent me notes. Even Anaïs had not gotten beyond writing to boys. These Jousserand girls are charming! I am not sorry for Dr. Dutertre if he still gets himself appointed official physician.)

We formed a striking group. One brunette on the right, the other on the left, Claudine's excited curly head in the center and the rosy-cheeked Apple rapt in innocent contemplation. Now bring on your old men! (I say "old men," but I know some young ones who— Renaud ought to be back soon.)

"Apple, look out of the window and see if the gentleman with the candy is coming."

"Is her name really Apple?" I asked Helen, whose pretty head rested confidingly on my shoulder.

"Yes, her real name is Marie Apple, but everybody calls her Apple."

"She'll never set the Thames on fire, will she?"

"Good heavens, no! She's a mouse-like person who agrees with everybody."

Losing their shyness, the two young creatures looked me over closely as I stood dreaming of the past. With an inquisitive glance and a gentle touch they examined my bobbed hair ("Her curls are natural, aren't they?"), my white doeskin belt, as wide as your hand ("See, you said wide belts weren't being worn any more!"), its dull gold buckle—a present from Renaud, like everything else I have—my Peter Pan collar and my pale blue lawn waist with wide pleats.

(The time is passing. I realize that I'm leaving tomorrow, that this is all merely a hurried dream. Jealous of the present, which comes so close on the heels of my past, I feel a desire to brand something or someone here with a sweet yet burning recollection of me.)

Drawing Helen close to me, I whispered almost inaudibly, "If I were your schoolmate, little one, would you love me as much as your sister loves Liline?"

Her Spanish eyes, drooping at the outer corners, opened large and almost frightened. Then the screen of her eyelashes came down over them and she straightened up stiffly.

"I don't know yet."

(That's all I need to know!)

Apple, at the window, cried out joyfully, "Bags and bags of it! He's got bags full of candy!"

After this outburst, Renaud's entrance was received with respectful silence. He had bought everything the modest Montigny candy shop had to offer, from chocolate creams to striped peppermint sticks and English candy with a flavor suggesting sour cider.

(Just look at all that candy! I want some, too!)

Renaud stood for a moment in the doorway, looking at our group with a certain smile I have seen on his face before. Finally he took pity on poor palpitating Apple.

"Which do you like best, Apple?"

"All of them," she ejaculated, beside herself with joy.

"Oh!" exlaimed the others, scandalized. "What a way to behave!"

"Apple," continued Renaud, bubbling over with enjoyment, "I'll give you this bag of candy if you'll give me a kiss—do you mind, Claudine?"

"Good Heavens, why should I?"

Apple hesitated a couple of seconds, torn between her gluttonous appetite and a sense of propriety. With an ingenuous expression in her golden-brown eyes, she looked appealingly at her hostile comrades, at me, at heaven and at the bags of candy which my sweetheart was holding out toward her. Then, with a certain naïve gracefulness she flung her arms around Renaud's neck, received her bag of candy and blushingly withdrew into a corner to open it.

Meanwhile I was pillaging a bag of chocolates, assisted noiselessly but quickly by the two sisters. Helen's little hand travelled back and forth tirelessly and steadily from the candy to her lips. Who would have imagined that her small mouth was so capacious!

A sharp tinkle interrupted our enjoyment and brought Renaud back to his senses. The little girls fled in terror without stopping to say "thank you," without even looking at us—like marauding cats.

Renaud finds the supper in the dining hall immensely entertaining. It rather bores me. Under the spell of that vague hour between daytime and evening, the purplish twilight which I feel coming on and settling over the woods, my thoughts wander in spite of me.

But dear Renaud is so happy! Shrewd old Mademoiselle has known just how to stimulate his curiosity. In this white hall, seated at the white oil-cloth-covered table opposite these pretty young girls still in their black pinafores—toying listlessly with their beef stew like children surfeited with candy—she talks to Renaud about me, lowering her voice at times when the Jousserand girls prick up their ears too noticeably. I listen with a tired smile.

"She was a terrible tomboy, Monsieur Renaud! For quite a while I did not know what to do with her. At fourteen and fifteen she lived most of the time up in the air—literally. Her chief preoccupation seemed to be to exhibit her legs clear up to her eyes . . . Occasionally she displayed the characteristic cruelty of children toward their elders." (That's a mean one!)

"But she was charming, as she still is . . . Although she was not any too fond of me, I used to enjoy watching her move about—such suppleness and yet such perfect control! The stairs leading to this floor—I never saw her come down them otherwise than astride the banister rail. Just imagine what an example for the rest of the school!"

The dishonesty of her motherly tone amuses me in the end. There comes into Renaud's eyes a dark and dangerous light that I know only too well. Looking at Apple, he sees Claudine at the age of fourteen, "exhibiting her legs clear up to her eyes." (Her eyes, Mademoiselle? The tone of the school is much more elevated than it was in my day.) Looking at Helen, he sees Claudine astride the banisters, gesticulating naughtily with her violet, ink-stained fingers. (It's going to be a warm night!) And he breaks into a nervous laugh when Mademoiselle turns from him to call out to Apple, "If I catch you again taking salt with your fingers, I'll give you five pages of exercises to write out!"

Helen watches me silently and looks away when our eyes meet. Her sister Isabelle is decidedly less good-looking—when she is not in a bright light that shadow of a moustache makes her look like a child whose face needs washing.

"Mademoiselle," asked Renaud suddenly, "will you permit me to give them all some candy in the morning?"

At this the voracious little redhead, who had licked the platters clean and devoured all the leavings from the supper, let out a muffled howl of gluttonous greed. And what a scornful look she got from the three older girls, gorged to the gills with sticky sweets!

"Certainly," replied Mademoiselle. "They don't deserve it, the mollycoddles, but this is an exceptional occasion. Why don't you say thank you, you little ninnies? Come now, off to bed, all of you! It's nearly nine o'clock."

"Oh, mmmzelle," I pleaded. "May Renaud have a look at the dormitory before the children go to bed?"

"You're still only a child yourself, my dear. Yes, he may," she consented. "And you careless girls, heaven help you if I find a hair-brush lying around anywhere!"

Gray-white, blue-white, yellowish white—the walls, the curtains, the narrow beds like rows of children strapped too tight in their swaddling clothes.

Renaud sniffs the peculiar odor floating about—an odor of healthy young girls, of sleeping bodies, the sharp, spicy perfume of a bouquet of water-mint hanging from the ceiling. His keen nose analyzes, enjoys and meditates.

Mademoiselle automatically thrusts a redoubtable hand under the bolsters in order to confiscate any half-gnawed piece of chocolate or forbidden dime novel.

"Did you sleep here, Claudine?" Renaud whispered, his feverish fingers tapping on my shoulder as on a piano.

Mademoiselle's sharp ears caught his question and she forestalled my reply.

"Claudine? Good heavens, no! Nor would I have wanted it. In what condition would we have found the dormitory—or the pupils—the next morning?"

(Or the pupils, eh? This is getting a bit thick! My modesty will not permit me to put up with these suggestive insinuations any longer. It's time we beat a retreat.)

"Have you taken it all in, Renaud?"

"Yes, dear, all of it."

"Then let's go to bed."

We hear whispering behind us as we turn to go. I can imagine what the little brunettes are murmuring: "Say, is she going to sleep with the gentleman in Mademoiselle Aimée's bed? . . . I'll bet it never saw a man before!"

Come along. I cast a smiling glance at little Helen, who is braiding her hair for the night, resting her chin on her shoulder. It's time to leave!

I remember the narrow, brightly lighted room—the lamp that gave off too much heat—the rectangle of pure blue night at the window—a cat creeping, velvety and ghost-like, along the perilous windowledge . . .

I remember the mounting ardor of my liege lord after brushing up against very young Claudine all evening—the nervous tension that stretched the corners of his mouth in a horizontal smile . . .

I remember that I snatched a little sleep, lying face down with my hands crossed over my back—"like a prisoner trussed up," Renaud says.

I remember how the dawn drew me to the window in my night-gown to see the mist floating over the woods in the direction of Moutiers and to listen more closely to Choucas' little anvil, ringing out its G sharp that morning as of old.

There is nothing I have forgotten about that night.

Not a soul in the school is stirring yet—it is only six o'clock. But Renaud wakes up, sensing that I am no longer beside him. He listens to the metallic hammering at the forge and unconsciously whistles a strain from "Siegfried."

Renaud is not homely in the morning—which is a remarkable quality in a man. The first thing he always does is to run his fingers through his hair, after which he makes for the water-bottle and drinks a tumbler of water. I can't see that at all—how any-body can drink something cold in the morning! And since I don't like it, how can he?

"How soon are we leaving, Claudine?"

"I have no idea. Are you in a hurry?"

"You bet I am! In this town it doesn't seem as if you were mine. You are more interested in all the noises and smells and old, familiar faces. You give yourself to every tree."

(I laughed but did not answer because I felt that there was some truth in what he said. And, since I no longer have a home here in Montigny—)

"We'll leave at two o'clock."

Reassured by this, Renaud looked for a moment at the candy heaped up on the table.

"Claudine, what do you say we take the candy and go and wake up the girls?"

"But suppose Mademoiselle should catch us at it?"

"Are you afraid she might give you an exercise to write out?"

597

"Hardly! Anyhow, what if she does catch us? It will be all the more fun!"

"I love your rebellious schoolgirl spirit, Claudine! Come, let me have a whiff of you."

"Ouch! you're mussing up my blanket, Renaud! Mademoiselle will be getting up herself if we don't hurry."

He in blue pyjamas, I white and tall in my long nightgown, my hair still falling in my eyes, we walk along silently, our arms full of candy. I listen before opening the door of the dormitory. Not a sound! They are as still as little corpses. I open the door gently.

How can they sleep, the wretches, in such a bright light, with the sun blazing in through the white curtains?

I look immediately for Helen's bed. Her pretty face is buried in her pillow, only her braid is visible, stretched out like a black snake.

In the next bed Isabelle is sleeping flat on her back, her long lashes resting on her cheeks, a modest, preoccupied expression on her features. Beyond her the little sandy-haired girl lies like a discarded jumping-jack, one arm here, the other there, snoring gently with her mouth open, her mop of hair making a golden halo.

But it is Apple that Renaud looks at with special interest. Feeling too warm, she is doubled up like a jack-knife in her long-sleeved nightgown, her head touching her knees. Her hair, pulled straight back Chinese fashion, is braided tight like a rope. One cheek is red, the other pink. Her mouth is shut and her fists clenched.

How sweet they look! How much more attractive these pupils are! In my time, the scholars would have inspired even that old woman-chaser Dutertre with a passion for chastity.

As charmed as I—and affected in another manner also—Renaud walked over to Apple, decidedly his favorite, and dropped a green pistache fondant on her smooth cheek. The cheek twitched, she unclenched her fists and stretched her pretty little body under its gauzy covering.

"Good morning, Apple."

Her golden-brown eyes opened big with astonished friendliness. She sat up bewildered. As her hand fell on the sticky green candy, she exclaimed "oh!" and gobbled it like a cherry.

Apple's cheerful "Good morning, sir!" and my hearty laugh caused a wavy motion under Helen's covers, the black snake moved slightly and she suddenly sat bolt upright in bed, as brown as a black-capped warbler. Waking with effort, she stared at us and tried to connect today with yesterday in her mind. Her amber cheeks became rosy-colored. With her left hand she pushed back a big lock of her delightfully tumbled hair which persisted in falling across her nose. Then she caught sight of Apple sitting up, her mouth full of candy.

"Oh!" Helen cried out, "she's going to eat it all up!"

Her cry, her outstretched arm and her childlike dismay fascinated me. As I squatted tailor-fashion on the foot of her bed, she drew her feet up under her and blushed a deeper pink.

Her sister stretched, muttered a few words and with a modest hand drew together her slightly gaping nightdress. Nana, the little carrot-top, down at the end of the big room, groaned with envy and wrung her hands as Apple ate on and on, conscientiously and tirelessly.

"That's cruel, Renaud! Apple is very attractive, I admit, but give some candy to Helen and the others."

Renaud nodded ceremoniously and stepped back a little.

"Very well. Now everybody listen to me," he announced, "I don't give out any more candy"—there was a palpitating silence—"unless you come and get it."

The girls looked at one another in dismay. But Nana had already stuck her stocky legs out of bed and was examining her feet to see if they were clean enough to be shown. Holding up her long nightgown in order not to stumble, she ran nimbly to Renaud in pattering barefeet, looking like the tousle-haired children in the Christmas chromos. Catching the bag of candy that Renaud tossed to her, she went back to bed like a contented pup.

Unable to stand it any longer, Apple burst from between her

599

covers and, indifferent to a well-rounded calf that flashed for an instant in the golden light, she ran up to Renaud, who held the coveted candy beyond her reach.

"Oh, I can't reach it," she wailed. "Please, sir!"

Then, since it had worked so well the night before, she threw her arms around Renaud's neck and kissed him. It worked again that morning, but I began to find this little game rather annoying.

"You go next, Helen," Isabelle muttered in an exasperated tone.

"I declare! Go yourself. You're older than I am—and you're greedier, too."

"I am not!"

"You aren't, eh? Well, I'm not going, so there now! Apple will eat them all up. I only hope she throws up, just to teach her a lesson."

At the thought of Apple eating all the candy, Isabelle jumped out of bed, but I held Helen back, grasping her slim ankle under the covers.

"Don't go, Helen. I'll get you some."

Isabelle returned victorious. But as she quickly clambered into bed, we heard Nana's shrill voice cry out, "Isabelle has hair on her legs—lots of it!"

"You nasty thing!" Isabelle retorted, covering herself up so that only two angry, flashing eyes showed. She called Nana names and threatened to get even with her. Then her voice got husky and she turned over and wept copiously into her pillow.

"There, Renaud, now see what you've done!"

He laughed so heartily that he dropped the last bag and it broke on the floor.

"What do you want me to put them in?" I asked my little Helen.

"I don't know. I haven't anything here. Oh yes, my wash basin, the third one over there on the washstand."

I gathered up the highly colored, indigestible stuff in her enamel wash basin and brought it to her.

"Renaud, go and have a look outside. I think I hear footsteps."

Meanwhile I sat on my little Helen's bed as she sucked and crunched, looking at me furtively. When I smiled at her, she blushed at first, then got up her courage and smiled back. She has a moist, white smile, fresh and appetizing.

"What are you laughing at, Helen?"

"I was looking at your nightgown. It makes you look like one of us, except that it's made of lawn—no, batiste?—and I can see through it."

"But I am one of you. You don't believe it?"

"No, indeed—and I'm sorry you're not."

(It's coming along well! I move up closer.)

"Do you like me?"

"Yes—a great deal," she murmured almost with a sigh.

"Would you give me a kiss?"

"No," she protested quickly, in a low, almost frightened tone.

I leaned over very close to her and whispered, "No? Sometimes people say 'no' when they mean 'yes.' I've done that myself."

With an entreating look she indicated her comrades. But I felt so wicked and curious! I was just about to torment her again, leaning still closer, when the door opened and in walked Renaud, followed by Mademoiselle in her wrapper—what am I saying?— in her house dress, with her hair already done up for public view.

"Well, Madame Claudine, do you feel tempted to come back to school again?"

"I admit it is particularly tempting this year, mademoiselle."

"Only this year? How marriage has changed my Claudine! . . . Come, young ladies, do you realize it will soon be eight o'clock? At a quarter to nine I shall look under the beds and, if I find anything at all there, I will make you sweep it up with your tongues!"

"Will you forgive this early morning escapade, mademoiselle?" I asked as we were leaving the dormitory.

Lowering her voice, she replied good-naturedly and yet ambiguously:

"Oh, in vacation time, you know.—Besides, as far as your husband is concerned, I prefer to regard it as merely a bit of fatherly indulgence."

I shall not forgive her that remark.

I remember the walk Renaud and I took before luncheon, the pilgrimage I insisted on making to my former home—dearer to me than ever since my stay in that detestable Paris—and the pang that gripped my heart as I stood motionless before the double flight of steps, with its black iron railing. I stared for some time at the worn brass bell-handle I used to pull on with all my weight when I came back from school. I stared at it so hard I could feel it in my hand. Then, as Renaud looked at the window of my old bedroom, I turned toward him with tear-dimmed eyes and said, "Let's go—it hurts me too much."

Moved by my unhappiness, he quietly led me away, clinging to his arm. I could not resist the temptation to twirl the catch on one of the ground-floor shutters. That was all.

I'm sorry now that I insisted on coming to Montigny, moved by a desire to see my old haunts again, also by love and pride. Yes, pride, too—I wanted to show off my handsome husband so as to spite Mademoiselle and her absent Aimée. (But is this fatherly lover, this sensual guardian, really a husband?)

And now (this should teach me a lesson!) here I am, feeling so little and heartbroken, uncertain where my true home is, my heart lying torn and bleeding somewhere between two places!

Because of me the luncheon was a dismal affair. Mademoiselle did not know what to make of my disheartened appearance—nor did I. The little girls, sickened by too much sugar, would not eat. Renaud alone laughed as he plied Apple with questions.

"Do you answer 'yes' to everything?"

"Yes, sir."

"You round, rosy Apple, I could not possibly pity the lucky men who may be attracted to you, for you have in you the promise of a happy future made up of serenity and equitably divided affection."

Then he looked to see if Mademoiselle was displeased, but she shrugged her shoulders and said in reply to his look, "Oh, that doesn't matter with her—she never understands."

"Perhaps I could explain in a more tangible manner?"

"You wouldn't have time before your train leaves. Apple never catches on until a thing has been done for her at least four times."

A signal from me checked the daring remark my wicked husband was about to make. My little Helen was taking it all in. ("My little Helen" is the name I gave her from the very start.)

And now good-bye to all this! For, as I am closing our bags, Papa Racalin's harness bells and oaths are making a din in the courtyard. Farewell!

I used to love—I still love—these re-echoing white hallways, this huge white building, with its red brick corners, the horizon hemmed in by trees. I liked even the dislike Mademoiselle aroused in me. I was fond of her dear Aimée and of Luce—who did not know I cared for her.

I stopped a moment on the landing, my hand on the cool wall. At the foot of the stairs Renaud was chatting with Apple. (Again!)

"Good-bye, Apple."

"Good-bye, sir."

"Will you write to me, Apple?"

"I don't know your name."

"That excuse won't hold water. My name is 'Claudine's husband.' Will you miss me, anyhow?"

"Yes, sir."

"Especially because of the candy?"

"Oh yes, sir!"

"Apple, your scandalous innocence fills me with enthusiasm. Give me a kiss."

I hear a faint rustle behind me. I turn around. My little Helen is there, looking so pretty, all white and black. She says nothing.

I smile at her. She wants very much to say something, but I know it is too difficult to express, so she simply looks at me.

Then, while at the foot of the stairs Apple calmly and obediently hangs on Renaud's neck, I slip one arm around this silent young girl who smells of cedar pencils and sandalwood fans. She trembles, then surrenders herself and lets me plant on her yielding lips a kiss of farewell to my girlhood past.

My girlhood past? Here, at any rate, I do not need to lie. My little Helen, who, trembling and already passionately aroused, ran to the window to watch me go, shall never know something which would surprise and grieve her—it was the memory of Luce which I kissed on her eager, inexpert lips.

In the train that bore us away I stood silently watching as the old tower, crushed beneath a mass of fleecy clouds gathering for a storm, disappeared behind the rounded outline of a hill. Then, unburdened as if I had said good-bye to someone, I turned once more to my dear, frivolous sweetheart, who looked at me admiringly (merely to keep up the habit) and put his arms around me. But I checked him with, "Tell me, Renaud, is it really so pleasant to kiss that Apple girl?"

I gazed earnestly into his eyes but could not fathom their mysterious bluish black.

" 'That Apple girl'? Can it be, my dear, that you are paying me the compliment of being jealous?"

"Oh, that's not much of a compliment, let me tell you! I could hardly regard Apple as a flattering conquest."

"My slender, pretty little woman, if you had told me not to kiss Apple, I could not have claimed the slightest credit for leaving her alone."

Oh yes, he will do anything I wish, but still he did not answer squarely my question as to whether he enjoyed kissing that Apple girl. He is very clever at not committing himself, at slipping out of situations and smothering me with evasive caresses.

He loves me—there's no doubt about that—and more than anything else in the world. And, thank heaven, I love him—that is also a certainty. But how much more of a woman he is than I! I feel so much more elemental, brutal, sombre—yes, passionate—than he.

I purposely refrain from saying "straightforward." A little over a year ago I could have said it. At that time I would not have been so easily tempted, there at the top of the dormitory stairs, to kiss those girlish lips, cool and moist like a crushed fruit, under pretext of bidding farewell to my girlhood past, to my black-pinafored childhood. I would merely have kissed the desk where Luce used to rest her obstinate forehead.

For the past year and a half I have felt going on in me the gradual, pleasant process of corruption that I owe to Renaud's influence. Looked at through his eyes, the important things become trivial, the serious side of life retreats, while useless and especially harmful futilities take on enormous importance. But how can I protect myself from the incurable and seductive frivolousness that sweeps him along—and me with him?

There is something still more serious—Renaud has initiated me into the secret of sensual pleasure both given and received, and now that I possess this secret, I take passionate delight in it, like a child with a deadly weapon. He has revealed to me the unfailing, inexhaustible power I can wield through my long, supple, sinewy body, with its firm loins, its small breasts and its skin as soft as an alabaster vase, my tobacco-brown eyes, which have gained in depth and in restlessness, my short, fluffy hair, the color of a partly ripened chestnut.

All this new power I use, but only half-consciously, on Renaud—don't I, though!—just as I would have used it on that charming Helen, had I remained two days longer at the school.

Yes, but don't press the point or I shall say that it was because of Renaud that I kissed Helen's lips.

4

"My silent little Claudine, what are you thinking about?"

I remember he asked me that question on the hotel terrace at Heidelberg as my gaze wandered from the broad sweep of the Neckar to the touched-up ruins of Schloss Heidelberg below us.

Stretched out on the ground, I rested my chin on my hands.

"I was thinking about the garden."

"What garden?"

"Oh, what garden? Why, the garden at Montigny, of course."

Renaud tossed his cigarette away—he lives amid clouds and perfumes.

"What a strange little woman! With such a view before you! Are you going to tell me that the garden at Montigny is more beautiful than this?"

"No, indeed! But it's mine."

That's the way it always goes. We have talked things over again and again but without coming to an understanding. Kissing me with an affectionate but slightly superior air, Renaud calls me "little lazy-bones"—his "stay-at-home tramp." With a laugh I reply that his home is in his valise. We are both right and yet I blame him for not thinking as I do.

He has done too much travelling—I not enough. With me it is only my mind that likes to wander. I follow Renaud about cheerfully because I adore him, but I like journeys that have a definite goal. He loves travel for travel's sake and is happy to wake in a strange land and to think that today he'll be off again.

He will be eager for the mountains of some nearby country, for the sharp wine of this or that region, for the artificial charm of some dolled-up, flower-bedecked watering place or the solitude of a hamlet on the mountainside. And he will go on his way again with never a regret for the hamlet or the flowers or the heady wine.

As for me, I follow him around. And I enjoy—yes, I too enjoy the pleasant town, the sun behind the pine trees, the re-echoing air of the mountains. But I realize that an unbreakable bond ties me to the old walnut tree in the garden at Montigny.

I do not think I am an unnatural daughter and yet I must confess that on my travels I have missed Fanchette almost as much as I have Papa. It was only in Germany that I felt a longing to see my worthy parent again. What reminded me of him there was the Wagnerian postcards and chromos adorned with Wotans, all of whom looked like Papa except for the eye. They were all handsome men and they brandished harmless thunderbolts, just as he does. Their beards were as wild-looking as his and they wore the same lordly mien. I fancy that their vocabulary, like his, contained all the robust expressions of the age of fable.

I wrote to him very seldom. His replies came at long intervals, affectionate and hurried, written in a deliciously hybrid style in which cadenced periods that would have enraptured Chauteaubriand (this is flattering Papa somewhat) concealed in their bosom —their august bosom—the most hair-raising oaths.

I learned from these extraordinary letters that everything was going wrong except as to Monsieur Maria, who was still playing the faithful, silent secretary.

"I do not know whether I should blame it on your long absence, you stubborn little mule," my dear father explained, "but I am beginning to find Paris loathsome, especially since that bit of human trash named X—— has just published a treatise on *Universal Malacology* stupid enough to turn the stomachs of the lions crouching at the door of the Institute. Why in hell does the Eternal Justice vouchsafe the light of day to such scoundrels?"

Mélie on her side did her best to describe to me Fanchette's state of mind since my departure, her heartbroken cries for days and days. But Mélie's chirography looks more like hieroglyphics than handwriting, so that it's impossible to keep up a steady correspondence with her.

Fanchette crying for me! The thought of this haunted me. Whenever in our travels some poor tomcat fled as we turned a corner, my heart gave a leap. A score of times I surprised Renaud by dropping his arm and running to caress a cat sitting gravely on a doorsill. Frequently the startled animal would draw in her chin and with a dignified air puff out her throat. But I would persist and add a whole string of onomatopoetic sounds in a shrill, minor key until the green eyes took on a sweet expression and narrowed in a smile. The cat would then rub her small, caressing head vigorously against the door jamb by way of friendly greeting and turn around three times, which signified clearly, "I like you."

Renaud never once showed any impatience over these attacks of cat-worship, but I suspect that he was more indulgent than sympathetic. (He is quite capable—the wretch!—of having been actuated solely by diplomatic considerations when he used to stroke my Fanchette.)

How I enjoy reliving this recent past! Renaud, on the other hand, lives in the future. This man, who is tormented by the fear of growing old and stops in front of every mirror to note with despairing minuteness the network of wrinkles at the corners of his eyes—this very same man is impatient with the present and feverishly hurries Today along into Tomorrow.

As for me, I like to tarry with the past, even though it be but of yesterday, and I like to look back, although it is almost always with longing. It would seem as if marriage—nonsense! I mean love—had brought out more sharply in me certain reactions that are older than myself.

This surprises Renaud, but he loves me and, whenever the lover in him fails to understand me, I take refuge in that other side of his character—the dear old fatherly friend! I am to him like a trusting daughter who leans on the father she herself selected and bares her inner soul to him—behind the lover's back, as it were.

But it goes even further than that. If lover-Renaud happens to try to come in between father-Renaud and daughter-Claudine, the latter treats him as one would a cat that had landed in the middle of a work basket. The poor fellow then has to wait, impatient and disappointed, until Claudine, refreshed and lighthearted again, returns to him with her feeble resistance, her silence and her passionate love.

Alas, in spite of all I have written here—somewhat at random— I still have not been able to make clear to myself just where the trouble lies. And yet, good God! I can feel that it is there.

5

HERE we are in our own quarters. The wearisome errands attendant upon getting settled are finished and Renaud's feverish desire that the new home should please me has been pacified.

He begged me to choose between two apartments which both belonged to him. (Two apartments are none too many for a Renaud.)

"If they don't suit you, my dear little girl, we'll get another still handsomer."

I resisted the temptation to say, "Let me see that one," and, seized with my chronic horror of moving, I examined them both quite conscientiously, sniffing of them with particular attention. I chose this one because I recognized the odor of it to be the more congenial to my sensitive nose.

Although the apartment had almost everything necessary, Renaud, with his attention to detail and his nature more feminine than my own, searched in every corner and racked his brains to make everything absolutely complete and perfect. Eager to please me— and watchful of everything which might displease his own too expert eye—he sought my opinion again and again.

My first reply, "I really don't care," was sincere. So was my second, on the subject of the bed—"the keystone of conjugal happiness," in Papa's lingo. I expressed my preference frankly.

"I would like to have my single bed with its chintz curtains."

Whereupon my poor Renaud raised his hands in hopeless despair.

"Lord have mercy on me! A single bed in a Louis XV room! Besides which, you cruel little monster, do you realize we'd have to widen it?"

Yes, I admit it, but how could I help it? I couldn't feel interested in a lot of strange, new furniture—not right away, anyhow. The big, low bed is now a good friend of mine and so are the dressing-room and some roomy, high-backed armchairs. But all the other things continue to eye me distrustfully, if I may put it that way. The mirror-front wardrobe looks at me askance as I pass. The drawing-room table, with its legs curving outward, tries to trip me up as I go by—and I return the compliment.

Two months! Good Lord, isn't that enough to tame a whole apartment? (I try to drown out the voice of reason which mutters, "You can tame a lot of interiors in two months, but not a Claudine.")

Would Fanchette be willing to live here? I went to see my be-loved white darling at Rue Jacob. They hadn't told her I was com-ing and my heart swelled to see her fawning speechless at my feet, while my hand could not count on her warm pink belly the excited beating of her feline heart. I turned her on her side and started combing her lustreless fur. At this familiar sensation she lifted her head with an expression full of many things—reproaches, lasting affection, discomfort joyfully endured.

Oh, little white creature, how close I feel to you because I understand you so well!

I saw my worthy father. He is as tall, generously proportioned and needlessly contentious as ever, with the same sonorous phrases rolling forth from his multicolored beard.

Although not very conscious of the fact, we are really deeply attached to one another and I sensed the genuine pleasure which lay back of his greeting, "Will you condescend to kiss me, you young good-for-nothing?"

I really think he has grown in the past two years. No joking! The proof of this is that he confessed to me that he felt cramped in the Rue Jacob apartment!

"The trouble is, I bought some old books at an auction sale lately—nearly two thousand of them—and, damn it all, I've had to put the cursed things in storage. This dump is too small. Now, in that back room at Montigny that we never use, I could—"

Plucking at his beard, he turned away, but not before our eyes had met in a knowing glance. I'll be damned—greatly surprised, I mean—if he doesn't go back home some day just as he came to Paris—for no particular reason.

I am dodging the unpleasant thing I have to report. Perhaps it is not so serious after all? If only that might be so! Here it is:

Yesterday they completed the work of decorating at Renaud's —at our place, rather. No more shall we have to watch the upholsterer fuss around with a self-important air, or the window-shade man, with incurable absent-mindedness, mislay his brass gadgets every five minutes.

Renaud strolled about, very much at home, smiling with satisfaction as he looked at a stylish little mantel clock, or energetically straightening a picture that was out of plumb. Giving me his arm, he led me on a tour of our estate. Then, after an expert kiss, he left me in the drawing-room (doubtless to go and work at his job on *The Diplomatic Review*—to settle the fate of Europe with Jacobsen and give Abdul-Hamid his just desserts), saying as he left, "Here, my little despot, you are monarch of all you survey."

Sitting there, with nothing to do, I allow my thoughts to wander dreamily for a long time. The striking of a clock brings me to my feet, uncertain as to the hour. I find myself before the mirror, putting on my hat hurriedly—to go home!

That was all—but everything crumbled in that instant. You say you don't understand? You are fortunate!

To go home? Where, pray? Am I not at home here? No, no! And that's the misfortune of it.

Go home? Where? Certainly not to Papa's apartment, where he piles my bed high with his musty papers. Not to Montigny, since neither the house nor the school—

Home? Then have I no home? No! Here I am living in a man's house—a man I am in love with, it is true, but still I am living in a man's house!

Alas, Claudine, torn from your native soil—had your roots struck as deep as that? What will Renaud say? Nothing. He can do nothing about it.

Where, then, can I take refuge? Within myself—plunging deep into my sorrow, my unreasonable, indefinable sorrow, and drawing it close about me.

Sitting down again, with my hat on and my hands tightly clasped, I draw my sorrow about me.

6

My DIARY hasn't much of a future before it! I left off five months ago in a gloomy mood and I cannot forgive it for that.

Besides, I haven't the time to keep it up-to-date. Renaud trots me around and shows me off in his social circle—and in others of a somewhat different stripe—more than I would choose, but since he is proud of me, why, naturally I can't hurt his feelings by refusing to go with him.

His marriage caused a stir—of which I was quite unaware—among the many people of all kinds whom he knows. No, he doesn't know them. An enormous number of people know him, but he cannot recall the names of half of those whom he shakes hands with cordially and introduces to me.

Dispersing his interests with incorrigible fickleness, he is sincerely attached to no one—excepting me. "Who is that gentleman, Renaud?" "That's—I declare! his name escapes me."

Well, it seems that his profession makes this obligatory, that drafting profound reports for serious diplomatic journals necessitates shaking hands with a lot of people who put on airs, painted and powdered women (ranging all the way up and down the social scale), painters, models, tactless and insistent would-be actresses and so forth.

But Renaud, with a tender naïveté really touching in this blasé Parisian, puts so much conjugal and paternal pride into those three words of introduction, "My wife Claudine," that in spite of myself I draw in my horns and smooth out the wrinkles of my frown.

And besides, I have other compensations—as, for instance, the malicious pleasure of replying, when Renaud vaguely names someone "Monsieur— Durand," "Why, you told me day before yesterday his name was Dupont!"

Consternation spreads over the swarthy face and the light mustache droops as he exclaims:

"I told you that? Are you sure, dear? Well, now I am in a fine fix! I confused both those men with—you know, that other fellow, the moron whom I have to call by his first name merely because we went to school together."

All the same, I find it difficult to get used to intimate friendships that are so hazy.

Here and there, in the foyer of the Opéra-Comique, at the Chevillard and Colonne concerts, at evening receptions especially —at the moment when the prospect of having to listen to music brings a shadow of dread over people's faces—I have caught glances and remarks that indicated not unmixed goodwill toward me. So people are talking about me? Ah, that's so, here I am Renaud's wife, just as at Montigny he is Claudine's husband. These Parisians talk low, but the ears of Fresnois people could even hear the grass growing.

They say, "What a young thing she is!" Or, "Too dark—looks bad-tempered." "How can you call her dark? She has chestnut curls." "That bobbed hair is just to attract attention! And yet Renaud has good taste!"

Or, "Where did he pick that up?" "She's from Montmartre." "Slavic—look at her small chin and wide temples." "She looks as if she had stepped out of one of Pierre Louÿs' uni-sexual novels." "But is Renaud really so old that he has begun to take an interest in little girls?"

Renaud, Renaud. It is significant that they always refer to him by his first name.

7

YESTERDAY my husband asked me, "Are you going to have a regular day for receiving visits, Claudine?"

"Good heavens, what should I do that for?"

"So as to gossip—to jabber, as you say."

"With whom?"

"With society women."

"But I don't care much for society women."

"Then with men also."

"Don't tempt me! No, I'm not going to have a regular reception day. Do you imagine that I know how to receive?"

"Well, I have a day at home myself."

"What, you? Very well, stay at home and I'll come and call on you. Believe me, that will be safer. Otherwise I'd be liable to say to your fine friends by the end of the first hour, 'Run along now. I'm sick and tired of this. You bore me to death.'"

Renaud did not press the point—he never does. He kissed me—he is always kissing me—and went out laughing.

My stepson Marcel heaps polite scorn on me because of the misanthropic tendency, the timid aversion to society which I have frequently proclaimed. This young boy, so callous to women, persistently seeks their company, talks sweet nothings to them, feels of their dressgoods, pours them tea without spotting their delicate gowns and gossips like mad.

But it is a mistake to speak of him as a "young boy." At twenty, one is no longer a boy and as for him, he will always be a young girl. When we returned to Paris, I found him as charming as before but somewhat the worse for wear—altogether too thin, his eyes larger than ever, with an unwholesome expression in them and three premature lines at the outer corners. Is Charlie responsible for all this?

Renaud's anger at the deceitful lad was not of long duration.

"I cannot lose sight of the fact that he is my son, Claudine, and that perhaps, if I had given him a better bringing up—"

As for me, I forgave Marcel because of indifference—indifference, pride and a desire (which I do not and could not well admit) to know more about the irregularities of his sexual life. And I take a mild pleasure, which does not grow less, in looking at the white mark that my nails once left under the left eye of this young man who should have been a girl.

But this boy Marcel astonishes me. I was prepared for unremitting rancor and open hostility on his part. No such thing! Constant sarcasm, yes—also contempt and curiosity, but nothing more.

His one absorbing preoccupation is himself. He continually looks at himself in the mirror and, pressing his fingers against his eyebrows, pulls the skin of his forehead up as far as it will go. I was surprised at this gesture, repeated so frequently as to amount to a nervous habit, and questioned him about it.

"I do it to rest the skin under my eyes," he replied in all seriousness.

With blue crayon he lengthens the dark shadow above his eyes. He sports turquoise cuff-buttons that are much too handsome. Ugh! At forty he will be a gruesome spectacle.

In spite of what happened between us, he feels no embarrassment in taking me partly into his confidence either through instinctive bravado or because of a steadily increasing moral depravity. Yesterday he was lolling about here, the picture of graceful lassitude, with his excessively slender figure and his face aflame with a feverish glow.

"You seem completely done up, Marcel," I remarked.

"Well, that's just what I am."

(An aggressive tone is customary between us. It is merely a game, however, and has no special significance.)

"Is it Charlie again?"

"Now, please! It is fitting that a young woman should be ignorant of—or at least ignore—certain mental abnormalities. I believe that is what you call them?"

"Why, yes, they do call them abnormalities, but I should hardly say they were mental," I replied.

"The physical is highly complimented madame. But frankly, there is nothing about my fatigue that Charlie can take to his credit—that weak-willed, vacillating fellow!"

"Oh, come now, Marcel!"

"Yes, really. I know him better than you do."

"I flatter myself you do!"

"Our friendship is now a closed incident. I am not trying to repudiate it—I'm simply breaking it off on account of certain rather unsavory incidents."

"What! Your handsome Charlie? Was it over money matters?"

"Worse than that. He left a bundle of letters from women in my apartment!"

With what disgust and hatred he snarled out this accusation! I gazed at him in deep meditation. He is an unfortunate, misguided, almost irresponsible child—but he is right. One only has to imagine oneself in his place—which heaven forbid!

It is written that everything shall happen to me suddenly—pleasures, disappointments, unimportant events. Not that I make a specialty of the unusual—my marriage excepted. But time moves along for me the way it does for the minute hand of certain public clocks. The hand stands still for fifty-nine seconds and then suddenly, with an ill-co-ordinated jerk, jumps abruptly to the next minute. The minutes seize it roughly—exactly as they do me. Not that this is always and unqualifiedly disagreeable, but still—

Here is my latest sudden jump. I went to see Papa, Mélie, Fanchette and Snail. The last-named, striped and splendid, commits incest with his mother and takes us back to the worst days of the legend of the Atridae. The rest of the time he strides up and down the apartment, arrogant, leonine and bad-tempered. He has not inherited a single one of the virtues of his amiable white mother.

Mélie rushed to greet me, holding her round left breast in her hand like Charlemagne holding the terrestrial globe.

"My little darling, I was going to write you a note. If you only knew how everything here is topsy-turvy—My! but you do look sweet in that hat!"

"Hurry up and explain yourself! Everything is topsy-turvy? Why? Has Snail upset his—spittoon?"

Offended at my sarcasm, Mélie withdrew.

"Oh well, if you're going to take it that way, go ask your father and you'll find out."

Puzzled and curious, I went into Papa's room without knocking. He turned around at the noise and disclosed an enormous box which he was filling with old books. An expression peculiar to him, a mixture of harmless rage, annoyance and childlike embarrassment, came over his handsome bearded face.

"Is that you, my little jackass?"

617

"So it would seem. What under the sun are you up to, Papa?"

"I'm—er—filing away some papers."

"What a queer filing cabinet you have there! Why, I recognize that box! It came from Montigny."

Papa determined to face the music. Buttoning his narrow-waisted frock coat, he sat down in leisurely fashion and crossed his arms over his beard.

"It came from Montigny and it's going back there. You understand?"

"No, not at all."

Puckering his bushy eyebrows, he looked me sternly in the eye, lowered his voice and let it all out.

"I'm going to get to hell out of here!"

(I had understood perfectly. In fact, I had felt this senseless departure drawing near. Why had he come and why was he going away, I meditated. Papa is like one of the elemental forces—he serves the purposes of hidden destiny. Without knowing it, he came to Paris so that I could meet Renaud and now, having fulfilled his function as an irresponsible father, he is going away.)

As I made no reply, my awe-inspiring father became more self-confident.

"I've had a bellyful of this town, do you understand? I am ruining my eyes in this dump. I have to deal with scoundrels, idiots and bums. I can't move a finger without striking a wall. I bruise the wings of my spirit against the universal ignorance. Damn it all to hell! I'm going back to my old hang-out. Will you come to visit me there with that tramp you went and married?"

(What a fellow Renaud is! He has fascinated even Papa, who sees very little of him but always speaks of him in a special tone of gruff affection.)

"Bet your life I will!"

"But—there's one very important matter I must discuss with you—what to do about the cat? The creature is accustomed to me—"

"The cat?"

(That's so, there's the cat. He is very fond of her. And Mélie will be there, too. Besides, I wouldn't trust Fanchette to Renaud's valet or his cook. My dear little daughter, I have another warm body than yours beside me at night now.)

I made up my mind.

"Take her with you, Papa. I will decide later on. Some day I may come and get her."

(What is uppermost in my mind is that, under pretext of doing my filial duty, I shall have a chance to see the old house once more, just as I left it, filled with enthralling memories—also the dear old school, with its shady reputation. At the bottom of my heart I bless my father's sudden departure.)

"Take my bedroom set, too, Papa. I will use it when we go to see you."

The bulwark of malacology crushed me with a scornful glance.

"Ugh! You would not blush to pollute my immaculate roof by cohabiting with your husband—as you women all do, foul creatures that you are! What do you care about regenerative chastity?"

How I love him when he is in this mood! I kissed him and came away, leaving him busily burying his treasures in the deep box and gaily humming a country song he adores:

"You know very well that I mean what I say,"
She said as she fondled her tra-la-la-lay.
  "You know very well,
    Not a word more I'll say."

So that's the Hymn to Regenerative Chastity!

"By the way, I'm starting my days at home again."

I learned this piece of news from Renaud while in our dressing room, getting ready for bed. We had spent the evening at Madame Barman's and, by way of a change, had witnessed a battle royal between that fat old hen and the loud-mouthed boor who shares her lot in life.

She said to him, "What a vulgar person you are!"

To which he retorted, "You bore everyone with your literary pretentions."

And they were both right.

He yelled and she squawked. The performance lasted quite a while. At a loss for invectives, he threw down his napkin, left the table and noisily tramped up to his room. Everybody sighed and relaxed and we finished our dinner in peace. When we came to the dessert, our hostess sent Eugenia, the chambermaid, to cajole the coarse fellow (by what mysterious means?). He finally came downstairs again pacified, but offered no apology. In spite of this, Gréveuille, the mincing academician, a faint-hearted soul, blamed his venerable ladylove, made a fuss over the husband and helped himself to the cheese again.

To this charming setting I contributed my curly head, my soft, suspicious eyes, a suggestively lowcut dress, showing a sturdy, well developed neck on a slender pair of shoulders, and a taciturn mood that embarrassed my table companions.

Nobody tries to flirt with me. My marriage is still so recent that it keeps people at a distance and I am not the type that is on the lookout for opportunities to flirt.

One Wednesday, at this same old Barman's, I was followed about —oh, very politely—by a goodlooking young writer. (The boy had handsome eyes, slightly inflamed, but what if he had?)

He compared me to Myrtocleia (my short hair, as usual!), to a youthful Hermes and to one of Prud'hon's cupids. For my benefit he ransacked his memory and the secret museums, quoted so many hermaphroditic works of art that I began to think of Luce and Marcel and he almost spoiled for me a heavenly *cassoulet*, a specialty at the Barmans', which was served in individual, silver-bordered baking dishes.

"Every man to his own bean-pot—amusing isn't it, sir?" Maugis whispered into Gréveuille's ear—to which the sixty-year-old parasite assented with a lopsided smile.

My young flatterer, aroused by his own suggestiveness, kept right after me. Taking refuge in a Louis Fifteenth high-backed chair, I watched him parade his literary knowledge but hardly listened at all to what he was saying. He gazed at me with his caressing, long-lashed eyes and murmured for only me to hear, "Ah, but your reverie is that of a childlike Narcissus, his soul filled with ardent desire and bitter sorrow!"

"My dear sir," I replied quite positively, "you are talking through your hat. My soul at present is filled with nothing but kidney beans and smoked pork."

He shut up as if struck dumb.

Renaud scolded me a little and laughed a lot.

"So you're going to hold receptions again, you dear fellow?"

He had planted his long frame in a wicker armchair, while I undressed with my customary chaste unconcern. (Chaste? Well, let us say free from evil intention.)

"Yes. And what do you plan to do, little one? You looked very sweet and tempting this evening at that hook-nosed Barman's."

"What am I planning to do when you start your days at home again? Why, I'll come and call on you."

"Is that all?" the disappointed expression on his chin inquired.

"Of course. What else would I be doing at your reception?"

"But after all, Claudine, you're my wife!"

"Who's fault is that? If you had been willing to listen to me, I would be your mistress now, all fixed up nicely in a quiet little hole in the wall."

"In a hole in the wall?"

"Yes, in a cozy nook somewhere, far away from all your social set, and your days at home could take their usual course. Go ahead and do just as if you were my lover."

(Good Lord! he is taking me literally! Just because I picked up with a nimble foot my mauve silk slip which had fallen to the floor, my tall husband has swung into action, all excited over the double Claudine he saw reflected in the mirrors.)

"Nay, nay, none of that now, Renaud! Shame on you! A gentleman in full dress with a little girl in her panties! Why, that's as bad as a Marcel Prévost description of high-class depravity."

(The truth is that Renaud takes great interest in what the gossipy mirrors have to tell with their naughty reflections, whereas I avoid them and ignore their revelations, preferring darkness, silence and ecstasy.)

"Renaud dear, we were discussing your day at home."

"To hell with my day! I much prefer your night."

8

SO PAPA has left the way he came. I did not accompany him to the railway station, not caring to witness the turbulent departure, which I could very well imagine. Left to his own resources, he will envelop himself in a stormy cloud and hurl invectives at the "filthy gang" of employees, whom he will scornfully tip with lavish generosity, while forgetting to pay his taxi.

Mélie was sincerely sorry to leave me, although the permission to take Fanchette along healed her bleeding heart "for the time being." Poor Mélie! she still cannot understand her "little girlie." Here I have married the man of my choice, I sleep with him as much as I want to—even more!—I live in a lovely house, have a man-servant and a car hired by the month, and I'm not more stuck up than that? In Mélie's opinion, a sense of superiority should manifest itself visibly.

For that matter, she may be partly right. When I am with Renaud, I think of nothing but him. He is more engrossing than a spoiled woman. The intensity of his inner life shows itself outwardly in smiles, comments, humming of airs, lover's demands. He reproaches me affectionately for not making love to him, for being able to read in his presence, for fastening my gaze too frequently on some point in infinite space.

When away from him, I feel embarrassed at being in an abnormal and illicit situation. Can it be that "the married state" was not intended for me? Still, I ought to be growing accustomed to it by this time. After all, Renaud is only getting what he deserves. He didn't need to insist on our getting married.

9

S PREAD the news! My husband has started holding receptions again.

The news spread all right!

What did Renaud do to the good Lord to bring down on himself so many friends? Ernest, the butler, ushered some two-score persons—men, women and Marcel—into the study, done in mulatto-colored leather and smelling agreeably of oriental tobacco, and into the long foyer, to which we had consigned the drawings and sketches from here, there and everywhere.

The very first time the doorbell rang, I jumped to my feet and ran and shut myself up in the comforting safety of our dressing-room. The bell rang again and again and every time it rang, I had shivers up and down my spine that made me think of Fanchette, who on rainy days has the same nervous spasms as she watches the big drops of water drip from the leaky gutter. Alas, we're a long way off from Fanchette! Here comes Renaud to plead with me through the bolted door of my hiding-place.

"Claudine, my precious child, I can't keep it up any longer. At first I told them you hadn't come home yet but, believe me, the situation is getting critical. Maugis maintains that I am hiding you in a subterranean chamber known only to God Almighty."

(As I listen to him, I look at myself in the mirror and laugh involuntarily.)

"People are going to think you're scared."

(The rascal! He's gone and said exactly the right thing! I brush my hair down over my forehead, feel to see if my skirt is hooked and open the door.)

"Can I appear like this before your friends?"

"Yes, yes. I adore you in black."

"That's no answer! You like me in any color."

"Especially flesh color, I admit! Come quick, dear!"

They had been smoking a lot in my husband's lodgings. The aroma of tea mingled with that of ginger—then the strawberries and ham sandwiches and pâté-de-foie-gras sandwiches and caviar sandwiches—how quickly a warm room gets to smell like a night club!

I took a seat and played that I was merely a visitor. My husband offered me some tea as if I were one of the regular guests and it was the pretty woman from Cyprus with the paradoxical name, Madame van Langendonck, who brought me the cream. It was great fun!

Here—at Renaud's—I met again the same mixed company I had been meeting at concerts and at the theatre—the big critics and the little ones, some with their wives, the others with their mistresses. Yes, they were all there. I had insisted with my husband that there should be no censorship—a horrid word—and the thing itself would have been even more detestable. And besides, as I have said, it was not I who was receiving.

Holding a wineglass full of kummel in his hand, Maugis was questioning with marvelously feigned interest the author of a feminist novel, who was expounding the thesis which his next book was to deal with. The writer talked untiringly and the listener drank unceasingly until, properly intoxicated, he inquired in a thick voice, "What did you say is the title of this masterly work?"

"The right title has eluded us thus far."

"Try to follow its example, my dear man," Maugis retorted, as he walked away stiffly.

From the large foreign delegation present I drew a Spanish sculptor with handsome horse-like eyes, a finely cut mouth and only a passing acquaintance with our language. He was especially interested in painting.

I confessed to him without the least embarrassment that I hardly knew the Louvre at all and that I wallowed in my ignorance without any very great desire to climb out of it.

"You don't know the Rubens pictures?"

"No."

"And you don't want to see them?"

"No."

Thereupon he stood up, struck an Andalusian pose and, with a deep, respectful bow, dealt me this blow:

"You are a pig, madame!"

A handsome woman who belongs to the Opéra troupe (and also to one of Renaud's friends) started and looked at us, expecting a scene. But she didn't get it. I had understood the character of this esthete from across the Pyrenées who has only one disparaging expression at his command. "Pig" is the only term he knows. We ourselves have only one word for "love"—which is quite as ridiculous.

As someone came in Renaud exclaimed, "I thought you were in London! Then you've sold it?"

"Yes, we've sold it and we're living in Paris now," replied a worn-out voice, with just a touch of English accent, barely noticeable.

A tall, brick-complexioned, blond-haired man stood talking to Renaud. He was square-shouldered and held his small head with its opaque blue eyes very erect. Square-shouldered as I have just said, and well dressed, he nevertheless carried himself stiffly, like a man who is continually remembering to stand up straight and look as if he were in robust health.

His wife and I were introduced but I did not catch her name. I was taken up with looking at her and I very soon caught on to one of the principal reasons for her charm—every motion, the swinging of the hips, curving of the neck, quick raising of one hand to her hair, circular swaying of the body while seated, formed curves so nearly round that I could discern the pattern of intercepting rings (like the perfect spirals of some sea shells) which her leisurely movements left traced in the air.

Behind their long lashes, her eyes, of an amber-shaded changeable grey, seemed darker by contrast with her wavy hair of feathery greenish-tinted gold. A black velvet gown of too rich material but simple design clung to her round, flexible hips and her small though not tightly laced waist. A tiny, star-shaped diamond clip twinkled among the folds of her hat.

Slipping her warm little fingers out of her fox muff, she shakes my hand quickly as she looks me over. I instinctively expect her to speak with a foreign accent. For some vague reason, in spite of her correct attire and the absence of jewels and even of a necklace, she strikes me as having something of the adventuress about her.

Her eyes have a foreign look. She talks—let us listen a moment. Upon my word! she talks without the slightest accent. How stupid it is to jump at conclusions! Her fresh, rosy lips, small when in repose, become tempting and full-blown when she speaks.

She immediately begins by showering me with flattering remarks.

"I'm so glad to make your acquaintance! I knew your husband would dig up a pretty wife somewhere who would surprise and charm us all."

"Many thanks on behalf of my husband, but aren't you now going to pay me a compliment that I can keep all for myself?"

"You don't need any," she replies. "Just resign yourself to being different from everybody else."

She scarcely stirs at all and then only with restrained movements and yet, merely to come and sit down beside me, she seems to turn around twice inside her gown.

Are we coquetting with one another already or are we sparring? Coquetting, rather. In spite of her flattering remark of a few minutes ago, I don't feel the slightest desire to scratch her eyes out—she is charming. Being nearer to her now, I count her multiple curves and spirals. Her hair obediently curls on her neck, her intricate, delicate ear curves around and around, her radiating eyelashes and the quivering feathers draped about her hat seem to be thrown outward by some invisible centrifugal gyration.

I am tempted to ask her how many whirling dervishes she numbers among her ancestors. But I must not—Renaud would scold me. And besides, why should I shock this attractive Madame Lambrook so soon after meeting her?

"Has Renaud spoken to you about us?" she inquires.

"Never. Are you well acquainted?"

"I should say so! We've had dinner together at least six times now, to say nothing of the receptions."

Is she making fun of me? Is she sarcastic or merely dumb? We'll find out about that later on. For the present, I am fascinated by her cajoling voice and gently drawling speech, in which from time to time a rebellious *r* lingers and purrs softly.

I let her talk on, the while she never takes her eyes off me, noting closely in a near-sighted manner but without embarrassment the color of my eyes, which match my bobbed hair.

She proceeds to tell me about herself. Inside of fifteen minutes I know that her husband is a former British officer, completely broken in health by service in India, where he lost his physical strength and mental activity. She gives one to understand clearly that there is nothing left of him but a handsome, hollow shell.

I learn also that she is rich, but "never, never rich enough," she declares passionately, and that her Viennese mother gave her beautiful hair, a skin as white as a morning glory blossom (I am quoting) and the name of Rézi.

"Rézi," I commented. "That is a strange name!"

"In this country, yes, but I believe that in Vienna it is a pet name about as stylish as Nana or Titine."

"It's all the same to me. Rézi. How pretty that sounds—Rézi!"

"It sounds pretty because you say it so prettily," she replied.

Her ungloved finger-tips glided over my bare neck so swiftly that I started, more as a nervous reaction than from surprise, because I had for a couple of minutes been watching the gaze of her restless eyes playing about my neck.

"Rézi—"

This time it is her husband, who wishes to take her away. He comes up to bid me good-bye and his opaque blue eyes embarrass

627

me. I fancy this "hollow shell" can still house quite a bit of jealousy and despotism, for at his brief summons Rézi gets up quickly without protest. He expresses himself in slow, measured terms—"as if he had to wait for the prompter every few minutes," Maugis says. Obviously he is watching his enunciation in order to eliminate any trace of British accent.

They agree that "we must get together often" and that "Madame Claudine is adorable." If I keep my promise, I shall call on this blonde Rézi at her home in Avenue Kléber, only a few steps away.

Rézi! Her entire person exhales an odor of ferns and iris, an unpretentious, straightforward, bucolic odor which surprises and charms one by its contrast—for I do not find anything unpretentious or bucolic about her. Nor, on my word, straightforward either—she is far too pretty for that! She talked to me about her husband and her travels and myself, but I know nothing about her save her charm.

"Well, dear?"

My darling husband, keyed up and contented, looks about with satisfaction at the drawing-room, empty at last. Dirty dishes, half-nibbled lady-fingers, ashes from cigarettes laid on the arm of a chair or the edge of a table (they sure have some nerve, these ill-bred callers!), glasses sticky with horrible concoctions (I even came upon one southern poet with classic locks who was engaged in mixing together orangeade, kummel, brandy, cherry cordial and Russian anisette! "A liquid Jezebel!" exclaimed little Madame de Lizery, Robert Parville's sweetheart, who informed me that at the Oiseaux school the pupils always called any dreadful mixture a "Jezebel.")

"Well, dear, you don't say anything about my reception."

"Your reception, my dear man? Why, I think you are more to be pitied than blamed—and you ought to open the windows. There are quite a lot of these cream puffs left. They look very inviting but are you sure, as my worthy father would say, that somebody hasn't wiped his feet on them?"

Renaud shakes his head and presses his temples. He has a headache coming on.

"Your worthy father is a very cautious individual. Follow his example, my dear, and don't touch these suspicious-looking victuals. I saw Suzanne de Lizery handling them with caressing fingers that had been—who knows where?—and bore signs of fatigue in their bluish nails."

"Ugh! Shut up or I won't be able to eat any dinner. Let's go and dress."

My husband had so many people at his reception today that I am frightfully tired. But he—my youthful, white-haired Renaud!—seems more full of life than ever. He goes here and there, chatting and laughing, comes and takes a whiff of me—which, it seems, is a sure preventive of headache—and circles around my chair.

"What's the matter with you? You're hovering about like a buzzard."

"A buzzard indeed? I don't know the animal. The buzzard represents to me a little brown animal with a hooked nose, who strikes with his hoof and has a rotten reputation. Is that it?"

This picture of a four-footed bird of prey threw me into such a fit of youthful merriment that my husband stopped before me, almost annoyed. But I only laughed the more and his eyes changed their expression and looked at me ardently.

"Is it as funny as all that, you little curly-haired shepherd boy? Laugh once more and let me see all that pretty mouth."

(Look out! I am in danger of being loved a bit too ardently.)

"Nay, nay, my lad—not before dinner!"

"Afterwards, then?"

"I don't know."

"Very well then, before and after. Don't you admire my skill as a conciliator?"

Weak-willed, too-yielding Claudine! He has a certain way of kissing that is an open-sesame, after which I have a heart for nothing but darkness, naked bodies and the silent, futile struggle to hold myself in check for one minute, one minute more, on the brink of ecstatic bliss.

"What kind of people are they, Renaud?"

(The lights out, I seek my place in the bed, my special spot on his shoulder, where the plump muscle of the upper arm makes a soft, familiar cushion for my head. Renaud stretches out his long legs as I press my chilly feet against them and, throwing his head back, tries to find the center of a pad of horsehair which he uses for a pillow—unvarying preparations for the night, which are almost as invariably followed or preceded by certain other ceremonies.)

"Are who, my little one?"

"The Rézi's—I mean, the Lambrooks."

"Ah, I felt sure you'd like the wife."

"Hurry up and tell me who they are."

"Well, they're a delightful but ill mated couple. What I specially appreciate in the wife is her neck and shoulders with their milky blue veins. She displays as much of them at private dinner parties as a young creature can who is solicitous about the happiness of others. I like also her insinuating coquetry—expressed in movements rather than in words—and her fondness for frequent changes of residence.

"In her husband it was the collapse hidden behind his square shoulders and correct bearing which roused my interest. The real Colonel Lambrook stayed behind in the colonies—only his physical shell came back here. He still leads a secret life out there. The minute anyone mentions his precious India, he ceases to reply and cloaks himself in haughty silence in order to conceal his emotion. What fascination of suffering, beauty or beloved cruelty holds him enthralled out there? Nobody knows. And that is such a rare thing, little girl, a soul so tightly closed that it can keep its secret from everyone."

(My dear Renaud, is it really so rare?)

"The first evening I dined with them—that was two years ago—in the fantastic bazaar that served as their home at that time, I was treated to a very fine Burgundy and I asked whether I could get some like it.

" 'Yes,' replied Lambrook, 'it is not expensive.' "

"He thought for a moment and then, raising his terra cotta face, added, 'Twenty rupees, I think.' "

"And he had been back in Europe for ten years!"

I remained silent and thoughtful for a moment, snuggling close to my darling's warm body.

"Does he love his wife, Renaud?"

"Perhaps he does, and yet he treats her with a combination of courtesy and brutality which does not make me very hopeful."

"Is she untrue to him?"

"My dear little question mark, how should I know?"

"Why not? She might have been your mistress."

The positive tone in which I made that statement convulsed Renaud with ill-timed laughter.

"Lie still, Renaud, you're mussing up my side of the bed. I didn't say anything as silly as all that. There's nothing shocking about the idea for either you or her. Do you know any of her women friends?"

"Why, this is a regular inquest—worse than that, a conquest! I never saw you so taken with a stranger."

"That's true, but you see I'm reforming. You accuse me of being unsociable, so I'm planning to develop some acquaintances and, having met a pretty woman with an agreeable voice and a hand it is pleasant to touch, I proceed to get information about her, I—"

"Claudine," Renaud broke in with mock seriousness, "don't you think there's a suggestion of Luce in Rézi's—er—skin?"

What a mean fellow! Why did he have to take the bloom off the whole thing with that remark? I flopped over like a fish and went off to sleep in a chaste and chilly region on the easternmost border of the big bed.

10

T HERE'S a big gap in my diary. As I have not kept the record of my impressions up-to-date, I shall surely make mistakes in summing them up now.

Life continues its regular pace and Renaud goes here, there and everywhere in lively fashion. It is cold and he drives me from one first-night to another, complaining loudly that he's sick and tired of the theater and disgusted with the coarseness of that "medium."

"But, Renaud," simple-minded Claudine inquires, "why do you go then?"

"Because—you're going to condemn me now, my stern little judge—because I want to see the people there. I want to see whether Annhine de Lys is still chummy with Willy's friend, Miss Flossy, whether pretty Madame Mundoe's Reboux hat is a success or not, whether that strange Polaire, with her seductive eyes like a love-sick gazelle, still holds the record for a wasp-like waist. Or I want to watch the lyrical Mendès recite his flowery patter at some supper-table after midnight, or have a good laugh looking at grotesque Mama with Gréveuille, her 'night errant', as Maugis calls him, or to gaze with admiration on the colonel's aigrette that tops that fat old weasel, Madame de Saint-Niketês."

No, I don't condemn him for being so frivolous. And, even if I did, it would be of no importance because I love him. I know that first-night audiences never listen to the play, but I do listen—with passionate interest—or else I say, "This is disgusting."

Renaud envies me for having such strong and simple convictions. "You're young, my dear," he says—but not as youthful as he! He loves me, attends to his work, pays calls, gossips, dines out, receives every Friday at four and still has time to think to buy me a sable bolero.

Now and then, when we are alone together, his charming, tired face relaxes and he holds me close and sighs with great sadness.

"Claudine, dear child, how old I am! I can feel the wrinkles growing deeper every minute. It hurts—oh, how it hurts!"

If he only knew how I adore him when he is in that mood and how ardently I hope that time will calm his feverish desire to be always on exhibition. When he is willing to give up being seen everywhere, then—and not till then—we shall really come together. Not till then shall I cease the effort to keep up with this forty-five-year-old livewire.

11

ONE day, recalling with a smile the Andalusian sculptor and his "You are a pig, madame," I took it into my head to explore the Louvre and admire those new Rubens paintings—without a guide. Togged out in my sable bolero and toque to match, I set out bravely alone, with no sense of direction and losing my way at every turn in the galleries, like one of Zola's wedding parties. For, whereas I am able in the woods to tell instinctively the time and the points of the compass, I get lost in a simple apartment all on one floor.

I found the Rubens pictures. They are disgusting. Yes, disgusting. For at least half an hour I tried conscientiously to get all het up literarily (Maugis' style is infecting me), but it's no use! That red meat, all that red meat! That chubby-cheeked, powdered Marie de Médicis, with her dripping breasts! And that plump warrior, her husband, borne away by a glorious and robust zephyr—bah, bah, triple bah! I shall never understand such art. If Renaud and his women friends should know! Well, what do I care? If they press me, I shall say just what I think.

Downhearted, I walked away with mincing steps, resisting the temptation to slide over the polished floor between the rows of masterpieces looking down on me.

Ah! this is more like it! Here are some Italians and Spaniards who amount to something. All the same, somebody had a nerve to label "Saint John the Baptist" that sharp-featured, enticing face by da Vinci which leans forward smilingly like Mademoiselle Moreno.

My God, that fellow's handsome! So at last I've met the lad who could have made me fall from grace! What luck that he's on canvas! Who is it? "Portrait of a sculptor," by Bronzino. How I'd like to touch that forehead under the thick black hair where it swells out just above the eyebrows, and kiss those eyes of a cynical page! That soft white hand molded statues? I'll try to believe it.

From the tones of the face I can imagine that that velvety skin was of the kind that takes on a greenish tint like old ivory at the groin and behind the knee—a skin that's warm at every point, even at the calves, and moist on the palm of the hand.

What am I up to? Awaking from my reverie and blushing red, I look about me. What am I up to? Why I've been untrue to Renaud, by Jove!

I'll have to tell Rézi about this æsthetic adultery. She will laugh with that laugh which breaks out suddenly and dies down gradually. For we have become good friends, Rézi and I. A fortnight sufficed. Ours is now what Renaud would call "a close acquaintance of long standing."

Good friends? Yes, indeed! I am enchanted with her and she finds me charming. I ought to add that we do not confide in one another to any serious extent. Doubtless it is still a bit too soon for that—at any rate, too soon for me, certainly. Rézi does not deserve that I open my soul to her. I let her have my company frequently, also my curly head, which she loves to comb out— a hopeless task!—and my face, which she seems to love without jealousy, as she holds it between her two soft hands while she watches my eyes dance, as she puts it.

With coquettish insistence she displays to me freely her beauty and her grace. For the past few days I have been going to her house every morning at eleven.

The Lambrooks live in one of those apartments on the Avenue Kléber in which the architect has sacrificed so much to the janitor, the stairway and the first and second drawing-rooms—rather fine woodwork and a good copy of the young Louis Fifteenth by Van Loo—that the private rooms get light and air as best they can. Rézi sleeps in a long, dark room and dresses in a hallway. But I like this inconvenient dressing-room, always overheated. And Rézi dresses and undresses there with fairylike magic, as I sit primly in a low armchair and watch her with admiration.

There she is in her chemise. Her exquisite hair, touched with pink under the dazzling electric light and showing a metallic green in the dim, bluish daylight, sparkles with fire when she shakes her head to fluff it up. Whatever the time of day, this deceptive double light from the inadequate window and the excessive electric illumination always throws its theatrical glare on her.

She brushes out her hair which resembles a billowing mist. One stroke of a fairy wand and the magic comb has gathered in all that gold, smoothed it out and coiled it demurely above her neck. What makes it stay up?

Open-eyed, I am about to beg, "Do it again," but Rézi does not wait. Another stroke of the wand and the pretty woman in her chemise now stands before me in a tight-fitting, dark gown with her hat on, ready to go out. The stiff girdle, the daring drawers and the soft, silent slip have come fluttering down on her like eager birds.

Rézi looks at me triumphantly and laughs.

Her undressing is no less enchanting. Her clothes fall off all at once, as if tied together, for this charming rival of Fregoli keeps on only her chemise and—her hat. How that hat does irritate and astonish me! She puts it on before she puts on her girdle and takes it off after she has removed her stockings. She says she even bathes with her hat on.

"But why wear your hat so religiously?"

"I have no idea. A question of modesty, perhaps. If the house caught fire some night and I had to flee, I wouldn't mind running out in the street entirely naked—but not without my hat."

"Well, I declare! The firemen would have a grand time!"

She looks even prettier than the first time I saw her and not as tall as I thought—with a white complexion only occasionally touched with pink and a dainty, well proportioned figure. Her nearsightedness, the uncertain gray of her eyes and her constantly moving eyelashes veil her thoughts. The fact is, I know her only slightly, notwithstanding her impulsive remark the fourth time we met, "There are three things I adore, Claudine—travel, Paris and—you."

She was born in Paris and loves the city like a foreigner—passionately fond of its cold and questionable odors, of the theaters and the streets and of the twilight hour when the lamps touch with red the deep blue of the sky.

"Nowhere else, Claudine, are the women as good-looking as in Paris! (We'll leave Montigny out of the discussion if you don't mind, my dear.) It's in Paris one sees the most prepossessing women of forty, made up and tight-laced to the limit, with faces of well preserved beauty, having retained a finely shaped nose and youthful eyes, women who are both pleased and embittered to be stared at."

Anyone who thinks and talks like that is no silly fool. That time, as though to thank her for turning her thoughts so prettily, I pressed her finely tapered fingers as they accompanied her words with spiral gestures. The very next day she stood before the window at Liberty's and thrilled with delight—over an obvious combination of pink and saffron satin!

Nearly every morning, shortly before noon, when I finally made up my mind to leave the Avenue Kléber apartment—invariably late—and the low armchair in which I would like to stay a while longer, and go home to my husband and lunch and to Renaud's eager embraces and his fondness for rare meat (for he does not live on meadow larks and bananas, as I do), the dressing-room door opens noiselessly and discloses Lambrook's deceptively robust figure.

Only yesterday it happened again and Rézi exclaimed, exasperated, "Which way did you come?"

"Along the Avenue des Champs-Elysées," Lambrook replied calmly.

Then he lingered, kissing my hand, examining my unbuttoned bolero and looking sharply at Rézi in her chemise.

Finally he said to his wife, "What a lot of time you waste putting your clothes on, my dear!"

Thinking of my friend's remarkable quickness, I burst out laughing. Lambrook never winced, but a slight shadow passed over his terra cotta face. He asked after Renaud, expressed the hope of having us soon to dinner and then went away.

"What got into him, Rézi?" I asked.

"Oh, nothing. But you shouldn't laugh when he is speaking to me, Claudine. He thinks you're laughing at him."

"Really? Well, I don't care if he does."

"But I do. I'm in for a scene now. His jealousy is getting hard to stand."

"Jealous of me? For what? What an idiot!"

"He doesn't like me to have a woman friend."

Can it be that he has his reasons for this?

And yet there has been nothing in Rézi's behavior that would lead me to think so. Sometimes she looks at me for a long time without blinking—the straight line of her eyelids making her near-sighted eyes look longer. Her small, closed lips open part way with a childlike, tempting expression. A slight quiver passes over her shoulders and with a nervous laugh she exclaims, "Somebody just stepped on my grave." Then she kisses me—that's all. I would have to be very conceited to imagine—

I give her no encouragement. I let the time pass as I study this iridescent Rézi in all her phases and await whatever is coming. I wait and wait—more from indolence than from virtue.

I went to see Rézi this morning—notwithstanding which she came hurrying impatiently to my house about five o'clock. She sat down after turning around a couple of times, the way Fanchette does.

Her dark blue tailor suit brought out the reddish gold in her hair. She wore an elaborate hat trimmed with birds, a veritable battle of gray sea-gulls, so lifelike that it would not have surprised me very much to hear shrill cries come from their entangled beaks.

She settled down as if she had come to take refuge, and sighed.

"What's the trouble, Rézi?" I asked.

"Nothing. I get so bored at home. The people who come there make me tired. One—two—three flirtations today, until I'm sick of it all. The sameness of these men! I could have hit the last one."

"Why that one specially?"

"Because the miserable fellow told me he loved me only half an hour after the second one had said the same thing and in the very same words! And the second one was merely repeating what the first had said. Those three won't see me again very soon. Good God, all these men who are exactly alike!"

"Take only one of them—there's more variety that way."

"Also more fatigue."

"But how about your husband—doesn't he get sore?"

"Why, no! Why should he?"

(Now, look here! Does she take me for a simpleton? What about her precautions the other morning and her warning hints to me? And yet she looks at me in the frankest manner, with reflections of moonstone and gray pearl in her eyes.)

"Come now, Rézi! Only the day before yesterday I wasn't even to laugh at anything he said."

"Oh, well!"—and her hand gracefully whips up some imaginary mayonnaise in the air—"But, Claudine, it's not the same thing, you and these men who come purring around me."

"I should hope not! Especially considering that my reasons for pleasing you could not possibly be the same as theirs."

(She darted a quick glance at me and as quickly looked away.)

"But tell me, Rézi, why you seem always glad to see me."

(Reassured, she put down her muff in order to be better able to emphasize with her hands, her head and her whole body what she wished to tell me. Then she settled back in the deep armchair and smiled at me tenderly and mysteriously.)

"You want to know why I like you, Claudine? I might simply answer, 'Because I think you're pretty,' and that would be explanation enough for me but it would not satisfy your pride.

"Why do I like you? Because your hair and your eyes, made of the same metal, are all that remains of a little statue of light-colored bronze, all the rest of which has turned to flesh—because your vigorous movements go well with your gentle voice—because you tame your unsociable nature for my special benefit—because you blush over some hidden thought that escapes you or that someone guesses, as you would over a brazen hand that slipped under your skirts—because—"

I stopped her with a gesture—a brusque one, I admit. I was annoyed and disturbed that so much of my inner self should show on the surface. Should I be angry with her—break with her then and there?

She forestalled any adverse decision by impulsively kissing me beside the ear. Buried in her furs and grazed by sharp wings, I had scarcely had time to inhale her fragrance, the deceptive simplicity of her perfume, when Renaud came in.

I stood there embarrassed, with my back against the chair—embarrassed, not at the position I was in, not over Rézi's hurried kiss, but by Renaud's piercing glance and the smiling, almost encouraging indulgence I read on his face.

He kissed my friend's hand and said, "Please! Don't let me interrupt anything."

"You're not interrupting anything at all—nor anybody," she

639

exclaimed. "On the contrary, come and help me mollify Claudine. She is displeased over a very sincere compliment I paid her."

"Very sincere, I don't doubt, but did you put sufficient conviction into your tone?" Renaud replied. "My Claudine is a very intense and earnest little girl who"—belonging to a generation that still read Alfred de Musset, he hummed the accompaniment to Don Juan's serenade—"could not tolerate certain smiles implied in certain words."

"Renaud," I protested, "no conjugal revelations, I beg you!"

Being vexed, I unconsciously raised my voice, but Rézi turned toward me with her most disarming smile.

"Oh please, Claudine! Let him go on. I am so interested! And it's really a kindness to corrupt my ears a bit—they're getting to a point where they scarcely know the meaning of the word 'love.'"

Hmm! This eagerness of a half-starved wife hardly seems to tally with the surfeit of flirtation, which she mentioned a few minutes ago. But Renaud doesn't know anything about that. Touched and sympathetic, he looks Rézi over from top to toe and I can't help laughing when he exclaims:

"Poor child! So young and already bereft of what gives life its color and beauty! Come unto me! Consolation awaits you on the divan in my sacrificial office and it won't cost you as much as to go to a specialist."

"Are you quite sure? I distrust these professional discounts to artists."

"You're not an artist. Besides, one either plays fair or one doesn't."

"And you don't. No, thank you!"

"You shall pay—whatever you wish to give."

"What is that?"

Half closing her smoke-colored eyes, she added, "Who knows but you might merely tarry awhile at the gate."

"I would far rather tarry within the gate."

Delighted with the sensation of being assaulted, so to speak, Rézi drew in her chin and swelled out her neck the way Fanchette does when she comes across an extra large grasshopper or a horned beetle.

"No, once more no, benefactor of the human race. I haven't reached that point yet."

"What point, pray, have you already reached?"

"Compensatory satisfactions."

"Which ones? There are several kinds—two, at least."

She blushed, acted more nearsighted than she is and turned to me with a sinuous gesture of entreaty.

"Claudine, come to my defense!"

"I will indeed—by forbidding you to let Renaud console you."

"Oh, really? Jealous, eh?"

She sparkled with a far from charitable joy that greatly enhanced her good looks. Sitting on the edge of her chair, one leg straight out and the other one bent at the knee, its rounded form showing under her skirt, she leaned toward me in a tense posture as though she were ready to flee. The fine down on her cheek was of a paler gold than her hair, and her eyelashes quivered unceasingly, as transparent as the gauzy wings of a wasp. Captivated by so much beauty, I replied very honestly:

"Jealous? Oh, no, Rézi. You are much too pretty for that. Now, if Renaud should be untrue to me with a homely woman, I could never forgive him the humiliation."

Renaud gave me one of those understanding, affectionate looks which bring me back to him whenever my unsociable nature or a particularly strong attack of aloofness or of woolgathering has carried me rather far away. I felt grateful to him for thus silently saying so many tender things to me over Rézi's head.

Meanwhile Rézi, the Blonde Queen—had she fully caught my meaning?—came over to me, nervously stretching her hands clasped inside her muff, and murmured with a pout and a shrug of her shoulders:

"I give it up. Your complicated psychology requires too great an effort for me and I'm hungry."

"Oh, you poor girl. To think of my letting you starve this way!"

I jumped up and rang for the butler.

In a few minutes the steaming cups and butter-soaked toast were exhaling an atmosphere of friendly peace and understanding.

As for me, I despise the tea of these fashionable folks. Holding a basket between my knees, I nibble at withered sorb-apples and squeeze and pick at flabby medlars, winter delicacies from back home, sent me by Mélie and smelling of the cellar and over-ripe fruit.

And just because a piece of toast, burnt and blackened, spread through the room an odor of fresh charcoal, I was immediately off for Montigny on the wings of my imagination, flying toward the hooded fireplace. I seemed to see—I do see—Mélie throw on the fire a bundle of damp twigs and Fanchette, sitting on the raised hearthstone, draw back a little, shocked at the boldness of the flames and the crackling of the green wood.

"My little daughter!"

I had been dreaming aloud! Renaud's amusement and Rézi's amazement made me blush and I, too, laughed, but from embarrassment.

12

THE debilitating winter drags out its warmish, decaying existence. January is nearing its end. In what alterations of haste and indolence the days pass by! Theater parties, dinners, matinées and concerts until the early morning hours. Renaud swells with pride and pleasure. As for me, I give in to him.

We wake late. Then a flood of newspapers submerges the bed. Renaud divides his attention between England's attitude and Claudine's as she lies on her stomach, wrapt in bad-tempered dreams, a hearty sleeper who is being robbed of too much indispensable rest by this unnatural existence.

A hasty luncheon—rare meat for my husband and all sorts of atrocious sugary concoctions for me. From two to five o'clock the program varies.

The one thing that does not change is my call on Rézi (or hers on me) at five. She is becoming more and more attached to me without concealing the fact, and I to her—my God, yes!—but I try to cover it up.

At seven o'clock almost every evening, as we are leaving some tea-room, or a bar where Rézi has warmed herself with a cocktail as I nibbled some too salty potato chips, I think to myself with suppressed anger that I must go home to dress, that Renaud is already waiting for me as he puts in his pearl shirtstuds. I must confess—although my modesty suffers horribly over it!—that, on account of my sensible bob, I seem to disturb the thoughts of both men and women alike.

The men, because of my shorn locks and my coldness toward them, say to themselves, "She prefers women." For obviously, if I do not care for men, I must have a special fondness for women— such is the simplicity of the masculine mind!

And the women, too—because of my shorn locks and my coldness toward their husbands and their lovers—seem inclined to reason the same way. I have noticed pretty glances—questioning, abashed and furtive—cast in my direction, sudden blushes when my gaze rested for a moment on an exposed shoulder or a perfectly shaped neck.

I have also had to bear the brunt of very frankly expressed advances, but these drawing-room professionals—one square-built dame of fifty or over, a dark-complexioned, bony young girl with undeveloped hips, a monocled woman who sticks her sharp nose into low-cut bodices as if trying to fish up a lost ring—these temptresses have discovered in Claudine a lack of interest that evidently shocked them. Which almost wrecked a reputation that was coming along fine.

643

On the other hand, day before yesterday I detected on the lips of one of my "friends"—that is to say, a young literary woman whom I have met half a dozen times—such a malicious smile at the mention of Rézi's name that I understood the whole situation. And it occurred to me that Rézi's husband is liable to kick up a jolly row when the gossip reaches his sun-baked ear.

Yet one day I unintentionally came near thawing out that gentle-man—who, incidentally, is a most unattractive individual.

With my nerves all on edge, I was unwillingly listening, at one of Renaud's receptions, to the yappings of a group of baldheaded young men talking literature with high-pitched animation.

"His last novel? Don't fall for the advertising bunk! They have put out six editions in all."

"No, eight!"

"Six, I tell you! And at that, editions of only two hundred, in-cluding the review copies—Sevin told me so."

"What do you expect? The publisher prints as many as he wishes, many more than you get royalty on, and there's nothing you can do about it."

"Take my *Dissection of the Soul*, for example. Floury alone used to sell twenty copies a day. Well, it netted me altogether six hundred francs. And to cap the climax, didn't they want to deduct a miser-able advance of a hundred and fifty francs!"

"When you think that we get no royalty on the complimentary copies, it's disgusting! As for me, I coolly graft some books, on the pretext that they are for reviewers, and I go peddle them at Gougy's."

"So do I."

"I do too, by God! We've got to protect ourselves somehow."

"My dear man, when the publisher allows the retailer forty per cent discount and fourteen to the dozen, he could very easily pay us twenty sous per copy sold and still realize a neat little profit."

"He could even hand over thirty sous without going broke."

"What a gang they are!"

They all talked at once with the earnestness of those who don't want to hear. Thinking of Kipling and his monkey-kind, I muttered, "Bandar-log."

At this Hindu word which he instantly recognized, Lambrook, who was sitting beside me, had an unnatural quivering of the jaws. His pale and lusterless eyes met mine. But Rézi's nervous laugh rang out at the other end of the drawing-room and he got up with a nonchalant air to go and see with whom his wife was having such a noisy good time.

A too well known novelist, whose specialty is boring deep into women's souls, came and settled himself in the place left vacant by the ever watchful husband. He whispered to me, with the attitude and expression (put on for effect) of a man breathlessly hovering on the brink of ecstasy, "What miserable weather!"

Accustomed to the mannerisms of this "Paul Bourget of the Poor," as Renaud nicknamed him, I let him deliver without interruption an extempore recitation—carefully rehearsed behind closed doors and rather skilfully modulated—on the enervatingly warm weather, the deliciously demoralizing influence of early twilight and the deceptive spring-like character of this winter month. A more dependable springtime (excellent transition here), one of moist skin and full-blown bosoms, throbs beneath heavy fur wraps.

It was only a step from that to the desire to help remove those heavy wraps and let them fall on the noiseless rug of a well arranged bachelor apartment. Being wound up, this half-baked artist was about to take that step.

Dreamily and submissively, as if won over, I murmured, "Yes, outdoors it is as though one were breathing the dangerously intoxicating lifeless air of a hothouse."

Then, assuming an exaggerated country accent on purpose to disconcert him, I added brusquely, "And boy, oh boy! Will the wheat be a-sproutin' early this year 'n' also th' oats!"

What a lunatic he must have thought me! I could have danced a hornpipe for joy. But now the fellow, offended at my behavior, will go about repeating everywhere, like the rest of them, as he puffs out his big fat belly, "Claudine? She prefers women"—adding to himself, "because she doesn't prefer me."

Prefers women, eh? The pack of fools! Let them come into our room at—well, let's say ten in the morning and they'll see if I "prefer women"!

A letter—pompous and heartbroken—has come for me from Papa. Notwithstanding the bats flitting about in the belfry of that happy man, he is irritated by my absence. In Paris he didn't care a rap, but down there the old house seems empty to him without Claudine. He misses the little girl, silently curled up with a book in her lap in the hollow of the big armchair bursting at the seams— or perched in the fork of the walnut-tree, cracking nuts with the noise of a squirrel—or stretched out full length and very flat on the top of a wall, trying to reach a neighbor's plums or Mother Adolphe's dahlias.

Papa does not write all that—his dignity would not allow it, nor would the loftiness of his style, which holds itself above such childish things. But he is thinking them. And so am I.

Trembling and moved to the depths of my soul with longing and memories of olden times, I ran to Renaud to hide in the hollow of his shoulder and find peace there.

My beloved man never grumbles, even though I take him away from his virtuous labors and he does not always understand the reasons for what he calls my "shipwrecks." He shelters me generously without asking too many questions.

At the warm contact of his body the Fresnois mirage became hazy and evaporated. And when, quickly stirred by my touch, he drew me closer and leaned over me his golden-streaked mustache, smelling of lily of the valley and Egyptian tobacco, I looked up at him and said with a laugh, "You smell like a blonde who smokes."

This time he replied teasingly, "And what does Rézi smell of?"

"Rézi?" I thought for a moment. "She smells of falsehood."

"Falsehood! Do you mean that she doesn't love you and is only pretending to have a crush on you?"

646

"Oh no, dear. I meant less than I said. Rézi doesn't lie. She conceals. She stores away. She does not tell everything in lavish detail, like pretty Madame van Langendonck—'I have just come from Les Galeries Lafayette' at the beginning of a sentence which ends with, 'Five minutes ago I was at Saint-Pierre de Montrouge.' Rézi doesn't bubble over and I am grateful to her for that. But I feel that she buries and neatly covers over a lot of dreadful little things with careful paws, the way Fanchette does in her pan—banal and revolting, perhaps, but well turned."

"What do you actually know about that?" Renaud asked.

"Nothing, I admit, if you demand proofs. But I know it instinctively. Besides, her maid often has a strange way of handling her a rumpled paper in the morning and saying, 'You left this in your coat pocket yesterday, ma'am.' One day I happened to catch a glimpse of what she had 'left in her coat pocket' and I would swear that the envelope was still sealed. What do you think of that postal system? Suspicious old Lambrook himself would not see anything but waste paper there."

"It's ingenious," Renaud commented aloud.

"So you see, dear, this secretive Rézi who arrives here all white and gold, with frank eyes that you can see clear through, who envelopes me in a fragrance of ferns and iris—"

"Why, Claudine!"

"What's got into you, Renaud?"

"Why do you ask what's got into me? How about yourself? Am I dreaming? My far-away, scornful Claudine is taking enough interest in someone, in Rézi, to study her, reflect and draw conclusions! Look here, young lady,"—crossing his arms and pretending to scold, the way Papa does—"can it be we're in love?"

Drawing away, I scowled at him, frowning so sternly that he became alarmed.

"Come, now! Angry again? I declare, you take everything tragically."

"And you don't take anything seriously."

"Nothing but you," he retorted.

He waited but I did not budge.

"Come here, little ninny! Dear me, what a lot of trouble this child causes me! Tell me one thing."

(I had curled up in his lap, silent and still somewhat tense.)

"What is it?"

"When you have to confess one of your innermost thoughts—even to your old father-husband—why do you balk skittishly, as embarrassed as if you had to expose yourself in a gathering of notables?"

"You naïve man! It's because I know my body is firm and pleasant to touch or gaze upon, whereas I am not as sure of my thoughts, of their clearness and of the way they will be received. My modesty very sensibly confines its attention to hiding whatever in me I fear is weak or ugly."

13

I UNEXPECTEDLY came upon Renaud this morning in the midst of a gloomy fit of deep anger. Silently I watched him rumple a lot of papers and toss them on the fire, then quickly make a clean sweep of an armful of pamphlets on one corner of his desk and heap them up on the crackling coke. A small ash-tray, thrown with sure aim, buried itself in the waste basket.

It was Ernest's turn next. For not having come quickly enough he was threatened with dismissal. Things were getting serious!

Sitting there with crossed hands, I watched and waited. Renaud's eyes fell on me and immediately took on a gentler expression.

"Oh, there you are, little one. I hadn't noticed you before. Where have you been?"

"At Rézi's."

"I ought to have guessed it. Forgive my absentmindedness, dear, I am not in a very happy frame of mind."

"Lucky for me that you hide it so well!"

"Don't make fun of me, dear. Come here close and comfort me. I have received some information about Marcel that is exasperating, even detestable."

"Ah?"

There comes to my mind the last visit of my stepson, who really goes too far. An incredible desire to show off impels him to tell me a hundred things I never question him about—among others the quite detailed account of an acquaintance he struck up in the Rue de la Pompe at the hour when the Janson school turns out into the street a swarm of young boys in blue berets . . . That day Marcel's account of his adventures was interrupted by Rézi, who for fully three-quarters of an hour tried on him in vain the full power of her glances and the entire gamut of her most expert twists and turns.

Tired out at last, she gave up the struggle and turned to me with a pretty gesture of discouragement which said so well, "Pshaw, I've had enough of this!" that I started laughing and Marcel (that disordered brain of his is anything but dull) smiled with infinite scorn.

His scorn quickly changed to undisguised interest when he saw the eclectic Rézi turn in my direction the entire battery—the very same one!—of her seductive devices. Affecting an entirely uncalled-for discreetness, he withdrew.

What new scrape can this lad have gotten into?

My head resting on Renaud's knee, I wait to hear about it.

"It's the same story over and over again, dearest. That charming son of mine is now bombarding with Neo-Greek literature a boy from a respectable family—. Have you no comment to make on that, little girl? I ought to be hardened to that sort of thing—alas!—but such doings fill even me with sickening disgust."

"Why?"

As I gently asked this question, Renaud started with surprise.

"What! You ask why?"

"What I meant, Renaud dear, was this—why do you smile with

649

such keen, almost approving interest at the idea that Luce was unduly fond of me and why do you hope—yes, I repeat it—hope that Rézi may prove to be a second and more fortunate Luce?"

Such a strange look on my husband's face at that instant! Marked surprise, a sort of shocked modesty and an abashed and winsome smile passed over it in waves, like the shadows of clouds scurrying over a meadow. Finally he exclaimed triumphantly, "It isn't the same thing!"

"No, not exactly, thank God!" I replied.

"No, it isn't the same thing at all! You may do anything you wish, you women. It is all charming and unimportant—"

"Unimportant?" I interrupted. "I don't agree with you there."

"But what I said is quite true," he insisted. "With you pretty little creatures it is only—how can I put it?—a consolation for what you have to submit to with us men, a restful diversion."

"Indeed!"

"Or at any rate a compensation, a very logical seeking after a more perfect mate, after a beauty more nearly equal to your own, in which your sensitiveness and your frailties may catch their own reflection. If I dared—but I don't—I would tell certain women that they need a woman in order not to lose their liking for men."

Well, I still don't understand. What a strange and pitiful situation, to love one another the way we do and yet feel so differently about everything! In what my husband has just said I cannot see anything but a paradox that disguises and puts a good face on his depraved tendency to enjoy watching the depravity of others.

14

R É Z I has become like my shadow. She is here at every hour of the day, enveloping me in her rhythmic movements whose spiral lines extend into infinity, enthralling me with her words, her glances, her turbulent thoughts which I expect to see burst like sparks from the tips of her slender fingers. I am uneasy, sensing in her a will power more sustained and determined than mine, which functions spasmodically and becomes dormant during the intervals between.

At times, irritated, exasperated by her insistent sweetness and her beauty—which she waves like a bouquet under my nose and parades, scantily clad, before my eyes—I am tempted to ask her brusquely, "What are you driving at?" But I am afraid she might tell me. So I prefer to keep quiet, like a coward, so that I may continue to have her company without doing anything wrong, for she has been for three months now a precious habit with me.

To tell the truth, there has been nothing to give me cause for alarm, aside from the insistence of her gentle grey eyes and the "God, how I love you!" that frequently escapes her naïvely and spontaneously like the cry of some little girl.

As a matter of fact, just what is it she loves in me? I am fully alive to the sincerity, if not of her affection, at least of her desire and I fear—yes, I am already afraid that she is animated only by this desire.

Yesterday, oppressed with a crushing headache and the melancholy twilight, I allowed Rézi to lay her hands on my eyes. With closed eyelids, I pictured her to myself standing behind me, the arabesque of her body bending over me, slender in its clinging gown of leaden grey—a grey that made one hesitate as to the exact color of her eyes.

That silence which is so dangerous settled down over us. She did not venture a single move, however, and did not even kiss me.

She simply said after several minutes, "Oh dearest, dearest!" and lapsed into silence again.

When the clock struck seven, I roused myself with a start and hurried to turn on the electricity. As the sudden light disclosed Rézi's pale, exquisite face, her smile bruised its dainty wings against my most unkind expression, set and brutal.

Adroitly repressing a little sigh, she looked for her gloves, felt to see that her irremovable hat was on straight, whispered "Goodbye till tomorrow," with her face close to mine and left me alone before a mirror, listening to her light footsteps as she fled.

Don't try to deceive yourself, Claudine! Your deep meditation as you stood leaning on one elbow before that mirror, your manner as if trying to analyze a growing remorse, was that not merely your uneasiness at finding unmoved that brown-eyed countenance your friend loves so well?

15

MY DEAR little girl, what are you thinking about?"

(His "dear little girl" is still abed, squatting tailor fashion, enveloped in a long pink nightgown, pensively and silently clipping the toenails of her right foot with the help of a dainty pair of ivory-handled scissors.)

"My dear little girl, what are you thinking about?"

I raised my head, with its short, snake-like curls, and looked at Renaud—who is already dressed and tying his cravat—as though I had never seen him before.

"I asked what you are thinking about. You haven't uttered a word since you woke up. You let me demonstrate my affection without paying the slightest attention to what was going on."

I protested with a gesture.

"I am exaggerating, of course, but you did take it in an absent-minded manner, Claudine."

"I am surprised, Renaud!"

"Not as much as I am. You had accustomed me to more conscientiousness in those pastimes."

"They are not pastimes."

"Call them nightmares, if you wish, but my remark still holds good. Where have you been all morning, little bird?"

"I want to go away to the country," I said after reflecting for awhile.

"Oh, Claudine!" he exclaimed in consternation. "Just look!"

He lifted the curtain—a torrent was running down the gutter and overflowing the rain pipe.

"Does this morning dew give you a hankering for the country? Stop and picture to yourself the dirty water running over the ground, wet skirts flapping around your ankles and cold drops falling on the tips of your ears."

"I'm bearing all that in mind. You have never understood the charm of rain in the country—the wooden shoes that swish as they come up out of their muddy tracks, the furry hood that spikes a pearly drop of water on each of its woolly hairs, the pointed hood that makes a little hut over one's face and into which one retreats with a laugh. It's true, the cold is piercing, but you warm your thighs with two pocketsful of hot chestnuts and you wear worsted mittens."

"You needn't finish! My teeth grate at the mere thought of woollen gloves against the ends of my fingernails! If you wish to see your dear Montigny again, if you really want to as badly as all that, if it's your dying wish"—with a sigh—"we'll go."

No, we won't go. As I talked, I began sincerely to believe what I was saying, but this morning I am not torn with longing for the Fresnois country. My silence is not due to homesickness. The trouble is something different.

The trouble is—the trouble is—that hostilities have begun and

Rézi's treacherous love-making has caught me irresolute and without any plan of defence.

I went to see her at five o'clock, since she is now the inseparable companion of one half of my life. (This both enrages and delights me, and I can do nothing about it.)

I found her alone roasting before an infernally hot fire. The light from the hearth seemed to pass right through her and set her afire. Her fluffy hair was like a halo of pink flame and the outline of her silhouette merged and fused into the copper and cherry red of molten metal.

Without getting up, she smiled and held out her arms to me so lovingly that I became apprehensive and kissed her only once.

"All alone, Rézi?" I asked.

"No—I was with you."

"With me? And who else?"

"With you and myself. That satisfies me. But not you, alas!"

"You are wrong, dear."

She shook her head with a swaying motion that extended to her feet, folded under a low hassock. And her sweet, pensive face, on which the dancing firelight etched two shadowy dimples at the corners of her mouth gazed at me searchingly.

What! Has it come to that? And could I think of nothing else to say? Before I allowed her to penetrate my very soul and become imbued with me in turn, could I not have reached a full and clear understanding with her? Rézi is not like Luce, who invited harsh treatment and would let you alone for twenty-four hours after a good beating. It's all my fault—my fault.

Looking up, she studied me sadly and said in a low voice:

"Why do you distrust me, Claudine? When I sit down too near you, I always find under your dress a defensive foot which, standing out from you as inert as the leg of a table, holds me at a distance. Yes, holds me off, Claudine! It hurts me that you should even think of physical defence. Have I ever, in kissing your dear face, committed one of those intentional errors which one tries afterwards to attribute to haste or the darkness? You have treated me like a deranged person, or a—professional whose hands one watches closely and in whose presence you have to be careful what pose you assume."

She ceased talking and waited. I said nothing. She began again, more appealingly, "My dear, my dear, can it really be you—sensitive and intelligent Claudine—who would confine affection within such ridiculous fixed limits?"

"Ridiculous?" I challenged.

"Yes, there is no other word for it. As though you said to me, 'If my friend, you may kiss me only on such and such spots, but if you are my sweetheart, all the rest is yours.'"

"Rézi—"

She checked the gesture I was about to make.

"Oh, have no fear. I generalize too sweepingly. There is nothing of the sort between us! But I do wish, dear, you would stop hurting my feelings by keeping your prudence on guard against me when I don't deserve it. Be fair to me," she begged, drawing nearer with a gliding motion imperceptible to me. "What is there in my affection for you that arouses your distrust?"

"Your inner thoughts," I replied in a low voice.

She is near me, near enough for my cheek to feel the radiation of the heat that hers had absorbed from the fire.

"Then grant me forgiveness," she murmured, "for loving you so deeply that I cannot conceal it."

She seemed docile, almost resigned. My breathing, which I restrained so that she should not detect how deeply moved I was, brought me the smell of overheated silk, iris and a still sweeter odor when she raised her arm to smooth the back of her mass of golden hair.

(Who will save me from losing control of myself? Pride forbids my having recourse to some too obvious diversion.)

Rézi sighed and stretched her arms in the pose of a Rhine daughter awaking under the waves. Her husband had just come into the room in the noiseless, indiscreet way peculiar to him.

"What! no lights yet, Rézi dear?" he exclaimed after shaking hands.

"Oh, don't ring!" I begged without waiting for Rézi to reply. "This is the hour I love, between daylight and dusk."

"With a slight preference for the latter, it seems to me," was the sly reply of that insufferable man.

Rézi said nothing, but followed him with a look of dark resentment. He walked at a regular pace into the dark opening leading to the main drawing-room and continued his promenade. His measured step brought him back toward us, where the fire threw a light upward on his hardened features and opaque eyes. When a couple of feet from me, he executed a soldierlike rightabout and strode away again.

I sat there, uncertain what to do.

Rézi's eyes took on a diabolical look. She measured her spring. Raising herself to me with a noiseless effort, she threw one arm about my neck and swept me away with a maddeningly sweet kiss. Her wide-open eyes, looking down into mine, listened to the retreating steps and her free hand, raised in the air, marked the rhythm of her husband's walk, while the trembling of her lips seemed to count the beating of my heart—one, two, three, four, five.

Her hold of me relaxed suddenly, as though a cord had been cut. Lambrook turned back. Rézi was once more sitting at my feet, apparently reading something in the flames.

Moved by indignation, surprise and distress over the very real danger she had just run, I could not restrain a quivering sigh and a muffled exclamation.

"Did you say something, madame?" Lambrook asked.

"Please make me go home. It is frightfully late. Renaud must be looking for me at the Morgue!"

"I flatter myself he will look for you here first."

(I'd like to beat that man!)

"Rézi—good-bye."

"See you tomorrow, dear?"

"Yes, tomorrow."

That is why Claudine is pensively cutting her toenails this morning.

Cowardly Rézi! Her adroit movement, the way she took advantage of my discretion, knowing I would not betray her, the unforgettable perfection of that hazardous kiss—all that happened yesterday plunges me into an oppressive reverie.

And Renaud thinks I am sad! Can it be that he does not understand—never will understand—that desire, keen, intense longing, voluptuous passion are always reflected darkly in my eyes?

Deceitful Rézi! Deceitful woman! Two minutes before she assaulted me with a kiss, her humble voice was reassuring me sincerely and telling me how it hurt her to feel my unjust suspicion. Deceitful woman!

In my innermost heart the suddenness of her manœuvre is an argument in her favor. This same Rézi, who complained of my misinterpreting, if not her desire, at any rate her restraint, did not hesitate to change her mind in an instant and run the risk of my anger and the brutal jealousy of that hollow giant of a man.

Which is she more in love with, danger or me?

Me, perhaps? I can see again that swift, animal-like movement hurling her like a thirsty woman on my lips—. No, I shall not go to her house today!

"Are you going out, Renaud? Will you take me with you?"

"Any time you want to come, darling child. So Rézi is engaged elsewhere?"

"Never mind about Rézi. I want to go out with you."

"A quarrel already?"

I replied merely with a gesture that dismissed the subject. Renaud did not press the matter further.

As thoughtful as a loving woman, he got rid of his errands in half an hour in order to join me in our car—a rented affair, somewhat the worse for wear but smooth-running—and take me to

Pépette's to have a cup of tea, some Chester cakes and herring and lettuce sandwiches. We were cozily and comfortably seated, talking the nonsense of badly behaved young married couples, when my appetite and my gaiety suddenly disappeared. Happening to glance at a half-eaten sandwich, I was suddenly stopped short by the memory of a small incident in the already distant past.

One day at Rézi's, scarcely two months before, I had—absent-mindedly or because I was not hungry—left some toast out of which I had bitten a crescent-shaped piece. We were chatting and I did not see Rézi's hand nimbly and cautiously steal this partly finished piece of toast. Suddenly I noticed her quickly biting into it and enlarging the half-moon made by my teeth. Realizing that I had seen her do it, she blushed and thought she could cover it up by saying, "What a greedy pig I am, eh?"

Why did this insignificant incident have to come up out of the past to disturb my peace of mind at this moment? And yet, maybe she really is grieving over my staying away from her.

"Claudine! Hey there, Claudine!"

"What is it?"

"Why, dearest, this is getting to be a disease. Never mind, my poor little bird, as soon as the fine weather comes, we'll set out for Montigny, your worthy father, Fanchette and Mélie. I don't intend to have you break down completely this way, my dear child."

I gave my dear Renaud an ambiguous smile which did not re-assure him at all. We walked home in that sticky weather which follows a rain, when pedestrians and horses alike slip and totter drunkenly on the greasy pavement.

At the house a special delivery letter was awaiting me.

"Claudine, I beg you, forget—forget! Come back and let me explain, if it can be explained. It was all in play, I was only teasing you and also I had a mad desire to play a trick on that man walking up and down so near us. His footstep on the carpet drove me crazy . . ."

658

What! Have I read it correctly? She merely wanted to play a trick on "that man walking up and down," as she says? And, like an idiot, I was going to walk into the trap. Only teasing me? I'll show her whether anybody can tease me like that with impunity!

My anger swept through me in waves like those on the belly of a suckling kitten.

I turn over in my mind cruel schemes for revenge. I dare not tell myself how much my wrath is made up of disappointment and jealousy.

Renaud came on me with the open letter in my hand.

"Ah! So she's running up the white flag? Fine and dandy! Remember this, Claudine, always let the other person do the surrendering."

"What a keen insight you have!"

From my tone he guessed that an outburst was coming and became uneasy.

"Come, tell me what has happened. Not something you can't talk about? I don't ask to know any of the details."

"Nothing of the sort!" I replied. "You're away off. We've had a quarrel, that's all."

"Want me to go and see if I can patch it up?"

The dear man! His sweetness and naïveté broke down my self-control. With a laugh that was half a sob I threw my arms around his neck.

"No, no. I'll go tomorrow. Don't worry."

Only teasing me!

16

A LAST remnant of good sense checks my hand as I am about to ring at Rézi's door. But I am well acquainted with that good sense because it is my own. When I am about to do a foolish thing, it enables me to enjoy the conscious pleasure of saying to myself, "This is a foolish thing to do." Thus forewarned, I go right ahead serenely, steadied by the reassuring weight of full responsibility.

"Is Madame Lambrook at home?"

"She is somewhat indisposed, but in your case that does not matter."

(Somewhat indisposed? Bah! Not enough for me to hold back what I wish to say to her. And anyhow, even if it does hurt her, what of it? "All in play," eh! We'll see who's going to play now.)

She is dressed in white crêpe de chine. Mauve rings around her eyes give them a bluish appearance. I stop still, somewhat taken aback and, I must admit, deeply moved by her graceful beauty and by the look she gives me.

"Rézi, are you really ill?"

"No, now that I see you again."

I rudely shrug my shoulders. But what is this? Stung by my sarcastic smile, she lets go of herself.

"How can you laugh? Go away from here if you wish to laugh!"

Unnerved by this sudden violence, I tried to get the upper hand again.

"Why, my dear, I was under the impression that you were very fond of *play* and of carrying your *teasing* rather far."

"Yes? You believed that? Well, it isn't so. What I wrote you was a lie, a miserable lie, told in the hope of seeing you again, because I can't get along without you. But—" her intense feeling gave way to a desire to cry—"but I did not write it in play, Claudine!"

Waiting timidly for my reply, she became alarmed at my silence. She did not know that I was overwhelmed with joy and that everything within me was a-flutter like an excited nest of birdlings.

I was overjoyed at being loved and at being told so, as happy as a miser over recovering a lost treasure—and triumphantly proud to feel that I was more than just an exciting plaything. It was a victorious retreat of my womanly honor—I realized that clearly. (But since she loves me, I can make her suffer some more.)

"My dear Rézi—"

"Ah, Claudine!"

Thinking I was about to yield, she stood up, trembling, and held out her arms to me. The same yellow light shone from her hair and her eyes. How strange, alas, that the things I love—this friend's beauty, the gentle charm of the Fresnois woods, the longing for Renaud's intimate caress—should rouse in me the same emotion, the same hunger for possession and close embrace! Does this mean that I am capable of feeling things in only one way?

"My dear Rézi, am I to believe from your feverish impatience that this is the first time anyone has resisted you? When I look at you, I can well understand why you have always found women you could enthrall and dominate."

Her arms, raised in an appealing gesture above her white gown, which wrapped itself tightly about her and then trailed off into the darkness like the equivocal train of Melusina—her upraised arms fell to her side. In this pose I saw that she was quickly mustering all her skill and wrath. She met my challenge with:

"The first time? Do you imagine that, having lived eight years with that hollow shell of a husband, I have not tried everything—that, in order to awaken love within myself, I have not sought that sweetest and most beautiful thing in the world, a loving woman? You, perhaps, value most of all the novelty and awkwardness of a first—misstep, but, Claudine, there is something better still and that is the seeking and choosing . . . I chose you," she added in a wounded tone of voice, "and you have merely endured me."

A last vestige of prudence restrained me from going to her—also an overpowering desire to admire her longer. Letting loose her passion, she had called into action all the resources of her voice and her graceful beauty. She had frankly declared, "You are not the first woman," because in such situations truth produces a more skilful effect than falsehood. I could swear that her very frankness was part of her strategy. But she loves me!

I stood and looked at her as in a dream and feasted my eyes on her. A certain movement of the neck evoked the old familiar Rézi at her toilet, half-dressed. A thrill ran through me. I realized it would be wiser never to see her thus again.

Wearied and irritated by my silence, she peered through the dusk to try to catch the expression in my eyes.

"Rézi," I said with an effort, "if you don't mind, we are going to lay all this aside for today and await tomorrow—tomorrow straightens out so many things! It was not that you had displeased me. I would have come to see you yesterday and I would have laughed at you or scolded you—if I cared less for you."

With the quick movement of an animal watching its prey, she thrust forward her pretty chin, cleft by an almost imperceptible vertical dimple.

"You must give me time to think it all over, Rézi, without surrounding me this way with your lovely presence and casting over me such a net of glances, persistent thoughts, impulses which you check just in time. You must sit down here beside me, your head in my lap, and not say a word or stir, because if you do, I shall go away."

She sat at my feet and laid down her head with a sigh, clasping her hands about my waist. With fingers that trembled in spite of me I combed her beautiful hair in ringlets which were the only shining thing in the dark room.

She did not move, but I caught the sweet odor of her neck, I felt the warmth of her fevered cheeks and the roundness of her breasts against my knees. I prayed that she should not stir. If she should see my face and my agitated state—

But she did not move and once again I was able to leave her without revealing my emotion so akin to her own.

Out in the sharp, cool air I calmed as best I could my bristling nerves. Is it not in precisely such situations that our self-respect, still intact, serves to brace us up? Yes? Well, in my case, I considered that I had been more or less taken in.

17

As they left the house today, I wager the habitués of my husband's at-homes must have said to themselves, "Why! Renaud's little wife is getting amiable—she is learning how to behave."

No, my good people, I am not learning how to behave, I am trying to forget. It is not for your benefit, this indiscriminate amiableness, this feverishness that makes me break the teacups! Those attentions of a young Hebe were not intended for you, old man addicted to Greek letters and Russian spirits. Not for you, self-satisfied novelist of socialistic pretensions, was the unconscious smile with which I received your proposal to come to my house (like the manicurist) to read me some Pierre Leroux.

Nor for you, Andalusian sculptor, my effort to follow the flood of half-Spanish invectives you spewed over contemporary art. My acquiescent attention was not directed solely to your æsthetic axioms ("All the talented artists died 200 years ago"), but was listening at the same time for the laughing voice of Rézi—her figure molded in a white cloth suit of the same dull, creamy white as her long crêpe de chine tunic.

You had to give up the attempt to convert me, my Andalusian sculptor, when I said, "I have seen the Rubens paintings," and in reply to your question, "Indeed! and what did you think of them?" I called them "a lot of tripe." How mild the term "pig" seemed to you and how you prayed that I be struck dead!

Nevertheless I am still living and living in a most sickening respectability. Rézi's violent infatuation, my sense of the ridiculous-

ness of it all and the futility of my resistance—everything conspires to make me impatient to go through with the affair, to drink
my fill of her until I shall be surfeited with her charm. And still
I resist and stubbornly hold out even while I despise myself.

Today she again went away, borne along on a chattering tide of
men who had been smoking and drinking and women flushed by
the physical contacts and the extreme heat of the drawing-room
in contrast with the cold outside—went away under the constant
surveillance of her husband, without my saying to her, "I love you
—I am coming tomorrow"—went away haughtily, the unkind
woman, sure of me despite my resistance, confident of herself,
amorous and foreboding.

When we were left alone at last, Renaud and I, we looked at
one another gloomily, like exhausted victors on a field of battle.
Renaud stretched, opened a window and leaned on the sill. I
went and stood by his side to drink in the cool evening mist, the
fresh breeze washed clean by a shower of rain.

Renaud's strong arm about my waist quickly recalled my thoughts,
which had been scurrying pell-mell or wandering disconnectedly
like idle tufts of clouds. Although he towers a head and a half
above me, I wish he were still taller. I should love to be the
daughter or the wife of a giant Renaud, so that I could nestle in
the fold of his elbow or in his cavernous sleeve. I would crouch
under the shelter of his ear and let him bear me away over endless
plains and through boundless forests. His hair, lashed by wind
and rain, would groan like the storm-tossed pines.

At a movement by Renaud—the real one, not the giant—my fairy
tale took fright and scattered to the wind.

"Claudine," said his rich voice, soft and velvety like his eyes,
"it looks as if you and Rézi had made up."

"Yes, after a fashion. But I am holding off for awhile."

"There's no great harm in that, Claudine, no great harm in
that," Renaud chanted. "So she's still crazy about you?"

"She is indeed. But I am going to keep her waiting a while
longer for—for my forgiveness. 'The longer the suffering—'"

"The greater the reward," his baritone responded, continuing his decidedly musical mood. "Your friend looked unusually pretty today."

"I have never seen her when she wasn't pretty," I replied.

"I can well believe it. Is the small of her back pleasing?"

"The small of her back?" I exclaimed in a startled voice. "Why, I don't know anything about it. Do you think she receives me in her tub?"

"Well, yes, I thought so."

"Those little traps are not worthy of you," I said, shrugging my shoulders. "You can count on my being honest enough, Renaud—and also sufficiently fond of you—to come and say to you squarely, 'Rézi has led me further than I meant to go'—whenever that day arrives."

"Ah, Claudine, so then—?"

On his face, as it bent over me, I read curiosity and eager interest, but not anxiety.

"So then you can see that day drawing near?"

"I have nothing of that sort to tell you this evening," I answered, avoiding his eyes.

I evaded the question because I felt disturbed and more palpitating than a hawk-moth, one of those little reddish brown moths with phosphorescent blue eyes, which hover over the asters and the laurels when it is in bloom. Its velvety body, when held in the hand, gasps and suffocates and its pathetic warmth is pleasant to feel.

(I have lost control of myself this evening. If my husband should wish it—and he will!—I shall be the Claudine who alarms and fascinates him, who abandons herself to love as though it were to be the last time and who clings tremblingly to his arm, helpless against herself.)

"Renaud, do you think Rézi is given to unnatural practices?"

It is nearly two o'clock in the morning. I am lying in pitchblack darkness, close beside Renaud. He is blissfully happy and quite

665

ready to plunge me back again into the delirium from which I have just emerged. Beneath my head I can hear the quick, irregular beating of his heart. My whole body limp, I plaintively revel in the swooning convalescence that follows a too intense moment . . . With the return of my reason, however, there comes back to me likewise the thought that scarcely ever leaves me and the mental picture of Rézi.

Whether she comes—wrapped tight in her white gown and holding out her arms to me—to illumine the black night in which my wearied brain sees multi-colored dots dancing about, or whether, seated at her dressing-table, listening to me with her arms up-raised, she turns her head away and shows me only her amber-colored neck merging into the pale gold of the first fine hairs—she is still and always Rézi.

Now that she is no longer here, I am not sure that she loves me. My confidence in her affection amounts merely to a disturbing desire to be in her presence.

"Do you think she is given to unnatural practices, Renaud?"

"I told you, you silly little girl, that I have never known Madame Lambrook to have any lovers."

"That isn't what I wanted to know. Having lovers is not un-natural."

"No? Well, then, what do you mean by 'unnatural'? Homo-sexuality?"

"Yes and no, depending on the form it takes. But even that is not exactly what I mean by 'unnatural.'"

"There's an unusual definition coming, I fancy."

"I am sorry to disappoint you. For after all, it is quite obvious. If I take a lover—."

"Hold on there!"

"This is only a supposition."

"But a supposition that is going to bring you a spanking!"

"If I take a lover without loving him, but merely because I

know it is a wicked thing to do—well, that's unnatural. But if I take a lover—."

"That makes two of them."

"Someone I really love or whom I merely desire—wait a minute, Renaud!—I am obeying a sound law of nature and I consider myself the most virtuous of women. To sum it all up, it is unnatural to do wrong without enjoying it."

"What do you say we talk about something else if you don't mind? All these lovers you've been taking on—I need to make you do penance for your sins."

"All right, bring on your penance!"

All the same, if I had talked of taking a woman for a lover instead of a man, Renaud would have considered my proposition quite acceptable. In his eyes, adultery is a matter of sex.

18

She puzzles me. In her studied gentleness, her deft precautions against arousing my distrust, I do not recognize the pale, impassioned Rézi who used to plead with me, melting into tears and consumed with feverish fire.

A glance from her, sparkling with mischief and loving challenge, has just revealed the secret of this discreet demeanor—she knows that I love her (that bald word fails to convey my exact meaning). She has perceived my agitation at our being alone together. When I give her a hurried kiss upon arriving or on taking leave (I dare not stop this now!), her thrill of ecstasy seems to pass over into my body.

Now she knows and she is biding her time—a threadbare

manœuvre, a pitiful lover's snare, as old as love itself, but into which, although forewarned, I tremble lest I fall.

You shrewdly scheming woman! I have been able to resist your desire for me, but can I resist my own for you?

"To abandon oneself to the intoxicating bliss of loving and desiring—to forget all past loves and begin to love anew—to grow young again in the freshness of a new conquest—that is the purpose of the universe!"

It is not Rézi who is speaking thus. It is not I. It is Marcel! His unconscious depravity at times attains a certain grandeur, especially now that the inspiration of a new love has stimulated his listless beauty and flowery lyricism.

Sitting in front of me slumped in a high-backed armchair, knees close together and eyes downcast, he rambles on as if in a trance, continually raising his hand with a nervous gesture to smooth his pencilled eyebrows.

He does not like me, that's sure, but I have never poked fun at his strange love affairs and that may be the reason for his confiding in me.

I listen to him more attentively than ever and not without emotion, "To abandon oneself to the intoxicating bliss of loving and desiring, to forget all past loves."

"Why must one forget, Marcel?"

"Why?" he replied, raising his chin as a sign that he did not know. "I have no idea. I forget in spite of myself. Today casts a shadow over Yesterday and eclipses it."

"For my part, I would rather bury Yesterday with its withered flowers in the perfumed casket of my memory."

(I imitate almost instinctively his verbose style, cluttered with metaphorical figures.)

"I have no desire to dispute that point," said he, with a gesture of indifference. "But tell me something about your Today and her somewhat sensually Viennese grace."

I frowned at him threateningly.

"Are people gossiping already, Marcel?"

"No, it is merely my own intuition. You know how it is—one gets the habit after awhile. But I say! you certainly have a preference for blonds."

"Why the plural?"

"Well, I declare! Rézi has the spotlight at present but the time was when you didn't dislike me!"

(What impudence! This conceited young fop is mistaken. Ten months ago I would have slapped his face, but now I am not sure if I am much better than he. He has some nerve, all the same!)

I scrutinized his face, fixing my gaze on his delicate temples which will soon become wrinkled and on the already tired-looking folds underneath his eyes. Then, having examined him minutely, I announced, "You, Marcel! Why, at thirty you'll look like a little old woman."

So, he had noticed it! Can people see it then? I dare not try to reassure myself by recognizing that Marcel has a special flair for such matters. The lazily fatalistic impulsiveness that determines my actions advises me in a whisper, "Since they think that is what is going on, you might as well be doing it."

That is easy to say! But although Rézi continues to make love to me silently by her presence and her glances, she seems to have given up any actual advances. She grooms her beautiful person in front of me as meticulously as one polishes a weapon. She waves her perfumes before me like incense and mockingly teases me with all her charms. She throws herself into this game with mischievous audacity and at the same time with a sincere restraint in her actions that I cannot find fault with:

"Look at my toenails, Claudine! I have a new powder that's a marvel. They are like little convex mirrors."

The slender bare foot is lifted daringly out of the slipper to show the delightful artificial pink of the nails glistening at the tips of the pale toes—then it disappears again at the very moment when perhaps I was about to seize and kiss it.

And then there is also the temptation of her hair. Rézi lazily entrusts me with the combing of it. I perform this duty to perfection, especially at the beginning. But the prolonged contact of this skein of gold that I am unravelling and which, charged with electricity, clings to my clothes and crackles under the tortoise-shell comb like burning fern leaves—all the magic of this intoxicating hair permeates and overpowers me. In cowardly fashion I drop the loose-flowing golden armful, whereat Rézi becomes vexed—or pretends she is.

Last evening at a dinner party of fifteen at the Lambrooks', while they were all absorbed in the difficult task of picking a lobster *à l'Américaine* out of its shell, she went so far as to throw me an adorable kiss—noiseless and complete—her lips first tightly closed, then half-parted, her sea-grey eyes first open and imperious, then half-closed.

I shuddered lest someone see her—and was even more deeply stirred with emotion.

At times she gets herself into difficulties with this exhausting game—as happened this morning.

In straw-colored girdle and slip, she was turning about before a mirror, trying to bend backward like a Spanish Montmartre dancer until her head was on a level with her waist.

"Can you do that, Claudine?"

"Yes and better than you do it."

"I don't doubt it, my dear. You are like a well-tempered fencing foil—hard and supple. Ah!"

"What is the matter?"

"Can it be there are mosquitoes at this season? Quick, look at this precious skin of mine. And just tonight when I am to wear low-neck!"

She made an effort to see a (pretended?) mosquito bite behind her bare shoulder. I leaned over her.

"There, a little above the shoulder blade, higher, yes—something has bitten me. What do you see?"

I saw—close enough to touch it lightly—Rézi's perfectly curved shoulder and her anxious profile and, below that, a youthful bosom exposed, round and divided, like those that are so familiarly mauled in the racy engravings of the eighteenth century.

I was contemplating all this, absorbed and speechless, not conscious at first of my friend's intense gaze fastened on me. When she finally caught my attention, I turned my eyes away to the unrivalled, shadowless, untinted whiteness of her skin and the breasts suddenly terminating in a pink that matched the polish on her nails.

Rézi victoriously followed the course of my glance. But when it fell on one spot and remained fixed there, she weakened in her turn and her eyelashes quivered like the wings of a wasp. Her eyes darkened and reeled and it was she who murmured, "No more! Thanks!"—as visibly agitated as I.

"Thanks!" By this whispered word, at the same time childlike and voluptuous, she did more to precipitate my defeat than she could have done with a profound caress.

19

WHAT a time to be coming home, little girl! And the one evening that we're dining together alone! Come on into the dining-room —you're all right just as you are. Don't go to your room under pretext of arranging your hair, dear. We would still be here at midnight. Come and sit down. I ordered for dinner that dreadful eggplant *au parmesan* you're so crazy about."

"Yes."

I heard without taking in what he was saying. Handing him my hat, I ran my hands through my curls to cool my head and then slumped into the leather-covered chair opposite my husband under the soft, friendly light.

"No soup, dear?"

I puckered up my nose in disgust.

"While you're waiting for me, you might tell me where you've been. You seem to be walking in a dream and your eyes are as big as saucers. You've been at Rézi's, eh?"

"Yes."

"You must admit, Claudine, that I'm not a very jealous husband."

(Not jealous enough, alas!—that's what I ought to have answered, but I confined myself to thinking it. His swarthy face, barred with a moustache lighter than his skin, leaned toward me, softened by a woman-like smile and so radiant with amorous fatherly affection that I dared not.)

To keep my restless hands occupied, I broke off golden crumbs of bread and carried them to my mouth, but my hand failed me —the fragrant odor that still clung to it made me turn pale.

"My precious child! Are you ill?" Renaud asked anxiously, throwing down his napkin.

"No, no—merely tired, that's all. Please, I'm very thirsty."

He rang and called for the sparkling wine I like best, Asti muscatel, which always sets me smiling when I drink it. But this time I was intoxicated before I had drunk a drop.

Very well, then—yes, I've been at Rézi's! I would like to cry out—stretch my arms until the bones cracked in order to relieve the exasperating stiffness in my neck.

I went to see her about five o'clock, as I do every day. Without making any appointment with me, she expects me faithfully at that hour and without making any promises, I arrive at that hour faithfully.

As I walk quickly to her house, I notice the days growing longer, the pavements washed by March showers, the violets from Nice heaped up on little handcarts and filling the rain-soaked air with their precocious springtime, rakish and intoxicating.

It is along this short path now that I study the progress of the seasons, I who, as alert as a wild animal, used to watch for the first leaf tip in the woods, the first wild anemone like a white sentinel streaked with lavender, the pussy-willows, little furry tails with a honey-like odor. Wild creature of the forests, a cage now hems you in—and you cling to your cage.

Today, as every day, Rézi was awaiting me in her white and green room, the bed painted a dull white and the tall late Louis Fifteenth chairs upholstered in almond-green silk with a white all-over pattern of little bows and large bouquets. Against this soft green my friend's complexion and hair stood out radiantly.

But today—

"How gloomy it is in here, Rézi! And no light in the hallway! Speak to me—I can't even see you!"

Her voice answered me petulantly, coming from the depths of a large armchair, one of those uncertain seats, too wide for one, too narrow for two.

"Yes, isn't it cheerful! Something happened to the electricity and it seems they won't be able to fix it till morning. Of course there's nothing on hand to take its place. The maid spoke of sticking candles into my perfume bottles!"

"Well, that wouldn't be so bad, would it?"

"Thanks. You always side with my bad luck. Candles! Why not church tapers? They look so funereal! Instead of coming to console me, you stand there laughing all by yourself—I can hear you! Come sit in this big armchair with me, dearest."

Without a moment's hesitation I went and nestled in the armchair. With my arms about her waist, I felt her soft, warm body underneath her loose dress. Her perfume enveloped me.

"Rézi, you are like the white nicotine flower which waits till nightfall to exhale its fragrance. When evening comes, one can smell nothing else. It puts the rose to shame."

"Have I really no fragrance until night comes on, Claudine?"

She dropped her head on my shoulder. I held her, alive and warm like a captive partridge.

"Is that husband of yours going to rise up again out of the darkness like an Anglo-Indian devil?" I asked in a muffled tone.

"No," she answered faintly. "He is piloting some compatriots about."

"East Indians?"

673

"No, Britishers."

(We neither of us pay heed to what we are saying. The darkness hides us. I dare not unclasp my arms now—and besides, I have no desire to.)

"I love you, Claudine."

"Why put it in words?"

"Why not? I have given up everything for love of you—even the flirtations that were my one escape from boredom. Am I not sufficiently unobtrusive to please you—sufficiently anxious not to displease you at any cost?"

"At any cost? Oh, Rézi!"

"That is just the word. To love and long for hopelessly costs, as you know."

(Yes, I know—how well I know it! What am I doing at this very moment but revelling in this needless suffering?)

With an imperceptible movement she turned more toward me until from shoulder to knee her body was pressed close against mine. I scarcely felt her move—she seemed to turn within her gown.

"Not another word, Rézi! I feel so lazily comfortable here—don't force me to get up. Imagine that it is night and we are on a journey. Feel the wind in your hair. Lean forward, that low branch might drench your brow! Sit close to me. Look out! the water splashes up out of the deep ruts when the wheels strike them."

With treacherous docility her entire body followed the play of my fancy. Her head resting on my shoulder, her unruly hair brushed my forehead like the branches imagined by my restless searching diversion.

"I am travelling," she murmured.

"But are we going to reach our destination?" I queried.

Her nervous hands gripped my free hand.

"Yes, Claudine, we shall reach it."

"Whither are we bound?"

"Lean over and I will whisper it to you."

Credulously I obeyed—it was her lips I encountered. I hearkened long to what her mouth had to say to mine.

She was right—we are nearing our destination. My haste to arrive is as great as hers—dominates it and forces it to yield.

Startled at the revelation of myself, I pushed away Rézi's caressing hands—she understood, quivered, struggled for one brief moment and then lay back, her arms hanging limp.

The faint noise of a distant door brought me to my feet. I could vaguely distinguish the dim figure of Rézi sitting before me, pressing her feverish lips against my wrist. With my arm about her waist I lifted her to her feet, held her whole body close against me, bent her head back and kissed her at random—her eyes, her moist neck, her tangled hair.

"Tomorrow, please!"

"Yes, tomorrow. I love you!"

I hurry along, my head swimming. My fingers still tingle from the slight roughness of the Valenciennes lace, they still feel the satiny smoothness of a flowing ribbon, the velvet touch of the softest skin earth ever knew.

The evening air, tearing away the veil of perfume she wove about me, cuts me to the soul.

"Claudine, dear, if you are cold even to eggplant *au parmesan*— I know what that means."

(The sound of Renaud's voice brings me back with a start. I was far away! It is true, I have eaten nothing. But I am so thirsty!)

"Aren't you going to tell me about it, dear?"

(That husband of mine certainly is not like other husbands.)

Embarrassed by his insistence, I entreated him:

"Don't tease me, Renaud. I am tired, nervous, uncomfortable in your presence. Wait till this night is over and, my God! don't imagine so many things!"

He said nothing more but all that evening he watched the time

675

pass and at half-past ten he pleaded an unbelievable need of sleep. Once in our big bed, he quickly sought in my hair, on my hands, my lips, the truth I refused to tell him.

20

Tomorrow, please," Rézi had pleaded.

"Yes tomorrow," I acquiesced.

Alas, that tomorrow never comes. I hurried to her house, sure that we were going to enjoy a longer and more complete happiness during the remaining hour of daylight and that I should find Rézi adorable and unresisting. That is how completely I had forgotten her husband!

The wretch interrupted us twice. Twice our eager, frightened hands parted at his sudden entrance. Rézi and I looked at one another, she on the verge of tears, I so blind with rage that, at a third intrusion, I had all I could do not to hurl my glass of orangeade in the face of that rigidly polite, suspicious husband.

And now, tremulous farewells, furtive kisses, stealthy caresses can no longer satisfy us.

What can we do?

On the way home I devised and discarded impossible schemes. I could think of no solution.

I went back to Rézi's today to confess my helplessness, to see her again and once more breathe her fragrance.

As impatient as I, she came running to greet me.

"Well, dearest?" she asked.

"No luck! Are you angry with me?"

Her eyes caressingly followed the curve of my lips as I spoke. Her own lips quivered and parted slightly. The radiation of her desire ran through my whole being. Should I seize her then and there, in that banal drawing-room, and caress her to the death?

She read my thoughts and stepped back.

"Don't!" she whispered hurriedly, pointing to the door.

"At my house, then, Rézi?"

"All right, if you wish."

I smiled assent, then shook my head.

"No, the bell is always ringing, Renaud keeps coming and going and the doors are always slamming. No, no!"

Rézi wrung her white hands with a little gesture of despair.

"Does this mean, then, that never again—? Do you imagine I can live for a whole month on the memory of yesterday?"

"You shouldn't have done it in the first place," she added, turning her head away, "unless you were going to be able every day to quench my thirst for you."

Pouting affectionately, she threw herself into the large armchair —the very same one. And although clad today in a woolen street dress of the same color as her blonde hair, as she lay there I discerned only too well the curve of her hips and the elusive outline of her thighs with their impalpable down of silvery velvet.

"I have it, Rézi!"

"What is it?"

"Our motor car?"

"Your motor! Think of the jolting about and the interruptions and how cramped we'd be and the inquisitive faces suddenly appearing at the windows, the chauffeur discreetly asking, without turning his head, 'Madame, the street is blocked, shall we go back?' or some slight accident and then the too obsequious policeman opening the door. No, Claudine, no motor car for me!"

"Very well, my dear, suggest a possible nook yourself. So far you've hardly suggested anything but objections."

Swift as a startled adder, she raised her golden head and darted at me glances full of reproach and tearful sorrow.

"Do you love me no more than that? You would never think of being hurt if you loved me as much as I love you."

I shrugged my shoulders.

"But why do you always put obstacles in the way? The motor car paralyzes you with fright and this drawing-room bristles with traps set by that husband of yours. Must we get the evening paper and look for a furnished room to rent by the day?"

"I'd be quite willing," she sighed ingenuously, "but all those places are under police surveillance—at least, so I was told by—er—somebody."

"What do I care for the police?"

"That's all very well for you with the husband you have!"

Her voice changed.

"Claudine," she said slowly and thoughtfully, "Renaud is the one person who can—"

I stared at her in amazement, unable to think of anything to reply. She sat there in serious meditation, looking so slender in her light-colored dress, with her girlish chin resting on her hand.

"Yes, Claudine, our safety depends on him—and you."

She held out her arms to me. Her impenetrable, loving face looked up at me appealingly.

"Our safety—well, dearest, our happiness—call it what you will. Believe me, I can hardly wait, now that I have felt your strength, now that Rézi is yours, with all her love and all her weakness!"

I glided swiftly toward those inviting arms and lips, ready to make the best of her tight, hampering clothing, ready to spoil our enjoyment by too great haste . . .

She tore herself from my grasp.

"Ssh! I hear footsteps!"

How frightened she was! Her white skin paled slightly. She leaned forward and listened, her eyes big with fear. Oh, if a chimney only could fall on that cursed Lambrook and get him out of our way!

"My golden darling, what makes you think Renaud would—?"

"Yes, he would. He's an intelligent husband and he worships you. You must tell him—almost everything, and his ingenious affection must arrange a retreat for us somewhere!"

"In his case, you aren't afraid he might be jealous?"

"No."

(There goes that little smile of hers again! Why did she, with a disquieting expression, a sly twist to her mouth, check my confidence just as it was rushing madly to her on the heels of my desire? But after all, it was merely a fleeting shadow and even if she should give me nothing but her sincere sensualism, the twofold sweetness of her skin and her voice, her golden hair which she entrusts to me and her feverish lips which enslave me—is not that enough? Cost what it may, I shall ask Renaud's help—not right now, a little later. I want to look around some more myself. For her sake I will humble my reticent, easily embarrassed nature and the loving pride I would have taken in myself discovering a safe refuge for our love.)

Nerve-racked fits of ill-humor, angry tears, tender reconciliations, tense, vibrant hours when the mere touch of a hand drove us mad —that is the sum total of this week.

I have not mentioned the matter to Renaud—it is so hard to bring myself to it! And Rézi is vexed with me for this.

I have not even admitted to that dear man that our affection— Rézi's and mine—is assuming a definite character that one cannot very well put into words.

But Renaud knows all about it in a general way and without details, and this certainly fills him with a peculiar restlessness. A strange, loving readiness to play the part of a procurer makes him urge me off to Rézi's and even seek to render me more attractive for her. At four o'clock, when I toss aside the book with which I have been beguiling my impatience, if he is near, he gets up and moves about nervously.

"Are you going over there?" he asks.

"Yes."

He runs his skilful fingers through my hair to fluff up the curls and leans over me till his long moustache almost touches me as he carefully re-ties my cravat of heavy braided silk and looks to see if my boyish collar is clean. Standing behind me, he makes sure my fur turban is on straight and holds my sable coat for me.

As a final touch, he slips into my amazed hand a bouquet of dark red roses—her favorite flower! I admit I would never have thought of this by myself.

Then, with a long, loving kiss, "Run along now, dear. Be a good girl. Be a little high-handed—not too humbly affectionate. Make her want you."

Make her want me? She does, alas, but that's not due to any strategy on my part.

21

W H E N Rézi comes to see me, the situation is even more irritating than at her house. I have her here in my room—which is, after all, our bedroom, Renaud's and mine. I would have only to turn the key in the door and we would be alone. But I am not willing. Above all, I don't relish the thought that my husband's chamber-maid (a girl who goes about as noiselessly as a shadow and whose flabby hands sew such loose stitches) might knock and mysteriously explain from the other side of the locked door, "It's about your blouse, ma'am. There's somebody here to fit the sleeves."

I dread also the spying eye of Ernest, the butler with a face like a wicked priest. These are not my servants. I employ them with discretion and repugnance.

And—for I must tell the whole truth—I fear still more Renaud's curiosity.

That is why I let Rézi unwind in vain in my room the long spiral of her seductions and run the gamut of her reproachful poutings.

"You haven't found anything for us, Claudine?"

"No."

- "And you haven't asked Renaud yet?"

"No."

"That's cruel of you," she whispered with a sigh, suddenly lowering her glance.

I felt my will power melting away. But at that moment Renaud came to the door and knocked gently as a warning. I hurled him a "Come in!" more brutal than a cobblestone.

I don't at all like the coquettish humbleness that Rézi affects with Renaud, nor do I like his way of sniffing of her to try to find out what we are concealing from him, of searching in her hair and her gown for the fragrant vestige of my caresses.

He did it again today—right before me. He kissed both her hands when he came in, just to have the pleasure of saying afterwards, "So you have adopted Claudine's perfume, that brown, sweetish Chypre, eh?"

"Why, no," she replied quite frankly.

"Ah! I thought you had."

He gave me a sidelong, knowing glance with the air of congratulating me. My whole being stamped with rage. I was tempted, in my exasperation, to yank at his long moustache until he should cry aloud and strike me. But no, I held myself in check and maintained the taut, well bred composure of a husband who sees his wife being kissed in some harmless parlor game.

And anyway, he made as if to go out, with the insultingly discreet manner of a waiter in a private dining-room.

"Stay, Renaud," I said, stopping him.

"Never, my dear! Rézi would scratch my eyes out."

"Why so?"

"I know too well, my curly headed shepherd boy, the charm of being alone with you."

(A shameful fear poisons my mind. What if Rézi's unstable and deceitful nature should develop a preference for Renaud! It just happens today that he is very handsome in a well-fitting frock coat, with his small feet and wide shoulders. And there she sits

681

—this Rézi who is the cause of all my trouble—wrapped in her sables, as blonde as a sheaf of rye, with her precociously springlike hat of lilacs and green leaves. I can feel welling up in me the brutality that used to make me strike and claw Luce. What a sweet and poignant relief to my tormented soul if I should see Rézi crying!)

She said nothing but looked at me, putting all she wished to say into her eyes. I felt myself yielding—finally I gave in.

"Renaud, dear, are you going out before dinner?"

"No, little one. Why do you ask?"

"I'd like to have a talk with you—I have a favor to ask of you."

Rézi sprang out of her chair joyfully, adjusting her hat at random. She had understood.

"I must be going . . . Really I can't stay this time. But tomorrow, we'll have a long visit together, won't we, Claudine? Ah, Renaud, how much you are to be envied for having a child like her!"

And she hurried away to the accompaniment of her swishing skirts, leaving Renaud bewildered.

"Is the woman crazy? What's got into both of you anyhow?"

(Dear me, shall I ask him now? How hard it is!)

"Renaud, I—er—you—"

"What is it, little one? Why, you're pale as a sheet!"

He drew me down on his lap.

(Perhaps it will be easier there.)

"Well, it's this way—Rézi's husband is very annoying."

"You said it—especially for her."

"He is for me, too."

"You don't say so! I'd like to see him start something! Has he been getting fresh with you?"

"No. Don't move, dear. Keep your arms around me. I mean that that Lambrook wretch is always popping in on us!"

"Oh, now I understand!"

(I knew Renaud was no fool! He's quick to catch on.)

"You dear little lovesick creature! So they're tormenting you— you and your Rézi? What can we do about it? You know very well that your old husband loves you so much that he wouldn't for the world deprive you of a little happiness. Your blonde friend is charming. She loves you dearly."

"Yes? Do you really think so?"

"I'm sure she does. And your two types of beauty complement one another admirably. Your amber tint has no cause to fear comparison with her skin, my dear. There, I made a rhyme without meaning to!"

A quiver ran through his arms. I knew what he was thinking about. And yet my tenseness relaxed at the affectionate—genuinely affectionate tone of his voice.

"What would you like, you dear little bird? Want me to stay away tomorrow for the whole afternoon?"

"Oh, no!"

After an embarrassed silence, I added, "If only we could—somewhere else—"

"Somewhere else? Why, nothing could be simpler!"

He jumped up, set me on my feet and walked up and down with a youthful stride.

"Somewhere else—let us see—of course there is—no, that wouldn't do. Ah! I have it!"

He came back to me, wrapped me in his arms and sought my lips. But I felt so ill at ease and embarrassed that I turned my head away a little.

"My charming little girl, you shall have your Rézi and Rézi shall have her Claudine. You don't need to worry about anything now—except how to wait patiently for a day or two. That's a long time, isn't it? Kiss your old sweetheart, dear. He will be blind and deaf as he stands guard at the door of your room with its little noises."

The joy and certainty of possessing Rézi with all the charm of her white skin and dainty perfumes, the sense of relief now that I have confessed our unlovely secret—all this does not prevent my feeling

683

another keen sorrow. Oh, Renaud, how I would have loved you if you had refused with curt disapproval.

I had hoped that this night of waiting would be a happy one, filled with gentle, rhythmic palpitations, half-unconscious dreams, through which should pass the figure of Rézi in a flood of blonde light. But it calls up another night of waiting in my little bedroom in the Rue Jacob, a night aflame with more youthful fire.

No, I am mistaken. I fancy this sleepless night must be more like the one Renaud spent, two years back. Will Rézi find me beautiful enough? Ardent enough, I am sure—yes, indeed!

Worn out with wakefulness, I disturbed my sweetheart's light sleep with my cold little foot and nestled my shivering body in his arms, where I finally dozed off.

Dreams followed one another, jumbled, hazy, indistinguishable. A supple young silhouette appeared dimly from time to time, like the face of the moon, veiled with clouds and then disclosed. When I called "Rézi!" it turned and showed me the broad, sweet forehead, velvety eyelids and small, full lips of little Helen, she of the white skin and black hair. Why did this girl, whom I barely saw and have nearly forgotten, come into these dreams?

22

R E N A U D lost no time. He came home to dinner last night, breezy, energetic and affectionate. "Send word to Rézi," he said as he kissed me. "Let that young sorceress perform her ablutions in preparation for tomorrow's orgy."

"Tomorrow? Where?"

"Ah, wouldn't you like to know! We will meet here and I'll take you to the place. It wouldn't be wise for you women to be seen going in alone. And besides, I will help you get installed."

This arrangement chilled my enthusiasm somewhat. I would have preferred that he give us the key and the address and then leave us free.

Rézi arrived ahead of time and full of anxiety. I said to her with a forced laugh:

"Will you come with me? Renaud has found a—er—bachelor—girl apartment for us."

Her eyes danced with delight and took on a deep golden shade.

"Ah! Then he knows that I know that he—?"

"Why, of course. Could I have managed it any other way! It was you yourself who suggested—with a persistence that I now thank you for, Rézi—that I ask him to help us."

"Yes, yes."

Her gray eyes, shrewd and caressing, uneasily sought mine. Raising her hand to the back of her head with a sinuous motion repeated a dozen times, she smoothed into place some unruly locks of her golden hair.

"I'm afraid you don't love me today, Claudine—not enough for —er—that."

She came so close to me as she spoke that I felt her breath. That was enough to make me grit my teeth and bring the blood rushing to the tips of my ears.

"I always love you enough—too much—madly, Rézi. I admit I would have preferred that no one should either permit or forbid us to enjoy an afternoon of seclusion and abandon. But if, behind some safely closed door, I can have for a few minutes the illusion that you belong to me, to me alone, to me above all others—I shall regret nothing."

She listened to the sound of my voice dreamily, perhaps without hearing me. We both started as Renaud came in and Rézi lost her composure for an instant. He put her at her ease with a knowing, good-natured laugh and said, as he mysteriously drew a small key from his vest pocket, "Ssh! Which of you is going to take charge of this?"

"I will," I replied, holding out my hand imperiously.

685

"No, I will," Rézi begged coaxingly.

"My — mother — told — me — to — take — this — one," Renaud counted off, as he laughingly put the key back in his pocket.

"Come on, children, the taxi is waiting."

Sitting opposite to us on the uncomfortable folding seat, Renaud only half-disguises his excitement over this escapade. When his eye happens to fall on Rézi, his nose turns white and his mustache twitches.

Rézi, not entirely sure of herself, tries to make conversation, then gives it up and, with an inquiring glance, seeks to fathom my glum, unbending impatience.

Yes, I am consumed with impatience—impatience to taste all the joys that the eagerness and entreaties of my friend have been promising me during the past hectic week—impatience, especially, to get there and put an end to this somewhat scandalous three-cornered pilgrimage.

What! We're stopping in the Rue Goethe? So close by! It had seemed to me that we had been driving for half an hour. The stairway of No. 59 isn't half bad. There is a garage in the rear of the yard.

We go up two flights. Renaud opens a door noiselessly. Even in the hall I notice the heavy, dead air of rooms hung with draperies.

While I am examining the small drawing-room in none too friendly mood, Rézi, like a prudent (I will not say experienced) person, hastens to the window and inspects the surroundings without raising the white tulle curtains. Apparently satisfied, she, too, wanders about the miniature drawing-room, which the freakish taste of some lover of Spanish Louis Thirteenth style has crammed full of carved and gilded furniture, heavy frames with huge ornamentation, figures of Christ agonizing on moth-eaten velvet, uninviting prayer-stools and an enormous glass-windowed sedan chair —now used as a cabinet—massive and handsome, with a harvest of gilded apples, grapes and pears carved out of its sides . . .

This sacrilegious austerity pleases me and puts me in good humor. A half-open portière discloses one corner of a bright, English-style bedroom, the brass knob of a bedstead and a comfortable-looking *chaise longue* covered with flowered chintz.

I am agreeably impressed after all.

"It's simply charming, Renaud!" declares Rézi. "Whose apartment is this?"

"Yours, Bilitis! Here's the electric switch and here's some tea, lemons, sandwiches, grapes—and my heart which beats for both of you."

How perfectly at ease he is and with what good grace he plays his questionable rôle! I watch him bustle about, set out the saucers with his deft, feminine hands and offer Rézi a bunch of grapes, which she nibbles at coyly.

Why am I surprised at him when he is not surprised at me?

I hold her close to my heart and pressed against my entire body. Her cool knees touch me and her little toenails scratch me deliciously. Her rumpled chemise is merely a wisp of gauzy silk. Her head rests in the crook of my protecting arm. I plunge my face into her billowy hair.

The day is drawing to a close. Shadows are beginning to fall on the bright foliage of these bed curtains, strange and annoying to my eyes. From time to time, as Rézi speaks with her face close to mine, her teeth gleam white like the belly of a minnow.

She talks in a fever of gaiety, one bare arm waving in the air, the forefinger emphasizing her remarks. In the dim light I follow the motions of this sinuous white arm which beats a rhythm for my lassitude and for the heavenly sadness with which I am intoxicated.

I wish she were as sad as I, as pensive and fearsome of the fleeting minutes—or that, if nothing else, she would leave me alone with my thoughts of what has been.

She is exquisitely pretty now. A few minutes ago, she was passionately beautiful.

At the first caress, as though wounded, she turned on me a

marvelous animal-like countenance—frowning brows, a scornful, hostile mouth, an expression at once infuriated and supplicating.

Then it all merged into an unrestrained offer of herself.

Now she is talking and her voice, dear though it is to me, disturbs this precious hour. The truth is, happiness makes her loquacious, as it does Renaud. Can't they get the joy of it in silence? Look at me, as gloomy as this unfamiliar room. What a poor companion I make after the embrace!

I roused my feelings again by clasping her warm body, which yielded to mine, following my every movement—her beloved body, so well rounded, despite its elusive slenderness, that nowhere did I feel its resisting frame.

"Ah, Claudine! you hold me so tight! . . . As I was saying, his marital indifference and his insulting jealousy are enough to excuse everything."

(Is she talking about her husband? I wasn't listening. Why does she need to talk about "excusing"? That word sounds out of place here.)

With a kiss I dam up the flow of her gentle prattle—for a few seconds.

" . . . But you, Claudine, I swear nobody ever before made me go through such a torment of waiting. So many weeks wasted, darling! Bear in mind that spring is nearly here. Every day brings us nearer the summer season, with its separations."

"I forbid your going away!"

"Oh yes, do forbid me something!" she pleads with irresistible tenderness, clinging to me. "Scold me. Don't leave me. I don't want to see anybody but you—and Renaud."

"Ah! So Renaud finds grace in your sight?"

"Yes, because he's so kind and has a woman's soul and understands and shields our privacy. Do you know, Claudine, I don't feel the least bit ashamed in Renaud's presence. Isn't that strange?"

(Strange, indeed, and I envy her. As for me, I do feel ashamed—

no, that isn't exactly the word for it. It's more that I'm—somewhat shocked. That's it—my husband shocks me.)

"Besides, dear, say what you will," she goes on, raising herself on one elbow, "we three are acting out a rather unusual little romance."

("Rather unusual!" "A little romance!" What a chatterbox! If I kiss her lips somewhat cruelly, doesn't she suspect why? I'd like to bite off her pointed little tongue. I'd like to make love to a Rézi who was dumb and docile—maintaining perfect silence, unbroken save for her glances and her gestures.)

I lost myself in the kiss I gave her, feeling her short, hurried breathing on my nostrils. It was getting dark, but I held her head in my hands as if it had been a fruit and mussed up her hair, which is so fine that just by the feel of it I could guess its color.

"I'm sure it must be seven o'clock, Claudine!"

Rézi leaped from the bed, ran to the electric switch and deluged us with a flood of light.

Shivering and lonesome, I curled up in the warm spot in order to retain the heat from Rézi's body a little longer and to let the blonde odor of her fill my being. (I have plenty of time. My husband is waiting for me without any anxiety—quite the contrary!)

Dazzled by the light, Rézi groped about for a moment without finding her scattered underclothing. She bent over to pick up a stray tortoise-shell comb and, as she stood up, her chemise slipped to the ground. Quite unconcerned, she put up her hair with that graceful celerity which always both amuses and fascinates me.

The hair under her upraised arms and on her youthful body is of such a pale, moss-like gold that in the bright light she seems to be as smooth as a statue. But what statue would dare to have those full, firm haunches, in such bold contrast with the slenderness of the torso?

Her hair neatly put up like a well dressed woman, Rézi planted her springlike hat on her head with a serious air and stood for a moment looking at herself, stark naked except for her lilac toque. My burst of laughter spurred her to hasten, alas! In quick order, chemise, girdle, diaphanous "panties" and dawn-colored slip came fluttering down on her as if summoned by a magic formula.

A minute more and modish Rézi stood before me in sable coat and ivory suède gloves, proud of her sleight of hand.

"My blonde beauty, everything is dark, now that all the white and golden color of you no longer vies with the electric light. Help me get up. I am powerless against these covers which are holding me down."

Standing up and stretching my arms to relieve the slightly painful stiffness between my shoulderblades, I studied myself in the huge, well placed mirror. I felt proud of my muscular slenderness and my graceful beauty, more boyish and cleancut than Rézi's.

She coyly slipped my upraised arm about her neck. I turned my head away from the double image, dressed and nude, reflected in the mirror.

I dressed quickly, assisted by my friend, who spread about me an aroma of love and furs.

"Rézi dear, don't try to teach me to be as quick as you. Compared with your fairy hands, I shall always seem to be dressing with my feet . . . Why! we haven't eaten a bite!"

"We had no time," Rézi protested, looking at me with a smile.

"Let's have some of those blue grapes anyhow. I'm so thirsty!"

"All right. Here, take some."

I sucked the grape from between her lips . . . I staggered with desire and exhaustion. She slipped out of my arms.

The lights are out. Beyond the half-open door, the re-echoing chilliness of the brightly lighted stairway. For the last time Rézi offers me her warm, grape-scented lips.

Then suddenly the street, the elbowing haste of the passers-by and, because of the unaccustomed hurried dressing, the shivering and slightly sickish feeling one has when one gets up while it is still night.

23

''C o m e here, dear child and let me show you something that will make you laugh," Renaud called out, interrupting the long morning ceremony of combing out my short hair. He is already laughing, ensconced in the wicker armchair.

"Listen! This morning a devoted individual who consents, for the sum of sixty centimes an hour, to keep the Rue Goethe apartment in order turned over to me an object which had been found among the storm-tossed bed-coverings. She had wrapped it in a piece of *Le Petit Parisien* and handed it to me with the words, "A part of your apparel, sir."

"! ! !"

"There you go, imagining right away something improper! Take a look."

He held up by the tips of his fingers a narrow piece of lawn finely pleated and edged with lace—one of the shoulder-straps from Rézi's chemise. I snatched it from him and shall not give it back.

"What's more, I suspect that concierge of supplying wisecracks to some of our most popular vaudeville entertainers. About six o'clock last evening, a bit uneasy over my darling's staying away so long, I went and discreetly questioned her about you two. With a respectfully reproving air, she replied, 'Those ladies have been waiting for you, sir, going on two hours now.' "

"And then?"

"Then—I didn't go upstairs. Give me a kiss as a reward."

24

THIS is not going to be Claudine's diary any longer, to tell the truth, because now I cannot talk about anything but Rézi.

What has become of the energetic Claudine of former times? Listless, sad, consumed with fever, she drifts along in Rézi's wake.

The days pass quietly by without other incidents than our meetings in the Rue Goethe apartment once or twice a week. The rest of the time I follow Renaud about as he fulfills his various functions—at first nights, dinners, literary receptions.

When we go to the theatre, I often take my friend with me—Lambrook tagging along—in order to have the cowardly assurance that during those few hours she will not be untrue to me. I am tormented with jealousy and yet—I do not love her.

No, I do not love her! But I cannot throw off the hold she has on me. And besides, I make no effort to do so. When I am not in her presence, I can without a shudder imagine her bowled over by a taxi or crushed in a subway accident. But my ears throb and my heartbeats quicken if I think to myself, "At this very moment she is giving her lips to some lover—man or woman—her head tossed back as if drinking it in and her eyelashes fluttering, in the pose I know so well."

What difference does it make that I don't love her? I suffer the same as if I did.

I find it hard to endure Renaud's sitting in as a third party the way he so willingly does. He would not let me have the key to the little apartment, maintaining—doubtless rightly—that we should not be seen going in there alone. And so each time I have to make the same humiliating effort to say to him, "Renaud, we're going over there tomorrow."

He shows us every possible attention, happy, no doubt—like Rézi —over the "unusual little romance." This need, common to both of them, to pose as immoral and up-to-date puzzles me. And yet I am doing the same as Rézi—and even more—and I do not feel immoral.

Renaud now has the habit of tarrying awhile when he escorts us "over there." He pours the tea, sits down, smokes a cigarette, chats of this and that, gets up to straighten a picture or snip a moth on the velvet covering of the praying-stools, and in general indicates that he feels quite at home.

And when he finally consents to go, pretending that he must hurry for some reason or other, Rézi is the one who always protests, "Oh, don't go—stay a little longer."

As for me, I say nothing.

I am left out of their conversation, made up as it is of gossip, scandal, jokes which quickly become suggestive, scantily veiled allusions to the tête-à-tête that is to follow.

Rézi laughs and helps to drag out this interminable proceeding with sweet, nearsighted glances and graceful turnings of her head and body. I give you my solemn word I am as shocked by all this— as annoyed and embarrassed—as a pure-minded girl before obscene pictures.

The ecstasy of love—as I conceive it—has nothing to do with this sort of flirting.

In the bright room, pervaded with Rézi's iris fragrance and Claudine's less delicate, sweetish Chypre, in the large bed scented with our two bodies, I mutely take vengeance for all these unseen, bleeding little wounds. Then, lying close to me in an embrace that is now blessedly familiar, Rézi talks away and plies me with questions, irritated at my short, simple answers, eager to know more and unwilling to believe that I have led a proper life until now and that my present infatuation is a new experience for me.

"But how about Luce?"

"Well, she was in love with me."

"And—nothing happened?"

"Absolutely nothing . . . Does that seem silly to you?"

"Not by any means, Claudine."

Laying her cheek on my breast, she seems to be listening to something within herself. Recollections rise out of the past and sparkle in her gray eyes.

If she speaks, I shall be tempted to strike her—and yet I long to hear her talk.

"You didn't wait until you were married, Rézi?"

"Oh yes, I did," she exclaimed, sitting up and giving way to the need to tell all about herself. "Such a ridiculous, commonplace initiation! My singing teacher, a charming blonde with the bony frame of a horse, who, because of her sea-green eyes, affected ultra-modern styles in dress and the mannerisms of an Anglo-Saxon sphinx.

"Under her tuition I cultivated my voice and the whole gamut of strange emotions. I was very young, newly married, timid and constrained.

"After a month—yes, exactly one month—I stopped taking lessons, having been terribly disillusioned by witnessing through a half-open door a scene in which the sphinx, wrapped in liberty scarfs, bitterly accused her cook of having cheated her out of something under nineteen cents."

Rézi became animated, swaying in undulating movements, shaking her head of silky hair and laughing at the ludicrousness of her reminiscences. Sitting close against my thigh, she leaned forward with one foot in her hand and her chemise slipping down. She seemed to be enjoying herself immensely.

"And then, Rézi, who came next?"

"The next one was—"

She hesitated, looked at me quickly, set her lips and decided to go ahead.

"It was a young girl."

I would have sworn from the look on her face that she had skipped someone—man or woman.

"A young girl? Really? That's interesting!"

(I could have bitten her.)

"Interesting—yes. But how I suffered! I never after that wanted to become friends with a young girl."

Dreamy and half-nude, with a sad expression about her lips, she looked like a lovesick child. How I would have liked to imprint my teeth in two little red semi-circles on that shoulder to which the dim light imparted a mother-of-pearl tint.

"You—loved her?"

"Yes, I did. But now I love no one but you, dear."

Whether through real affection or instinctive apprehension, she threw her pure white arms about me and buried my face in her loose-flowing hair.

But I wished to hear the rest of the story.

"How about her—did she love you?"

"How could I tell? Claudine, dearest, nothing equals the cruelty, the coldblooded and imperious curiosity of a young girl (I refer to those of good character—the others don't count). They have no understanding of suffering, no feeling of pity, no sense of justice.

"That young girl, although more eager and hungry for pleasure than a widow of a year's standing, used to keep me waiting for her weeks on end, would never receive me except in the presence of her parents and contemplated my unhappiness with cold, hard eyes and a naïve expression on her pretty face.

"Two weeks later I would learn why I was being punished in this manner—I had kept her waiting five minutes or had had too lively a conversation with one of my men friends. And what mean remarks, what cutting insinuations made out loud in the presence of others, with the sharp, brutal boldness of those who have not yet been softened and chastened by their first misstep!"

My heart, gripped and constricted, beat rapidly. I would gladly have annihilated this woman who was speaking. And yet I thought more highly of her for her spontaneous and truthful confession. I prefer her turbulent eyes, darkened by memories of the past, to the provocative, childlike expression she assumes as she looks intently at Renaud—or any man—or woman—even the concierge.

Good Lord! how I have changed! Perhaps not fundamentally—I hope not—but outwardly. Spring is here—the Paris springtime, slightly consumptive, somewhat corrupted, easily wearied—but never mind, it's spring!

And what do I know of it except what I gather from Rézi's hats? Violets—lilacs—roses have successively bloomed on her charming head, opening to the glowing light of her hair. She has presided in a domineering manner at my sessions at the milliner's, annoyed to remark how ridiculous certain "ladylike" hats looked on my curly bobbed head.

She dragged me to Gauthé's, to have them gird me in a coat of mail of overlapping ribbons, a pliable girdle that yields to the rhythm of my hips . . . Very busily she picked out from among the dress-goods the blues that go well with the yellow of my eyes, the pronounced pinks that bring out so peculiarly the amber of my cheeks.

I am wrapped up in her—filled with her presence. I have difficulty withstanding the desire to strike her, and I fear lest I displease her. Before crossing her threshold I throw away the bunch of wild narcissus I had bought of a peddler. Their too strong, southern odor is dear to me but Rézi does not like it.

How far from happy I am! Where can I find relief from the sorrow that is crushing me? Renaud and Rézi are both indispensable to my life and I haven't the slightest idea of choosing between them. But how I would like to separate them—or, better yet, how I wish they were entirely unknown to one another!

Have I found a cure for this situation? At any rate, it is worth trying.

Marcel came to see me today. He found me in a strange mood, depressed and at the same time aggressive. This was because for the past week I have been putting off an appointment that Rézi is begging for—Rézi, so fresh and eager, stimulated by the springtime. But I can hardly stand any longer Renaud's being there with us.

How is it he does not sense this? The last time we were at the

Rue Goethe apartment, his affectionate, slightly morbid curiosity met with such brutal surliness from me that Rézi, growing uneasy, got up and gave him some signal or other, whereupon he left at once.

This sort of private understanding between them exasperated me still more. I became stubborn and Rézi for the first time left without removing her hat, which she takes off after her chemise.

Marcel accordingly twitted me on my dour face. (He long ago uncovered the secret of my anxiety and my joy. He goes straight to the sore spot in my soul with an unerring instinct that would astonish me if I did not know my stepson.

Today, seeing that I was low-spirited, he maliciously kept harping on the cause of my unhappiness.

"Are you jealous of your friend?" he asked.

"Are you?"

"I? That depends . . . Do you keep an eye on her?"

"Is that any of your business? And anyhow, why should I?"

Leisurely adjusting his necktie, which reflected the iridescent tones of a scarab, he cast a sidelong glance at me with a disdainful expression on his sharp, pencilled and painted features.

"Oh, for no special reason. I admit I know her only slightly. On a superficial acquaintance she strikes me as a woman who will bear watching."

I smiled sardonically.

"Really? I defer to your wide experience with women."

"Charming of you," he remarked without emotion. "That was a nasty dig, but entirely justified, I grant you. I saw you three, by the way, at the first night at the Vaudeville Theatre. Madame Lambrook looked bewitching—her hair done up a little too tightly, perhaps. But what exquisite grace and how she seems to love you—and my father!"

I held myself rigidly under control and showed nothing outwardly. Disappointed, Marcel got up with a swaying motion of the hips—for whose benefit?

"Good-bye. I'm going home. You would give a humorous writer the blues—if they weren't already so dismal, all of them."

"On whom are you going to bestow your company now?"

"On myself. I am enjoying a honeymoon in my little apartment."

"So you've a new love affair?"

"Why, hadn't you heard of my emancipation?"

"No, those fellows are all so discreet."

"Who do you mean?"

"Your very special friends."

"Their occupation requires it. Yes, I have a regular kept woman's apartment, a tiny little place—just room for two if they stick close together."

"Which they certainly do, don't they?"

"Have it your way, my dear. Any chance of your coming to see the place? I'd just as soon, however, you didn't bring my revered father. As for your girl friend, if that would amuse her—why! what's the matter?"

(I had seized his wrist sharply, struck with a sudden idea.)

"You're never out in the afternoon, I presume?"

"In the afternoon? Why yes, I am. Thursdays and Saturdays. Now don't think I'm going to tell you where I go," he added, smiling coyly like a modest young girl.

"I'm not interested in that," I replied. "Tell me, Marcel, I don't suppose anyone could go and look at your little resting-place in your absence?"

"My little tiring-place, you mean?"

He raised his wicked-looking eyes, their blue streaked with dark gray. He had caught my idea.

"Why yes, at a pinch," he continued. "She can hold her tongue, your pretty Madame Lambrook?"

"How can you ask!"

"I'll give you a key. Don't break any of my little gadgets, I'm attached to them. The electric tea-kettle is in a green cupboard to the left as you go in. You can't miss it. All I have is a study, bedroom

and bath. The crackers, Château-Yquem, arak and ginger brandy
are in the same cupboard. Thursday, then?"

"Yes, next Thursday. Many thanks, Marcel."

I admit he's a young rascal, but I would gladly have thrown my
arms around him. Boisterously happy, I stride from one window
to another, my hands behind my back and whistling noisily.

That fellow lets you have the key!

25

I CAN feel the lump made by the little latchkey in my handbag. I
am taking Rézi to the apartment in the mad hope of finding a way
out of this situation. To see her secretly, to eliminate from this
entire affair (which does not concern him at all) my dear Renaud,
whom I love so deeply—I do, indeed!—that I cannot see him mixed
up in this business without feeling terribly upset—

Rézi docilely accompanies me, much amused and glad that my
sternness has melted at last after a week of staying away from her.

It is a warm day. In the taxi Rézi unbuttons the mannish jacket
of her suit of rough blue serge and sighs for air. I furtively study
the outline of her clear-cut profile, the childlike nose, the eyelashes
through which the light shines, the blonde, velvety eyebrows.

She holds my hand and waits patiently, leaning forward a little
now and then to look at a flower-laden cart that flings its moist
fragrance into our faces, or some shop window or a well dressed
woman walking past . . . She is so gentle! You would think she
loved no one but me, desired no one else.

Chaussée-d'Antin—a large inner court—then a small door and a
diminutive, well kept stairway with landings where you almost had
to stand on one foot.

I climbed the three flights without resting and then stopped. It smelt of Marcel already—sandalwood and fresh-cut hay, with a dash of ether. I opened the door.

"Wait a minute, Rézi. Only one can go through at a time."

Yes, it was exactly that way. The doll-like apartment immediately struck me as hugely entertaining. An embryonic hallway led to a mere suggestion of a study. Only the bedroom-parlor-etc. was of normal size.

We crept in like two stray cats, stopping at every piece of furniture and in front of each picture. Too many perfumes, too many perfumes!

"Claudine, look at the aquarium on the mantel-piece!"

"And the fish with three tails."

"Oh, there's one with fins like the flounces on a skirt! What's that—a perfume-burner?"

"No, an inkwell, I think—or a coffee cup or something."

"What a fine old piece of goods, dear! It would make a delightful facing for a spring jacket. That fascinating little goddess who stands with folded arms—"

"That's a male figure."

"Why no, Claudine!"

"You can't see very well because of the flowing garment."

"Oh, come quick and look, little shepherd boy!"

(I don't like to have her call me "shepherd boy." That's one of Renaud's pet names for me. It hurts me for her sake and especially for his.)

"Look at what?"

"His picture!"

I joined her in the bedroom-parlor-etc. It was indeed a portrait of Marcel, dressed up like a Byzantine lady, a rather unusual pastel, bold coloring on a weak drawing. Her reddish hair coiled over her ears and her forehead loaded down with jewels, she—he—oh, fudge, I give it up—Marcel, then, was holding away from him with a stilted gesture one long panel of the stiff transparent costume of gauze embroidered with pearls, hanging as straight up and down as a shower and disclosing between the folds glimpses of a pink thigh, a calf, a slender knee. A thin, sharp face and scornful eyes, bluer yet by contrast with the reddish hair—it is Marcel sure enough.

Standing dreamily with Rézi close beside me, I saw again the suggestive-looking, dark-complexioned lad whose striking portrait by Bronzino in the Louvre once captivated me so instantaneously.

"What pretty arms that child has," sighed Rézi. "Too bad his tastes should be so—"

"Too bad for whom?" I asked with a flash of suspicion.

"Why, for his family, of course!"

She laughed and gave me her parted lips to kiss. Which started me on another train of thought.

"But say, where does he lie down?"

"He doesn't—he sits up. It's bad form to lie down."

Nevertheless, I did discover behind a rose-colored curtain of panne velvet a sort of narrow alcove, a couch covered with the same pink velvet, on which large, five-pointed leaves had left their outline in grayish green. Pressing an electric button, I amused myself flooding this altar with the light that streamed down through an inverted crystal flower.

The decadent young pansy!

Rézi pointed with her slender finger at the cushions strewn over the couch, as she remarked, "That alone would indicate that no woman ever laid her head or anything else there."

I laughed at her penetrating wit. The carefully selected cushions were all made of rough brocade, embroidered with spangles and gold and silver thread. A woman's hair would be mercilessly curry-combed by all that.

"Come, Rézi, we'll take them away."

"Yes, let's get rid of them, Claudine."

Perhaps this is going to be the sweetest recollection of all our intimacy. I am more yielding and less fiercely dominant than usual.

Rézi brings her customary ardor and her submissive docility, while the inverted flower diffuses its opaline glow over our brief moment of rest.

After a while, in the apartment below, a tinny, spavined piano and a broken-down barbershop tenor join forces to pound out with conviction:

Jadis—vivait—en Nor—mandie . . .

At first I find it annoying to have such a strong sense of rhythm. But one gets used to this by degrees and in time it is no longer annoying—quite the contrary.

Jadis—vivait—en Nor . . .

If anyone had ever predicted that a ballad from "Robert le Diable" would one day move me so deeply that it clutched my throat! But a special combination of circumstances is necessary for that.

Toward six o'clock, just as Rézi, all desires satisfied, was dropping off to sleep with her arms about my neck, the doorbell rang imperiously enough to wreck our nerves. Rézi, terror-stricken, smothered a cry and dug all her nails into my neck. I raised myself on one elbow and listened.

"Don't be afraid, dear, there's nothing to fear. It's somebody at the wrong door or one of Marcel's friends. He can't have notified them all that he would be away."

This reassured her and she uncovered her pale face and lay back in the most thoroughly Versailles-eighteenth-century state of disorder imaginable. But once more, *trrr.*

Rézi leaped from the couch and began to dress, her scurrying fingers not the least paralyzed by her fright.

The ringing continued insistently. It took on a teasing, insinuating character and even played tunes. I gritted my teeth with nervous irritation.

My poor friend, pale and already dressed to leave, clapped her hands over her ears. The corners of her mouth quivered every time the bell started up again. I felt sorry for her.

"Come Rézi, it's evidently one of Marcel's friends."

"One of his friends? Why, can't you hear the spitefulness, the mean intention of that unbearable ringing? Believe me, it's someone who knows we are here. If my husband should—"

"You're not very brave!"

"Thanks! It's easy to be brave when one has a husband such as you have."

I made no reply—what was the use? I slipped on my girdle. As soon as I was dressed, I tiptoed over as noiselessly as a cat and held my ear close to the door. I heard nothing but that interminable bell.

Finally, after one last, long ring—a sort of exclamation point—I heard light footsteps departing.

"He's gone, Rézi."

"At last! Let's not go out for a while yet, they might be watching for us. If you ever catch me here again—!"

What a wretched ending to this meeting that will never have a morrow! My pretty, scared friend was in such a hurry to leave me and get away from the house and the neighborhood that I did not dare ask if I might go home with her. She went down the stairs first while I extinguished the inverted crystal flower and picked up the spangled cushions. Marcel's portrait, with its disdainful chin and rouged, tightshut lips, looked down at me from the wall.

26

I HAVE standing here before me this afternoon, in a very short, tight-fitting black coat, the original of the compromising Byzantine pastel. He is bursting with curiosity, as in the days when he was so intrigued about Luce.

"Well, how about yesterday?"

"Why, thanks a lot. You have there a small temple quite worthy of you."

"And of you also," he replied with a bow.

"You are too flattering. Your portrait—er—interested me particularly. I am glad to learn that you have a feeling for things as they were in Constantine's day."

"It's quite the rage just now . . . But say, you aren't either of you very gluttonous. My Château-Yquem, a present from my grandmother, doesn't seem to have tempted you."

"No, all our other instincts were paralyzed by our curiosity."

"Oh, curiosity, eh?" he queried with the skeptical smile of his portrait. "What a good pair of housekeepers you are! I found everything in perfect order. Nobody disturbed you, I hope?"

(A flash of a smile and a swift glance that quickly turned aside—ah, the villain! So it was he who rang the bell—or got someone else to do it! I should have suspected it. But you're not going to catch me off my guard, you young rascal.)

"No, not at all. It was as quiet as any well kept house. Somebody did ring once, I believe—and yet I'm not sure they did. I was at that moment all absorbed in contemplating your little hermaphroditic goddess, the one with her arms crossed."

(There, that will teach him a lesson! And since we are both good sports, he puts on the air of a well pleased host.)

27

A LETTER from Montigny that I have to read aloud in order to understand it, the spelling is so hieroglyphic.

"Arnt yu comin dowen this way attall yung ladee. The big ramler is alreddy to blosum and the wepin ash has groan a lot. Yur father is abowt as usule."

That my father is "abowt as usule," Mélie, I don't doubt in the least. That "the wepin ash has groan a lot" is fine. And the big rambler is about to blossom . . . It is so beautiful! It mantles an entire wall. It is always in a hurry to bloom and does so ceaselessly and generously, exhausting its strength along toward the autumn by beginning all over again in spasms of sweet-scented renascence —a thoroughbred that will die in harness.

"The ramler is alreddy to blosum." At this news I can feel the fibres that attach me to Montigny coming to life again, juicy with sap. It is ready to blossom! I throb a little with joyous pride like a mother who has just been told, "Madame, your son will win every prize!"

All my relatives in the vegetable kingdom are calling me. My ancestor, the old walnut-tree, is growing old waiting for me. Under the clematis there will soon be showers of white stars.

But I can't go to them—I simply can't! What would Rézi do without me? I don't want to leave Renaud near her—my poor boy is such an inveterate lover and she is so lovable!

Take Renaud with me? And leave Rézi all alone in a dry, scorching Parisian summer—alone with her wild fancies and her liking for intrigue? She would never remain faithful to me.

Good heavens, is it true that, hour by hour, between kisses and quarrels, four months have already gone by? I have done nothing during all that time, nothing but wait. When I leave her, I wait for the day that shall bring us together again. When I am with her, I wait for the voluptuous pleasure—which comes to her sometimes slowly, sometimes swiftly—to deliver her into my arms more beautiful and more sincere than before. When Renaud is with us, I wait for him to go, and wait for Rézi to leave so that I may talk awhile without bitterness or jealousy with my Renaud, whom it seems to me I love more than ever since Rézi came into our life.

28

I MIGHT have known it would happen! I fell ill and now three weeks have gone for nothing. Influenza, a chill or over-exertion— let the doctor who is tending me call it whatever he wishes, I have had a lot of fever and pain in my head. But I have a sturdy constitution at bottom.

Dear old Renaud, how precious your tenderness was to me! I was never so thankful to you for talking in that rich, low, melodious voice.

Rézi also took care of me, in spite of the dread of appearing homely to her which made me hide my burning face in my hands. Sometimes her way of looking at Renaud and then sitting down— for his special benefit—on the edge of my bed, one knee raised like a woman riding side-saddle, with a hat of broad braided straw and a velvet-belted gown of English embroidery—the whole performance, too coy and affected for a call on a sick person, shocked me.

Under cover of my fever I could exclaim, "Go away!" She thought I was delirious. It seemed to me also that I saw Renaud smile when she came in, as one does when one catches a whiff of a cool breeze.

They chat in my presence of things I have not seen and their conversation, which I have trouble following, offends me as if it were a secret language they had made up between them.

I felt vexed at my friend for the clear, fresh, velvety beauty of her cheeks. And although she very gently laid some long-stemmed dark red roses along the edge of the couch on which I was recuperating, after she had gone I took the hand mirror hidden under my pillow and thought of her with jealous resentment as I gazed long at my pallor.

"Is it true, Renaud, that the trees on the boulevards are seared and brown already?"

"Yes, it's true, little girl. Do you want to come with me to Montigny? You'll see greener ones there."

"They're too green . . . I could go out today, Renaud, I'm feeling so well. I ate the entire eye of a chop besides my egg and I drank a glass of Asti and nibbled some grapes . . . Are you going out?"

Standing at the window of his "temple of toil," he looked at me undecided.

"I'd love to go out with a handsome husband like you. That grey suit is very becoming to you and the white piqué vest gives you that imposing mid Victorian air I like so much . . . It is for my benefit that you look so young today?"

He blushed a little under his swarthy skin and stroked his long silvery moustache.

"You know very well that it hurts me to have you talk about my being so old."

"Who's talking about your being old? On the contrary, I'm dead scared that your youthfulness may last as long as you do yourself, like some disease one has had from birth. Take me out with you, Renaud! I feel as if I had strength enough to startle the universe!"

My grandiloquence did not sway him.

"No, no, Claudine. The medicine man told you, 'Not till Sunday.' This is Friday. Forty-eight hours more to wait patiently, little bird. Hello! here comes a friend who will be able to make you stay in the house."

He took advantage of Rézi's coming in to slip out himself. He doesn't seem at all like my dear man, usually so anxious to please me, regardless of consequences. That doctor is an idiot!

"What are you pouting over, Claudine?"

She is so pretty that I can't help smiling this time. Blue, blue, blue—the color of mist and soap bubbles combined.

"Rézi, the elves have dipped their garments in the water of your dress."

(She smiles. Leaning against her thigh, I gaze up into her face. A long dimple like an exclamation point divides her wilful chin in two. The outline of her nostrils forms the simple and symmetrical arabesque I used to admire in Fanchette's nose. A sigh escapes me.)

"Can you beat it? I wanted to go out and that jackass of a doctor won't let me. You stay with me anyhow and let me enjoy your freshness, the cool zephyrs that play hide-and-seek in your skirts and toy with the leaves on your hat. Is it a hat or a crown? I never saw you so irresistibly Viennese, dear, with your hair as light as the foam on a stein of beer. Stay by my side and tell me all about the streets and the parched trees—and the tiny remnant of affection you still have for me after our long separation."

But she refused to sit down and as she talked to me with a cajoling voice, her eyes traveled from one window to another as though seeking a way of escape.

"I'm simply broken-hearted, sweet one! I'd have loved to spend the whole day with you, especially if you are to be alone. Your lips so long ago forgot their love for mine, Claudine dearest."

She leaned over me, baring her moist teeth for me to kiss, but I turned my head away.

"No. I must smell feverish. Go take a walk—I mean, go out for a walk."

"I'm not going for a walk, dear. Tomorrow is the anniversary of our engagement—don't laugh!—and I'm in the habit of giving my husband a present on that day."

"Well, what of it?"

"Why, this year I forgot my duty as a grateful wife, so I've got to run around in order that Mr. Lambrook may find under his cone-shaped napkin this evening a cigar case or pearl cuff-buttons or a dynamite scarfpin—it doesn't matter what, so long as it's something. Otherwise there'd be three weeks of icy silence and irreproachable dignity.

"Good God!" she exclaimed, raising her clenched fists, "when men are so badly needed out in Africa, why is he hanging around here?"

Her voluble, forced jesting filled me with distrust.

"But Rézi, why don't you entrust this purchase to the thoroughly reliable judgment of a valet?"

"I thought of that," she replied. "But, except for my Mädchen, the servants are under my husband's control."

(It's evident she is determined to go.)

"Run along, virtuous wife. Go and celebrate Saint Lambrook's Day."

She had already lowered her little veil.

"If I get through before six o'clock, would you like me to drop in again?"

(How pretty she is as she leans over me this way! Her skirt, wrapped around her in a spiral by the sprightliness of her movements, reveals her entire figure. A purely platonic admiration stirs me . . . Possibly because of my convalescent condition, I no longer feel the tumultuous desire of other days beating its great wings within me . . . And besides, she turned down my request that she give up Saint Lambrook's Day for my sake.)

"It all depends. But come in anyhow, you will be rewarded according to your desserts . . . No, I tell you, I smell feverish."

So now I'm alone. I stretch—read a few pages—walk about. I sit down at my dressing-table and glance at the mirror from time to time as one does at a clock.

I don't look so badly after all. My curls are rather good this length. This white collar and blouse of red lawn with fine white stripes suggest going out for a walk. I read in the mirror what my eyes have determined on. It is soon done! A black-ribboned straw hat on my head and a jacket on my arm so that Renaud shall not scold me for my imprudence—and I am in the street.

My! how warm! I'm not a bit surprised that the rambler took it into its head to blossom. What a horrible place this Paris is! I feel light, I have grown thinner.

The open air goes to one's head a bit but one gets used to it as one walks along. I have hardly any more thoughts in my head than a house dog taken out after a rainy week.

Without intending to do so, I automatically turned into the Rue Goethe. Nothing surprising in that!

I smiled as I came opposite No. 59 and I threw a friendly glance at the white tulle curtains hanging at the windows on the third floor.

Ah! the curtain stirred! That little movement transfixed me to the sidewalk as rigid as a china doll. Who could possibly be in our apartment? It must have been a draft from one of the rear windows that lifted up the curtain.

But while I was trying to reason logically, my instinctive self, goaded by a suspicion and then suddenly infuriated, guessed rather than understood.

I dashed across the street and up the two flights in a sort of nightmare as though on cotton-padded stairs that yielded and sprang up again under my feet. I shall press with all my might on the brass button, ring the bell loud enough to bring the house down. No—they wouldn't come to the door!

I stood still a minute with my hand over my heart. That poor little commonplace gesture recalled to my mind with cruel force something that Claire, my foster sister, once said: "Real life is the same as what's in books, isn't it?"

I pressed the brass button timidly, startled by the unfamiliar noise of the bell, which had never rung for us. For two long seconds, seized with a little girl's cowardice, I thought to myself, "Oh, if only nobody would answer!"

The sound of approaching footsteps brought back all my courage in a flood of wrath. Renaud's voice asked crossly, "Who's there?"

Choking for breath, I leaned against the imitation marble wall, which felt cold to my arm. At the sound made by the door as Renaud opened it a little, I wished I might die.

But not for long. I must go through with it! I must! After all, I'm Claudine! I threw off my fear like a cloak and said, "Open the door, Renaud, or I'll scream."

I looked him square in the face as he stood in the doorway, fully dressed. He started back with surprise but merely remarked quietly, "I'll be damned," like a gambler annoyed at his bad luck.

A feeling of being the stronger of the two braced me up still more. I'm Claudine!

"From the street I saw someone at the window," I said. "So I came up just to say hello."

"What a dumb thing I've gone and done," he said as if to himself.

Without making the slightest move to stop me, he stepped aside to let me go by and then followed me in.

I passed quickly through the little drawing-room and pulled aside the flowered portiére . . . Ah! I knew it! Rézi was there sure enough, putting on her clothes—in brassière and step-ins, with her lace-trimmed slip over one arm and wearing her hat, just as she used to with me.

I shall never forget that blond face which, as I continued to stare at her, became convulsed with fright and seemed ready to die. I almost envied her for being so terrified.

She looked at my hands and I saw her thin lips turn pale and parched. Not taking her eyes off me, she groped for her dress with one hand.

I took a step toward her. She almost collapsed and raised her elbows to protect her face. This gesture, revealing the silky down under her arms in which I had so often buried my face, let loose a hurricane within me.

I had an impulse to seize a carafe and throw it—or even a chair. The outlines of the furniture danced before my eyes like heated air over a meadow.

Renaud, who had followed me in, touched my shoulder ever so lightly. He was undecided what to do—a bit pale but above all annoyed. I said to him, speaking with difficulty, "What—are you doing here?"

He smiled nervously in spite of himself.

"Why—er—we were waiting for you, dear, as you see."

(Am I dreaming or is he losing his mind?)

I turned toward the woman standing there. While my eyes were off her, she had slipped on the dress of sea blue in which the elves had dipped their garments. She would never dare to smile, not she!

"Real life is the same as what's in books, isn't it?"

No, gentle Claire. In books the woman who comes seeking vengeance fires two shots, at least. Or else she goes out slamming the door and hurling her scorn at the guilty ones in a crushing remark.

Whereas I can think of nothing to say. The truth is, I haven't the slightest idea what I should do. You can't learn offhand, in five minutes, how to play the part of the outraged wife.

I was still blocking the doorway. I thought Rézi was going to faint. How strange that would have been!

Renaud, at any rate, was not afraid. Like me, he watched with less emotion than interest, the successive manifestations of terror on Rézi's face and seemed at last to realize that there was something incongruous about the three of us meeting here in this manner.

"Listen, Claudine. I want to explain—"

With a gesture of my arm I cut his sentence short. And anyhow he did not seem particularly anxious to finish it, but shrugged one shoulder with a more or less fatalistic gesture of resignation.

It's Rézi I am angry with! I walk toward her slowly. I can see myself advancing upon her. This dual personality which comes over me leaves me in doubt as to what I intend to do. Am I going to strike her or merely intensify her fear and shame until she falls in a faint?

She steps back, slips around behind the table on which the tea stands and reaches the partition. She is going to get away from me! Ah! I won't allow that!

But she already touches the portière, gropes for the doorway, walking backwards with her eyes always fixed on me. Unconsciously I stoop down to pick up a stone—there is none. She has disappeared.

My arms fall to my side, my spirit suddenly is broken.

We stand there, the two of us, staring at one another. Renaud seems in his usual good humor—or nearly so. There is a grieved expression on his face and a slight touch of sadness in his handsome eyes.

My God! he is going to say "Claudine . . ." If I give voice to my anger, if I let the strength that is keeping me up dribble away in reproaches and tears, I shall go out of here on his arm, plaintive and forgiving.

I will not! I am—I am Claudine, after all! And besides, I would never forgive him for my forgiveness.

I waited too long. He came toward me and said "Claudine . . ." I rushed to the door and instinctively fled like Rézi—except that in my case it was myself I was running away from.

I did well to run away. The street and a glance at the telltale curtain revived my pride and my resentment.

And moreover, I now know where I am going.

To rush home in a taxi, grab my overnight bag and leave after tossing my house-key on the table took less than fifteen minutes. I had some money—not much, but enough.

"Gare de Lyon, taxi."

Before going aboard the train, I dashed off a telegram to Papa and then dispatched this message to Renaud: "Send to Montigny clothing for indefinite stay."

29

THOSE cornflowers on the wallpaper, faded from blue to grey, mere shadows of flowers on a still paler background—that chintz curtain with its fantastic pattern (sure enough, there's that grotesque apple with the two eyes!)—I saw all that scores of times in my dreams during those two years in Paris, but never so lifelike.

This time I certainly did hear, from the depths of my semi-conscious sleep, the creaking of the pump!

As I sit bolt upright in my little bed, my childhood room smiles its greeting and releases within me a flood of tears—limpid tears like this sunbeam that dances in golden spangles on the window-pane, tears as sweet to my eyes as the faded flowers on the grey wallpaper.

So it is really true—I am here, in this room! I have no other thought in mind—until I come to dry my eyes on a little pink handkerchief that never came from Montigny.

A wave of sadness checks the flow of my tears. I have been cruelly hurt—beneficially, perhaps. I am almost ready to believe so, since after all I can never be entirely unhappy at Montigny, in this house.

Oh! my little ink-stained desk! All my school copybooks are still in it, "Mathematics," "Rhetoric"—for under Mademoiselle's régime we never wrote "Arithmetic" or "Spelling." "Mathematics" and "Rhetoric" were more distinguished, more "higher education."

Sharp nails scratch at my door and rattle the latch. A distressed, imperious "meow" summons me to open the door.

Oh, how beautiful you are, my dear child! My brain is in such a turmoil that for a moment I had forgotten you, Fanchette. Come up on my bed and into my arms. Press your damp nose and your cold teeth against my chin, so glad to see me that your paws, with claws extended, "knead dough" on my bare arm.

How old are you, anyway? Five—six—I have no idea. Your white fur makes you look so young. You will be young till you die—like Renaud. There now! that reminder has spoiled everything . . . Stay here under my cheek, Fanchette, and let me forget my troubles as I listen to your purring machine vibrating at top speed.

What must you have thought of me, arriving so suddenly and without any baggage? Even Papa suspected something.

"Well, how about the other idiot, that husband of yours?" he inquired.

"He will come as soon as he can spare the time, Papa."

I was pale and absent-minded. I was still back there in the Rue Goethe apartment, with those two people who had hurt me so. Although it was after ten, I refused to sit down at the table. All I wanted was a bed and some warm, secluded corner where I could dream and cry and hate.

But so many kindly little ghosts of my past were hiding in the recesses of my old familiar room that deep and comforting sleep came to me along with them.

Slippered footsteps come shuffling along the hallway. Mélie enters the room without knocking, having fallen right back into her old habits. She is holding the worn little tray in one hand—yes, the same old tray!—and supporting her left breast in the other.

She is faded and untidy, always ready to be the go-between in dubious affairs. But the mere sight of her refreshes my soul.

This homely servant is bringing me on the battered little platter a steaming cup of "the philter that annihilates the years." It smells like chocolate. I am famished.

"Mélie!"

"What is it, my darling?"

"You love me anyhow, don't you?"

She sets down her tray in a leisurely manner before replying, with a shrug of her shapeless shoulders, "Guess I do."

I know she does. I can feel it. Standing beside my bed, she watches me eat. So does Fanchette, stretched out on my feet. Both of them gaze at me with unlimited admiration.

However, Mélie shakes her head and, balancing her left breast in her hand with a disapproving air, remarks:

"You don't look any too well, my child. What have they been doing to you?"

"I had the flu. I wrote Papa all about it. Where is he anyhow?"

"In his cubbyhole, I bet. You'll see him in a little while. Want me to fetch you a tub of water?"

"Why for?" I ask, falling into the dear old ways of speech.

"Why, to wash your little behind and all the rest of you."

"Yes sirree! And make it a big tub."

At the threshold she turned around and asked me point-blank, "When's Monsieur Renaud coming?"

"How do I know?" I replied, "No doubt, he'll notify you in advance. Now run along!"

While waiting for the tub, I leaned out of the window. One could see nothing but a long line of roofs sliding down the street. On account of the steep slope, the second story of each house was on a level with the ground floor of the house above it.

I declare, the incline has become steeper during my absence! I can see the beginning of Convent Street which leads straight— I mean zigzag—to my old school. I've a notion to call on Mademoiselle. No, I'm not looking pretty enough. And besides, I might run into little Helen, that future Rézi.

No, no more friends of that sort—no more women! And I shook my hand, the fingers wide apart, with the slightly sickening aversion one feels for a long, snaky hair caught on one's fingernails.

I slipped barefooted into the sitting-room. The old armchairs smiled at me through their rents and tears. Everything was back in its old place. Two years of exile in Paris had not bent their round backs with sorrow or their dainty Louis Sixteenth legs, on which bits of white paint still showed.

What a blockhead that Mélie is! The blue vase that for fifteen years I was used to seeing on the right of the green one she has gone and put on the left!

I quickly set things to rights, tidying up and putting the finishing touches on this room which had been the setting for almost my entire life. Truly nothing was lacking—except my happy mood of days gone by, my joyous solitude.

Out there beyond those shutters, closed to keep out the sun, is the garden. No, dear garden, I'm not going out to look at you for an hour or so. You move me too deeply, merely by the murmuring of your leaves. It is so long since I have eaten any of your green things!

Papa thinks I'm still asleep. Or else he has forgotten that I am here. Never mind, I'll go to his den in a little while and make him swear a bit.

Fanchette follows right at my heels, as if she feared I might try to run away. Don't be afraid, my dear. Remember, my dispatch read "clothing for an indefinite stay." (What does that mean? I haven't the least idea. But it seems to me that I am to be here a long, long time ... How good it is to transport one's sorrow to another clime!)

My short morning slipped quickly away in the enchanted garden, which seemed to have grown up. The tenant had not touched a thing—not even the grass in the paths, I really believe.

The huge walnut tree has thousands and thousands of heavy nuts. And as I crushed one of its leaves, the pungent, funereal odor made me close my eyes in ecstasy. I leaned up against the giant who stands guard over the garden and yet at the same time plays havoc with it, for his cool shade kills the rosebushes.

What of it? There is nothing more beautiful than a tree— especially that one. At the end of the garden, against Mother Adolphe's wall, the twin pine trees bow in stately fashion, standing stiffly in their sombre, year-round raiment.

The wistaria scrambling all over the roof has shed the blossoms of its charming clusters. So much the better! I find it hard to forgive that flower for having once adorned Rézi's hair.

Lying prone at the foot of the old walnut tree, I can almost hear myself becoming a young growing thing again. Quail Mountain over there looks blue and far away. It will be fine weather tomorrow if Moustiers is not overcast ...

"My little girl, here's a letter for you!"

A letter! Already! How short the respite has been! Couldn't he have let me alone for a little while to enjoy the sunshine and this animal existence? I feel so small and frightened in the face of the sadness that is going to come down on me now. Oh, if I could only wipe out all the past and start a new life—alas!

"My darling child . . ."

717

(He might just as well have let it go at that. I know everything he is going to say. It's true, I was his child! Why did he deceive me?)

"My darling child, I cannot cease sorrowing over your unhappiness. You did exactly right and I am only a most wretched man who loves you broken-heartedly.

"You surely realize, Claudine, that it was only stupid curiosity that drove me to do what I did and so that is not what I blame myself for. I am telling you this even at the risk of turning you still more against me.

"But I have made you suffer and I can find no peace.

"I am sending you all the things you asked for. I entrust you to the care of the country you love.

"Remember, dearest, that you are my one true love and my only source of happiness. My 'youth'—as you used to say in the days when you still laughed as you raised your eyes to mine—my pathetic youth of an already old man disappeared the instant you went away."

How miserable I am! I sob as I sit leaning my head against the rough bark of the old walnut tree. I am unhappy over my own sorrow and unhappy—alas!—over his.

I never before knew what it was to have "an unfortunate love affair" and now I have two and I am even more heartbroken over his than over my own. Renaud! Renaud!

I am falling into a stupor here, my grief is gradually becoming deadened. My burning hot eyes follow the flight of a wasp, the whirr of a bird, the erratic course of a beetle.

How blue that blue monk's hood is! What a strong, healthy, everyday color! Where did that honey-sweet breath of air come from, as fragrant as Oriental perfume or rose cake? It is the big rambler waving its incense before me. Enchanted, I spring to my numbed, tingling feet and hurry over to it.

So many roses! So many roses! I'd like to say to the bush, "Take a rest, my dear, you have bloomed enough, worked enough, given lavishly of your strength and your perfume."

718

The bush would never heed me. It wants to beat the record for roses as to both quantity and fragrance. It has endurance and speed, it gives every ounce that is in it. Its countless offspring are pretty little roses like those in religious pictures, the edge of the petals tinted with a heart-shaped spot of bright carmine. Singly they might appear rather childish—but who would ever dream of criticizing the mantle humming with bees with which they have covered this wall?

"God damn it! That foul beast vomited up by the devil himself should be skinned alive!"

There can be no doubt about it, that's Papa making his presence known.

Delighted to see him and to be diverted by his eccentric ways, I ran toward the house. I caught sight of him leaning out of one of the second-story windows, the library window. His beard had grown a little whiter but still flowed over his chest like a tri-colored river. He breathed fire from his nostrils and his gesticulations struck terror to the heart of the universe.

"What's the matter, Papa?"

"That filthy cat walked all over my beautiful wash drawing and ruined it! I've got to throw her out of the window."

(So he is perpetrating wash drawings now! I tremble a little for my Fanchette.)

"Oh, Papa, did you hurt her?"

"Of course not! But I could have and I should have, the ill-begotten wench!"

(I breathe easy. Seeing him so seldom, I had forgotten how harmless his fulminations are.)

"And you, my little Dine, how are you?"

At the infinite tenderness in his voice and that pet name of my earliest childhood, springs of remembrances started flowing within me. I listened to the gentle rippling of clear and fleeting memories.

(Ah, there he goes thundering again!)

"Well, you little idiot, why don't you answer?"

"I'm very well, Papa dear. Have you been busy?"

719

"It's an insult that you should even have any doubts on the subject. Here, read this. It came out last week. All my good for nothing colleagues are bellowing with rage over it."

He threw down to me the issue of the *Proceedings* which carried his precious communication.

(Malacology! Malacology! You bestow upon your worshippers the blessing of happiness and indifference to humanity and its misfortunes.)

As I turned the pages of the journal, with its pleasant rose-colored cover, I discovered all by myself the true snail, this word which dragged its fifty-four slimy letters across the page: *Tetramethyl-monophenil-sulfotripara-amido-triphenyl-methane.*

(I can hear Renaud laughing at such a discovery.)

"Will you let me keep this, Papa? Shall you need it?"

"No," he replied from his window with Olympian majesty. "I have ordered ten thousand reprints from Gauthier-Villars."

"That was a wise precaution. When do we lunch?"

"Inquire of one of our menials. I am pure brain—I do not eat. I think."

And he slammed shut his window, on which the sun beat fiercely. I know him well. For a man who is "pure brain," he is soon going to be "thinking" a respectable beefsteak.

30

I AM passing the whole day seeking out, step by step, bit by bit, my childhood scattered about in the recesses of the old house, and watching through the gate, twisted out of shape by the mighty wistaria vine, how far-away Quail Mountain changes color from pale green to deep purple.

The dense woods, of a rich, opaque green that turns blue toward nightfall I don't want to love until tomorrow. Today, I am tending my wound, nursing it in seclusion. Too much light, too many fresh breezes and the green-leaved, pink-blossomed briars might tear to shreds the slight protective covering which my bruised sorrow is wrapping about itself.

In the reddening glow of eventide I listen to the kindly garden preparing itself for sleep. Above my head zigzags the noiseless, black-winged flight of a bat. A pear tree, eager to give lavishly of its store, lets fall one by one its full, rounded fruit, quickly over-ripe and carrying down in its fall tenacious wasps—five, six, ten of them boring their way into a single pear and continuing to eat as they fall, merely beating the air a little with their amber wings. In the same manner Rézi's golden lashes used to flicker under my kisses.

The thought of that treacherous friend did not make me shudder with the painful shrinking which I had dreaded. As far as she is concerned, I already suspected that I did not love her.

On the other hand, I cannot, without a cruel start, without wring-ing my hands in anguish, recall Renaud's tall figure as he stood in the shadows of that flower-decked room, awaiting anxiously my decision, his sorrowful eyes dreading the unanswerable . . .

"A telegram for you, my child."

(No! this is too much!)

I turned around threateningly, ready to tear the message to pieces.

"The answer is prepaid."

I read, "Beg you to wire news of your health."

That's all he dared say, having in mind Papa, Mélie and Mademoiselle Mathieu, the postmistress.

I thought of them, too, as I replied, "Good trip. Papa well."

31

I CRIED in my sleep and yet I cannot remember my dream, although it made me wake with an oppressed feeling and sighing convulsively.

Day is just beginning to break, it is only three o'clock. The chickens are still sleeping. Only the sparrows can be heard, making a noise like pebbles being rattled around. It is going to be a fine day, the dawn is blue.

I want to do as I used to when I was a little girl—get up before sunrise so as to go and capture the nocturnal flavor of the cold spring in the Fredonnes woods and the last shreds of night which, retreating before the first rays, plunge deep into the thickets.

I jump out of bed. Fanchette, dislodged from between my knees but still asleep, rolls over and over like a snail without opening an eye. Whimpering faintly, she presses her white paw tighter than ever against her closed eyes. The dawn, moist with dew, does not interest her. She likes nothing but the clear nights when, sitting erect and dignified like an Egyptian cat-goddess, she watches the white moon roll on its endless course.

My hurried dressing and the uncertain hour of early dawn took me back to the winter mornings when, as a scrawny little girl, I used to get up shivering and leave for school through the cold and the deep snow. Courageous under my red hood, I would crack boiled chestnuts with my teeth as I slid along in my pointed little wooden shoes . . .

I went out through the garden and over the spiked gate. With a piece of coal I wrote on the kitchen door, "Claudine has gone out, will be back for lunch." Before picking up my skirts and climbing over the gate, I smiled back at *my* house—for there is no other so completely mine as this rambling old dwelling of grey granite with its trustful windows throwing wide their unpainted shutters day and night.

Patches of low-growing, golden lichen gave a touch of beauty to the purplish slate on the roof. Two swallows perched on the arrow of the weather-vane puffed out their throats and offered their white shirt-fronts to be stroked by the first darting ray of the sun.

The unwonted sight of me in the street at that hour disturbed the dogs in their task as attachés of the street cleaning department. Grey cats slinked silently away. Safely ensconced over a doorway they followed me with their yellow eyes, waiting to climb down again as soon as the noise of my footsteps had died away around the corner.

(These Parisian shoes are no good for Montigny. I'm going to get others, heavier ones with little hobnails.)

The exquisite cold of the blue dawn stung my unaccustomed skin and nipped my ears. But overhead light veils of mauve-colored gauze floated by and the roofs suddenly became edged with flaming orange pink.

Half-running toward the light, I reached the Porte Saint-Jean, midway down the hill, where a cheerful, tumble-down house, set off all by itself on the outskirts of the town, stands guard at the entrance to the fields. I stopped there with a deep sigh.

Have I come to the end of my suffering? Shall I now hear the echo of that brutal blow die away? In this valley, as narrow as a cradle, I used for sixteen years to rock to sleep all my dreams as a lonely child. It seems as if I could still see them sleeping, wrapped in the veil of a milky white mist which ebbs and flows like a wave.

The banging of a shutter thrown open drove me from the heap of stone where I sat musing, into the wind, which felt cold on my mouth.

It is not the people of Montigny that I came out here to see. I am going to go down the hill and through that blanket of mist and climb the sandy, yellow road to the woods, now touched at their tips with fiery pink. Let's go!

I walked on and on, hurried and troubled, scanning the base of the hedges as though seeking there some healing herb.

It was past noon when I got home, more used up than if I had been assaulted by three poachers. But while Mélie wrung her hands, I gazed in the mirror with a listless smile at my hair matted with burdocks, my tired face scarred with a pink scratch beside the lip and my wet skirt embroidered all over with the shaggy green pellets of the wild millet. My blue lawn waist being split under the arms, I caught the same warm, moist odor which used to turn the head of Ren—no! I am determined not to think of him any more.

How beautiful the woods are and how soft the light! How cool the dew along the grass-fringed ditches! Even though I did not this time find under the thickets and in the fields the fascinating army of slender little flowers—forget-me-nots and wild pinks, narcissus and spring daisies, even though the Solomon's seal and the lilies of the valley had long since shed their hanging bells, at any rate I was able to plunge my bare hands and chilly legs into thick, deep grass, sprawl wearily on the dry velvet of mosses and pine needles, lie in unthinking restfulness under the burning rays of the rising sun.

Like a room opening on a garden, I am filled with sunshine, astir with soft breezes and resonant with the song of the locust and cries of birds.

"What a mess! And such a pretty dress, too!" Mélie scolded.

"What do I care? I'll get others. I don't think I'd have come home at all, Mélie, if I hadn't had to eat. I'm simply famished."

"That's good. It's all cooked and ready . . . But what a crazy thing to do! Your father has been hunting all over for you and going on like a sick cow. You're the same as ever, you little tramp!"

I had done so much roaming about and looking and loving all morning that I spent the whole afternoon in the garden. In the vegetable garden, which I hadn't yet visited, I feasted on warm apricots and sharp-flavored peaches, which I ate slowly as I lay on my stomach under the big pine tree with an old volume of Balzac open between my elbows.

Dear me! I feel so care-free, so deliciously tired out, it seems as if the happiness, the forgetfulness and the joyous solitude of former times had come again to me!

I might easily have thought so, but no, Mélie is wrong, I am not "the same as ever." As the day declines, restlessness begins to show again, uneasiness returns—a tormenting uneasiness which keeps me constantly moving about, shifting from one room, one chair, one book to another, as one seeks a cool spot in a feverish bed.

I wandered about the kitchen and hesitated a long time . . . I helped Mélie beat up a mayonnaise dressing which refused to whip. Finally I asked with an air of indifference, "Weren't there any letters for me today?"

"No, pet, nothing but your father's newspapers."

I went to bed so weary that my ears hummed and the over-tired muscles of my legs twitched spasmodically. But my sleep was not restful, being disturbed by troubled dreams through which ran a nerve-wracking feeling of expectancy. Consequently I am lingering abed this morning between Fanchette and my chocolate, which is getting cold.

Fanchette, convinced that it is for her alone that I have come home, has experienced perfect joy since my return—a little too perfect perhaps. I do not bother her enough. She misses my insistent teasing of former days, when I used to make her sit up on her hind legs, hold her up by the tail, tie her paws together and swing her to and fro, calling out, "Here you are, an eight-pound white rabbit!"

Now I am merely affectionate with her, I stroke her without

pinching or nipping her ears. But really, Fanchette, one can't have everything. Look at me, for instance—

Who is coming up the front stoop? The letter carrier, I think. If only Renaud hasn't written to me!

Mélie would have brought me the letter by this time. I don't hear her coming, although I strain ears and nostrils to listen . . . She isn't coming. He hasn't written. Well, so much the better. I only want him to forget and let me forget.

Why that sigh? It was a sigh of relief, I feel quite sure. And yet, for a woman whose fears have been allayed, I seem to be trembling a good deal.

Why didn't he write? Because I haven't answered his letter— because he is afraid of irritating me still more—or else he did write and then tore up the letter—he missed the mail—he is ill!

I jump out of bed, pushing away the dishevelled cat who, rudely awakened, squints at me through half-opened eyes. Moving about brings me to my senses and makes me ashamed of myself.

Mélie is so disorderly! Maybe she left the letter on a corner of the kitchen table, near the butter which they bring wrapped in two large green leaves. The butter will make a grease spot on the letter. I ring a bell that lets loose a racket like a gong in a convent.

"You want your hot water, my dear?"

"Of course I do . . . Tell me, Mélie, did the postman leave anything for me?"

"No, my darling."

Her blue eyes wrinkle with a mischievous tenderness.

"Ah, I see! Getting impatient waiting for your man? There's a real bride for you! Hankering after something, eh?"

And she goes off laughing to herself, while I turn my back to the mirror so as not to see the expression on my face.

Recovering my spirits after a time, I went upstairs, preceded by Fanchette, to the attic which was so often my refuge during rainy spells. It was a huge, sombre place. Freshly washed sheets hung from the rungs of the clothes-horse. A pile of partly worm-eaten books filled one corner. An old-fashioned night-stool, minus one leg, gapingly waited to minister to some ghost.

Tucked away in a large wicker hamper were short ends of wallpapers dating from about 1830—a bilious yellow background with plum-color stripes, or green lattice work up which climbed an intricate vegetation, while improbable cucumber-green birds flitted about.

All that was jumbled up with the remains of an old herbarium whose fragile skeletons of rare plants brought from all over I used to marvel at—and then ruin. Some of them were still intact and I turned the pages idly, inhaling the pleasant old dust which smelt somewhat of a pharmacy and of musty paper and dead plants or like linden blossoms gathered a week ago and spread out on a cloth to dry.

When I raised my head to look out, the open sky-light formed a frame, just as it used to do, around the familiar little landscape, far away but complete—woods on the left, a sloping meadow, a red roof in the corner—carefully composed, sentimental and charming.

There was a ring at the door downstairs. I listened to the closing of doors, the sound of indistinct voices and something heavy, like a piece of furniture, being dragged along.

(Poor bruised Claudine, how little it takes now to get you stirred up! I can stand it no longer. I would rather go down to the kitchen.)

"Where under the sun have you been, my darling? I looked all over for you and then I thought you had gone for a tramp again. It was your trunk which Monsieur Renaud sent by express. Racalin took it up the backstairs to your room."

The sight of this big leather trunk depresses me and irritates me as though it were a piece of furniture from *back there where he is*. One of its sides still carries a huge red label with white lettering: HOTEL DES BERGUES. It is from our wedding journey. I asked that this label be left on, as it made it easy to recognize the

trunk from a distance at railway stations. At the Hôtel des Bergues
—well, it rained all the time and we didn't go out.

I raised the lid with a vigorous motion, as though I wanted to
throw off the dear, burning memory that rose before me with
hopeful countenance.

At first glance it seems to me that the maid has not forgotten
much. The maid? I notice traces of other hands than hers. It
was not she who placed the little green jewel case under the summer blouses on a bed of fine, fresh, newly ribboned underwear.

The ruby Renaud gave me glistens in the casket, limpid, blood-
red, like sweet, rich wine. I hardly dare to touch it. No, no, let
it sleep in its little green casket.

In the bottom of the trunk they had laid my dresses—empty
waists and discouraged sleeves—three plain dresses that I can
wear here. But shall I also keep this antique vermilion box which
he gave me, just as he gave me the ruby and everything I have?
Someone has filled it with the candy I love—excessively sweet
chocolate creams and caramels. (Renaud, wicked Renaud! If you
only knew how bitter candy tastes when moistened with hot tears!)

I hesitated to lift each fold, where a bit of the past lay hiding and
over which hovered the tender, pleading solicitude of the man who
had been false to me. It was all full of him. With his own hands he
had smoothed out the folded garments and knotted the ribbons
of the sachets.

My eyes misty with tears, I tarried long over emptying that
reliquary. Would that I had tarried still longer! At the very
bottom, a white letter is rolled up and stuck into one of my morocco
leather slippers. I know very well that I shall read it, but how
cold this folded paper is! How unpleasantly it crackles under my
trembling fingers! I must read it, if only to put an end to that
detestable noise.

"My poor little girl whom I adore, I am sending you every last
bit of you that I have here, everything here that still retained the
fragrance of you and something of your presence. Dearest, since

you believe objects have a soul, I hope these things may speak to you of me in a kindly spirit.

"Will you ever forgive me, Claudine? I am desperately lonely. Give me back, dear—not now, later, whenever you will—not my wife but just the dear little daughter you took away.

"For my heart is heavy with sorrow when I think of your pale, earnest little face smiling at your father, while all that I have left is Marcel's cruel countenance.

"When you are less sad, I beg you to remember that a line from you will be as precious and welcome as a promise."

"Where are you goin'? And lunch waiting on the table!"

"Well, it's out of luck, that's all. I'm not going to have any lunch. Tell Papa—anything you wish—that I've gone for a walk to Quail Mountain. I'll not be back till evening."

As I spoke, I feverishly crammed into a little basket a piece of bread broken off the loaf, some autumn apples and a leg of chicken which I stole from the platter.

(I most certainly am not going to lunch here! If I am to clear my confused mind, I must have shadows streaked with sunlight and the beauty of the woods to give me counsel.)

In spite of the blazing sun, I walked without stopping along the road to Vrimes, a ditch rather than a road, deep and sandy like the bed of a stream. The sound of my footsteps scared away emerald-green lizards, so timid that I have never been able to catch one of them. The common butterflies, beige and brown like ploughmen, rose before me in clouds. A larger one flew past and barely cleared the hedge in its zigzag flight, as though it had trouble lifting any higher the heavy brown velvet of its wings.

Here and there a slender track had made a winding furrow in the sandy roadbed. An adder had passed that way, slate-color and glistening. Maybe it was carrying aslant in its tortoise-like, flat little mouth the still struggling green legs of a frog.

I looked back frequently to watch the Saracen tower edged with ivy and the dilapidated *château* grow smaller and smaller. I wished to go as far as the game-warden's cabin which some hundred years ago lost its flooring, its windows, its door and even its name. For hereabouts it is called "the little house with all the dirty things written on the walls"—just like that. And it is quite true that never were there so many obscenities, so many naïve, vulgar jokes carved and chalked up and down and crosswise, all run together and illustrated with sketches done with a knife or a piece of coal.

But I was not interested in the little hexagonal house which serves as a place of pilgrimage on Sundays for the insulting country yokels and the sly groups of girls. I was seeking the woods it used to guard, not befouled by the young people in their Sunday best because the growth is too dense, too silent, interspersed with boggy spots whence ferns shoot out luxuriantly.

Half-starved and with my mind deadened, I ate like a wood chopper, holding my basket between my knees and enjoying to the full the sensation of being an animal keenly alive and responsive only to the pleasant taste of crisp bread and a mealy apple. The peaceful landscape awakened in me a sensual delight akin to the rapture of the hunger I was appeasing. The even-topped, sombre woods suggested the flavor of the apple, while the fresh bread was cheerful like the pink-tiled roof that broke their continuity.

Then, stretching out on my back, my arms outspread like a cross, I awaited the coming of blissful torpor.

Not a soul in the fields. What would anyone be doing there? None of the land is cultivated. The grass grows up, the dead limbs fall to the ground, wild game is lured into the snare. Little girls released from school pasture the sheep along the roadside. Everything at this hour is taking a noon-day rest, as I am doing. A briar thicket in blossom diffuses its deceptive odor of strawberries. The low branches of a stunted oak make a roof-like shelter over me.

As I wiggle about to find a fresh bed of cool grass, a crackling of rumpled paper drives away the sleep that was near. Renaud's letter is throbbing its tender entreaty within my blouse.

"My poor little girl whom I adore . . . the dear little daughter you took away . . . your pale, earnest little face . . ."

He wrote that without weighing his words, without literary pre-occupation—perhaps for the first time in his life, he to whom usually the repetition of a word two lines apart is as shocking as an ink stain on his finger.

I wear that letter next my heart like a young fiancée. That and the one that came day before yesterday are the only love letters I have ever received, because during our brief engagement Renaud was always close beside me and since then I have always followed— joyfully, docilely or with indifference—his liking for travel and for social affairs.

What have I done during these eighteen months that was of any benefit to him or to myself? I have found joy in his love, have been saddened by his inconstant nature and shocked by his ways of thinking and acting—but I said nothing, avoiding any discussion and still blaming Renaud more than once for my own silence.

I made it a matter of selfishness to suffer without seeking any remedy and of unthinking pride to accuse him in silence. And yet what would he not have done at my request? I could have obtained anything I wished from his devoted affection. He loved me enough to have guided me—had I first pointed the way. And I asked of him —a bachelor apartment!

We shall have to start fresh again. Thank God it is not yet too late. I will say to him, "My beloved man, I order you to dominate me!" And I will tell him—many things besides.

The hours are passing, the sun is sinking, the delicate moths on their hesitating, prematurely nocturnal flight are coming out of the woods. A timid owl, friendly and dazzled by the light, appears too early at the edge of the woods and sits there blinking. As the day declines, the thicket becomes alive with a thousand uneasy noises and little cries. But I lend only a distracted ear and far-away, loving eyes to all this.

Suddenly I stand up, stretch my benumbed arms and cramped

legs and flee toward Montigny, pursued by fear of getting there too late—yes, too late for the Paris mail. I want to write a letter—a letter to Renaud.

I have made up my mind. Ah, how little effort it cost me!

"Dear Renaud, I feel embarrassed in writing to you, because this is the first time. And it seems to me I shall never be able to say all I want to before tonight's mail leaves.

"I want to ask your forgiveness for having left you and thank you for having let me go. It has taken me four days, all alone at home with my sorrow, to come to understand something you could have convinced me of in a few minutes.

"Nevertheless, I do not think these four days have been wasted.

"You wrote me of your great love for me, dear, without mentioning Rézi, without saying, 'You did with her what I myself did with such a slight difference.'

"And yet that would have been very reasonable, only the least bit defective in its logic. But you knew that *the two things were not the same*. And I am grateful to you for not having said they were.

"I should like never, never again to cause you any sorrow, but you will have to help me, Renaud. Yes, I am your child—not merely that—a too dearly loved daughter to whom you should sometimes refuse what she asks.

"I wanted Rézi and you gave her to me as you would a piece of candy. You must teach me that some of the things we are greedy for are harmful and that anyhow one should beware of imitations.

"Renaud dear, don't be afraid of hurting your Claudine's feelings by scolding her. I enjoy being dependent on you and standing a little in awe of a sweetheart whom I love so dearly.

"I want to say this, too—that I shall not go back to Paris. You entrusted me to the care of the country I love, so come and join me here, love and keep me here. If you should sometimes leave me, by choice or through necessity, I will wait for you here faithfully and trustingly.

"In this Fresnois country there is enough beauty and sadness so that you need not fear to be bored if I am by your side. For here I am more lovely, more loving and more straightforward.

"And then, too, come because I cannot stand it any longer without you. I love you, I love you. This is the first time I have ever written that to you. Come!

"And remember, darling husband, that I have been waiting four weary days for you no longer to be too young for me!"